THE MING STORYTELLERS

Laura Rahme

THE MING STORYTELLERS

Paperback - ISBN: 978-1479296187

ePub - ISBN: 978-0-9872937-1-8

Cover Artwork and Title Font
Caryn Gillespie
www.gillespiefox.com

Beijing Imperial City and Palace Illustration
Celeste Ramos
www.celesteramos.ca

www.laurarahme.com

Foreword

This novel draws on Early Ming Dynasty historical events and figures. I am indebted to historians and academic researchers whose work has informed this novel, including Louise Levathes, Albert Chan, Shih-shan Henry Tsai, Victoria Cass, Timothy Brook, Hua Mei, and Gavin Menzies.

Location Names

Locations in this novel are referred to by their 15th century Chinese name. U-Tsang refers to Tibet, Ku'Li refers to what is now Calicut in Southern India, Bengshi is the ancient name for modern day Baisha, a village in the province of Yunnan, Nonguzhi is the ancient name for what is now Lijiang in Yunnan, and Annam now equates to Northern Vietnam. The Chamadao (cha = tea, ma = horse, dao = way) and Tiger Leaping Gorge are still well known today. The Northeast Chinese provinces of Liaoning, Jilin and Heilongjiang are referred to as Manchuria though this translated term did not arise until the Qing dynasty.

China, Mandarin, Folangji

The country name, China is thought to derive from the Persian *Cin* and from names used by people in South-East Asia and India, such as the Malay term, *cina.* These terms influenced early Europeans, including Marco Polo in naming the country China.

The Chinese themselves call their country, Zhong Guo. This novel uses the term Middle Kingdom which, together with "middle country" is the equivalent of Zhong Guo.

The language of mainland China is known in the English speaking world as mandarin. But the Chinese do not call their language, mandarin. This term derives from nouns used by the Dutch, Portuguese and Malays to denote a Chinese bureaucrat, that is, a scholar who could read and write.

Today, mainland Chinese refer to their language as *putong hua* or "common speak". The English term, mandarin generally applies to Beijing Hua which is the Beijing dialect.

This novel uses the terms Nanjing Hua and Beijing Hua to denote the Nanjing dialect and the Beijing dialect of 15th century China.

Since the crusades, Muslims have called all Europeans, *Franques* (derived from the Franks who lived in France). In turn, after contact with Muslim traders, South-East Asians began to use the term *ferengi* to denote all Europeans, including the Portuguese. Similarly, Ming Dynasty documents indicate that the term *folangji* was used by the people of the Middle Kingdom. This novel refers to all Western foreigners beyond Arabia as Folangji.

Name Conventions

A Chinese person's full name normally begins with their surname or family name. However it is not uncommon for Chinese people to address others by their surname. For clarity, the characters in this novel are mostly referred to by their full names.

Measurements

Following 15th century China convention, distances are measured using the Chinese *li* which is equivalent to half a kilometer. Height uses the Chinese foot which is the close equivalent of a foot (1.1 foot). The Chinese calendar makes use of lunar months with the first lunar month commencing in mid-January to early February depending on the year. For clarity, this novel refers to Gregorian calendar months. In the Beijing imperial city, the passage of time is denoted by the striking of a bell with night being divided into five *geng,* each marking about two hours. The first and last night *geng* are also accompanied by the sounding of drums. The first *geng* signals the Hours of the Dog (7-9 pm) while the last *geng* signals the Hours of the Tiger (3-5am). In turn, a *geng* divides into three *dian.*

Characters

*Historical figure

Zheng He* - Grand Admiral of the Ming fleet, born Ma He, also known as San Bao
Min Li (Li Guifei) - a palace orphan, Zhu Di's concubine
Zhu Di* (also **Prince of Yan, Yong Le emperor)** - Middle Kingdom emperor
Zhu Gaozhi* (also **Hongxi emperor)** - eldest son of Zhu Di, heir to the dragon throne
Minister Xia* - Xia Yuanji, a talented Finance minister who served Emperor Jianwen, then later Emperor Zhu Di, his son and grandson
Princess Xia - Min Li's adoptive mother
Shahrzad - traveler from Zanzibar with Omani and Persian lineage
Kareem - envoy from Zanzibar, Shahrzad's cousin and fiancé
Old Yu (Yu Ling) - physician on board the Ming fleet, Zheng He's personal doctor
Zhijian - eunuch from the province of Yunnan who performs menial tasks in the palace
Shin - palace eunuch appointed by the *Silijian*, Zhijian's mentor
Ji Feng - shady, high-ranking eunuch
Hua Xue (also **Xue Guiren, Xue Guifei)** - rival concubine to Min Li
Lan Wong (Wong Guiren) - Min Li's bedchamber companion and friend
Mai Zhou (Zhou Guiren) - greedy concubine
Mei Guifei, Xun Guifei - senior concubines
Yin Dao - Embroidered-uniform Guard appointed by the Eastern Depot
Huang-Fu - street thug from the Port of Tanggu
Ping - Huang-Fu's gambling friend
Jun - seamstress and storyteller on board the treasure ship
Mustafa - Omani business man living in Zanzibar, Shahrzad's father
Zhou Man* - Admiral, present on the Ming fleet during the sixth Ming naval expedition
Yang Bao - Assistant Admiral on Zhou Man's treasure ship

Jamma - blind woman living in the village of Nonguzhi
Bei Lan - mysterious stranger who arrives in the village of Nonguzhi
Namu - Nakhi villager, friend of Bei Lan
Sonam - tea-horse trader from U-Tsang
Ekbal - a native of Ku'Li
Giri, Balraj - Ekbal's assistants
Lieutenant Deng - officer on board the Ming fleet, assigned to torturing traitors
Jin Hong - carpenter supervising the construction of the Imperial Palace in Beijing
Shen - convict who works on the construction of the Imperial Palace in Beijing
Chou - Shen's drinking friend
Mai - Princess Xia's chamber maid
Amira - Shahrzad's devoted maid
Semi - a slave master

**

Other Historical Characters

Zhu Yuanzhang (Hongwu emperor) - Zhu Di's father, founder of the Ming Dynasty
Jianwen - Hongwu's chosen successor, deposed by his uncle, Zhu Di
Ma Huan - official writer on board the Ming fleet
Empress Ma - Consort to emperor Hongwu
Empress Xu - Consort to Zhu Di
Xu Miaojin - Empress Xu's sister, later a nun
Zhu Gaoxu - troublesome son of Zhu Di, brother of Zhu Gaozhi
Zhu Gaosui - third son of Zhu Di and of his consort, Empress Xu
Zhu Zhanji (also **Xuande emperor**) - Zhu Di's grandson
Xie Jin - Grand Secretary, commissioned by Zhu Di to compile the *Yong Le Encyclopedia*, assisted the election of Zhu Gaozhi as heir, assassinated through the influence of Zhu Gaoxu
Minister Yang Shiqi - Grand Secretary; compiler of the *Ming Shilu* and later Minister of War
Yishiha - high-ranking eunuch who is reputed to have led nine expeditions to Manchuria

Arughtai - leader of the Eastern Mongols against whom Zhu Di led several campaigns
Prince of Xian - one of Zhu Di's brothers
General Fu You De - one of Hongwu's generals during the Yunnan campaign
Nguyen An - Annamese eunuch and architect who designed the Imperial Palace of Beijing
Niccolo da Conti - well-traveled Venetian living in South Eastern Asia
Lady Wen - Zheng He's mother
Princess Xianning - daughter of Zhu Di and Empress Xu
Ji Gang - Commander, appointed by Zhu Di to head the Eastern Depot

Beijing Imperial City and Palace Map

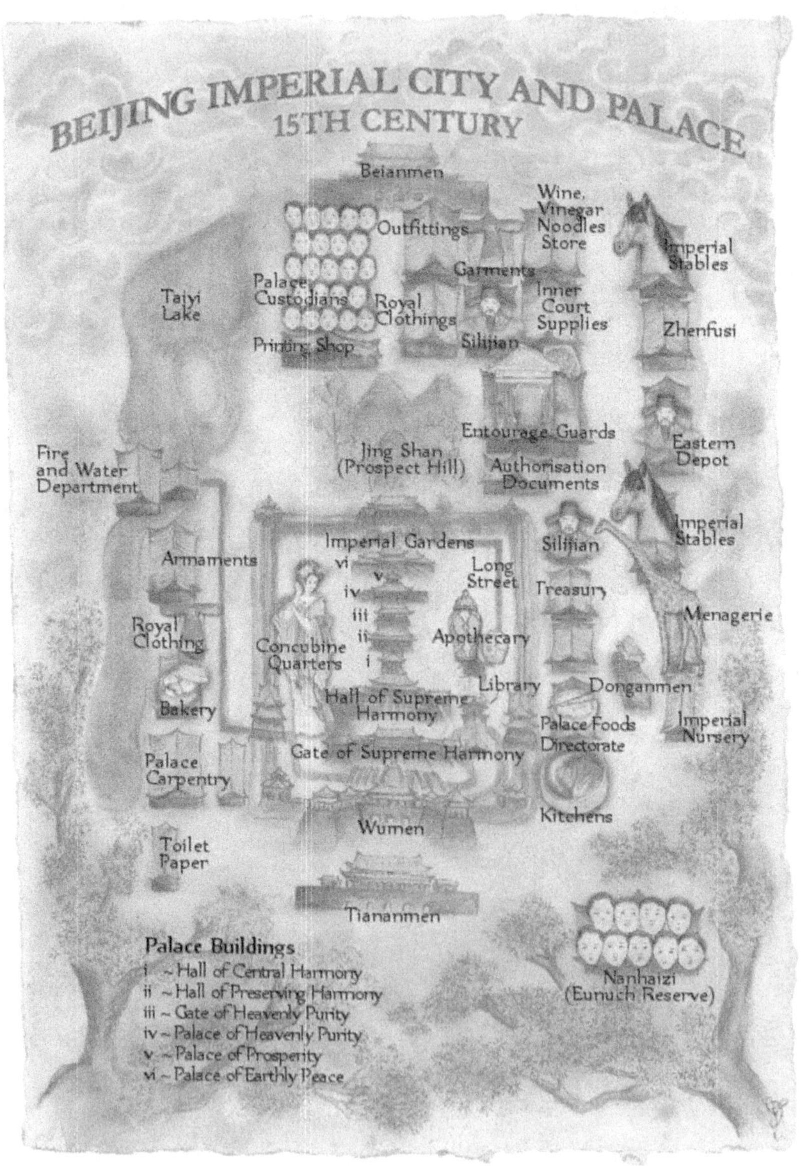

The Ming Storytellers

para Isabel
"Errar e humano"

For Isabel
"To err is human"

Fire in the Beijing Palace

It has been written, many years ago, that the imperial city fire of May 1421 began when lightning struck the highest point of the palace.

It was from the Hall of Supreme Harmony where two months earlier, the usurper, Zhu Di stood before an assembly of thousands that the raging flames sprang to life.

Before the eunuchs could reach it, the fire swept through the palace, incinerating the three Great Halls on its path as though they had been vulgar *hutongs* cramped in some Beijing back alley. From here, it knew no respite. Rising twenty feet high, it advanced towards the west and into the ladies' apartments.

This monstrous blaze yielded to none of the eunuchs' efforts to extinguish it. As much as the castrates strained themselves to the vast copper urns whose water content was soon exhausted, still, the fire's fury continued.

As the western wing burnt, a wasted, pale woman of about five and twenty slumbered in her prison. Several days earlier, she had been locked out of sight to be starved in the back chamber of the concubine compound. There, she waited a slow, agonizing death. Her cruel punishment would serve as an example to concubines who dared defy emperor Zhu Di.

What to say of this treacherous creature, save that while she lay on the cold floor, her long raven hair ravaged by mites, her fingertips pecked by rats and her dried lips curled in a feverish pout, she looked no less sensual than if she were naked on a bed of roses.

Yet if she had once felt the shivering cold of her dark cell, now a rising heat stirred the woman from her dreams. The fire had made its way into the concubine compound. Already, horrifying screams rose from beyond the chamber.

As her eyes opened, she could not remember where she was. Unaware of the violence outside, she smiled as though her lover were nearby and she were reminding him of their mutual secret. But he was not here. She was alone. She remembered that she had been alone for years.

She studied her surroundings. Her eyes lifted to the wooden beams framing the high ceiling. They ran down the scarcely painted walls. At last, intent on discovering the reason for this great noise, they rested on the door where a curious haze had lifted. About a foot's height on that door, a tiny slit glowed like burning amber.

Using her elbows, she crawled towards the light. At first, she did not comprehend. But as her nostrils twitched and her lungs grew indignant under the assault of smoke, the unsettling realization struck.

She peered through the slit into the orange-lit corridor. A waft of ash stung her eye. She blinked. The cats had grown insane. They scurried past, hissing and screeching in and out of the concubine chambers. She frowned. Where were they all? The Guirens, the Guifeis... All the emperor's ladies?

The rooms seemed vacant if not for the resonant shrieks in the corridor. Though she could not see them, she could imagine the concubines sitting still, stiff with fear, in their doomed chambers. They all waited for the fire.

For there, directly ahead, amidst collapsing timber and clouds of ash, the advancing flames engulfed everything in its path. In time, it would burn them all.

She had to escape.

Surmounting another urge to cough, the prisoner pressed herself against the door.

"Lady Xue! Lady Xue, help me." Her voice was muffled by the thick wood. "I beg you, help me!" She banged on the door with her tiny fists. "Please! Can anyone hear? Please help!"

There was a fluttering of red silk, ten feet ahead. A familiar haughty figure emerged, two rooms from her prison. Like a silent ghost, the woman in the red skirt stood transfixed by her chamber's doorway. It was Lady Xue.

Lady Xue had bound feet and could not run. She seemed lost in a daze. Only a moment ago, two other lotus feet concubines had attempted to force through the advancing flames. They had crept on all fours, like two animals. Alerted by their screams, the eunuchs rushed to unlock the front doors of the concubine compound. But when these unfortunate ladies burst out into the courtyard, none of the eunuchs from the Fire and Water Department could recognize them.

The hapless eunuchs who witnessed this calamity later reported seeing strange animals contorting themselves on the ground. They recalled how these blazing figures had rolled across the tiled pavement, piercing the air with their shrieks, their voices consumed with reproach and rage. At first the castrates failed to recognize these virtuous concubines, so alarming were the sounds that the creatures producing them could not be human.

And now, Lady Xue knew well that she was trapped. She would never be favorite concubine. All her efforts had been in vain. As she turned to face the prison door, an unmistakable expression of rage glistened on her terrorized face. And then her shrill voice rose like biting venom.

"This is all your doing! You wrought this upon us! May you be cursed by the Heavens, Min Li! Cursed!"

Horrified, Min Li jerked herself from the door. In a wild panic, she searched for an escape that did not exist, had never existed. Her coughing redoubled. Sobbing, she hurled herself at the door, slamming violently at the stubborn wood. She tried again, and again, tears streaming down her ashen face.

And then she heard... She heard the monstrous, inhuman cries from the other side. It chilled Min Li's bones even as sweat ran down her brow and her damp skirt clung to her sweltering breasts.

She dared one last look through the hole. She saw... Lady Xue's charred skull was on fire. And how she danced in the corridor...

Min Li cried out. Now the flame dragons would come for her. Now they would eat her the same way they had eaten the other concubines.

She stumbled to the back of the chamber, refusing to look. A sob knotted her throat as she clamped her hands to her ears.

There was a sound. Perhaps the crackling of the door being set ablaze. Already, the skin on her fingers burnt but Min Li dared not open her eyes. Instead she curled herself into a tighter ball.

Not a whimper rose from her lips, only a lament.

"My dearest Admiral...you were right. We could never be."

And then darkness.

The Children of the Middle Kingdom

Across this vast land known as the Middle Kingdom, the Mongol powers, the pride of Genghis Khan, have long waned. Once they ruled on horseback, invincible on their Mongolian horses. It was told that these fierce riders, long hardened by life on the steppes, learned to ride as young as two and could thrive for days by drinking fresh blood from their horse's cut veins.

In the beginning they spread from Mongolia, sweeping terror across the west, pillaging the cities and women of Baghdad, Herat and Samarkand.

In the Middle Kingdom, even the Great Wall, this northern stronghold that for centuries had kept the Mongols at bay, could not stop them. For it was from the southwest, in Yunnan and Sichuan provinces, that the invaders traveling at an unfathomable speed of up to two hundred *lis* per day forced their way in.

The invasion would take sixty years. For sixty years, the people of the Middle Kingdom clung to their freedom, battling an enemy that surpassed them in horsemanship and archery, battling a wave of death, famine, pillaging and cruelty. In 1272, the triumphant Kublai Khan proclaimed his capital at Yuan Dadu. The Yuan Dynasty had begun.

Empires rise and fall. The year is now 1380. Decades ago, a great change has swept in, stirred by mighty troops eager for freedom, eager to oust the foreigner.

The newly formed Ming armies, led by the once famished Anhui peasant, Zhu Yuanzhang, have risen to oust the Mongol invader. Emboldened by their revolutionary leader, loyal to their land, animated by vivid memories and tales of years long past, the Ming soldiers have regained control of the Middle Kingdom. In the city of Yingtian, Zhu Yuanzhang has seized the dragon throne. They call him, Emperor Hongwu.

After almost one hundred years, the Yuan Dynasty is no more. In its place is the Ming, the Bright.

There remains however, a Mongol stronghold further down towards the South in the province of Yunnan.

Honored reader, the boy you are about to meet is, according to Ming soldiers, a petty Mongol partisan. To be sure, he has never harmed anyone and his family is for the most part, peaceful. For this reason, we should bow in silence and humbly excuse ourselves. We should say, instead, that the little boy was a Hue which is how the Han natives of the Middle Kingdom called his people.

As a Hue, the boy was also one of the Semuren, the colored eye people. Many years before the Mongol invasion of the Middle Kingdom, the boy's ancestors had traveled to Yunnan from their native Bukhara in the western land of the Uzbeks. But his family was also believed to be descended from Kublai Khan's followers. This was why the Ming soldiers now drove their horses south. They would conquer the Mongol partisans.

Honored reader let me draw you into this mountainous land of Yunnan, a land of many tribes and many tongues. Here, in the village of Kunyang where our story begins, the gentle hills descended into a leafy valley. It was a clear afternoon and the summer light lent warmth to a lakeside clearing. How lovely it all was!

Yet if the boy had known that danger loomed, he might have not played at all.

Ma He was his name. At this tender age, being a Hue was only interesting to him because it meant that one day he would sail like his father on the Mongol fleet. Ma He looked up to his father. His father was his world. But this would change.

It had rained heavily the previous day. To Ma's great joy, the clearing was muddy and spotted with shallow ponds of water. To other children, playing in the mud was a reckless pastime but for Ma He it was an adventure that he approached with caution, never wanting to soil the clothes his mother had lovingly pressed.

Today he had on a white head cap and a pair of blue cotton pants. A long-sleeved cobalt tunic with fine red embroidery completed his prim outfit. Ma He crouched at a prudent distance from the edge of the largest puddle. With his arms stretched out, he glided a toy-sized wooden ship on the surface of the water. As he played, sunlight caught auburn strands in his dark hair. Ma He was nine. Good humor already shone from his deep set eyes.

Close by, concealed behind a pine tree, a younger girl observed him with a smile. It gave her much delight to watch him so absorbed by his game. She was a Mosuo from the Mosha-yi tribe. Her long brown hair was parted in two and braided to her hips. She wore a full-length pleated white skirt under a red tunic. Around her tiny waist she had wrapped a colorful sash. A fine string of turquoise beads dangled from her tanned neck and though her arms and hair were adorned with silver jewelry, she kept a modest bearing. She was listening.

"I am the captain of the ship! I order you to surrender!" shouted Ma He, unaware of the smiling intruder peeping behind him.

How delightful he was. But she could not see him well. She would have to sneak across, maybe to the other tree so that she could best observe this fascinating Ma He with his puddle and boat game. The next time he raised the boat and shouted out, she would dart across. She hoped his voice would hide the sounds of her tiny footsteps on the grass. With a bit of luck, he would not see her.

"We are sailing into the seas. Into the Arabian Seas we sail!"

Ma He froze and looked up. The girl was startled.

"Oh, it's you," he said, not without reproach. But he forgave her intrusion as one welcomes a break from solitude. "Have you seen my boat?"

She blushed and made a pout, avoiding his gaze. Still crouching, Ma He was eager to share his future plans.

"When I grow up, I'll sail away, just like my father!" He weaved his boat with pride.

"I, too, will cross the Arabian ocean!"

She approached him. As she moved, her silver bracelets jingled as though she were a colorful bird and had been born with singing jewelry. She sat beside him, her little slippers hidden under the folds of her skirt, making herself as tiny as possible. Her timidity was endearing.

But it was not so much timidity but rather knowledge that one is a little different and sometimes not welcome, that endowed this lovely oval face with a soft glow.

The girl may have had a name but to Ma He, she was just the Mosuo girl. Aside from the rare occasions where he had seen her scouring for plants and seeds for her mother's healing potions, or heard his parents scorn Mosuo witchcraft practices, Ma He knew nothing of her.

He had been warned by parents and schoolmaster alike not to play with the child. There were times when he had witnessed the other boys poke fun at her outside school. Of course she never attended school because the Mosuo were different. He had stood there that day and said nothing while the boys teased her. But back at home, he had felt weary remembering her silent tears, as though the burden of protecting innocents fell on his shoulders. And now here she was, watching him like a besotted admirer.

"Do you want to play?" he asked, a little confused at himself by his sudden compassion. "Come closer. I want to show you something. It's a secret, ok? Promise you won't tell. You promise?"

He reassured himself that no one would give weight to her words and that his secret would be safe. He immediately regretted this belittling afterthought and blushed. Then he smiled and faced his model.

"Watch this!" he announced. He pulled a lever on the side of the ship and behold! Below the stern, was a little hole the size of a finger. "You see this cabin?"

Her mouth parted in astonishment. He welcomed her response, happy with himself and his toy. He pressed his index finger to his lips.

"Hush! It's my secret cabin. That here, will be my cabin when I grow up!

Her little black eyes widened.

"Your cabin?"

"Yes, my cabin. I will be the captain!"

She smiled. Ma He had shared his precious little toy with her. And she, most of all, knew well how precious it was to him. She was moved by his kindness.

Satisfied that he had pleased the girl, Ma He resumed his game. This time he swished around the puddles for effect. He felt a need to entertain her. The poor girl was probably lonely. She needed to understand that he was not like the other boys.

It was then that she chose to speak.

"It's very small your cabin," she began. "How will you ever fit in it?"

"It is only a game. It's not real. Don't tell anyone, ok?"

"I won't..."

Ma He played on while his companion watched, fixated on the wooden boat. She seemed lost in a daze. He glanced in her direction to assess whether his antics were still keeping her amused, or perhaps to feed his own curiosity, he wasn't sure.

And then an uneasy thought took hold of his mind. Had not his parents warned him? That little girl and her mother are not like us, they had said. They have strange ways. Remember to keep away.

But it was too late. And she was indeed different. She began to speak again and Ma He noticed that her voice had changed to a deeper, almost womanly tone.

"You know... You will be almost seven feet tall, Ma. I've seen you..." Her voice trailed. "I've seen you," she repeated in a manner that made him shudder.

At once, he looked up. He even forgot his boat so that it tipped over and fell flat on one side. A little wary but now pretending he had not heard her, he picked it up and shook it to let the water drip.

"So...who says I'll be seven feet tall?" He observed her dark pupils. They danced like little seeds washed down in the rain. She had no idea what she was saying. Or did she?

"I've seen you in the years to come! You'll be gigantic!" she said, still staring ahead of her with that joyful smile. It seemed as though a puppet show carried on in front of her eyes, one that only she could see. "I've seen you Ma He!" she repeated, almost ecstatic.

"Hush! What is it with you?" He jumped to his feet, boat in hand and stared at her with reproach. "Didn't they tell you to keep quiet? Don't you realize that no one will ever want to play with you if you act this way?"

He bit his lip and mentally repeated the phrase, *act this way*. Act how? He could not describe it but it wasn't normal. His parents were right. What strange people they were. Only Allah could see the things to come.

But after his outburst, he noticed that the girl was no longer smiling. It was sad to see.

"I'm sorry," she said, her head lowered in shame.

He does not understand, she thought. I had better leave. She pushed her little hands against the soft wet earth to bring herself to her feet and was about to leave when Ma He, alarmed that he had hurt her feelings began to shout.

"Hey girl, don't go! Please..."

She tilted her head to the side and turned to face him. Ma He remained transfixed. The two children stared at each other in silence.

A gale had risen, stirring the tree branches. Ma He's clean cap was tossed to the ground. The cotton fibers drew muddy water. He ignored it. He continued to observe her, a little fearful, as though she was some foreign animal from a land where his father may have sailed on a journey to the Arabian lands. And yet, he realized she was not at all frightening. She looked so pretty with those two braids framing her broad tanned face.

Taking a deep breath, he came closer. Then he leaned towards her and brought his lips within whispering distance of her tiny ear. "Go on and tell me... What else did you see?"

Time has a way of disappointing the curious, cutting short life's pleasures. For an instant, Ma He felt that she was close to answering but she merely shook her head.

"No. I can't tell," she said.

It was then that he heard the shrill sounds of his mother's voice. Noble Lady Wen seemed to leap out of nowhere, followed by three servants. They had alerted her after spotting the two children in the clearing. Upon sighting her son in dubious company, Lady Wen gasped. She shuffled in agitation towards him. His arm was clamped in her iron grasp while he tried in vain to retrieve his cap from the ground.

"I told you not to play with the Mosuo! Come along!" She turned to the girl, "What did you tell him? Don't you go round putting curses on my boy, do you hear!"

The mother hurried away, shielding her son under a protective arm. She continued to cast fearful glances behind her until they had both disappeared from the clearing.

Left alone, the little girl hid her pain. That hard lump in her throat, she knew it well. Sometimes, like now, it was bitter and it hurt to swallow. She knelt by the puddle, picked up a stick and resumed the boat game, alone, in her most enchanting voice.

No one could hear what this precious daughter of Yunnan was saying, lost in her daydreams. And yet, even if they had heard, they would have certainly shaken their heads in disbelief and walked on.

"I am Ma He, the Grand Eunuch!" she invented in a soft voice. It was lovely. The game could still be fun even if she did not have a boat to play with.

Yet over time, her playful thoughts became muddled. And very soon, the game had merged into something else, something familiar to her.

I must try to control *it*, she thought. But *it*, whatever it was, became pressing, more urgent. It would not let her mind be free. The Mosuo girl looked ahead and froze. Carried forth from some distant plain, a speck of red dirt settled on her nose. Her nostrils twitched.

She could smell the change closing in. It screamed at her with the mingled voices of women and children.

She shifted her head to the left. The vision rose from nothingness, stirring the earth's soil under whip lashes and racing hooves. She thought they were gods with metal harnesses and tasseled round helmets on their heads. But they were men, men on horses, men with swords, bows and arrows. They rode the plains with their lances raised high. She followed the vision, shifting her head towards the right. She saw the streaming triangular banners with their fierce dragon embroidery, flapping against the wind. What were they?

Somehow she knew. They were coming. In three more moons, they would be here.

She blinked. The black mane horses galloped in a mist of red dust, sweating under the fury of unrelenting soldiers.

She trembled from the power of her visions. She wanted to escape their grip, to go on playing again. She wanted to continue impersonating the boy, shouting out the name Ma He as he had done before. But no, this was no longer his name. Now, what was his name?

"I am... I am...Zh...Zheng..."

"Zheng He," she repeated, surprised by the foreign word as it brushed her tiny lips.

Yes, that's what they would call him when he became a man.

The fierce wind rustled a bed of dried leaves. Rising high, they swirled around her, in a furious vortex.

And time began to pass.

Book One: Metal

The Ming Emperor

"Metal overcomes Wood"

Chapter 1
The Emperor's Glory

Beijing, March 1421

Ode to the Imperial Palace

Come, honored traveler. Enter the Purple Palace, enter.

At the mighty Wumen, this five-arched Meridian Gate, the hefty red doors of the west gateway have swiveled open. Do not stand here after your long journey. Today, just today, you must enter. For now the red-walled palace is revealed. It beckons you.

Hear now, the clashing cymbals. Hear now as drums are struck to honor this auspicious day. Cross; cross one of the five marble bridges and over the Inner Golden Stream. Let the thousand echoing voices guide you.

Here, flanked by husky banner carriers, the busy eunuchs attend to the celebrations. Watch as they escort foreign visitors through the majestic Gate of Supreme Harmony. Follow them. Cross the large square to this king of all gates. Pay heed, traveler, pay heed. Behind this gate awaits a place where pretense meets with incomparable splendor and nothing is what it seems.

Behold the colorful sea of guests where brocaded silks, gold threads and ebony buns vie for attention. Ming royalty, ambassadors, military and court officials, all have come to pay their respects to the usurping emperor. They stand in their full-length robes, their glistening jewels of beads and pure jades, their sumptuous embroidery of flowers, phoenixes, dragons and cranes. First they bow to him. Now their faces tilt up towards the heavens. They gaze at a round bearded figure, perched high upon marble steps.

Do you see him?

Watch this man. This one, he calls himself Son of Heaven. But we know him as Zhu Di, Prince of Yan and bitter son of Zhu Yuanzhang. For what son is not bitter when his father does not choose him for an heir? An usurper, Zhu Di may be but who can contest his ascension to the dragon throne? Not you, honored traveler, not I.

For now, feast; feast your eyes on the hundreds of copper-skinned drummers, beating with all the vigor of their toned limbs. In that resounding throb, recognize the dark rhythm that has led you here.

Watch the sylphlike dancers fly into a swirl of ribbons. How daintily they float as they adopt one figure after another. Steal an erotic glance at their tiny feet while evanescent silk graces the air and flirts with their fragile form. But you are dizzy now. It is time. Look up!

Perched high above three levels of white marble paving, Zhu Di towers before the assembly. A mist of sandalwood-infused vapors rises around him. No less than eighteen bronze incense burners are lit for him. Zhu Di absorbs almost through his nostrils, the euphoria of his triumph.

And what triumph it is. Envoys from as far as Zanzibar and Persia have come to pay tribute to the emperor. And like you, they have seen nothing like this place before. There he stands, the master of time and space, Son of Heaven. His face beams before the torrent of echoing hails. There he parades, giddy with pleasure, in his finest gilded robe, before the Hall of Supreme Harmony.

But murmurs travel fast, here, among those assembled. The excited voices cannot be silenced as they whisper a new name and follow a new shadow. For Zhu Di's subjects have glimpsed a new interest.

Ah... Do you see what I see now, honored traveler?

An unusually tall figure strides up the marble steps. It is a rare honor, a privilege that Zhu Di bestows to only a few. And why not, since this man has once saved his life. And if it were not for this man's courage and ingenious mind, who knows, perhaps Zhu Di would not be standing here today; perhaps his nephew would still be emperor.

The tall man approaches. Though he appears in his late forties, he is much older. In him, there is dignity and confidence, someone still reaching towards lofty goals. But look within. Look closer. It is a man still eager to prove his worth, in the familiar manner of one who does not yet know his real worth.

He wears a full-length red robe and a black high hat. He is a eunuch. If one were to look closely, one would notice a large embroidered panel across his chest and back. It bears the insignia reserved for the highest ranking military admirals – the Lion. And by the side of his thick waist, rests a jade-hilted sabre. It is as green as the jade dragon buckle on his belt.

He reaches the marble platform and bows before his emperor. He seems to seal now and forever, the unique ties he has shared with Zhu Di for over thirty years. Like the dutiful eunuchs who serve the Ming emperor, this man, perhaps more than all others, is known for his loyalty.

His name is *Zheng He.*

***

The Lord of the Seas

Zheng He ascended the steps until the two men were almost level. Though it was spring, season of dust storms and dry winds, today only a thin gray mist hovered over Beijing. From the Hall of Supreme Harmony, the view over the palace's yellow-tiled roofs was breathtaking.

"Do you see, now?" asked Zhu Di. "Nanjing was nothing compared to this! Nothing! Oh, we know what they are thinking... They've never seen anything like this palace before. Almost ten thousand rooms! We have surpassed all expectations."

Zheng He seemed to blush as the assembly hailed him. "Your Majesty honors me," he whispered, bowing low.

"The Grand Admiral is too modest."

The emperor and Zheng He were now seated. Zhu Di would have sat beside his beloved empress but she had died at least fifteen years ago and he had never remarried. He had tried to marry his sister-in-law but the rejection he had suffered when she fled to a convent had since curbed his interest in electing another empress. As consolation, he told himself that he had no need for another empress. After all, he already had four sons and believed that unlike him, they were all useless.

Zhu Di's gaze lingered over a row of princes, princesses and other nobles of the court, all seated at the bottom of the steps. Aside from his son, Zhu Gaozhi, and his beloved grandson, Zhu Zhanji, he had no time for court matters today. Let those Hanlin academics bicker, oh, he would show them. He searched in the audience for his son, Zhu Gaozhi.

Even if one were close to him, it was impossible to intuit the emperor's thoughts. A seasoned military commander with years of experience on the field, he concealed his designs well. At this instant, he hid his disappointment. There was no sign of Zhu Goazhi.

Could it be? The heir apparent was not present. Curse him.

Zhu Di's seemingly impassive gaze continued to the right where a coterie of elegant women knelt in their fine silk robes. Secluded by a screen and rows of eunuchs, they could only be seen by the elevated emperor and his highest admiral. Zhu Di's eyes rested on one of these women.

Hers was an arresting, enigmatic beauty. Yet one that was unsettled by a gaze of fierce resolve. Every few moments, her eyes probed the assembly as one seeks danger within. It seemed as though a darker truth inhabited this creature, as though she could see beyond what those present could ever see.

Her silken hair was secured into a bun by a tortoise shell comb. As she kowtowed to the beat of the drums, Zhu Di studied the slender curve of her back. Reaching her neck, his possessive eyes savored her tender lobes from which hung exquisite beaded earrings.

Zhu Di bit his lip. Min Li had raised her face towards Admiral Zheng He. For a short moment, he watched the concubine's vermillion lips move apart. A deep frown was etched on Zhu Di's up to now, inscrutable forehead.

The colorful processions unfolded in honor of the new Beijing palace and to farewell foreign ambassadors on their journey home. A group of stocky men bedecked in full-length robes now marched towards the marble platform. Like Zheng He, they wore a tall, winged hat fastened below their chin. They carried a sword attached to their hip. All eyes were on them. From the top of the steps, Zheng He was one of the first to notice them.

"Your Majesty! The admirals are here!"

If these had been men, they would have had no need to stand with such feigned pride. But they were not men. They were eunuchs. Each wore the long-sleeved red uniform. Each sported the magnificent square embroidery, the *buzi*, across his chest and back. One of these depicted a lion, another, a tiger. Such was the honor reserved for the commandants and navigators of the Ming imperial fleet.

Marching at the sound of the drums and preceding this bedazzling procession were several tasseled banner carriers. They left no doubt that the emperor had vested much power in his admirals. And it was also this which sparked envy among the other, lower rank eunuchs.

As for Zheng He, he was beaming and could not contain his enthusiasm.

"Together at last! Two years since we escorted the ambassadors to Beijing..."

But Zhu Di had ceased listening. He stroked his beard, an absent expression on his face. He had caught Min Li steal yet another glance towards Zheng He.

The admirals moved into formation. Before the marble steps, they presented their respect to the emperor while the heavy drone of the drums redoubled in intensity.

"Zhou Man is here! Can you see him, Your Majesty?" whispered Zheng He.

He had failed to notice the frown across his emperor's brow.

"Yes, yes...We can see... How they adore you..."

Zheng He gave him a questioning side glance. In response, the emperor forced an abrupt smile. Then he stood.

"Let our guests be entertained. Come Admiral. We wish to discuss your next voyage."

Swift on his feet, Zheng He followed but not without noting the foreboding manner in Zhu Di's next words.

"We are curious to know where our son is."

***

Zhu Gaozhi

Of the three great buildings in the center of the Purple Palace, the Hall of Central Harmony, nestled between the immense Hall of Supreme Harmony and the Hall of Preserving Harmony was the smallest. It was in this sparsely furnished hall where lay a golden throne that the emperor liked to rest before large ceremonies.

Zheng He's face was still flushed from the attention he had received but he grew more somber as they entered the dim building.

Unlike what they had expected, the hall was not empty. As the celebrations ensued, the heir apparent, Prince Zhu Gaozhi had summoned the six ministers, and today, of all days, they conferred around the golden throne, their indignant voices echoing in the hall.

The ministers declined to wear lavish attires like the imperial family. They preferred a simple full-length gown with a black rimmed collar and broad long sleeves. When they moved, they seemed to glide sinuously on their high felt boots. They were scholars and members of the Hanlin Academy, men who had ascended the highest echelons of learning and excelled in the Central Examination. They were well versed in many fields with an emphasis on Confucian ideologies and the upholding of strict moral values. They were also proud of their learning, preferring to grow their fingernails long so that it was obvious to all that they did not engage in manual occupations.

Just like his father, Zhu Di relied on them as aids in governance. But Zhu Di was less amenable to being told how to rule and how best to uphold Confucian tenets.

Hongwu had been all too eager to prove his intellect and transcend his humble background of Anhui peasant. He had sought to impress the scholars. He had listened to their advice and worked hard on his Ming code and other moral documents.

Not so Zhu Di. The Prince of Yan was not intimidated by the scholars' sharp tongues. An expansive, military man, he was fond of more controversial ideas. And where these ideas were likely to be rejected by the conservative scholarly clique, he happily relegated his designs to his loyal eunuchs.

"They detest me," he whispered to his admiral. "All of them, without exception are jealous of you, Zheng He. Watch them..."

Zhu Di liked the dual structure in his government because it allowed him to manipulate his subjects at his will. The two men advanced towards the throne.

"We can be certain," pursued Zhu Di, "that if these men confer, it is to vent their pent up frustrations. They believe they can rule the kingdom better than we can."

It was on the golden throne that the fat prince, Zhu Gaozhi, not yet Son of Heaven, sat among the venomous scholars. Seeing his father approach, the prince silenced the Hanlin academics with a subtly raised hand.

"My son will always be a fat slob," murmured Zhu Di while he and the admiral were still ten feet away. "I love him but he puts me to shame."

At this instant, Zhu Gaozhi recognized his father's companion and fumed. As for the admiral, he expected Zhu Di to grow red and vociferate but the emperor did no such thing.

Zhu Di was unpredictable these days. It was a side effect of that Taoist elixir he had begun taking ever since his partial paralysis had set in, three years ago. Zheng He had heard the drug concoction was so potent that it often caused his emperor to lash out in anger. For this reason, one could never know how Zhu Di would behave. Zheng He observed his emperor smile with affected nonchalance. Zhu Di stroked his pointy beard.

And now, the ministers bowed before their emperor. Yet their eyes roamed towards Zhu Gaozhi as if preparing to seek support from the prince who would one day lead the empire.

They knew too well that Zhu Di did not tolerate their conservative political sermons and while they feared that he may put them away in his newly re-opened Eastern Depot prison for none other than this clandestine conference, they also knew that the best defense in their favor was an unflinching support in the Confucian ideals. They felt safe as the guardians of tradition.

Like a bird circling towards his prey, Zhu Di paced towards the golden throne. The thread of his yellow robe reflected the light seeping through the latticed window panes and he emanated the glow of a man who thinks himself beyond reproach and who cannot help wonder why anyone would choose to turn against him.

"Ah! Here is one who will have no willing part in our celebrations. Look, Zheng He. Our heir prefers the company of the Hanlin to that of his own father."

The admiral failed to offer any replies. In response, he felt the curse of Zhu Gaozhi's murderous stare.

Zhu Di's head lolled to the side. "My son, is that seat to your liking?"

Zhu Gaozhi stepped away from the golden throne.

Zhu Di continued, "You see, dear Prince, the Son of Heaven has yet more to achieve. Oh...Xia," he added, facing his finance minister, "we have need to discuss future Mongolian campaigns once the admiral's fleet departs. Be sure to report to us with an account of your proposed military budget early next month."

The minister grimaced.

"Oh, and Xia..."

Xia Yuanji waited, his eyes transfixed on the ground.

"We will *not* take no for an answer."

The minister bowed, disgusted at the thought of another campaign. He shot a nervous glance at Zhu Gaozhi as though prompting him to dare express their grievances.

Zhu Gaozhi stepped forward.

"If you must know, Father, we were discussing matters highly relevant to these excessive festivities—"

"Oh, then do enlighten us."

"...inflation Father. Nobody can afford anything these days. Do you know, Father, do you know, of the rampant starvation in several provinces while we gorge ourselves on rich foods off the backs of our peasantry?"

"If you are talking about the famine in Anhui—"

"That's one such province."

"We dealt with it. You should know. Grain relief was distributed and a standard two year tax exemption will follow."

"Only a short term solution. There is, Father, a more pressing problem—"

"The threat of Mongol invasion *is* a pressing problem, Zhu Gaozhi. One cannot while time in one's private chambers reading book after book. One needs to actively defend the empire. And this, my dearest indulgent son, requires riding horses and putting on our armors."

"That is precisely our contention, Your Majesty. We are wasting resources. Your army feeds off the food which it does not even grow—"

"My army is self-sufficient! The majority of conscripts are tilling the land, as they always have since your grandfather's days!"

"Your Majesty, if you could look at the reports you will find that this is no longer the case. Between those soldiers that desert us and those posted along the Northern border, your army is no longer self-sufficient."

The corpulent Zhu Gaozhi paused to catch his breath.

"We tax heavily to feed your army, do we not? And who do we tax, Your Majesty?"

"Enough!"

"And as you no doubt know, pepper is hard to get by these days...wouldn't you agree, Grand Admiral?"

The emperor was quick to come to his favorite eunuch's rescue.

"What are you trying to do? Have you not had enough for today?"

But Zhu Gaozhi was too incensed to let the matter drop. And he had reason to be. The paper money introduced by Emperor Hongwu had descended to almost one thousandth of its original worth. Pepper was most valuable, sold by the grain and often used as replacement currency. Whenever receiving tribute pepper from the South Indian port of Ku'li, the Ming government hoarded supplies in its warehouses to that intent. But as Zhu Gaozhi had noted, it was now more expensive for Beijing's inhabitants to appropriate themselves with the currency.

The scholars attributed the tight government hoarding of pepper to the cost of Zhu Di's extravagant projects. This included global expeditions which they saw as the cause of many of the country's ills.

Zhu Di had heard it all before. The ministers sought to curtail him in his vision. Having failed to persuade their ruler through intellect, they had turned his heir, his own son, against him. Curse them.

And now, out of breath, his plump cheeks burnt to crimson, Zhu Gaozhi persisted.

"I have been toying with a riddle, Father, the riddle of the Ming. So you no doubt know that famine is killing our countrymen, that some are reduced to eating mud. Does it not seem farcical to you? Here we have, the Ming in all its glory, starving its own civilians! Today our peasants cannot even afford to buy the very products that your treasure ships hoard as tax!"

He examined Zheng He.

"And what is it, I hear? Are we yet to invite more tributary traders into our shores? Your Majesty, with all due respect, you cannot continue to entertain the belief that this is to our economic benefit!"

"You've said enough," warned Zhu Di.

The prince turned to Zheng He. "I hear you are embarking in the next fortnight," he remarked, knowing the answer only too well.

Zheng He's hand tightened on his sword, outraged at the fat prince's outburst. It was odd because the admiral had heard nothing but praise about Zhu Gaozhi's generous, humanistic ways. Today's behavior was out of character perhaps.

Once again Zhu Di was quick to admonish his son.

"You disappoint us, Zhu Gaozhi. Yes, the admirals are sailing soon. But, why hold such resentment towards those who, really, ought to inspire your admiration? Have we perhaps held you, heir apparent, in more esteem than you deserved?"

Zhu Gaozhi's lips trembled into a bitter pout. But he recomposed himself.

"I am at fault, Your Majesty. I have made reproaches unworthy of the dragon throne. I shall attempt to follow Zheng He's example." He paused. "After all... Why ponder over domestic economics when naval engineering and foreign trade offer all solutions."

Before Zheng He had the time to reply to this tirade, Zhu Gaozhi bowed and marched out of the hall with injured resonance.

The admiral was not ignorant of the rampant poverty. He had heard that in the winter months, Beijing beggars slept in manure to keep warm until they died of pestilence. He understood well the prince's discourse. But he dared not contribute to Zhu Gaozhi's argument, preferring instead to affect that it was the prince who had insulted him. He watched Zhu Gaozhi leave the hall and stumble towards his waiting sedan chair. After lifting the prince, the four sedan carriers moved towards the Inner Palace.

The ministers had since dispersed, leaving Zhu Di and Zheng He alone.

"Do not blame him, Zheng He. Aside from frolicking with his Korean concubines, our son has no grasp of the world outside the Middle Kingdom. Vision, he lacks."

Zheng He had known for years that he could not disagree with his emperor.

***

The Visitors

Behind the three Great Halls, there stood a large gate attended by palace soldiers. This, the Gate of Heavenly Purity led to the Inner Palace where one could find the private quarters of the emperor, princes and concubines. On this day, due to the sprawling number of guests, the entrance to the Inner Palace was even more heavily guarded.

Soldiers stood on both sides of large bolted doors, barring the way to any royal family member who did not qualify as either prince or duke. Only highly ranked military officers, those below the second grade, such as Zheng He, or officials of the third grade were permitted to penetrate the gates without a memorandum.

While court members were turned away, two guards recognized the prince's sedan.

"Make way, make way."

A guard suddenly called out.

"Stop! You there! Stop!"

Zhu Gaozhi's disciplined carriers hesitated. They were still a good six yards from the gate. Ahead of them, the soldier had interpolated two foreign visitors.

At first Zhu Gaozhi paid no heed to his halted sedan chair. Nor did he notice the translator being ushered into the courtyard to parlay with the foreigners. His mind remained in the Hall of Central Harmony where his father had humiliated him before the admiral.

He knew that their views on state policy diverged but that is not what had vexed him. No, that, he could ignore because one day, he would be emperor and he would change this defiled, corrupt government.

What troubled Zhu Gaozhi was Zhu Di's bitterness and the nagging references the emperor enjoyed making about his son's lack of military involvement. Why does he always behave as if I have failed him?

Years ago at the siege of Beijing, they had all thought him clumsy and sickly. But he had proved them wrong. He had distinguished himself. Had his father forgotten?

Zhu Gaozhi felt confused that Zhu Di could have chosen him as heir and yet failed to truly see him or understand his ideas. His mind wandered to that year when he had defended Beijing against Emperor Jianwen, who his father had since deposed. Emperor Jianwen had sent General Li to take Beijing, but Zhu Gaozhi had held on to the city. It was now twenty-two years ago. But he remembered it as if it were yesterday. The anger he had felt...

In the aftermath, it was Zheng He who had taken most of the credit. Ingenious, they had said. The young Ma He, barely twenty then, had dug a dike, the Zheng village dike. This had disrupted the flow of enemy supplies and delayed General Li's troops. The Zheng village dike had bought enough time for his father, the Prince of Yan, to arrive and charge onto Li's confused soldiers.

That's when it had all begun. If one listened to the rumors, Ma He could *wade through boiling water and scorching flame*. And then his father's favorite eunuch had been renamed Zheng He. Since then, he had been one of his father's closest confident.

Zhu Gaozhi felt sick. He wanted to lie down in his bed with his concubines. But when the sedan failed to pursue its course towards the imperial chambers, he lifted the yellow drapes to evaluate the situation.

"What is it? Why aren't we moving?"

"Your Highness, we apologize for the delay. There was an intruder."

"I see." His eyes pierced across the square towards a broad, white-clad figure. He looked like one of the foreign merchants who had arrived two years ago and who had enjoyed the imperial hospitality at the expense of...

He waved away those unpleasant thoughts.

"Your Highness, we have advised the man that his female companion may not enter without a memorandum. But he insists. The translator is useless. The man is saying that his companion will be very upset and he implores that she be allowed to visit the palace."

"Upset? Whatever for?" cried Zhu Gaozhi. I need to lie down now, he thought.

"They are from Zanzibar, Your Highness. They say they are returning home without having seen the new palace. It is a very long journey... The man says, without having seen this beautiful place they feel that they will never return and that—"

The prince wiped his sweaty brow. "Enough, Enough. My father's palace seems a veritable attraction these days. Move along!" Then he let the curtain drop with a grunt.

The sedan carriers resumed their passage through the Gate of Heavenly Purity. As they did, the prince attempted to forget his dreary thoughts. He distracted himself by regarding the foreigners.

The man was comely, thick around the waist with long dark locks framing his anxious face where black hair grew in abundant curls. They were hairy these barbarians, noted Zhu Gaozhi with tired amusement.

But it was the man's companion who attracted the prince's attention. The woman was veiled from head to toe and yet stood in a commanding manner. Zhu Gaozhi could only see her eyes. He was moved by the silent way in which she watched him pass with what seemed like envy and interest.

The hirsute man attempted to nudge her away but the veiled woman would not desist. She remained there, staring at the gates, animated by a grave purpose. There was something dignified about this Arabian woman. Zhu Gaozhi had always been impressed by them, as with all women if truth be told. He peered out of the sedan.

"Halt there for a moment. You!"

A young soldier ran towards the prince and bowed low. Zhu Gaozhi handed him a slip of paper with his personal seal.

"See to it that the woman is given a memorandum. Just the woman, no man must enter."

***

Min Li's Chamber

The sun had no sooner flitted behind the yellow-tiled roofs of the Purple City that two women of the court held a secret meeting in the concubine quarters.

The first, a lady in her late thirties was clad in black silk from head to toe. She wore a full-length skirt and a circle cape. A purple sash was wrapped many times above her waist. Its long threads were tied into an intricate knot from which hung all manner of jade amulets in deep set greens and purples. The lady wore no jewelry save for two emerald jade pendants that hung from her long lobes.

There was a stern air on her defiant face and it did much to mar her charm. She stood behind a mirrored vanity cabinet in a chamber sprawling with cats. Beside this royal princess, Min Li sat on a stool, much occupied with her toilette, a cat curled at her feet.

The princess could not suppress a glance over Min Li's pale breasts, bound tightly as they were beneath a sheath of red silk. Her clandestine gaze fell upon two tender mounds before caressing the concubine's neck and reaching her bewitching oval face. Min Li's detangling gestures were like a dance. One could very much lose oneself...

She averted her gaze just as Min Li suddenly turned around, flicking her hair back in protest. As though sensing the tension, the black cat raised its ears.

"My mind is made up, Princess Xia. I will not go."

"The emperor—"

"For this once, let us assume that favorite concubine has been beset by a sudden female inconvenience."

"And what sudden inconvenience could afflict this concubine?" replied the princess, sliding the jade pin into Min Li's bun. The dangling beads rattled above the concubine's earlobe.

"You forget one thing, Min Li. He is expecting no other."

Princess Xia reached for a lacquered box, removed the lid and pressed two index fingers onto the rouge. After warming the pomade with her palms, she began to apply this make-up onto Min Li's cheeks. Her fingers moved with slow intimate movements, loving the face and gazing intensely into the concubine's eyes.

But Min Li averted her gaze.

"It is perhaps improper but the emperor may have to be deceived this once," she said.

Princess Xia jerked herself away from the commode, startling the indignant cat to its paws. "There is nothing we could do. And even if it were possible, I will not. You know that this is beyond my power and I would be infringing all the court protocols."

"I beg you to intercede on my behalf. You could have the eunuchs dispatch Zhou Guiren instead of me. I wager she will be only too willing."

"And that she would! But how does that advance you? And what do you expect of the emperor once he has ears of your stratagem? No. It is far too impudent."

Princess Xia paced the room picking up clothing with her slender, transparent hands. Maids should have performed this task. But the two women had dismissed them. They always did.

Princess Xia frowned. "And you will be caught. Whatever it is you are plotting... You will be caught."

She paused.

"When you were younger you were always running around. Always making trouble..."

She caught a glimpse of Min Li's insistent gaze in the mirror. "Min Li, what is this ploy? Have you considered the consequences?

"I have."

There was a long silence before Princess Xia replied with a hiss, "This concubine is very stubborn. They should have bound this concubine's feet."

She spun around.

"You think I am cruel to you if I do not help you? I am not cruel. Ever contemplated the pain other women face? Look around you, Min Li. Women of the palace are intimate with pain. They understand pain and they do not ask for more than their lot. They have long learned to cherish what they have and to accept their roles. It is virtue."

Min Li was amused by Princess Xia's tone. She observed with much indignation that even with her bound feet, the princess was far from an obedient woman. She was about to share this but she held her tongue, out of respect.

At last, she smiled, belying her inner turmoil.

"You suspect me of strategy. What strategy do you speak of?"

"What fool does not know her own daughter?" replied the princess in a tired voice.

"I don't know what you mean," said Min Li, looking away.

"Min Li, do you remember that snowy night with the Grand Admiral? What you told me? I saw a flame burn in you, one that has yet to burn out."

Min Li winced.

The lady continued. "I have always suspected it. Always! But the Purple Palace makes one mute. After many years, I have learnt to keep all that is not spoken, unspoken. We are all very good at it. Aren't we? But I have more experience than you, Min Li. Believe me. What you are planning is dangerous. If he catches you..." The princess bit her lips. "If he catches you, I can do nothing for you."

Still Min Li did not reply. She had already gone to a place where even Princess Xia could not reach her. *Yes, I am very good at it.* But Princess Xia was wrong. Experience had nothing to do with anything. One could learn so fast in the palace, age scarcely mattered.

A distant drum resounded, marking the first *geng*. The two women froze. Min Li looked alarmed.

"It is time," she whispered. "My mind is made up and I will not turn back. I implore you, Princess Xia. Please, help me."

Her adoptive mother approached. She held the concubine's little hands into her own and smiled. She ached to hold Min Li close but maintained her position. Her face grew severe. An icy expression had replaced the loving gaze.

"Tonight, the eunuchs shall come to your chamber to escort you to His Majesty. When they come, I shall greet them. Zhou Guiren will be sent in your place. She has always coveted my emerald pendant. I am certain she will find the arrangement to her favor. As for the emperor," she sighed, "let us hope that he is too drunk and too enamored of his own grandeur to notice the difference."

Min Li dropped at Princess Xia's feet, embracing her gratefully. They were interrupted by the arrival of a servant eunuch who tapped on the door. Min Li rushed to greet him and Princess Xia saw that hidden below his tunic, inside a little brocaded pouch, he carried red ink and paper.

"So then, it is as I suspected," said the princess, her voice colder still.

"Will you help me?" asked Min Li.

"I know a eunuch who will do it. When you give the signal, tonight, the eunuch will approach Zheng He," said Princess Xia. "You do remember, don't you? What I taught you?"

"Yes."

As the stationary eunuch left, Min Li took a careful glance outside to assure that none had seen him. The courtyard was empty. Good.

But as she was about to close the door, she glimpsed a figure behind the wooden screen of the left wing. It seemed to be waiting for something before it finally stirred and walked away. The figure was veiled so that Min Li could not identify the owner's face. Her heart skipped a beat. She observed the smooth, gliding gait and watched an olive-skinned hand adjust the owner's black robe. Min Li held her breath.

The stranger hastened away, her furtive footsteps barely audible on the courtyard tiles. Min Li knew instantly. It was a woman. A woman who does not belong in this palace, pondered the concubine. How very strange.

She closed the door. She could not be certain who this woman was. She hoped it was just a servant and nothing would come of it. To hell with it, she thought, I cannot stop now.

She would go along with the plan even if it meant her death.

Chapter 2
Porcelain and Intrigue

Two blue-clad eunuchs busied themselves not far from the three main halls of the Imperial Palace. The one with a brown birthmark on his left cheek moved silently past the vast copper urns. He had a melancholy air about him. He took his time, verifying that the urns were filled before making markings on his wooden tablet. A fire was the last thing they needed tonight.

"Zhijian!" called out his companion. "Do you take me for a fool? You've been checking those urns for the last hour now. I know you well enough. You'd do anything to be in that hall and take a peek at her. But we're not supposed to be here!"

Zhijian continued his inspection. The other eunuch sighed.

"Enough. We must leave. Everything is ready. Make haste!"

The two eunuchs shuffled towards Xihuamen, the Western Gate. They saluted the guards and made their way out of the palace. But Zhijian, upon passing the central archway, his wooden tablet in hand, appeared to hesitate. He gave one last longing glance towards the three great halls. His companion turned around and gave him a friendly nudge.

"Come on, lover boy. Cease your dreaming."

They disappeared towards the Fire and Water Department to close their shift.

Everyone in Beijing knew that the new Imperial Palace was rife with celebrations tonight. For days, the *Silijian*, the Directorate of Ceremonial had worked under pressure to organize this stately banquet, dispatching orders to the relevant departments in the imperial city.

The eunuchs were intent on making it a glorious success. They had been told that the emperor wished to farewell foreign dignitaries from many parts of the world before these were to leave the Middle Kingdom. For this prestigious gathering, and to honor the inauguration of his prized palace, Zhu Di had elected to hold a banquet in the Hall of Preserving Harmony.

Red, oblong lanterns lined the roof eaves of each building. On this misty night, they floated like incandescent ghosts in vaporous state. The palace eunuchs had erected torches along the majestic path, starting from the Meridian Gate then up the marble stairway to the Hall of Supreme Harmony all the way to the Hall of Preserving Harmony. It was along this wondrous path that groups of lowly eunuchs carried official sedan chairs loaded with guests. As they reached the hall's entrance, the carriers lowered the rectangular canopied chairs while officers greeted the attendees.

Thousands had been invited. Half were couched inside the Hall of Preserving Harmony. Officers above the third grade and foreign merchants of modest repute remained outside, under temporary sheds erected for the occasion.

Inside the hall, guests were arranged around low square tables. These radiated outwards from the imperial throne where Zhu Di sat before a spacious table. Before being seated, each attendee kowtowed five times before the emperor.

Despite the large congregation, it was in fact, a restricted gathering. Those present included the heir apparent, Zhu Gaozhi and his family, the emperor's higher ranking concubines, the other princes and their wives, a select number of ministers, the higher ranking civil and military eunuchs and the soon to depart foreign delegates who sat beside official translators. As chance would have it, perhaps a large enough gathering for Min Li to execute her plan without raising attention.

***

Min Li Watches

If he had observed her early at the banquet, the emperor would have noticed that Min Li was nervous.

She sat beside Xun Guifei and Mei Guifei, two ladies of noble virtue and refined talent who tonight were more concerned with their coiffures than talking to a second ranking concubine. Every few moments, these ladies exchanged understated glances only to resume their silent evaluation of Min Li, eyeing her like two possessed demons. But Li Guifei did not notice this. Her mind was elsewhere.

Because at the far western edge of the room, opposite her and sitting upright like an impenetrable tower, was the woman she had spotted this very afternoon in the courtyard of the Inner Palace. This realization made her uneasy. Whenever Admiral Zheng He disappeared from her line of sight, Min Li switched her focus to steal carefully concealed glances in the intruder's direction.

She was veiled, save for a pair of magnificent green eyes lined with kohl and generous curled lashes. Her gaze was underlined by a curious blend of pride and compassion. It pierced through a horizontal slit, spanning from the base of her brow to the middle of her nose and linked by a filigree silver chain. A broad tasseled ornament crowned the woman's veiled forehead. As the torch lights reflected on that silver mesh, colored shadows seemed to dance inside those green eyes giving them a warm, humid glow.

Early in the evening, the banquet official had introduced the barbarian woman as a tributary envoy from some country whose name Min Li did not recognize but which only served to further pique her curiosity. Everything about that woman, from her dark kaftan whose collar and broad sleeves were stitched with silver embroidery, to her tanned wrists, even the dark ivy-like patterns on her palms and fingers, all fascinated Min Li.

But it was the poised yet provocative manner of the barbarian woman that both outraged and captivated our concubine. The foreign woman sat with one wrist dangling carelessly on her raised bent knee, while the other leg was folded beneath her. There was something unpolished, yet terribly at ease with this woman.

Although none in the Hall of Preserving Harmony could see the foreigner's face, it seemed to Min Li that all the other palace ladies and even the military officers present also scrutinized the veiled woman. And they probably noticed the same thing, she thought. All the time, while her table companions spoke, the veiled barbarian remained silent while her eyes vibrated with a stealthy alertness that put their own curiosity to shame.

Min Li's contemplation was interrupted by the appearance of the catering eunuchs. The dishes were finally being served. The imperial banquet officer pronounced a few words, prompting good cheer from the audience. Guests presented their cup to the emperor who evinced a faint smile before drinking from his own.

And then began to appear, dishes that drew praises from every table. Servants ushered in hundreds of sumptuous, colorful platters prepared with the finest fresh ingredients. Hungry eyes soon feasted on the glossy lacquered ducks, the sweet almond chicken on its bed of ornately cut vegetables, rich venison, aromatic steamed buns filled with mashed beans and sweet meats, crispy pork, still drizzling from the imperial oven fires and yard-long fish braised to perfection.

Dishes came in hundreds, all resting on renowned Ming blue porcelain and gilded black enamel plates of various sizes. Jade bowls offered bird's nest soup and hearty pig trotters' soup, while skewers of spicy mutton imported from the North Western lands formed pyramids on red enamel platters. A sunflower-shaped jade bowl, heaped with sticky dumplings, emanated a fine ginger aroma on every table. It found its place beside a generous mound of white steamed rice towering over a heated porcelain platter. As guests partook of these lavish dishes, the room echoed with a crescendo of clicking lacquered chopsticks.

Min Li was too absorbed with her plan to think much about eating. It was her good luck that the secluding screen reserved for concubines consisted of several loosely hinged wooden panels. She had changed the angle of her body so that the slit between these panels gave her a unique view of the other tables in the hall. Through the bevy of eunuchs serving guests and offering wine, she could and was still watching Admiral Zheng He. Occasionally, her right hand fiddled with the gilded threading of her table mat where rested a set of barely touched porcelain saucers and bowls.

Tonight, she thought, my appetite will betray me. So for the remainder of the evening, she called the servants requesting this and that dish. When they arrived, she neglected the previous one for some imagined defect and eyed the new platters with a feigned air of gourmand envy.

The truth was that she had lost her appetite months ago. *After that night*, after what she had seen, anyone would lose interest in food. But she could not allow the two heavily rouged phoenixes who shared her table to suspect her preoccupations.

There were few moments when she could see him. And this, she reflected, may very well be the last. He ate quietly the Grand Admiral. He engaged the other admirals with a reserved yet understanding air. She guessed that they were discussing the upcoming journey. At times he would laugh and a tender dimple on the right side of his lips appeared, giving him a joyous air that rendered him younger than his years. Min Li noticed he enjoyed the mutton and the ginger dumplings, which he ate with relish.

At times he spoke slowly, just a few sentences but it captivated the attention of the other high-ranking eunuchs and had them nodding in profound agreement as if they shared a secret pact or a language that others would never understand. Perhaps it was the language of the sea, or the language of men who are free, she contemplated. She envied them. She wanted so much to talk to him but tonight, she had no place there.

Halfway through the evening, he had ceased eating, losing himself in a private reverie. He appeared engaged with the rest of his circle but Min Li speculated that if she had been able to look into his eyes at this very moment, she would have noticed, what she wanted to believe, that he was not happy. But she was weary of projecting her own melancholy onto him. How long since they had last spoken? Three, no... Over three years.

His eyes sparkled at the arrival of dessert. Zheng He had a sweet tooth. She smiled. When we met, you were biting into an almond sweet. I remember, she thought. I so like watching you, but you, you do not even see me, she sighed.

Her attention turned towards her emperor. How different they were. Since she had little to lose now, she found herself comparing the two.

As per tradition, Zhu Di sat alone before a two-tiered table laden with an array of dishes. Her expression darkened as she watched the man who had controlled her life for over ten years. She watched him carry out his precious dining rituals.

At the introduction of each dish, Zhu Di waited while a trusted eunuch dipped a few drops of a gray substance inside his food to test it for poison. Satisfied with the test, the emperor would reach out into the dish with his chopsticks and bring colorful morsels of food into his appreciative lips. Min Li wondered where he had found this new appetite. She knew very well that he fasted often. All this opulence, this magnanimity, this largesse with guests and the princes, yes... All that was pure show. She had since realized but at what cost? How many years had it taken? She bit her lips.

Tonight could very well change my life. It is tonight or never. *Now, dearest Princess Xia, I will show you how brave I am or I will die.* And she smiled, thinking about Zheng He.

The banquet was well advanced now. And then, during the parade of sweet cakes and fruit, when the room became filled with a pleasant mellow ambience, Min Li's heart skipped a beat. She noticed Zheng He stand and make his way to the envoy table in the back. Her heart beat faster. The Grand Admiral was walking towards the barbarian woman.

"Why, you seem so ashen, Little Sister. Are you not well?"

Xun Guifei was staring at her. The violent red of her lips seemed suddenly accentuated.

Seeing that Min Li did not respond, Mei Guifei also took up to the game.

"Do you know," she began, still chewing her duck with a faked insouciant air. "Do you know that the seafaring eunuchs have taken quite a liking for the foreigners they escort?"

"It is what I heard," agreed Xun, knowing well that Mei had only made the remark to stir Min Lin.

"It is because they share the same religion," attested Mei as she now tucked into the dessert dishes with a malicious glimmer in her eyes. "They understand each other well."

"One must suppose they would if we consider that they have traveled together all these years," confirmed Xun, scrutinizing Min Li for any signs of jealousy.

I have nothing to fear, thought Min Li. Even if they had seen her observe Zheng He, only Princess Xia knew of her devotion to the admiral.

"Xun Guifei, I do not think anyone can understand these eunuchs," she dismissed. "Let alone put up with smelling them for an extended period of time," she quipped. It was an allusion to the incontinence problem that plagued some eunuchs all their lives, following their major operation. Her joke had the desired effect. Her rouged companions were soon engaged in peals of laughter.

Min Li scanned the court ladies in search of Princess Xia. Meanwhile, Zheng He was now in full conversation with the envoys. The musicians were enthralled by their own performance while all eyes were on the exquisite desserts. She resolved to forget about the veiled woman even if this one had heard something. There was no turning back.

It was time to execute her plan. Min Li sought the princess. She had always thought Princess Xia was like a cat. She would often dress in black and her limbs moved like those of a cat. That and she seemed to have the gift for sensing when she was being watched and knowing where that gaze came from.

It did not take long. Princess Xia raised her powdered face from her wine glass and the two women's eyes met across the hall. It was time. In response, Min Li touched her right jade earring. Then she used her right hand to touch the wrist of her left arm. Princess Xia nodded.

***

The Clumsy Servant

At the larger envoy table, discussions were rife about naval trade.

"It is rumored that the Folangji have grown interested in our affairs," the opulently robed Kareem said in Arabic.

It was a language that Zheng He understood and the translator did not bother to intercede. Zheng He had met Kareem and his family when he had first visited Zanzibar in Eastern Africa. That was now seven years ago and since then, a mutual trust had been established between the East African merchants and the Ming empire.

Zheng He seemed at ease as they conversed. The two had sailed many days together.

"The Folangji could very well present us with some difficulties, it is true. It is not a question of competition. I believe that competition is healthy for trade."

"They are bandits!" protested Kareem. "Bandits and barbarians! They take what isn't theirs but they take it in the name of their God." He shook his head with gravity. "No, my friend, it is a most unpleasant business."

"But to date, I do not believe the Folangji are aware of our route around the East African coast," offered Zheng He to reassure him.

"And what calamity if they did! I am certain they would like nothing better than to sail across the oceans and take over our trades."

During this animated exchange, the veiled woman remained impassive. Her eyes searched the room. The woman intrigued Zheng He and he had always felt uncomfortable around her. Kareem was now speaking passionately.

"San Bao, there are those who say the Folangji are working together. It is said that they have dispatched a spy in our mist. It is believed this person is well aware of our navigational patterns, our routes, our contacts. He knows us well enough and could even take hold of your navigation maps. Imagine the consequences – what this would mean for trade in our seas..."

Zheng He laughed at his friend's lavish conspiracy theory. "Surely you do not mean, Da Conti?" he asked. "The eunuchs' report is very clear in this respect. He is a most cultured, virtuous individual with no political aspirations. I can assure you that your suspicions are unfounded."

"But it's most certain! That is the very man, I assure you. He is highly determined and influential. He even speaks fluent Arabic. Almost as good as yours! Who knows what his true intentions are. I'd keep a watchful eye on your maps if I were you."

"Rest assured. As always, those maps will be closely guarded, my friend," said Zheng He. "I will take no chances."

At this moment, a Zamorin merchant who had followed the discussion through his translator now intervened.

"Pardon me, Admiral, supposing that they, the Folangji, do set out as far as you have, do you think... What do you think will happen to us?"

"Much is said of their ways," said Zheng He to the dark man sitting opposite Kareem. "It is said they do not share our vision of the world. As you know, our imperial fleet is diplomatic. Aside from thwarting off dissidents and pirates, we do not bend others to religions or ways of being. From the accounts I have heard, one cannot say the same of the Folangji."

But the Zamorin merchant, though his main source of income depended on trade with the Ming and the Arabs, was not convinced. He did not understand the generalized view of foreigners held by the unduly self-righteous people of the Middle

Kingdom. He believed in the progress of global trade and that all people, regardless of where they came from, were animated by honest intent. When his translator had finished speaking, the dark man thought for a moment before replying.

"Then perhaps...these Folangji you speak of, perhaps, they too, are just eager to trade?"

"We can only hope. *Insha'Allah*," replied the admiral.

It seemed to Zheng He just now, that the veiled woman gave a sudden jerk, almost as if she had been stirred from contemplation by something unpleasant. That something was unrelated to their political conversation because her eyes remained anchored to the other end of the room.

Kareem extended a benevolent smile towards her. "My dear cousin, you are very quiet tonight. Is the quality of the food not to your liking? You have not eaten much. Are you finding this night tiresome?"

Kareem was often brazen and in his comfortable friendship with Zheng He, he had no qualms about exposing his fiancée's discomfort, even if this undermined Ming hospitality. It was his honest manner, jovially speaking his mind while meaning no harm that Zheng He appreciated.

Zheng He looked to the lady across him and he noted the glint in her eyes in response to Kareem's remark.

"On the contrary," she mused, placing careful weight on each word. "I am enjoying this night very much."

Her Arabic was graceful. When she said the word for night, *leil*, her l's resounded sensually, like smooth, flowing water. Deep murky waters nevertheless, felt Zheng He. This impression, he kept to himself. But he could not help shuddering when he heard the rest.

"And you know..." she added, pausing dramatically, "the night is about to take an even more interesting turn."

At this solemn declaration, Kareem shrugged his shoulders and resumed eating his sweet buns. As for Zheng He, he could not bring himself to comment. The woman always seemed to belong to another time and often, she would utter words as though she expected everyone to have returned from the same mental journey, as though her shared observations were the most natural thing in the world. Kareem seemed used to it. But for Zheng He who understood her less, it was most puzzling. The lady was unfathomable.

It was while Zheng He was considering whether to return to his table or to further question his female guest that a eunuch presented himself to their table with a platter of sesame seed pastries. The servant sought to lean over and offer the platter to the admiral first but in his eagerness he seemed to trip on the carpeted floor. The platter landed with a loud clamor, knocking over and spilling the contents of a wine carafe.

"Oh, so sorry, so sorry, so, so sorry," muttered the servant in a profusion of kowtowing, all the while shaking his head and dabbing a cloth on the wet table. He moved in a deliberate motion and managed a clumsy brush past the admiral's sleeve as he re-ordered the platters.

At this, Zheng He suddenly recoiled from the servant, his face flushed with anger. In a flash, he leapt from his seat. His fingers curled around the jade hilt at his waist. The servant cowered under the admiral's furious gaze.

"Traitor!" whispered Zheng He, drawing out his sword under the befuddled glance of several onlookers. The servant's face grew ashen. A collective murmur overcame the surrounding tables.

Unaware of the scene, the emperor had not flinched. He continued to eat. But at the far end of the hall, Min Li blanched and sat up on her seat. Under the table, the skin on her knuckles grew white.

"*Salaam*, my friend," said a voice while the owner's hand was placed calmly on the admiral's forearm. It was the veiled woman. The admiral hesitated.

Without a word, he re-sheathed his sword. The servant hurried away. Zheng He spun on his heels and faced the front of the hall. He glared at the wooden partition. Through the narrow slit, Min Li saw the look of contempt in his eyes. Her breath halted. She clutched the jade pendant around her throat, swallowing painfully.

As though remembering where he was, the admiral bowed towards the emperor and sat back down with reluctance. His table companions remained in an awkward silence, confused by the incident. They exchanged furtive glances, not knowing what to say and when to say it.

Only Kareem had found the courage to resume talking. He was self-engaged in a series of "ohs" and "ahs" as he dipped into the desserts, marveling at the different sweets with delight.

As for Zheng He, he stared at the dessert platter with a grave expression. It appeared to most of them that he also blushed but they attributed this to his embarrassment. Then, without warning, he stood, bowed with great dignity and returned to his table.

As he left, the veiled woman, again, shifted her position. Behind the opaque shroud shielding her face, not a soul could hope to glimpse the smile that now formed slowly but generously, on her lips.

***

Zhu Di Broods

Up to now, everything the emperor ate, he could not taste, so enthralled was he with his appearance and the way his guests perceived his grandeur.

The vexation he had endured earlier at the whim of his pedantic son, no longer perturbed him. After all, he had elected Zhu Gaozhi as his successor in the certainty that the prince would soon be succeeded by his son. In retrospect, there was little he could say to Zhu Gaozhi without them both descending into a disagreement of some sort. He had long since given up.

Halfway through the meal, Min Li caught Zhu Di's attention and he forgot about his son. She was becoming so skinny. One glance at the dishes left untouched before her and he surmised that the concubine's mind was at its most industrious.

To further fuel Zhu Di's scorn, she was ceaselessly fidgeting and peering at the far side of the hall. Another ruler may have overlooked this capricious female behavior but the astute Zhu Di knew well that in the last six months, his concubine had grown aloof.

He followed her gaze towards the back of the hall. An insipid sensation of discomfort clawed its way across his chest. Did the insolent bitch believe that no one would notice the direction of her glance through that wooden screen?

What is she up to? Whatever it is, he thought, I will find out tonight.

Chapter 3
The Princess and the Baby

Honored reader, let us leave the Beijing celebrations a while and discover a little more about this Min Li, for it is she who drives our story.

In 1368, Hongwu's army reconquered the city of Dadu from the Mongols. He renamed the city, Beiping. The existing Mongol concubines who had not fled or committed suicide became prisoners. Releasing them would invite treason or risk revealing imperial secrets. They were sent to do laundry outside the palace walls where they were supervised and lived miserably. It was not uncommon for Mongol captives to find themselves in the seedy, aptly named *education district* of Beiping where they would forever live an unchaste life.

In 1370, Beiping became the seat of Hongwu's son, Zhu Di. Ten years later, perhaps intrigued by the beautiful concubines he had seen in Beiping, Hongwu sought out new concubines from the North Western lands and had them brought to his capital. A feisty girl of fifteen years, Min Li's mother was taken to the palace of Yingtian where she joined Hongwu's Royal Chamber as a lesser consort. What became of her life and if she was ever happy, we will never know.

On June 24, 1398 when Min Li was barely five moons old, Emperor Hongwu died. Min Li's mother was destined for immolation in accordance with remnant Mongol customs. She, along with thirty-eight concubines, would follow the late emperor into the afterlife.

But days before the ceremony that would claim her life, the doomed woman created a scandal. Upon learning of Hongwu's death, she gave a wail and threw herself to the ground. She refused to bathe, dress or eat. She rocked forth and back, twisting her hands as though possessed.

Little remained of this broad-faced temptress who once inflamed the Mongols' lust. Years before, she was an exotic prize plucked from the fertile lands bordering the Altai Mountains. A prize fit for an emperor. Like her Hun ancestors, she remained fair but the waning light in her face now merged with the pallor of death. The seven braids that in her flirty youth she had once worn long were gone. Her hair was now a knotted mess veiling her tear-streaked face.

For six days before her immolation, during which she was pushed into Hongwu's grave, she haunted the grounds of the palace like a roaming ghost, unfed, distraught and uttering nonsense.

They let her be. For at the time, more serious trouble threatened Yingtian. In the days following Hongwu's death, vigilance reigned supreme in the imperial stronghold. The fortified Yingtian walls and ramparts were thick with soldiers, armed to the teeth. Hongwu's grandchild, Jianwen, heir to the dragon throne, was determined to protect his ascension. In an attempt to ward off contenders to the throne, he explicitly forbade his uncles, the late emperor's sons, to attend the funeral.

But the daring Prince of Yan did not heed this warning. Unrelenting, Zhu Di advanced his main guard unit towards Yingtian. And so the hysterics of a mad widow, a lowly concubine at that, was of no concern to the palace. Indeed, they let her be until her last moments.

Jianwen had only permitted the Prince of Yan's sons to attend the funeral. Escorting Zhu Gaozhi, Zhu Gaoxu and Zhu Gaosui, was Ma He and several other military eunuchs. Ma He was no longer the little boy from the clearing that we met earlier. He was now twenty-seven. He had been educated in palace etiquette and had spent years living in army tents in the Northern steppes while honing his military skills. Jianwen knew little of Ma He's close friendship with the Prince of Yan. To him, Ma He was just another eunuch.

The Prince of Yan's representatives reached the palace two days before the funeral. What happened then remains unclear. But on their arrival, while Ma He was being escorted by two other inner court eunuchs to his designated chamber, an agitated hunched figure shuffled along the Imperial Gardens and sprang up towards them.

The hideous form wore no makeup. She had not smoothed or combed her long black hair. Her eyes were haggard. They could smell her from afar because she had not bathed for days and had exerted herself. Her dirty skirt hung loose round her bruised flesh as though she had fallen many times and taken little care of herself. She came closer. Closer still... And then her eyes focused and she gave a sigh of relief.

"San Bao! It is you!"

"Hold, you should not be here!" shouted a guard trying to push her away.

She evaded him, shrieking like an animal. At once, she flung herself at Ma He's feet, speaking rapidly, her words erratic and disjoint. The young eunuch was taken off guard by this inappropriate display of emotion, more so given the delicate political circumstances.

Following his shattered youth in war-torn Yunnan, he had only known sword, battle and discipline. What to do then, with this broken woman who would not let go of his robe.

"We should find the other concubines," he advised. "They will calm this one."

The guards hesitated.

"Do not worry," said Ma He. "I will remain here until you return. You have my word."

Ma He was known for his charming, easy going nature and he was convincing enough.

The guards left him. Once alone, he gathered his courage.

"You are afraid of death. It has made you lose your mind. Stop this. Be strong."

"Oh, no San Bao, I go to my death with a light heart and no fear. But it is my little one... My poor little one..."

"You have a child?"

"A little daughter...a baby...my poor baby...they will take my baby!"

Ma He looked askance to see whether the guards had returned. The commotion had stirred the other ladies who now shuffled to the courtyard to see what was happening. Two princesses appeared in the doorway of a nearby building.

One of them, a young girl no older than twelve observed Ma He with vengeful eyes. When he noticed this girl, Ma He froze. She seemed older for her years and there was in her gaze something hateful and dark, as though she were reading his mind and mocking his weaknesses. At last, remembering the shadow at his feet, he spoke up.

"We could hide your baby," he lied.

The concubine at once lifted her face, delighted with the idea.

"Oh yes, yes! Hide my baby! Please, hide her!"

Ma He nodded, relieved with the idea but not at all convinced that he could carry it out. "She shall be raised in the palace and no harm shall be done to her," he continued, eager to calm the woman. It seemed to work because she loosened her rabid grip around his leg. She stared gravely at the eunuch.

"I have not made a choice, San Bao. But my daughter will. Please, help her, San Bao!"

How did she know his nickname? Ma He was about to ask but rising voices interrupted him. The concubine, too, was startled. She stood in fear and shuffled away towards the concubine chambers. Ceremonial officers chased her, resolved to control her frightful fits and prepare her for the burial rituals.

Ma He watched the eunuchs take her away still pondering over the name she had used to address him. At the far end of the courtyard, the young princess was still glaring at him with an insolent silence. Feeling self-conscious, he re-arranged his robe and adjusted his belt before following the eunuch escort.

"This is Princess Xia," one of them explained, sensing Ma He's awkwardness.

"Go back! Go! Go play!" riled the other one as they passed the princess.

Ma He noted that her eyes continued to shoot arrows in their direction.

"What is wrong with that girl?" he asked.

"Who knows..." replied the guard.

Two days later, the drugged and well-fed concubines were led to the burial chamber where they jumped into Zhu Yuanzhang's tomb. There, they were buried alive with him.

Ma He made plans to visit the nursery at the far Eastern end of the palace and become acquainted with the little baby. But when he again tried to enter the Inner Palace, he was turned away for security reasons. Disappointed and troubled for the child, he left. His concern for the baby girl, however, did not last.

There were other matters at stake. The Prince of Yan was determined to seize the throne from his nephew. Soon he would enter into battle against Jianwen's army.

"Ma He, you are the only one I trust with my secret. Conceal it well," confided Zhu Di when his loyal eunuch had returned from the burial ceremony and divulged security information.

No one knew what the scheming Prince of Yan plotted. For now, Zhu Di laid low, belying the wilful forces within him. He lived as a vagrant in the streets of Beiping. The rumors spread. In Jianwen's court and beyond, the news made a sensation. A beggar, the prince! They all thought he had gone mad.

But Ma He knew better. It was just a matter of time, he thought, just a matter of time. As the court would later find out, it was a grave mistake to ever underestimate how far the ruthless and wilful general could go. Years later, Zhu Di laid siege on his nephew's palace. He marched through Yingtian. In a near paranoiac bloodbath of mass murders and strategic imprisonments, he purged the royal family of its Jianwen supporters.

And what of the little girl? About a year following Hongwu's death, after her princely family perished in a mysterious fire, Princess Xia survived the flames. Once settled in her new home in Beiping, she soon found and adopted the child. How very odd it was to see this wilful girl focus her solemn gaze towards an infant and indeed, to have found her calling as mother of an orphan much like herself. Visiting the nursery gave her purpose.

Princess Xia had no time for anyone but for this little one, she had all the time in the world. It was still unclear who the father had been and it was assumed that, not Hongwu, but rather one of the princes may have had a clandestine encounter with the unfortunate concubine.

There was an understated belief in the palace that Min Li was special. Since her mother had demonstrated loyalty to the emperor, this little girl, born in the first lunar month, in the last year of the reign of Hongwu, would be raised with care.

Yet for now, she remained insignificant. It seems she was never officially registered as one of Hongwu's twenty-six sons and sixteen daughters.

Chapter 4
The Pain of Children

Five years after Emperor Hongwu's burial, during an official visit to Yingtian, Ma He once again found himself embroiled in a rare, sordid incident.

As he emerged from a private hearing with Emperor Zhu Di, and passed through Yingtian's Inner Palace, a pig-tailed little girl appeared. At first he was startled by a flash of rose tunic and red slippers. This little angel seemed to be on a frantic chase, stomping her tiny feet across the private courtyard just behind the Imperial chambers. Two flowery tassels pinned to her dark hair bopped up and down as she ran. There was great distress in the girl as she looked for an escape in every direction and emitted short sighs to catch her breath.

But more perplexing were the girl's pursuers. Encumbered by their full-length silk robes, a string of flustered and cursing eunuchs, led by a heavily powdered nursery matron chased after the child. Further afield, stumbling on her bound feet was the distraught Princess Xia, now in her late teens.

At that moment, Ma He was beaming from a recent promotion. During the New Year celebrations, Emperor Zhu Di, still jubilant from his victory over Jianwen, had showered him with attention. The emperor had given his loyal Hue eunuch a new name. It was the promise of a new beginning. It opened doors. And Zheng He was a fine new name.

Zheng He's service as supervisor of Civil Engineering had been highly commended. Over the years, his knowledge of weapons and ship construction had surpassed expectations. All at the court were impressed at his ascension. And today had been the best day of his life.

Today, he had been once more summoned by his emperor. He had been given the imperial order to build and lead a navy of a hundred thousand strong and use it to ward off the marauding Japanese pirates. The emperor had cited Zheng He's practical and progressive mind as perfect for the task.

For all his recent awards, our Zheng He found himself distracted by the little girl's cries. Glorious images of potential success, of journeys as far as Arabia, images that anyone in his situation would have entertained with relish, vanished as the girl approached.

It happened fast. He was knocked off balance by the desperate child who clung to his robe. Responding to an impulse, he leaned forward, lifting her with his long arms. The exhausted girl found herself warmly cushioned by the eunuch's welcoming chest. She eagerly gazed back into his face to better take in the giant before her. Her untidy locks dripped with sweat. She seemed ready to doze off after her strenuous escapade.

"Well, little one. This is no way for a palace lady to behave."

The girl tightened her grip around his neck and buried her tear-streaked face in his cape. She thought for an instant that he smelt sweet and absorbed the aroma that only children can discern and judge as good or bad. He smelt so good.

The nursery eunuchs gathered round Zheng He. They bowed in deference stifling their frustrations.

"You will hand the child over!" pronounced the matron.

"So much running cannot be good for the palace peace," remarked Zheng He, waiting for an explanation.

"Little pest ran away from the nursery... Ran off, just as we prepared the foot lotion!"

"These things happen all the time. But she is a clever one," added the other eunuch, reaching forth to grab the girl.

But Zheng He stepped back and glowered at him.

"I see. You mean to bind the girl's feet."

Neither the Mongols nor his own people in Yunnan bound their women's feet. Due to his upbringing, he himself was adverse to foot binding. Seeing women toddle in the streets by the portside or in the marketplace made him cringe. He hesitated. Following Ming rule, the practice had returned, even spreading to the countryside.

He remembered what an old Hue nurse had explained to him, back when he was a little boy. "The city women of the Middle Kingdom have their feet bound at a very young age," she had explained. "The little girls' feet are tightly bandaged, like so. Their toes are broken then bent in, right under the sole."

She had described how the bandages were tightened every four days so that soon enough, the second, third, fourth and fifth toes were merged under the sole.

"What happens then?" he had asked, horrified.

"Their feet will cease to grow. Sometimes their toes will fall off."

He had grimaced at this. Recently, his own physician had explained it all in ghastly details. "The lack of *qi* flow to the feet means that they begin to stink. The flesh rots. The women suffer pain for much of their lives and yet, they submit."

He had also learned that the pain did not end at feet. It spread to their knees, hips and shoulders. Old Yu's account had unsettled Zheng He.

He pressed the girl to his chest. What to do? It was not his place to defy palace order.

"Can you not see that she is afraid?" he asked. But he was not sure what to do as this situation was at odds with his military experiences.

"Foot binding can also be a form of discipline, Your Eminence," warned the eunuch matron through his pursed red lips.

Zheng He did not like the way he had said that. He felt himself grow tense as the matron continued.

"This child is most insolent! She can no longer remain in the imperial nursery. Let us bind her feet so that she may be betrothed to a prince or a marquis."

"So you see foot binding as a punitive measure then?" replied Zheng He coldly.

"No whippings are enough for this brat. It will do her good. Her own slut of a mother did not have bound feet. And look what happened to her!" puffed the matron.

"It is what is best for the child, Your Eminence," soothed in another eunuch in a honeyed voice.

"It will calm her roaming Mongol temperament," said the matron.

"Lest she lose her mind like her mother did," continued the other, reaching out once more for the girl. But Zheng He refused to let go.

"Her mother?" he asked. "Her mother was a Mongol?"

"A concubine with no name, Your Eminence..." dismissed the eunuch.

A vague memory stirred in Zheng He's mind.

"How old is this child?" he asked.

The eunuchs looked at each other, confused by the question.

"Well? How old is she?"

"Five years old, Your Eminence, but..."

Zheng He observed the child's features and understood who her mother had been.

"We will take her now. Give her back."

But Princess Xia who had finally reached the group began to shout, eyes ablaze.

"You will not take her! She will never return to the nursery, do you hear me?"

Seeing a royal princess take the child's defense, Zheng He understood what to do. Ignoring the matron's protests, he turned towards the child and pressed a finger on her nose.

"What is your name?"

"Min Li," she said with a pout.

"Very well, Min Li. Princess Xia will take care of you."

The princess rushed forth and took the child in her arms.

Zheng He turned towards the nursery attendants.

"Listen to me carefully. You will not bind her feet. I shall bring this incident to the attention of the director in charge of your department," he lied.

"But Your Eminence, this is against protocol! All children must—"

"Enough! Do not make me report you."

Zheng He's face had flushed red as he pronounced these words. Yet he ignored what had come over him and why he even felt a tinge of anger. It was this inner confusion that now prompted him to abandon the scene as soon as possible.

He began to pace towards the Northern palace gates where his sedan chair and carriers awaited. As he passed Princess Xia, he tried to avoid her gaze. They both remembered the promise he had made to Min Li's mother before she died. But as he later reflected, no one but the princess could have taken better care of the late concubine's child.

He saw himself with more important naval goals to attend to. Besides, he knew that it was not his place to guard infants. Women were better at this task. He felt at peace thinking of the pig-tailed girl in Princess Xia's steel arms. It gave him a strange comfort.

From the moment Min Li had come running towards him, he had wanted to help her. And while he would not have mustered the courage to do this had not Princess Xia also intervened, he secretly praised himself for his action.

No matter that thousands of other girls faced this pain every day, in almost all the provinces, they were remote from view. As such, he could ignore them since he was powerless to change these widely accepted cultural practices.

But when the girl's tiny arms had encircled his neck and she had buried her little nose on his shoulder, he had been unable to ignore her. He had felt her vulnerability, as if it had been his own.

And his own, he remembered it vividly. Like one remembers being bled alive.

He had promised himself he would never be that vulnerable again. But he could not forget. During daylight, the past lay dormant but at night it came in dreams and in sweaty chills to haunt him. This pain was etched so deep in him that, try as he might, he could not forget it. Yet he spoke to no one about it. What was there to tell?

For centuries, the Middle Kingdom had castrated its war prisoners like vulgar criminals. At least, he had lived, where his father, the great Ma Haji, disciple of Kublai Khan had been executed by Emperor Hongwu's commanders.

It was in 1381, soon after General Fu Youde's army had taken Kunming that his world collapsed. Boys of his age had been rounded up, chained and taken to the soldier camps. Ma He had been one of them. For days they were forced to march across the forest of the Southern provinces. They were shackled like ox and made to do menial work for the soldiers. Some were raped. Others disappeared in mysterious circumstances or were sold off to brothels. These boys were children but they were forced to be men. They endured the hunger, the thirst and the cruelty of the soldiers who taunted them in a manner so often observed in those who are fuelled by hatred and empowered by conquest.

These soldiers, they were young too and perhaps this war made little sense to them. And even if they did not at first hate their captives, they began to loathe them. For it was the only way they could give meaning to this senseless war. And so they beat them and kicked them forward, always towards the East.

Ma He saw the sun rise and set for many moons before General Fu Youde, recognizing the determination in Ma Haji's son, took him under his wing. He was sent to a smaller camp. There, at night, the elite boys cried for their slain families. They knew what would become of them. They were to be castrated and some of them would be sold off as slaves to wealthy households while others would be transported to coveted posts in the imperial cities of Beiping and Yingtian.

Back then, the little Ma He had a vague notion of what castration entailed. He understood that it must be something shameful and that only bad men were castrated. He knew enough about it to realize that it would forever engrave him as one who had been defeated and made prisoner. In future years, he would be reminded of that day when he had looked for support and for help but instead, had found himself alone, an orphan in this brutal world.

Ma He had never imagined that life would turn out this way for him. It seemed like only yesterday, rather than months ago, that he played with his boat alongside the Mosuo girl. Oh, the joy of that afternoon! What he would have given now, to listen to the chimes of her silver bracelets as she moved about in her pretty skirt. And it saddened him to recall how on that day, she had tried to tell him something and he had snapped at her. What had she said then? Ma He's tears rolled down his sunburnt cheeks. That he would be very tall. What a silly girl she was.

He drew in his chained ankles to keep his body warm. He wondered what had happened to her. He looked around in his cell, where some boys whimpered quietly while others moaned from the day's labor and the miserly food. Like him, they were all hungry and frightened. They grieved the loss of family, the loss of their home and the safe world they had known.

He felt small and miserable. Nothing could be worse than this. He could only pray, he thought, just pray. Pray to Allah that he would be safe. These were the longest nights in his life. They were spent waiting, and again waiting. Waiting for that day, and praying.

They came for him one morning. "Ma He, son of Ma Haji!" they announced and when he fearfully raised his hand, they dragged him, his weak legs dangling, out of the dirty cell. They led him to another building and then to a moist, dark chamber where he was asked to remove his clothes.

As he entered, his terror-filled eyes sized up the room. Four men stood there, waiting for him. Two of them carried themselves with authority and wore uniforms with a square insignia across their chest. Ma He assumed that they were surgeons or some sort of medical men. He saw a table where unknown objects were laid out. He saw a bench. His heart beat faster. In preparation for the surgery, he had only been allowed little water the night before and so his mouth was parched dry and he felt dizzy.

"Undress!" repeated the older surgeon.

He removed his tattered tunic and his worn trousers even folding them neatly as his mother had taught him. His pristine white cap, he no longer had. There were still two soldiers present and they eyed him, making lurid jokes. He knew from his parents' teaching that modesty was a virtue and that man should be well covered. As a reflex, he clasped his little hands in front of him to hide his nakedness. Recognizing his discomfort, but more likely as part of procedure, one of the surgeons ordered the soldiers to leave. But Ma He was far from relieved.

Once the soldiers had left, the surgeons began to prepare a dark brown concoction on the table. One of them, a young man who looked to be in his twenties approached Ma He and asked him to lie down on the broad bench. Taken aback, he watched the other surgeon tie up his hands while the two other assistants, held his legs spread on the bench. They moved in silence. They were focused and worked with swift decisive movements. They each knew what had to be done to ensure a castrate lived.

When he felt the ropes dig into his flesh, Ma He panicked. He could feel the blood thumping in his temples. He remembered what his father had taught him about the lot of criminals in the Middle Kingdom. But Ma He knew that he was not a criminal. He felt a need to protest. In vain, he tried to tell himself that what was happening to him now, on this bench, had nothing to do with what criminals endured. That it was only a medical inspection.

He began to cry, his breath short and fast. I am not here, reassured his inner voice. I am still in the clearing, playing with my boat, my precious wooden boat. Where is it now, he wondered. His family had fled Kunyang to seek refuge in Kunming. They had left their house by the lake and somewhere in that house, he knew was his boat.

They spread a brown paste across his loins and between his thighs. The sensation was warm and smooth but to Ma He it felt unnatural. They rubbed the paste in until he felt numb. After a while, he could no longer feel what they were doing to him. This terrified him even more. To avoid thinking about his ordeal, he attempted to remember the details of his boat and the sailing techniques his father had taught him.

And then he saw the knife. It was a curved knife with a blunt edge. Ma He grew faint. He could no longer think. All he could do was close his eyes and pray that he would pass out. He was too tired to scream and besides, screaming was not an option as he knew that no one, not a soul remained that could or would help him. He understood this well and the injustice hurt him even more than the knife ever could.

As numb as he was, he still felt the pressure of the knife. He felt it slide across, bringing with it waves of stinging, relentless pain. But at this point, Ma He's spirit was elsewhere. He was in the green leafy clearing and he was running towards the little girl with the silver bracelets. She had been crying. He had wrenched himself from his overprotective mother and had run back to console the Mosuo girl. "Please do not cry little girl. All is well now, I will play with you. I will be your friend. I will be your friend", he kept repeating over and over again. But as the pain intensified, and as his body jerked from side to side while still under the firm grip of the assistants, Ma He screamed until he lost consciousness.

In the dark comforting world of dreams, the little Hue found himself floating and in this carefree spirit state, it dawned on him that he did not even know the little girl's name. And soon it was too dark to think or feel.

The surgeons revived him. His hands and legs were freed. He looked down and could make nothing of the bloody mess. They reached out below his navel, dabbing him with a solution that stung like fire. He yelled from the pain.

"Boiled pepper," one of them said. "Just scream if it stings."

Ma He screamed pitifully, tears streaming down his blanched face. The boiled pepper solution was used to wash his wound three times before a tiny pewter plug was inserted where he would normally urinate. When the plug was pushed in, Ma He had already been through too much. He did not flinch.

The young assistant watched as Ma He's head lolled from side to side. The boy seemed to observe the treacherous world through an increasingly blurred vision. He barely emitted a whimper. The young assistant understood that he was in shock. He gestured to the others. They gripped the boy and held him up. Then they covered his wound with a cloth and asked him to stand. Trembling, his mouth parched, Ma He began to mutter inaudible requests for water.

The young assistant took pity on him. He held up Ma He's face and asked gravely, "Son of Ma Haji, do you want to live?"

Upon hearing his father's name, Ma He opened his eyes. Then, remembering where he was and that the man he loved and could never hope to emulate was dead, he swooned. The young man's grip was firm on his weak arm, sustaining him upright.

"Do you want to live, son of Ma Haji?" he repeated, locking eyes with him.

As waves of darkness beckoned him, Ma He could hardly make out the assistant's round face. Still, the young man's voice called to him. It was soothing. Finding a rope to hold on to, Ma He's eyes lit with hope. He held on.

"Yes, I do."

"Then wait. And do exactly what I tell you. Understood?"

Ma He nodded again. He sensed an ally in the assistant. In later years, that same man would become his personal physician, Yu Ling. But right now, it was a stranger's voice.

"Now listen to me. The hard part will be the coming days. Listen carefully. You must not drink for three days. Here, put your weight on my shoulder. We are going for a walk."

"Walk?" repeated Ma He with disbelief. The last thing he wanted to do was walk. He began to cry. But tears or no tears, the assistant held him up and walk they did, for almost three hours. Three hours that seemed like three days to Ma He. At the end, he felt that life had been drained out of him and he collapsed.

The next three days were unbearable for Ma He. He was given sparse food and was refused liquids no matter how much he begged for water. He was kept in a hospital bed alongside dozen others like him. He awoke on the second day to see the bed beside him empty. The boy next to him had died. Ma He understood that his life hung precariously between determination and despair. He promised himself that he would live and then he closed his eyes.

On the fourth day, they removed the pewter plug and for the first time, he looked at his mutilated body. There, between his legs, there was nothing left. Only thirteen years old, yet he was overcome with great shame and sadness.

When he urinated for the first time, the physician nodded and he was pronounced "fit to live". Others were not so lucky. Failing to urinate at all, meant impending death from organ failure. And those who could not urinate were beaten. The fear that the beating inspired compelled the boy to relieve himself but sometimes, even fear could not ward off the inevitable. Scores of young boys died.

But Ma He lived.

And now as a grown man, if he had contemplated what he had endured as a little boy, he would have glimpsed the reason for wanting to spare the lovely Min Li his own agony. She would one day discover the putrid feet and handicap of other women and she would be quietly glad.

But for Zheng He, there was no such gladness. Nor in fact was there the same sadness and shame that he had felt after his operation. Gone was the despair that had brought tears to his eyes when his father had died and when he found himself alone in General Fu Youde's camp. These days, Zheng He no longer reflected on his pain for very long. There was no point. After all, there were so many like him in the palace. And how they thrived!

This was life. He shunned the past. For the future was so much more promising and every month, every day, he climbed higher and higher. There was so much that could be achieved. Besides, over the many years at Zhu Di's service, the little Ma He had since forgotten the mysterious Mosuo girl. So too, did he blank out the memory of his parent's house by the lake and the little wooden boat that had once given him such delight. Why should he remember these things?

For now, he was Zheng He and he was no longer afraid. He was going to build a fleet.

Chapter 5
The Great Game

Yingtian, 1411

The Performer

While it is true that Min Li had escaped the pain of foot binding, she would later encounter pain of an entirely different sort. Because there exists many a torment in the path of human existence and those of the mind are often of the worse kind. But forgive your humble servant, honored reader. We are glimpsing ahead and we should perhaps begin from the beginning.

It is said that in the time of Zhu Di, there lived in Yingtian palace no less than two hundred concubines. Some had been plucked as young as thirteen from nearby *hutongs*. Indeed some of the most beautiful girls were said to originate from several districts in the palace's vicinity. Many had also been offered as gifts to the emperor. In some cases, these gifts were demanded as tribute to the Son of Heaven and the oppressed subjects would not dare refuse, obliging the ruler of the Middle Kingdom with great resentment.

The beauties of the palace had come from as far as the Jurchen tribes in the Northeast, from Korea, from Annam in the South but also locally, from reputed places like the Fujian province of the Middle Kingdom. Most of these beautiful women, unlike Min Li, had bound feet. The tradition of foot binding may have appalled the ruling Mongol women during the Yuan dynasty, but it nevertheless resurged under the Ming as it had in the Song Dynasty.

When Min Li was thirteen years old and, as Princess Xia's protégé, lived a blissful existence in the Yingtian palace, Zhu Di noticed her. It was an agreeable afternoon long after holding court and he was returning from a visit to the Directorate of Stationary where he had inspected new writing products. He had chosen to be escorted through the Imperial Palace Gardens. To what purpose, it was not known.

Through the drawn curtains of his higher vintage point, he could observe forty odd concubines whiling time in the gardens with the imperial princesses. Their faces shielded under colorfully painted bamboo parasols, the women idled in small groups, lost in animated discussions. The younger ones sang or climbed up stone structures, while others played hide-and-seek behind cave-like stone figures that gave life to this artificial landscape.

A large congregation caught the emperor's eyes and he ordered his eunuchs to come to a standstill. Several feet ahead, encircled by an audience of senior ladies, Min Li was talking with dramatic verve.

He could not hear but he could see. There was something highly convincing and enthralling about her delivery. She seemed to captivate others and mouth her words as if on a stage. When she talked, Zhu Di noticed that her hands free flowed about her as if to accentuate each idea and convey her passions more fully to her listeners. He noticed how she raised her right eyebrow in an erotic, yet playful way to engage her older friends. He noticed that her laugh, the only sound he could hear, had a troubling genderless quality. But there was nothing overtly boyish about this young girl. Her motions, while lively and certainly more energetic than those of her older counterparts, seemed all the more graceful in their fragile fluidity. A true performer, thought Zhu Di.

"Princess Xia's little friend," whispered one the escorting eunuchs who had at last caught on to the halted sedan. "She is His Majesty's half-sister."

Zhu Di waved his right hand with nonchalance to signal that the eunuchs could lift up the sedan chair and resume their return to his quarters. But his nuanced gesture also indicated that he wanted to have a closer look at the young girl. As they complied, edging closer to the group, the female congregation dispersed, making way for the emperor and his guards. The ladies bowed in respect, some hiding coyly behind their fans, others waving their handkerchief in a flirtatious gesture.

Min Li had ceased talking now. Alerted by the imperial presence near her cub, Princess Xia stood. The emperor's sedan remained for a short instant. But it was enough. Min Li bowed low towards her emperor. But no sooner had his sedan chair passed that she lifted her head and gave a furtive glance towards the man who, because he still peered through the drapes, was confronted by her insolence.

Princess Xia extended a warning glance towards Min Li until this one shifted her eyes away from the sedan. The princess was highly protective and while she put up with Min Li's nonsense from time to time, she complied with limits. No one should make eye contact with the emperor.

But Princess Xia was also a woman of infinite perception and her distressed gaze followed the sedan long after it had already disappeared into the main living quarters.

As for Min Li, she was enthralled by her cheeky encounter with her emperor and failed to see the troubled expression in her adoptive mother's face. She felt proud that he had halted his sedan to look at her.

In truth, while Zhu Di was mostly drawn to her clever manner, he was not immune to the titillating charms of this budding peach, this playful nymph who pouted her way among the belles in the court. Like her Mongol mother, Min Li had inherited shapely locks that graced her temples and refined her broad oval face. Beneath arched eyebrows, her long lashes flittered above sensual pools of the deepest brown. Often, as when she smiled to reveal two rows of pearly teeth, the outer corners of her eyes drooped gently to the side so that even the eunuchs found her irresistible. Narrow-waisted but deliciously ripe, she was already showing signs of blossoming in all the right places.

In his sedan, Zhu Di smiled with satisfaction. After witnessing this little performer with his own eyes, an idea had germinated in the astute general's mind. As they halted in front of his private chambers, he was all too eager to put his plan into execution but he did not let this show. He hailed his escorting eunuch and spoke with calculated vagueness.

"Have Princess Xia bring the little prostitute to us."

By this, it was clear that *the little prostitute* was a general term meant for a girl whose name the emperor did not know. But the eunuch had read his intentions and knew well who the emperor spoke of.

In fact Min Li was well known by both the servant eunuchs and the ladies of the palace. As a vivacious, bouncing little girl, she had been the delight of the older princesses and the bored concubines who relished in taking turns to coddle and sleep with her. At five, she was like a kitten they had somehow rescued from the nursery. A cheerful, independent child, she never made a fuss or threw tantrums. Her temperament appeased the delicate imperial ladies.

It was unwise to suppose, however, that Min Li would be docile as she grew up. That she had, until then, concealed her inquisitive streak together with an urge to explore or challenge her environment to the point of rebellion would only be significant in future years.

Several days later, in one of the Inner Palace courtyards, two Royal Chamber officers approached Princess Xia while she sat on stone steps, combing Min Li's hair. The officers wasted no time. After bowing, one of them said exactly what the princess had feared.

"His Majesty has summoned the girl to participate in the Royal Chamber selection process."

"And you, Excellency," added the other, "have been ordered by His Highness to present the girl for inspection by tomorrow morning."

Much to their vexation, Princess Xia continued to comb Min Li's hair as if she had not heard. Her expression had turned cold.

The eunuchs eyed each other in silence.

"Princess Xia," pronounced the tallest, "the emperor will recompense you for your loyalty."

Without as much as a reply, Princess Xia's left hand continued its resolute, detangling strokes through Min Li's hair. Min Li bit her lips. She could not see her adoptive mother's face but she had sensed her reluctance. Her first impulse had been to leap up to her feet and spin her heels towards the officers, so honored had she felt at the request. But she dared not cross the woman who had taken care of her for so many years. So she remained quite still.

"Name your price," persisted the eunuch with a tinge of exasperation.

Princess Xia ignored him once more. Min Li wondered what she could possibly be thinking and was surprised that there was a side of Princess Xia that she did not know.

The eunuch breathed a sigh of contempt. "Do you defy the emperor?"

Princess Xia froze. The comb fell to the ground. Yet the princess remained still, staring in silence at Min Li's crown. Her right hand was still cupped on Min Li's shoulder. Feeling the tension, Min Li drew away from the embrace and stood.

The eunuchs looked at each other, satisfied with the authority that their position afforded them and almost grateful for Min Li's cooperation. The first one announced, "Min Li, you are to present yourself to the Chief Directorate of the Royal Chamber Affairs. Be present tomorrow. Princess Xia, His Majesty orders that the girl be bathed and in her finest attire. You will be recompensed by an increase of five piculs to your monthly stipend."

They shuffled away. Princess Xia lowered her head.

At last, she turned towards the smiling Min Li and spoke in a tenebrous voice.

"Now, you will learn to know this place."

And Min Li, who had barely heard the remark and who still felt the blessing of the eunuchs' visit, promptly embraced the noble princess as if to brush away her motherly fears.

***

The Selection Process

The idea of competing with hundreds of other girls seemed at first amusing to Min Li but it later filled her with anxiety. She already knew that the eunuchs had performed a pre-selection two days ago. Of the initial three thousand candidates, half of these had been eliminated, either for being too short or too tall. And now, in the course of three days, she would be compared to two thousand girls. This prospect did not fail to stir Min Li into an un-welcomed exercise of self-analysis.

She had in her possession, a small palm-sized mirror framed in a red and black cloisonné. This was a gift from one of the princesses, following Min Li's first menstruation. This mirror was too small and she could not see what she wanted to see. If only she could view her entire figure from the head down. She set upon exploring the immense palace for a mirror that she had once glimpsed in one of the bedrooms. This was one art in which Min Li excelled, exploring.

She knew the Yingtian palace well. For when the ladies of the palace were absent from their chambers, she would quietly enter their elegant, carpeted rooms and admire the jewelry, the furniture and any clothes that she found lying around. She would push her large feet in their minuscule smelly slippers and play at being a princess. She was not a mischievous little girl, only a curious one with a deep need to experience her world. And this palace, albeit old and with only a hundred rooms, was spacious enough for her secret escapades and fantasies.

Some of the palace eunuchs had even become her playful accomplices, promising to advise her if a room was empty or to warn her if a princess approached in the corridor. The eunuchs knew her games were harmless and they played along to indulge her. After all, she always cheered them up and the thought of her extravagant follies alleviated the drudgery of their everyday housecleaning duties.

The early afternoon *geng* sounded. Min Li eclipsed herself from the courtyard and stole into the princess quarters. In the far chamber, a tall cloisonné-framed mirror leaned against the side wall. She entered, casting a careful glance behind her shoulder.

In her excitement, Min Li failed to take note of a eunuch who busied himself in the corner of the room. While she pouted and adopted seductive poses before the mirror, the eunuch carried on with the emptying of bedpans. Having completed his task, he rose to his feet, catching hold of his breath. By then, the provocative adolescent had forgotten all attempts at modesty. The eunuch gasped.

Min Li was far from startled. Servant eunuchs were a common sight in the palace and she was not frightened. For an instant, she froze, smiling at both their reflections. He stood quietly in the shadow but she could just discern the dark coloring on his cheek. As he fumbled towards the door, looking somewhat guilt-stricken, she spun round and called out to him.

"Am I beautiful?"

The young eunuch was accustomed to being ignored. He gave her a furtive downcast look. She noticed the birth mark across his left cheek. He was straining for words. He smiled back.

"They say...you are the most beautiful in the palace."

There was a melody in his voice. It filled the room and appeased all her doubts.

She watched as the eunuch stumbled out with his equipment.

After this brief encounter, Min Li's nostrils flared with pride and she felt more hopeful about her chances.

Not until the next day, when she was shuffling among hundreds of other girls in the Royal Chamber Selection Hall, did the eunuch's words haunt her. Who exactly were *they*? Why had *they* not talked to her directly before? Who knew her and what else did they think of her? Was it all good? What if it wasn't all nice things? And what would such an insignificant eunuch know of those things anyway?

And so on the first day, as a pointy beard officer inspected her ears, eyes, nose, her hands, ankles and feet, Min Li entered an inner contemplation. With it, came the realization that in the home she had known, in this palace where she had gamed all her life, there was another game, a far greater one, being played.

Min Li was flawless. By the examiners' standard, she had exquisite complexion, a product of having remained indoors for so many years. She was almost a little too pale but that did not matter. Almost six hundred years ago, during the mid-Tang dynasty, a fashion had been introduced of wearing no rouge on the face. The only make up allowed was the black lipstick which gave its wearer a deathly pale complexion. This had given the style a name, "weeping make up" or "tears makeup". The examiner marveled that Min Li's skin was a pure as jade and white as glistening snow.

"This one has the skin the emperor is fond of," he noted approvingly.

To which the other eunuchs nodded in agreement.

She liked how they approved of her and it gave her more confidence.

In another chamber, she was stripped naked and examined by an old woman to ascertain that her limbs were neither too fat nor too thin and that she had no unsightly moles or ugly scars. She had none. The eunuchs then measured her hands and feet.

Finally, a eunuch approached her with several questions. He, of course, knew the answer to each of these questions. But he wanted to hear her speak.

"Your name?"

"Min Li."

She observed him with a manner that comes from knowing that one has lived for years in royal surroundings and has not been fished out from some dinghy *hutong*. But this was only an act. She was terrified.

"Place of birth?"

"Yingtian."

"Year of birth?"

"Year of the Earth Tiger...last year of Hongwu."

"Month?"

"First lunar month, Month of the Tiger..."

The examiner frowned and shook his head.

"A double Tiger for a concubine? What next!" he muttered under his breath.

"Look at it this way," said the other one, "at least, this will ward off evil spirits from the Royal Chamber."

"But tigers die violent deaths—" pondered the first.

"Silence!"

It was the sonorous voice of the Royal Chamber director who tried in vain to quieten the other girls. He was so agitated from overwork that the side wings of his black eunuch hat vibrated as he moved. The examiners promptly finished their markings on Min Li's record. She was then ushered out to the adjacent room while the next girl was summoned.

"Wait!"

Min Li froze.

The wiry director rose from his stool and shuffled anxiously towards her. He stooped down as though sniffing at the ground beneath her and then frowned in disgust.

"Your feet!" he reproached. "They are too large!" He said this as though implying that Min Li had tried to dupe him.

Conscious of the oversight, the other examiners shook their head, looking blankly at the recorded figure beside Feet Length. The chief examiner turned abruptly towards them.

"Why was this not noted, you dumbasses! Feet too large... Note it here, note it!"

"Am I eliminated?" asked Min Li.

"Silence! Do not speak unless spoken to! Insubordinate girl!"

Then turning to the clerk, "You! Write this down."

Min Li said not another word but she was petrified. She left the room looking regretfully at her feet, feeling uncertain. Would this mean that she would not become a concubine?

Until then, she had sized up the others and was assured she had a good chance. All the girls she had met so far possessed flaws. One of the girls stuttered, another accidentally spit when she said her name, another had bad teeth and a good portion sounded nasal or vulgar. As expected, these girls were eliminated.

But now Min Li began to worry. Perhaps she too, would be eliminated shortly due to the size of her feet. She had always felt grateful about being spared the pain and inconvenience that foot binding entailed. Unlike her, the ladies of the palace could barely squat on the chamber pots without assistance.

One peek at Princess Xia's smelly, disfigured stubs made her nauseous. Besides, the added fact that Princess Xia had never had a male suitor persuaded Min Li that no matter if a woman had small feet there were other conditions that determined whether she would remain unmarried for the rest of her life. Min Li clung to that conviction and it gave her hope.

Certainly she often ached to have lotus feet too but when she watched the other ladies of the palace lull about in their chairs and waddle awkwardly, she felt privileged for her ability to hop, climb, squat, and wander. How she loved to wander! Princess Xia had explained that it was because of her restless nomadic Mongol blood.

She loved hearing Princess Xia recount the story. "Many years ago, one of the influential palace eunuchs found you running away from the nursery matron in the Imperial Gardens. He scolded the nanny and gave you to me. He told them not to bind your feet."

"Tell me more about this man!" she would cheer on with glee.

The possessive princess, eager to give the girl a father figure that was not too accessible, had briefly mentioned that this elusive eunuch was her adoptive father. It was her deepest, yet unmanifested desire, that Min Li should never meet Zheng He. Years later, when Min Li was eight years old, Princess Xia had nevertheless embellished the tale, so eager was she to enchant her protégée.

"Your adoptive father is commanding the emperor's fleet now. He has just left on a faraway voyage on a giant ship." And she regaled Min Li with drawings of the Ming fleet, depicted above the ocean's swells.

From that day on, unknown to the princess, Min Li began to regularly wonder where her mysterious father was and why he had never come back to meet her.

Once I become concubine, surely he will notice me. I know he will, she thought with a smile.

She was ushered into another room where another hundred girls waited. One by one, they were to walk to a table, sit on the stool facing the table and then return to their starting position. It was an etiquette exercise, aimed at determining their grace, manners and balance.

Min Li had taken it for granted that she had a gracious gait and knew how to move in a titillating sway. But in this room, there were all manner of clumsiness. One of the girls had lived all her life in a farm and did not know what to do with the strange stool. Others walked as if they carried a heavy load, bent forward at the hip with their backside up and shoulders sloping. Two Korean girls exaggerated what they perceived to be proper court mannerisms, appearing haughty and older than their years.

A racket had degenerated. Whenever a girl began her short journey to the table, the female congregation stifled a nervous giggle or two. A few girls were unable to contain their anxiety and began shedding miserly tears. The incessant girly whispers about this one for being so lovely yet clumsy, or that one being a dunce for knocking the table, or the other for failing to walk in a straight line, irritated the director. He mechanically tapped his walking stick to the ground, grunting the word, "Silence!" This had absolutely no effect and the giggling, sobbing and commenting continued within the next round. In the end, the examiner abandoned his disciplining method and his voice was lost in the cacophony.

It was in this rowdy assembly that Min Li, burdened by the realization that her feet were too large and unhappy at the memory of her adoptive father, took her turn on the manners test. Her moody mind had flitted elsewhere and she was trying to tell herself that she no longer cared for anything. An inscrutable blend of thoughts painted her face.

As she approached the table, the examiner, one of the rare eunuchs who could write, noted her impeccable ghostly manner and her detached sullen air. He frowned. He could not capture the essence of her personality in his notes. At last, when he was inspired with what he thought were the perfect words, he scribbled, "Has the charm of a remnant."

But soon enough, Min Li came to her senses. Realizing that all eyes were on her, she blushed. The examiner noted all this with appreciation. As she sat timidly on the chair, an erotic color rushed to her cheeks. The examiner was now a little flustered.

At last, fully conscious of her charm and intent on being selected, Min Li emerged from her previous apathy. She had seen these country girls, submit one by one to a crude routine all for the honor of being selected and she now felt indignant. Hadn't she lived in this palace all her life? If anyone will bed the emperor, she thought, it will be me. And I will make my adoptive father so proud that he will take me away on his big ship. Yes, he will!

Her confidence revived, she rose from the stool and walked with marked arrogance to her starting position. Halfway through, eager to cause a little mischief, she peered over her shoulder at the unsuspecting eunuch. He had barely finished scribbling, "Very erotic" and wondered why the room had suddenly reverted to silence. As he drew away from his notes to meet Min Li's daring gaze, he froze.

The audacious girl was staring at him with a provocative pout. The examiner blinked. Then he stared blankly at the notes he had previously written. That would never do, he thought. He had only just formulated the next characters when her delicious cherry lips curled into a pearly smile of the most dazzling white.

The examiner was taken aback. He was now uncertain what the sum of his evaluation should read. The girl seemed like three different personalities in one. He scratched his head uneasily and contemplated for a moment. At last, divinely inspired, the eloquent eunuch scribbled a few more characters in his document.

By the end of the fifth day, Min Li was officially summoned to compete with the remaining hundred girls. She was overjoyed. The final stage of the process no longer frightened her. After all, since her large feet had not disqualified her, nothing else would stand in her way. She breathed a sigh of relief.

On the second last night, she shared Princess Xia's bedchamber. It was to be one of the last times they slept together because potential concubines slept in another quarter of the palace. Much to Min Li's surprise, Princess Xia was particularly distraught that evening.

Instead of congratulating her, the lady brooded. In fact, the princess had secretly harbored the belief that Min Li would be summarily rejected on the basis of her feet. For some reason, her prediction had not come true.

While the excited teenager expounded on her day, recounting all that had transpired and describing all the beautiful young girls she had seen today, Princess Xia maintained a forbidding silence, refusing to share her thoughts.

That night, long after Min Li had given up on any response, Princess Xia snapped.

"But how could they let you through? They ought not to!"

This of course was the last thing that Min Li wanted to hear.

"My dear princess, are you saying that I am not worthy of the emperor's choice?"

"No. I am not saying that."

"Then it is my feet? You also think they are too big for the emperor?"

"No, that is not what I said."

Princess Xia looked away to hide her distressed features. "It's just... Something is wrong. They should not have let you through. All this is Zhu Di's doing. It is him. One of the examiners has been bribed."

Min Li frowned. There was Princess Xia, staring out through the window into the moonlit courtyard, crisping her jaws tight when she should have been proud of her adoptive daughter. How could her beloved princess be so against her achieving an honorable place in the palace? How could the princess not see that even her father, this elusive navigator, would be honored if she rose to the emperor's favor?

"They wanted you to pass but I ignore why," continued the princess.

Among her concerns was the unsettling notion that while Min Li had been born from a low-ranking concubine, she was also of royal blood. Was this no longer in the records? How could it be so grossly ignored? *What was Zhu Di plotting?*

Princess Xia shook her head and looked away preparing herself for bed. Min Li tried to reassure her adoptive mother all the while convincing herself that the outcome was positive.

"Well nothing bad can come of it. Soon I will be concubine. Surely this will be better for me than living in the palace as a nobody, won't it? Or being wedded to an old marquis... Now, I will finally have a name in this place."

Princess Xia said nothing. Min Li made another attempt.

"You will always be my special princess and I am grateful for all you have done for me."

Still Princess Xia said nothing and lowered her gaze.

"We shall remain close. Won't we, Princess Xia?"

She was met by more silence. Min Li was out of ideas.

"Do not worry. I will be happier once I am concubine. The emperor will take care of me."

At this, Princess Xia's raucous voice rose in the chamber.

"Will he? You do not know what you are saying, Min Li."

Then she extinguished the oil lamp and drew her quilt over her head to annul the conversation. Min Li was beginning to worry but soon enough, in the darkness, as if nothing had happened, she heard Princess Xia's voice soften, easing away her doubts with some welcomed advice.

"Tomorrow I vouch that they will inspect the way you smell. If you want to be concubine, do not eat onions or spices early in the morning. Mint tea is best. And wash yourself very carefully down there." She hesitated. "But not too carefully. Keep it...natural."

"Why?"

"The choice of concubines depends on compatibility in odor. Your scent should never offend the emperor. Even the most attractive face will not compensate for displeasing odor. Sleep now."

The next day, female examiners began a thorough, more intimate inspection of the remaining candidates. One of the examiners sniffed Min Li's armpits and recorded the odor. The other asked her to breathe out multiple times as she smelt her breath.

A meticulous scribe indulged in mouthing out every word that she wrote down in the candidate's file. This meant that Min Li knew exactly what the old woman reported. It appeared that they were numerous ways to describe breath and armpit odor. In her fascination with the entire process, Min Li forgot to be embarrassed even though she was now completely naked.

It was the next part of the examination that had her blushing. Naked as she was, she was asked to lie down on a couch. The examiner then approached with a date. Min Li wondered what the woman was doing with the fruit. Before she had the time to protest, the small date was pushed in the opening of her vagina. Min Li was too shocked to move. She remained perfectly still waiting for what seemed an eternity. After an awfully long time, the date was retrieved with ceremonious care. To her dismay, the examiner touched her nose to the date and sniffed it three times. Min Li was stupefied to see the examiner nod approvingly and scribble even further descriptive passages in her notes. So it seemed that the emperor did not favor sweet smelling concubines and Min Li's natural secretions were considered sound.

The entire process did not last long but as they emerged from the chamber, the girls looked at each other with blank self-preserving expressions. Some had tears in their eyes from the invasive measures that they had endured. But Min Li felt reassured. This was exactly what Princess Xia had described.

When Min Li left the selection hall that day, she was too anxious to return to Princess Xia. I must find out if I have been selected, she thought.

Knowing that the officers were busy escorting the other candidates to their lodgment, she ran across in the opposite direction and followed the director, creeping behind him and his four assistants until they disappeared in their working cabinet. On all fours, Min Li hid behind a large wooden screen in the ante chamber and listened. Soon, muffled voices rose from behind the thin wooden door.

She listened as the director gave orders and sat down to give an evaluation. One after the other, she heard the director call out the girls' names. Each name was followed by a hesitant pause and soon after, by either a ceremonious tap or silence. The tap was rare. She quickly understood. The officials were stamping a seal of approval on each of the approved girls' file. When she did not hear a tap, she knew the girl would not be admitted to the Royal Chamber. Each time she heard a name, she mouthed a number, counting with her fingers. Fifty names had now been called and she had not yet heard her name.

"Hey! What are you doing here?"

"I..."

A eunuch had emerged from the adjacent cabinet. His sharp eyes had caught sight of a pink form huddled behind the ornamental screen. She'd forgotten to tuck her skirt under.

"Get out of here!" snapped the eunuch.

"I...I got lost," protested Min Li, bowing profusely in an attempt to hide her face. She heard another tap inside the cabinet. Sixty.

"I'll teach you to snoop around!"

The eunuch grabbed her wrist. Conscious of making any further noise, she evaded him, running past to the door opposite the cabinet. She tried to open it but it was locked.

"Now I've got you, hmm, you little brat!" spit the eunuch. Sixty-four.

She attempted to wriggle free but he gripped harder, dragging her by force to a nearby stool. There, he sat, panting. He seemed eager to molest this peachy creature. Sixty-eight. She struggled, emitting timid little cries, afraid to raise the director's attention. If he found out that one of the candidates had followed them, she would be finished. Still protesting quietly, she wriggled again, but the officer was strong.

"I'll whip your backside until it's raw, you little slut!" He fondled beneath her skirt, maintaining her face down on his knee with his other hand. Min Li's face flushed with indignation. Finally she screamed, giving way to her anger.

"Let me go! Let me go now!" she cried, kicking in all directions.

Before the eunuch could react, she had rolled to the floor and leapt back to her feet.

At this, the cabinet door opened. The director emerged, mouth agape.

"What is the meaning of this?"

"This servant girl is snooping in the hall, Director. I was teaching her a lesson, hmm."

"This is shameful. Shameful! Shame on you both!"

"I...I got lost," repeated Min Li, this time on the verge of tears. The counting had stopped at seventy.

One of the attendants appeared, still holding his seal in hand. He took one glance towards Min Li and had a moment of recollection.

"This is no servant girl, Director. This is the girl with the big feet."

The director gasped then craned his neck, eyeing Min Li's feet with horror. At once the indignity of the situation overwhelmed the already stressed man and he began to run after the officer, waving his walking stick menacingly.

"Ji Feng! I'll teach you to soil His Majesty's girls!" he yelled. He then proceeded to cane the insubordinate officer who raised his hands to protect himself from the blows.

Min Li did not stay a moment longer in the anteroom. When the flustered director had finally given Ji Feng his due punishment and dismissed him, he collapsed with exhaustion on the very stool where moments earlier Min Li had been so ruthlessly exposed. The old man wiped his forehead and looked around the room. Min Li was nowhere to be found.

"What shall we do?" asked the attendant, eyeing his director with concern.

"Bring me her file," ordered this one.

***

When Min Li returned to her shared chamber that night, Princess Xia was not home. She lay on her mat, the afternoon's events churning in her mind. She had ruined every chance to win the emperor's favor due to her indomitable curiosity. Later, she shared her doubts with the princess, taking care not to reveal her escapade in the Royal Chamber director's bureau.

"My child," replied the princess, "even if you do not enter the Royal Chamber, it does not mean you are not precious."

Min Li was troubled. Thirty girls remained to be named and based on her calculations they had yet to select two more concubines. After this afternoon's incident though, she knew she could never be one of them.

She slept badly that night. A crushing feeling of doom submerged her as she curled her body into a tight ball and tried to forget that she had barely escaped a rigorous beating. Tomorrow would reveal if the director had reported her behavior to the emperor. And if the emperor was displeased by her lack of virtue, perhaps even Princess Xia would be too? Perhaps they would send her away from the palace and she would have nobody.

As always, she had not been capable of resisting the thrill of discovery. It was silly, really. The joy of venturing through the palace, unknown from others had once again taken precedence. She knew it was her fault. Now she would pay the price.

No sooner had the emperor begun holding court the next morning that the Royal Chamber director was summoned to pronounce the results of the latest selection process.

"Have we found what we were looking for?" asked Zhu Di, stroking his beard.

"We have, Your Majesty."

He presented a silver dish where lay ten jade tablets.

Ten concubines had been selected. It would have surprised Min Li to know that of the ten names etched on those jade tablets, it was her name the emperor eyed with marked satisfaction.

Chapter 6
The Castrates

How quickly Min Li forgot her encounter with the soft-spoken eunuch from the mirrored chamber. However kind and uplifting were his words, Zhijian remained invisible, one of the countless castrates in the palace.

Yet he, on the contrary could not forget her. It seemed that his entire life had found meaning from the mere glimpse of her. He felt more alive now than he ever had since his appointment to Yingtian palace.

It was three years ago. He remembered it well. It was the year he had met Shin.

"How long have you been at his majesty's service?" had asked the chubby Korean.

He eyed the timid recruit as they walked side by side into the Eastern palace grounds.

"I was castrated when I was twelve years old. It's about a year now..." replied Zhijian in a barely audible voice.

"And did you always want to serve the emperor?" enquired the senior eunuch, leading him to a service cabinet by way of the kitchens.

"No, I... It was my father's wishes. My father is from Yunnan."

"Oh? So you're a Southerner then?" Shin seemed to mull over that thought. "So many former Mongol prisoners in the palace these days. Here, take this broom. Let's see... I think you have everything. Now follow me to the Halls."

"I didn't mean it like that," contradicted the naive Zhijian, grabbing the cleaning equipment in one hand. "I was never made a prisoner. My father...we needed the money. So I agreed to become a castrate. It's complicated. My father's name is Jin Hong," he added with a hint of pride. "He is an imperial carpenter for the Ministry of Works."

Everyone knew that the Ministry of Works was headed by the very talented Annamese architect, Nguyen An, the man rumored to be designing the new Imperial Palace. Whoever Jin Hong was, thought Shin, he was a lucky man.

But after pondering this, the Korean glanced severely towards the handsome youth. He was accustomed to fancy references and fabrications from ambitious recruits. While Zhijian seemed trustworthy enough, the senior eunuch could sense when a story lacked coherence and where it was better to keep one's own counsel.

But there was something in Zhijian's countenance, his dreamy eyes and soft, young body that appealed to the older Korean. He looks a little out of place around here, he thought. Maybe this one will turn out alright.

"Volunteering is one noble act but self-mutilation is forbidden," he replied. "If that had been the case, you, my little one would have been sent to serve in Zhu Di's army at the border. Now that would have taught your father a lesson!"

Not wishing to again contradict his mentor, Zhijian changed the subject.

"Is it true then that there are eunuchs from all over the world in this city?"

"I'm afraid so. Just to add to the confusion and make communication difficult," replied the Korean bitterly. "We have all come from faraway, Mongolia, Korea, Annam, the Khmer lands, Siam... Ha! Some fare better than others."

They reached the Gate of Heavenly Purity.

"Well, look who we have here, hmm!" said an oily voice emerging from the Inner Palace.

Its owner was a tall, thin man. He had a jaundiced complexion exacerbated by sinewy eyebrows of the blackest night. Like the other eunuchs, he wore a winged black hat secured below his chin. The man's high hat only accented his long face and pointy jaw. What distinguished this eunuch from the others were the two black strands he wore loose and which framed his bony temples. His sharp, stained teeth were splendidly matched to his complexion and when he smiled, more of his gums were exhibited than was bearable for the world to see. He had observed the two eunuchs from afar and now emerged from the gates, eager to make his presence known.

"Shin! It is you!" he said. "In what dark corner of the palace have you been hiding, hmm?"

"Zhijian, I want you to meet Ji Feng. Bow low, now. Good boy. Ji Feng, this is Zhijian."

Zhijian kept a respectful silence while the two senior eunuchs spoke among themselves.

"You have a new uniform," said Shin, eyeing the *buzi* on Ji Feng's robe with curiosity.

"Oh, this? A recent promotion," dismissed Ji Feng, satisfied that Shin had noticed the egret on his chest. Then, he gave a disdainful look at the new recruit. It pleased the long haired Jurchen to know how fast and far he had climbed in the last years.

"A promotion? Are you still in the *Silijian*?" asked Shin, still staring at the egret.

"Deputy 6a, in charge of communications…among other things," smiled Ji Feng.

Zhijian noticed the man's teeth and felt a bizarre shiver run down his spine. He watched Ji Feng rant about his new post and his many varied roles.

"I do like it you know... I am working as a liaison now. I mediate between the Inner Court and the Ministry of Works. We are, to say the least, very busy at the moment, hmm, yes, notably with the new imperial city. I vouch you have heard all about it so I will not bore you, hmm?"

Ji Feng knew only too well that news of the new Beijing capital raged and that his role, together with the picul stipend it assured, was much coveted. He paused for a moment as if to ascertain that none of his words had gone amiss.

"And what about you, Shin," he condescended, "still processing court documents?"

He meant to remind the Korean that he was still a 7b grade eunuch and that, unlike Ji Feng, he had not progressed. Shin was quick to understand the nuance.

"Yes, still in the Directorate of Ceremonial. Someone has to keep a watchful eye over proper etiquette," he smiled. "We still need to ensure that our new recruits are following proper protocol and wearing the correct attire. Of course, you are right, I still keep record of their birth, their job classification, their rank...that sort of thing."

"You always did have a good eye for detail, hmm?" chirped Ji Feng with sly satisfaction. Then eyeing Zhijian, "And where is our new recruit heading to?"

"He just completed his training. He will begin in the Palace Custodians Directorate shortly."

"I am to clean the halls and sweep the courtyard," explained Zhijian very simply and with a humility that Shin promptly noticed.

"We all must start somewhere," said Ji Feng, pleased with himself. "I must leave now. I need to make my report and close the shift. But we shall meet again, hmm? No doubt."

At this, he began his proud stride towards the *Silijian* building. Zhijian noticed how he held his head high, strolling along with his wooden tablet under one arm. Ji Feng's clenched fist seemed to mirror the eunuch's icy determination. Or perhaps, observed Zhijian, it was ready to pound anything that dared jeopardize the Jurchen's promising career.

As for Shin, as soon as Ji Feng had left, he noticed that Zhijian was lost in a reverie and wondered whether the young man might not be a little wishful. His heart warmed.

"Let me share a secret with you," he said. "If you want to get ahead around here, you will need to make strong connections with those eunuchs in more senior positions than you. That is how Ji Feng was promoted so quickly." Then he frowned. "Although I hear he also became the little protégée of some influential palace women. That also helps. Another perfect example is Yishiha."

"Who?"

"Yishiha. I am surprised you have not heard of him. He is gaining much power with the court...Much like Zheng He who, as I speak is preparing for his third expedition. Anyhow, Yishiha is our emperor's new hero. There are talks of him being dispatched as an envoy to Southern Manchuria next year to improve our relations with the Jurchens in the North. Yishiha is of Jurchen origin you see, and one of the reasons I believe he did so well with himself is that he was initially appointed to serve the Manchurian concubines of the palace."

Shin paused. He put his hand on the young boy's shoulder as though to wrap up his short lesson.

"You see, Zhijian, if you can earn the trust of the palace women, you will go far. But that is not to say that *you* should trust the palace women. The two are very different."

The Korean had been quite passionate in his expository on palace politics. He had spoken as if to persuade Zhijian that life as a eunuch promised notoriety and that loyalty to the emperor would be well rewarded. When he had finished he paused to examine the effect of his words on the young man. But much to his surprise, they had very little effect on the boy.

"I will bear this in mind. But for now, I will be pleased to fulfil my duties as palace janitor," Zhijian replied with accented fervor.

Shin was taken aback. The boy was either very cunning in dissimulating his ambition or else extremely stupid.

"Little one, you need to understand something. No one likes this job you have been assigned. It is reserved for the lowest paid eunuchs. Take it from me, during the colder months, sweeping the courtyard is true penitence. This, you will probably discover yourself. And when you do," he smiled at him with benevolence, "come and see me and I will see if we can find something more interesting for you. In the meantime, start at the wall there, and make your way around each hall until you reach the Inner Court again. Don't speak or rest until your shift is completed. Now... Oh, yes, pay attention to the sounds of the *geng* and the *dian*. You'll be beaten if you waste any time. Now, off you go."

***

This was how Zhijian began his service at the Yingtian palace. Back then, he had little idea about the mind-baffling variety of posts available within the eunuch institution. Nor was he too keen to explore the opportunities available to him. He recalled the confident Ji Feng with his new silk uniform and his impressive gait. Strangely, the eunuch with his mottled face and sharp eyebrows had evoked little in him save for a nauseating fear.

Besides, what did he care for such promotions? He felt himself different from the other eunuchs. The very thought that a man, usually a commoner with no chance for a better life, could willingly castrate himself at the risk of death to aspire to a post in princely establishments or rub shoulders with the emperor himself, filled him with revulsion.

Back at the castrate reserve camp, he had met many such young men. It was in this large complex that he had been detained before his admission to the Imperial Palace. There must have been thousands of new castrates waiting for an appointment. Most were Annamese and Mongol prisoners of war. Others were gifts from Korea or Yunnanese like himself. But others were wretched children from the local peasantry, all desperate to make a decent living. Zhijian remembered how these famished boys even limped and dawdled miserably as they contributed to their daily chores within the reserve units.

He shared sleeping quarters with hundreds of other eunuchs, all of them waiting to be interviewed by the palace directors. The foul tang of uncontained urine and feverish sweat permeated the air. It was worse at night. They lay side by side, their meagre possessions next to their mats. Each without an exception carried with them an urn which contained none other than their severed body parts. This urn would be with them forever, a grim reminder of who they were and a much prized treasure to take with them in the afterlife.

In the first month, he blamed his father. But Zhijian had a humble nature. If he ever despised anything it was always himself. It made it all the more difficult as he observed those others, like him. The horror that he was one of them was too much to bear. He had even wanted to desert but this, he knew, would break his father's heart.

Luckily an interview had already been secured for him and he never remained in that horrendous stench-filled camp for too long. But back in those days, at the tender marriageable age of fifteen—for he was much older than what his father had told the officials—Zhijian wept bitterly. He wept for days, mortified by the new ill-shaped body that he no longer recognized and sometimes could not control. He wept until he tired himself to sleep and then only then, he would find peace.

In his dreams were visions of beauty and peace, well beyond the soiled sleeping mats, the rotting camps, beyond the stench of excrement. It was radiant with sunshine.

In the Yingtian palace, he understood the difference from the very beginning. They lived and aspired to nothing but success in this world. But he didn't. This world now meant nothing to him. He had wanted to die ever since his father had asked him to sacrifice his manhood. The entire experience filled him with despair and revulsion but he had relented.

He had accepted the humiliating operation usually reserved for prisoners and criminals and now, consigned to work in the palace grounds, he would never again see his village at will. Nor would he ever enjoy the sensual pleasures that he had once savored on a couple of occasions with the tavern women so eager to contribute to his education. Now those illicit memories were a treasure to him. He could recall every detail as though the thought of being with a woman, something he had once taken for granted, was close to paradise. Excited as he was, he had refused them, then, telling himself that all this *yang* energy must be preserved and shared only with the right woman.

And now, he would never feel any of it again. Neither would he find a wife that would be willing to serve him as man, since after all, he would be utterly useless. And worse, he would never have children of his own. He would never see them grow and extend their filial devotion to him just as he would have given them his life. Everything had lost its meaning.

In the early days as he writhed in his bed trembling from pain, he had regretted not rebelling, not running away. He reproached himself for being too young to really understand how ugly the eunuch existence could be; too young to visualize the enormity of the eunuch machine, its rules and its injustices. And then that haunting question would arise every night. Was he even a man? What exactly was he? A slave? An animal? It was unspeakable.

He could not answer these questions. Over time, he lost himself in the routine of work. Work made everything more bearable. And there were others, like Shin who had initially been his mentor, who also helped. They intrigued his mind and worked to distract him from his troubles. The bureaucratic Shin had been only too eager to explain the way the imperial city eunuch agencies were organized.

"There are a total of twelve directorates, four departments and eight bureaus," he had commenced. "The most important of these which you should remember is the *Silijian*. You should study the different insignias carefully. They will help you recognize the eunuch ranking and greet other eunuchs appropriately with due regard. Understand that this is to your benefit as are all well maintained work relationships."

Shin had given him a grand tour of the Yingtian imperial city and explained each department and bureau to him.

"If you are ill, report to the special eunuch infirmary, if you need authorization to enter the Inner Palace grounds, head to the Documents Department. From now on, you shall receive ten piculs of rice as your monthly salary. If you damage your uniform or require additional supplies, you are to report to the Royal Clothing Directorate. You have four days off per month and your shifts will be scheduled by the Palace Custodians where you must report daily."

By the time he completed his training, Zhijian fell into a numb, depressive state.

He felt as though he were floating outside his body. As if it were not really him in that maimed shell surrounded by like shells. He seemed to have reconciled himself to his condition. If he could not live happily like this, he could at least pass time. When you are kept busy, he thought, time did pass so very quickly.

To the many palace dwellers and even from the perspective of the other eunuchs, Zhijian did not exist. Though he was there almost every day, crouching, sweeping and scrubbing his way in and out of the palace grounds, though he regularly cleaned each of the buildings, courtyards and halls throughout the Imperial Palace, somehow Zhijian came and went without as much as being noticed. A remarkable ability of those we deem too insignificant is that they will consistently fail to attract our attention.

Shin had been right, reflected Zhijian. Being associated with important figures assured promotion within the palace. Perhaps that is why no one wanted to be associated with him.

And yet, he, more than any other eunuch in the establishment, developed a growing attachment with the Yingtian palace. Life buzzed around him wherever he went. Life was outside while he slowly died inside. Life, as it passed him was a sort of alien, unwelcome realm. He grew fascinated by it and all the more alienated from it.

Face down along the ample hallways, inside the many pavilions adorned with flowers or in the bustling courtyards, his vision of the palace was unique. There were the faceless whispers, the equally enigmatic conversations of which he could barely make out the gist, the felt footsteps emerging through swishes of fabrics which passed him by and sometimes shoved him aside as he obstructed their path. There were the horses' hooves, the sedan carriers that lent him shade from time to time, the drum rolls, the imperious bells.

He did not begrudge sweeping because when he swept, he could dream and forget himself. Often he watched the rays of the sun deflect through the lattice of a palace pavilion and create diffused light spots on the courtyard tiles. He scrubbed the surface clean in a ritualistic motion. He would become so entranced by his tasks that his existence seemed suspended while the patterns danced on each tile. He would follow those sun spots, until his very sanity hinged on their presence.

When the sun began to set and he neared the completion of his shift, he watched shadows advance across the pavements until they spanned several tiles. The sudden dimness mirrored the despair deep within him. The sun would disappear and a limp blanket enveloped the cool, spotless courtyard where life, his activities and his meaning came to a halt. The chill of the stone would haunt him.

Then he would awake from that pleasurable dream. He would reluctantly put away his broom and his cleaning materials. Finally he would shuffle to the outer palace compound where he slept and took his many meals.

Every day was the same. There were special days during his Imperial Palace shift where he would find himself close to the women's quarters and he enjoyed hearing them laugh or share pleasantries. These hours would find a smile on his absent-minded face. But they were rare.

During one of those rare moments, Zhijian saw a young girl enter the Inner Palace. She was dressed like a servant yet after having seen her before in the Imperial Gardens, he remembered how she had embraced one of the princesses. At the time, he had assumed she was also a palace maid. But a servant would not dare hold a princess the way she had. Nor could a servant enter the imperial quarters without one of the court ladies. Zhijian was intrigued.

Later he asked Shin to explain. Shin simply said that the girl was Princess Xia's protégé.

"I noticed she has not had her feet bound."

"You did, did you? Well that, I should think, is one of Princess Xia's many whims. Horrible woman. But you never heard it from me. If that girl is anything like the Princess she may turn into a veritable tyrant."

After a moment's reflection, Shin added, "One must never irritate the ladies of the palace. Do you hear me?"

"But why would I—"

"They are bored, lonely, vain, and spiteful women. Above all, boredom makes them dangerous and malicious. Do not cause yourself any indignity from being too close to them or engaging with them. Only woes will come from it."

"Is this young girl a concubine then," asked Zhijian.

"No. But she is very beautiful and no doubt will soon be one. Now just remember what I said."

"How do you know?"

"Let's just say I know the right people," Shin whispered. "You see, Zhijian, we have secret eunuch councils where trusted members meet to exchange information. It keeps us sane. If you would like to join, I can arrange it for you. I think you'd like that and it might make you a little bit more...worldly. I've seen the way you look at everyone with your dreamy eyes. You need to sharpen up, boy."

"Is Ji Feng also part of this council?"

At this, Shin emitted a loud belly laugh but did not reply.

***

Ji Feng was not part of the trusted eunuch council.

Ji Feng was not what the people of the Middle Kingdom called a *tong jing*. This means that unlike Zheng He, who was castrated before puberty, Ji Feng was not "pure from childhood". And unlike Zhijian, who had reluctantly submitted to castration under dire straits in order to uphold filial piety and duty to family, Ji Feng was a willing castrate. He was one of those clandestine adults who had taken matters into their own hands and illegally self-castrated in order to advance their careers at the emperor's service.

Ji Feng had several reasons for choosing to become a eunuch. The first was that it would eventually secure him an important place in the Imperial Palace. There, he could hope to distinguish himself over the years and acquire the status, financial comfort and prestige that he so badly craved.

Astute in his enterprising ideas with a thorough eye for detail, he was not a man without talent. Unlike many of the eunuchs who had begun their service in their earlier years under the rules of the Hongwu emperor, Ji Feng could read and had worked in a library before his imperial appointment. He had read many books and acquired knowledge on a variety of subjects. He of course told no one that he could read so well. But this knowledge and his remarkable adaptability to learn on the job soon served him well.

The second reason that had compelled Ji Feng to present himself for service to the emperor was a strong, instinctive desire for self-castration which manifested quite early in his late childhood. There are and there still exists, even today, men born with such desire that cannot be explained. This, coupled with Ji Feng's inherent aggression inclined him to sever his manhood in an act so brutal as to be incomprehensible for the majority of men.

To Ji Feng, the self-aggression was not only a necessary act, one he had coveted for many years during his adolescence. It was also a form of catharsis that somehow freed him to become the person he felt it his destiny to be.

He writhed and sweated on his blood-soaked bed for several days following his self-mutilation. But no matter how contortioned his glacial body, no matter how gut-wrenching the pain that seared through him for days, he, rather than regretting his traumatic ordeal, managed to extract from it a sense of victory. He bathed in the euphoria of his newly found freedom.

There was one last factor in Ji Feng's nature that distinguished him from other eunuchs.

It was simply that Ji Feng, ever since he had been a little boy, deeply loathed and despised all women. Perhaps it was because his toothless wretch of a nurse had been so cruel to him in his younger years or because his miserable mother, agonizing over her bound feet, beat him too frequently for petty insolence. Whatever the cause, Ji Feng's indignation had been aroused numerous times at the hands of women.

Not only did this hatred distance him from them but, in his eyes, it further justified the absolute futility of remaining whole as a man. Since he would never seek to be with a woman, life as a eunuch seemed the rightful course to follow.

This was then, Ji Feng. And even if the other eunuchs bowed low before the embroidery on his chest and even as he thrived in his role within the palace, his many vices, his general antipathy and obvious self-interest, all alienated him from the friendly eunuch organizations and from acquiring the full trust of his colleagues.

The imperial eunuchs had suspected for years that Ji Feng profited illegally from many activities within the palace but they could not speak for fear of being the only persons to speak up against him. It was this communal silence, then, rather than any real authority over others which protected Ji Feng. And this phenomenon, whereby one person of dubious character rises in importance despite misdeeds that continue unreported is not isolated in history.

***

Zhijian had since joined Shin's secret council. This consisted of several eunuchs who were on courteous terms with each other and held different posts at various levels. After their long day, they would meet in inconspicuous places outside the Imperial Palace. Revived by drink they would talk about their day, the latest palace news, share anecdotes or else bicker about rival eunuchs and palace women. Through such a council, Zhijian learnt many things about the mysterious girl.

Whether the information was fact or hearsay was not known. To begin, he learnt that Princess Xia was no other than the emperor's niece, the daughter of one of Zhu Di's twenty-four brothers, the Prince of Xiang. During a highly politically charged climate, when the Prince of Yan was the most skilled general in the Middle Kingdom, Emperor Jianwen knew he was too militarily weak to dare confront his uncle directly. Instead, Jianwen set about attacking the other less important princedoms.

Zhijian found out that the first such confrontation was with the Prince of Zhou, an intimate of Zhu Di, who after being stripped of his title, was coerced into testifying against his brothers, listing various fabricated accusations. This caused a rippling effect among Zhu Di's brothers. As a result, in June 1399, the enraged Prince of Xiang was said to have set fire to his own palace.

And so it was that the Prince of Xiang, together with his entire family, perished in the fire. But several days later, it was rumored that Zhu Di's troops had found a survivor among the palace ruins. It was the twelve year old Princess Xia.

Zhijian pondered over this fantastic tale for many days as it was both so tragic and extraordinary. In another interesting twist, he learnt that the name Xia was in fact a diminutive for Xiang and that after being brought back from the Xiang palace ruins, she had been adopted by Zhu Di's wife, the future Empress Xu.

According to those who remembered, the orphaned Xia had been spoilt and doted upon by both the empress and her sister, now a nun at Water Moon monastery. Zhijian thought it was curious that many years later, Princess Xia herself, adopted the mysterious orphaned girl who now captured his imagination, day and night.

Zhijian paid close attention to anything he might hear about her. Some of the eunuchs worked closely with the female palace servants and often shared anecdotes about the palace women. From time to time the girl's name was mentioned and it was clear that she was a charming and witty personality and that her embroidery was exceptional. For her young age, it was thought that she was well read and very clever.

"Ah, but her feet are too big," observed one of the eunuchs with distaste.

"She'd be right at home with the peasants!" laughed another.

Oddly enough, the maimed could still laugh at others' imperfections, thought Zhijian cynically.

It's true, her feet were not bound. Zhijian had never really thought about this. The other eunuchs were still laughing and he felt a strong urge to come to her defense. But not wanting to raise their suspicion, he abstained himself.

Another much older eunuch interjected at this point. "Big feet? Humph! Do you think that will discourage the emperor?"

"Lower your voice! Don't speak of His Majesty so loudly," replied the others.

The older man waved his hand as though the petty subject of concubines' feet tired him. He proceeded to shovel rice into his mouth with his chopsticks.

"It's true enough. You're quite right," observed another. "Emperor Hongwu's consort had huge feet too."

Seeing the confused look on Zhijian's face, the older eunuch stepped in. "You see, the emperor's mother, Princess Ma was of Mongol descent. Her feet were never bound."

"The first Ming empress?" asked the incredulous Zhijian.

"That's right, Zhu Di's mother. At least, the woman His Majesty likes to believe is his mother...but we all know differently," he added, alluding to the rumors that Zhu Di had been born of a Korean concubine. "Now, see, Empress Ma was a true soldier's wife, could ride horses, mend shirts, bake bread... You never saw her with bound feet! Hongwu could have had any woman but he chose her."

"That's because she was very intelligent and she was the only one who could control his temper!"

"Yeah, that's right! She sure could Serve the Gentleman!"

"From what I heard, people in the court still poked fun of Empress Ma. They didn't do it in front of her, of course. But everyone knew that her feet were unsightly."

"If I were the Hongwu emperor, I would have summoned my lotus feet concubines every night to try to avoid Empress Ma."

Their laughter redoubled and Zhijian blushed because he could not bring himself to join them. He pretended to be too busy adding meat pieces to his half-empty rice bowl.

The eldest eunuch raised his voice to bring an end to the discussion. "In the end, Hongwu was a soldier. He knew what was best for him. And Zhu Di's much the same. Military stock; both of them. Generals need real women, not dainty little things."

These words troubled Zhijian. He began to wonder more about the young girl. He pondered over whether Zhu Di would really choose a girl with unbound feet to become concubine. How could this palace girl ever arouse his interest in the first place? And if she did, what would become of her? But Zhijian kept all speculations to himself.

Soon, they had enough of discussing about palace women. Gossip was entertaining but only to a degree. Perhaps the mention of women reminded them too much of what they had become. The conversation would usually veer to different topics and eventually the subject of promotion would awaken their ardor.

And so the meetings went. They occurred regularly, whenever the eunuchs could find the time and unchecked by the eunuch police and much later, hidden from the rumored and greatly feared Eastern Depot.

Aided by recommendations from his new friends, Zhijian soon found himself progressing through several appointments in the imperial city.

In one of these roles, he delivered toilet paper around the palaces. Not as prestigious as the other department roles, but it was better than the endless, exhausting janitor work. From the Toilet Paper Department, he would load his small one-wheeled cart and push it along on the very tiles he had previously spent months sweeping. He wheeled his little cart everywhere, supplying all the buildings that sheltered lavatory facilities with stamped, imperial toilet paper. Now he knew his way around in and out of the palace and in the many streets and alleys of Yingtian.

It was autumn 1411, when Zhijian was finally assigned to a new important promotion. He became engaged in the Fire and Water Department.

Only this morning, Zhijian had entered the princess quarters to replenish their coal supply. The bite of winter had surprised them this year and they would need to heat up the rooms earlier than planned.

In the middle of his shift, he had felt a warm presence in the room. It was the young girl that he had once mistaken for a servant and about who he had heard so much. She was gazing at herself in a full-length mirror and adopting various poses. Determined to remain as long as he could in the chamber, Zhijian began to empty chamber pots.

How she had grown! When she finally noted his presence and asked him a question, he replied, his voice quivering with adoration.

Then, overwhelmed and blushing profusely, he parted from the beautiful young girl, feeling as though his chest would burst and that his spirit floated high above him. In his confusion, he almost forgot the reason why he had visited the chambers and found himself erring corridor after corridor, trying to replay the encounter in his mind.

He tried to visualize her again. She was about his height. She was much more lithe and white than he, considering his outdoor duties. He visualized her pouting in front of the mirror.

Her full-length peach skirt was tied with a blue silk sash, high above her budding breasts. The silk billowed round her slender form as she spun. Smiling at her own vanity, she had draped a cape of sheer red silk over her porcelain shoulders. He had dared to rest his eyes on those shoulders and then up...

The double bun above her slender neck peered through a lattice of coiled braids and high above her delicious brows, behind each shapely ear, were two apricot peonies stained with crimson streaks.

In his entire life, either in or out of the palace, he had never glimpsed anything so precious. The vision tore at him.

As of now, even with his limited experience, he could vouch that this creature was the most beautiful thing in Yingtian, if not the whole world. Unlike him, she seemed animated with joyful wonder and touched the world with her graceful whimsicality. Perhaps because she was so delicate and moved with insouciance, the contrast reminded him of the very prison that had kept him locked day after day, inside his ugly, deformed shell.

Yet somehow, he felt certain that she was perhaps the loneliest girl in the world. This is then, how he saw the young girl. Like a faltering bird in a cage. He saw her as one sees a young lamb about to be slaughtered and shuddered at the thought.

Yet it comforted him to think of her. For days, months and years later, while his colleagues jested about his obsession, he would replay the encounter in his mind and pine for a new exchange.

Chapter 7
The Royal Chamber

Kittens

"Welcome, Li Guiren!" came the girly cheers. As Min Li proudly entered the concubine compound, a row of porcelain skin creatures, cradling kittens in their slender arms, approached with beaming smiles.

She recognized some of the other girls she had already met months ago in the palace gardens. They were thrilled to see her and proceeded to show her those rooms she had never seen so as to make her at ease in her new home.

The largest rooms were reserved for the Guifeis, the higher rank concubines. Each of the Guifeis, due to their seniority, had their own room. Meanwhile the lesser concubines, including those who were like Min Li, a Guiren, or fifth ranking concubine, shared a room.

"You want to be a Guifei! The Guifeis receive the best quality silks and the prettiest jewels," indicated a slender girl by the name of Mai Zhou, a tinge of envy in her voice.

On average, four women could live in one room. They slept on a low wooden bed which doubled up as a couch in the day.

"My name is Hua Xue," smiled a slender, elegant girl with a dimple in her left cheek. "You'll be sharing a room with me."

Hua Xue or Xue Guiren was her palace name, one she had been given following her arrival from Korea at the age of fifteen. Selected among thousands of virgins from her native Korea, Hua Xue was a tribute gift to the Middle Kingdom emperor in exchange for her people's protection from pirates. She was three years older than Min Li and had an equal affinity for prim Siamese cats and ginger sweets. Her breasts had soon given her a salacious reputation, for, not cloth-bound from an early age, they were perched high and ripe as delectable mangos. In return, Hua Xue enjoyed nothing more than pointing out the other girls' physical faults.

"Well, did you all see that? I bet I could fit my leg in Min Li's shoes," she boasted, sighting the new girl's feet. Exposing the newcomer's flaws was only an attempt to protect her own fragile ego from envy. Nothing was more reassuring for Hua Xue's competitive nature than seeing real or imaginary faults in other girls. It is unfortunate that this petty mind was also married to sharp wit, together with a general disposition for bragging and slander.

These traits, no matter how far they departed from Confucian virtue, somehow did not prevent Xue Guiren's advancement. For while she was despised by the princesses, she would become as perplexing as this may seem, one of the most called upon courtesans in the Royal Chamber. This was secretly attributed to Hua Xue's hunger for sensual delights something that Min Li would witness much later. For at night, when she thought her companions fast asleep, the clearly imaginative Hua Xue devised wicked erotic games with her kittens. On several occasions, Min Li was kept awake into the night, so distracted was she by the muffled sounds of Hua Xue's moans.

The other girl in Min Li's room was an Annamese that went by the name of Lan Wong. Wong Guiren was as soft as a cotton ball to the touch and fearful of most things which too often gave her hiccups. She was especially fond of collecting ribbons and other accessories. Lan Wong was among the first courtesans to wear a silk waist coat with the latest craze: those tiny porcelain buttons.

A sentimental, Wong sought hard after the affection of all women and when this did not succeed for who in this world is liked by all, she would descend into spells of neurotic gloom. In the years to come, Min Li would, on several occasions, witness Lan Wong in tears whenever this one felt that the emperor had not called upon her for months and that she must have fallen in disfavor.

As Min Li inspected the concubine quarters, she crouched at intervals to caress the dozens of cats idling in the corridor and on the furniture. She rapidly understood that some of these chambers were more inviting than others. Each room seemed to reflect the energy of its occupants.

What Min Li ignored for now was that the veritable force driving the Royal Chamber's energy was the emperor himself. He could, with just a few sharp words, or else by his lack of attention towards one or more girls, create a dynamic at will.

Left in her room, Min Li noted the sparse furniture. There were wooden stools and low lacquered tables where rested all manner of mirrors, combs, jewelry boxes and other permitted belongings such as family gifts. In one of the Guifei chambers, she had glimpsed elegant porcelain vases with garden flowers and other trinkets hanging by the latticed window pane.

She knew that little was kept inside the concubine chambers since on demand, the eunuchs rushed about to bring forth whatever else the women desired whether this be parasol, needle work, embroidery, foot warmers and bath tubs.

A permanent fixture of each chamber was the bedpan or commode which concubines used to relieve themselves. This was then spread with coal ash to absorb moisture and remove unpleasant odors from the room. But unlike their counterparts in the Middle Kingdom, the emperor's women were supplied with toilet paper. This luxury was made inside the palace and each sheet meticulously bore the imperial stamp. Every day, the lowest of eunuchs would clean out the bedpan and remove its contents to an area outside the palace, often joining the rest of the waste in the Yingtian river moat.

These daily rituals were familiar to Min Li who had lived in the palace since childhood. Yet one ritual given particular attention by the concubines was bathing.

At bath time, maids brought heated water to fill wooden tubs. The eunuchs provided palace made soaps, perfumes and towels but during bathing, they retired and maids attended to each concubine. The girls would be bathed and dabbed with a cotton cloth dipped in jasmine-scented oil or imported Persian rosewater.

While smelling good was imperative to please the emperor, fragrant satchels were also worn to ward off evil spirits. The girls sewed pouches under their sleeves, giving off effusions of magnolia, jasmine, cinnamon and clove as they wafted past in the Inner Palace.

They did not lack fine clothes. The Clothing Agency regularly dispatched eunuchs to ensure that each had enough clothes and shoes and that their attire was appropriate for the relevant ceremonies. Laundry maids collected worn or dirty clothing and these would be returned days later, carefully washed and steam pressed and if required, mended, ready to wear.

Min Li, who was already well versed in reading and writing, thanks to Princess Xia's tutelage, soon found out that not all of the girls knew how to read. Since Empress Xu, Zhu Di's consort, had died several years ago, Princess Xia, along with other princesses, often lent their support to the concubine education. Their rich knowledge supplemented the official teachings that childless maidens, hired from the township of Suzhou dispensed to the Royal Chamber.

Princess Xia held lessons almost every month, much to Min Li's delight who never went too long without seeing her adoptive mother.

Those imperial concubines who could already read were fond of sharing books. When Min Li first entered the Royal Chamber, the other girls proceeded to interrogate her on the works she had read and the poetry verses she could recite.

"To begin," declared one of the senior concubines, excited by the prospect of a challenge, "let us ask her whether she has read Empress Xu's Domestic Lessons."

"Of course she has! Haven't you, Min Li?" cheered Lan Wong.

Min Li nodded. As a dozen pair of black eyes rested on her, she sensed a competition, not unlike what she had felt during the concubine selection process.

"The Domestic Lessons are part of the Four Books for Women," she announced, knitting her brow with learned confidence. "Do you think I would be here if I had not read these," she quipped. "The eunuchs were very thorough. They asked me the same question. I told them I had read all twenty sections. But whether or not I applied them was another matter..."

Her eyes sparkled, as she gauged the effect of her wit on her audience. The other women looked at each other with foreboding. Min Li's sense of humor alarmed them.

"Let's see, what were they?" continued Min Li, determined to prove herself. "Virtuous Nature, Self-Cultivation, Care in Speaking, Scrupulous Conduct, Diligent Encouragement, Restraint and Moderation... I forget what comes next..."

"Accumulating Good," whispered one.

"Moving Towards Good," volunteered Lan Wong.

Min Li smiled with good cheer, "I always forget these two!"

They laughed, secretly relieved that she was not entirely perfect.

"Well as long as you never forget Serving the Gentleman you will no doubt prosper, Little Sister!" observed a beautifully braided Jurchen with the tiniest feet Min Li had ever seen.

Min Li continued to enumerate all the sections of the Domestic Lessons that Zhu Di's empress had once written. To the ladies of the Royal Chamber, Empress Xu represented the pinnacle of perfection, an embodiment of virtues that they knew none could hope to attain.

When she had finished, there was a glow in the room. The other women had warmed to her modesty and learning. "Excellent!" they cheered. "Well done, Min Li!"

But they were eager to test her in the manner reserved for all newcomers.

"Min Li," whispered Xue Guiren one afternoon. She bore a wicked smile that was exacerbated by the rouge on her dimples. "Do you read Chantefables?"

The girls had gathered inside the most senior Guifei's chamber. Their eyes now shone with complicity while they giggled amongst themselves, eyeing Min Li mischievously.

The noble Guifei had remained quiet until then. She had been too busy attending to the crane taking flight on her embroidery and the left wing was giving her grief. But upon hearing Xue Guiren's question, she grew distracted and pricked her finger with the needle. She pursed her lips and looked up with a stern gaze. "Tut-tut! Shame on you, Little Sisters," she said with a demure, velvety voice.

Even on this non-eventful day, Mei Guifei's face was caked with makeup. Her dangly arms were laden with jade bangles and other jade ornaments. Though not first concubine, she was currently one of the emperor's favorites which meant that the women treaded carefully around her.

"Chantefables?" asked Min Li. She was intrigued as much by the discussion as by the woman sitting on a patchwork quilt, needle in hand. "What are those?"

"Sordid tales," replied the Guifei with a wrinkle in her nose. Yet her eyes glistened. "Rhymes, love stories," she cooed with an absent tone, still fixing her crane.

"I think they're just lovely," protested a pouty Annamese.

"Now, now," replied the Guifei, prodding the needle deep into her work so that she nearly tore the silk, "that's just what I mean. Lovely things are not always welcome." The needle pierced the crane's eye with a pop. "Are they?" she added, watching Min Li closely.

Min Li grew tense with apprehension. At this, two concubines grabbed her hand to lead her into their chamber where she could better preview the books in question. If they had at all sensed the Guifei's understated meaning, they did not let it show.

***

Chantefables

"So many books!" mused Min Li. She inspected the wooden cases in which rows of leather bound publications were kept side by side. Here was a treasure trove of classic novels, almanacs and moral guides received from the princesses and the late empress. These were gifts. Such books, notably the classics, were favored for instructing women to respect the order of all things and behave in accordance to Confucian principles.

But there were other books, those forbidden for their immoral or distasteful nature. No sooner had they closed the door that Hua Xue slipped out a cloth bound publication from underneath her couch. She stepped forth, a look of defiance on her face, and ceremoniously presented Min Li with the illustrated book as though daring the newcomer to take a gander. Two other concubines fixed their insistent gaze on Min Li who, now amused, began peering through the first few pages. She emitted a gasp. The other girls giggled at her dismay.

These books contained a collection of narratives, or folk stories that had originally been told in colloquial verse by ambulant storytellers in several provinces. Print merchants in nearby Fujian had seen an opportunity in these hugely popular oral street tales and they soon compiled them into the written form for distribution. No ladies of the palace were permitted to read these publications because many years ago, they had been decreed immoral by Zhu Di's mother, Empress Ma.

One would have thought that the concubines would be highly influenced by Empress Ma's verdict, so eager were they to emulate virtuous conduct. On the contrary, the secret longing for precious, forbidden literature and the thrill of finding one that had been dissimulated into their room by a worldly, trusted eunuch, afforded the concubines with a glimpse of the danger and adventure that their lives lacked.

Min Li met one such eunuch on a cold evening, soon after dinner, while the younger concubines were gathered in the warmest chamber they could find. She soon recognized him.

As he slinked in, unannounced, the girls quietened and sat up. Some of them eyed each other, their mutual silences charged with understanding. Intrigued by this, Min Li observed both the visitor and the effect he had on the Royal Chamber.

He had entered, ever slowly, much like a snake among doves as it searches for prey. His sharp eyes pierced through the large room, feeding on every detail with a raw hunger. He watched the lazy limbs stretched out on cushioned bunks and onto improvised couches. He watched the lotus feet barely hidden beneath peach and azure silks. His quick gaze contoured the gentle curves undulating beneath sheer and silken fabrics. They writhed before him, those feminine forms, entwined as they were, among the cats, like the cats, to keep warm. Like the many feline creatures he encountered, idling and stretching in this infernal compound, there rose from these sprawled female forms, a titillating sensuality that irked him savagely.

As he absorbed that sweet, musky odor rising from the room, the man's upper lip curled into a faint sneer. Min Li could not discern whether the twitching on his lips betrayed repugnance or something else, something more predatory. Given her earlier experience with this eunuch, her senses were awakened by a warning that she could not explain but it sent a cold chill down her back.

Now whispers rose around her. Ji Feng is here! It's Ji Feng! It was as though the women were all back in the selection hall and the Royal Chamber director were tapping on his cane, vying for their attention. In this case it worked. The concubines interrupted their idling and sat upright on their knees, attentive to the visitor.

Ji Feng raised his head high, assessing whether all eyes were on him and perhaps, intuited Min Li, as a show of his power. Still, that unmistakable sneer remained on his lip as though he were afraid of being contaminated by the occupants in the room but all the while enjoyed breathing them in.

Xun Guifei shuffled towards him with apprehension. "You were not to come until the next day," she reproached quietly, looking behind the door to ensure that no other eunuch lurked in the corridor.

"I, alone, choose when I come."

"But you said—"

"Times are difficult. You should be pleased that I managed to come at all," hissed Ji Feng.

Xun Guifei said nothing then. She lowered her gaze apologetically.

Up to now, Min Li had dismissed the rising tension in the room. But as the Guifei's gaze became resigned to the carpet, the young concubine looked around only to see that all the other women were submissively eyeing this Ji Feng. She couldn't believe it. Here was the officer who months earlier had tried to beat her in the Royal Chamber director's bureau. Disgust mounted inside her. Yet she reasoned that if she were to reveal him, her own conduct would come to light. So she chose to remain silent.

At last, he slowly unfolded the bundle he held in his wiry arms. With a glimmer in his eyes, he smiled, revealing a row of yellow-stained teeth that further repulsed Min Li.

"The latest tales from the printing houses of Fujian," he began, presenting the first book for all to see. "What do you think, hmm?" breathed Ji Feng, waiting for their response. "Ah, yes, and this one!" He licked his lips. "This one is my favorite! Chantefables from the South! Hmm?" His knotty fingers ran down the book's spine like a hideous caress.

Ji Feng fed on his audience's wonder. A savage glow lit up his pimply complexion and his eyes darted to every corner of the room, savoring every beaming face.

And it was like a magic spell. Min Li watched the concubines emit gasps and smile with glee. She watched them lick their lips, eager to devour every page and be transported into worlds they would never see or experience. Ji Feng had them captivated. And they paid him well. Each would raise a little of their stipend and hand them over to Guifei Xun.

When he had received his due and made motion to retire, Ji Feng's eyes surveyed the room one last time and saw a figure he had not previously noticed. Min Li returned his gaze, hinting that she was no longer afraid of him and confident in their mutual understanding. She had remained to the far corner of the room, her knees drawn up towards her chin, a kitten resting on her warm lap, her eyes partly concealed behind a rebellious hair strand.

She knew that her large feet had caught his eyes. She responded by hiding them beneath her skirt, not out of shame but out of fury that he had dared to regard her. Foreign to the ritualized delivery of forbidden books, she showed little enthusiasm, remaining quietly in retreat while the other concubines leapt to their feet and scrambled to take a look at their three new treasures.

Ji Feng observed her, a calculated smile etched on his face.

"This is Min Li," explained Xun Guifei. "One of our new girls this month...Min Li, come and say hello to Ji Feng."

"Come and see what Ji Feng has brought for us," cheered one of the concubines.

Min Li did not budge. She feigned somnolence, closing her eyes to wish the man away.

"Ah, she is too shy," lied Mei Guifei in Min Li's favor. "Min Li...Where are your manners?"

As though he accepted the Guifei's apology, Ji Feng tilted his narrow head with a mixture of feigned lenience and damaged pride. But Min Li saw through his charade. In the last glance he shot at her, she sensed his raging resentment.

It seemed Ji Feng had some power over the concubines and enjoyed this. But she wasn't keen on letting herself be intimidated over mere trifles like Chantefables. So she met his eyes with a defiant glare that would have made Princess Xia proud.

And when he had gone, Min Li promised herself she would not succumb to the spell he had evidently cast on the other women.

Honored reader, it may seem to you a contradiction that Ji Feng came to be trusted and commerced with the very beings that he considered abject and for whom he secretly entertained passionate violent impulses.

It is often the very beings we loathe or feel envy for who seem to exert a fascination in us. This was also true of Ji Feng and his intrigue for palace concubines.

***

Waiting

Min Li soon discovered that Life in the Royal Chamber was an agonizing wait for eventful days. Reading provided the fantasy and excitement so lacking in the women's lives.

Boredom was the norm. And for lack of freedom to explore the world, till the land, cook, or raise their own children, the concubines had to endure much idleness for an average of ten to fifteen years. After this period, they could be released back to their families or find an occupation as a laundry maid.

Aside from literary pleasures and spending long hours perfecting their embroidery, the concubines were fond of collecting pretty trinkets of all sorts, hair pins, combs, jade bracelets, charms, many of which were gifts from the emperor himself.

Playing in the winding alleys of the garden was another pastime. Surrounded by cypress trees, pines and flowers, the ladies idled all day long or played hide-and-seek behind the stone formations.

And then of course there were the official duties. It was the duty of every concubine to participate in religious ceremonies or take part in the lunar festivities at the start of each month. These were the rare times when the ladies could venture away from the palace, dressed in beautiful fabrics inviting the eyes of the world to glimpse their elusive forms always shielded by the escorting eunuchs. They were fond of organized sorties with the worldly princesses, the rare monastery visits, the short stays in the other palaces.

On those occasions, Min Li longed to finally pass the palace gates and breathe the mixed auras of Yingtian. For hours, she would gladly abandon herself to the enduring sway of her caravan as it moved across the marketplace and traveled to the nearby palaces. Propped on brocaded silk cushions, a thin veil of sheer fabric covering her face, she peered avidly through the sedan curtain for a glimpse of the world that some had known while she could only imagine. And to think that her adoptive father commanded the emperor's fleet and that he could take her away to see this world if he so wished. Where was he now?

After being secluded day after day within the palace walls, any escapade was welcome. And so the women were eager to please the emperor because it meant that they would be chosen to accompany him on his rare frivolous sorties.

But most of all, the ladies of the palace were fond of cats. These creatures wandered in and out the long carpeted corridors and were found perched in every corner of the rooms.

It is not a surprise if these creatures were pampered and fussed about. The cats entered the Royal Chamber as gifts from the emperor and princesses, and all too soon became substitute children for these bored, affection craved women who passed time as best they could.

As one would expect from any human congregation where movement and freedom are limited, gossip, exciting news and all manner of lengthy philosophical discussions kept the Royal Chamber girls occupied. And because there were girls with different personalities and different origins, cliques were formed so that secrets were held by different groups and these groups rivalled for the emperor's attention.

To be privy to secrets, meant that one belonged. No sooner had Min Li passed several tests of conduct and obtained the approval of the other concubines that these relaxed in her presence. It was easy. In all her social encounters, she demonstrated enough reserve, saying only what was necessary and always remaining humble about her knowledge and abilities. There was no need to arouse jealousy, she thought. Soon, she was privy to the rumors.

One such rumor was that they would soon move to a bigger palace. The new palace would be located in Beiping because this had once been the princedom of their emperor. One of the eunuchs whose father worked for the Minister of Civil Works had told them so.

"A bigger palace? Oh, just think, we would each have prettier rooms and more space!" said a beaming Lan Wong.

"And more cats! Imagine a room full of cats!" added Mai Zhou, ever eager to fill the void in her loveless life with more possessions.

"I should hope for a larger garden, I do tire of this one. I know its every plants, now."

"There will be one," assured another concubine. "A eunuch told me that we are to play in Jing Shan!"

"Whoever told you this nonsense, Little Sister? Eunuchs cannot be trusted," chided Mei Guifei, offended that she had not herself been advised by the said eunuch.

"Jing Shan?" asked Lan Wong with apprehension. "What is that?"

"It is a mound on the site of the new palace where there are lovely views."

"What I heard is that Jing Shan is good Feng Shui. It will protect the new city from northern dust storms—"

"Dust storms!" shrieked one. "Are there dust storms in Beiping? It sounds horrible! I don't want to go! Imagine not being able to go outside all day. I shan't like that at all."

Min Li had not said a word up to now. There was, she thought, an air of gaiety and excitement from all the women but it belied their real emotions. As for all new matters deciding their fate, the concubines were often left in the dark. It was up to them to cajole the eunuchs or the emperor, if they ever could, to draw information, and hence obtain some control over the course of their lives. Living in the palace was about survival so as not to be too surprised if something dramatic like the arrival of a tempestuous newcomer should come to sweep their lives.

Apprehension and insecurity were rampant among the women. Always on their guard, they feared the ire of the paranoid and vengeful Zhu Di. All change, even if it stirred their excitement, was also viewed with suspicion. They would one day leave Yingtian, to be escorted in a procession of imperial sedans, flanked by retainers on horseback, all the way to Beiping. They did not know what to expect and when. They did not know whether some of them would be left behind.

Min Li who since then, had pondered over largely different matters, spoke at last.

"How do we know when we are to meet the emperor?" she asked.

The others turned towards her. They observed her with calculated silence. Since Min Li's arrival, they had forgotten that she had not yet spent the night with the emperor. They wondered how she would be received by Zhu Di. For a passing moment, they both feared for Min Li's wellbeing and saw a threat in her.

It was the pragmatic Xun Guifei who finally answered.

"On the day you are chosen, your name will be written on the board outside by the afternoon. The eunuchs do not bother on special mourning days though..."

"And on special fasting days," continued another older concubine.

"The emperor is not so demanding," chuckled one.

"Silence!" warned Xun Guifei. Then she turned again to Min Li. "If you are ill, you shall advise the eunuchs and they will make the necessary arrangements to call onto someone else. But we cannot see a male physician. You must write down all your ills and have them noted by the eunuch who will then speak on your behalf to an imperial physician."

"And we may never leave the palace!" added a chubby concubine for good measure as she buried her nose in a furry kitten that was all but strangled in her tiny arms.

"She already knows this, silly," reproached Mei Guifei with her imperative velvety voice.

It seemed to Min Li that Mei Guifei wished that it were otherwise and that Min Li was indeed, well away from the palace grounds.

Chapter 8
The Emperor

Several months later, just after dinner on a cold evening, the emperor selected Min Li's name from the silver tray of tablets bearing his concubines' names. The eunuch took away the tray and rushed off to advise the Royal Chamber officers. After months of checking for her name in vain, Min Li saw it written on the board outside the concubine compound. It was her first night of meeting the emperor. It happened a fortnight after she had barely turned fourteen. She felt a rush of excitement and swelling pride.

Two servant girls shuffled into the preparation chamber. Each carried a bucket of heated water. A third maid brought a tray of rolled towels heaped into a pyramid. Min Li sat naked in a wooden tub while the maids dipped towels in the water and washed her limbs. They rubbed palace-made soap all over her body and rinsed away the lather. Finally they used the remnant towels to pat her dry. Sitting Min Li on a stool, the maids oiled and combed her hair for braiding. When they had finished coiling and pinning braids around her double bun, they retired.

No sooner had they left that two concubines entered to assist with the makeup. Min Li had slipped into a full-length sheer robe. Now the girls tied long blue ribbons around her braids and arranged little flowers in the crown of her hair. Next they plucked and drew in her eyebrows into dark crescent moons. After applying a white powdered base, they proceeded with the rouge. One of the girls dabbed red pomade on Min Li's cheeks while the other spread a lighter shade of powdered vermillion on her eyelids.

"Now," said the first, "we will teach you how to paint your lips in the erotic fashion."

She dipped a tiny brush into lip balm and pressed it across the center of Min Li's lips. She stood back and offered her a mirror.

"Like this! See? The red is vivid in the center of your pout. Just like a ripened cherry."

"We're almost done, now," said the other. "Give me your hand."

Gently, the girl dipped her fingertips into a dye that Min Li had never seen before. It was an odd blend of egg whites, beeswax, Arabic gum and balsamic dye and it had soon colored her nails and her fingertips with a flirty tinge of red.

Min Li floated in a giddy euphoria. She knew not what to expect but felt very special. Did all concubines feel as special every time they were to meet the emperor? They probably did. She thought of how proud she had felt when the Royal Chamber eunuch had advised her of the emperor's choice. She had soon pictured Hua Xue, her obvious rival and wondered whether she could outdo her.

When the other concubines had left, she examined her reflection in the full-length mirror. Then, without hesitation, she removed the flowers, and loosened her hair out of its braids. She wanted it to fall above her shoulders. Yes, like this. It was perfect.

She stood still before the mirror, practicing her pout. A strange thought crossed her mind. There was, it seemed, a curious desire within her to inspire the emperor's favoritism and topple the older concubine, Xun Guifei. It rose out of nowhere such that she hardly recognized herself and questioned her desire.

She contemplated the rules of the game in her new life. For the courtesans, there was only one choice. It was to compete with other women while at the same time, strive to win their affection. Somehow, she knew that concubines needed one another to thrive in the palace. But she also knew that a courtesan was nothing if she lost her emperor's favor. And hence there existed a double game, here, in the Inner Palace.

The first evening *geng* sounded. Min Li's heart skipped a beat. She felt that thrill again. It promised adventure, the unknown. It would be easy, she thought. I can do this.

Darkness blanketed the imperial city of Yingtian. And as it happened, every night, the emperor had retired to one of his bed chambers. Each night, no one save for the dozen or so eunuchs in charge of attending to him, knew of his exact location within the hundreds of room in the Imperial Palace. These were measures aimed at protecting his life.

No sooner had he dismissed his entourage and sat to savor his tea that two Royal Chamber eunuchs presented themselves. Between them, they carried a load high on their shoulders. It was a rolled feathered rug. When the emperor had given the sign, they carefully offloaded the rolled cloak onto the carpet. In silence, they pressed their brows to the ground before their emperor. At last, they eclipsed themselves.

The chamber was now perfectly still but for two distinct sounds. The first of these was sharp and regular, like two lacquered surfaces hitting against each other at intervals. The other sound was fast and erratic. It was not unlike faint whistling. It seemed to come from the rolled red fabric that the emperor was now eyeing carefully while he toyed with his Tao balls in one hand.

The clicking came to a halt. He put the Tao balls away and continued to watch the feathered roll before him. Now he could better discern the nervous breathing emanating from beneath the fabric. He smiled.

"You can come out now."

The breathing halted.

"Come out," the emperor repeated.

The mysterious thing inside the red rug stirred and appeared to stiffen as though still deciding. The emperor fixed the rug eagerly. Then, with an understated violence, the mass unfolded onto the floor. Soon a sea of red down unfurled across the carpet and its contents began to take human shape, revealing first, an alabaster leg then another, followed by a jet of entangled black hair and at last, two exquisite nipples perched arrogantly on soft, milky breasts. The released nymph panted from the effort. Then, sensing the imperial presence, she rose up on her palms looking up like a fierce cat between two black strands. She was terrified.

The emperor's voice rose, deep and poised. Through her temples, she felt the quickening pace of her racing heart.

"You must understand. It is not our intention to embarrass your modesty."

He advanced towards her, his towering mass pounding the ground with every step.

"But security matters to your emperor. The eunuchs had to ensure that you did not come armed or carried anything that could harm me. When you leave tonight, you will also leave in the same state. Here, wear this."

He reached out for a silken robe and covered her shoulders.

"On your feet, Min Li," he ordered.

He observed the trembling teenage girl as she pushed one arm through the sleeve. While she dressed, his eyes lingered casually across her little breasts and down to the black patch between her thighs. He caught sight of her feet.

"You remind me of my mother," he said.

He stood back to examine her with a distracted air. "But you are very beautiful."

Even his compliments inspired dread.

Min Li glanced at the man who had just seen her completely naked and felt the fire rise to her cheeks. He was easily in his late fifties, still strong and rightly proud of his powerful mass. He was of medium to tall height. A long, stiff beard pointed down from his chin and a thin moustache protruded arrogantly from either side of his mouth. When he talked, his sharp, scheming eyes often squinted under plush eyebrows. This gave him the appearance of a man who was astute but careful at hiding it.

"I would like us to become good friends, Min Li," he said.

Without hesitating, he reached out an arm to touch her. He stroked her chin. Min Li's eyes widened with apprehension. All those well-practiced seduction tricks, those she had never in fact used on any men but believed she somehow possessed, seemed to vanish from her mind.

Under his caresses, she could no longer think. She noticed the room was thick with incense, perhaps giving off what the concubines had referred to as an aphrodisiac. Smoke fogged her vision. It rendered less severe the lines on the old emperor's face. His ruthless traits were softened under the glowing mist.

With a resigned sigh, she inhaled the incense. He drew her close and continued to stroke her neck with his coarse, soldier palms. Seizing her jaw in one hand, he forced her to face him until their eyes met. It was a violent encounter one she knew was forbidden but it was precisely why this thrilled him. She read something in those eyes, danger...the unknown.

His breathing came like a series of grunts as he savored the display of her young, shapely body. Min Li grew more alarmed. She sensed that perhaps the emperor could read through her. She felt small and stupid. She felt foolish, completely at his mercy.

Now as they faced each other, he clawed her left breast and toyed with the nipple. With his other hand, he caressed her smooth thigh, brushing his fingers from her knee up, all the while, hungrily licking his lips. She felt the blood drain from her limbs. She tried to avoid his gaze to at least calm her racing heart. Yet she understood that to resist was death.

Now he was tugging at the sash around her waist. He wanted to disrobe her all over again. She stared at him with alarm. His caress grew more demanding. His fingers were hard between her thighs. The vice like grip hurt her arm and she looked at him in protest. Then, just as she felt tears of shame well up in her eyes, the pain eased. The emperor cursed. He released her.

She did not understand what had happened. It seemed something had gone wrong and the emperor was not happy. Fear, once more, set in. She drew the red silk robe back over her shoulders and waited. She watched him pick up the teacup and pour some *pu'er* tea. He inhaled the aroma and sipped it quietly.

She was still standing there, in the middle of the room, not certain what to do or think. Was he finished? Could she go now? She expected him to summon the eunuchs to take her away. But he did not. The emperor drank. He poured another cup. It seemed as though he really had forgotten her.

Then, without warning, he looked in her direction and pronounced with a tart, reproachful voice, "Your feet are far too big."

It was like a slap. Fear was replaced with anger. Her pride simmered inside her but she knew to say nothing. Better not argue. Just observe and learn, she thought.

But the emperor had other ideas. In fact, talking and elaborating his plan was exactly what he wanted to do, at least for now. The problem is that he had not attempted these new designs before and he ignored the best way to begin. True, he often used his knowledge of the Art of War to destabilize his ministers during confrontational discussions about state matters. And he could easily convince himself that a concubine would be no match for his mind games.

But this... This was a different matter. How could he trap this woman? How could he best use her?

There was one thing he understood about concubines and that one thing was evident also in Min Li. They all wanted to please him. Thanks to his late consort's insipid books on womanly virtues, he found himself doted on by spineless, soft women who bent to his will and did all they could to satisfy him. All of them without exception, wanted his approval and the good behaviors they apparently manifested was only a facade aimed at indulging their emperor and gaining from it. So much for virtue, he thought. Luckily he had soon learned to use their craving for approval to his advantage. He knew that to take it away meant to destabilize them. Fear worked in most, if not all, the cases.

He lowered the cup and looked up with an air of having had great expectations that have just been deceived. "You are very quiet, Min Li."

Min Li swallowed nervously, wondering what to say. Everything was not going the way she had thought. She was beginning to doubt her suitability as concubine. She felt small.

"Have the Guifeis ensured that you met with your educators?" he asked.

She did not have time to reply. "They are some of the most intelligent, most talented women in the country. Well versed in literacy and the arts. You must learn from them. We want you to spend regular hours finessing your skills. We must develop this fine mind of yours."

"Yes, Your Highness."

"Very good, we shall see to it that you are well instructed."

He took a sip from his tea. "You must learn how to write well. It is of high importance. You see..." He sipped the semi-fermented tea once more. "Min Li, do you know why you are here?"

"Yes... I mean, no."

The emperor nodded. "What happened tonight will no doubt happen again. But with you...With you, I want something...*different.*"

Min Li listened, bullied by his coarse expressions. She wasn't sure what the emperor was trying to tell her. Would she be asked to dance perhaps? Or maybe recite poems? She was at loss. What was she supposed to do? Maybe the emperor was after a special form of coupling? She panicked. She tried in vain to recall the scandalous illustrations she had seen when the other concubines had lent her their most prized illustrated book; the one they had sworn never to mention in front of the princesses. In those saucy vignettes, the naked figures brandished wooden toys and the women straddled the man in the most original manner. That was all she could recall because at the time, she had been distracted by the way her bed companions giggled at every turn of the page. She swallowed hard.

The emperor continued to talk forcefully, luring her away from her thoughts. "You are beautiful, intelligent, and I have heard, cunning."

Min Li said nothing. She remained perfectly still. She continued to listen.

In the shadows of his partly open robe, she could discern the hair on his broad chest and the bulge of jagged scars. She understood that this was and always would be a man of the field, a man who was not afraid of battle. She continued sizing him up as he spoke.

Meanwhile, Zhu Di was equally fascinated. She resembled her crazy mother. It made him uncomfortable but he had to continue with this. It was important.

"I need someone like you," he said, interrupting his long monologue. He watched her carefully for changes.

Min Li felt that something was wrong. But she could not say what. What did he mean by all this? And had he really been put off by her feet? It was something she had envisaged would happen. But she had hoped perhaps that her charm would compensate. But now, she dreaded the thought that she would never really compare with Xun Guifei. Her head throbbed from all the tension and the long anxious hours she had waited today.

"Min Li!"

"Your Highness."

"At last," smiled the emperor with mellow indulgence, "I thought you would refuse to speak to me."

He stroked his beard and nodded again with appreciation.

"You and I shall soon become very good friends, Min Li. I shall teach you many things and you shall become useful to me."

But I will be patient, he thought. *First things first.*

"Tell me, my girl, have you made friends with the other concubines yet?"

"Some of them, Your Highness."

"Good! And what do you think of them?"

"They are—"

"Yes?"

"Beautiful, Your Highness."

"Of course. Of course. And did you like your tutors? You must show respect for the noble women of Suzhou. They have come all the way to the palace to instruct you. They are highly cultured women."

"I have met one about a month ago..."

"Good, this pleases me. You shall learn how to sing, dance..."

He eyed her feet.

"That should not be too difficult for you. I hear you already know how to read..."

"Princess Xia taught me."

"Did she, now?" The emperor had turned grave at her words but he forced himself to smile. "That is excellent," he said. "And we shall be able to converse and talk poetry. You must know all about the arts of conversation. It is, how shall I say this…the most important part of your education. Do you understand?"

Min Li did not understand but she was ready to agree to anything. She lowered her head and nodded.

The emperor stood.

"And... Do you know your way around the palace?" It was an interesting question. He already knew the answer.

"I... Yes. Yes I do," replied Min Li proudly.

"And you are familiar with the eunuchs of the palace?"

Min Li did not understand. Well of course she was. She'd lived here all her life hadn't she? She knew about their ranks and the work they did. She knew some by sight for years. And she could remember the names of the directors. What kind of a question...

"Some of them, Your Highness," she replied. Then, seeing that he was not satisfied, she added, "I know of the important ones".

The emperor caressed his beard again, nodding approvingly. He was inscrutable, so unlike the people she had since met in her short life inside the palace. Min Li's mind was now working overtime.

Zhu Di was pleased but weary at the upcoming task before him. This would be a long night, he thought. She needed to trust him first and he would slowly, over the months, years even, make her trust him.

She would be perfect.

He could see her trying to seduce him already. If it were not for his damn problem he would have had her already. He did want her, even with her impossibly huge feet. But he told himself that she would strip his already depleting *yang* if he was not careful. Besides, he had better ways to use her, far better ways.

"Tell me, Min Li, how far would you go to please me?" he began.

Min Li's eyes widened. The invitation in the emperor's voice seemed promising.

"What does my emperor wish?"

He smiled.

"I seek someone special, someone who is not afraid. And what I ask of her will take her time even outside the night chamber."

She sensed it. This fulfilled all her wishes. It was a test, a demonstration of her unique devotion, an opportunity to surpass the other concubines and finally impress her adoptive father. She rose from the bed, leaving the robe behind so that she now stood proud and haughty in her naked beauty. She looked him straight in the eye.

"How far does Your Majesty wish me to go?"

For a moment he pondered over how she could appear so shy one moment and so self-assured the next. It seemed like the girl was different person at different times. He had a fleeting afterthought, a glimpse of an omen that had him almost reconsider his plan. But he ignored the superstitious thought. He was a soldier and would not back down. The opportunity should not be wasted.

She is perfect. This is what I have wanted for many years. It must be with her.

***

In the Hours of the Tiger, when the eunuchs escorted Min Li back to the concubine quarter, she was exhausted. Her head throbbed like never before. She found herself sleeping well into the afternoon. At around midday, when she was almost awake, she thought she saw Xun Guifei watch her closely through the doorway. When she opened her eyes, the chamber was empty.

Later the next afternoon, when the other concubines had been officially dismissed, a high-ranking eunuch approached her alone with a tray.

"The emperor would like you to have these."

Min Li's eyes widened with curiosity as the eunuch raised the contents of the tray. They were coin-shaped jade earrings mounted on gold with filigree pendants so fine, they seemed like golden hair.

"A gift from the emperor," declared the eunuch.

She did not think twice. Victory made her smile. This had been a challenging night and it seemed she had proven herself. Once she was alone, she set one of the dangling jewels to her earlobe and watched the reflections dance in the mirror.

This would be the beginning of many rewards for Min Li. In the meantime, there was much work to be done. She breathed a sigh of satisfaction.

Chapter 9
The Qilin

Yingtian, 1415

Cosmopolitan Yingtian burst with life. In the imperial city, a procession of travelers from far beyond the Middle Kingdom had arrived after a long journey aboard Admiral Zheng He's fleet. Colorful posters were pasted onto every wall of the city, and those who could read joined in the collective praise for the admiral and the glory of Ming.

It was a tribute bearing ceremony. The emperor looked on from the Gate of Supreme Harmony as visitors from beyond the seas kowtowed multiple times. To the emperor, the envoys knelt three times before prostrating themselves nine times. To the crown prince, they prostrated eight times.

Those who submitted to this symbolic ritual were indeed blessed. For was not their sole intention to trade with the most industrial country in the world. And for this privilege, they left their homes for months, sometimes years, and brought gifts with them, obliging even the emperor's whims. What would they not do for profit? Ming hospitality offered a restricted but nevertheless advantageous trading schedule in Yingtian. Loyalty to the Ming meant business profit. It also ensured the Ming's protection.

To be sure, the trading foreigners had to first prove that they were state representatives. Yet some of these were hardly ambassadors. They had not sighted or signed a single diplomatic document in their life. Not that it mattered. Business was what they sought. And the Ming tributary system favored their business.

Once all tribute bearers had paid their respect to the emperor, fierce drum sounds rose again and a gong announced the arrival of a man they all waited for. The tall red-clad rider emerged, sitting with dignity on his giant white horse. He advanced through the large gate flanked by a procession of soldiers, each bearing a tasseled Ming banner.

The emperor had sat idly, watching from atop the gate building. But as the man crossed the gate, Zhu Di stood to welcome him. Inside that very building, from where the shielded concubines looked on with disinterest, one of the women rose from her languorous mood and gazed through a lattice pane. She observed the rider below with somber intent.

He wore a jade-hilted sword. A giant jade buckle sealed his belt. He was large at the waist yet still moved with agility as he steered his horse to the side to make way for the rest of the procession.

The horses gathered into a formation. What followed drew even more excitement from the crowd. Into the palace, there came a file of exotic animals each tied to a leash and each drawing gasps from the audience. They came in, one by one, each led by a skilled eunuch. First a lion, then a tiger until there, amidst the wondrous sighs, another spotted beast with its tall neck and funny ears followed suit. While the enthralled assembly sighed, praising the mythical beauty of the *qilin*, Min Li only saw him.

He looked more vigorous than his forty four-years. She noticed the high cheeks and the broad, intelligent forehead. As he lifted his head towards his emperor, her avid gaze found his large glaring eyes and elegant nose. A mixture of envy and bitterness rose through her.

"Min Li, who are you looking at? The animals are over there," chided one of her companions, pointing towards an African elephant.

"Admiral Zheng He."

They squeezed together beside Min Li, determined to take a gander through the pane.

"He looks so handsome!" cheered the girls as they pressed their faces against the wooden lattice.

"For a eunuch he isn't too bad," said one.

"And what a lovely horse!"

"He is so tall!"

All they knew of him was through his reputation. Always by Zhu Di's side, some said Admiral Zheng He was the cleverest and most loyal eunuch that the emperor had. The scale of this man's achievements invited admiration.

Min Li looked on. A moody pout drew itself on her lips. It galled her to watch him. She had quietly recalled the admiral's repute and dismissed all stories told of him. There was, however, one story she did not forget, one which Princess Xia had told her and of which she was most fond.

Only it seemed that *he* had forgotten it.

The animals were led away towards the menagerie. With the gong and drums fading into a distant rhythm, the procession ebbed. Palace eunuchs and sedan chair carriers motioned to escort the emperor, together with his imperial court, to their private chambers. Before long, visitors returned to their idle palaces on the outskirts of the city.

While the melee of noisy guests left the palace, still, one of the women waited. She had not left her chamber with the intention of watching the procession. There was much that Princess Xia preferred to do rather than waste her time honoring a giant goat. That's what the *qilin* was for her, and she found it amusing how this long-necked, ugly animal had acquired mythological properties among the court. If she was at all present today, it was because she was anxious to speak with Min Li.

She shuffled towards the large gate, eager to embrace the young woman. In her haste, she tripped on the hem of her skirt and gave a startled cry, latching onto the first thing in her grasp to avert her fall. To her disgust, this happened to be Ji Feng's robe.

"Princess, you ought to be more careful, hmm," warned the wiry eunuch in his smooth, oily voice.

"I am unharmed!" barked Princess Xia putting her hand to her hip to ward off further pain and pushing the eunuch away. "How dare you touch me!"

At this, Ji Feng kowtowed dispassionately and stepped aside, his mouth curling in disdain. A cheerful voice made Princess Xia forget her indignation.

"Princess Xia! Did you hurt yourself, my princess?"

"It is nothing. My knee giving me grief, as usual. These celebrations exhaust me. Standing all day on my bound feet to watch tributaries bow all day pleases no woman. His Majesty seems to have a fondness for inconveniencing court ladies."

"So then," she added, clearing her throat, "have the Guifeis been kind to you since the last time I saw you? You have been well, I hope."

"Princess Xia, I suggest we retire from here," whispered Min Li. Princess Xia gave a furtive glance towards her right where Ji Feng still stood, watching them with his haughty eyes.

"Why, the insolent! To the gardens then! Come with me. Ji Feng sends a shiver through my spine, too. He has, I hear, some thriving business with the princesses."

Princess Xia hobbled along still holding Min Li's sleeve as she spoke. "It has given him airs these days. I tried to talk sense into those other ladies but they all dote on him. There's nothing I can do."

"He has acquired influence," remarked Min Li in a tone that the princess hardly recognized. "I believe he is to be promoted. I do not like him. But he shall soon manage concubine education and well, here's the thing, Princess, I have seen the manner in his eyes when he looks at us."

Princess Xia's eyes narrowed with vengeance. "Keep your wits about you. The impudent tried to lay hands on me, not a moment ago. I despise eunuchs! But he is certainly the worst of them."

They reached the Imperial Gardens at last.

"Ah, here we are," sighed the princess. "I can finally sit. So, now that we are alone at last..." She looked around her as if to better ascertain that fact. "Tell me everything. It is everything you hoped for this year, isn't it? Being His Majesty's concubine is a privilege."

"Oh, yes," said Min Li a little too evasively.

Princess Xia suppressed a frown. "And... His Majesty?"

"Oh, you mean, my very energetic lover?" giggled Min Li.

"What you wrote to me is true then!" exclaimed Princess Xia. "The princesses say he's as limp as—"

"Hush!"

They exchanged a knowing glance.

"The emperor has only just returned from his last tryst with the Mongols," continued Min Li. "So I suppose that court life has been more interesting since. But...well, nothing new apart from—"

"What of your relationship with the other girls? Hua Xue?"

"Caustic as always."

"You must never trust that girl."

"I never do. Not after the necklace incident."

Princess Xia nodded, remembering how Min Li had almost been caned for supposedly stealing the necklace that Xue Guiren had herself hidden.

"Now what of the senior ladies...Xun Guifei still haughty in your regard?"

"She's learning to keep her distances. The emperor's growing generosity towards me has seen her virtue flourish."

Princess Xia frowned.

"Generosity?"

"I have now earned a beautiful gilded phoenix," cheered Min Li before immediately biting her lips.

Princess Xia nodded quietly.

"His Majesty seems to find you deserving of gifts. What is your secret, Min Li?"

The concubine blushed and lowered her gaze.

Princess Xia waited for Min Li to reply but the young woman remained silent. There was something unsettling about her silence. Princess Xia contemplated the concubine with an uneasy expression before changing the subject.

"You have pleased His Highness. I am though most pleased about the girls. Last year, your existence was made unbearable by the other Guirens, but you have earned their trust. It is not easy. And what of that chamber eunuch you've mentioned to me several times?"

"He is loyal. I can trust him."

"Excellent. You must cultivate these alliances. You never know when they can come to good use. And are you practicing the code?"

Her eyes glowing, Min Li sprang up from her seat and onto her feet. She stood confidently in front of her adoptive mother and composed a demure, elegant pose. Then without warning and keeping her eyes ahead of her, she pressed her thumb to her right ear and then raised it gracefully to brush the outer edge of her right eyebrow.

"Very good," smiled the princess. "Anyone would believe you were grooming yourself. It was excellent. I will teach you more hand gestures tonight, at the banquet. When the others are fussing about Admiral Zheng He, we shall meet. I miss our time together..."

She sighed, observing her adopted daughter with joy. "We should do this more often," she said, overcome by a youthful enthusiasm that Min Li had not noticed in her before. "We should meet here and talk like we used to."

But the concubine's expression had changed on mention of the admiral. She, who had been so content demonstrating her secret code earlier, had now resumed a gloomy air.

Noticing the seventeen year old's changed expression, Princess Xia grew tense.

"What is it?"

"Oh, nothing," muttered Min Li. "I probably should not speak of those things."

Princess Xia stared at Min Li with unveiled intensity.

"Please tell me. What is troubling you?"

Min Li sighed. Her eyes looked reproachful.

"Princess Xia, why could you not tell me?" she began.

In response, the princess's eyes widened. She grew pale and began to stutter.

"I...I... Tell you what?"

"Please, you know what I am talking about."

"I... It is not what you—"

"It was Zheng He all along! Yet you did not tell me!"

Princess Xia knit her brow. She was now more confused than flustered.

"You knew he was like an adopted father to me," continued Min Li, "and you hid it from me. Oh, Princess, everyone knows him just as he casts me aside."

Princess Xia suddenly understood and, far from remaining disconcerted, her traits relaxed. Min Li did not notice this transformation or question Princess Xia's response. Instead, the concubine continued speaking animatedly about her absent father.

"All these years, the admiral visits the palace and is celebrated in great pomp as if he were a mighty hero. It is all about him. You saw what happened today! It is not the first time a *qilin* is presented to the emperor. The Bengal ruler sent one a couple of years ago but today, did you see? Did you see? Zheng He this, Zheng He that. All this time, they say he's the emperor's new hero and everyone, everyone knows him. Everyone..."

"My child, calm yourself..."

"I feel like a fool. Princess Xia, he is known by everyone. I'm just a shadow in all this fanfare. He cares so little, not even enough to enquire about me. Or maybe visit me..."

Princess Xia sensed bitterness.

"Yes, it doesn't seem very fair does it? But the admiral is very taken by his duties. You know he would be suspect if the emperor found him giving you, or any other concubines for that matter, too much attention. You must calm yourself."

Min Li shook her head. "I have to make him see me," she sighed. "Do you think the admiral has forgotten his promise to my mother?"

"His promise... Oh, Min Li. It was not even official. Your mother was selected for the burial ritual... She did not know him... It was—"

"But he gave his word! He did! He promised he would take care of me, did he not?" cried Min Li, as if she had herself been there on that day. "That's what you told me. Why did he lie?"

"He has had affairs of the state in mind. He has other adoptive children...in Yunnan... Why, he is barely in the palace these days..." *And he is a cursed eunuch,* seethed the princess. But she silenced those thoughts and wrapped her long arms around Min Li's shoulders.

"I only want him to notice me and to ask about me. Just once!" said Min Li burying her face in Princess Xia's silk robe.

"I know how you feel, Min Li," whispered the princess holding her tight and inhaling her lovely hair.

"He knows about me...but he carries on and avoids me as if I do not exist! He fails in his promise to my mother."

Princess Xia released Min Li, astounded by the girl's imagination. How could the girl infer those things about a man she had never met? Had she been foolish to tell her that Zheng He was like her father? She bit her lips.

"Min Li, let him be. Listen, you must know something. I have never mentioned it because there was no need to. You are a grown woman now. You do not need him. And the emperor takes good care of you, yes? I know how pleased he is... Listen. There are rumors, Min Li. The princesses, the Guifeis, me...we believe that you will be named Guifei very soon..."

Min Li had heard the word Guifei. A small part of her stirred with interest yet she continued to pout and did not respond.

The royal lady was troubled. How could the girl entertain so much anger towards a man she had never met? Where could such misplaced passion lead to, wondered Princess Xia, alarmed by the concubine's outburst. And from whence had it come?

Princess Xia was wise enough to know that only one person could be held accountable for Min Li's emotional state. And so the person she found herself thinking about was none other than Zhu Di. She thought about this man and what he was capable of.

She recalled how he had murdered countless royals upon ascending the throne. And what he had done to her years ago. She swallowed hard trying to push away those memories. And now Min Li was in this man's bed. The realization struck her.

She would have to keep an eye on the girl and ensure they met more often. She knew even *that* would gall the emperor. But she had no choice. She had noticed a more troubled Min Li and was determined to save the girl's spirit.

"The admiral does care enough for you, sweet child," she resumed in a cheerful tone. "When you run around and play, like a monkey in the gardens...you remember every day, don't you, that if it wasn't for him, you would have bound feet, just like the rest of us."

"I do remember that day," replied Min Li who had reconstructed Princess Xia's tale many times in her mind. A glow of hope lingered in her eyes.

"Well then, hold fast to that memory and be happy. It is his gift to you. That is all you need from him. Now, let him be. Do not afflict yourself with pursuing his affection."

They were both silent for a while. And then Min Li began to sing in a happy tone. Princess Xia smiled. That's much better, she thought, as she joined in, reaching even higher notes. But unknown to her, an idea had sprung in the concubine's mind.

And as Min Li hummed lofty notes, the clever idea was forged into a plan. She would have to talk to Zhu Di first and he may not like it. But it could work.

Talks of the fifth expedition were already circulating. Zheng He would no doubt disappear to the ship docks for months. Then just before his departure, he would return to the palace and be treated to yet more honorary banquets with the other admirals. The fleet's

Grand Eunuchs would linger in the imperial city for the celebrations. She would have her chance then.

She would confront Zheng He. She would show him what a woman she had become, without his support and how wrong he had been to dismiss her as a little girl. Such were the thoughts marring Min Li's spirit. They were far removed from those of the young girl who had once amused the ladies of the palace with her playful antics.

Even if Princess Xia's insights were correct, it was impossible for her to guess the full extent of Min Li's change over the last four years. Nor to what force this change could be attributed.

***

"What are you plotting?" asked the emperor with his military bluntness.

It was well past the third *geng* and they lay close, smoldering in the steamy chamber.

"Only this," replied Min Li, "consider that the admiral is absent more frequently. This could be the perfect opportunity." she declared. "His Highness can put the loyal admiral to the test. And I will have a glimpse of this world I know nothing of."

He did not reply. She responded by gently running her fingers through his coarse chest hair. She already sensed the tension within him. The idea had pleased Zhu Di. But he felt a lingering irritation. At last, he frowned and pushed her naked form to the side, raising himself from the bed.

Min Li lolled in the sheets, still thinking. She knew not to react. Remain firm, she told herself. The emperor was too paranoid to reject her offer.

His voice finally rose, tense but injected with strategic nonchalance, "Guiren, do you think we are that foolish? You ask us to watch while you frolic with our naval eunuch?"

She replied with an unwavering silence.

Zhu Di grunted and reached for his robe.

"We have no answer to give. I am leaving now," he added, adjusting his sleeves with a strange fury. "I have to meet someone."

Seeing his haste, she rose and began to dress. To her surprise, the emperor raised a hand to stop her. "No. Stay here. It is not yet daylight," he said, moving to the adjacent room.

Min Li sat on the bed, pondering over his strange behavior. When he had partly closed the door behind him, she leaned forward, just in time to glimpse a blue-clad visitor. The two men talked for a while until the felt footsteps brushed past the door again with a swish of fabrics. It was now the fourth time she had breathed the odor of tobacco in the emperor's chamber. The man entered without a sound and left just as quietly. It was as though he had never been there at all.

When he had gone, Zhu Di once again made an apparition. He did not meet her gaze but walked straight to the bed. His traits were severe. She watched him disrobe and slide quietly by her side.

She dared not move, wondering about his visitor and what had been spoken. The emperor found her breast and flicked his hard fingers, inflicting a sharp pain on her cherry-sized nipple. The flicking continued while she moaned. His fingers grew harsh. He breathed heavily and seemed to have forgotten his encounter with the smoking visitor.

"What did you decide, Your Majesty," she cried as he parted her thighs.

"It is an excellent idea, Li Guiren," he said. Then he pushed his fingers deep inside her.

Chapter 10
The Embroidered-uniform Guard

The emperor suspected nothing. Soon she would have the chance to converse with the admiral during his stay in Yingtian. Yet while she relished the thought, another more sinister obsession had crept in her mind. From the moment she had left the emperor to return to the concubine quarters, she had not ceased mulling over the visitor with the felt boots.

Who was he? And why had he, on occasion, chosen to meet with the emperor precisely when she was his selected concubine. Did he also visit when the emperor spent the night with the other girls? She did not know. She set upon questioning the eunuch chamber attendant that she had taken care to identify the night before.

Finding him in the Imperial Library one afternoon, she cornered him with a smile.

"I am searching for a book about the Tang dynasty," she began, "the one Princess Xia likes so much. Do you know where I can find it?"

The eunuch nodded in recognition, moving furtively between shelves to find her the book. At last, eager to please, he placed the large volume inside her hands with a delicate bow.

She pressed the book to her bosom, tightening her cleavage into plump mounds. The eunuch licked his lips. He could not detach his eyes from her breasts.

"You are very smart," she said. The eunuch listened avidly. "Not at all like the other eunuchs," she added.

At this, he grinned ear to ear, still fixating her breasts. She seized her chance.

"I tried asking the other eunuchs about the emperor's visitor the other night. None of them could tell me much. They are ignorant and would not know a traitor if they saw one..."

She observed his changed expression.

"I hate the smell of tobacco, you see," she smiled, still discerning for a reaction.

The young eunuch's face had paled. He lowered his gaze.

"Do you know who I speak of?"

He shook his head.

"Is the emperor in danger from this man?"

"No!"

"Then you know who he is?" she insisted.

"Please," replied the young eunuch, shaking his head furiously. "I don't know him. No one does..."

Min Li frowned.

"He comes often and he scares me," she confided.

At this the eunuch softened. He gestured silently towards the corner of the library and began to whisper with great apprehension.

"He frightens us all. He is an Embroidered-uniform Guard... They have a lot of power." He swallowed, afraid that he had shared too much.

"I shall tell the emperor never to let him in when I am selected. Do you think he will listen to me?"

The eunuch shook his head. He looked around with fright.

"Oh, why not?" she pouted, looking much offended. "He is a horrible man. And he smells horrible!" she added, with a tone she purposefully wanted childish and ignorant.

"Guiren...no. The emperor will not listen to you. The guard is from the Eastern Depot." He bit his lips.

The sounds of approaching footsteps interrupted them. The eunuch became pale. "Excuse me, Guiren," he mumbled, shaking beyond belief as he moved past her.

Min Li watched him leave the library to regain his shift.

"The Eastern Depot," she mouthed, as though the very words were forbidden.

***

"It is one dangerous game you are playing at, Li Guiren."

The man who had spoken reeked of tobacco. He had not raised his voice yet she discerned his accusative tone, echoing under the moonlit gateway. He had imposing shoulders and nervous limbs.

Right now, he leaned against a wall at the Donghuamen, the Eastern Gate of the palace, watching her from the corner of his eye while he lit a smoking pipe.

It had seemed like just another night. But after the third *geng*, unable to sleep, she had left the concubine compound and followed the screams for over an hour. No sooner had the figures disappeared behind the nine-bolt doors of the Donghuamen that the Embroidered-uniform Guard had reentered the Imperial Palace. And now he stood there, watching her quietly.

It startled her. She took a step back, away from the gate, pretending that she had not followed him and the other two guards, pretending that she had not heard the commotion in the Inner Palace. Yet she knew. Someone had been imprisoned tonight. She knew she would never see them again.

"You…You recognized me…" she whispered, trembling despite herself.

"Don't let that trouble you," answered the man, his face shielded behind a waft of smoke.

She knew that voice. He had not come into the emperor's chamber for a while. Perhaps the emperor still met him secretly. To what design, she knew not.

They observed each other in the dark, like two opponents, each sizing up the other. She wanted to run away, return to the Inner Palace but he had such magnetic power that she remained fixed on the spot.

The eunuch from the library had been right. The man was dangerous. Somehow he had seen through her servant disguise. For years, she had worn that disguise at night and had never once been recognized.

"I won't be telling anyone, Li Guiren," he reassured with a wily smile. "There would be no *gain* in that."

Despite not understanding his last words, she sighed with relief, adjusting her skirt before walking off. Her nonchalant gait belied the defeat she felt from having her disguise revealed.

"I am glad we have finally met," he called out.

She froze, spinning back to face him with a cold stare.

"Who are you?"

He exhaled, pausing before answering, "My name is of no consequence to you. But here is something of interest, Li Guiren. There is an Annamese eunuch who comes to your compound at the end of each fortnight. He changes linen. If you wish to talk to me, do it through him."

"And why would I?"

He inhaled another whiff from his pipe.

"Why would I want to speak to you?" she repeated.

"Oh, I think you would."

Then he looked ahead, not prepared to elaborate. There was an uneasy silence. She glanced up nervously. She could see the silhouette of the south eastern turret from afar, glowing under the moonlight. She wondered whether the archer had spotted them. Even so, something told her he would not reveal them. So she paused, careful with her next words.

"What had these men done?"

He inhaled the tobacco quietly and then lowered his head as though pondering on something and savoring its flavor. She saw the glint in his eyes and shuddered.

"He was a high-ranking eunuch, wasn't he?" she continued, still waiting for a response.

"Good night to you, Li Guiren," came the reply. With a swift gesture, he signaled to the gate keepers. The soldiers responded at once, unlocking the doors for him. She watched him as he walked out of the palace, leaving a dense fog in his wake.

She stood there for a while. For the first time in years she was assailed by a deep doubt. Something about the way he had said that *she would want* to speak to him. How did he know that?

She stole into the night, weaving her way back to the Inner Palace. None of them knew her behind that disguise. Then how had the mysterious guard known it was her? She promised herself she would meet him again. But for now, she set her mind on Zheng He.

Chapter 11
Admiral Zheng He
January 1417

Warfare

On the eve before his fifth expedition, Admiral Zheng He returned to Yingtian. It was as Min Li had predicted. Celebrations ran in full force to honor his upcoming grand voyage. This time, the admiral would be sailing as far as the Arabian Coast in the port of Hormuz and then onto Africa. The Ming fleet would skirt the African East coast, passing through Zanzibar before returning to the Middle Kingdom through the Indian Ocean.

An uplifting atmosphere reigned in the city, not due entirely to the upcoming expedition but because the emperor was euphoric from his recent military triumph. Indeed, the Mongol hordes, the scourge of the Northern border, had dissipated during Zhu Di's last campaign. Their respite came following the death of their leader, Mahmud. It was a peaceful time, the perfect moment for Zhu Di to enter into his next military strategy, relocation.

Despite the recriminations of the Hanlin ministers, the emperor was forging ahead to relocate the imperial capital. He would return to his beloved Beiping together with his court. He would rename the city, Beijing, North Capital. Yingtian would be officially renamed Nanjing, Southern Capital.

Zhu Di was decided and nothing the ministers could say would change his mind. It was from Beijing that his military defense against the Mongols would be more effective. No one could protest against thc general in Zhu Di.

The eunuchs distributed media leaflets throughout the entire imperial city in preparation for the crew's farewell banquet. They praised the admiral's fleet in prose and inflated the merits of the expeditions. They hailed the tributary countries, affirming their decisions to pay homage to the Ming emperor. They evoked the prestige of the Middle Kingdom with eloquent description of the country's wealth and industriousness.

There was a joyful air in the city. Some of the concubines had already begun their journey to Beijing where they would be relocated to the new city. Min Li along with others had remained back. Zhu Di had accepted her proposition.

And so the emperor was not in the least perturbed when the woman he had newly titled as Li Guifei chose to attend the night's banquet among the admiral eunuchs and other hired concubines. Meanwhile, his man of the moment, Admiral Zheng He, not quite knowing who she was, found her to be most entertaining company. Several times throughout the meal, he observed her from a distance with a mixture of curiosity and wonderment. She was well versed in many subjects including religion, literature, history, fine arts and seemed to have a good grasp of current politics. As expected, she never spoke unless spoken to but her replies were always well formed betraying a sharp mind that was not devoid of a striking sense of humor. Still, Zheng He was weary of imperial etiquette and he kept strict distance between himself and the young woman. That is, until one afternoon.

Zheng He savored the last quarter of an almond cake. He had bid farewell to the other revelers and was heading to a chamber reserved for high-ranking eunuchs. Now as he paced swiftly through one of the anterooms adjourning the Hall of Preserving Harmony, his long red robe swished on the carpeted floor. And where the winter's long shadows met the rays of the sun, he discerned the young woman several paces ahead, leaning against the gilded doorway. She had an air of dignity and defiance even as her indolent body rested on the gold frame.

He quickly brushed the crumbs away from his lips knowing that he would have to pass through that door. He recognized the concubine from the banquet. Earlier in the day, she had been entertaining his colleagues on several occasions. They had been introduced but she had merely nodded, sipping her tea in an absent manner.

A tart voice drew him out of his recollections.

"So this is Zheng He, the famous soldier of the Zheng dyke!" The woman raised herself from the doorway, her haughty demeanor belying her youth. The admiral smiled at the challenge.

"I am that soldier. Well, that is to say, I was."

"Everyone knows what you did to save Beijing."

"And what would the Guifei know of warfare," reproached Zheng He, rather amused by her overture.

She scarcely acknowledged the rebuke. Her voice echoed across the hall with stinging arrogance.

"That it is best played out in the bed chamber or else spoken by the ruthless tongues of women."

With quiet elegance, she glided towards the admiral, her eyes still on him, taking her time, wanting him to have a full view of her.

"That warfare relies solely upon strategy..."

Her gaze remained steady. He noticed that she walked without a limp.

"And that one must often concede loss, in order to eventually claim victory."

She came to an abrupt halt, raising her oval face towards him. Her dainty fingers traveled to her waist. They halted at the knot fastening her dark blue *beizi* and there, they played with much insolence. She seemed to understand the sensual lure of her gesture.

The admiral watched the creature before him.

"Well spoken. But these are not battles in which I would ever find myself engaged in the coming months," he replied in a dry tone. "Suppose you continue to strategize in the confines of the bed chamber and avoid those subjects in the presence of the military."

Min Li did not blink once or look down. Her mouth curled with disdain.

"Do you always speak for your emperor rather than for yourself?" she chided.

Zheng He felt the blood flush his cheeks as she continued.

"What if Admiral Zheng He were trapped in my bedchamber?" she said with a cunning smile. "Or are his principles perhaps too precious to consider defeat by a woman?"

It was out of place to engage the Guifei into an argument.

"Illicit relationships do exist between court women and eunuchs," began the admiral in his famed diplomatic style. "Or so I have heard... But, in defense of eunuchs, what sort of artifice could they possibly employ to fascinate women? We are...of a different kind," he added, feigning pride. "And we serve only one purpose – our emperor."

"How honorable! I am put to shame."

Her lips had melted into a warm smile. It softened her face even as it gave her a knowing glow, well beyond her age.

"Forgive me for saying this, Admiral, but you are mistaken. Eunuchs, it appears, have many artifices. At least those living in the palace... Perhaps one would say that it is your status as eunuch that serves you best. Let me explain. If illicit relationships do exist between women of the palace and eunuchs, then they are scarcely suspected. After all, isn't that why eunuchs are admitted to the Purple City?"

"Guifei, are you accusing me of potentially deceiving my emperor?"

"No. But it might be worse to deceive one's self, wouldn't you say?"

He was speechless. She conceded that self-preservation was very important for this man.

"I apologize, Grand Admiral," she said, melting into a seductive smile.

"There's no need. Your words have...enlightened me."

"I am Min Li." Her voice quivered, as though she were apologizing for her recent affront.

"I know your name," he replied walking behind her, onto the marble paving.

She was hurt by the casualty in his voice. She had secretly hoped that he would evince emotion knowing who she was. Yet his face remained inscrutable. There was a momentary pause as she quickly recovered, smiling anew.

"I have heard many things about you. You are the most famous man in this city, apart from His Highness. You and His Majesty go back to Jianwen's time I believe."

They moved through the Inner Palace and he escorted her quietly towards the garden. She was not as petite as he had thought.

He could still make eye contact without slouching forward as he often had to with court women.

It could have been his imagination but he believed that her smile acquired more warmth as soon as they were alone. How long had she been a concubine? Five years, maybe six. There was no trace of arrogance now. The eyes were absent, vague almost.

She eludes me, he realized. *That is why I'm still here. I ought to have retired by now.*

He frowned. He could not stop looking at her. His eyes lingered on her lips. She was lost in a sort of monologue that captivated him.

"I do like it when the ministers hold court with the emperor."

"Why is that?"

He sat by her side, enraptured by her dreamy manner.

"Then this place changes. If His Highness holds court, and as you know, this happens about three times in the day, some parts of the palace appear to stand still. Like now, you see? All the energy of the palace flows into one area, one of the main halls where the ministers convene."

Her hands were talking, they moved with grace to illustrate her ideas. "That is where the grand state discussions take place. And me? Well I come here, to think. Sometimes it is like standing outside above the palace and observing it like a bird. I am here, but I can travel elsewhere..."

Zheng He had not said a word but sat there, listening. She was a different person now. She had acquired a childlike quality.

"As though I were floating high above this place," she repeated. "I watch life go by and I become shapeless...as though I was dead and a floating spirit. Everything looks different..."

Every time she smiled, he noticed that the corners of her eyes slanted generously towards her temples. It was subtle but it tore at him.

"...the servant eunuchs are busy going about their chores. Outside, the noise of the marketplace is buzzing. The guards steal a game of dominoes when they think no one is watching. It is at these times, that I enjoy my strolls. I usually walk alone. The other concubines like to rise late, you see. They will gladly ignore *dian* after *dian* at times. I don't know how they do it."

From the corner of his eye, he watched her clasp her own hands nervously. Odd the way she twisted her fingers...

"...I can't sleep. I can hear the trees, the birds. Sometimes, I can almost, almost make out the voices in the marketplace beyond the palace gates. Foreign voices even... I can, you know. I think I'd like to go out like Princess Xia one day. Just...disappear." Her voice trailed. She pressed her palms flat on her knees as though wiping away something. She seemed to rebuke herself for what she had just shared with him and her voice became cold again.

"How long have you been in Nanjing?" she asked, startling them both from their daydream.

"A few months..." He paused. "Li Guifei, you have the privilege of serving His Majesty. Leaving this palace is not something you should ever contemplate. It can never happen."

She nodded. "Yes, yes, of course."

Then, staring ahead, she pronounced the words that she had practiced several times in front of her mirror.

"The emperor would like you, Grand Admiral, to keep me company during your stay in Nanjing. It is part of my education you see. The idea was mine... I have expressed a desire to know more about the world."

"You are mistaken. There is nothing a man like me can teach the emperor's concubines."

"Ah, Admiral! What modesty! Surely the world you have seen must be fascinating! I saw the *qilin* you brought back a year ago. I've never seen anything like it," she added, fully aware that it was a lie. "And to think that those mythical creatures exist..." She sighed again.

Zheng He frowned. It was something he would have to verify with Zhu Di. But then, what if she had lied and was punished for it? He did not want to cause her pain. And if she had lied, he could not imagine her reasons. Yet, he conceded, she was very clever. She had clearly given him an alibi to continue talking with a royal concubine while still demonstrating his loyalty to Zhu Di. He had only to take it and he would not lose face. His curiosity took over.

"What would you like to know?"

***

The Baths

For days the wine had flowed and thousands of dishes had been consumed. And it came, the last joyful evening before the admirals' departure. They all drank heavily that night. Even Admiral Zheng He had been drinking and the dimples in his cheeks spread merriment with all that shared his table. More than anyone, he was imbued with the happiness of his emperor, who, no longer burdened by marauding Mongols, had also abandoned himself to elation. It was a rarity.

There was another reason, aside from the upcoming voyage why the admiral was pleased with himself. But no one, it seemed, noticed the fascinated glow in his pupils whenever he addressed the lady beside him.

He had spent the last fortnight in admirable company. It was unplanned entertainment and at first, conscious of imperial etiquette, he'd tried to avoid it. In the end, it was delighting. The emperor had not protested. Indeed, it was peculiar that Zhu Di had never questioned it.

Min Li was a charming courtesan with genuine interest in his travels. She was curious, lively and spirited. There were times when she would enjoy repartees and mocked him gently while at other times she would resume her childlike pouts and sink back into her coddled youth.

At last, the emperor raised himself from his lonely table to retire. He was cheered by the prospect of his new palace plans and at peace, knowing that his fleet was in trusted hands. Min Li, along with other concubines, were escorted back to the Inner Palace.

The last few days had taken an unexpected turn for Min Li. Her initial plan had been to punish the admiral for his neglect. She had wanted to taunt him. But he was so kind to her, so diplomatic, so eager to answer all her questions and she could see that he genuinely liked her after the first day. Hearing his travel accounts had moved her with wonder and the respect she had for him had grown. But it was the manner in which other men, notably his old friend, Admiral Zhou Man, had spoken of him that had defined the admiral. His colleagues, even the somewhat cynical navigator Yang Bao, all knew that he was a remarkable man and yes, now she could understand it, a hero of the Middle Kingdom.

Thick snowfalls covered the Great Halls as the naval party broke up. They dispersed, some to their lodgings within the imperial city and others to a special eunuch dormitory within the palace.

Having verified that Lan Wong was fast asleep, Min Li slipped on a heavy brocade coat over her skirt and pushed her feet in her padded felt boots. She had swirled her hair up and fastened it loosely with a large wooden comb. All the concubines slept as she traversed the corridor and stepped out into the cold.

Aside from the faint glow of burning oil lamps in several buildings, it was dark. The unrelenting snow discouraged anyone but the most dutiful eunuchs.

Min Li did not fear the cold. It was the sun that tired her. Winter loved her. But tonight she wanted warmth and she sought it from the man who had captivated her all evening. She wanted to play too. And most of all, she wanted to *forget.*

Moving swiftly from one pavilion to the next, she stole out of the concubine compound. She hid by the side of a building adjacent to the Gate of Heavenly Purity and waited for the admiral to surface.

She waited, her ear listening in for sounds of footsteps and voices. For how long did she wait? She waited until the snow iced her hands, numbing her fingers and until the hem of her skirt was soaked in ice.

At last, she heard the guard. She stiffened. The voices at the gate no sooner rose that they quietened. She realized, then, that he was walking alone. The impulse took her. As he emerged from the gate, she ran towards him, the sound of her footsteps engulfed by the thick layer of snow, her nose, swollen red from the biting cold.

The admiral ambled towards his chamber rugged up in a red woolen cape and a domed fur-lined hat. He saw then, in the distance, this nymph that the night brought forth in a flurry of transparent silks and shiny satins. She was so lithe that she seemed to float on the blanket of snow, the bellowing fabric of her skirt glowing under the blue moon. He rubbed his eyes in disbelief.

"What madness is this? You ought to be in your chamber, Li Guifei," he cried when he finally recognized her.

But Min Li was having a joyous time. The last thing she wanted was to do was return to bed. Besides, the emperor would not need her tonight. He was busy with Xue Guifei. She was determined to enjoy her last evening with the admiral. She stopped running only two paces away from him, examining him as though pondering on a fate she knew well.

A smile was etched on her red lips. Evanescent blue smoke rose up in the space between them as she caught her breath. Zheng He was too puzzled to speak. Seeing his face, she began to laugh.

"Min Li, what...what are you doing here?"

"I wanted to show you something!" Her voice was smothered by the thick falling snow.

"It is so late," protested the eunuch, conscious of the brew's effect and scolding himself for his weakness at supper.

"Oh please, please, you must come!"

"Come where?"

She emitted a chuckle.

"I have the key. But you must not tell!"

Her laughter rang in his ears. Through the thick snowy mist, Zheng He watched the once haughty concubine's giddy smile as she dug into the pocket of her coat and revealed a wooden key.

"What are you doing? Silly girl! I will have you return to your chamber at once," he chided with an amused grin on his tired face.

"No. Not my chamber. The bathing room! You must come, Admiral. It's heated. You'll see. It's lovely. Run. Run now, Admiral! We should head there quickly before the second *geng*. The guards will not see us."

In other circumstances he would have scorned at her plan. Unthinkable that he, a Grand Eunuch, could venture into these baths, whatever these were, with an imperial concubine in the middle of the night. For a moment he felt the terror of incurring the emperor's wrath. Yet, he surmised, astounded that he could still reason despite the murkiness of his alcohol imbued head, surely the beauty before him belied her agile mind. And what a mind it was. It left him bewildered and estranged at the same time. As though it were not a nymph whose footfalls now imprinted themselves on the silent snow but an all knowing ghost and an orphaned child all at once.

Somehow, he found himself running, enraptured by her laughter and intoxicated by drink. Still troubled by the prospect of being found, he glanced around with apprehension. But she seemed to know exactly when to pause, when to hide and when it was safe to run. Why, this little minx knew the palace back to front. How often had she done this?

He watched as she gestured forward towards the West chambers. She grew silent as they entered a cramped courtyard at the back of the women's palace. An arched door at the far end was locked. There were no eunuchs in sight except for a meek chamber maid with a pile of towels under her arms.

"She'll report us," warned Zheng He.

"No... It is safe. Hide your face and crouch a little. Yes, like this. She is almost blind. She will not know you."

Min Li tippy-toed towards the maid and embraced her. She slipped a silver coin in the old woman's hands and whispered, "For your trouble." Then, the towels bundled under one arm, she grabbed the eunuch's hand and led him towards the back of the building. As they halted at a service door and she pulled out her key, he hesitated.

"Min Li, if the guards—"

"Hush!"

"What is the meaning—"

"Hush, will you. I warn you, we will be found if you speak. Really, you are much too noisy, Admiral," she added, scolding him a little. She opened the backroom with her wooden key and entered. He peered through the door.

"On most days, no eunuch is allowed in here," he heard her say as he followed.

The concubine's voice had vibrated like a watery echo. At first the admiral could not see. He distinguished a deep sound resonating around them. It was the sound of water. There were porcelain gargoyles fixed at regular intervals along a curved wall opposite the door. From each of these ducts, steamy water gushed into a spacious, oblong pool.

He grew accustomed to the dim light then looked around him as though in a dream. Through the vaporous glow of four oil lamp burners standing at each corner of the large vaulted room, he could discern the shiny surface of the water. He realized what it was, a room filled almost entirely by a yellow marbled bathroom. The high domed ceiling encouraged echoes so that inside this room, one could easily forget the outside world.

Peach, red and yellow petals floated on the pool's surface. There was a sweet rose scent emanating from the shimmery pond. He felt himself relax, welcoming the reprieve from the icy chill that had slapped his cheeks a moment ago.

"Isn't it beautiful?"

"It is..."

Speechless, he admired the beauty of the many carvings on the wall. His eyes caught phoenixes spreading their wings among petals and blooming branches, a crane taking flight towards the crest of a sunlit mountain. The carved walls glowed with a translucent alabaster light. It was beyond imagining.

"The princesses used to come here all the time. Sometimes we would join them. Even some of the Arab foreigners have seen it. They try to replicate what you see here, in their palaces, but the princesses say that none of them have."

"Thank you for showing me this room. I've never been here before. I ignored its existence!"

"And wait until you feel the water, Admiral! It will revive you."

"What are you doing?"

"I want to go in. Bathing in these clothes will not do."

She had removed her shiny coat. Now, she untied the silk sash that bound her sheer skirt above her small round breasts. He tried to avert his eyes. She seemed to pay him no mind.

"I want to feel the water on my skin!" she chirped.

At last, she unwound the cotton straps wrapped around her breasts. Zheng He's pulse quickened. He stepped back onto the marble tiles, suddenly engulfed with panic. His head spun. Before long the slender Guifei stood before him, her nakedness at once vulnerable and threatening.

"You'll see how nice this is," she cooed stepping down the marble steps.

Her perfectly shaped tiny body glistened in the glow of the dim lamps and was soon fully submerged in the scented waters.

"Oh, it's lovely. So lovely and warm!" she splashed.

"I will retire now," said the eunuch, feeling faint.

"Oh no, please! Please stay!" She swam towards him and sat up. "You'll see how nice it is when you enter the water," she reassured.

The skin on her shoulders glistened with heated rose water. The admiral relented. He felt eager for something that he did not want to name. Somehow, he found himself disrobing quickly, removing first his boots, then his cape and finally his long robe. He kept the cloth around his waist. Then he entered, feet first, into the pool, smiling like a child. His body relaxed in the heat.

He filled his nostrils with scents of rose, vanilla and other flowers that he could not name. It felt so wonderful and he had to admit that it was one of the most pleasurable sensations he had felt perhaps in his entire life. But he was mistaken. There were so many things he did not know and believed to be out of his reach. There were so many things that he could not name.

They were soon gliding in the waters, relieved by its warmth. For a while they played, several arms' length from each other. He watched her disappear from one end of the pool only to appear further up at the other end. How he liked hearing this girl laugh.

After several rounds, Min Li came to a halt in the middle of the pool.

"I must tell you something, Admiral," she smiled out of breath, "I always wanted to swim here, ever since I was a little girl." There seemed to be a distant pain in her voice.

"I should have told the princesses to let you in this pool in the same way I scorned that matron many years ago," replied Zheng He.

She smiled, delighted by what he had said.

"Yes, you should have. You should have stayed here to protect me, Admiral."

He looked amused.

"Protect you from what?"

For a while, she did not answer. She sported, suddenly flushing water in his face.

"Protect you from what?" he laughed.

The intensity of her gaze startled him.

"My sweet Admiral, you know so little."

She said no more. But he continued to fix her lips, waiting for more. In her eyes, moist with passion, it seemed as though a question were forming. He ached for her to speak. He did not understand that the question had no words and could not be asked.

Her wet hair floated like smooth silk around her face. He saw her then, reaching across, edging her body closer to his. He was now scarcely breathing. The quiet sound of the water alerted him to her every movement. He let her approach, unable to pull back.

She was closer, her naked limbs at arm's length. He closed his eyes, trembling with desire. He felt her soft breasts against his chest. Her tiny arms embraced him. He felt a soft pressure as she cradled her head against his warmth, holding him with clinging arms. He sighed and gave a cry of alarm.

"I can hear you breathing," she whispered.

She caressed his back as if to further reassure him.

"Let me," she asked in a voice he had not heard before. She was neither the child nor the concubine, she was someone else altogether. She was Min Li.

He obeyed. He wrapped his long arms around her, delighted with the perfect arch of her lithe back. Enraptured by Min Li's scent and the warm contact with her soft body, he pressed her swollen breasts tightly against his aching chest. He breathed in her hair as though he were inhaling life and his own perdition all at once. In the moments that followed, he understood that nothing mattered except her. His hands traveled to places he could not name yet somehow he knew all of them. She moaned.

Finding the nape of his neck, she reached up to whisper in his ear, "Yes, like this. Now, Admiral, we can forget the world."

And strangely, it was exactly what he wanted. He closed his eyes and in that moment, he forgot the world. For another world opened itself now, beckoning, urging him to put to rest the senseless reserve and abandon himself to much reckless savoring. He had drawn away at first to gaze at the fierce desire in her eyes. Astounded by what he saw, he pushed one finger and then two, through her parted, hungry lips. The forbidden wetness of her sweet tongue greeted him as he cried. How well those delicious lips embraced him, how well that hot torrent of a mouth devoured him as he slid further, watching her eyes dim with pleasure. The taste of the rose water on her lips excited him all the more. He ran his hand over her glistening body, delighted by her gentle curves.

As he leaned back against the edge of the pool, he understood that she waited for something. Her eyes demanded it. Sensing that he was confused, she held his hand down, pressing her thighs against him. She moved forward until his palm found what she wanted him to find. And it seemed that he had been wrong about the wetness of her lips. For what other pleasures could exist, beyond this tiny pink tongue, beyond the salt of her exquisite mouth. What joy to lift her up and sit her tiny body on the marble ledge before him so that he could find this new wetness and devour its secrets.

Now this was better because he could watch her, arched as she was before him, he could caress her, taste her and hear her delighted cries, muffled as they were by the sound of the gushing gargoyles. As she panted out his name, he felt wanted. He felt cherished. Never had the sound of his name given him such pride.

She was so perfect. He glanced down at her ankles, eyeing her pretty feet with their tender arches and delightful toes. She sat up with a hungry smile and watched him run his tongue between her toes. Holding her foot adoringly, he now caressed the arch with his finger. He wanted to take each toe in his mouth to savor it. How lovely they were. These were perfect toes and they were his.

Chapter 12
A New Palace
March 1418

Goodbye Nanjing

"Min Li, I cannot find my red ribbons."

"What red ribbons?"

"Those I weaved through my braids... You know, at the New Year ceremony last month."

"Look under the couch, Lan."

While her friend agitated herself, Min Li sashayed in the room, in her silk *dudou* and skirt. She was loading a large leather crate with her jewelry boxes, dresses and slippers.

"Oh, pretty... Is this new?" asked Lan Wong, eyeing Min Li's red box with avid curiosity.

"This one? No. I've always had it," dismissed Min Li. "Just a gift from the princess."

"Oh really? I've just never seen it before..."

Lan Wong crouched on all fours to inspect the carpet underneath the couch. She pouted.

"Not there. I must have lent them to Guiren Chong."

Min Li contemplated those words in silence. Trembling, she reached for her silk sash and wrapped it around her thin waist. She began tying her bow with deliberate motions.

"Well," she replied after a moment's reflection, "why don't you run off and ask her if she still has your ribbons?"

Lan Wong had already limped out as fast as her bound feet could take her. Min Li bit her lips. She slipped on a rose-colored cape and adjusted the bun with her wooden comb. That would do. She slammed the crate shut and gestured to the eunuch outside.

"I'm ready."

"Excellent, Li Guifei."

"And be gentle with that," she warned as the eunuch picked up the crate and passed it over his shoulder.

As more eunuchs came in to pick up luggage, she heard carefree voices rise in the corridor. Two concubines were heading towards the courtyard where the sedans waited.

"Goodbye Nanjing!" enthused one of them, a dimple in her smile.

"Goodbye Nanjing!" cheered the other.

They went off with giggles, beaming with excitement.

The new palace was waiting. In and out of the compound, eunuchs shuffled to and fro, dizzy with concubine orders, rushing about to fetch clothes, capes, parasols, books, crates and to execute the concubines' whims. The Inner Palace was abuzz with the shrill voices of women enlivened by the prospect of their journey from Nanjing to Beijing.

Standing at the doorway, Min Li glanced across her empty room. She would miss Nanjing. She would miss the baths... She'd heard they were to be demolished soon and it saddened her. Her eyes rested on Lan Wong's crate. It lay on the floor, still opened, beside her things. She heard Lan Wong's voice in the distance and frowned.

"Min Li!"

The Annamese was hobbling fast through the corridor. She seemed agitated. Two Guirens towed in behind. Both seemed pained.

I'm so exhausted, thought Min Li as she watched them approach.

"What's wrong? Did you find your ribbon?" she asked in a dry voice. "You ought to hurry up!"

"Oh, Min Li! You will never, *never* believe what has happened."

"She's gone!" cut in one of the other Guirens.

"They've sent her away!" cried Lan Wong.

"Who is gone?" asked Min Li without surprise.

"Guiren Chong! She's been sent out of the palace!"

"She is no longer with us..."

Min Li shrugged her shoulders. "Well it looks like you'll never see your ribbons again, Lan Wong."

"I guess not," replied this one with another miserable pout. She moved to her crate to continue packing her treasures.

"Who knows where that ribbon is now," continued Min Li as she adjusted her double bun and fixed her comb in place for the second time.

Then she gave one last wistful look at the room.

"You'd best pack your things fast. The sedans are waiting," she called out, avoiding eye contact with her chamber companion. Then she hurried along the corridor.

"She's upset at me for wasting time. We're to share a sedan," explained Lan Wong, her tender heart broken by Min Li's petulant attitude.

"Of course not. She's not upset at you."

The Guirens lowered themselves on their knees to help their friend pack.

"She's sad, that's all. That's all there is, I'm sure. You know, I think Li Guifei was friendly with Chong Guiren."

"You think so?"

"Yes, I would see them together many times. She used to speak with Chong Guiren a lot. And now the Manchurian girl is gone. We never know who remains and who leaves...do we..."

"Yes, these things happen. Chong Guiren must have been found lacking. Maybe the emperor had her dismissed."

"Maybe you're right," replied Lan Wong, no longer caring much about her ribbons.

***

Sweets

"Get away! Away with you!"

Alongside the caravan's path, the long-robed men with their funny looking winged hats scurried left and right, unable to keep up with the scrawny legs. A band of barefoot children in filthy rags, their faces smeared with grime and snot jeered at the castrates. Judging from their language, it was astounding how much children could know about eunuch anatomy.

Min Li peered through her sedan drapes, amused by the commotion. She saw another child run towards her, his little hands stretched out with a spirited smile. There was a huge gap in his mouth where his two front teeth should have been. She smiled back at him, digging into her silk pouch. As the escort eunuch turned round with a litany of curses, Min Li cheered and tossed another flavored sweet in the child's direction.

Looking back, she watched the boy's dimples while he sucked on the tea drop. It was a pity Lan Wong was still asleep, thought Min Li, she would have enjoyed this game. She observed the stream of saliva running down the chubby concubine's lips. Lan Wong was no doubt dreaming about her dear family back in Annam.

They had journeyed north for the past three days. Min Li's legs ached. But she refused to sleep. There was so much to see.

It was the first time she had been as far away from Nanjing. She had thought the world and its people were as orderly and lavishly dressed elsewhere as inside the palace but all her assumptions were rudely contradicted. Beyond Nanjing, everywhere she looked, her attention was drawn to the poverty around her and the people facing much strife. At night, while they slept in large imperial tents, she had spotted a family of beggars being hushed away by the eunuchs. The eunuch's voices were louder but Min Li heard one of the beggars protest and utter something about the famine. She did not know what a famine was. And so the next day, she had asked one of the eunuchs. With a certain pride, he had promised that his uncle would send a eunuch tutor to explain this to her. His uncle was an adviser to finance minister, Xia and he would not mind instructing the concubine about these matters.

The original plan had been to transport the concubines on large ships along the greatly expanded Grand Canal all the way to Beijing. But the idea was abandoned due to the heavy canal traffic. It had been decided that the safest and most efficient route for the ladies would be to make the journey by caravan.

They were flanked by an escort of soldiers to the front and rear but remained wary of bandits and gang lords. The eunuchs cursed whenever curious onlookers drew too close. A caravan of court ladies was easy prey and the castrates took seriously their responsibility of safeguarding these women from kidnappings or attacks. During the day, it was the children who made things unbearable. They carried on chanting, teasing and attracting more attention to His Majesty's cortege. It was a battle to shoo them away. But Min Li felt sorry for them.

Another child looked in her direction. Not far, a saddled eunuch shot her a disapproving glance. Undeterred, she reached into her pouch for another sweet. The boy clapped his hands with excitement and ran towards her sedan. She bent her elbow, ready to throw the tea-flavored drop.

"Catch!"

A vicious grip held her wrist and the rider's breath was hot on her face.

"Li Guifei you should not encourage the wretched demons!"

It was Ji Feng. He was riding alongside the concubine procession and had watched with a sneer as Min Li amused herself. She wrenched her arm away holding her painful wrist with an indignant pout.

"They are hardly demons! I've not seen children as skinny as these. Look at them! They are famished!"

"We should refrain from making a spectacle of His Majesty's Royal Chamber, Guifei," hissed Ji Feng, whacking the children with his leather rod.

He came after the toddler, descending a shower of blows in his direction. The child ran away screaming.

"Stop it! Stop this! Please, you are frightening them!" cried Min Li, raising herself from her cushions so that the sedan chair nearly toppled to the side.

She watched the children shrivel to the side of the road. Horror spread on their little faces under Ji Feng's cruel gaze. From this moment on, the eunuch kept his horse so close to Min Li's sedan that the children grew discouraged and began to disperse. Min Li looked back towards them with disappointment.

"Look what you've done! Could you not see they are hungry?" she scorned.

She wished he would just gallop away and leave her alone. But Ji Feng remained there, perched on his black horse. Min Li retreated in disgust. For the next few hours it seemed the eunuch's horse had found a niche, right beside Min Li and he was making it his duty to ruin her view and her journey.

"It is not virtuous behavior," he hissed as his shoulder all but brushed the drapes. He eyed the loosened sash above her breasts.

"And how else should I feel at ease in these cramped cortege?" she snapped.

He continued to fixate the soft mounds swelling beneath her sheer blouse.

"You are showing too much flesh," he spit. "His Majesty would not be pleased to discover that the relocation of his favorite concubines had become an erotic display for all peasants."

In reply, Min Li drew her curtains with a sharp tug.

***

The Great Within

When the concubines arrived in their new abode, they were impressed to find that a familiar layout existed in the new palace. Indeed, for its nine hundred and ninety-nine rooms, Beijing's palace remained modelled on the palace of Nanjing. Naturally, the rooms in each compound were more numerous and the great Halls in the Outer Palace, larger. There were also other differences and these were immediately apparent to the ladies of the court.

On the far Western wing of the Inner Palace, there existed a long, narrow building whose exterior walls were visible to all but which only the emperor and eunuchs could enter. The thin rectangular structure was the new concubine quarters. It housed a long corridor flanked on each side by an agglomeration of rooms of varying sizes.

This long building was accessible via two known entrances. The front entrance was guarded by two heavy doors, both painted red with nine ornate bolts. During the day, these doors remained opened, allowing the inhabitants of the building to walk in and out freely and into the Imperial Gardens. But late during the night, the doors were locked. Only selected eunuchs possessed the keys. At all times, the emperor and other high-ranking eunuch officers could also gain access to this rectangular complex by means of a side entrance adjoining the corridor to the other imperial buildings.

This was then the new concubine complex. When the concubines began to settle in their new rooms, they noticed something odd. At the very back of this long compound, were two smaller and badly lit rooms that remained permanently locked and empty.

Eager to seem worldly and assert their control over the fearful concubines, some of the eunuchs spread rumors. They asserted that these two back rooms were prisons, reserved for insolent concubines who dared to invite the emperor's scorn. One of the eunuchs added that immoral women could be thrown without food or water in these rooms to serve as an example for the others.

This of course sparked giggles and incredulous stares from the concubines who chided the eunuchs for their impertinence. More likely, had added the newly promoted Xue Guifei, these were spare rooms or storage rooms.

Min Li ignored them. She was tired after the journey and found herself brooding in her new chamber. She thought it strange that she had not been given a new room for herself like Xue Guifei and still had to share with Wong Guifei. After all, she had been a Guifei for over a year. And since most of the concubines were now in Beijing, crowding should no longer have been the Royal Chamber director's concern. She observed Lan Wong with a cloudy expression. The quiet Annamese had been reunited with her favorite kitten after the four day journey and was eagerly massaging its belly.

Min Li rose. Still in thoughts, she paced the corridor towards the back room. She pulled on the latch. The wooden door remained locked. Returning with a stool from her chamber, she pushed it against the door and raised herself on her toes to take a peek through a tiny lattice opening. It was pitch black but she could just make out the interior.

Unlike the other rooms, the two spare rooms were not carpeted. Their walls were devoid of tapestry. There was no furniture, no couch and no windows. Even the ceiling was not painted. These rooms were barely finished. Min Li's gaze lingered over the more spacious of these two chambers with a certain apprehension. Dust and musty odors could quickly find a place in those rooms, she thought.

***

Demons in the Night

"What is the trouble? Why aren't you asleep? Are—"

"Listen... Can you hear that noise?" asked Min Li.

They listened. There it was again. Like swift running feet, the thumping sound she had heard. It seemed to near their chamber. Min Li opened their door. There was no one.

"What are you doing?"

"Hush... There! It's louder when I draw close to the back room but as I near our chamber...not a sound... And look! There is no one in the corridor."

"What do you mean? You're frightening me, Min Li..."

"It means that the noise is coming from elsewhere. We should check the back room."

"What? The...the back room? Do...do you think the...the eunuchs have locked someone in there? Like...like an old concubine maybe?"

The thought revolted them. Old concubines were usually sent home or became laundry maids for the rest of their days. Lan Wong and Min Li had bid farewell to a few of them over the years. These older women were, in truth, scarcely thirty but they were no longer wanted.

"The sound does appear to come from there..."

"I'm scared, Min Li. What do you think it is?"

In their excitement the two women forgot that they were no longer whispering. The door across opened to reveal Xun Guifei stepping out into the corridor without her makeup. A horrible sight indeed, thought Min Li but she was too distracted to dwell on it.

"What is the matter with you, two? Must we all hear what you have to say?"

"Xun Guifei, Older Sister, you are up! You must have heard that sound," said Min Li.

"I heard nothing save two selfish girls keeping me awake in the middle of the night! Now go back to sleep!"

"There! Can you hear it now?" interrupted Min Li.

At this, Xun Guifei squinted. Her lips pursed together with a scorn. She had indeed heard something but she was determined to put her rival back in her place.

"Li Guifei, I've known you for years now but I did not think you foolish enough to be afraid of a cat," she scoffed.

"It is not a cat. A cat does not shuffle that way. There's something...someone in the back room."

"And I tell you it is only a cat!" screeched Xun Guifei. "Now return to your chamber at once!"

She shot Min Li a murderous look before lowering her oil lamp. She was her senior concubine and Min Li knew better than to irritate her. Besides she had to show respect only because the woman was older than her. Min Li didn't mind being punished but she wouldn't wish it on her companion.

"You are right. It's probably just a cat."

"Well, that's better. And turn off that lamp! You'll burn us all," warned Xun Guifei's from across the corridor. She all but slammed the door behind her.

When the entire complex had grown silent again, Lan Wong turned her moonlit face towards Min Li and observed the frown on her friend's forehead.

"You don't really think it's a cat, do you, Min Li?"

Min Li shook her head. It was strange, but to Wong Guifei, Min Li did look so tired.

"I shall tell you a secret, Lan. But you have to promise me that you will not speak of it."

"What...oh. I...I promise. I will not tell a soul."

"This is not the first time I hear the noise. I heard it when we first moved here, on the first night. I thought perhaps it was the eunuchs moving things, you know, getting everything organized. But...the days after, it was there again. And now..."

Lan Wong's eyes widened with horror. She shriveled under her quilt. "But... But...if it's not a cat...is it a demon? Or a hungry ghost?"

Min Li smiled despite herself. She was not superstitious like her bed chamber. The last thing she wanted was to alarm her friend.

"A demon? No, of course not." Then she reflected for a moment. "Hey, you know what? Xun Guifei is right. It has to be a cat. Come. Let us go to sleep."

Min Li spread out her long hair over her wooden neck rest, glancing aside to ensure her friend's hair was not entangled. They lay side by side, arms entwined. In the distance, the third *geng* sounded. Min Li watched Lan Wong's eyelids flitter in the dark until the Annamese was fast asleep. She smiled, a little envious. Then she stared at the crossed beam above, determined to shut out the noise. She stared and stared, eager to imagine something, a vision outside those walls.

Slowly, the beam began to take shape. She thought of the *qilin* with its elongated neck and the neck lengthened and lengthened until it became a mast and soon there were nine tall masts and red sails that she had heard described but never seen. Then she saw his face. She felt the gushing warmth through her chest and the familiar ache that she could not describe. She held on to that memory, tasting its bittersweet embrace. But even as she visualized his face, it faded. She watched her vision fade and fade. Her heart sank.

She listened. Silence.

The backroom was still. A tear pearled down her face. It was still. Still like the walls of this chamber, still, like the corridor, still, like the palace, still again like the walls and the imperial city gates. There was only stillness.

***

The Long Street

And there were days where she would feel it; the longing for his mouth, his hands and his breath. It was made worse now that she had realized what she felt for him. Some of the more seasoned court ladies had once told her that the eunuchs made wonderful lovers. She had shrugged them off, amused and disinterested. The work she did for the emperor was more important. She was aware that a couple of the older concubines secretly continued to have eunuch lovers despite Zhu Di's witch hunt several years earlier. She had a fair idea of who they were but she told herself never to mention their secret.

And now, as she remembered the night in the baths, she understood what the older concubines had meant. What the eunuchs could not do for lack of their severed member, they more than made up for it in other ways. Min Li's curiosity had been satisfied but it was not the reason why she had lured Zheng He into the bath chamber with her.

She had initially wanted to punish him for ignoring her all these years and for failing to live up to the promise he had made to her mother. She had anticipated that her nakedness would confront him and frustrate him.

But in the warm scented waters, she had felt a surge of happiness. Through this voluptuous sensation, her secret tormented life had suddenly flashed before her eyes, in all its ugliness. It was she who had swallowed the truth about the void in her life. Tears had welled up in her eyes as she touched him for the first time.

She felt confused. Had she sought his warmth just as one seeks a mother after being frightened too long, or had she wanted to quell the burning passions he had stirred despite her will. And now, while walking alone in this new garden, she realized it was both.

She was certain the emperor suspected nothing of what had gone on in the bath last year. Yet for several months later, Zhu Di, in morose contemplation of his waning manhood, repeatedly mulled over her night with Zheng He and demanded to know what she had learnt.

"He is loyal to you, Your Highness. Be assured that the Grand Admiral behaved righteously."

And then to her great concern, Zhu Di heard rumors about his loyal eunuch, Zheng He. It was said that before leaving for the fifth expedition in 1417, Zheng He had become strangely moody and aloof. According to one of the accountants, the admiral may have become sullen upon learning that such and such persons had been accused for ill sayings against the emperor and imprisoned by the Embroidered-uniform Guards. The Grand Admiral had, according to several accounts, sent copious amounts of rice to the prisoners' families.

After sharing this, Zhu Di tormented Min Li with questions.

"What should we do with the question of the Grand Admiral, Zheng He? For all my tolerance for those Hues, perhaps I am wrong to trust them. Perhaps you saw something that I have not glimpsed. If word be true, he conspires against me."

She shook her head.

"Such yapping tongues know no respite, Your Highness. Let me tell you that jealousy these days, for want of honor and riches, speaks ill of many a dutiful servant. I would say Admiral Yang Bao had a hand in this. I saw the envy in his eyes at the banquet. Would you have men less worthy take comfort from the Admiral's demise? To be sure, this Zheng He filled my head with talks of religion such that I wanted to run away at the end of the night. But never once did he speak ill of his emperor."

"Yet he provokes us by comforting our enemies."

"The Huis are generous to the poor, Your Highness. Their religion demands that they share their wealth with those less fortunate. It may be clumsiness on the admiral's part."

She had spoken well. The charges had been dropped. What had Zheng He known of her devotion? He was far at sea. He was not even aware that for months, she had worked at his liberty and his reputation, showering the emperor with his own greatness, soothing Zhu Di's ego, impressing words upon him, words that had allegedly been spoken by his humble servant, Admiral Zheng He.

Her thoughts were interrupted by a mild rustling. She paused, looking around beyond the trees, ready to smile to hide her sad thoughts. There was no one in sight.

She realized that she had been walking to the edge of the garden, an area she was not familiar with. The new palace was immense and while with her unbound feet, she had ventured further than the other concubines, she still had much to explore. She saw, then, the long red walled street that adjourned the Imperial Gardens and turned into it.

Zhu Di must have been holding court. The street was almost empty, save for a few eunuchs who went about their duties. Others hurried along, carrying wooden tablets, ready to pass them on to eunuchs on the next shift.

As she veered into the street, Min Li again heard the shuffling sound behind her. She saw it. The tall figure with its proud *buzi*, advanced menacingly towards her. Her heart skipped a beat. She recognized the long greasy hair and the pimply face. How long had Ji Feng been following her?

Their eyes met. He knew that she had seen him. As she moved hurriedly down the empty street, Ji Feng's silent footsteps were close behind. The familiar chill ran through her spine. She dared not look back to meet his cold, cynical smile. She kept her eyes locked straight ahead, trembling despite herself. She could hear his breathing as he quickened his pace.

She realized that something was wrong. The street was too quiet. Her desperate eyes traveled ahead searching for workers, other eunuchs, maids perhaps but the long walled street remained resolutely empty. It would only be a trap for her. She realized that she had no choice but to turn back soon to regain the concubine compound.

Ji Feng's steps picked up speed with a resolve that terrified her. Now he knew that she was afraid. She pressed her hand to her chest, alarmed at her uncontrolled heartbeat. She had to turn back. Turn back now and run, she thought. She pivoted on her heels. In a flash, he had blocked her passage. He grabbed her wrist.

"Let me pass," she warned.

"You little bitch!" he sneered.

She struggled but his grip tightened.

"What a surprise, I remember you! You are Min Li, hmm? The impetuous peach in the sedan chair, I recognize you! Now, what is it? Feeling afraid?"

"Let me go!"

"Now, now...what is it? Hmm? I know! Not as haughty as you were the other day perched inside your sedan, hmm? You don't look well. Are you lost?"

His breathing was heavy. A dangerous light shone in his eyes. The more she struggled, the more he twisted her arm.

"Let me go!" she roared.

There was a loud clamor behind them. Zhijian stood, several feet back. On the way to his shift, he had dropped his wooden tablet. He hurried to pick it up before shuffling past.

Ji Feng released Min Li and stepped back.

"Have a good afternoon Li Guifei. Have a good afternoon," he bowed, half-mocking.

As she ran back towards the gardens, his eyes followed the concubine. A cruel rictus formed on his lips.

Chapter 13
Shin Talks
Beijing, 1419

It was one year following relocation to Beijing that Shin came to see the then twenty-eight years old Zhijian with an offer that sounded highly promising.

"One of the 5a intendants to the Fire and Water Department will be retiring due to illness. There is a position available to fill his place. I can put in a word for you if you are interested."

Zhijian was happy hearing this. Perhaps he would finally make his father proud. He thought for a moment and decided that he did not want to look too eager.

"Let me think about it," he replied. "When do you need to know?"

"The role is to be filled by mid next year. There are several changes taking place with the new departments in Beijing. The role remains in planning stage for a while. Let me know."

"Thank you Shin, I am honored."

"I have not seen much of you lately. I fail to understand how someone could take so much pleasure in their work...We should share a drink. What do you say?"

They soon found a noisy inn, not far from the imperial bakery beyond the Western walls of the palace. After much drinking, the senior eunuch began to lose his sense of propriety. He spoke everything that was on his mind and did not care for the consequences.

"Zhijian," asked Shin gravely, "did you know that Ji Feng has been demoted?"

"Ji Feng? No, I had no idea."

"Can you imagine the blow to his pompous face? He will never recover. The latest news is that he is no longer attached to the palace."

"What happened to him?" asked Zhijian as he poured more wine in Shin's goblet.

"It's those women. Did I not tell you? They are trouble! No good can come of them."

"What about the women? You are not making much sense."

But Shin did not answer. He looked around as though inspecting the tavern for the source of noise. Zhijian could see that he was distracted. Shin cursed.

"Damn those yapping gamblers upstairs! Someone should lock them up."

He hesitated.

"So you want to know about those women? Alright my boy, listen..."

He knelt forward across the wooden table and lowered his voice.

"He was up to no good that Ji Feng. Mingling with the women of the palace—"

"What do you mean, mingling?"

"Well here's the thing. You know the publishing house attached to the *Silijian*? That odd looking building? He was printing illegal books, was what our Ji Feng was doing! Selling publications on the side and trading several copies per month to the concubines. But you never heard it from me, do you hear?"

Zhijian's brow narrowed.

"What sort of illegal books?"

"Astronomy, folk tales, immoral rubbish...the lot! Our Ji Feng was setting up his own little business on the side, he was. Lucky for him he could not read and pleaded innocent when found out."

Shin seemed flustered. He nearly spilt his wine with his clumsy movements.

"Astronomy! Can you believe it? Astronomy is a state secret. Zhu Di should have had Ji Feng locked up and flayed. Ah, but the emperor was too lenient. That new palace has filled His Majesty's head...that and all the nonsense about Admiral Zheng He coming back and everything. Zhu Di wants to put on a show of mercy and impress the foreign envoys. You see, there is another problem. Ji

Feng has always managed a good reputation. He has served the emperor well...so..."

"Where is he now?"

"...soon to be waving hello to the U-Tsang traders at the Sichuan border. They've put him in charge of the *chamasi* at Baidu station. He'll be suspended from the palace for a few more months, complete his training and then move to the South West. Let's see how he likes it there. Countryside will do much good for his insufferable complexion. Good riddance, don't you think?" He gulped another goblet of wine.

"I never liked him much," agreed Zhijian.

"Me neither," Shin replied making a face. "But he's better than those devils."

"Who?"

"Well don't you know?"

"What devils?"

"Boy, you are thick. Who else but the women who sold him? One of them did it. All it takes is one slandering bitch. They turned him in, him and the concubines who were reading that filth. You can bet they did."

Shin grew more agitated. He kept shuffling on his wooden seat. So much so, that Zhijian began to suspect that the Korean might be secretly wetting the incontinence cloth all sensible eunuchs attached to their loins and concealed beneath their robe.

"I cannot imagine concubines reading astronomy, Shin. That's ridiculous. Isn't that a little too complicated?"

"Perhaps... But then Ji Feng was without a doubt selling astronomy books elsewhere. Which as you would agree is even more troubling for the emperor. Well, as much as I didn't like the Jurchen, I pity him. I'm telling you, young man, court women are all witches! They wanted to ruin him and they found his weakness just as they profited from it."

"Were any of the concubines punished too?" asked Zhijian, feeling suddenly anxious.

"They were, if you can call that punishment. Two of them were escorted outside the palace. They were forced to walk between several city gates. You should have seen them agonize with every step. It was ghastly. Bound feet may be erotic but it's not meant to get you far. They'll be recovering for days."

Zhijian caught on to those last words and his eyes widened as if he had just realized something. It seemed to appease him.

"That's punishment enough," he replied. "But if I may speak my mind, Shin, I am not persuaded that any of these women were guilty of turning in Ji Feng. I mean...well...what do you think?"

"Don't you, now...Well that's where you and I are a little different. See, I like you, Zhijian but you are far too naïve. I'm telling you these women are devils. Maybe they don't start up that way. But they sure end up that way."

Chapter 14
The Eastern Depot

September 1420

They were in the Imperial Garden, all of them. At first they were timid. They flirted with the warm sun's rays filtering through a thin blanket of clouds. Then, alarmed at the heat on their cheeks, they called out for the eunuchs to fetch parasols. In a thin file, they tippy-toed onto the tiled pavement and into the garden.

Autumn hues greeted the women, their chatty red lips barely visible under peach and white parasols. Like fragile birds released into the wild. Slender porcelain hands reached out with delight; they cupped the orange tinged leaves before tossing them high. The slanted eyes gazed in wonderment as though discovering the garden for the very first time.

Min Li remained inside the compound feigning a headache. The ever suspicious Xun Guifei passed her chamber with a dispassionate inclination of the head. She enquired about Min Li's health and asked whether Li Guifei would be joining the audition held in Princess Xianning's honor. The princess was to sing this afternoon and the women were eager to give her audience and praise her talent. In response, Min Li moaned in her bed. Xun Guifei left but not without pursing her lips in outrage.

And when they were gone, Min Li waited. She knew this game. She knew it well.

Would Princess Xia notice that she was not at the audition? She would. The princess would demand after her. The eunuchs would explain that Li Guifei was deeply unsettled. An unmanageable headache, it was. Xun Guifei would cut into the eunuch's apology with one of her acerbic remarks, deploring the frequency of Min

Li's headaches. The venomous concubine would not miss an opportunity to draw royal attention to herself, adding that "Li Guifei ought to eat more pork to revive her dwindling *qi*" and that those headaches were surely a sign that "Li Guifei was incapable of having children". This of course would amuse the princesses, notably Princess Xia, who knew only too well that Zhu Di could not sire another child.

At the very moment when Min Li mulled over the effects of her absence from the audition, a mysterious black-clad eunuch traversed the inner quarters of the palace, sweeping the carpet of leaves with his long silk robe. Unlike the odd servants that he occasionally passed and who dared not raise their fearful eyes to his level, the eunuch had an imposing gait. His swift, powerful demeanor denoted strength and cunning. This, together with the half-hidden *buzi* beneath his long jacket alluded to his military background.

When he reached the concubine quarters, his tenebrous eyes shifted sideways inspecting the building's long shadows for any hidden presence. Having ascertained that there were no witnesses to his clandestine visit, he stepped quietly into the long corridor.

The sound of rustling leaves rose Min Li from her contemplation. She leapt, fully dressed from her couch rolling her quilt to the side. Her ears pressed to the door, listening for female sounds within the concubine compound. None; save for the felt footsteps drawing near.

Min Li turned towards a small wooden cabinet where the oil lamp rested. She moved quickly, her heart pounding. Removing the lamp, she lifted the silk cloth to reveal the handle of the first drawer. She pulled on the brass handle, and one by one, lifted out three boxes. It was the last one that she sought. It was a carved red lacquered box. The rectangular front face was incised and gilded. It featured a sinewy dragon with a long flowing mane, horns, a prominent beard and whiskers.

Her hands trembled. She dug underneath her *beizi*, tugging at the woven silk string around her neck until she held a set of brass keys. She pushed one of the keys into the gilded brass lock until it was unlatched and the box opened.

The emperor's gifts glistened. It had been nine years, she thought, eyeing the treasures with mixed feelings. It would be a risk and a death sentence but she had to take that risk. She caressed the gems. Nine years of her life were in that box.

Who were you then, Min Li? She swallowed hard, biting her lips to muffle the sobs deep within her lungs. Not now. Don't think of this now. The little Min Li is no more. The young girl who lusted after those jade beads, those rubies, those pearls... She sank her palm inside the box, feeling the cold stones. How hideous her hand with its red balsam-painted nails. She would not go on. Her lower lip curled in disgust. Now, she wondered, wary of the felt footsteps closing in, what would please the eunuch most? Ah, yes. She found the brooch. She lifted the gilded phoenix whose plumage fanned out into sixteen blood-red rubies. Enough to fetch a large sum, she thought.

A tap at the door alerted her.

"Who's there?" she cried, eager to replace the three boxes.

She spread the cloth back over the cabinet and shifted the lamp to its original position before reaching for the door. But just before she turned the handle, she locked her eye into a tiny peephole one inch wide on the lower panel of the door. She had found a weakness in that portion of the wood and created the hole years ago. It gave her a preview of her visitors without their knowledge.

He was not armed. He had come, it seemed, without his uniform. The only aspect of his dress that distinguished him from the other eunuch officers was the ring he wore at his index finger, the seal of the Embroidered-uniform Guards. But it was not the ring that Min Li noticed first. It was the eunuch's long pointy boots. They were well dissimulated beneath the guard's robe but she noted the soiled, dirty leather.

Her left palm on her chest, she felt her own terror. She blinked but remained pressed against the peephole. Behind the door, the guard's feet became hesitant, shuffling on the spot as though to leave.

She could hear his breathing even through the *nanmu*. A dangerous man, he was. She felt as she had on that night at the Donghuamen in Nanjing. Another tap. This one was more ominous than the first. Min Li swallowed hard and moistened her lips, defiant until the end. The door swiveled opened.

When the eunuch entered, pacing the room with calculated movements, Min Li had regained her composure. She was unreadable. She stood tall, facing him, her eyes darkened by the knowledge she had gathered in the previous instant. If she felt fear, she did not show it. Her eyes followed the military officer as he infused her chamber with a sharp tobacco scent. He stopped short and folded his powerful arms.

"How did you know I would come?"

"I knew." Her voice was firm.

"Ahuh. And you also know, then, in what grave danger you run into, Li Guifei."

"Do not say my name," she retorted. "We've never met."

He smiled, visibly intrigued by her resolve.

"Yes, yes. These are fine terms. Well then, nothing in this palace comes cheap. I will expect the payment..."

She extended a palm towards him. She watched the scarred hand whose knuckles were swollen with red calluses, as it seized the bundle. Something about that hand revolted her. Now this very hand was raised as the eunuch admired the phoenix and she could not decide which of the two were more hideous.

The officer smiled again. Like Zhu Di, he had a full grown moustache with tapering ends. It framed his cracked lips and reached to just beneath his chin. A deep scar marked his right temple.

"Your director does not know you are here," she advanced. It was not a question, but a bold request.

"That is correct," agreed the eunuch, complying with the arrangement. His teeth were sharp and stained by excess tobacco.

He replaced the phoenix in its pouch, drew the string and tucked the pouch inside his left boot which disappeared beneath his black tunic. She remembered her own gesture with the tablecloth a moment earlier. We are so similar, she thought. How is this possible?

She resumed their written conversation. "Do we have an agreement?"

He did not reply. Instead, he turned on his heels and leaned against the door with one raised knee, still folding his arms as though collecting his thoughts.

Min Li stared at the guard with alarm, waiting for his answer.

She knew she could not force him into anything. She knew he could take the brooch and simply walk away. The only hold she had over him is that at this very moment, he was in the concubine chamber. At any moment, he could be found and she could incriminate him just as he could accuse her of treason. It would be his word against hers. They both wanted something. He wanted money to reward his underpaid efforts. And she wanted something else. Something only he could give her.

The eunuch seemed to mock her with his richly stained smile. She could tell he was of Mongol stock. Like me, she realized. His cynical smile chilled her once more.

"Li Guifei, I know what you want. I warned you years ago that you would seek me."

"Do we have an agreement," she repeated, her voice rising and trembling against her will.

He did not notice the quiver in her voice. He began speaking with a slow, deliberate pace.

"Li Guifei, this...this palace where you live, is it not to your liking? Is there...something missing perhaps? No, no, do not answer."

His voice chilled her. Trembling within, she ran her cold fingers against the jade beads round her neck.

"Li Guifei, there are times when it is best to accept our roles as His Majesty's subjects and not try to uncover too many truths. You are a very well cared for woman, privileged and respected in the palace. Even I – and you may not believe this – but even I... I have respect for you."

Min Li closed her eyes, dismissing his words.

"I want us... I want us to go on with what we agreed," she replied, almost choking.

"Yes, yes, of course. You are as foolish as you are dissatisfied," he mused.

"I care very little for what you believe. Do we or do we not have an agreement?"

There was a glint in his eyes.

"Tonight, you will meet me after the third *geng*. Be at the Donghuamen. You must come alone," he warned.

"That gate will be locked and guarded," she observed.

"And so it will be."

"And...What of the soldiers at the eastern turret? What of the guards outside?"

"Leave that to me. Drape yourself well. No one here must notice you leave this compound. And no one, no one, must recognize you at the gates. We will cross the new moat towards the Eastern Gate of the city—"

"The Donganmen. What then?"

"Then my lovely, I will show you the guts of this city and you will leave reeking of it. And when we are done, poor, foolish woman, you will beg me to make you forget, though it will not be in my power to help you."

"These are just words, Officer. They do not frighten me. Invent what you will to dissuade me from this. It will not change my mind. Part of reality is in your boot, in that bundle I gave you and tonight, tonight when I see the other side of reality, everything will be clear for me. Forgetting plays no part in my designs."

"Aha, yes!" sneered the eunuch. "And is that what you think? A mere glimpse of the emperor's secrets and then you can return here, at his side? You think then, that you will find it easy afterwards to play in your pretty garden? Or sit by your embroidery perhaps?

You think that you will continue to work for your emperor—and yes, *I know* about your work, Li Guifei, it is well documented—you think afterwards you will simply return to this life and say to yourself with relief, Ah, now I know! You think you will feel content with yourself? That you will happily grasp onto that knowledge and not burst for want of sharing what you know with someone else?"

"So that's it!"

"What?"

"You reproach me for wanting to soil my happiness with the mysteries of this palace. You scorn me in advance for the pain I will endure from the lack of a confidante. But you see now? You see what you must do? You, yourself, are desperately in need to share what you know with me! On the surface you mock me, Officer, perhaps you feel privileged and enjoy my need for truth. You like the power it gives you. But underneath..."

She looked through her grilled window as though gazing at the garden. "You think that I care so much for happy garden games, so much so that it would ruin or mar my existence if I knew what you know? Well let me tell you that I've not looked at the flowers, climbed the trees or danced in the rain for years. You think if I did,

I would be the brand of woman to part from the phoenix I just gave you?

"You say you know about my work, so then, you must also understand that for me, nothing is the same as for those other women of the palace. What do I care if through what I am to discover, I am changed or troubled. You must know that nothing is worse for me than to serve my emperor in the manner I have served him and not know what I have done, in what design my work has been used. Play in the garden? No. Any woman in my position would abandon those foolish games if she knew the burden of my existence."

He pursed his lips. "Then I shall show you what you want to see."

"Yes! Because you want to," she snapped. "I can see how much you desire to fill me with the same dread that consumes you."

"Ah, maybe so... Maybe so, Li Guifei. But you shall find, in time...that we are different."

"Not so different. You are a stranger to me, but I believe that today you showed me more of yourself than what you've shown many others."

"I've told you nothing," warned the eunuch.

"Oh no? You are desperate for money. That I know. You are a tormented man, I know that too because you hesitated in coming here. Yes, it is so, do not deny it. What else? You have a secret that burdens you enough to wish warning me and deterring me, me, a complete stranger, from ever being privy to its nature.

"You play this power game of knowledge, but the truth, Officer, is you derive little pleasure from what you know and no matter how eager you are to unload your burden, no matter how much *yang* fire burns inside you, you'd rather shield me from your secret than burden me with it. This very reluctance betrays the horror you live.

"We're not too different. I have never told anyone about what I feel about my work. Here we are then, two strangers. I do not know your name and you, you will not speak mine. But you know, now, everything about me, and tonight, yes, tonight, I will know everything about you too."

The eunuch had listened attentively. The cynical smile had vanished from his lips. Instead there was a painful grin that Min Li could not decipher.

"Very well then," he began, opening the door to leave. "Tonight, Li Guifei. At the Donghuamen. Do not be late."

***

She was familiar with the night. The clear autumn skies set the stars to shine for her like beacons. She moved swiftly from building to building, hiding below the eaves of each doorway and hunched like a maid whenever a figure, often a servant preparing for the upcoming day's work, loomed in the distance.

As she approached the long walled street beyond the Imperial Gardens, her felt footsteps were muffled by the resounding third *geng*. Her heart skipped a beat. She had a moment of doubt, a violent realization of the danger she placed herself. But she brushed it off and began to run. She could not be late. He had warned her not to be late. She picked up her pace, running along the red wall, her long cape trailing behind her, giving her the appearance of a ghost floating beneath the waning moonlight.

She observed the large building ahead. There it was, the Donghuamen, the Eastern Gate of the palace. Four guards stood by the doors. She looked around. There would be guards inside and outside. Yet she saw no sign of the stranger with the upturned boots. Where was he? She could not hesitate now. To hesitate may mean her arrest and her death.

She exhaled moist air preparing to speak. The guards watched the slight shadow approach, the owner's face partly hidden beneath her hooded cape.

"Open the gates," she ordered in a firm voice.

She waited with bated breath, alarmed at her own boldness. And a most strange thing happened then. The guards obeyed. They moved in silence but with decisive movements as if made awake by the urgency in her voice. They lifted the wooden planks and pushed open the heavy doors. They kept their eyes down as if they had been ordered not to look at her or question her presence. As though she were not even a woman, she thought.

The Embroidered-uniform Guard stood a few paces behind on the other side of the gate building. She ran across. In a moment, she emerged outside the Imperial Palace. Any other night, and this would have felt strange. The air that greeted her outside was dense with gloom. It seemed colder out here.

He had been smoking a pipe and smelt of opium. He looked unwashed. His tired eyes sank beneath his brow, giving him a stern, intense gaze. He wore the same self-contained expression but it was underlined by a cynical smile belying the terror in his eyes. He noticed she had swapped her embroidered slippers for plain felt slippers like those worn by the chamber maids and her feet tapped noiselessly on the tiles. He nodded approvingly.

"This way, Li Guifei."

She climbed inside a sedan, her face well hidden from the curious sideway glances of the carriers. The guard stepped inside. She refused to look at him. They crossed over the moat ditch that imperial workers had begun digging and continued onto an unlit road.

Her heart beat savagely with each sway of the sedan chair. In that short journey which to Min Li seemed to last for months, they passed myriads of buildings and red lights beyond the Imperial Palace. But she saw nothing. Unfolding in her mind were the many years she had spent as Zhu Di's concubine, locked inside the walls of Nanjing and Beijing palaces. And as the night chilled her limbs and fogged up her senses, it seemed to Min Li that this sedan journey was the culmination of all she had ever lived in her life. That everything she had ever done or said, every path she had taken so far in her life had led to this road and to the gate that now towered before them as the carriers sighed and lowered their loads. The Donganmen.

The guard watched her descend. She kept her eyes fixated on that gate. Under the glow of raised lanterns, it seemed to call out to her.

The imposing Donganmen had three archways. It was a single-eave building, housing twenty rooms. It was covered with glazed yellow roof tiles. Beneath each arch, lay a pair of large gold-nailed red doors, guarded on either side by two well-armed soldiers.

"Welcome to the Donganmen, Li Guifei," said the guard.

He motioned towards the side archway, signaling towards the soldiers. They crossed the gate, emerging outside the imperial city. Min Li was trembling.

They turned towards the left, passing two large buildings and a remote courtyard. Another uniform guard saw them approach. He glowered at the tall woman before walking past them and disappearing behind mulberry trees. Now they neared a large building. She stared fixedly ahead, stifling her growing fear. Her cape flouted about beneath her shoulders. She had so far walked with her head held high as though she had been here before, as though the place had never been a secret for her. But this was not all pride. True, she may not have known about the building, but deep inside, she had always known of its existence.

The building was new, she calculated, smelling the wood and the fresh paint. It was clear that the emperor had only recently commissioned it for his Eastern Depot. But it was the idea, the symbol that was well known to her. For it represented the emperor she knew. It embodied the paranoiac tendencies she had observed in him for years. It embodied all the work she had done for nine years now. And so while the new building was clearly unknown to her, it belonged to a world that was only too familiar.

At the entrance of a square building, ten officers of the ninth grade played dominos around a table. For them it was routine. Min Li ignored the men and stared at the large insignia hanging inside the building. The rising dawn bathed the hall, allowing her to just make out the characters as she entered. A glacial shiver ran down her spine.

The plaque read, "Heart and Bowels of the Court".

The eunuch sensed her tension.

"I shall only show you what concerns you, Guifei. Nothing more."

"No. Show me everything," she declared, her eyes ablaze.

"Very well. See that cabinet on the left? It is the principal security office. The emperor interrogates Eastern Depot officers and confers with the Depot Commander here. It contains documents."

"Many documents," he added, looking straight into her eyes. "Your file...is also in there."

Min Li frowned. "What do you know about my work?"

He smiled. "Over the last nine years Guifei, the intelligence you supplied led to the arrest of sixteen people under suspicion of treason or *secret meeting without apparent cause*, thirty for misconduct towards his majesty and of these, twelve have been tortured, five have been executed. My congratulations, Li Guifei."

She had heard but gave no sign of understanding. Her eyes hovered suspiciously over the corridor at the other end of the building.

"Why all that information?" she asked coldly.

"You want to know the truth, Li Guifei. The truth always begins with one's self. Since you've come this far now, I will indulge your curiosity, my Lady.

His voice rose.

"You have been a powerful assistant to the Eastern Depot. We owe you some revelations. You need to know everything, don't you? That's why you came? Then I propose to tell you now before dawn finally breaks and the emperor holds court, what you have always suspected.

"His majesty knows no bounds to protect the dragon throne from traitors. We work here every hour of the day and night to safeguard His Majesty's life. We inhale his paranoia and ingest it inside our very guts. Because how else do we protect someone unless we learn to sense threat in every word, in every whisper, in every nuance and in every raised eyebrow. Your eyes tell me that you are familiar with what I'm saying Guifei? Yes, I see that you are. There is no peace for people like us. Is there now?"

He spun round.

"But come. Come now, I cannot show you the building on the left. It is the Inside Depot. It is highly secure and only criminals and dangerous men are kept there. Not a place for a woman."

"I want to see what you did with the people I had arrested," she interrupted. "Show me."

The guard paced the hall, rubbing his moustache. He wondered what drove this woman. Was it truly curiosity? Or did she also seek to gauge the power she had held over the years? That wonderful power...of being trusted and playing a defining role in the lives of others... He understood that only too well. As much at is consumed him and tug at his soul, it revived him and gave him a sense of purpose.

And then he began to understand this deluded woman. A sense of purpose is what Li Guifei craved and had always craved. Poor Guifei. He smiled, pleased with the profile he had finally made of the only woman ever appointed to the Eastern Depot. The emperor had chosen her well.

"Take me to their cell," she insisted.

"They are not here, Guifei. They are either in detention or *dead.* What do you think the emperor does to traitors?"

He watched her grow pale. Reality had set in.

"Where does this corridor lead to?" she mumbled.

A thin smile belied his scorn as he followed her to the adjacent building.

"It leads to hell on earth, Li Guifei."

"Take me to this place. I want to see what you did with the people *you* arrested."

"Ah, yes. You want to see the Bureau of Suppression and Soothing."

Her brows met.

"The Bureau of Suppression and Soothing? The Zhenfusi," she whispered.

"It is a monstrous building, my Lady. I could not take you in there without leading you into despair. Are you sure you have the strength?"

"Strength is irrelevant now," she replied. But her voice quivered.

"And so it is. *Trees have already been made into a boat*, what is done cannot be undone. But your spirit may not survive what you will see."

She reached the rectangular building. It was guarded by a wooden gate with an oversized lock. A loud echo resonated from inside. She listened for the howling sound. It was a moan, something barely human rising from the brick wall.

"Open that door."

"Ah, no. I can't do that."

"But you must. You promised to show me the very essence of myself and the very essence of my work, did you not? So now, hold fast to your word."

"This place is a stench," sneered the man. He spat on the floor to emphasize his point.

"But you know it well and you can lead me inside. You've read my file, you've access to this building and you know it inside out."

"Yes, yes. I go in there every day! And I've no interest in increasing the frequency of my visits so that you can indulge your curiosity, Li Guifei."

"What is this place?"

"It is a torture house. Nothing more, nothing less."

"Show me."

"Foolish woman."

"Open the door."

"Very well. But you've been warned."

He fumbled for his buckle, pulled two keys from his belt and turned the lock. The heavy doors creaked open.

She entered an antechamber lit by lamps attached to the walls on either side. The echoing voices rose from the corridor.

She reached for a torch and raised it to scrutinize the path ahead. Now she advanced into the arched brick passage.

"What is that smell?" Her voice was strangled by a gut-wrenching wail echoing ahead.

He ignored her questioning side glance and walked behind her, his voice, aloof.

"You know, Li Guifei, we've invented nothing that has not been tried since the Tang dynasty. Oh, certainly we have refined a few...techniques."

A drawn out wail rose up ahead. It was followed by the muffling sounds of gushing water. It was like being inside a living organ. *The guts and heart of the palace.* The phrase resounded inside her mind. Her terror-filled eyes widened, eager to consume her surroundings. They passed more locked doors along several corridors. Her senses protested, nauseated by the air's sharp tang. It was a blend of sweat and macerated urine, of putrid vomit and something else...What was it?

They passed by locked cells which carried hellish sounds to her ears. And then there were those grilled cells through which she could see and these were the worst. What had the man with the moustache said? Hell on earth. It was befitting. In one of these, soldiers dressed like her companion held a bloodied man down onto a spiked rack. They moved quickly, loading heavy bricks on his body, ignoring his pleas and his agonizing screams. In another cell, where rose more horrifying screams, a disfigured man, his flesh hanging in shreds on his reddened back, suffered the scorch of a burning iron rod. Min Li looked away, her face ashen.

She gasped, out of breath, refusing to believe.

"Torture rooms, all of them. Why waste your time, my Lady?" came the guard's irritated voice.

Min Li came to a halt. She could hardly breathe.

"We should go now," said the guard with increased contempt.

She took a step back. She stared at him as though she had only just seen who he was. Her back hit the wall behind her. She spun around. And then she saw it. It was the first cell without a solid door. She could see through the grilled bars.

"Ah, the human pig..." sighed the exasperated guard.

Inside, the walls were smeared with feces and blood. On the glistening coarse tiles, human entrails floated in a slosh of red liquid. Blood. This was the smell she had been unable to recognize. She suppressed an urge to retch. And in the butcher's cell, was...she could not see.

"You understand, now. This is only for extreme circumstances..."

There was something not human in there. She heard the strange yelps. Min Li discerned nothing until the two guards inside stepped away. And there it was. It writhed before her in such a manner that Min Li could scarcely believe what she saw. She pushed her cheeks across the iron bars.

"Barely recognizable...do not even try," said the guard.

Min Li stared at *it*. Not a sound escaped from her choked throat. Yes, it was human. It *had* been human. She could see from the two severed breasts that it had been a woman.

"Let me know if you recognize her."

Min Li watched the body closely. The woman's breathing was labored and erratic. She had little time left. She was completely shaved so that even her eyebrows were gone. Her pubic hair was also shaved.

"One of your bedfellows, I believe... A Manchurian."

Min Li gasped. She wanted to scream but no sound came. The Manchurian's limbs had been sawn off, leaving bloodied pulps jutting from her torso. Caked blood trickled from ugly orifices where once had been her sensual almond eyes, her bulbous nose and tender ears. Out of her lipless mouth, poured another torrent of blood from a recently severed tongue. Min Li suppressed another urge to vomit. The mutilated form writhed on the bench, torn between the agony of living and the defeat of death.

Min Li could take no more. She screamed; she could not but scream; she had to scream only to release her horror of what they had done. What *they* had done!

In the cell, the two soldiers raised their heads. They had seen her.

The Embroidered-uniform Guard responded fast. He leapt from behind, placed one arm round her neck and clamped her lips with one palm. He wrenched her away from the cell door and drew her back to the corridor.

"Foolish woman!" he spat.

His brutal shove had sent her to the ground. She felt the odious slime under her legs and hands. Her skirt was drenched in a slosh of urine. Gripping the bars of one cell, she heaved herself up, shivering with shock.

"What you saw, Li Guifei was a rare case. That woman was a Manchurian spy!"

"You're murderers! You've made her into this...this—"

"You've seen enough!"

"Why did they hurt her? Why?"

"Do not be so naive! Actions lead to reports! Reports lead to arrests! Arrests lead to questioning! Questions lead to answers or more torture!"

"You...you...you are one of those monsters, aren't you?"

Without responding, he seized her arm and pulled her out of the building.

She was angry as they reached the courtyard. "Is that your work? Answer me!"

He ignored her, pushing her towards the gate.

"You've been in here long enough," he spit.

She had surprised him. He had been so sure she would leave the building on her first encounter with the stench. Even the first cell, ought to have scared any Guifei away. But not her. Remarkable, she was. But she had found her limits.

"You've interrogated the people I reported? Is that your work? What did you do to them? What did you do to the Guirens? And to the others?"

"Do not tarry in guilt. Those you denounced have always been found lacking, in one way or another!"

She shook her head.

"But I didn't... I didn't—"

"You *have* been an impressive ally to the Eastern Depot, Li Guifei."

"No. We're both monsters...monsters..." she whispered. She could not stop shaking.

The soldiers at the Donganmen would be advised never to mention the presence of this distraught lady at the Eastern Depot. She was a shadow and nothing more.

Min Li passed the gate's arch once more. And it was as though she had sprung from a womb, as though the Donganmen had birthed a new woman. As frail as a newborn, she stumbled blind into the imperial city. The blood had drained from her face.

When they reached the sedan chair, she turned back, awestruck. She watched the soldiers seal the red doors. In the ripping silence of dawn, the Donganmen stood before her, proud, insolent and foreboding. Yet now, thought Min Li, it held no more secrets.

The Embroidered-uniform Guard seemed to have read her mind.

"You are an expert at drawing confidences from willing others. You adapt your manner perfectly based on the situation."

She could not respond.

"It is evident, isn't it? People trust you easily. It is all in your file. It was in your file from the moment you became concubine. From the very first day you were summoned..."

He watched the surprise mount in her eyes.

"What do you mean?" She could not believe what he was saying.

"Get in!"

He pushed her into the sedan chair and glowered at her. She felt his horrid breath on her face as he paused before drawing the curtains.

"And as for me, Li Guifei, I am adept at uncovering the truth by force from those who would not tell me otherwise. All methods are valid."

She clasped her palms to her ears but it was no use. The deafening cries from the Zhenfusi gnawed at her soul.

The sedan meandered back to the palace. She saw nothing of the road ahead. The sun would rise in moments. The fourth *geng* must have sounded long ago, while they were still at Donganmen.

Somewhere in the palace, the emperor was having his first meal. He would be holding court soon.

The guard escorted her towards the Eastern palace gate. She moved silently, twisting her palms, exhausted from her ordeal.

"Make haste. The guards at the Donghuamen will be replaced soon. You do not want to have to explain how you came to be outside the palace, do you?"

"An expert at drawing out the truth...what is that?" she asked pitifully.

"Goodbye, Guifei," replied the guard in a final tone. "The palace is on the other side of this gate. Rest assured. You will not have to do this for much longer now."

His words came like a slap. She winced.

"What do you mean?"

He looked exasperated.

"Li Guifei, I deal with traitors and despots every day. Do you think I would have permitted you to come here today, unless I was assured that you represented no threat to His Majesty?"

"But... I thought we had an agreement..."

"To hell with our agreement! His Majesty comes first. I sympathized with you, yes. I showed you what you wanted to see. But you irritate me, Li Guifei. You've no sense of your work and its meaning yet you've been so diligent all these years. Why? I know I'm a demon and I've killed and maimed people but when I do something, I do it with a complete understanding of where it leads and how it affects those lives that are handed to me.

"But you, you're so completely blind to our purpose. Are you so selfless that you would sacrifice your cherished virtue to please an emperor? An emperor that your spirit does not veritably serve...or else it would not have been so repulsed by our methods. Yes, it's hell on earth! But without it and without the work that you've seen today, the dragon throne would not be as safe. But that means nothing to you, does it?"

"I...I never wanted to kill anyone... I did not know... I did not know they would do this to the Guirens..."

"No, you did not. But see now, how different we are. I'd kill and maim anyone who threatened to overthrow the emperor and I'd kill to draw out information that I could use to protect him."

She stared at him in disbelief.

"You're a monster..."

"Ah, yes. Well it's just as well, Li Guifei! Just as well you've realized what you're not. Luckily for you, it will all end very soon."

"What are you saying? What do you mean by that?"

They had reached the Donghuamen building and she stood there, refusing to re-enter without hearing the rest. He remained silent for a moment as if preparing himself for his next revelation.

"Tell me what you mean!" she screamed, out of herself.

"As you wish. Your file has been under review, Li Guifei," he said in a grave voice. "Your services will no longer be required. The Eastern Depot is being officialized as the only security and spying agency as of the end of this year."

"What! You're lying. There's something else isn't there? Something else?"

"It means this, my Lady, all peripheral agents not falling under the supervision of the Embroidered-uniform Guards and our Commander Ji Gang are being disposed of."

"Disposed of... I...I do not understand."

"I can only surmise that His Highness has a fondness for you that extends beyond his security needs. But if I were you, Min Li," he hissed, "I would enjoy those last moments I had left in the Imperial Garden. I'd breathe every flower and try to wipe the stench you've inhaled today. If you move in the wrong direction or utter a word against His Highness, he will have no recourse but to get rid of you. You're of no use to him now."

"You lie! Liar!"

She lashed out at him, scratching at the air in vain. Again, he reacted with brute force, grabbing her wrists and twisting them in his coarse fingers.

"My part of the bargain is fulfilled. I gave you the truth. Now you know everything. And if that pains you, Guifei, if that pains you, then there's nothing I can do."

He pushed her away and moved hurriedly back towards the sedan. She stared at him long after he had gone. Once he had disappeared from view, she moved like a sorry figure across the hall of the Donghuamen.

Halfway through, she paused. And then, resigned to her fate, she re-entered the palace, her life prison.

How dense the walls now seemed round her as she dragged her feet along the long street. She barely acknowledged the eunuchs as they rushed past the kitchens for their early morning chores. The street seemed endless. It was like traversing time and moving through a corridor that spanned years. She felt those years. She felt them stripping her bare with each step towards the garden.

The fifth *geng* resounded from afar. She winced from the first rays of the sun. As she reached the gardens, she found a flat stone beside a flaming cypress. She sat there, breathing quietly, her eyes vacant. She had a vague sense of the sun's gilded rays bathing the garden stones, but it did not matter.

She knew not for how many hours she remained on that stone, breathing the morning as though to wipe the hell of dawn from her senses. Her skirt had been torn and her hands were dirty from clenching the bars inside the Zhenfusi.

Around mid-morning, as Min Li still sat in the Imperial Gardens, her shoulders sunken under the weight of despair, she noticed a lithe figure strolling towards her in the distance. It was the young concubine who had joined the Royal Chamber this summer. She was thirteen. She had a radiant smile on her face and held a bunch of peonies in her right hand. Upon seeing Min Li, the girl walked as fast as her tiny feet could allow until she reached the stone where the Guifei sat.

"Guifei Min Li", she chirped, unaware of the correct way to address her elder. "Look, look what Princess Xia gave me! Are they not precious?"

Min Li smiled and reached out to caress the young girl's plump cheek.

"Guifei Min Li," continued the animated young girl as though the place filled her with exuberance and wonder, "wouldn't it be so beautiful if the entire garden was filled with these?"

Min Li nodded quietly. Her smile had faded. She let her hand fall back to her lap. In that gesture, her cape slipped to the floor. The young concubine caught a glimpse of Li Guifei's dirty hemline and was startled.

"Your skirt...what happened to your skirt, Guifei Min Li?"

"I fell," replied the Guifei.

And her voice came like a whisper.

Chapter 15
The Invitation
Beijing, March 1421

And now, honored reader, you know as much as we do about Min Li, her world, how she came to be Zhu Di's concubine, her work and her longing for Admiral Zheng He. We return now, to that Beijing spring evening on the eve of the foreign envoys' departure.

On this misty night, shortly after Min Li and Princess Xia had plotted in secret, hours after prince Zhu Goazhi had collapsed into an indulgent afternoon nap to soothe himself from the unfortunate argument with his stubborn father, and almost half a day after Zhu Di had praised his favorite admiral before an adoring audience, a lavish farewell banquet was held at the Palace of Preserving Harmony. And when it ended, Admiral Zheng He retired for the night.

After dismissing his escort, Zheng He walked briskly towards his chamber beyond the Northern Gate. As he passed the Genggufang, the Night Drum room, the second *geng* resounded through the imperial city. Hearing this, he hastened until he reached the *Silijian* complex where a chamber had been reserved for him. The servant eunuch greeted him with a deep bow. Zheng He dismissed him with a nod.

The scent of warm *nanmu* lingered in the air as he entered the new private chamber. His belongings had been delivered and arranged as expected. His night robe lay on the bed beside a bouquet of flowers. It was a nice touch. He removed his military hat and sword and unbuckled his heavy jade belt before collapsing on a newly appointed silk divan.

Since his encounter with the clumsy servant at dinner, he ached to remove the rolled parchment carefully concealed within the left folds of his sleeve. But he was wise and had preferred to wait until he was alone. He knew it was from Min Li.

Since returning from his fifth expedition, he had heard unpleasant rumors. Some eunuch officials claimed that according to medical records, it was believed that Min Li could not sire children. Others went as far as supposing that unknown to Zhu Di, Min Li was having an affair with one of the Korean eunuchs. Decidedly, all yapping tongues had fertile imaginations, sighed Zheng He. Despite knowing this, he felt a tinge of jealousy.

But most alarming was a rumor that had leaked among high-ranking eunuchs, a rumor that Zhu Di himself had secretly appointed Min Li as an agent for the Eastern Depot.

Aside from intense surveillance of the emperor's subjects, the Eastern Depot had of late been associated with torture and brutal methods for extracting confessions from suspects. They arrested countless innocents, including some of Zheng He's old time friends. This, Zheng He knew from his high-ranking position, though it was never spoken. He understood Zhu Di's political fears but he did not approve of his methods.

When the rumors had reached him upon his arrival two years ago, he had denied it. It was terribly discomforting to contemplate given what had happened between him and Min Li before his fifth expedition. If the rumors were true, exactly how long had she spied for Zhu Di? These were the very thoughts that had driven him away from her.

He heard the distinct sound of a bronze bell announcing the second *geng*. Night advanced, and still, he had not even glanced at the clandestine missive. He distracted himself with forced purpose, gazing at diplomatic documents across the lacquered rosewood table. His lazy fingers traced the elegant frame of an old compass.

At last, overwhelmed by a familiar longing ache in his chest, he drew out the tiny parchment that the shrewd, yet apparently clumsy servant had slid in his right sleeve earlier in the night.

It was from the palace. It bore the imperial seal like all paper manufactured in the imperial city. Zheng He was amused that Min Li had dared use red ink. Aside from the emperor, the use of red ink was forbidden.

After ascertaining that all his eunuch attendants had left, Zheng He read.

"In memory of old times, please allow me to farewell the Grand Admiral. I shall be waiting, just after the third geng. To my chamber, will you come?"

This was followed by instructions explaining how to reach Min Li's private chamber.

Zheng He crushed the parchment in his fist as though it had suddenly become detestable. If the emperor learned of this, he would be finished. He dipped the tiny scroll in the oil lamp and watched its ink dissolve until the ominous parchment shriveled to ashes.

He remembered the day she had gazed at him from the garden, enamored of the *qilin*. But she cared not a grain of pepper for the *qilin*. No. She had looked at him, with her wicked eyes not even attempting to hide her seductive game. He had known this all along. But he had played. It was easy to play with drink. Because he was weak and he wanted her. And that had been the beginning of everything. And when it was over, he went away.

The thought of that night and its secrets made him blush furiously. No good could come from visiting that woman. And now, with those rumors that she was the emperor's spy, even less good could come of it.

In an attempt to keep his mind off Min Li, Zheng He summoned a private guard and entrusted him with sealed scroll containers. They were navigation maps that he had verified and collected from his desk. He had taken care to order three new starmaps. Starmaps were astronomical charts several yards long, crucial for identifying sighted stars. Without the starmaps, the fleet navigators had no way of gauging their latitudinal position from the home port. Any charting was out of the question.

"Organize an armed escort and have these shipped to the fleet in Tanggu, immediately."

The guard nodded and disappeared. Despite himself, as soon as he was alone again, Zheng He's mind fleeted back to the secret missive.

What did she want?

She wanted to see him. It was clear. *I should pull back. Forget her while I still can.*

But he could not.

The third *geng* announced midnight. It resonated throughout the imperial city like an omen, or so Zheng He felt as his heart pounded from within his chest. Each time he sought to keep away, he grew pale and shivered.

One word from her, one note, and look at me, he thought. I am swept into the ocean's depths. I am the emperor's servant while another usurps him.

So then, why should I find those allegations so surprising? Perhaps there is some truth in them. Even judging from her effect on me, the woman is as adept as she is cunning.

Min Li could have been working for the Eastern Depot all along. The thought taunted him again. It rose to a pitch, enough to gall him for all the injustices he had since learned.

***

At this very instant, deep into the Inner Palace, Zhu Di waited. Two eunuchs reached the room where, following his security ritual, His Majesty had secretly elected to spend the night. The door was opened and a frightened concubine was pushed in.

Avid for royal gems, Zhou Guiren had eagerly accepted Princess Xia's bribe and agreed to fulfil Li Guifei's duty. But now, as she entered the incense-filled room, trembling despite herself, the realization that Zhu Di would not be fooled weighed heavily on her conscience.

Zhu Di after all, had waited a long time for Min Li.

During the banquet, vexed by his restless concubine, he had half shut his eyes, giddy with wine, savoring the soon to be had sensual pleasures of the night.

Tonight, in his unsurpassed feeling of omnipotence, his smug contentment with all he had achieved before the world, Zhu Di felt an uncontested supremacy. Tonight the warrior in Zhu Di had awakened and he hoped this would stir his stubborn, dormant loins.

As a deluded impotent, he thought himself capable of reaching the summit of ecstasies if only he were given the appropriate stimulation. According to ritual, concubines were to be rolled naked in a feathery garment and carried to his chamber by the attending eunuchs. But was this not depriving him of all sense of intrigue?

If he had long been so astute to observe a hidden strength in Min Li, was it not proof that he sought and preferred this quality in women? And would it not rob him of his pleasure to watch this concubine already stripped of all defenses so that she was no different from the docile others?

He had fondled every part of her body but it was never enough. To date, there had been something in Min Li that he had never once attained. After so many years and hundreds of tries, still, the general had failed. He imagined this unspoilt entity to be an obscure power that Min Li had, one to which he owed his persistent lust and in which he longed to bury himself.

To hell with naked beauties, he thought. This time, he wanted her bedecked in rubies, her long raven hair set high above her alabaster neck. She would enter the chamber, drawing out each step like a dangerous opponent and pout her way in a show of arrogance into his bed. She would mistakenly believe that there would be no more than usual to their encounter.

Had it not always been this way? They would talk. They would exchange secret information and then he may or may not toy with her delicious curves before drifting to sleep.

Ah, but this time it would be different. He could see her fight him and perhaps he would enjoy that too. It would only make the thrill of seeing her fallen, more enticing.

Still, one question had taunted him the entire evening. What was she hiding? The suspicions gave rise to an ill feeling, one that demanded vengeance. Almost at once, he was overcome with the delicious notion of revenge and relished the thought of reviving his jade member. He savored these unpleasant feelings and even urged them on.

Just let the bitch deceive me so that I may punish her.

He surprised himself in the realization that he wanted to be cruel. He wanted to dig his hands round her neck as she cried out from fear. While he insulted her white flesh with his coarse assaults, he would see her moan in the admittance of her own treacherous, depraved nature. He imagined the red welts he would leave on her skin. He would tease this befallen tower of pride and vanity until she panted like a frightened kitten. He would taunt her. He would be the one to slip out the wooden pin from her bun and tear off her silk dress. And on it went...

No sooner had he left the banquet that Zhu Di had sent an urgent order to his trusted apothecary. He had chewed and swallowed copious amounts of pulped ginseng, a plant reputed for its aphrodisiac properties. He cherished the prospect of finally reviving his limp member.

There was a tap. He paused, out of breath. Sweat glistened on his forehead. The moment had come. The door opened and here she was his wretched victim. But she was not Min Li.

With one swift stride, Zhu Di descended from the platform where the canopied bed presided. His face was twisted with rage. He reached the cowering concubine, slapping her hard. Zhou Guiren collapsed in tears, her lips bloodied by the revengeful strike.

***

In the Northern part of the imperial city, the admiral rose. He carefully re-opened his chamber door. He cast a glance outside. The courtyard was empty. He shut his eyes.

Rather than continuing to run away as he had in the last two years, he would endeavor to face her once and for all. Nothing, nothing could be better than to confront those things that most threatened his integrity. If she is the emperor's spy then she is truly a peril to me, thought Zheng He. *But what if she wasn't...*

"Don't you understand," he repeated. "All things must have their place, Min Li. It is the Confucian way. Yours is alongside the emperor. Please understand."

For a moment, he reconsidered but the longing tore at his soul. Feverish with passion, Zheng He stepped out of his chamber and into the night.

Honored reader, it is dark. And there he goes our admiral. Folds of darkness envelop him and shield him from our sight. And the accomplice night keeps still even as the demons wrestle within him.

Where is he going, our proud, self-preserving admiral and what tidings does his visit to Min Li bring?

Alas, honored reader, you must have patience. The night is discreet, and so must I be.

Soon, Zheng He will return, just before sounds the fourth *geng*, before awakes the wrath of our emperor; and soon, very soon, our journey begins.

For now, honored reader, forget.

Book Two: Fire

The Punishment

"Fire overcomes Metal"

Chapter 16
Tanggu Port

March 17, 1421

The Man from the Inn

It was a sweaty two-story winehouse with a winding wooden stair case that creaked under every step. A balustrade overlooked the eating area below, a spread of plain wooden tables and stools. The owner who also cooked and managed a money laundering business on the side rented three of the filthy rooms upstairs to anyone who could afford a cheap concubine. In the fourth room, he kept his family, that is to say, his wife, mother-in-law and his three scrawny children.

The hearty fare restaurant had retained the same old menu for years, not because the regulars lauded it but rather because the owner was a miserly cook. He liked his little underground world as it was, tucked away in one of the seedy alleys of Tanggu port not far from the docks. Its dismembered wooden sign dangled pitifully underneath the dirty eaves of the red-tiled roof. The characters were so soiled by weather and grime that the exact name of the wine-house remained unknown.

Outside, as the heavy downpour subsided, the dawn was breaking. The sun had not yet appeared but alongside the maze of cargo crates, horses and other stock, coolies in their hundreds busied themselves on the port.

Oblivious to the bustle outside, there sat in the winehouse a group of rowdy gamblers, miserly clad in tattered pants and shirts. They had spent a cheery night barely closing an eye. What did they care that hundreds of Ming ships were soon to set sail loaded with treasures from the Middle Kingdom. For these men it had been just another fun night. They cared not a grain of pepper that hundreds of yards away, the world's mightiest fleet prepared to plough the oceans, armed to the teeth.

As daylight broke, the sun's rays filtered through the windows, drawing their game to an end and diffusing the feverish gambling spell that had animated them during the moonlit hours. As always, the break of dawn filled some players with dread while others rejoiced over their gains. Slowly, the players dispersed, leaving their dues and eclipsing themselves from the suspicious inn.

But at the center of the room four men continued to bark round a dirty table, still clutching their cards, determined to persist to dangerous ends. Only two tables were left, reflected Huang-Fu, eyeing his companions. Across him, he watched the eunuch smile like a coon at his hidden hand. Huang-Fu sighed. The eunuch wiped his brow for what seemed the fiftieth time since last night. What a poor devil, thought Huang-Fu. Would he never learn?

"Aaargh!" cried Shin when it was all over. He showed his hand with a grimace.

Laughter rose from the table. With a sweeping arm gesture, Huang-Fu amassed his dirty wins. The defeated Shin collapsed across the table, cupping his head in his trembling hands. The others eyed one another with a knowing look. The senior eunuch sat there for a while, lamenting over his losses. Then, exhaling pitifully, he was on his feet, his knees wobbling from having sat too long on the hard stool.

"Why the sour face? Another game tomorrow and you'll win it all back," consoled the tall skinny man who straddled a stool across Huang-Fu.

"N..no!" stuttered the ashen-face Shin. "I must return to Beijing tomorrow. I should not be here," he mumbled, barely making eye contact as though fearing he might succumb once more to his vice.

With a bitter pout, he adjusted the perfume satchel attached to his waist. It seemed that losing had only increased the shame he felt for having accidentally wet himself overnight. He then shuffled to the door with a beaten expression in his sorry eyes. He had not worn his uniform but most of the inn regulars knew well where he worked.

"What does he do?" whispered one of Huang-Fu friends as the man left the winehouse.

"A high-ranking eunuch, I'm told. He's always losing money," chuckled Huang-Fu. He assembled the cards and sorted them for the next night. "But that doesn't stop him. You watch, Ping, he'll be back next month. Sorry ass."

"He'd squander all the jewels in the palace if he could come back for one more game!"

"Did you see his face at the end of that fourth round?" laughed Chou. "I thought he'd figured everything out!"

"Bunch of cheats," jeered Huang-Fu very aware that the eunuch stood no chance. Then he laughed and spit his amusement on the soiled floor.

"Steal from the rich and give to the poor. I'm doing a good thing," chirped his lanky friend, eagerly licking a drop of spilt wine off the corner of the filthy table.

"But you're cheating, Chou. Cheating the eunuch dry, that's what you're doing. You bald ass!" scorned Huang-Fu, pushing his precious cards in his torn pocket.

"Prove it!" the mightily drunk Chou laughed. Then he happily spat on the ground.

Huang-Fu shook his head still laughing. He stretched up from the stool where he'd crouched for hours, his legs spread, kneeling forward on the table to scrutinize the players. His muscles felt stiff from the prolonged concentration effort.

"Alright I'm done for the night," he announced. "It's almost time for breakfast. Clear the tables. Who wants eggs?"

"Oh come now, just one more game. Don't be like that."

"I said put away your cards and clear the tables. My cunning master won't be long coming back and the officers are prowling all over the port looking for a place to eat. I want no trouble with anyone."

"You're no fun!"

"Just one more game, don't be a chicken," cried Ping.

Huang-Fu eyed both men. He was tired and had little patience. Moving towards them, he suddenly swept his toned arm across the table sending the *mahjong* pieces flying across the floor and leaving the three men cursing.

"Hey!"

"Now pick that up and get out," warned Huang-Fu. "My boss is coming now. Clear those tables for your own good."

But just as he pronounced these words, two government eunuchs and four naval officers entered the inn, escorting the said boss inside. Huang-Fu nudged his friends who began to frantically pick up the suit pieces lying on the floor. But the officers had already been forewarned.

"It's them two!"

The fat inn owner signaled towards the crouched gamblers, ignoring Huang-Fu.

"Well, well, well," began one of the civil officers.

Huang-Fu's jaw dropped just as two soldiers advanced towards his friends. They were young and eager to use their authority to give themselves importance.

"You filthy gambler," spit one of them, grabbing Ping by the collar.

It was out of proportion and Huang-Fu knew it. He'd seen it before. Even innocent men could be intimidated and made to feel as if they'd done something wrong.

"Do you know the penalty for gambling!" roared the soldier.

"I wasn't—" protested Ping shriveling in his torn shirt.

"Don't believe them. They come here almost every night, I've seen them," assured the innkeeper while Huang-Fu gasped. "These low-lifers are turning my respectable restaurant into a den for gamblers."

"Rest assured, we shall sort out these vermin," declared the most senior officer as he grabbed Chou by the collar.

"Where are your arrest warrants, Mr. Eunuch?" protested Chou, mock-punching the air.

"I'll show you my warrant, it's on the boat, now move it," said the accompanying naval officer, drawing out his sword.

But Chou wriggled out of the eunuch's grip and leapt across the table like a demon.

Taking advantage of the flurry, Ping sent a sharp kick into the soldier's shin and sprung up on Chou's tail using the table as shield.

"Arrest them!" yelled the red-faced, civil officer as he raced to catch Chou. The four soldiers advanced, one of them still limping from the blow Ping had given him. Huang-Fu rolled on the floor and leapt before his friends to protect them, landing on his heels with an unconvincing praying mantis pose. In response, the soldiers drew out their swords in unison.

"Get them now!" continued the irritated government official.

At this, a much disheartened Huang-Fu watched as the officers rounded up his companions and shuffled them towards the door.

"Hey wait!"

"Shut up!" called out the innkeeper as he received his reward and let the coins drop into the folds of his tunic.

"Oh no, you don't!" hissed Huang-Fu under his breath. "Not this time! These are my friends, you son of a bitch!"

"Don't say another word, you fool!" warned the greedy boss, giving Huang-Fu's sleeve a vicious tug.

But Huang-Fu wrenched himself away and called out to the naval officer. "Listen, you. Stop! Don't listen to him, these men are innocent. I'm the only gambler in here..."

Feeling that he was hardly believable he added, "...and my partner's worse. He just left. Just left a moment ago..." Who cares about that damn eunuch, he thought.

At this instant, a bespectacled old man entered the inn. Deep worry lines were etched on his face as he squinted towards the back of the winehouse. Spotting the guest seated at the far corner table, he shuffled past the soldiers, shaking his head in disapproval.

"So there you are! I have been looking all over for you!"

Meanwhile the officers looked to Huang-Fu with amusement.

"Very well," said one. "So you say these men are not gamblers. Be very careful. The penalty for gambling is heavy caning. But only when I am in a good mood. Today though I'm in a dog of a mood and I believe exile on the Ming fleet ought to teach you just the lesson you need. So then, what shall it be? I can lock these three men up or I can lock you up. You choose."

"Well, I—"

"Hurry up now. We haven't got all day. So you tell me, how far does that friendship of yours extend?"

The officer gave a wicked grin. Huang-Fu suddenly regretted his impulsive show of loyalty. He looked around for witnesses. No one. Well except for the tall, silent man who sat in the far corner by the window and who'd remained aloof all night. Was he even drinking? He'd entered the place well after midnight and just sat there for the entire morning. He'd not said a word after eating his oxtail soup.

He'd but remained there like an old hermit not even stirring as they cheered on and whiled the hours with furious licentious gaming. Huang-Fu could hear the old man as this one tapped the hermit's shoulder.

"Is that where you have spent the night? And then you will complain to me about your poor kidney *qi*. What is this?"

The old man eyed the hermit's goblet, sniffing with disgust. Still the hermit kept to himself. Huang-Fu noticed that he looked sickly and cared little for his surroundings. They could have laid down tavern maids on the table and caroused all night and the man might not have noticed. Until now, Huang-Fu had almost forgotten about him.

"So then, you will admit you are a wretched gambler and that your friends are innocent?" bellowed the officer, startling Huang-Fu.

The innkeeper mouthed silencing words in Huang-Fu's direction. The young man took fright. "I...ok, no... I did not gamble." He glanced apologetically in his friends' direction. His boss was a greedy rat and he should never have trusted him.

The innkeeper melted into a honeyed smile. He proceeded to usher the officers out, eager to protect his reluctant accomplice. Business was good and he did not want any more trouble than merely using his restaurant as a trap house.

"Wait..." It was Huang-Fu having second thoughts.

"What now? Changing your mind again?" mocked the officer.

Damn, thought Huang-Fu, glaring at the newly stern-faced innkeeper. But his boss played no part in his change of heart. There was no way he'd get on that boat. He liked it too much on land. So he rubbed his neck with a sheepish expression and replied with flippant good cheer, "Nah, I'm far from a gambler."

And Huang-Fu would have remained happily on land had the tall man in the back corner not suddenly raised his face and called out in a strong voice. "Are you sure about that? You see, I've been here for a good number of hours to know what you did all night."

Huang-Fu stared back, speechless. The old spectacled man stepped aside as the hermit stood. Seeing this tall man approach, the lead officer scoffed with self-importance.

"And who might you be?" he asked.

"I have seen enough of these men to properly advise you, Officer," replied the hermit.

"Shut up!" interrupted the officer.

A soldier sprang forth, sword in hand, eager to bully the hermit back into his corner. At this, the old man gasped behind his spectacles and called out, "You fool! Do you know who you are speaking to?"

"Hush! Leave this to me, Old Yu," said the tall man, silencing his friend with one hand. It seemed, then, that a ray of light filled the tavern because the officers gasped. The brazen soldier nearly dropped his sword then recovered, only to bow profusely before the hermit.

"Let one of these men go," ordered the tall man.

Huang-Fu stared, incredulous. The officers released Chou without hesitation. Then, mouth agape, they stared at the stranger as if somehow awaiting his next order.

"Excellent. This young man will take his place," continued the hermit.

Huang-Fu shot him a vengeful look. What was he? A rich merchant? A scholar? A darn monk? Who the hell was he? Was he paying the officers? He looked at his master but this one shrugged his shoulders.

"Who asked you?" he scorned at last, aware that the man had influence but still determined to defy authority with his last breath. He had little to lose.

"Watch your mouth!" cried out a soldier, menacing Huang-Fu with his blade.

The hermit was leaving, flanked by Old Yu but he paused halfway through the door. Then he turned, walked back towards Huang-Fu with a resolute gaze and with alarming gentleness, he whispered so that the others did not hear.

"I admire what you were going to do."

He was indeed tall...rather handsome with a dignified gait. His words, even as he whispered, resonated pleasantly. Yet the man's charisma only irritated Huang-Fu.

"Yeah, well that's great, that's just great!"

"I've watched you try to help your friends. That was a brave thing to do. But...you doubted. Why did you doubt?"

"Why? To hell with you! I'm happy here and I won't get on that boat even if they drag me out in a cangue!"

The man smiled. Yet Huang-Fu noticed that it was a painful smile and that the man's eyes were bloodshot. Hermit clearly wasn't used to staying up all night. Either that or something else. Maybe the man was ill. Ill or not, right now he was staring at him with a grave expression. Then he gestured to the officers. "And you might want to search that young man's pockets. You may find a colorful set of Ma Diao Pai cards."

"Damn you!" yelled Huang-Fu with clenched fists.

"It's not so bad on the boat," said the man. "But you know what is worse? Living in fear. Living in fear is terrible."

Huang-Fu was ready to pull his hair out.

"What? Hey, who are you? I don't even know you! Ok, ok, so between you and me, you saw what happened tonight. So what if I was brave? I've had a sudden change of mind! I'm staying. They can go and sail halfway to the end of the world, I don't care. I'm not going!"

The man closed his eyes as if absorbing the incoherent outburst and letting it slide. Then he opened them and observed Huang-Fu carefully as though pondering over his character.

"You have no choice," he finally replied.

"Says who?"

"I do. I will tell the officers to take you away and you will get on the fleet," replied the man with a firmness that shook Huang-Fu.

"So that's what you've been doing all night then? Spying on me? That's great. Fantastic."

"I was not spying on you," replied the stranger in his unflinching manner.

"You didn't even drink! Sat there for the entire night and you did not drink!"

"I had no heart for drink," replied the stranger. "Besides, many Huis do not drink. And as for you, you should honor the Confucian precept, *a gentleman does not gamble.*"

Huang-Fu rolled his eyes to the ceiling. "A sermonizing Hui, that's all I need! Cursed Heavens!"

"Enough. I will leave you now. I have a long day ahead of me. You, young man, you've a chance to change your life. I am giving you that chance. Just then, you revealed courage and a great deal of loyalty. I tend to think you are capable of much more. So if I ask you to get on that ship, and believe me you shall get on that ship, I am doing you a greater service than you know."

Huang-Fu stared, dumbfounded.

"You are doing me a service?" he asked, incredulous.

"Hold fast to that chance, young man. Do not be a fool."

"Oh! Because you're not a fool?" cried a disbelieving Huang-Fu glaring at the stranger with reproach.

Four feet away, the officers' alarmed expression warned him that the man ought not to be addressed this way. But Huang-Fu did not care. He was fuming.

The tall man did not reply at first and Huang-Fu noticed that his eyes had watered. They couldn't be tears, he promptly dismissed. Yet there, he saw it again, right at the corner, there was...

"Yes. Yes, you could say that I am one," replied the stranger at last.

Had the situation been entirely different, Huang-Fu would have warmed to the stranger but his indignation had risen to rage. On what should have been a routine morning that saw him prowling the streets of Tanggu for sorry debtors, his life was being decided for him and that was the last thing he wanted.

***

The Emperor in Disguise

After his encounter with the boy from the inn, Zheng He was eager to rejoin the fleet. He had not slept for days since his arrival in Tanggu.

The Ming officers scoured the port. They sifted through the scum of narrow alleys and seedy dens for additional head counts. The scorn of society in these parts were the gamblers and the thieves.

Gambling was forbidden. The Ming exercised strict control over any gathering where gamers could gamble large stakes. But the pleasure was too well ingrained in the people and they continued to indulge these illicit pastimes. If found, these gamblers often provided the extra crew members that were required to keep the daily fleet operations running smoothly.

For their petty crimes, these men were lent to the fleet as kitchen hands, animal attendants and cleaners. They would exist as the guts of the ship. They would be seen neither on the upper decks, nor in the richly decorated cabins nor the gentle lanes of the treasure ship.

Theirs was a pitiful lot and they had little choice but to do what no one else would. They could choose to go to exile or provide their services to the Ming fleet. If their conduct improved, there was chance of a better life and maybe a promotion at sea. For the most part though, they toiled under the heat in the salt and in the wretched humidity, all too often dying at sea. Petty thieves, gamblers, scum; they were seen as easily replaceable.

But the boy had been different. Zheng He saw a chance to have him promoted eventually. After years at sea, the admiral had learned to discern those who could be trusted and those who would fail to mend their ways and improve themselves. He recognized that life dealt a poor hand to many people in the Middle Kingdom and that on the fleet these men could amount to better things. Perhaps they could even ascend to a proper life and improve their status in society. This idea ran against Confucian tenets but Zheng He felt that if he could help others, it was worth defying the order of things.

Yet this morning, the admiral was tormented. As he approached the treasure ship, he promised himself not to brood over his last night in the Imperial Palace, to put it behind him once and for all, and to never look back. But there was the emperor... The emperor suspected.

Since arriving in Tanggu, the admiral had heard a rumor. It was believed that the emperor had suddenly left for a short visit to Tanggu. He had left Beijing in secret and reached the port two days ago. And it was today, shortly after Zheng He left the inn and performed his last prayers on land, that an officer brought sobering news. The emperor's whereabouts were confirmed.

Zheng He frowned. If Zhu Di was in the port, he could be anywhere.

The admiral recalled Jianwen's short time on the dragon throne when the Prince of Yan had taken to the streets dressed like a vagrant. Zhu Di was unrecognizable as he wandered the streets of Beijing, even sleeping in the gutters. For months, none saw through his disguise. How he'd liked that. He had ingested too much of Sun

Tzu's Art of War and embraced this game of seeming weak to hide strength. How far could he go?

Zheng He felt uneasy. How often did Zhu Di resort to subterfuge, even today? Just like Hongwu, his father. They were the same. Zheng He had once reflected that both emperor Hongwu and now, Zhu Di, knew well how to make a dramatic performance, one posing as a monk before suddenly pouncing to take on the Mongols, the other one feigning madness to avoid arousing his nephew's suspicions. And it went on. If rumors were true, Zhu Di liked nothing better than to visit the ports, the markets and the provincial counties, unseen and unrecognized. He was dangerous that way.

Trying his best to remain stoic, the admiral surveyed the activity on the port. They were loading cargo, water, grain and other produce onto the fleet. It would take a further two days before the ambassadors arrived.

He was so lost in his thoughts that he did not see a figure approach.

It was Zhu Di. The emperor was disguised in a ragged robe. He had improvised by tying a coarse sash around his well-fed waist and his feet went bare in monk sandals. Zheng He could just make out the heavily armed imperial escort eyeing them several paces behind. The Son of Heaven was not taking any chances.

Zheng He winced.

"Behold, the glory of Ming!" mused Zhu Di. He was sporting an overly passionate smile on his tired face. He seemed jubilant with his surprise visit.

Zheng He placed his hands behind his back as though to hide something, a gesture that Zhu Di took care to notice. They both faced the sea but Zhu Di peered at him from the corner of one eye.

"Welcome, Your Highness. Yes, it is indeed beautiful—"

"Aaah...we were not speaking of the fleet, San Bao. But of you! We know well that this enterprise is nothing without our trusted Grand Admiral." Again he smiled.

Zheng He nodded, a little wary. Was Zhu Di feigning good humor? He was conscious of the emperor's insistent gaze in his direction. A full head shorter than him, Zhu Di remained one of the few men with the power to make him feel small.

It was fortunate that no servant was permitted to look at the emperor in the eye. Etiquette could prove useful. But the admiral knew he had to work on his voice. Much emotion could be discerned through voice and Zhu Di was listening carefully. So the admiral remained silent, observing the port for a while longer as though he were quietly absorbing the emperor's praise with profound humility.

Ahead, on one of the smaller ships, new reluctant recruits lined up behind a counter manned by two soldiers. The soldiers filled in documents. In the far left, Zheng He also distinguished a short, hooded woman burdened by three large boxes who disembarked from an unstable Fujian barge. Five soldiers approached her speaking with great verve.

Zheng He found himself distracted from his predicament as he observed the woman. The soldiers roared with good cheer and seemed to be arguing about who would escort her to the treasure ship. Zheng He allowed himself an internal smile but it soon faded remembering his emperor's presence.

The general's voice rose.

"What are you thinking about, San Bao?"

"I wondered, Your Majesty..." From afar, he observed the vivacious young man from the inn into whose hands a bundle of clothes were shoved. The boy made a sour face before joining other recruits for a tour of the ships. "I wondered how many ships would return from this journey. In the past, we have lost many ships and countless men have died. I surrender to Allah and pray daily to the Heavenly Mazu but when ill happenings strike, I always feel at fault."

Zhu Di melted into an affected smile.

"Now, now! You know as much as we do that such a sacrifice is indispensable to our imperial mission. Think of the lands you will encounter. Think of the people whose path yours will cross. Go to the ends of the world, San Bao! Tell them that Ming is great!"

He was smiling as he casually stroked his long beard. Zheng He watched the coarse fingers penetrate into the wild pointed tuff. Even in his disguise, the emperor could not conceal this telling gesture, one that belied a man deeply engrossed in his calculations.

"We really ought to find you a concubine or two for those long journeys," said Zhu Di, rising from his contemplation. "Perhaps a refined, well-spoken lady, someone who could keep the admiral company during the long months..."

He emitted a diabolic laugh as though delighted with his own suggestion. Zheng He's expression darkened. But Zhu Di was only just beginning. He was suddenly light-hearted, enthralled with his idea and seemingly amazed that he had not thought of it before.

"Come now, San Bao, you are no doubt well aware that some of the senior eunuch officers have taken to bringing their own concubines aboard? Highly trained ladies with all round talents are well sought by your colleague admirals. We have heard the journeys are much shorter that way."

Zheng He crisped his jaw and replied in a tone he wanted brief.

"Your Majesty knows that his humble servant cares neither for the fickleness of women nor for idle pleasures."

"Yes. Yes. Quite so," replied Zhu Di.

The emperor began to remove imaginary specks of fluff from his green garb. It seemed he had completely forgotten that he was not dressed in fine imperial attire and that today he was passing for a traveling monk on the port.

"We have often wondered, Zheng He, ever since you were a scrawny, teary captive...oh, a very long time now... we've often wondered..."

The emperor disposed of the last speck of fluff. "*What is it* that Zheng He seeks in a woman?"

Zheng He was trembling now.

"Your Majesty places much thought into matters of no consequence."

"Is that so? We are hardly naive, Admiral. Men like you...men in your position still present much intrigue to women of the palace. Why, only a year ago, if you remember, we had to execute several concubines for having had illicit affairs with our so called much trusted eunuchs. It is fortunate that there still remains a handful of loyal advisers who respect our Royal Chamber..."

Zhu Di watched Zheng He. The admiral's jaws tensed up.

"...But aside from the Royal Chamber, the ports of Guangdong abound with beautiful courtesans and it is a well-known fact, San Bao, that the crewmen are quite fond of them..."

Zhu Di frowned. "You see, San Bao, in all these years after our abject nephew was deposed...and after your skirmishes with a few pirates, we've not seen you take arms. You know that a man who spends years away from battle becomes restless. His *yang* accrues. Soldiers away from the field always seek women if only to keep active... We assume, then, that even though you are *maimed*," he cruelly stressed, "you have had occasions to...to..."

He looked towards Zheng He's silent, inscrutable face.

"Tell me, San Bao, my trusted San Bao, why have we never known you to pine for a woman? Or could it be... Have we been so blind? After all, even Li Guifei is not, how shall we say, unattractive. Or perhaps..."

The blood had drained from Zheng He's face.

The emperor paused. "I wonder... Are we the fool?"

Zheng He bowed.

"Your Majesty, *lusting after women ruins a man*," he quoted, still trembling. "My only wish is to serve my emperor. The fleet is my company... I care for nothing else."

At this instant, three battalion commanders approached flanked by the fleet navigators. The emperor quietly replaced the hood on his head. Zheng He began delegating orders.

"You, you will organize for the ambassadors to be escorted upon arrival. They are to embark the treasure ships and be led to their quarters. Ensure they lack of nothing."

"And you," he added, turning to another commander, "you are to convene the admirals to my cabin for tomorrow's meeting. Bring the chart copies and distribute the starmaps."

He turned sharply to the navigators.

"You have the instructions for synchronizing our ships. Familiarize the men with our procedures. I will send a courier two hours before our departure."

The admiral's voice continued to disseminate orders, strong, unperturbed and visibly in control. The Ming expedition was set in motion. Zheng He was now in command and all the emperor could do was return to his palace. When the officers had left, Zheng He turned towards Zhu Di who had remained a hooded figure three paces away.

"It is time, Your Majesty. Foreign vassals await the honor of your fleet's visit."

Zhu Di face convulsed with a frightening violence. The man he most wanted to question was also the man to whom he had entrusted the sixth Ming expedition. The Ming fleet could not wait.

Simmering with rage, the emperor signaled to a courtier several feet away. The courtier, in turn, ushered in a group of sedan chair carriers.

Zheng He watched the emperor's sedan fade towards a remote barge. He knew he would have to face the emperor on his return to Beijing. For now, there was nothing to be done but to continue on his course.

A sudden wooden clamor interrupted his thoughts.

"Forgive me, Admiral!"

In his anguish to leave the port, he had collided with the short woman from the quay. Losing her balance, she had fallen to her knees. Her three cases landed with a bang, startling them both.

The boxes split open. Bobbins of silk thread, more silk fabrics, and strange tools were hurled forth onto the wet platform. A seamstress...

The unfurled silk grew dark, soaked by the previous night's downpour. The short, well-formed woman recognized his uniform and kowtowed several times.

Zheng He was too shaken by the emperor's visit to give her further notice. He hastened to the treasure ship, eager to put a divide between the quay together with all that had transpired there and his own naval realm.

Behind him, the apologetic seamstress remained crouched on her knees. She gathered her strewn fabrics and shoved them into her work boxes.

And then, when she was certain that the giant man in the uniform was far enough and could no longer see her, she paused. She watched him board a shuttle and head towards the flagship. Forgetting about her cases, she fixed her determined gaze on this one man.

Hers was a curious expression, one that was at once weary and dreamy. But none of the couriers and crewmen who passed by gave the tiny woman any notice.

For how long did she remain on her knees, staring at the ship that she would board in a few days, she did not know. But the very thought of what she sought to do and the enormous effort it would take, for days, months, perhaps a year...all this, warned her that she would need to summon the last of her strengths.

***

The Gambler

When Huang-Fu emerged from the winehouse, his head giddy from lack of sleep, he had barely three copper coins in his pocket and a packet of cards. And now he had another object in his possession. It was the horrible knee-length white robe that the naval officers had given him. They had ordered him to follow them to the docks where he was to register and embark on one of the peripheral vessels escorting the treasure ship.

He was all too familiar with the bustling port, having observed the harbor many times. Life at sea frightened him, partly because he could not swim. He liked to know his foot was on solid earth.

His mother, a sleazy, toothless prostitute had abandoned him in the port of Guangdong as soon as he could walk. Growing up by the seaside, he had become used to the imperial fleets as they made their way down the Yellow Sea and into the south west, eagerly recruiting cheap concubines for the long journey.

Journey to hell, he brooded, spitting on the quay.

As a teen he had planned to escape Guangdong's seedy ports and join the army. He longed to enlist in the cavalry, to ride a fierce Mongol horse and learn archery. He wanted to fight alongside the deserting Mongol eunuchs at the North-eastern border and serve his emperor.

A fine dream that was. But these dreams only come true for other people, not for me, he thought.

Because at sixteen when he had traveled to Nanjing in an attempt to enroll, he had soon found out that military conscription was reserved for certain families only. Not only that but with his shady background, the most he could aspire to, if he was lucky was to become a foot soldier. That was the end of it.

No one had ever told him. Not that he had asked. He had assumed that if he showed interest and bravery during training then that ought to be enough. But the civil military officer had clearly explained as though it were the most natural thing in the world, that if a man was not born in the right family, he could not hope to enlist in the cavalry, at least, not in a legitimate way.

Those were the *weisuo* military rules. They had been like this since Hongwu and therefore, had declared the officer, Huang-Fu should know better than to challenge them. Since Huang-Fu did not know the identity of his father, he had no legitimate name. Nameless, he fitted under no registry and according to Ming military rules he could not hope to ever join the cavalry unless his father before him and his grandfather before that had both been in the cavalry.

It wasn't fair. The thought of being a foot soldier, of spending his days making oat bread and cultivating land along the Northern Wall did not appeal to him.

If I had wanted to be a farmer, I wouldn't try to enlist in the first place, he had thought, indignant at the prospect of tilling land. And I want much more than to be a mere foot soldier. Who wants to patrol the Northern Wall and light beacon fires once a month? Not me.

So that had settled it. He had not joined. This was why Huang-Fu had remained a street thug. He had traveled north, visiting the eastern cities of Fuzhou, Nanjing and Beijing before settling in Tanggu. He had taken a role in one of the local gangs attached to the illegal gambling houses. He would spend his nights networking and chasing up debtors.

Familiar with every joint in the port and nimble on his feet, he was clever at his job. There was not a man he could not find, not a crook he could not hunt down. He'd built a respectable reputation in the port and had a solid relationship with his stingy master who was the scum of this earth, in every possible way, a cunning swine at that.

And now this had happened to him. It was sickening.

Huang-Fu sighted the docks and tried to suppress the seaside nausea mounting in his chest. The smell of salt reminded him of Guangdong, back in his old hole.

So this is it, he thought, I'm going to die at sea. He stared at the ships.

The silhouette of hundreds of vessels extended to the horizon. The forest of masts rose against a fiery orange sky but he remained unimpressed. He'd seen them countless times before. They haunted him as a child. Somehow he associated the masts with the pangs of hunger he'd felt then.

And then Huang-Fu's heart leapt in his chest. It couldn't be! Huang-Fu looked closer. It was unmistakable. The tall Hui was now in a white uniform. He was kneeling on a private platform. He appeared to face the West, lost in prayer. Huang-Fu watched the hermit quietly press his face to the ground and then raise himself again. His white silk robe flapped gently in the cold wind.

Huang-Fu fumed. If he didn't have to board this damn fleet, he would have liked an encounter with the Hui. This time, though, he would teach him to mind his own business.

Chapter 17
The Ming Fleet

The Grand Eunuchs had arrived, proud in their admiral uniforms. There were five to accompany Zheng He on this voyage. Each was to head a treasure ship with Zheng He commanding the flagship.

These great men included the illustrious Hou Xian, Zhou Man, Zhou Wen, Hong Bao and Yang Qing. Aspiring admiral, Yang Bao also arrived flanked by the other assistant admirals.

And then they came, the physicians, the writers, one of which was named Ma Huan, the navigators, the accountants, the boatswains, the civil officers, the concubines, the merchants, the naval officers, the sailors and other petty crewmen. They boarded barges in their hundreds.

Barges and sampans weaved through the labyrinthine fleet and came to rest near the hull of their selected ship. The barge occupants climbed up side ladders all the way to the gangplank and onto the towering decks.

Each vessel was destined for a particular ship according to the rank and profession of its passengers. In smaller barges came the caulkers, sail makers, scaffolders, servants, seamstresses, the carpenters, most of whom had worked on the reconstruction of Beijing's imperial city and who now would find a new purpose. And even if they feared death at sea, they had little choice. Life on the continent meant hunger.

Aside from barges ferrying passengers to and from the ships or between ships, there were also large boats stocked with water and floating gardens of fruits and vegetables. Some stored livestock, including pigs and barking dogs destined to be eaten on board during the long journey.

And then there were the larger barges, decked with red brocade awnings and yellow ribbons. These were manned by two long-robed eunuchs who smoothly glided the foreign ambassadors and their entourage towards Zheng He's treasure ship.

It was in one of these elegant boats that the veiled woman from the banquet was seated, propped up on silk cushions with her head held high under her black muslin veil. She observed the scene in her usual impassive silence. She appeared much out of place in this throbbing landscape.

Across her, Kareem evinced a nervous smile. He adjusted his kaftan and wiped the sweat off his brow. She did not share his discomfort. If she remained silent, it was not because she was overwhelmed or made frigid by all the noise. If she sat still, it was not because she feared the barge's vigorous side to side motion.

No. She remained silent because she was quietly sad to leave the Middle Kingdom and also because she loved and lived for this journey. As the barge drew closer to the large treasure ship, she relished the days to come.

She would absorb the smells, the sights; she would hear the gong as it announced each period of the day and prompted the crew to take their shift positions. At every port, she would look out for the beat of resounding drums as they serenaded the fleet's departure. At first, the men struck at long intervals, spaced out by an ominous silence. And then these intervals grew shorter, as departure drew near. The mounting sound of the drums would rise into a furious crescendo as though it announced to the rest of the world that the Ming fleet, the might of the ocean, once again intended to make its way through the Southern seas and beyond the Indian Ocean, dwarfing all vessels in its path.

Her pulse quickened with the anticipation of the upcoming moment when all ships would move out from Tanggu port in an awe inspiring synchronized scale. She felt never more enthralled than in this moment, letting drum rolls resonate through her body, watching the crew members shout orders at one another in many tongues, Hindu, Malayalam, Arabic, Beijing Hua, Nanjing Hua, and others. They came from all parts.

There were no less than a thousand men aboard Zheng He's flagship. The voices of hundreds of sailors rose up in near cacophony as they worked on the rigging deck or hauled cargos of grains, animals and luggage into compartments. She loved this madness.

The red awning barge came to a halt at the prow of the treasure ship. The veiled woman stepped to the side and sat in a wooden crate reserved for important guests. The crate began to rise. Above, a band of sailors hoisted the crate by means of a pulley system.

As she rose higher and higher onto the luxurious vessel, she looked up, in time to glimpse three carrier pigeons circling above the masts. The finely trained birds seemed oblivious to the buzzing motions below. They ignored the raucous clamor of wooden planks as compartments were sealed. They paid no heed to the signaling bell chimes and loaded drum sound. These flying couriers set out with purpose, sweeping across at swift speed from one treasure ship to another, enabling messages between the navigators.

The foreign woman's head swooned from the hazy glow of the afternoon sun. As she stepped onto the ship, she gripped her escorting eunuch's arm more tightly. Then she turned around to glance back at the sea. She gasped with sheer delight. Below and beyond, it seemed as though a virulent army of black creatures covered the sea in a vain attempt to swallow the giant treasure ship. The horizon's ochre backdrop lent each ship a menacing silhouette. None, though, appeared as solemn as the nine masts towering above her and which now waited patiently, as a warrior waits.

"This way, please."

A sturdy officer who she believed to be one of the lieutenants bowed low before leading the way towards their cabin. She and Kareem moved towards the stern, passing a large group of sailors on the rigging deck. They ascended via two flights of wooden staircases and emerged onto the upper deck.

As she crossed the cabin area, her hand running along the carved railing, she remembered the ship where she had lived while on her first journey to Beijing, a couple of years ago. This vessel was noticeably larger and of course, much cleaner. The fresh smell of pine permeated the corridors and she realized it was newly constructed.

She crossed a long canal flanked by lush plants and arrived to the bridge where the grand admiral's cabin was situated. Below, was a row of cabins designed to house the ambassadors. There were about sixty cabins, each well-tended by two servants. The lieutenant halted outside a door. She peered inside, curious to venture into the dwellings where she would be housed for months.

It was exquisitely furnished with a curtained canopy bed, silk beddings, embroidered cushions, two lacquered tables and an ornate vanity cabinet. A set of tall-back chairs were arranged around the larger square table. The lieutenant placed her luggage at the door and bowed again. At this point a long-robed eunuch officer stepped in. He assessed the room with satisfaction.

"A cabin assistant will be at your disposal for emptying bedpans," he began. "Oh, and a maid will be at hand should you need assistance in bathing, my Lady. Please let me know if you need anything else, my Lady," he said before ushering out the lieutenant and closing the door behind both of them.

Alone with Kareem, she nodded her approval, inspired by the celestial scalloped dish in the center of the table. She approached to grab a peach while still admiring the blue and white porcelain artwork on the dish.

"Almost looks Persian," she quipped.

"It is designed with the Persian customer in mind, My Eye. Their cargo holds are filled with similar porcelain," said Kareem, taking off his slippers and collapsing on the bed with a grateful smile.

"Is the blue, Persian?"

"Imported cobalt, yes. Worth twice as much as gold. They've called it, *hue qing*, Muslim blue. Amusing."

"It is."

She remained standing in the center of the cabin, lost in pleasant thoughts. Her hennaed fingers played with the fruit's velvet skin.

"Well, here we are then. At last," she said, "my only chance to speak with *him*."

Kareem's exhausted voice rose from behind the curtained canopy. "*Insha'Allah*! Then we can go home!"

Chapter 18
The Merchant and his Daughter

The woman who had captivated Min Li on the night of the banquet was the daughter of a reputable Arab merchant. She came from a mixed line of wealthy Persian and Omani traders who had migrated to the East African coast since her father was a child.

While the family's booming Oman-based business continued to grow frankincense in Dhofar and traded in Muscat, Mustafa had built himself a solid enterprise in Zanzibar. He was immensely wealthy and respected. His own brother was a delegate of the Zanzibar envoy.

Mustafa had only one daughter. The girl was still at the unveiled age when her mother, a green-eyed beauty of Persian descent, had died of a mysterious illness during their visit to Kenya. Some said the lady was cursed with the evil eye, perhaps by an old hag in the markets of Malindi. It was while her husband left to inspect ivory goods for a shipment destined to Muscat that his wife had suddenly grown weak and perished.

The merchant was inconsolable. He could have easily remarried and his wealth would have brought him four wives if he so wanted, but the loss of the love of his life marked him forever. To his only daughter, he turned all his hopes and bestowed all his love. In business though, he was ruthless and cunning. But in the privacy of his well-tended home, his daughter became his world.

She grew spoilt but aware of lost love and grief. This combination of limitless bliss combined with familial doom contributed to her solemn, indomitable character. Not having a sister or brother, she invented her own friends and indulged in games of her imagination. Her father took her everywhere with him as he would not lose the one thing that remained to him from his short lived marriage.

And so this little girl traveled on merchant dhows to the ends of the known world, from the Strait of Hormuz, to Melaka and from Cordoba in the former Al-Andalus to the canal city of the prosperous Venetians. In Melaka, she played with the children of distant relatives and even met the local children while her father attended to business. While in Venice, she cruised along the canals and under hundreds of bridges with her cousin, Kareem. Enraptured by the perfumeries and eager to inhale every scent, they spent hours sighing at the precious glass vials with their magic swirls of color. Mustafa noted this. When his daughter was older, he bought her several vials of perfume from one of the most prestigious Venetian perfumers.

From the souks of Yemen and Oman, Mustafa scoured bookstores and loaded his dhows with yet more gifts for his beloved daughter. She loved to read, mostly in her native Persian and had also been trained in Arabic calligraphy from an early age. She recited the Qur'an at seven and found its meaning at nine. From then on, she saw meanings in all things and her thirst for knowledge and books became insatiable. There was little she would refuse to do for her father yet she was herself progressively more demanding in her search for books and travel.

Whenever he visited their ancestors' home in Oman, her father filled crates with jewelry and with other finds from the souks of Muscat. He would amble pleasantly through the market stalls, haggling with shopkeepers. He praised their precious silver jewelry enriched with brass and gold designs, an Omani specialty. Then he would abandon himself to hours of indignant bartering, gesticulating as all respectable customers should. Among the treasures he brought back, there were amulet holders, kohl boxes, incense burners, hair ornaments and all manner of heavy necklaces and dangly bracelets.

One piece treasured most by his daughter was a circular hair ornament with a six-sided star in the center. The lower half of the circle spawned little chains, each holding *hamsas*; the hands of the Prophet Mohammed's daughter, Fatimah. The girl loved this ornament as it was good luck in many parts of the Arabian world where Fatimah was venerated for her strength and healing abilities. Under Fatimah's protection, a home could never succumb to fire.

But for this bright girl, the greatest jewel of all, were the ships from the East. It was during a business trip to Hormuz, then gem of the Arab world that she first encountered the Ming fleet. At the time, she came face to face with the giant eye painted in bold colors on one of the Ming ship's prow. For a moment she remembered the curse on her own mother and felt safe around this protective eye. She also wondered how it was that even the Ming, who came from so far away, also painted large eyes to ward off evil spirits.

The Ming visitors had been eager to trade their porcelains for beautiful Arab jewels. Meanwhile, the rich Arabs were keen to trade for massive amounts of porcelains pieces, favored even by the Sultan of Constantinople. How many porcelain pieces could there be stocked up inside the guts of those ships, she wondered? They were immense.

Accompanied by Kareem who was her male escort at all times and an eager companion for her many escapades, she had skirted one of the treasure ships and brushed past the Grand Admiral himself. They called him San Bao. In Sumatra, Calicut and Melaka, it was all the same. Everyone was in awe of him. The Ilkhans who ruled Hormuz had invited San Bao and his high-ranking crew for a dinner. The people of Hormuz were cultured and generous, their manner, inviting. The admiral could not refuse.

It was 1415. She was nineteen and already heavily veiled. It was during one such opulent dinner that her father met Zheng He. Their exchange was easy because the admiral spoke some Arabic. But mostly they used interpreters. And she noticed that Zheng He spoke Arabic quite well. And then a wonderful thing happened. Her father, along with ambassadors from East Africa, had been invited to sail back to the Middle Kingdom and trade there. She would soon sail on the Ming fleet. It was a dream come true.

Soon, her hennaed palms were caressing the engraved ship railing; she admired their upholstered spacious cabin and marveled at the gardens on board. For Kareem and her it was an extension of their courtship. It was a journey into a world that surpassed their expectations. And Admiral Zheng He was ever present, conversing with ambassadors and receiving them at banquets on board.

They remained one year in the Middle Kingdom.

In 1416, she returned from Yingtian on land via an escorted caravan; from Hormuz, they sailed home to Zanzibar. Her mind was pleasantly filled with her encounters with princesses, eunuchs and concubines. She dreamed of the forbidden chambers in the palace of Yingtian. She and her father had been lodged in a huge complex in Chang'an Street with the other foreigners.

Eager to trade, her father had managed to persuade the court of his legitimacy as an ambassador from Zanzibar. As a result, they were treated favorably and given the best meals and lodgments. As for all the foreigners, they were given wooden identity cards whenever they left the complex and they were only permitted to trade at the guest house for several days. But during this time, she had gazed in wonderment at this cosmopolitan city and its bustling foreigner's market.

This, she had realized was indeed the largest and most industrious city in the world. The Middle Kingdom produced goods in unimaginable quantities whether this be, porcelain, silks of all different weaves and tints, quality craftwork or jade figures. One could find almost anything in the streets of Yingtian. At times, they would visit the city, closely escorted and she would breathe smells she had never known before, even in Venice.

She shared her thoughts with Kareem. Where Venice was the place where West and East merged into a dance of seduction, this place was the pure, unfettered East, far removed from illusions. Where Venice dazzled as the major port of the western seas, this city seemed to her to be the center of the whole world. Where Venice was richly enticing, promising sensual pleasures, this place was intoxicating. It swallowed you whole. Where Venice's charms were subtle, this place was vibrant with energy. This is how she saw it.

Ah, how she remembered, then, what she had felt. *Only a young woman and I knew. I knew what I wanted to do most with my life.* She reflected on her home in Zanzibar. Little Pemba island with its daunting, lush forest seemed so fragile in comparison to the Middle Kingdom. Back then she had thought of the tiny island as insignificant at best. But now, after *the incident*, she was not so sure. Now, it resembled a forbidding body of land, a sort of nightmarish monster feeding off the ocean. She never dwelt on that vision for too long but it was there, like a secret memory, buried in the recesses of her mind, as veiled as her face.

Back on Zanzibar, the happiness of many years ago was now long forgotten. Yet, she conceded, there had been happy moments after they had left them all: the Middle Kingdom, Zheng He and his wonderful fleet. But it did not last.

When she first returned to the island with her father, she would sit with him at night and speak of their discoveries in the Middle Kingdom and elsewhere. Or they would quietly face the sacred stone of Mecca, say their prayers and later enjoy the dancing sun, setting across the beach.

He was a well-traveled man with a stern, yet welcoming face. Deep, dry lines were etched either side of his lips but they softened as he spoke. He enjoyed those moments with his daughter, a daughter that he believed was as bright and spirited as if she had been born a man. And she, in turn, took pleasure in his trust and the freedom that his wealth and position afforded her. Conversations were easy because despite their ages, they spoke the same language. And everything she said, Mustafa would easily understand and when she said little, he also understood that she was deep in thought.

But a shadow loomed over the island.

When she was twenty-three years old, Mustafa's daughter suddenly withdrew into herself. Inexplicably, she ceased speaking with him.

He did not understand.

She spent more and more time with her travel companion and cousin, Kareem, whose curious combination of comical antics and intellectual aloofness had always delighted her. Kareem enjoyed life and saw pleasure in every sensual experience, food, marketplace, women and art. But mostly he enjoyed this woman's mind because she was interesting and loved to dissect everything to the point where there was no art left. This fascinated him inasmuch as he felt deep respect for her.

They were to be engaged but she continued delaying their marriage and he indulged her because he was in love.

While still on excellent terms with Kareem, she continued to avoid her father.

But one day, upon learning that her uncle could not attend the upcoming Ming emperor's celebrations for health reasons, she breached her silence. She asked to be sent to the Middle Kingdom in his place.

"And Kareem will be coming with me," she added quite simply.

It took the old man by surprise to hear his daughter's curt voice. Hers may have been a request, but it was pressing and forbade any refusal. There was also, at least, as far as he could detect much nuance and reproach in that voice. It cut through him. He recalled that these were the only words she had ever spoken to him for months. Despite her cold tone, he listened avidly, ready to grant anything.

He regretted that she was so eager to leave. He had planned to take her on a safari to Kenya and rekindle their father daughter relationship. He had pondered for months about her sudden silence and thought perhaps that she had suffered a quarrel with her betrothed. But Kareem, as he had noted with a pang in his chest, was devotedly at her side at all times. And she was now always out with her fiancé. Mustafa had grown jealous a number of times. He envisaged that the wild beauty of Kenya with its endearing lion cubs would remind his daughter of the tragic loss of her mother and perhaps draw her near him again, at least in commiseration if not anything else.

The thought of his daughter traveling again to Nanjing exasperated him. How many years would she be away? And what could she possibly do in Beijing? He had heard of Beijing being redeveloped to supposedly surpass Nanjing but he did not believe it. What if she did not like Beijing? Powerless in the face of this woman who was now a stranger to him, he complied.

With his reputation, he managed to obtain seats on the departing Ming ship. A fortnight later, she sailed with Kareem and the rest of the Zanzibar delegation. This was in 1419.

It had been almost a couple of years now since their arrival in Beijing and her journey to the Middle Kingdom drew to a close. But it had given her much joy. This she kept to herself. In fact, all through their voyage in the Middle Kingdom and except in the privacy of her cabin with Kareem, she rarely spoke unless asking questions.

Even Zheng He had been surprised at how the young woman he had met in Hormuz, one he had joyously noted was imbibed with a rare passion for careless and exuberant discovery, could have become so guarded. They had developed a brand of quiet friendship, if at times a little tense. Often while they were at sea, she watched him. At times she read quietly. Often, she explored the treasure ship and still other times, in several ports, she would vanish, only to reappear again after unexplained absences.

While in Beijing, she had managed to gain entrance into the Inner Palace and was given a clandestine tour of the concubine quarters. There was nothing she would not want to see or touch and if refused, she would insist. With her towering height, her confident demeanor, her hennaed palms and her black veiled form, it could be said that she inspired fear.

Yet while braving cultural etiquette and shamelessly stripping the Purple Palace of its protocol, she remained dignified and detached in her world. Perhaps then, Zheng He was not mistaken when he felt unease around her. Perhaps he sensed that this woman would drill into his very soul.

It should be noted that during the farewell banquet, while Min Li could scarcely detach her eyes from the veiled woman, she would never have imagined that the curiosity had been mutual. Even later, on the way to the port of Tanggu, while the veiled woman sat inside a barge, pulled along the Great Canal by large harnessed horses on the shore, she thought of that night. She relived images in her mind, of the palaces she had seen, the chambers she had passed and the words she had heard spoken during her stay in Beijing.

She remembered furtive glances exchanged during the final banquet, feminine gestures that though concealed, had been deliberate, forced even, much like secret codes between accomplices.

And most of all, she remembered clumsy servants that were not at all clumsy.

All this, she kept to herself. Her name was Shahrzad.

Chapter 19
Min-Li

Huang-Fu was not mistaken. There had been tears in Zheng He's eyes as he'd left the inn. For days, the admiral had tried to forget. He had tried to drown his sad thoughts until these became a flimsy memory, one that all too often, a man burdened with responsibilities can make his duty to forget. But as the ships left the Middle Kingdom, Min Li came back to haunt him. As the majestic bamboo sails were raised, and the vessels pushed forth into the rolling ocean, the memory of that night relived somehow, sinking the admiral's mood.

It found form, this sorrowful vision. It sprang up like a floating mist draping the Yellow Sea. Like an unpleasant dream, serenaded by the voices of the crew, the echoing bells, the drone of the drums, it stung at his ears and burnt his temples.

And as the red bamboo sails stretched taut across their battens, as these leviathan ships demanded their due, bursting forth like gods, leaving behind the port of Tanggu, time, it seemed, stood frozen. Zheng He remembered everything.

***

All was still that night, as he ventured back into the Inner Palace through the Northern palace gate. The guards saluted. Upon sighting the lion on his chest, they did not check his papers.

Just as well, Zheng He thought, because he would not have known what to tell them. Lying was not what he had envisaged.

He advanced towards the western chambers of the palace. On his way to the Imperial Gardens, his quiet footfalls echoed in the empty street. The blue moonlight followed him, cold and moist like a ghostly trail.

As he passed the concubine playground, the grotesque stone structures appeared to come alive, writhing into twisted demonic figures. He felt the energy of those hideous stones. They seemed to warn him. Of what, he wasn't sure. But he knew that there was no turning back. As he approached the Hall of Gathering Excellence, he could hear giggling and muffled conversations. The princesses were passing time, he thought. At least no one would hear him.

He entered through the West alley, a street leading to the concubine pavilions. He continued down that street, all the way to the Hall of Mental Cultivation. Then he cut to the right.

A muffled footstep alerted him. He froze, listening in for the sound and pressing his body against a wall. There was no one. He had not seen a single servant eunuch and this worried him. He expected that one of them, perhaps on a night errand to deliver urgent toiletries for the princesses, would suddenly appear and identify him. But he saw no servants that night. Had they been prompted? It would not surprise him. Min Li, he recalled, was always prepared.

He peered through the main entrance of the concubine building. The double doors should have been locked but they were not. Had Min Li planned this?

He stepped in. Before him was a long narrow corridor, merging effusions of mustiness and confinement. It ran for at least twenty-eight yards ahead with shut doors on either side.

He advanced quietly, passing each closed chamber. He grew conscious of the oppressive feel inside the concubine compound. But he attributed this sensation to a childhood fear of being locked in. And as he ignored this crushing feeling of confinement, he gave himself reasons as to its source. Tonight, he was breaching all the laws he knew and if he felt uneasy, or trapped or slightly nauseous, it was surely because of guilt.

The admiral advanced, conscious of every breath and wary of every sound. To be found here would amount to death. There would be no excuses. He had no business here.

At last, he reached her door. He was trembling. He tapped only once but it opened, almost immediately.

She smiled. He met her eyes. It stripped him of his reserve for what seemed far too long. As he entered, he gave her a brief, inscrutable nod. He saw that she was beaming. It seemed as though a blinding ray of hope shot out of Min Li's chamber and into the dark corridor.

"You have come."

"I have."

"You are very brave," she smiled happily.

"I would say I am very foolish."

She eyed her chamber as though she were looking for an anchor to calm her emotions. Perhaps she was concerned that her surroundings would not please him. She was sensitive to this, as she was of her appearance. While it was soignée she had removed all her imperial jewelry and adorned her hair with flowers. He could smell their sweetness and it made him giddy and afraid. She looked more beautiful than he remembered.

"I wanted to see you because..." Her voice trailed. She fumbled across to the teapot. "Would you like some tea? I will prepare some tea."

"Min Li, I've not much time. Why the invitation?"

Without saying a word, Min Li walked towards him placed her small hands on the *buzi* and traced the lion with her fingers. He felt faint but let her.

"On your arrival...two years ago, why did you push me away when I tried to—"

"You know why."

"I do not."

"You are an imperial concubine. You should know your place."

"This is not your true meaning," she smiled, waving his abrupt tone.

"It is my meaning."

"Ever since that night, I have not ceased thinking about you. I have not."

"Li Guifei, women all over the Middle Kingdom would be grateful for the honor of being in your place."

She shook her head.

"The women you speak of, they are mad. I once felt like them. But I was wrong. I was so wrong."

"You disgrace your emperor. And you offend me."

Her smiled faded at his rebuke.

"I...I do not wish to offend you. I know you have little time... but...oh, let me say what I hoped to say and then you can choose to do or believe whatever you wish. But please, listen.

I think of you when I am with His Highness. I think of you when I awake, when I am close to falling asleep, in my dreams even, I think of you. I do not understand life without you. It is true, I know so little of the Grand Admiral. But I would like to know him. I would like to be his friend and for him to trust me. I would like so much for him to spend time with me the way he did...in the baths."

She paused to gauge his reaction. His jaws had stiffened.

"Min Li, I cannot let you cherish such hopes. What past do you speak of? You were only a child when we spent time together...you yourself said it was part of your education, did you not? What part did I not understand? We both know that you sought to appease your curiosity...and that I was fulfilling my duty."

"Is that what you honestly believe?"

"What?"

"That you were fulfilling your duty?"

"That, and nothing more."

She stared at him. Her lips quivered.

"You lie."

"I never lie."

"Everyone lies. Zheng He, I have learnt enough in my years as a concubine. Serving our emperor all these years, I've learnt enough. Isn't it true? Isn't it true that the only way to survive in this place is self-preservation? Don't look at me like that. Everyone, everyone in this palace, without exception, lies. Everyone!"

"Except me."

"No, Zheng He... Except that you lie to yourself!"

In all response, he paced the room. He felt her watching him. His jaws tightened and his lips twisted into a disdainful grimace... Now he glowered at her.

"Speaking of lies, Min Li..."

She was startled. Perhaps she knew what was coming.

"...are you or are you not entrusted to the Eastern Depot?"

"I...I ignore what you speak of," she said, in a choked whisper. Tears welled up despite her efforts to appear calm.

"Answer me."

"But...is that all you wish to know? Is that it?"

"Answer my question, will you. Is it true then? Is it true that you have worked for the murder and torture of innocents?"

She bit her lips.

"Yes. Yes, Grand Admiral. That is correct." She lifted her chin to face his cold, placating stare. "I did this. I spied for him. We are alike, you and me. We are the eyes and ears of the emperor." A bitter pout had twisted her lips.

Zheng He shook his head in disgust, "Do not dare compare my work to yours! How long have you been in this position?"

"Years! For too long. More than I can remember."

"How long?"

"The year I met him—"

"So young..."

"And it went on, on and on! Year after year! Are you happy now?"

"Even when we were in the baths?"

"That was different."

"And recall that it was your idea, wasn't it? What did you plan on that night? What did you tell the emperor after you had your fun with me? You set a trap for me and I, the foolish one, followed you to my perdition."

"No! It was never like this!"

"Then how? How was it? How long will it be before my skin is sliced from my bones? How long before the Eastern Depot guards raise their swords to arrest me? Do not underestimate him, Min Li!"

She shook her head. "Believe me, I wanted it to end. Just after we were together on that night, I wanted it over with."

"How could you do this? I do not believe a word you are saying."

"Please! I told him nothing. Nothing!"

He looked into her face and sought to divine what motives she had, what deceit could exist. There was a part of him that saw not a trace of treachery. No sign that she had been lying to him. How did he know this? How was it, that part of him believed that there, in her eyes, moist with tears, there was only love? She loved him. It glared at him. How he hated her love. He saw in it, only an impasse.

He felt that he wanted to hate her. Without this hatred, he would be lost. He had to hate her. There was no other way...

"And do you like what you do, Min Li?" he asked.

"I don't know. What sort of a question is that? Do *you* like what you do?"

"It is an honor for me to command the Ming fleet."

It was her turn to reply and she did so half-heartedly.

"It was fun at first. It filled the days. Being a concubine is a tedious affair."

"Fun? You've murdered innocents and you've blood on your hands. You say you did it out of boredom?"

"No. That is not why I did it. You know that. We are the same you and me! We are his slaves."

"I am no slave! And you... How many men have been thrown into prison because of you?"

"Don't say anything...please..."

"Are you even aware of what you have done? Of what dishonor you've wrought upon yourself?"

"There are so many things you don't know about me...you misunderstand me."

"On the contrary, I see you clearly now. You would have stopped at nothing to be favorite concubine. Now you have what you want!"

He moved to the door.

"Zheng He! Please don't go! Look at me, please. I am not who you think I am."

"Even now, you behave like a child. Tonight is just one of those whims. Do you understand the peril into which you placed yourself? What am I saying? The peril that I went through to come to you?"

She was smiling now. A shrill laugh escaped her throat.

"What do you speak of, my love? Peril? Danger? Fear? I am beyond these things now. Zheng He, are these then the only things you feel? What about what you feel for me? Won't you tell me? I have often wondered what it is that you wanted. I yearned to know what you thought of me, before I was made favorite concubine, before your last journey, before... I have always yearned to know what you wanted."

"Does it matter?"

"Yes! Yes it does. Won't you tell me?"

There was a long pause. The impasse weighed on him. He stumbled for a moment.

"Min Li. What you did, all those years and what you are doing now – it is all wrong."

"You know so little about the real me, my love. How I long for what you are, what you have. What I would give to have that one shred of freedom. To sail the seas, meet new stars, journey to foreign lands. Not to have my soul trespassed at whim by the man you call your emperor. No, let me finish. I must say this once and you must hear me. I long to be free to love the only man who has ever inspired my trust, the only man who has only to look at me for my bruised soul to flutter in its cage for want of another life. For every time I think of you, it hurls itself against its cage and wants to die. Every time you leave this palace, it dies a little."

She paced the cramped room, biting her lips. She seemed fearful of what she was about to say. But Zheng He understood that she was trying to desert the palace and come with him.

"Have I said too much?" she asked.

Then without warning, the beautiful Guifei was at his side lovingly pressing her little hands on his arm. It burnt him.

"Zheng He, my love, I could come with you," she whispered, her lips trembling. "Other concubines do... I could disguise myself and...and leave this place. I...I know a eunuch who would help me. It would be easier than you think."

She looked up to him but to her surprise, she saw little but scorn in his eyes. With a slow, deliberate motion, he had drawn away. And now, his head tilted in disbelief, he stepped back to better watch her.

His next words were cold.

"You are foolish. It would never work. Every man and every woman has their place. Yours is here."

"No..."

"...in this palace, with the emperor. It is an honor. Realize what you have. You are truly a fortunate woman. You must understand that the dreams you maintain are—"

She stared at him. She could not believe it.

"Zheng He...why? This is not like you! It is not what I have heard about you. For every religion you show tolerance, for every culture you extend a blessing, for every foolish man you forgive their flaws, for every woman you show respect...but for me, there is nothing, nothing but the basest reproaches. Tell me why!"

"You ask for too much! This expedition is too important for me to put your life and mine at risk. The admirals need me! What would they do if I was suddenly lost to them? What of our emperor's orders? Please...end this! End this foolishness, Min Li! End it at once!"

"Was I foolish to seek love from the Grand Admiral? For if I was, and if I erred in doing so, I deserve to know."

"If you would embrace the truth, then you would know. You would know that whatever you see in me, whatever you believe me to be, I am not. I am not! It is only illusion."

He shook his head as though he did not believe in the illusion himself. Then he moved to the door to take his leave. His hand paused on the door while she sobbed on the carpet.

Perhaps now that he remembered this moment, he could see that a small part of him had wanted to turn back, to kiss those tears and take her in his arms but he knew that it could never be. Instead, he remembered saying the one thing that she did not want to hear. Because it was the only thing he felt himself capable of saying.

"Now, please understand. We could never be."

Then without warning, the door shut behind him and he was gone.

He did not know this, but she waited. Because surely he would turn back... He would return and rescue her as he had when she was a little girl. She stared in disbelief at the door and pressed her two palms against it, pressing against it, pressing and listening for a sound.

Oh, she listened.

And as time passed, and the empty corridor echoed loudly in her temples, it seemed to the Guifei that her limbs were foreign to her and that the blood had drained from her body. Her vacant eyes met the four walls of her chamber and she made not a sound.

For resolve can be silent.

Chapter 20
Favorite Concubine
Beijing, April 1421

Honored reader, night falls, draping us once more in its heavy blanket and thus trapped, in its embrace, we cannot run.

Min Li's scheme to evade her nuptial duties and meet with Admiral Zheng He would bring grave consequences.

If Princess Xia and Min Li saw no sign that the emperor was outraged by the Guifei's absence on the night of the banquet, it was hardly because he did not perceive their stratagems. Zhu Di was, after all, a strategist who had a long experience in the military and his reaction to the deception was therefore calculating and thoughtful.

That Princess Xia would do anything for Min Li, including arranging a replacement concubine to visit him, of that, he was certain. To begin, however, the motivation must have come from Min Li. But why?

He carefully examined all he knew. Had he convened her recently about a task where she could be useful? No.

While Min Li was an asset to the Eastern Depot and he had at times made requests to have her speak to such and such eunuch, or obtain information from such and such official or prince, he had not made such request recently. It followed that her deliberate absence on that night had nothing to do with her assigned duties. No, it must have been a whim, a woman's whim. She had chosen to disobey her own emperor. His jaw crisped savagely as he pondered on that thought.

It was mid-morning as he held court outside one of the three Great Halls. He sat before a pompous array of Hanlin scholars who were all too eager to show him that his soon to depart expedition was a mistake. As always, the devoted Minister Xia led the attacks with his overzealous honesty. Zhu Di showed little interest. He flipped through documents that he scarcely read. Min Li's charade taunted him.

"Your Highness, we must once again urge you to reconsider these military campaign. The treasury is plunging into grave deficit."

The insipid tongues were tireless.

"There is still time to put an end to the expeditions. Here are the reports detailing the resources that could be saved."

"We've come to an agreement about the economic situation, Your Highness."

He saw the reports but barely glanced at the words imprinted on them.

One question continued to taunt him.

What sort of whim could a woman like Min Li have? One would think she had everything. He recounted these things, one by one. There was a certain degree of power acquired through her relationship with her emperor, power conferred to her through the Eastern Depot. Then there were the gifts...the most exquisite silk fineries, the gold, pearls, jade and silver jewelry; the attention and devotion of royal benefactress Princess Xia, albeit, he mused to himself, the nature of which Min Li hardly suspects...

And, he realized, grandly vexed, I genuinely adored her. I had put her on a pedestal ever since that afternoon in Nanjing, in the gardens. What a young peach she was. Just like her mother...

He remembered that afternoon, that scene in the garden where a teenage Min Li conversed with other court ladies. He replayed those old images, examining every detail, as if wanting to remember his first impression, to define every trait that had attached him to her but at the same time revisiting her face, her mannerisms so as to perhaps perceive aspects of her character that he had until now, overlooked and which now found themselves at the core of her recent deceit. Have we been misguided, he asked himself.

While Min Li's refusal to visit him after the banquet could be officially attributed to illness, he remained dubious. He recalled that there had been something particular about her behavior throughout that entire night. Her eyes had been riveted onto the far merchants' table and she had barely eaten.

Min Li normally had a good appetite. She belonged to those ladies who eat without a care about being watched and she had a fondness for sweets. He remembered how they had once spent the warm summer nights pulling off sweets and chilled fruits from the baskets that the eunuchs suspended on the ceilings. She made a sport out of eating. But that was when her mind was not distracted by other things. And so it was clear what had happened, that night.

She had been distracted.

And Zhu Di, following his visit to the port of Tanggu, suspected what had distracted Min Li. He had, over the years, assembled many pieces and they fitted well.

Soon after becoming Guifei, he remembered that Min Li had spent a number of evenings with the admiral. It had been at her request and it was also a test on his part to see how well she would serve the Eastern Depot. And now, he remembered how later, Zheng He had avoided Min Li. It was two years ago, following the fleet's arrival but the emperor had noticed. Zheng He seemed aloof. But not Min Li.

Zhu Di had caught her several times, watching the admiral. He had attributed her casual obsession to mere curiosity, the curiosity that one feels after being dejected by someone that we mistakenly thought that we could entrap or seduce.

Min Li was naturally seductive. She enjoyed cajoling people. It was her way of being; an extension of her chameleon personality. To be ignored by the Grand Admiral was possibly a vexation for this bewitching concubine. Perhaps she did not understand that the admiral cared little for women, the emperor had thought, that is, until now. Yet at the port, the admiral had denied everything.

He would find another way to weed out the traitors.

"Tell us," he asked Zhao Guiren, one of the fifth ranking concubines, "did Li Guifei receive a visitor on the night of the banquet?"

"Could it be that Your Highness has a rival?" teased the concubine, giggling as he stroked a red feather down her spine and deposited a wet kiss on her fine rump.

Then later, when they were both exhausted, she had replied. "Min Li slept alone on that night. She refused any of the eunuchs' assistance. I do not recall a visitor entering."

But before Zhao Guiren left at dawn, she advised the emperor that Xue Guifei might have more insight given her room was adjacent to Min Li's. The emperor smiled.

So on this sunny day he had summoned Xue Guifei during the gift ceremony to supposedly impart her with a token of his affection. Outside the gift storeroom, the eunuchs presented their emperor with a pair of gray-haired kittens and he offered the animals to the haughty Xue Guifei who was very fond of cats since they, like her, were sensual and playful and knew how to scratch when provoked.

"Be sure that they do not pester Min Li," warned the emperor. "She is often not herself around cats. They make her ill," he confided.

Seeing that the concubine did not respond, he ventured into more urgent matters, "How is Li Guifei since her illness by the way?" He said this while withholding one of the kittens which he stroked gently with his free hand. But while he did so, he also forced a glance into Xue Guifei's eyes as though to imply that they both knew Min Li had not been ill.

Xue drew away from the royal gaze. She hesitated. "Oh yes...yes, she is...much better, Your Highness." She gave a weak smile.

The emperor leaned towards her and placed the cat in her arms. "We have heard it is the company she keeps that has a healing effect on her."

"The company... I... Oh, thank you, these are just so lovely. I am honored."

"It is our pleasure. You know you can always send the eunuchs to us if you lack anything. We believe Li Guifei would do the same, as we keep nothing from each other. It is why, after all, she is one of our favorites," smiled Zhu Di.

Xue Guifei who, since then had not seen it in her interest to divulge information about Min Li when it was clear that she would be dismissed for slandering a favorite concubine, contemplated the offer.

She understood by the emperor's nuance that he knew nothing of Min Li's visitor. If she revealed what she knew then she would have to bear Princess Xia's scorn. This was not something she favored because Princess Xia was well liked among the royal princesses. She calculated. To fall into disfavor with the royal ladies was certainly one thing, but to please her emperor could open up new doors for prestige and assured success in the palace.

Xue Guifei pondered all these things in silence. She stroked the kittens with affected gaiety while an angelic smile remained painted on her lips. She was aware that the emperor was now fondly watching her while also scrutinizing her for any change in conscience which may bring some truth to light and reveal her as the more loyal concubine. She decided to be as elusive as possible in her revelation such that Min Li's fall from grace could be assured but so none of the princesses could ever suspect that she had caused her downfall.

"Your Highness, I am concerned for Min Li," she confided. "I have never once heard her talk in her sleep before. But on that night, I must admit she seemed so agitated and even changed voices a number of times...as if she were both man and woman. Of course, I may have imagined it." She emphasized the doubt in that last sentence to gauge whether or not the emperor had caught her meaning.

"It would have been quite late... and I suppose a night of banqueting and wining is the reason for much illusion," continued Xue Guifei.

"You may have been dreaming," suggested the emperor, urging her to press on.

Xue Guifei stifled a laugh. She was near hysterics and clung joyfully to the invitation.

"I found myself sleepwalking in the corridor to see whether the voices would somehow manifest themselves into a vision. I peered through my chamber door..."

"And...? Did...did this *illusion* have a form?"

Xue Guifei laughed even more nervously. She was entering into a dangerous ground and she knew it. The knowledge she possessed would inculpate more than one person and one of them had immense power. She dismissed her previous words.

"Oh, I really could not say... I saw no one, Your Highness. I believe it was probably just a eunuch come to check up on her..." She paused, avoiding the emperor's gaze, then added, "And... he left shortly after."

Zhu Di suddenly grasped Xue Guifei's shoulders.

"Which eunuch?"

There was a sharp miaow as one of the kittens fled her right hand and leapt to the floor.

Xue Guifei shriveled with fear.

"I...I do not know… It was a dream."

The emperor regained his composure.

"Xue Guifei," he announced, "the dreams that visit you fascinate us. We are intensely curious about these dreams. You say you imagined someone leaving Min Li's room and immediately, you felt, even in your dream that he was a eunuch. Now, why is that? Was he dressed like all servant eunuchs?"

The insistent manner in which Zhu Di said the words *like all eunuchs* betrayed his wish that this should be true. A servant eunuch may have come to tend to the concubine and perhaps bring some herbal relief but if he were not dressed like a palace servant then it would imply other things.

Seeing the concubine hesitate, Zhu Di seized her by the shoulders.

"Xue Guifei. Perhaps you are unaware that sometimes dreams have a predictive quality. So you must warn us if you feel that Li Guifei will come to harm in one way or another. As you know, we are fond of her. We would be greatly grieved if anything unpleasant should happen to her."

He did not mean any of this but it was his last ruthless appeal to withdraw information. The tone of his voice also implied that Xue Guifei should not remain silent if it were in her power to forewarn the emperor. She had no choice. She chose her words carefully.

"Oh, Son of Heaven... The man I saw...he would never harm anyone! Still, if you should know... it was not a common eunuch come to check on Min Li. I thought he was a eunuch because, well, he reminded me of the Grand Admiral. He...he was wearing a red uniform..."

Her voice faltered. Zhu Di eyed her with a demonic expression.

"That's all I remember Your Highness!" she cried, terrified by the glint in his eyes.

Zhu Di released her.

"Your Highness, please forgive your humble servant. Our dreams can be unclear and difficult to interpret."

Trembling and gathering the kittens in her arms, Xue Guifei was no longer pleased with herself. She had seen the rage across her emperor's brow. She wanted to disappear.

Long after she had shuffled off on her tiny feet, carrying her new litter with her, Zhu Di remained motionless, stunned to stone.

They had spoken outside the palace gift storeroom, flanked by two lower rank eunuchs four feet behind. He was certain they had heard nothing, but he felt so spiteful that he promised himself to have them imprisoned as soon as the opportunity arose.

And so Zhu Di had finally disproved the naïve assumptions he had made all these years about Min Li and Zheng He. In a single moment, only a fortnight after that fateful banquet, the comfortable illusion he had long created to nurse his ego was dispelled.

The admiral had lied.

He had lied to his own emperor. The thought was strangely painful. So then, the saying is true, thought Zhu Di. *There are even those who are dear brothers in the morning but who have already become enemies in the evening.* It befitted the admiral perfectly.

Soon after a routine dinner, Zhu Di informed the Royal Chamber eunuch about his choice for the night. The eunuch glanced at the tray and was startled by the tablet selection.

"What is it? You seem to think that we have made a mistake?" asked Zhu Di, after placing the jade tablet faced down with barely a moment's hesitation.

"It is...Your Majesty, very singular... There are so many other concubines. And besides, she has not been well since your last request. But...I am sorry. I will carry out your orders. I...I just did not expect it."

"We did not expect it either," replied the emperor.

Chapter 21
An Assassin in the Palace

Everyone wears a mask on occasion. Some of these masks are more inscrutable than others. The most effective of masks is not, as one would think, the mask worn with intent. It is not the mask we wear to deceive others, or to conceal one's true nature.

No. Such masks are an imperfect art.

In the Imperial Palace masks arose from rigid moralities, the pressures of abiding to protocol, the eunuchs' deep anxieties, and the fear of expressing one's true opinion and incurring the wrath of the emperor. These masks circulated in the palace, afflicting each wearer, either with a loathsome secret or a smug sense of superiority. They afflicted those who experienced the mask with the tragedy of a stifled truth.

They were those masks worn every day. But they remained ineffective because they were all well-known and well-practiced. Everyone recognized the other as an actor.

What is then the perfect mask? What is the masterful, elusive act?

Honored reader, it was the one Li Guifei wore on that night. It was one of those masks that manifest near the final act, at the end of the play, just after the last line, when the actor is too tired to perform and has withdrawn from center stage, when the actor, no longer wishing to arouse interest from her audience or to imbue the stage with her presence, becomes one with the elusive moment.

And while the actor's expressions are untamed and free, while they now reveal every truth with no intent to conceal, still, the sum of his past expressions remains imprinted in the audience's consciousness and it fails to see this new truth.

They think he goes on playing but he does not. They erroneously believe that he has now reached the summit of his art. They cling to this belief because they expect performance and do not suspect that he would reveal much truth. Transported by the raw beauty of the actor's lines, the audience misinterprets the person for the mask.

It is such a mask that Min Li wore when Zhu Di entered the nuptial chamber. He dismissed all servants and approached the bed where she sat, waiting for him. Something in her appearance surprised him.

She wore midnight on her pale skin and it suited her.

She did not turn to greet him. Her eyes stared impassively ahead. They were cold as death.

She was decked in regal elegance, her silk *beizi*, heavy with its gilded brocade. There were no less than twelve dragons woven into the garment. It was a deep blue, a color that no commoner could wear. The long sleeves were graced with broad black rims and the full length disclosed only a hint of the white silk skirt underneath. The front closure was secured with black silk ribbons into which several jade ornaments were intricately entwined. Her ebony hair sat low on her head. She had twisted it into an opulent bun and secured it with a ruby-encrusted hairpin.

She wore midnight on her pale skin and it suited her. She wore no rouge on her cheeks and no makeup, save for the black stain in the core of her lips and the shimmering vermillion on her lids.

She wore midnight on her pale skin and it suited her. There was no pretense from the start. They both knew she had avoided him nights ago. The unspoken between them set the mood for the night. It charged the room.

Zhu Di approached and sat beside her. Leaning forward, she began serving tea in absent, ritualistic movements. He broke the silence first.

"I was remembering…my father, how much he despised eunuchs..."

Min Li stood. He instantly reached for her arm, drew her back and sat her down on the bed. Then in silence, he sat up and began to untie her hair. It fell, obscuring part of her face. He continued to speak and caress her hair.

"One day, he heard that his concubines were plotting with the eunuchs...do you know what he did? He had them buried alive. They were all buried alive..."

Min Li stared at him.

"Concubines are buried alive at the emperor's death. Perhaps the time came earlier for these women," she replied. Her tone was vindictive.

Now this amused him.

"Always the clever girl," he smiled.

He ran his fingers through her hair until it was disheveled. He seemed to enjoy himself immensely.

"Your emperor is a very lonely figure. He is like a bee trapped inside a plotting hive. The ministers continue to vex me, you women mock me... Oh, I know. I know," he repeated, ignoring the look of protest on her face.

He was seething inside, she could see that. His voice had now risen.

"And those stinking eunuchs... Put them in charge of the state affairs and they think they rule the empire... They circulate in my palace like rats, plotting against each other..."

Zhu Di knew that everything he said up to now was private. It would never reach the Ming Shilu, the official record of the Ming. None of this would. He knew that he had to deal with treason in the best way he could and right now, much like his father, he saw treason everywhere.

There was much plotting. They were without a doubt all conspiring against him: his nephew, wherever the bastard was hiding, his own son, Zhu Gaozhi – even though the thought of the prince doing anything else but gorging himself and impaling concubines was laughable – the high-ranking eunuchs, the concubines, Princess Xia... *That* one, he seethed, he would see to it! He would wipe her devilish name off history. It would be as though she had never existed. This secret resolution gave him instant comfort. He smiled.

"Tell me, my girl, do you remember that first night, the night you were brought to me? Oh what is it now, eleven...maybe ten years ago? Ten years!"

There was a dark glimmer in his eyes.

"It was in Nanjing. Your first time... Do you remember what we spoke of? What your life depended on?"

She remembered only too well.

"I see you remain silent... Let me refresh your memory. You are my eyes and ears. You do not exist."

At least, I believed it would be a good idea at the time, he thought. Back then, he reluctantly conceded, it was ingenious. She was young, vulnerable and more importantly, she was a fresh concubine, plucked from the palace.

But that was not all. Everyone trusted her. He knew from the moment he had seen her in the gardens that day. He would watch her engage with the others, watched how she changed her expressions and her tone of voice, how she could appear to be different people in one. He knew that she could be useful to him. And she had been useful.

He stroked his beard, reflecting with a smile.

He had been right. Because she was a concubine, no one had suspected a thing. That was the genius. And no one had known right up until today.

He would summon select eunuchs to pass on messages to her and she would burn them at night using the oil lamps. In the summer, she would swallow the letters. When they talked, it was in his chamber, unheard by the servants who were usually dismissed. She told him everything, never omitting the details as though she sensed that he could find them useful. And they usually were. A prodigious mind, she had.

If he wanted to spy on this and that lady, and if that lady was wary of the eunuchs, as most of them with any sense in them were, he sent Min Li. There were few secrets that she could not unearth.

When she was young it was easier because she was eager to please and thought it was all a game. She enjoyed feeling useful. She enjoyed winning. And he knew how to use that. But later... Ah, later... Military strategies had a way of backfiring.

He should have seen it coming. She was probably disillusioned after many years. She was probably working against him and protecting the others. And she knew too much. Six months ago, she had been sighted around the Eastern Depot headquarters. They had been torturing a eunuch and his lover concubine. It was Min Li who had informed on them. Had she even known of the consequences of her action? What had she learnt from her little escapade with the guard? He had never asked Inspector Yin Dao. But he kept her under close watch now. This, she did not even suspect.

Now, he thought, recalling the night of the banquet when she had surely met Zheng He, the situation was becoming dangerous. He could no longer trust her.

He stood.

"What have your clever ears heard, my dear?"

Min Li emitted a sideways glance and prayed for the third *geng*.

Slowly, she began to speak of what she had heard from some of the eunuchs last month. It was nothing important but she was too tired to sift through it all.

"Manchurian noble groups are planning another uprising in Nanjing. Their numbers are growing... One of the eunuchs in the palace is spying for them. But I can't be sure if this is merely gossip...founded on jealousy...or whether it is truth."

"Then, I would say it is all three," replied Zhu Di. "Although, jealousy does compel people to commit the cruelest deeds..."

He was not in the least interested in the Manchurian uprising. Min Li began to fidget, losing her calm. She stood and moved away from him. What could she say to encourage this hellish evening to end?

"The Annamese—" she began.

"Don't bore me with the Annamese! They are lost to us. Cursed Southerners! What else?"

"What you ignore, Your Highness is that even the Annamese eunuchs have had enough of our careless logging."

"They can go to hell..."

"And if it were not for Ming's hunger for Annamese timber we would have left them well alone."

"Your tongue is very sharp, tonight."

"I'm only stating what everyone knows, Your Highness."

"And what is that?"

"That the Ming fleet, the pride of the Middle Kingdom, has been sucking Annam dry and killing our peasants."

Zhu Di felt a seething tightness in his jaw as his teeth clenched. He was prepared to go to full length tonight. He knew he would win. He would put her back in her place.

"Do I sense...resentment in your voice, Li Guifei? I should think the importation of timber from Annamese soil and matters of the Ming fleet should scarcely be any of your concern. Have I have been mistaken? Tell me...is there perhaps something else troubling you about this expedition?"

That tone chilled Min Li to her core. She knew that tone well. Her voice quivered.

"Princess Wong is pregnant but she took care of it... They think it is her own brother. The eunuch in charge of medi...medicinal herbs claims that Princess Wong asked for a lot of my...myrrh a fortnight ago. He swears that it was to...to treat the miscarriage..."

She was losing confidence. Zhu Di roared with laughter. "Ha! I knew it! That slut!" His traits contorted into a cruel smile and his eyes glowed with sadistic anticipation. He slapped his thigh. "What else? What else is the beehive hiding?"

Min Li trembled. She searched for more tales, more sordid stories that she could use to regale and appease his paranoid mind and yet, nothing came. She began to mutter senselessly.

"The villagers... people are dying in Fujian, Your Highness. The people... It is the worse epidemic we've had in years. They say...they say...that hundreds...thousands of corpses are rotting like animals in the fields...that the emperor's soldiers..."

Zhu Di stood and walked towards her, his gaze ablaze. He cupped her chin forcefully.

"What do they say about the emperor?"

"I overheard it from your accounting officer. The Ming expeditions are a waste!" she spit. "You starve your people while no-lifers and lunatics board your fleet to humiliate the rest of the world!

"Shut up!"

"Oh, you can be proud! Releasing those monster ships...all this, while famine rages in the North! Sending thousands of men to their death! Here and on the ships – for what? For what?"

"My expeditions are for the glory of Ming! The world must pay tribute to the Ming!"

"Your expeditions? Oh! You mean Admiral Zheng He's expeditions! You sit here doing nothing while your puppet sails away. They respect him more than they respect you!"

He struck her with so much force that her hair comb fired across the room. She collapsed on the bed. For a moment, she lay in shock. Then she began to sob.

Zhu Di rushed to the bed. He eyed the concubine as if to decide what to do with her. Then he took pity on her and reached for her sunken shoulders. It was a strange feeling, this pity. He fed it by his longing desire to hurt her over and over again.

He reached for her face, forcing her to look at him.

"Famine? What famine do you speak of? What haven't I done for you?"

And again, he repeated while she tried desperately to look away, "What haven't I done?"

His ruthless fingers tore at her hair while he attempted to remove each strand from her tear-streaked face. He felt her recoil in obvious disgust but it only excited him. His impotence had made him look for different forms of pleasure and he wanted to explore this power struggle for as long as he could. It drew him out just as it had on the night of the banquet. Like a soldier on the field, he felt the lust for battle and it tore at his useless loins.

He abandoned himself to a mixture of pathos and lust as he began to embrace her, like a child who clings for sympathy, all the while tormenting his mother. He knew how terrified she was and he loved that sensation.

"What's this? What do you know of life outside this palace? You speak of hunger... Do I not feed you? I saved you from your miserable existence as a palace whore. I have given you everything! Everything! You don't know what I know... You don't know," he repeated.

He buried his face in her neck. He clawed at her breasts.

The night was only just beginning, thought Zhu Di. He may just find himself again. Yes, he could. Min Li could serve another purpose now that he could no longer trust her. It was a purpose that the cursed Zheng He would thankfully never experience. He felt himself avenged by this thought.

Now that *we dream different dreams on the same bed*, she would have to be used just like the others. After all, it was the purpose she had been officially destined for... But I can go further, he thought, I could lock her up in a private chamber... I could...

He gasped and pressed one hand on his heart. His breath was heavy. Sweat pearled across his temples. It trickled down his swollen cheeks, seeping into each strand of his beard. Zhu Di ambled to the table and grabbed a tea cup.

"Here. Drink!" he ordered.

Min Li held the cup in her hands but did not drink. She seemed to manifest a sudden interest in her emperor. Something had stirred her. On the night of the banquet, she had made a pact with Princess Xia in exchange for her help. Yes, it was dangerous but at the time, she would have agreed to anything.

Min Li's eyes widened as Zhu Di poured more tea. She watched the black liquid as it flowed into the teacup, filling it with its secret essence. She saw him lift the cup. Saw him draw it to his lips...

"Your Majesty!"

It was the shrill in her voice that set him on edge.

Zhu Di froze. The cup slipped from his fingers. The night's spell was broken. To his great vexation, Zhu Di felt himself shrivel. All sense of renewed potency left him. The thrill he had sought was replaced with outrage.

Min Li was in tears.

With seething fury, he looked to where the cup had fallen. A trickle of black liquid seeped through the carpet fibers to reveal a green residue.

"You dared!"

Chapter 22
Princess Xia

A woman tried to run across the palace tiles, her disheveled form glowing under the moonlit skies. Her hurried bound feet traversed the royal apartments, stumbling clumsily into the courtyard. As the pain seared through her hips and spine, she let out muffled cries, drawing the attention of guards and eunuchs alike.

Yet she did not stop. They saw her hobble through the Imperial Garden and weave through the stone statues towards the Western palaces. As she entered the emperor's quarters, her hair had come undone, dropping to her waist.

An Embroidered-uniform Guard barred the way. He was armed to the teeth. She flashed dagger eyes in his direction. The guard squared his shoulders.

"Princess! I apologize but...but you cannot enter!"

"Out of my way!" she shrieked, pushing through the guards who dared not touch her.

The princess reached the door, only to come face to face with a mustached guard with a scar on his right temple. He reeked of tobacco. Now he observed her with contempt.

"Stop her, Yin Dao!" cried the others.

But Yin Dao, after a moment of reflection, merely stepped aside. He knew what the emperor wanted.

They followed as she burst into the imperial chamber. Inside the spacious room, two guards held Min Li. In the far corner, there stood Zhu Di and a further three Embroidered-uniform Guards.

Princess Xia did not flinch. She observed the scene, her eyes seeking Min Li. As she advanced, stumbling on her broken feet, the guards whispered to one another. She knew they spoke of her.

And something unforeseeable happened. The princess blushed. Her cheeks were burning but she remained composed and swallowed hard, her face defiant.

As Zhu Di turned to her, Princess Xia stood proud and straightened her robe. But it was no use. It was all too evident that she had been running. That she had fallen, too. The emperor noticed that her silk sash was loose at the waist, that her skirt was slit to reveal that the princess had grazed her knee and that it bled. He noticed that her hair had fallen out of her bun. He noticed her haggard countenance. All this, he noted with great satisfaction.

"Ah, Princess Xia," he began with an amusement that disconcerted even the guards. "*It appears that our roles are reversed.*"

With the exception of Yin Dao, the guards watched, perplexed, as their emperor addressed Princess Xia. This drew more blood to her face and she placed her hand on her stomach as though to protect her soul from further abuse.

There was, it seemed, an understanding between the two.

"Xia, you are here! We are most pleased. Come, come, we want you to see this," intoned Zhu Di.

Xia obeyed. She moved slowly, placing her hand on her throat as though to gauge her heartbeats.

"There, now, you see this charming creature you have taken under your wing? Look at her, Xia. Look at her. Tell me, isn't she beautiful?"

He caressed Min Li's cheek.

Xia looked pained.

"Well? Isn't she?" continued Zhu Di.

"She is," answered Xia in a barely audible whisper.

"Ah, but Princess Xia, you are like vermillion. *And he who stays near vermillion is soon stained red.* It is all your doing, Princess. You sully everything you touch."

Princess Xia's face blanched. She had seen through Zhu Di. After all these years, he was still out for retribution.

"We have always believed that beauty was an artful snare. That one could be deceived by her charms and lured to perdition. We were right. But tonight, tonight beauty has reached the very peak of its farce. See for yourself, Princess. This teacup..."

Zhu Di presented the empty cup, still smeared with arsenic. "What do you make of this?"

Xia took the cup and stared wide-eyed into it. Nothing could save Min Li now. This meant death. The princess was seized with panic. She looked frantically in Min Li's direction.

The concubine just stared ahead, seemingly removed from this world. Sensing Xia's gaze, she arose from her dreamlike state and gave a weak smile.

"It is all true, Princess Xia. All true," she said in a faint voice.

"Silence!" warned one of the guards.

Min Li's voice faded but she continued to smile at the princess.

Princess Xia's tears flowed all the more. She had noticed with what little conviction Min Li had said those words, how tired and withdrawn her voice sounded.

Princess Xia buckled to her knees.

"Your Majesty! I beg you! It was not her doing! It is not her! You know, you know yourself that it was not her idea!"

"Now now, Princess... Would you have us spare this woman after her wretched attempt on our life?"

"It was not her!"

Zhu Di addressed the guards.

"You shall lock her up in the back chamber. We are tired. We wish to retire."

"What shall you do?" asked Princess Xia, raising herself and stumbling towards Zhu Di.

"*An ant may well destroy an entire dam.* What do you think I shall do?"

Yin Dao stepped in.

"The penalty for attack on His Majesty's life is death," he announced.

Princess Xia gasped. Her face whitened.

Zhu Di sneered at her.

"Perhaps I should follow my father's example and have her flayed. Would that please you, Princess?"

"No! You cannot do this! I beg you! I beg you, do not do this!"

Zhu Di gestured for the men to leave. Only remained Yin Dao and the two guards who held Min Li.

"The Heavens will curse you!" roared the princess.

"Be silent!" cried Yin Dao.

Princess Xia's sobs tore through the chamber.

Zhu Di edged closer. His face brushed past so that none but her could hear his words.

"I *know* of your vile habits," he whispered.

Xia lowered her head. He seemed mildly satisfied.

"Have you ever wondered why we spared your life? Do you think we would have hesitated a moment longer fifteen years ago? How dare you grovel to us for mercy!"

He stepped aside, still staring at her with contempt.

"I never forget," he added, as he walked away.

And now, Min Li stirred. She watched the distress on Princess Xia's face.

"What is it, Princess Xia? What does it all mean?"

Still, her adoptive mother sobbed, refusing to answer. But Zhu Di gloated.

"Shall we tell her, then? Oh yes, you must tell her!"

"No..." cried the princess. "Please..."

Min Li had never seen Princess Xia in such a state. What strange powers the emperor possessed. His words remained an enigma.

"We thought perhaps years of penance would change you, Xia. But you are vile. It is you and your filthy nature that has enraptured Min Li. Perhaps we should imprison both of you. But that would please you now, wouldn't it? You disgust me!"

He thought for a moment before pursuing.

"No. I shall do no such thing. I shall fulfil my side of the bargain. With Min Li gone, you shall only suffer more, Xia. You shall remain in this palace until I am sick of you."

Min Li had not the slightest idea what bargain the emperor alluded to. But now she felt the guards tighten their grasp on her arms as Zhu Di's order shook the room.

"Take that slut away and lock her up!"

And as the guards marched Min Li to the door, the Guifei turned round one last time. She wanted to see the princess before she went to her death. Would Princess Xia even look at her? What was the matter with her? Why would she not raise her face? Princess Xia, so proud, so dignified was now reduced to this state of shame. Why?

Please look at me. I beg you to look at me.

Min Li contorted herself, dragging her feet behind to gain time. And then something took hold of Xia. She raised her face towards Min Li. The two women's eyes met. It was a brief instant but Min Li would remember it for years to come. What she felt through Xia's eyes warmed her being but frightened her beyond comprehension.

How beautiful it was to look at those eyes. It is as though I have been blind all along. How familiar this all is, thought Min Li. How familiar...

I know you, Princess and yet, I realize, I do not really know you. What am I to make of this? It is the last time I see you and yet, it is the first time. How quickly it ends then, our encounter.

Well, goodbye Princess. And thank you.

***

Locked away in her cold prison, Min Li was dreaming. Sweat covered her brow because the place where she had floated to, deep in her memory was damp and warm.

Clouds of vapor surrounded her. She could hear the echoes of shrill, excited female voices resounding throughout the marble cave.

That's what she called it then, the marble cave. She was only five and so young, too young to understand. As usual, she was forbidden to enter the waters of the bath chamber. She had to remain seated on the ledge and play with the kittens.

Across her, on the other side of the steamy, rose-littered pool, she watched silk garments unfold and drop. She watched unbound hair cascade from their buns onto porcelain shoulders. The women's black hair strands rested on their proud breasts. And below their slender waists, they flaunted a mound of thick black curls.

The princesses had turned into nymphs. Their robes and sashes lay strewn on the glistening marble floor. Broken feet advanced, dipping into the warm water. As their maimed limbs entered the bath, the princesses sighed.

Princess Xia waited. Resplendent with youth, she had long shed her clothes. She stood in the bath, encircled by fiery rose petals.

Min Li thought it strange the way Princess Xia addressed the others. Often her voice was raspy and dark. It was a voice that made one ache to obey, one that promised corruption and dangerous thrills.

Min Li raised her tiny head to observe the scene through a vaporous mist.

The other three princesses entered the pool. Two of them eyed each other with cheeky expectation. Their black eyes glowed with playful malice and a hunger that Min Li could not understand. They reached out for each other, hungry, their hands eagerly searching under the warm fluid.

On the edge of the bath, Min Li gave a frustrated kick into the water. But the women paid no heed. One of them arched her back to wet her hair. Her exposed moonlike breasts swelled under the heat. Min Li watched those breasts with a detached sullen pout. She watched Princess Xia set a kiss upon them and heard the arched princess moan. At first playful, the moans rose to a higher pitch. And higher still as Princess Xia's assaults grew fierce.

Min Li held her breath. The little kitten squirmed in her tiny hands. She watched naked limbs entwine on the steps across the pool. Princess Xia's backside rose above the water and she lowered her head onto one of the moaning princesses. Soon they would take turns and it would go on and on. Little Min Li was bored. She wished they would let her swim too.

Min Li awoke from the dream.

She lifted her head from the mat. It was cold and damp. This room, unlike the others, was not heated. And she had no food. And only a little water. How long had she been sleeping? She felt weak. Her mouth was dry.

Their voices carried from the concubine apartments but they could not hear her.

She knew where she was. The very room where she had heard noises once, the room that had once terrified her would become her death room. The emperor sought her death. The Embroidered-uniform Guard had been right.

She recalled her plan over the last six months after her encounter with the guard. Still, it was not the sole reason she had longed to see Zheng He. Everything she had told him was true. But Zheng He had not believed her. And now he was long gone and nothing mattered.

She fought hard to wrest herself from the dreams; to wrest herself from the guard's infernal grip. But he came to her, shaved, eyeless, his ears and nose cut out and vomiting blood.

Like a human pig.

Like a nightmare.

Chapter 23
The Imperial Palace Burns

As Min Li lingered in her cell, she had little idea of what had become of the last man she had so ruthlessly betrayed during her final year of serving the Eastern Depot.

Indeed, soon after her grim encounter with Ji Feng along the Eastern street, Min Li had resolved to protect herself from the eunuch that both she and Princess Xia so despised.

"I hear some ladies of the palace are reading books they do not understand," she told Zhu Di. "What sire, are we too poor to afford quality literature these days?" she mocked.

"You evil creature," replied the emperor. "There is a shipment arriving shortly from Fujian."

"Let us hope the new books are of a higher standard. The current publications are a farce. Why, they are barely comprehensible."

And she handed a set of erotic vignettes together with one of the newly bound astronomy volumes, for the perplexed Zhu Di to peruse.

Flipping open the cover, the emperor ran his eyes across the lewd vignettes and gasped.

"Where did you find this?"

"I found it in one of the rooms, I think one of the ladies must have left it there," she lied, knowing full well to whom the book belonged.

But if Zhu Di could condone erotica, he would not tolerate illegal dabbling in matters of state. Waving the astronomy book in one hand, he nearly choked.

"This...this is absolutely forbidden! What demons does my Royal Chamber harbor...?"

But Min Li did not wish to harm any of the concubines.

"Surely whatever its contents, none of us could make any sense of it, Your Majesty," she assured, dismissing the book with pronounced disinterest. "Besides, it's that eunuch's fault for even daring to venture in our chambers with these depraved literary works. The ladies do not know the difference, Your Majesty, they are bored."

"What eunuch?"

"Oh, see, now I have irritated you," she cajoled.

"Witch! Do not try to save these dissenters. Speak now, what eunuch was it?"

"Your Majesty, I could not say," she replied, brushing a comb over her long hair.

"Your eyes have never betrayed you before."

"Yes but my lips would not dare bring dishonor on a servant you trust."

"If he has erred somewhat he will be punished. Now speak! Who was it?"

To Min Li's great relief, Ji Feng's punishment saw him banished from his treasured imperial post and demoted by several ranks. He was forced to take on a new post in the Western province of Sichuan. In his appointment in one of the many tea-horse trade bureaus, or *chamasi*, he would be responsible for checking tea trader licenses.

To have worked years as a high-ranking Imperial Palace eunuch and to find himself suddenly relegated to a menial clerk job at the *chamasi*, of all places, severely injured Ji Feng's pride. The shame only aroused more of his anger.

After his dismissal from the Imperial Palace he was put under surveillance for training until his transfer to Sichuan. It did not take Ji Feng very long to hire a greedy eunuch within the palace to track Min Li's movements. Ji Feng was a patient man and he calculated that perhaps, one day, he would gather enough information to avenge himself from the concubine.

If a man had been responsible for Ji Feng's demise, our egotistical eunuch would have been as enraged and perhaps stalked him to the ends of the earth. But as fate would have it, his downfall had been plotted by one wily woman.

"The bitch will pay," he swore. "Even if it takes me years, I will get her back. Even if I have to wait until the emperor tires of her and sends her out to the laundries, she will pay."

***

On this very evening, while a dry wind blew on the desolate palace, a withered Princess Xia approached Xihuamen, the Western gate, her little maid in tow. She had not slept.

The young woman by her side must have been about fourteen, perhaps younger. Her eyes glared wildly around her while she clung to Xia's long silken sleeve.

"Don't say a word now, my sweet," whispered the princess, her tapered fingernail caressing her companion's nose as though to reassure her. Let me handle this.

"I am afraid..."

"There is no need to be, I have done this before, many times. Now hush. Hold my hand."

But Princess Xia's plans were interrupted by deep drum sounds rising from the opposite end of the palace. Becoming aware of the ominous noise, the guards at the gate left their posts and shuffled forward, barely looking in the women's direction. Their attention seemed captivated by the alarm.

"What is it?" cried Princess Xia, unsure of the drum sound's origin.

"It appears, Princess, that there has been an accident," replied one of the guards in a most courteous voice.

"I trust you have been advised of my special request. I need to leave tonight."

"My instructions were clear, princess, you may leave the palace, yes, but except under unusual circumstances."

"But—"

"We must first determine the reason for this alarm," dismissed the guard.

"You leave me much in the dark with all this nonsense. I have arranged for a sedan chair and an escort..."

The guards were not listening. They stared beyond the princess, their eyes scrutinizing the commotion ahead. The drum sound resounded further while in the distance, eunuchs ran from all directions towards the eastern palace.

Intrigued by the guards, Princess Xia turned around, only to see a short pale eunuch stumbling towards the gates, memorandum in hand. He seemed to be the only man running in their direction.

Sweating profusely, he raised his hand towards the soldiers. "Open the gates! Something has happened!" The eunuch's voice trembled despite the urgency of his message.

The guard squinted.

"Why it's—"

"It's Zhijian from the Fire and Water Department!"

"The imperial kitchens have been set ablaze!" urged the eunuch. "I must hurry and raise the alarm! Open the gates now!"

"Immediately!" ordered the captain, gesturing to the other guards.

The pale eunuch sped through the gate's building. Meanwhile the guards left the red doors opened, waiting for further instructions from the Fire and Water Department.

"You may as well be away from the palace in these conditions, Princess," whispered one of the guards. "The kitchens are far from here, but you never know with this wind. Good journey. And make haste!"

Princess Xia was startled by the turn of events but she did not hesitate. She adjusted her veil and traversed the gate building towards the awaiting sedan chair. The guards extended a foreboding glance towards the Eastern end of the palace.

"This could well be a long night," said one.

As the women shuffled through Xihuamen, their bound footsteps echoing in the passage, Princess Xia noticed that the eunuch who had run ahead a moment earlier was now standing at the far end of the gate. She watched the young man hesitate under the arched doorway. Just behind his dark form, were the bustling sounds of red-lantern lit Beijing. As the princess neared him, she saw that the eunuch was staring back at the palace.

She had been annoyed at his intrusion into her nightly escapade but the curious expression on his face made her forget her resentment. As she passed the gate's arch, still holding her lover's tiny hand in her own, she was perplexed by the curious blend of sorrow and terror on the young man's face. She also noted the large birth mark on his cheek and how he stood in retreat as though he surveyed something ahead. He had regained his breath but sweat continued to trickle down his knotted forehead.

Surely he should be given another role, if fire terrifies him as much, thought the Princess climbing into her sedan. Her own remark startled her. Why, she thought, I am much mistaken! *It is not horror I saw on the boy's face.*

Realizing her mistake, the princess bent forward and whispered something in her maid's ear. The little woman nodded and, partly relieved to be released from her clandestine duties, she walked away from the sedan chair to follow Xia's orders.

Seated in the waiting sedan, the princess reflected. Then she raised her curtain for one last view. The eunuch was now running up the street towards the Fire and Water Department. She beckoned the hesitant maid to follow him.

Satisfied, she called out to her carriers.

"Do not tarry, I need to be at the monastery by tomorrow nightfall."

Then, swayed by the gentle motion of her carriage, the princess closed her eyes.

"Farewell my dearest, my sweet Min Li," she whispered, through her tears. "Please forgive me. Forgive me..."

And as the mysterious sedan moved out of the city, leaving Beijing's lights for the provinces, Princess Xia sighed in her sleep. She saw Min Li's beautiful face smiling at her. A sharp pang traversed across her chest so that the princess awoke, stung by another realization. "Ah, Min Li," she gasped, "this guilt I saw on that young man's face was but my own."

***

No one knew for sure what set off the palace fire. They saw it as the anger of the Gods.

On that night, glorious visions that were dreamt became undreamt and the ashen face of the Imperial Palace sat in gloom, long after the next day like a grand lady who has not slept and whose hair now falls in wisps on her withered face.

As though driven by some heavenly designs, the flames had been unpredictable, changing direction to suddenly rage through the Halls. And when they reached the ladies' apartments, advancing into the side corridor, the rescuing eunuchs took much fright. For under Zhu Di's strict orders, the entrance to the compound had been locked. Eunuchs rushed into the courtyard to unlock the doors but it was too late. Many women died on that night. They burnt alive.

It was believed that Min Li also died in the flames.

Trapped in the back chamber, Min Li had curled into a corner and given up all escape. Haunted by Xue Guifei's chilling screams and grief-stricken by Lan Wong's sure death, she had first fainted.

Alas, she was never unconscious for long. There would be no escape in sleep. Ahead, the blazing door collapsed. With a sob, she pressed her hands to her ears.

And then something else happened. She thought she heard the muffled sound of rattling wood several paces ahead. Through the dense smoke, she could discern a shadow unfurling from the ground and creeping towards her. A shadow that seemed to rise out of nowhere, like death come to take her.

The death spirit was hunched and strong. It carried a cloak. Min Li saw it loom over her in the darkness. Out of breath, she felt her pulse falter. Her head lolled to the side. She smelled the rough cloak as it smothered her. In protest, she pushed against the fabric.

She had a thought that Zhu Di must have sent one of his henchmen to suffocate her. She struggled in vain but the long arms were strong and found ways to restrain her. Finally, exhausted, her lungs whistling under the cloak, she succumbed, embracing her fate.

When dawn rose in the imperial city, the first eunuchs summoned by the much afflicted Zhu Di were officers of the *Silijian* and the Directorate of Palace Works. They were to inspect the damage inflicted by last night's fire and commence all building repairs.

Mortified by Heaven's displeasure, the emperor fell into a stupor of self-reproach that would last several months. Clearly, the fire was a sign. The Son of Heaven had offended his ancestors.

Remembering his prisoner, Zhu Di dispatched an Embroidered-uniform Guard to perform a thorough search of the women's pavilions.

Yin Dao presented his report. The back chamber had completely burnt down. No trace of Min Li had been found.

It would seem that she had found her death, much like dozens of other concubines that night. Her consumed body was nothing more than a mist of ashes carried forth by the dry whirlpools that now swept through the grim entrails of the Imperial Palace.

Book Three: Water

The Ming Fleet

"Water overcomes Fire"

Chapter 24
Secrets on the Treasure Ship

The day following the fleet's departure, a commotion occurred on Zheng He's flagship.

On the lower deck, a group of brawling sailors crowded outside the cargo compartment. They jeered and tossed amongst themselves what appeared to be a small wooden box.

"Please! Please stop!" cried a middle aged woman. She waved her arms towards the box.

Though her face was marked by the lines of time, and her dark complexion betrayed her countryside upbringing, still, her cheeks were full moons of incredible smoothness. Even her swift movements as she tried to reclaim her possession, emanated a most charming and youthful appearance. It was almost impossible to determine her age.

She wore a blue tunic and white apron. In her agitated frenzy, her raven hair had come loose from its bun and cascaded down to her comely waist. At last, she mustered all the courage she could find and cried out in the Beijing tongue. "Please give it back!"

"So, you do speak our language then?" mocked one. He held the box in his two stubby paws and jerked it away from her reaching hand.

"And you know that suspect baggage is forbidden on board? I say you stole the box!"

"I say we open it!" cheered another.

Cheers greeted the suggestion as the woman pleaded. The men broke off into peals of laughter. They did not see the admiral approach.

"Who's in charge here?" asked Zheng He.

The sailors froze. They stared, speechless at the towering figure before them.

The woman had also fallen silent. But her face was now far from distressed. It was as though a veil of hope had passed over that face and caressed away all fears.

Zheng He had been touring a horse ship with Kareem and Shahrzad. While escorting his friends back to their cabin, they had heard the woman's cries.

The young recruits had never met Zheng He in person. While they had barely ingested an abridged training program, they understood naval discipline. They were terrified of being thrown overboard. One of the sailors spoke up.

"We...err, Grand Admiral, found this sealed box in this err...this woman's cabin. We were just—"

"I heard you clearly," pronounced Zheng He. "Perhaps I should draw my sword and see how far you and your pitiful companions will ingest a dose of your own petty bullying."

He grabbed the first man by the collar, lifting him up like a vulgar package.

"If I catch you once more tormenting the women on board, you miserable rascal, I'll skin your neck!"

He released the young man who landed on his bottom, cowering in fear. Zheng He turned to the rest. "Your behavior is deplorable! You are dismissed. Give me this package!"

One of the men handed the box over and retreated with a set of apprehensive bows.

"Enough! All of you! To your posts!"

When the men had dispersed, leaving their victim behind, one of the naval officers at Zheng He's side, cleared his throat.

"Pardon, Grand Admiral, I know this woman. She is the ship's seamstress. The men, it seems, wanted to know what she kept inside this box. She claims it is hers yet will not let us open it. Pardon your men, as they were merely obeying orders about suspicious luggage."

"They should know better than to turn procedure into sport. Show me this box."

Zheng He examined the traveling box. If indeed it belonged to the seamstress, he could understand why it had stirred the men's suspicions.

Even for a man as well traveled as the admiral, it was an unusual box. And what seemed more curious was that a mere seamstress should carry this object with her aboard a Ming expedition. Zheng He observed the design. The box could also have been Mongol, judging from the gold damascene on its iron fittings. It was made of wood and covered in reddish brown leather. The lotus design on each face had been made using an oil-based paint.

"Do you have the key?" he asked.

The woman nodded.

"You know the policy about personal belongings?" warned the admiral. "No sale items or weapons ought to be carried aboard a diplomatic ship without authorization."

Seeing that the seamstress did not answer, he continued.

"I am sorry but I am going to have to ask you to open this box."

At once, the seamstress eyes widened. She said nothing but her lips quivered. Zheng He was perturbed. She seemed to be hiding something.

"Alright then," he said, "you will give me the key or I will ask my officer to break it."

At these words, the said officer advanced towards the ashen woman who drew more labored breaths and collapsed on her knees. She seemed on the verge of tears.

It was at this moment that Shahrzad who had since then, remained a little in retreat, decided to intercede. She had observed at length and somehow extracted the meaning of this odd scene, choosing to remain silent until now. She glided towards the admiral, set a hand on his arm and in a tone that struck Zheng He to the core, she whispered close to his ear.

"It appears, San Bao, that we all have our secrets," she said.

Zheng He felt as if the Arab woman's hand had scorched his flesh and whipped him with hot sand. He turned abruptly towards her. The shameless green eyes stared back at him. This exchange had gone almost unnoticed by others. But Zheng He felt as though the ground below had opened to swallow him up and the whole world now gazed in his direction. It took him a good moment to regain his composure before turning back to the seamstress.

"What is your name?" he asked.

"Jun, Grand Admiral, my name is Jun."

There was a pause. Zheng He cleared his voice.

"Jun, where have you found this box?"

"It belongs to me, Admiral."

"And are the contents of this box in order?"

"They are, Grand Admiral. They are," replied the seamstress, her eyes lighting up.

Under Zheng He's signal, the officer returned the key to its owner.

"Good, Jun. I will respect your secret. But to avoid any further unpleasantness on my ship, I will confiscate this box. You shall have it when you are dismissed from your duties. Do you understand?"

Jun sprang to her feet. Her dark eyes seem to smile.

"Yes, I understand."

Before they disappeared, Jun extended a grateful gaze towards the Arab woman whose face she could not see. And though she sensed at once that the veiled woman's heart was marred by murderous designs, she still smiled.

Chapter 25
The Map Thief

Disarmed, the soldier scrambled to the railing, grimacing with pain. He looked up in disbelief.

"Hurry! Come quick! Stop that...aaargh!"

The silent figure in black raised his sword. The blade made a clean sweep as the soldier sobbed. He clutched at the gaping wound in his chest. Blood spattered on the upper deck.

A second soldier emerged at the bridge and gazed in terror. Then he bolted forth.

"Die, you cur!"

But the assassin spun round. In a flash, the soldier was folded over by a swift roundhouse kick. A cry escaped from his lips as the masked man's blade whipped through the air and sent him to his death.

Another naval officer had run up from the lower deck.

"Fight me! What are you waiting for?"

The figure remained still, concealing his intentions. Then without warning, he dashed down the staircase, slashing the officer's throat in passing.

Panic had spread on the lower deck. Alerted by their captain, a group of soldiers ran feverishly in all directions, seeking out the admiral. They found him discussing reports with the fleet writer, Ma Huan. The admiral raised his startled face.

"What is the cause of this commotion, Captain? Ma Huan cannot do any work in these condi—"

"Admiral, all hell's broken loose! A thief broke into the navigation cabin."

"What are you saying?"

"He's killing our men!"

"By my sword! The maps! Have you checked the maps, Captain?"

"They are intact, Admiral. But the man is armed. He's killed a dozen men so far. He's unstoppable!"

"Calm yourself. Where is he now?"

"He was last seen heading towards the gardens on the upper deck."

"Where are your men? And why was the drum not sounded?"

He looked up. A flailing body flew across, landing on the deck. Zheng He felt the blood course through his veins. He motioned towards the cabins. The thirty men moved fast, felt boots racing past the long corridor and up the stairs.

Ahead, undeterred by the melee of soldiers, the masked figure traversed a leafy corridor. The admiral bolted in that direction. He saw a black figure slinking past the luxury cabin doors. The assassin was heading towards the ambassadors' quarters.

"Not on my ship," muttered Zheng He, gripping the hilt of his sword. He drew out the blade and motioned to his captain.

"Inside! Advise our guests to lock their doors and remain inside!"

"One soldier for every cabin! Hurry!" ordered the captain.

Zheng He sped into the narrow corridor. Halfway through, at his feet, a bloodied mass was sprawled across the wooden planks. The admiral frowned. The man's wound was deep. The killer's sword had gone for the vitals with blunt precision. Perhaps this was no mere thief...

He scrutinized ahead. He glimpsed a flutter of fabric as the black form glided past Kareem's cabin. Zheng He followed. The thief was a block ahead. He turned the corner. The admiral paused, pressing himself against a door, watching.

"Admiral, look up!" shouted the captain.

The masked figure leapt across from a cabin balcony. He took a shot at the admiral's neck. Zheng He spun aside, evading the lethal blow. The thief rolled head first onto the planks. Zheng He's blade missed. His jade-hilted sword swept forth once more. Zheng He cursed. The assassin moved too quickly. Again, Zheng He prepared his attack. Each blow was matched by his skilled opponent.

But the thief was tiring. He had lost his footing and fallen back. The jade-hilted sword snipped a piece of black fabric. The captain raced across.

"Who are you? Show your face, coward!" he spit, drawing out his sword.

"Leave this to me," said Zheng He.

Without warning, the ever silent thief raised himself on his feet. He evaded Zheng He's blow. He tried to move past the captain and met this one's fist.

"Now we've got you!" roared the captain.

In all response, the thief leapt forth, hurling himself against a Zheng He. Shoving back the admiral, he prepared an escape down the staircase. The jade-hilted sword switched hands as Zheng He motioned to execute his secret feint. The thief gasped. He met the admiral's long blade with a stifled cry. But just as Zheng He clutched a snip of blood-stained fabric, his opponent wriggled free and ran down the corridor, leaving a red trail in his wake.

Zheng He rushed to the portside railing. He scrutinized the rigging deck. The thief was nowhere to be seen. He surveyed the soldiers gaping up at him from below. They'd seen nothing. His eyes hovered towards a row of sampans in the ocean below.

Perhaps he had jumped. Zheng He scrutinized one sampan then another. He searched in vain for the black form. Below, sitting in a stock barge laden with chickens and crowing cocks, an old peasant with a broad-rim straw hat and a gaping hole on his front teeth, smiled back at him. Not a feather stirred.

Wherever he was, the thief was wounded. And that's if he was still alive.

"Admiral! The navigation cabin! Come see for yourself."

Sheathing his sword, Zheng He followed the soldiers upstairs to the bridge.

The thief had forced himself inside the cabin. He had opened every drawer and searched through documents. Scrolled papers lay scattered on the carpet. Stools had been knocked over. A young soldier lay on the carpet, his neck, broken.

"We stopped him...Just in time," stuttered the navigator.

"The question is," interrupted the admiral, "how did this man cross the bridge without raising suspicion. And what did he want?"

The captain appeared confused.

"What do you mean, what did he want? San Bao that man almost killed you!"

"I can take care of myself."

"And I won't stand for your murder, Admiral. I will have my best men at your side."

"Your best men could not catch this assassin in time," reproached Zheng He.

"But surely—"

"That won't be necessary," protested the admiral.

"By my sword," grunted the captain, "that man was after you more than after anything else..."

In all response, Zheng He brushed past and entered the rummaged cabin. He inspected it before turning to his captain.

"From now on," he ordered, "none but I and your men are permitted on this bridge. Officer!"

"Yes, San Bao."

"Prepare your swiftest pigeons and have the same orders dispatched to the other ships. Double security when we enter the ports of Melaka."

"Yes, San Bao."

"Captain, does Old Yu know about the wounded?"

"He's already summoned a team of physicians."

"Excellent," said Zheng He.

He stared at the hundred masts stretching out before them. The Ming fleet seemed endless, a floating labyrinth, a perfect place for an assassin to hide.

"He may still be among us," he warned. "Be vigilant."

Chapter 26
Old Yu's Diary - Part One

The third lunar month is at its end already and we have been at sea for almost two months. Today has been the most eventful. I've had to nurse several men after a violent thief went on a killing spree on the upper deck. None of the soldiers survived and we had to dispose of their bodies at sea. Luckily Zheng He was unharmed.

I shall try to describe the happenings on board but I am afraid that I am no Ma Huan.

Let me introduce myself. My name is Yu, Yu Ling. For the past twenty years, I have joined the Ming fleet amongst the one hundred and fifty other physicians and apothecaries who also take part in Admiral Zheng He's expeditions.

My specialty is research in exotic medicines. You see, the Middle Kingdom may be rich, but we are lacking important medicines. It requires men like me to take part in long journeys across the ocean, to Hormuz, Melaka, Ku'Li, Malindi and other ports. Once there, I organize the purchase and cataloguing of new and known herbs that can be used in medicinal concoctions or other treatments.

On board, I attend to our foreign ambassadors and occasionally see some of the naval officials when none of the other physicians are able to help.

I also work in the many medicinal cabins in the lower decks. There, I supervise the steaming, soaking and drying of herbs so that their properties are preserved for the duration of the journey all the way back to the Middle Kingdom. As part of this work, I administer new concoctions to crew patients to see if these have any effect. It is a long and exacting process in which I have much experience. I try to avoid harming these patients though often the herb dosage is out of balance and causes more ills. But I do not want to bore you. Very few people understand the long process of herbal preparation let alone their complex effect on the patients.

Mostly and most importantly for the success of this fleet, I look after the admiral's health. I supervise his *shen*, his spirit. I am his personal physician.

There are many of us physicians serving on the fleet and so there are times in between port visits when I have nothing to do. Those times are few but when they do arise, I will be writing my thoughts inside this booklet.

I must admit that it was with poor confidence that I saw Zheng He pursue yet another one of his expeditions. But he is a most stubborn man and he will ignore me if I utter the words "rest" and "sleep".

I visit the admiral every fifth day to ensure that he is in his best condition for the long voyage. Such is his self-control that to most, it is not visible that this great man is beset by so many woes.

It has been a while since I last attended to him, back when we returned to the Middle Kingdom two years ago. There are still the same dark circles under his eyes, a symptom of the kidney trouble he has had. He often appears swollen. But this is usual for eunuchs.

In summary, these are the symptoms I have noted and which are common to many of the older castrates:

Poor Jing – his Vital Force or kidney *qi* is low

Persistent aching lower back – this is due to his kidney problems

Incontinence – this has only lately become a problem for him but is very frequent among the castrates.

Blurred vision – again this is due to his kidney problems

Dizziness – this I observed but he refused to mention it

Frequent thirst

Burning in the groin – this has always been present and again is common among the castrates. The herbs I give him alleviate the pain somewhat. The admiral is highly dependent on these herbs without which he cannot function.

Hearing problems – this is becoming more frequent but should not affect his duties

Restless sleep – this is new

I have begun applying needles on the acupuncture points of the Leg Shao Yin channel. Notably, I focused on the points along both sides of the groin. Correspondingly, I stimulated the arms along the Arm Shao Yin channel. Both of these channels relate to kidney harmony and will help stimulate this organ.

I will do this regularly and report on improvements for my fellow colleagues in Beijing as this is a relatively new technique and might interest them.

In order to maximize the blood flow and health of his kidneys I have asked him to avoid sitting awake during the hours of the Rabbit. This is known as the period where kidney blood flow is at its peak. To take advantage of this natural process, I have stressed that it is imperative that he remains at rest during that time.

Sadly this is to no avail, as he is an early riser and will be on the bridge by the early morning drum.

I have prescribed long walks along the upper decks. This should help to regulate the frequency of his bowels which his cabin assistant tells me are infrequent.

Zheng He has taken my advice and during the periods where his assistant takes over, the admiral is now walking. He does not walk for long as he is too restless and is galled by the thought of an escort. Yet this will have to do for now. I need to find something that will motivate him to take walks…

***

I have added this footnote here because I cannot sleep.

That veiled woman is unbearable. She puts her nose in affairs that do not concern her. Her partner would not bother me except that he does everything she asks him to.

I would be glad if we were to drop both of them off for good at the next port but the Grand Admiral seems quite content with their company.

He dines with them at every night banquet and they all speak together in Arabic which means I am left out and cannot take part in the conversation. Most of the time, I end up leaving early and going to bed.

If only San Bao could see what she was up to during the day! Oh, and that Kareem – what an unusual name, I still can't pronounce it – eats far too much. I would not be surprised if he came down with some stomach excess condition in the next couple of months.

Chapter 27
The Folangji

As the treasure ships coordinated their journey towards the South Indian port of Ku'Li, the constant movement of vessels streaming from one ship to another had intensified.

It was aboard one of these smaller ships that an exclusive contingent of soldiers escorted Admiral Zheng He. The escort ship weaved its way across the dense sea traffic, towering over noisy farm barges, couriers and other sampans. At last, it reached one of the other treasure ships from where Zheng He had been summoned earlier this morning.

As the admiral crossed the deck, he caught site of a sturdy well-formed man of five feet, who scrubbed the deck, his tunic wet with filth. He carried his head low but Zheng He recognized him. It was the gambling boy from the inn. He looked pitiful as he flushed sea water on the planks and shuffled on his grazed knees.

"Hey! When you're done Huang-Fu, go empty the latrines," shouted a sub-lieutenant from below. "Dat'll do you some good. You're a stinker!" he added. Then, catching a glimpse of the admiral's white robe, and realizing his error, the soldier fumbled to his post.

Zheng He glowered at the soldier before continuing to the upper deck.

***

In the navigation cabin, seated on a *nanmu* chair was the tall assistant admiral, Yang Bao. Beside him was the white-bearded Zhou Man, still ill since their departure from Melaka.

With a sour expression, Yang Bao observed the two officers before him. Their work was crucial to the fleet's security. They scoured the port of Ku'Li, interviewing Folangji and natives alike.

Dark, hirsute, themselves of mixed blood, they easily mingled with the crowds, employing skilled Ming translators to collect local tales, rumors and to keep the fleet informed.

After bowing, they sat on lowly stools.

"Your report?" grunted Zhou Man. He had reviewed the fleet's budget and was vexed by the mounting court admonitions. The fleet was sailing at a loss.

One of the blue-clad officers opened a scroll container. He reached inside to remove its contents. Unfolding the scroll, he presented it to the assistant admiral. It was a large portrait sketched on imperial paper.

"Who is this man?" asked Yang Bao upon examining the portrait.

"His name is Niccolo da Conti. He is a Folangji from Venice. He has been living in the local islands for a couple of years. Admiral Zheng He will soon meet with him upon our arrival in Ku'Li."

The other officer continued.

"Niccolo is amicable with the locals and...he has also converted to Islam."

"Most unusual," pondered Yang Bao rubbing his rugged chin.

But he seemed distracted. He cast a glance at the fully consumed incense sticks by the side of his book shelf and realized with bitterness that Zheng He was late.

"A Folangji, you say? And a Hue?"

The officers nodded. Yang Bao gave them a hard look before dropping the portrait.

"It is not a crime for foreigners to convert to Islam. What is your contention, officers?"

"Forgive us, Admirals, but this man also speaks many tongues. He is believed to be knowledgeable about the Ming fleet."

Zhou Man sat back, while Yang Bao crossed his arms before him, closing himself to their suggestion. They both appeared reluctant to address the report.

Zheng He had finally made an appearance. The second officer continued.

"We believe that the Folangji are seeking to probe further into our navigation methods. This Niccolo da Conti has been asking questions. The subject of his interest is none other than the whereabouts of the Ming fleet."

"Officer, what is it you are suggesting?" mocked Yang Bao.

"We believe he could possibly represent a threat to the Ming naval supremacy."

"Nonsense! The Folangji? Cursed Heavens! They are hardly a threat. Have you seen their ships?" The young admiral shook his head in disgust. "Ridiculous! They're no match. Is this why you urgently called our attention today? To present your...your prejudices? Surely your spies have been on these land expeditions long enough to make distinctions between ill formed rumors and meaningful threats! Incredible! Precious Ming money wasted for this trash of a report. And then no wonder we have the ministers behind our back! What a farce."

During Yang Bao's rant, Zhou Man had been coughing and nodding. But Zheng He merely leaned on the edge of the desk, examining the portrait with dark scrutiny. He had remained quiet since entering.

"Did you hear this, Zheng He? I was aware that Ku'Li was rampant with sordid stories but this one is by far, a crazy tale."

Yang Bao turned towards the officers.

"Niccolo...what did you call him? No matter his name. He is a traveler is he not? If he wishes to change his religion it should not be a concern of ours. Should it follow that a Folangji who embraces local beliefs be considered a suspect?"

"Admiral...may I say something," interrupted one of the officers.

"You've wasted our time so far," grunted Zhou Man.

"You know the saying. *No wind, no waves*," interceded Zheng He, at this point. "Admiral Zhou Man, Yang Bao, I see that you might be concerned about spreading our resources thin. But the recent violence on my ship leads me to believe that there may be some grounds to these rumors. Please continue your report," he added, facing the intelligence officers.

Yang Bao shot a glance at Zhou Man only to sink back in his seat, glass in hand. The officers hesitated.

"With all due respect, Admirals, it is not the man's religion that raises suspicion but rather, his allegiances."

"Continue," said Zheng He.

"Our spy believes that Niccolo da Conti has been corresponding with a man active within the Folangji government...a man who is well connected. Some sort of religious man...someone linked to the barbarian courts in the West and who would be in the position to benefit Folangji expeditions. To date we ignore this man's real name. But he is a priest of some sort in the place they call Venice."

"This is rich," protested Zhou Man. "As far as I know these barbarians are battling it out between each other as we speak! Isn't that right, Zheng He? I doubt they have any time for building ships."

But the spy continued, undeterred.

"Our correspondent in Venice assures us that Folangji relations with the Northern Hui states have turned so sour that Folangji traders could soon be barred from the Eastern end of the Silk route."

"Explain yourself," said Zheng He.

"Admiral, if the Silk Road is barred, it will cripple Folangji trade. For any trade to continue, they would require a sea passage to the Middle Kingdom. One can only imagine what the greater Folangji presence would signify for our oceans—"

"Bah!" interrupted Yang Bao. "Little ships have never inconvenienced our ports. I'm sure we can accommodate them. I say, let them come!"

"Do you have proof of this?" inquired Zhou Man, frowning despite the nonchalant response of his younger colleague.

The officer nodded.

"Admiral Zhou Man, one of our Ku'Li spy is well acquainted with Da Conti's servant household. A month ago, he had dinner with the courier, a local he knows well. This one had managed to intercept some of Da Conti's correspondence. He was initially reluctant to reveal its contents but our spy insisted."

"What did those letters contain?"

The officer did not reply at first. He let out a sigh.

"It would seem that the Folangji are seeking a path to the Indian Ocean."

"What do they want?" asked Zheng He, pressingly.

"A trade advantage, Admiral."

"But their ships are ill equipped to begin with!" launched Yang Bao.

"No mention of ships, Admiral. The spy believes that the Western barbarians have dispatched informers to interrogate our crew."

"It's a waste of our time," moaned Yang Bao, pouring himself a second drink. Zheng He raised his hand to silence him. He continued to listen intently to the report.

"We ignore what they seek, Honorable Zheng He. But Niccolo da Conti's men are in the port of Ku'Li as we speak. We are certain of it. If our suspicions are correct, they have planned to intercept crew members during our stay."

Yang Bao cleared his throat with a sip of strong brandy. "What could they possibly want? I'm sure a compass would make them happy, let them have a compass and be off to their Western courts," he quipped.

Zheng He remained pensive.

"It is the curse of those who are prejudiced to see others in a cloudy light," he whispered finally. He had spoken without facing the other man as though to express disapproval.

"You think I am blind, Zheng He, is that it?"

"My friend, you are convinced that the Folangji are incapable. Power has made you haughty. You see them as backwards and barbaric. You remain proud and certain of the Ming supremacy. All this blinds you. We must remain open. Open to change. Change arises quickly. Remember what happened to our friends the Arabs over the years. They were once the masters of these oceans. But then came the Song and the Yuan...our power on the seas rose swiftly and now, look at the Ming today. Do you see? We should not be so conceited. Remember, it is possible for the small rat to outwit the mighty tiger in his blind fury."

The younger admiral frowned.

"What I believe, Zheng He, is that we should remain loyal to our mission. The Folangji seek to trade just like everyone else. So what if they are curious about our fleet? After all, this fleet is a most remarkable achievement. You yourself should be proud of your own work after the amount of years you spent in the shipyards of Longjian."

"I can see the value of your argument, Yang Bao," replied Zhou Man, conscious that his assistant might be losing face, "but I do not consider for one moment that we should take our prestige on these oceans for granted. By my sword, that is a copious amount of brandy you have here..."

"Keeps my head clear," retorted Yang Bao. He paused. "As you wish, Admirals. What do you suppose we do?"

"We need to brief our men with leaflets," pronounced Zhou Man. "No man leaves this fleet and touches land without strict control over their word. No man discloses the fleet's contents or the methods we use."

Zheng He nodded.

"We are not to engage into doubtful exchanges with foreigners," he added. "We are here to trade, stock up on tributes, meet our envoys and engage the local rulers, not to discuss the fleet or our navigation methods."

"Very well, then," relented Yang Bao. "Officers, you are dismissed."

The two men bowed respectfully and withdrew. Yang Bao reflected a moment.

"What threat do you mean, Admirals?"

Zheng He eyed Zhou Man with uncertainty. This one nodded.

"Change when it is uninvited can take one by surprise," began Zheng He. "How would the Ming fleet encourage tributes and obeisance to the Middle Kingdom if it were to no longer reign as master of the world's oceans?"

Yang Bao raised his voice in disdain.

"That's absurd and you know it! The Ming will always rule the seas for as long as I live. And this will continue for years to come. Are we not well ahead of the rest of the world? It is absurd to see it any other way."

Zheng He shook his head not bothering to answer. Zhou Man stroked his beard pensively. Finally the gray-haired admiral spoke.

"As men of strategy, change is the only certainty that we must envisage. The imperial aim is to maintain uncontested supremacy over these oceans. Understand this, Yang Bao, we must protect what has become synonymous with the Ming."

"Our emperor would want us to do no less," agreed Zheng He.

But Yang Bao was not moved.

"Tell me, Admiral, this fear of change, it costs the fleet a lot of silver, wouldn't you say? Surely, you of all people know that fear is ruthless. It sees threat in remote corners and takes the life of innocents."

Zheng He was startled. There was in Yang Bao's reproach, a truth too close to home. But the Grand Admiral refused to compare their naval strategy with Zhu Di's methods.

"This is not fear," he retorted. "It is survival."

Chapter 28
The Storyteller

She always began her tale the same way, her eyes staring ahead, her pupils glistening with fondness. By the light rhythm of the gliding treasure ship, when the sea was smooth and the winds stable, her usual audience consisted of a couple of worn out sailors taking a well-deserved break, and the ever present Old Yu. But today, it was different. The seamstress, it seemed had found another interested listener. It was none other than Zheng He.

The admiral sat, a little in retreat, contemplating the sea while he listened carefully to her every word. On medical advice and soon after leaving Fuzhou's port, he had begun his daily walks up and down and along the ship decks. Often, he would find the seamstress seated there, on the lower deck, speaking with her delightful accent as she worked on her mending in full light. Old Yu would sit by her side, while making notes in his journal and giving the passing admiral a sharp, evaluative glance.

It was on this warm afternoon that Old Yu hailed him. "Good, very good! Why not take a rest now, Admiral? Take a rest!"

"Thank you Old Yu, but no. I have to return to my duties."

"Navigation worries again? All this contemplation is not good for your spleen..."

Zheng He laughed.

"San Bao," continued Old Yu, "why do you go on troubling your mind like this? Let the other admirals do some of the work. You see now, this lovely woman. She is also a slave to the rudiments of her trade. Watch as she pricks her finger again and again in an attempt to fend for this entire ship. But look closer, and unlike you, Zheng He, her mind is free."

Encouraged by his old physician, Zheng He walked towards the long wooden seat on the portside of the deck. He eyed the seamstress and recognized her at once. He understood the curiosity that had drawn him to her voice during his long walks. It was the woman with the strange wooden box who had created such a stir on board.

He thought Old Yu's comparison was a little audacious but said nothing. Old Yu was prepared to go full length in his exposition of Zheng He's lifestyle imbalances.

"Go on, now. Your spirit needs attention just as much as much as your body. Besides she is a good storyteller, this one. Oh, I am not the only person who says so. I've heard her entertain the sailors after supper. She puts to shame all those lazy concubines we've picked up in Guangdong. I hear that many of the soldiers find her entrancing."

He turned towards the seamstress. "Isn't that right?" he asked, a rare smile on his lips.

When the physician began speaking of her to Zheng He, Jun had absorbed herself back into her needle work pretending not to hear. She had kept her head bowed in a show of diligence. Now she ceased her mending, raised her head and bowed meekly towards Zheng He, her solemn expression belying her reputation as fine storyteller. Old Yu frowned.

He leaned forward to better whisper. "Daughter," he reproached, "you are most ungrateful. I introduce you to the admiral, my patient, who it is in your best interest to impress, and you, you refuse to share your talent with him. Now...please do not be shy. I know what you are capable of."

A little flustered, he coughed and since he was not wearing his Arab glasses, he frowned again to determine whether Zheng He had moved on or was still by the portside. The admiral had not budged. He was still leaning against the railing.

Old Yu called out, "As your physician, I do recommend you rest, Admiral, but I will not begrudge you if other matters are pressing you."

Zheng He approached, unsure of where to place himself. He felt conscious of the immense social barrier between himself and this woman. He didn't belong here. Even the sailors were uncomfortable seeing him there.

"Ah, that is so much better!" praised the learned man. "You will see for yourself how delightful she is." Then, turning towards Jun, "Why don't you continue your tale, now? Go on."

"Oh, I could not."

The seamstress had put aside her mending and now stared ahead in deep thought.

"Huh? Why not?" cried Old Yu.

"Well, I have a better one," she explained as a beaming smile lit her face.

"Oh!" squealed the old man. "Well, well! You see, San Bao, what I have been telling you? It's all true. She is so full of wisdom, this one! Well, go on. What are you going to narrate today?"

"It is about a place where I come from."

"Aha!"

At this moment two sub-lieutenants approached and sat beside the physician. They had been relieved from their shifts and were about to retire for a nap but the prospect of entertainment lured them to the little Southern woman. Very soon, however, they noticed the Grand Admiral standing nearby and hesitated, preparing to withdraw. Seeing their indecision, Old Yu beckoned them forward.

"Please, please," the old man gesticulated. "We are all here to listen to this tale and enjoy this pleasant morning. You are all welcome to join us."

"Where are you from?" asked Zheng He, eyeing Jun in a manner that made her shrivel.

"Yunnan," she whispered. Her voice trembled with emotion.

For a passing moment, a sad veil clouded the admiral's face.

"Where in Yunnan?" he asked.

"In Nonguzhi. It is my village. But I come from..." She swallowed. "Elsewhere."

"Well Jun, I myself, was born in Kunyang. Nonguzhi is a new town in the mountains. I have heard of it but I still long for the pleasure to see it. It is a most beautiful place, I have been told. The royal princes are fond of their holidays there. Old Yu tells me you are well versed in Chantefables?"

"I... Yes. Yes, I am," she admitted. "But Admiral, this storyteller implores you. Her tales are not the usual street side *small talk* that the virtuous Hans so deplore. You will see for yourself, if you lend her an ear."

"I am pleased, Jun," replied Zheng He. "For I would not listen to *roadside gossip.* But on this ship, mark my words, any entertainment recommended by Old Yu is welcome. Do begin your tale."

Jun took a deep breath and smiled. Then she sat perfectly still, her silence falling like a blanket on her attentive audience. The sound of a drum rose from the upper deck, soon muffled by the roaring flush of waves breaking against the prow. They waited, with bated breath, longing for a change, for a tale that would enliven their day and transport them to another world. And then her voice rose. It was clear, pure and strong.

***

Chantefable One: The Village

In the southern land of Yunnan, about seven days journey from Kunming, there is a green village nested so high and so well hidden by Jade Dragon Snow Mountain that there was a time, many years before the Yuan reign, when no outsider knew of its existence. In this secret village, the Nakhi live and have now lived for over a hundred years.

They built charming wooden houses along the canal. You see, the mountain water flowed down like a miracle, gurgling through the village, a gift from the gods. Even today, we say the snow water from Jade Dragon Snow Mountain is like the blood of the city. This water is precious. It gives life.

Lining these narrow canals are the gentle weeping willows that lend shade to the paved granite paths by the water. The air may be cool and often icy in these parts, but the sun shines almost every day bathing the people in its rays such that their skin turns a darker color and their eyes soon tire.

Oh, how breathtaking these mountain people were. They were like you have never seen.

Storyteller, if what you say is true, then do tell us, how is it that these people differ?

They do not care for wealth and are most hospitable.

And they do not dress like you and me. Take the women. They wear long flowing skirts below a tunic. The older women have a sheepskin cape with seven panels on their backs. These represent the stars in the sky. From each of these panels, tassels are hung so that to most Hans, the Nakhi women look strange. And strange too, are the ways of the Mosuo, the cousins of the Nakhi who came here long ago from the land of the U-Tsang.

And now, this storyteller will tell you about one such woman, a Mosuo living among the Nakhis of this village that we call, Nonguzhi.

In Nonguzhi, there lived an old woman who had never seen the sun since she was a child. This woman had erred throughout Yunnan for many years before settling in this gentle city. No one knew how old she was when she first arrived in Nonguzhi. Back then, the people came in small groups, until the town grew with each new arrival.

All began as strangers.

Now this woman... Some say she was over one hundred years old, some thought, maybe older. But one thing was certain, no matter that she was blind, she knew her way round the maze and bends of the city. With her walking stick, she would prod and feel and find her way. It was with a certain pride, that she busied herself daily with her morning duties, first fetching water from the city well then washing vegetables, walking along Qiyi Street all the way to the Market Square to do her business. All day, she made baba cakes and tended to her fire oven without any assistance.

At night, she made dinner. Later she danced with the older ladies, just as their ancestors had done for centuries, around a large circle. On special days, they would greet the passing tea-horse traders and celebrate in the Market Square. Often the women sat by Yulong Bridge and talked at length of village affairs. They would share stories, gossip and tell jokes about the Han eunuchs who managed the tea-trade.

Just like the other women, she too, wore a tasseled sheepskin cape. Yet unlike the Nakhi women, she never followed the laws of the Dongba, the great priests. The other women knew well that she scorned priests and their teachings but they said nothing. For despite their own beliefs, they knew that their friend was wise and her reasons were pure.

And at dusk this determined little woman would amble home, past the Mu chief family residence, past the spiral staircase leading to the Three Wells. She would enter into a narrow alley where countless other wooden homes existed side by side, their doorways lit by red lanterns, their wooden doors ornate with colorful symbols. In the still night, she, more than anyone in the village, listened out for the trickle of the canal waters and as the sounds grew louder, she knew that she was close to home.

And if she happened to overhear or sense a frog on the path to her modest home, she would be sure to change her course to avoid disturbing the sacred animal. For the frog is the mightiest of all Nakhi animals. And it is the frog that is the symbol of the Nakhi people. Sometimes one finds glistening green frogs beside the canal and this is a most reassuring omen. In those moments one must remember never to injure the animal and respect the symbol of this god.

You will find the Nakhi a superstitious people perhaps. Most Hans do. But that would be unwise, because the thriving of frogs in any abode, even to the non Nakhi person will tell you whether men and women exist in harmony with nature. The frog will tell you that, here, there is water to drink and here, the earth is green.

At this Jun paused. While extolling the virtues of this little creature, her voice had risen and was tinged by a fervent emotion. Her eyes hovered ahead as if to ensure that she had the attention of her audience. It was as though all shyness had disappeared and even Zheng He found himself in awe of her eloquent manner.

So you see, to you, even this frog can have meaning. But to the Nakhi, who revere nature and respect the beauty of life surrounding them, the frog is the most important god.

Storyteller, storyteller, you forget to tell us one thing! What is the woman's good name?

Honored listener, this is something you must know. Her revered name is Erche Jamma. I will call her Jamma.

Now Jamma, just like all Mosuo women, had many tender lovers in her long life before she reached Nonguzhi. But after so many years of keeping these lovers, these *azhu*s, as the Mosuo call them, Jamma, well, she only had one daughter. As all Mosuo children do, her daughter lived with Jamma from birth. She traveled with Jamma and was her closest companion.

The most precious thing Jamma had was her daughter. And year after year, she took care of her. Even with her blind eyes she raised this little girl and shared with her all she knew.

Many years passed. One day, her daughter, on the eve of her forty-fourth birthday, did not touch her baba cakes. She had grown restless. She had ceased eating altogether. And after many moons of this restlessness which consumed her mind and drew her away from the land of dreams, she touched her mother's shoulder and said, "Mother, I am leaving you. There is something I must do."

She bundled up her things and loaded up her boxes overnight. The next day, she was gone. She left Nonguzhi on horseback. She traveled away from this beautiful mountainous landscape and Jamma was never to see her for years. It was painful for Jamma. But now I must tell you this. Before she left, she told her mother a secret. And when Jamma learned of this secret, she understood that her daughter would never return.

Again Jun paused.

How is this true Storyteller?

How did Jamma know that her daughter would never return?

How she knew this I cannot tell you yet. But the thought of not seeing her daughter, of not hearing her voice which filled her silence and formed a bridge between her and the rest of the world was a heavy burden for the blind woman. But many moons had passed. And she continued to live her life as she had always done.

And a day came to pass, a day when something very unusual happened in Nonguzhi. A stranger arrived who was to change Jamma's life and become her new companion.

This is what happened.

On that morning, a man who seemed in his fortieth year rode into Nonguzhi. He came with a woman. He was a carpenter. He was much renowned for his fine work in the new Han capital of Beijing. It was said he had worked on the Imperial Palace itself before becoming a tradesman. When this man rode into the Market Square, the women did not dance, nor did they sit by Yulong Bridge talking about so and so as they would often do. Instead, they crowded around him as he dismounted and they fussed around his pale companion.

What is to be said about his companion, storyteller?

She is the very reason for this story.

Where the Nakhi women had brown skin, hers was as fair as snow and ice. Where the Nakhi women were short and a little stumpy, she was tall and slight. Where the Nakhi women were happy and strong in their knowledge that in this village, they were masters of their own destiny, it soon became apparent that this young woman, for she was quite young, had no soul.

Her eyes, although Jamma could not see them, she was told of this, were tired. Like two ponds of dark liquid where not a ray of light reflected, an opaque mask that watered now and then but scarcely glistened. It was as if she were filled with immense sadness. And just as she thought, so too, she moved. Her movements, they were slow and dreamlike.

She could not even farewell the eunuch who had brought her in. Maybe she never knew him. The craftsman convened with the Mu leader of Nonguzhi, paid him a large sum of money before leaving and that was all.

None but the mysterious carpenter knew who the woman was or from where she had come. All that Jamma knew was that as the most senior woman and on account of her daughter having left, it fell upon her to take in the newcomer.

If only she could have seen her. But she could not. As for the visitor, she did not speak. It was an amusing arrangement; an old, blind woman and her young mute guest. But she was not mute. It is just that she would not speak.

At least for a while, she refused to speak.

At this Jun was quiet.

"This storyteller returns to work now," she smiled. "But come again, to listen to her tale."

The small crowd clapped their hands in good cheer. As Zheng He rose in silence, preparing to leave, Old Yu noticed the disappointment in the admiral's eye. He smiled, knowing that the admiral would return for the rest of the tale.

That will do him some good, he thought, pleased with himself.

Chapter 29
A Certain Khanjar

The passenger Old Yu had chosen to call the veiled woman had been busy with reinforcing her notions of the colloquial Beijing tongue. Often, she would sit on the upper deck talking to the concubines. Grateful for the fresh air and the sunshine, she enjoyed the merry song of the bells, the drums, the crewmen and the laughter of pleasure women. It was through this and through books that she had borrowed from the ship's library, that she could learn new phrases.

Often, she was restless. Obsessive thoughts invaded her mind, memories mostly, and whether Shahrzad was running away from memories or creating new ones, she wasn't sure but she dreaded those moments.

And then whenever she spotted San Bao she tried in vain to engage him in conversation. She had been eager to speak with him since they had left the port of Fuzhou. She bided her time, waiting until the religious ceremonies that usually accompanied the fleet's departure from the Middle Kingdom had subsided.

There was one problem, however. The admiral seemed to avoid her. Such a peculiar man, he was. Always getting flustered and doing his mighty best to regain his composure. Did he think she never noticed?

She had discussed her speculations with Kareem. She called it, her female intuition, a sort of hunch she had about the admiral. Kareem was always impressed by her powers of deduction and he delighted with her ideas. If truth be known, San Bao exerted a fascination that she had not known with anyone. She almost loved him. That is, as one loves their own creation, she would tell herself, a being for whom one imagines a past, a present and a future and who one somehow comes to believe that they know. Yes, sometimes, I think I do know him. And if I love him it is only because he keeps my imagination so enraptured. Oh, she was fond of telling herself that.

Recently it seemed that Zheng He had gained a nervous body of entourage guards. Shuffling in tow of this naval giant who seemed more exasperated than relieved by their presence, the armed guards eyed the decks cautiously, fussing over the admiral's every moves. On this rare occasion, he had dismissed them.

"Peace be upon you, San Bao," she called out, in Arabic.

Zheng He was startled.

"Good morning. Peace be with you too, Shahrzad. What brings you on the bridge?"

"Well, I was wondering if you could have the ship searched for something."

"Oh." He frowned. "Please explain yourself."

Shahrzad hesitated. "I seem to have misplaced something of much value to me. I do not want to trouble you but it is upsetting me."

"Very well, tell me what it is and we will try to find it," replied Zheng He walking with pronounced hurry but with enough tact to reveal genuine concern.

Shahrzad sighed before launching into her prepared speech.

"It is a vexing problem. You see, back in Beijing, I had it on me on the night of the banquet, unknown to your security guards naturally... Not that they would dare search a woman. And then I remember taking it off...placing it in a drawer...or maybe under the bed? But now I cannot recall whether I wore it again before we took to the boats and went down the canal to Tanggu."

Zheng He reflected for a moment. His pensive traits took on a stern expression.

"I take it you have misplaced your khanjar, my lady?"

Her eyes glowed with humor. "Why yes, how do you know? Have you found it?" she smiled behind her veil.

"Well then, that should be a lesson for you to know that women should not carry knives... and certainly not in the presence of the emperor."

At this, Shahrzad took offence. Unperturbed, the admiral continued to walk ahead to his navigation cabin while she was left standing behind, lost for words. But Shahrzad was determined to carry out her plan. She hastened after him, entering the navigation cabin under the alarmed gaze of the assistant admiral. Two guards silently moved across, sword in hand, refusing to let her pass. She peered over their shoulders.

"You would be surprised, San Bao, that I made this one myself. I prize my khanjar for this very reason."

Ignoring the guards, she glanced inside the spacious cabin, examining the floating compass and the map scrolls on the lacquered rosewood table. A small bronze incense burner, inscribed with Arabic calligraphy, presided before the admiral's desk. Books were stacked to the left among shelves and boxes. Her fast gaze found a set of thirty leather-bound volumes which she guessed to be the Qur'an.

The admiral seemed distracted. Perhaps he sought something. She had hoped to impress him with her self-made khanjar or at least that he would find interest in her craft but he glanced at a wooden shelf beside his desk and failed to reply.

Did he suspect? Could it be that he knew she was hiding something. True, she conceded, her missing knife was not the reason she had approached him. In fact, her khanjar had gone amiss on the night of their departure and back then, she had deliberately omitted to mention its loss out of respect for her hosts.

She knew well that searching the ship would yield neither scabbard nor blade. This she understood, much to her regret. But her misfortune had provided an opportunity to engage the admiral into conversation. So far, though, he had made himself scarce.

Zheng He, after a pause, arose from his contemplation and walked out of the cabin. He brushed past the guards, refusing to make eye contact with her.

"May I ask where you are going, San Bao? Do you intend to look for it?"

"At this instant? I am setting off for a walk. Rest assured, Shahrzad, I will do my best to look on this ship for your khanjar. Perhaps you could describe it...yes... Send me a courier with a detailed description... Now, please, *foreigners* are not permitted on the bridge. Please return to your cabin."

She did not like the way he had pronounced that word.

"May I join you for your walk?" she offered.

"Impossible," he replied, not bothering to hide his reluctance.

Still they walked side by side with Zheng He growing uneasy at her insistence. The guards were now following, much to their mutual frustration. A battalion commander approached and he began talking with the admiral in Beijing Hua.

She waited until he disappeared before speaking again.

"San Bao, may I ask you a question?"

"Yes, what is it?" he frowned.

"Who is Min Li?"

At this Zheng He's expression hardened.

"Li Guifei?" he replied, a slight rasp choking his voice, "You want to know who Li Guifei is, is that correct?"

"Yes. Yes I do," replied Shahrzad, hoping to place little emphasis on the subject for appearance's sake.

"The daughter of a late Mongol concubine," replied Zheng He with an evasive tone. "One of Zhu Di's favorite concubines."

"Oh. And your relation to her?"

The admiral tensed up. "Shahrzad why are you asking me these questions? Do you realize I have work to do? Look, we are half a day from the port of Ku'Li. It is a very busy port and I am a very busy man."

"But you said you were going for a walk..."

"Well it is almost complete and I shall return to work shortly. Be assured that I will advise my crew to look for your missing dagger. Is there anything else you need?"

"San Bao, forgive me, you know by now how curious I am about the women of Beijing," she explained.

"So I have heard," replied Zheng He through his teeth. "So curious that you would disobey imperial rules and make intrusions into the Inner Palace."

"Oh! So you know about that. Ah, but you are mistaken! I did not break into the palace. I was officially admitted. I had authorization. From the prince, in fact."

"Of course, you did. I continue to be amazed at your impertinence. You've not ceased your infamous little escapades ever since you arrived in Nanjing two years ago."

"But it is all true! It was the prince! You are not troubled by our discussion, I hope, San Bao... Are you perhaps vexed at my question relating to this...this Min Li?"

"No. Why should I be?" He shot her a blunt look.

He could have fooled anyone but the whiteness of his knuckles as he gripped the jade buckle on his belt had caught the Omani's attention.

"You find me relieved, San Bao. I would not want to vex you. But," she added with a well dosed tinge of amusement, "why the reluctance to answer, my friend?"

She felt that by reminding him that they were friends he could not take affront at her audacity. She could not have been more wrong.

"It is none of your business," dismissed Zheng He in a manner he wanted detached. "Why don't you regain your fiancé and I will see you both tonight at the banquet."

But Shahrzad did not like being told where to go. Besides, she was a guest on this ship and she intended to indulge in the admiral's hospitality just as she had indulged herself in the Middle Kingdom.

"You are right, I am impertinent. But is it so wrong of me to seek truth?"

"When truth compromises others, yes, it is wrong, Shahrzad. Some things are not for scrutiny. Has your father not taught you this?"

She did not reply immediately. Her sprightly walk had come to a halt. For an instant, she faced the ocean with disdain.

"There are many things that my father failed to teach me," she finally answered. Her insouciant tone had disappeared. She was once more demure and inscrutable Shahrzad. "And look now, who is being impertinent?" she rebuked in a dry tone. "You have no right to speak this way about my father. He is not...he is not a bad man."

"I did not imply that he was."

There was an uncomfortable pause before Shahrzad spoke again,

"No, you didn't. Very well, it is my fault. I apologize for rushing into your private business."

She felt flushed from her previous outburst. The black *hijab* had grown heavy under the sultry Indian Ocean sun. They both paused to catch their breath at the railing. Then she did the unthinkable. She raised her veil.

The admiral squinted, becoming aware of a fine red scar above her right eye. It was not, as he first thought, kohl that she might have smeared, in haste or through sweat. There was indeed a red scar. It sprang from her forehead and skirted the arch of her eyebrow, narrowly missing her eyelid. Zheng He's memory assured him that this scar was not present when he had first seen Shahrzad's teenage face years ago. It could only mean that she had fallen or hurt herself recently.

"Very well, then I will ask you a less intrusive question. Have you ever...perhaps...fallen in love with a palace woman, Zheng He?"

Showing their faces was not something Arab women did lightly. What was her purpose in removing her veil? He realized then that she was trying to express her trust. He hesitated.

"No, of course not."

"Eunuchs have affairs all the time. I know all about that. After all, San Bao, there are eunuchs in the Arab lands too. They existed long before the Ming. And as for the Ming eunuchs, I've discovered a great number of things during my year in Beijing. But you, you are different."

"Well then, let us say that I am," confirmed Zheng He. "Is this all you wish to know?"

"No."

Zheng He looked away. He seemed eager to avoid the wilful Semuren with her flashing green eyes. Shahrzad's insistent voice rose behind him, "You are a man who has so much power. You can make any choice."

"Is that what you think?"

"Oh, I know that. You have but to ask and it will be given to you. Is that not the privilege of the Grand Eunuch?"

Zheng He made no answer. He ached to rejoin Old Yu and listen to Jun's tale. But the seamstress was ill today.

Shahrzad's voice startled him once more. "Zheng He...Who is Min Li?"

"Is there anything else I can do for you, Shahrzad? I have already answered that question."

"It appears that I am dissatisfied with the response."

"Shahrzad," said Zheng He between his clenched teeth. "Please regain your cabin. I need to think."

She drew the veil over her face and cheered, "I will see you at the banquet tonight, then."

"No more questions."

"Oh but I have one more."

"I will not answer any further—"

"Have you visited Mecca?"

The eunuch was taken aback.

"I...have not been able to," he replied.

"Ah, that is curious."

"Why?"

"You see...I would have thought that a man with your influence could afford a pilgrimage to Mecca. It seems to me that sailing as far as the Arabian States, something you have done more than once now, without a visit to Mecca...well, it is perplexing."

"My only wish is to serve my emperor."

"Of course...Well, that would explain it."

"It explains nothing, Shahrzad. I will ask you to desist on this matter. Do not say another word."

"It explains your reticence to tell me more about this Min Li."

"I am warning you Shahrzad, if you so much as persist for a single moment, I will have you locked in your cabin. You will not be permitted to leave it until we reach Zanzibar. And if I catch you once more on the bridge, I will have both you and Kareem put on watch. Do I make myself clear?"

Shahrzad's eyes were reproachful.

"Quite clear." She glided away, carrying the insult quietly with her.

***

Later, while Zheng He reviewed the proposed Ku'Li diplomatic schedule, a eunuch tapped at his cabin door.

"Grand Admiral... A gift from seamstress, Jun. She says she is grateful to the Grand Admiral for not destroying her wooden box."

Zheng He did not reply. The eunuch placed the cloth on the desk and left.

Zheng He had been ruminating. But he began to feel guilty for his outburst towards Shahrzad. After all, she was his guest. And she had the sensibility to remind him of it.

He turned to the gift. It troubled him that the seamstress would give him a gift. She gained face for it. He would have gladly forgotten the confiscated wooden box but she was reminding him of it. Such a strange woman, he thought. But he couldn't think much ill of her. After his outburst towards Shahrzad, he felt too much remorse and he wanted to prove that he was, after all, a patient, generous man, if only just to himself.

He allowed himself a moment of appreciation for the folded white cloth. He willed himself to soften up and to feel grateful. It was easy. The craftwork tugged at his curiosity as much as everything about its creator.

He observed the pattern. The design was somewhat familiar but he could not say how. Perhaps since Jun came from Yunnan, he may have seen this brand of embroidery before, perhaps in his childhood.

It ran across the cloth like a dense array of ants crawling in a disorderly fashion. There were oblique, irregular lines, curves and circles. The embroidery resembled no living thing or object. He tried to make out animals or plants but was forced to reach a blunt conclusion. The pattern made no sense.

Maybe it represented some language. He had learnt that the people of Nonguzhi used a peculiar pictographic language...but this was different. There seemed to be no regularity to this pattern. Its lines were brutal and scattered, almost as if the seamstress had been testing her embroidery skills, stopping there only to start stitching again, further up and to the side. Like a mad woman.

For all her eloquence and talent for storytelling, she is certainly clumsy at embroidery, thought Zheng He. Even so, the admiral could not say how but the pattern was strangely familiar.

Chapter 30
Chantefable Two: The Stranger

And now honored listener, where did this storyteller leave you? Ah, yes! The stranger.

On the first night, the stranger cried as she lay on her thin mat in her new home. She cried all night in careful, muffled sobs that no ordinary person could have heard, save that Jamma was no ordinary person. She could hear and smell almost everything. But come the morning, the old woman respected the newcomer's privacy and asked no questions, nor did she mention the crying.

This went on for a couple of nights and still, when the morning came, Jamma said nothing. But after she had left the young visitor at home to rest, and loaded her soft ham and baba ingredients into the Market Square she convened the other women of the village.

"She cries at night," she said simply.

"How sad this is."

"Why does she cry?" asked one.

"I dare not ask."

"The Mu clan's instructions were very clear."

"Yes, we must never ask her where she comes from."

"Can she at least talk?"

The old woman thought for a moment. "Not yet. But tonight, I will try speaking with her. If she is to live here with us, then we must do all we can to make her feel welcome."

"You could teach her to make baba cakes?"

"I hear of a need for more helping hands at the Bengshi corn farm, maybe she could work there occasionally? She has solid limbs, if only she were to eat a little more."

"And you could send her to fetch the water at the Three Wells. You are far too old to be doing this. You can barely carry the water up a few steps. You'll fall one day."

"Yes, yes," replied Jamma overwhelmed by the excited suggestions. "But let us take our time. She has only just arrived. Tomorrow, I would like one of you to show her around the village. It is easy to get lost in this maze of streets. Ensure she knows her way."

Because she remained silent for days and would not introduce herself, it was decided that they should give the woman a name, one suited to her pale complexion. Since she came from the northern region of the country, they agreed on the name Bei Lan or Northern Orchid.

It was, Jamma declared to her astounded friends, the wish of her long gone daughter that the stranger be named Bei Lan. No one questioned this. But no sooner had Jamma said this, that Bei Lan raised herself from her stool. Hers was a strong accent.

"I have not met your daughter," she asked, speaking for the very first time.

Jamma did not recognize the voice but she sensed its owner. Yet she revealed no surprise at hearing Bei Lan speak.

"She is not here," she declared. "She's left me about a year ago."

"What was she like?" asked the pale woman suddenly very curious.

There were murmurs among the women as they recovered from the shock of hearing Bei Lan speak. The blind woman silenced them with her stick. It made a sharp tap onto the paving. Then, she took Bei Lan by the hand as though to quieten her. "It is getting late now, don't you think. We should head back to my home. Why don't you lead the way, we will see how much you have learnt today. I hear you are very...observant."

Bei Lan blushed.

As they walked, she continued to ask questions in a timid voice. "What is that language you were speaking with the other women?"

"You mean when I am not speaking that absurd Nanjing dialect of yours? It is the local tongue. We speak it only among us."

"What is wrong with my dialect?"

"Nothing. I am being cynical. I like to blame others when I am furious. And I suppose the greedy Hans are always begging to be blamed. Don't pay any attention to a grumpy old woman. Continue walking, you are doing fine. I can feel my way perfectly with my walking stick, I assure you. If you make a mistake, I'll let you know."

"I notice some strange symbols on the doors of some houses..."

"Ahuh...did you, now? Keep left, Daughter, don't go steering into the canals, are you trying to drown me? Yes, that's good, onto the second street, excellent. So you've noticed the door markings, have you?"

"Is that your language? I mean... Is that the way you write? Can you teach me?"

"You certainly ask a lot of questions now that you have found your tongue. Yes, that is now our language. It is our way of writing it. And why on earth would you want to learn it? What is wrong with the Han dialect?"

"Oh, nothing. It's just... I thought you said... Never mind... Your writing symbols, they are so beautiful. Really, I've never seen anything like it."

"Hmm. Well, I won't be much help but that can be arranged. Ah! Here we are then! Where are you off to? We've arrived, don't go off plodding further. Come in."

And so Bei Lan came to live with the strong-headed Jamma. The young woman soon learnt of the village and its people.

Their most important possession was water. When it had been built over two hundred years ago, the elders had elected this plateau surrounded by mountains and sheltered with leafy trees, because of its abundant water. Crystal clear water from the mountains flowed in narrow canals through the village. The villagers depended on this heaven sent water for all of its activities. The water glistened like a giant pattern marbling its way through a slab of jade. This was the reason this area had once been called Dayan Zheng, meaning Town of Big Ink Slab.

In her first month, Bei Lan quietly explored the village's intricate lanes, ambling along the canals and traversing the many newly built bridges. There were hundreds of these, carefully laid out across the canals. For days she wandered, losing herself in this gentle maze of narrow streets that often merged into large public squares where the village activity bustled.

Spiraling up higher into the core of the village, she climbed dozens of steep steps all the way up to a large Ming temple and there, on a platform that overlooked the city, she saw the many rooftops of Nonguzhi side by side, extending for several *li*s. How beautiful it all was.

She admired each one of these charming homes with their spacious courtyards, their large wooden doors, their gentle red eaves. More often than not, the front doors were ornate with elaborate carvings and painted with strange colorful symbols. She did not know the meaning of those symbols. But still, how lovely were those houses with their two-story timber fittings, their tightly stacked mud-brick walls laid out in an intricate wooden framework and topped with a modest tiled roof.

Each adobe consisted of a main house flanked with three smaller houses and a large wall facing the main house. Each compound had five courtyards, one in the center of the four houses and the other four in one of the sides of each house. It was in these courtyards that the villagers outshone one another in the decoration of their homes.

Peering through partly ajar doors, she glimpsed the inside of these courtyards with their colorful drapes hanging against the interior white walls, and their ornate sculptures. She noticed the ground was laid out with cobbled stones. Her eyes ran up and down and far into the courtyard. It seemed to be the general practice to carve the screen wall's main beams into hideous demon heads. And this she noticed while peeping into several courtyards and it gave her much fright, so much so that she recoiled, in sheer terror but also in wonderment.

A month had passed. A shift seemed to have taken place in the newcomer. The women could now discern the quick intelligence animating Bei Lan's sharp peepers. They also noticed how conscientiously she attended to her morning chores and assisted Jamma. They liked how fast she had found her own way through the maze of streets and how she knew each and everyone one of their names. She had quickly understood the unspoken rules of the village, keeping to their group and at first refusing to speak to male villagers.

But the subject of male companionship was broached one afternoon as the women sat in the marketplace and a handsome lad perched high on his saddle trotted along. He was dressed like the other village men, save for a thick sheepskin coat and cow hide pants. His sturdy long haired horse was a burnt sugar color with a long white mane. It, along with its fine rider, had soon captured the attention of the entire square.

"What a solid mount that is," mused one of the old ladies crouched beside her freshly laid out vegetables.

"Watch your tongue. He may be taken," warned her companion.

Bei Lan's eyes widened in surprise. She glanced at the group of women but remained silent, pretending that she had not heard their odd remarks.

Her nearest companion, whose name was Namu, had not failed to notice Bei Lan's discomfort. She was not malicious but the sight of this innocent foreigner, so unfamiliar with their way of life, only added spice to her cheek.

"Perhaps we should ask him to visit both of us. I'll receive him first!" she giggled. They collapsed into laughter and Bei Lan's profuse blushing only redoubled their outburst.

"It's very simple here, Bei Lan. If you are interested in a man, and him in you, you two may become *azhu* and he is welcome to visit you at night and have sex with you. If you two have children, he helps take care of them but they are yours and they come to live with you.

"I know what you think, it is different in the Northern provinces. But here," she smiled broadly, "women are in charge."

At this, Bei Lan stared blankly at Namu.

"I don't think she understands you, you've confused her," said another. "Look Bei Lan, we women can take as many lovers as we want. Provided Jamma consents to this, if a man likes you enough to become your *azhu*, then it is permitted for you to—"

"Oh, be quiet!" protested Jamma. "You are troubling her! Can't you see she is almost reduced to tears?"

"I do not understand," said Bei Lan in a cold tone.

More laughter followed her outburst.

Jamma knit her brows while the lines on her face grew dark. "Be quiet you three!" She shook her head and continued roasting her sweet potatoes, turning them over her coal stove. After a long moment, her firm voice broke the silence, "You younger women are always playing the field. Perhaps Bei Lan has no wish to have an *azhu*."

A couple of new moons after Bei Lan had arrived, this incident was soon forgotten. The women no longer pestered her and she seemed to smile more often. Jamma also noted that Bei Lan no longer cried at night. She noticed that the newcomer was a woman of diligence and much talent. When it was discovered that she could embroider and use the spindle, she found a way to make herself useful.

Early in the morning, her first duty was to rise with the sun and join the other villagers who made their pilgrimage to the main well. Armed with her two buckets, she would step down a broad spiral staircase to the Three Wells.

Once there, she would kneel across the surface of the drinking well in search of her reflection. Sometimes the mountainous sun was hidden and she saw nothing. At other times, she could just make out that her skin had darkened and that her hair was marred by auburn tinges from the assaults of the sun. She would watch those sad eyes staring back at her like two lifeless moons dancing in the ripples.

Then she would tilt her head, questioning the pond, disdainful of her own reflection. Sometimes children came down to the well with their fathers and she would be stirred away from her reverie by their joyful giggles. She would turn her head towards those happy, shrill voices as their owners came bouncing down the steps. Seeing that she was no longer alone, she would promptly sit up and fill her two buckets. With a sigh, she would place them on each end of the rod that she then lifted across her shoulders. Without a word, she would ascend the steps back to Jamma's house.

There was an unwritten rule in the village that all drinking water must be drawn early. When the sun had risen high in the sky, only then was it permissible for villagers to wash their clothes and vegetables. And so later, when the sun was high enough in the sky, Bei Lan would wash her clothes and those of Jamma. Later, she would set off to the markets and buy vegetables and help clean them for dinner. And long before the sun set, she had spun cloth and tended to laundry or sometimes helped Jamma grind corn and make pancakes.

***

At this point in her narrative, Jun paused to catch her breath.

Old Yu who, until then, had remained silent was taken aback by the turn of her story. Raising himself from his seat, he asked in a grave tone whether she knew women who behaved this way in her village.

"Yes, it is reasonable behavior," assured Jun. "Women are the head of the household in my village. They make all the decisions too."

There was a general gasp of horror in the small audience. It was as if Confucian order had been defiled. Some of the men shook their heads in disgust.

The physician tilted his head to the side and silently contemplated the facts as if he sought to examine them before consenting to listen any further to Jun's tale.

The entire concept seemed absurd. It threatened to corrupt his Confucian moral system. In no way did he wish to be embroiled in this or accused of entertaining similar convictions as those Jun had bluntly exposed. But he was a medicinal man and as far as enriching his knowledge, he felt entitled to this exchange of ideas, no matter how vulgar this roadside gossip of a tale now revealed itself.

Besides, he remembered his military service in Yunnan years ago, when he was but a mere physician's assistant. Life had taught him that there existed more vulgar, ugly things to be outraged about. All things considered, this talk tale was not short of entertainment. And hadn't Jun said that she lived in such a village? If it were indeed true that there were such morally depraved people in her village, he wanted to find out! Such were the conflicting thoughts that possessed our physician as Jun interrupted her narrative.

As for Zheng He, he said nothing. He merely gazed intensely at the seamstress. It was hard to discern the admiral's thoughts. There was something in Jun's tale that had fascinated him. Something that spoke to him on an entirely different level and he was not sure what to make of it. All this seemed to him as foreign as that embroidery gift she had given him.

Even more puzzling, he felt that Jun's story had been designed with the intention of luring him into her audience. It was as though whenever she spoke each word, employing a most artful expression enriched by her lovely Southern accent, she were focusing on the admiral more than anyone else. To Zheng He it seemed that as far as Jun was concerned, he was the only member in the audience. But he could not explain how he felt this.

He looked uneasily at Old Yu, and then at the two officers. He noticed the passing foreign envoys who, even with their limited grasp of the Nanjing dialect had gathered to hear her tale in an attempt to break from boredom. Did they also feel the same way? Was it his imagination running ahead of him? Even now, while she sat in silence, as though to gather her thoughts, he felt overwhelmed by her previous words.

He wanted to know more about that village. He wanted to hear the wise blind woman speak and most of all, he wanted to know more about this mysterious Bei Lan.

He moistened his salty lips to speak. In truth, he had no desire to say anything but since he was the head of this vessel, he felt compelled to say something. He felt it his duty to utter the state of things, to make an observation that would officially announce how the tale had been received by all even though deep down he knew that his words were at odds with what he felt and perhaps would even jar with what others felt.

But not speaking may give the wrong impression that he had not enjoyed the tale and that was the last thing he wanted because it would scare off the seamstress and discourage her to continue. And so the admiral chose his words carefully.

When he managed to speak, his tone, while controlled, sounded almost too playful.

"What a fascinating old woman! I am now intrigued!"

The admiral had needed to affect enthusiasm because he was not accustomed to such public displays.

At once, Jun caught his words, almost as if she had pre-empted that he would speak to her. She nodded in agreement.

"Yes, yes she is..."

"I take it she is your favorite character then," ventured the physician observing Zheng He with some interest.

The admiral felt uncomfortable with the general attention that he was now receiving. Unlike Jun, he could not speak to a large group of people unless he felt secure in his authority. He did not know which role to take in this unofficial gathering. Somehow, he felt that his voice was weak in this assembly led by the eloquent seamstress. This was new to him, to express himself and the things he liked without some seal of imperial endorsement and it made him feel awkward. At last he chose to regain control in the only manner he knew.

"I should return to my duties now."

"And Bei Lan? What will happen to her," asked Old Yu, returning his attention to Jun and ignoring the flustered admiral.

Hearing this question, Zheng He, who had begun walking towards the bridge, froze and lent an ear in their direction.

"You will see," replied the seamstress.

Chapter 31
Shahrzad Talks to Kareem

Kareem licked his index finger to reveal the next page of the illicit *Hazar Afsanah*. He braced himself for the sixth night's tale which the young heroine, Shahrzad, had promised to deliver to King Shahryar. It was a popular volume, not least the final instalment in these most creative series and he had so far been transported by the magic of each tale.

What most appealed to Kareem as he licked his lips to turn each page, were the sensual nuances in each of the thousand tales and the moral richness transpiring through the main characters.

This colorful world of roaming *jins*, magic, hashish-induced visions, abundant red wine and beautiful treacherous women had no sooner lured Kareem in its voluptuous embrace that a loud clamor forced him to lose his grip and the book tumbled out of his hands.

He glanced at the cabin door just as Shahrzad entered, emitting a disdainful grunt. Kareem picked up the volume, found the lost page and pretended to read. He assumed an entranced expression but not without first casting an apprehensive glance in Shahrzad's direction.

The veiled beauty let out another grunt. She sat beside him at the edge of their bed and almost immediately sprang up to begin pacing the cabin.

Oblivious to his fiancé's frustration, Kareem had regained the paragraph where he had left off. It was the paragraph where the delicious vizier's daughter began her next tale.

At this instant, Shahrzad removed her veil and flung it to the other side of the room. This was enough to jerk Kareem away from his literary cocoon. The heavy book slipped again from his grip to join the carpeted floor.

"My dove, what is it?"

"I cannot fathom this man."

"Shahrzad, keep your voice down... Our cabin is adjacent the Zamorin's cabin. Please..."

Shahrzad pondered in silence.

"What has happened?" asked Kareem, raising himself from the bed. Shahrzad sat back down and lowered her head to her raised knees. She was ruminating. It was a bad omen, thought Kareem. She would not speak for a fortnight now that she had latched onto morose thoughts. The fun and frolic was over, he brooded. Enter, *One Thousand Tales.*

"By the Sword of the Prophet, Peace Be Upon Him, what troubles you, Shahrzad?"

"He refuses to speak with me, Kareem. That is all. He refuses."

"What? Now, now, what have you been up to? Chasing *jins* again?"

"It's no use."

This was only the beginning, observed Kareem. The philosophical theorizing would soon follow. Through a mental exercise that would have pained Aristotle himself, she would let loose to her intellectualization of all sordid emotions so that she could sleep better at night. Oh, but she did look so dark.

"Did I hear this correctly, my Eye? You...you tried then? You asked about..."

She batted her kohl-lined lashes at him. Enough said. The realization made him wince. "By the Hand of Fatimah! By the Sword of the Prophet! Shahrzad, what did you say to him?"

He felt his pulse quicken. He tried to name what he felt. Jealousy? No. Intrigue. He would always have more time later to be jealous but for now, he was curious. He wanted to know. This was better than *One Thousand Tales* after all... He approached and took her hands.

"So...what happened then? What have you learnt?"

"Oh, where does one begin," she sighed, lowering her face in defeat.

Kareem waited with abated breath, eager to absorb the details of her encounter. He loved their ability to speak of anything. Yet part of him remained wary. Did she perhaps favor the eunuch? After all, over the last four years, she had given the admiral far too much attention. It had begun as a vague pastime until it had swallowed her mind. Was there perhaps more to this? Had this new plan, as she called it, been nothing but a ploy to enter into an amorous liaison with the eunuch? He brushed those thoughts aside.

"Kareem, are you listening to me? You feel no jealousy, I hope."

"No, I'm not jealous. It was part of your plan. I understand."

"Good. Listen, I have a theory."

There was a pause.

"If something happened to you, something awful...to...to your manhood..."

Kareem nodded.

"If something earth shattering like...that...happened to you and you never made that choice, what would you feel?"

Kareem blushed preparing to speak.

"No, do not answer. Listen. We are talking about a man who has only one way to justify his existence according to what has befallen him and that is to serve his emperor. If one were to listen to his dribble, his life's calling is to pay allegiance to his Ming majesty!"

"I dare say, he means that, Shahrzad."

She shot him a reproachful look. "Even in your book, no one is so shallow. If we were to believe his words, San Bao is convinced that imperial devotion leads to happiness."

She was more interested in expanding on her theory than soothing his jealous soul, reflected Kareem.

"I am certain that there is a San Bao that we do not know. Yes, yes... I am certain of it," she added.

"Oh, so you know him, now, do you?" asked Kareem, a little vexed.

She began to reflect. "The Grand Admiral, Zheng He. Once a little boy, cut from his father, his village, his people, then castrated... He meets Prince Zhu Di at age twelve and you really believe that after all he endured, that he could be so entirely devoted to his emperor? I doubt it."

"Well it has been many years...they grew up together...the two are very good friends, I must tell you. They slept in tents together...went to war together..."

Shahrzad shook her head. "I have seen their friendship, Kareem. You forget that I, too, was there in the Ming palace. Let us be honest. That place is suffocating! Do you remember the tedious number of times we had to prostate ourselves to His Majesty? I could have retched. No, no, there may be friendship but it is all part of court etiquette. It is all rigid."

"And so what if it is? Surely they must be fond of each other by now?"

"Do you know what I think? About Zheng He... I think that he so despises himself, that for all his achievements and his rank, he is still crippled by his losses. That's what I think."

She was so satisfied with herself upon saying these words that even Kareem forgot his own preoccupations.

"Most men like him would be," he remarked. "I have heard the most dreadful things said of the eunuchs. And in Constantinople, they are much worse...power hungry, jealous, petty...much worse! Did I tell you that there is a eunuch in the book I'm reading, *Hazar Afsanah*—?"

"Not now, Kareem. See...those eunuchs, they embrace their new life by serving the Ming majesty. But with San Bao, I am ready to wager that it is different."

"How so?"

"Beneath the pride, we may find a man in much denial. Who knows, maybe he lives in secret contemplation of what he could have done and would have done."

Kareem shook his head. He picked up his book and flicked through pages.

"I do not understand you, Shahrzad. What are you trying to tell yourself?"

"The admiral has moved forth all his life and reached pinnacles of success in every domain. Why should he wallow in self-pity when he has only to reach out and further praises are showered down onto him? Oh, it's such a perfect, perfect life. Why ruin it? Are you following me?"

"Yes, you are saying that Zheng He would seek to avoid the truth about his condition?"

Shahrzad nodded. "What I suggest is that any introspection would remind him of his pain. So he shuns it. Do we agree?"

"Very well, he would avoid thinking too much..."

"Precisely! Imagine it, he may even wound another to evade his own emotional pain."

"I think I understand."

She raised her face. Kareem noticed the dark circles. He was mortified thinking back to all those nights when Shahrzad had laid in bed, drifting into morose contemplation while he read *Hazar Afsanah.*

"I've seen the way you look at me," she said. "What do you see? No, do not answer. I know what you see. This man has twisted me, hasn't he?"

Kareem reached forth to take her in his arms.

"My sweet dove, why do this to yourself?"

"It is my mind that loves, Kareem. Nothing else. But I want to share this with you. This man, yes, he will shun too deep an introspection in his soul. Because it would hurt him and he does not want to be reminded of pain."

She paused.

"But now, let us examine what I've just said. What would he do if someone gently let him see inside him? Someone... Someone who could reveal to him, perhaps love, or lust, or attraction? What a terrible situation that would be, don't you think? To love when you believe that nothing can come of it, or to sense attraction with your entire body and feel like a fool for it."

At this, Kareem stared at her intently, forgetting all his woes and feeling pity for the Grand Eunuch. It was absurd to feel pity for such a great man. If anything, he had long envied the admiral...ah, but the admiral could not sire children. What Shahrzad was saying made sense. Kareem was confused.

"Do you understand what I'm saying, Kareem?"

"I am not sure..."

"Well I was thinking that should there be a woman who loved Zheng He...then...she would perhaps be the saddest woman of all. And not as a result of his limitations, Kareem, not at all! What I am saying is that this man may hurt her, but only to avoid facing himself. It is self-preservation. He would prefer to reject her than to face his own shortcomings."

"Surely the admiral is not so cruel..."

"He is not a monster, Kareem, just a wounded man. And that is one way he protects himself. I have been thinking for many days. I've not slept much, Kareem, it's terrible."

"Why torture yourself?"

"Ah, wait. There is something else. Do you remember several moons ago when we boarded and the admiral took away a box from one the crew members?"

Kareem nodded. "I remember. It belonged to that indigenous woman."

"Yes, the ship's lead seamstress."

"He had her luggage confiscated..."

"Yes. The rules on board specify that he should have opened the box to reveal its contents. But instead, he confiscated it. Do you realize why he did this?"

"I heard what you told him, Shahrzad. You do have a way of making others self-conscious, my dove."

"True. But only in the instance where they have something to hide..."

She was silent for a moment. Kareem knew nothing of what she had heard and seen in Beijing's palace.

"He knew he was trespassing on that woman's secret. He knew this just as *he guards his own.* And then as we walked off, he must have felt guilty. I know this because he could have given the box to one of his officers. Instead he carried it away to the safety of his own cabin! It's still there! I saw it today when I followed him to the bridge."

"By the Hand of Fatimah..."

"Strange box that one. I saw him glance at it many times before he rushed out."

"Are you sure it is the same object, Eye of my Life?"

"It is the same box. There are not many like it. And there it was, among his things when I was trying to talk to him this morning. He kept brushing me off...you know, the usual. Well, I admit I did not make easy conversation. But the box distracted him, Kareem. That box and whatever is in it was the very thing that drove him into the cabin because I can tell you right now that he had little to do once he entered it!"

Kareem raised himself from the bed. "Are you sure of this?"

Shahrzad nodded.

"Do you think he's opened it?" he asked, his eyes aglow with wonder.

"I don't know. But it and whatever it contains, are not the reasons why I pondered over the incident. Don't you see? The man is proud, Kareem! He knows he's done the wrong thing by that seamstress but he can't give the box back now. He, of all people, would lose face. He'd feel shame for having taken it in the first place. Ah, but that box torments him. It does." She reflected on this. "Perhaps for more reasons than one..."

"Pride is in all men, Shahrzad."

"It is more than pride. You forget that it is a eunuch we are speaking of. Eunuchs who fall in love may suffer from pride all the more."

"You are troubling yourself, my sweet." He sat beside her on the canopied bed, pulling her close to his chest.

"I have been thinking, you know, about the one thing that could save him," she said.

"Hush..."

"One more thing and I promise I will let you read your wonderful book of magic tales. Oh, Kareem, my Kareem, you must think I'm mad. But people are my mystery and that journey has been most enriching. The only thing that will save Zheng He..."

"Yes?"

"It is perhaps absurd..."

"What?"

"Well...What if someone could reach the child that lives in him? Soothe the child..."

For reasons that will elude you, honored reader, Shahrzad's words made Kareem wince. Speechless, he reclined against the cabin wall, still holding his beloved. He caressed her hair as though every stroke sealed their understanding.

Chapter 32
Ku'Li Nights

Huang-Fu was a happy man. Two days before reaching Ku'Li, he, along with thirty other low life crew members, were approached by one of the battalion commanders. They assembled in a cabin where an officer handed them a modest allowance and a briefing.

The instructions were simple. They were to report the Folangji or any foreigners who expressed undue curiosity about the Ming fleet.

"If you see one, do not hesitate. Report him immediately," stressed the battalion commander while the men picked their noses and rubbed their taut chests, eager to rejoin land. On the question of what these Folangji looked like, the naval officer frowned. Unlike the admirals, he had never truly known a Folangji. What he did know sprang from rumors of the most ill-informed sorts.

"They have sickly white skin," he replied as though it were obvious.

Huang-Fu glanced at his companions with a bemused expression.

"They are hairy," continued the naval officer. Huang-Fu thought him ridiculous. "And they stink!" added the officer, before spitting on the floor.

If at first his strange assignment perplexed Huang-Fu, he shrugged it off. He was not about to ruin his chances. Why, this was the opportunity of a lifetime! He would be free to explore the famed port of Ku'Li and let loose his recently curtailed pleasure seeking habits. Anything was better than his occupation aboard the fleet.

Attached to Zhou Man's treasure ship and reporting to a rude boatswain who liked nothing better than scream orders to give himself importance, Huang-Fu spent his days bent over the most wretched, menial jobs. He scrubbed the decks clean, emptied chamber pots and regularly threw buckets of amassed dung overboard. Often he was sent to the eight-masted horse ships where he had little choice but to endure the smell of horse dung all day.

He had found life on a Ming treasure ship worse than any sweaty whorehouse in Tanggu. He was well fed but slept in the balmy, filthy lower decks. He felt dirty at all times. The salt in his hair and on his body reviled him.

And worse, he missed eating chicken meat. Aboard the Ming fleet, all chicken stock was reserved for interpreting omens.

"I tell you what, Ping," he told his friend. "If those bastards feed me fish balls one more night, I'm going to eat that horse dung."

But the fish kept coming and Huang-Fu resigned himself. The greatest injury was that he was confined at sea as punishment for gambling yet it was common knowledge that all crew members gambled on board. Cards, dice, the fleet was a floating gambling den! Huang-Fu conceded that the stakes here were much lower since beads and shells were used instead of money but he was resentful nevertheless. Nothing made much sense to him. He felt like a slave ripped from his life. And he missed the streets, missed scouring the dark alleys, climbing up the thatched roofs lining the port and leaping on unsuspecting debtors.

He longed for the thrill of his previous life. He wanted to be back on land where he felt in control of his life, safe from the threatening waters that surrounded him daily.

So when the officer explained that Admiral Yang Bao was seeking men with knowledge of port life, he had leapt at an opportunity to regain solid ground. When I reach the shore, I'll kiss the ground, he thought.

And finally, they arrived in Ku'li. Huang-Fu watched as the sailors busied themselves to the windlasses on the rigging deck. They worked in groups at the main sail, raising the lowest bamboo spar so that it stood almost erect against the towering mast. On the treasure ship, folding over the main lugsail was no easy feat as this one weighed a good five tons. While Huang-Fu contemplated the rigging crew, still, others dropped the mooring anchors at the stern and bow. Already, shuttles had been sent to shore to carry back supplies of fresh water.

Standing on the upper deck, Huang-Fu had a sweeping view of what seemed like a sprawling mass of foreign carriers. The sights and smells, blanketed by the intense heat were nothing short of oppressing. He had never seen anything like this. During the journey from Melaka, he had made enquiries and learned that Ku'Li was the Indian Ocean's most important port, the land of the wealthy Zamorins who extended their legendary hospitality to the Ming fleet.

No sooner had they moored that the Zamorin merchants, proud to be back on their fabled land, bustled about on the upper deck to organize guest houses, courtesans and servants. The envoys were overjoyed. These generous invitations promised to make their Ku'Li stop more enjoyable.

Huang-Fu descended along a rope ladder at the gangplank and found an algae-matted seat in a rocking barge. Gripping tight to the rim of the boat, he watched in apprehension as the barge became packed with his fellow recruits. He wondered how many could board before the vessel sank.

When they reached the shore, they were all staring, overwhelmed by the sights. "Look there!" exclaimed one of them. Their eyes riveted to the landing deck where merchants from Zheng He's treasure ship were disembarking. Near naked slaves with fully grown beards attended them. The black slaves now raised parasols over the wealthy men's heads.

Huang-Fu was astonished. He scanned the port. There were dark men everywhere. They crowded the harbor, unloading and carrying cargo crates and other goods from the ships' holds and leading them to the warehouses. These men went around almost naked with only a bandage-like cloth, wrapped around their waist and dangling to their knees.

Along the shores, were a gaggle of warehouses established by the Ming officers. According to what he'd heard, Admiral Zheng He had already organized his brigadiers to escort all trade cargo to those large buildings.

More here than in the Port of Guangdong, Huang-Fu discerned many foreign tongues. The translators were barely keeping up with what was being said and to whom. Each group of merchants was to be escorted by a translator yet as Huang-Fu was soon to discover, translators were not needed in Ku'Li's marketplace.

"Where are the inns around here?" asked one of the youths, eyeing the port with greedy expectation.

Another gripped his crotch.

"I could lick a lotus foot right about now!" he boasted, grinning from ear to ear.

"Lotus feet will be hard to find in these parts. Besides, you've only got a few coins, don't squander them!" mocked Huang-Fu. He had already spotted a promising tavern not far from the warehouses.

Bored by the rudimentary life on the fleet, they decided that a squandering was in order.

They did not speak a word of Malayalam but it did not matter. After forming groups of three to five, they scattered towards various parts of the port, jeering and singing as though the mere act of being in a foreign place absolved them from good conduct.

What a joyous picture! When the sun had set, Huang-Fu swam in a rapturous state. Roaring with laughter, he was sprawled on multi-colored silk cushions, betting on his fifth card game in the hearty company of a raucous bunch of sailors who, equally ravished by sweet ale, fondled willing tavern girls with glee.

What an adventure, what bliss! Huang-Fu did miss the narrow, ill-kept streets of Tanggu where he had whiled away seedy nights and consumed ale in many a shady inn. But Tanggu offered nothing compared to Ku'Li's immense warehouses, its pulsating esplanades and its intense, cosmopolitan nights.

After a splendid night on the port, Huang-Fu rose in the late morning. His head still throbbing, he set off to visit the town center.

There, he stood, transfixed at the majesty of the opulent Zamorin palaces.

Huang-Fu sighed. The envoys were no doubt indulging in the comfort of these huge mansions. After a formal greeting by the Shah Bandar, they would have been escorted to their rooms and invited to a lavish, welcoming banquet. For him there would be no such luxury. Nor was there a guest house waiting for him alongside the beach, on the fine Silk Street. It was in one such guest house that Admiral Zheng He was no doubt sheltered in preparation for his official diplomatic visit to the Zamorin ruler.

The second night, after wasting all his money on drink and the pleasure of a kiss from one of the tavern whores, Huang-Fu found shelter near one of the warehouses. Due to the pervasive pepper dust floating around the building, he sneezed all night long. Long before dozing off, he spent a good time musing about the man who commanded the fleet.

Huang-Fu had never seen the Grand Admiral but he knew that he was well known and respected on the ships. A few soldiers had regaled him with tales of the admiral's bravery at the Zheng dyke and how this unknown castrate had proved himself worthy of a new title and become the emperor's loyal admiral. Huang-Fu liked the story very much.

The following afternoon, abandoned by his joyous companions, he lay there, wondering what to do with his day and how to survive on the few taels he had left. He was soon joined by a contingent of soldiers from one of the escort ships. They were assigned to guard Ming rice, porcelain and silk merchandise from thieves.

"I thought the Zamorin port was a secure port," riled Huang-Fu.

"Sometimes," said the soldier lighting a cigarette. "But you can never be too careful in these parts, dumbass."

Huang-Fu nodded.

"Are you stranded here?" asked the guard, puffing in Huang-Fu's face much to this one's irritation.

"Stranded? No, I am on an important mission for the admirals," lied Huang-Fu. He proudly waved his letter of appointment in the soldier's face. The soldier shrugged.

"What do you mean by stranded?" asked Huang-Fu, folding the paper away under his tunic.

"Didn't they teach you anything? Whenever it rains, here, in the afternoon, nobody can board the ships. Haven't you noted the way the sea churns later in the day?"

"I did notice that nobody is boarding now."

"No. It's like this every day, you nit," replied the officer with a superior air. "You can't board at this time. The sea current is too violent. The crew do all their disembarking and embarking before the mid-afternoon. After that, nobody on land can return to the ships and no one on board disembarks."

"And why ever not?"

"Cause it's dangerous, is why. But that's what makes Ku'Li such a safe harbor."

"I don't understand," frowned Huang-Fu. "That doesn't seem very safe."

"Thicker than a bamboo pole, you are. It's simple. Pirates cannot operate in turbulent seas either. All ships are anchored out some distance from the shore. Doesn't matter where they're from, they just have to wait. Anyone who ventures out in this mad current is just crazy. You're not thinking of trying anything are you?"

"I have no reason to," replied Huang-Fu moving away from the bad-tempered soldier.

The next morning, after stealing some garlic-flavored flat bread to quell his gnawing hunger, Huang-Fu toured the bustling spice market. He was astounded to see foreigners from many parts including Arabs, Indians, Malays and Ming traders. It was the Arabs, they told him, who drove Ku'Li's trade. They were powerful and came from all parts, including Yemen, Persia, Oman and other East African states.

As he entered the marketplace, gorged with goods and crowded with people from all over the world, he stared in dismay. From afar, he recognized a man that he had heard called Kareem. He remembered him as the Arab envoy who often visited the horse ship with a veiled woman. The officers would organize a barge to escort the couple from the treasure ship and onto the horse ship. Once aboard, the veiled woman would work herself into a frenzy, wanting to see the merchandise. Huang-Fu would often let them feed the stallions destined for the Sultan of some Arab state whose name he could not remember.

Now as Huang-Fu watched, this Kareem had taken a towel from one of the side pockets in his garb and right in the middle of the Market Square, he was now immersed in a strange ritual. Huang-Fu squinted. The Arab clasped a spice merchant's hand. All the while, both men maintained their hands locked under the cloth, away from view. It did not take the puzzled Huang-Fu long to notice that everyone in the marketplace took part in this peculiar ritual. A voice rose behind him.

"Confused?"

It was one of the older lieutenants taking a break from his escort duties. During the trip to Ku'Li, Huang-Fu had played a game of Ma Diao Pai with him a few times.

"I am Deng," said the lieutenant. "Remember me? We shared that horny concubine on board a couple of nights ago? A great night...we should do it again sometime. Three is better company than two."

"Oh yes, a fun night... Deng, what is all this? What are they doing?"

"Oh, that. It takes a while to get used to. But I've been here a couple of times," Deng said proudly. "These are secret finger codes."

"Never seen that before. How does it work?"

"Well it depends. See that cinnamon trader over here? He has his own rules. Let's see, if I were to offer him four pepper grains for one sack of his cinnamon, I would have to grab four of his fingers and tug at them. But if I only wanted to offer three, I would only grab three fingers. The bargaining rules vary based on the merchandise and the trader."

Huang-Fu fixated Kareem, unconvinced. "Looks strange..."

"But it works! These merchants are clever. They stand there with their fingers locked under the towel and they make faces at each other...Just look, their expressions are so subtle that unless you come here every day, you would not understand what they mean. You'd have to be very smart to know what they have agreed upon. That's the idea. You should never gain an unfair trading advantage by knowing what others are up to, keeps everyone honest."

"That's amazing...they hardly speak to each other..."

"Brilliant, isn't it? Everyone can trade here. You don't need to know the language. That's the best thing about Ku'Li, save from low Zamorin taxes of course. It's your first time?"

"First time," replied Huang-Fu, growing weary of his mission.

"Well, don't get lost. There are two Jammu mosques not far from the bazaar. Keep a look out for them if you don't know where you are. That'll get you back on track. Let me know if there is anything I can help you with. By the way, if you're up to it, I know this great inn! It's right behind the Ming guest houses near the edge of the city...the best Indian courtesans pay regular visits. You'd love it!"

Huang-Fu pursed his lips. There was something about Deng that made him uneasy.

"Thank you but no," he replied, belying his last three nights spent in debauchery. "Tell me, if I was after a group of Folangji, where could I find them?"

"Folangji? Sorry, I don't know. There are not many of them."

Huang-Fu looked around with an expression of doom. He was surrounded by a maze of hefty spice-filled bags, agitated merchants engaging in secret finger codes or gesticulating in the local tongue. He needed to quench his unbearable thirst... He would have welcomed a good drink.

"Why are you after them anyway?" interrupted the young lieutenant.

"Oh, I have a message from...from Zheng He," lied Huang-Fu.

"Is that right?" The lieutenant scrutinized him. "Well, I'd best be off. My break is almost over. See you tonight if you're game!"

When the soldier had left, Huang-Fu escaped the market. There was, to be sure, a lot more fun to be had if only he was free to explore beyond the center.

After wandering aimless for another hour in the main part of the city, he decided to relent and meet Deng at the inn. On his merry way to the port, he turned a corner beside a colorful fruit stand and glimpsed a shining light. It caught his attention at once. So too, did the forceful giggling as a young girl ran into the alley.

He peered into the narrow passage only to be met by a smile, a set of white pearls on a bronze face. It was the darkest girl he'd ever seen. Adorning her delicate form were swirls of color and silver. She wore a close fitting brocade shirt that exposed her taut midriff. A pink gauze fabric was draped tight around her body such that its embroidered edge looped across her left shoulder and trailed behind her back. He noticed the tiny mirrors embroidered in her dress and understood that it was the sun's reflection that had first caught his eye.

The Hindu girl was still smiling but as he approached, she eclipsed herself and merged with the crowd. Huang-Fu set off to chase her. He followed her more from curiosity than because of a familiar ache in his loins. In his eagerness, he did not see the giant man signal to his accomplice as the two bolted after him into the narrow alley.

Huang-Fu continued after the mysterious girl, running past several stone archways. He looked up at the cramped terraces above. He'd entered some world he knew nothing of. As they reached a corner, she paused. She pressed her tiny hand against one of the house's worn walls. Then she batted her long lashes and smiled again. He shook his head.

"Alright, I get it. So all this time, you knew I was following you..."

She giggled, hiding her teeth with her hand.

"I am Huang-Fu! What's your name?" he said, pointing to himself and then to her. "Huang-Fu," he repeated. She stopped laughing and flitted like a bird into a side alley. Huang-Fu followed her down a sloped path into yet more labyrinthine streets.

He forgot everything and plunged deep into the city. He glimpsed the two large men who eyed him from afar but he did not recognize them. To Huang-Fu, they all looked the same those dark men, the darkest men he had ever seen. No sign of the Folangji here, he remarked with a tinge of irony. Here too, the stately Muslim merchants in their magnificent robes were nowhere to be seen. Huang-Fu had been told that most of the Arabs had larger estates and farms further into the countryside. Here, in the town's cramped alleyways, Hindus went about bare-chested, some with their long beards reaching down to their navel.

He wondered how far the port was from here and whether he might be able to regain the ship early enough to make his unfruitful report and obtain a reprieve. But he was fascinated by his new surroundings. Those narrow streets were a different world. One could get lost just like in Tanggu. He stopped to catch his breath. He desperately needed a drink...

The girl waved at him.

No matter how many times she ran away, he pursued, delighted with the effect she had on his body. He felt the pulsation under his pants and a delicious notion invaded his mind. He realized that he had only ever bedded women from his own country. Mostly whores, he conceded. There had been a few porcelain-skinned treasures but he'd paid a huge sum for those. And women were far more appetizing on land, he thought, remembering his cramped encounters with the drunken concubine in the lower decks.

The Hindu girl liked teasing him. It pleased him. He imagined himself kneading her delicious brown breasts. He licked his parched lips before another sweet thought. There lay the young girl, her honeyed legs slightly parted, her hair unfurled on red silk sheets. In his vision, she was smiling and beckoning him with her toned arms. Then, he was standing before her, flashing his eager member between her tanned thighs and pushing himself inside her, furious with desire.

The sound of a closing door dissolved his fantasy. Leaning against the wall, he paused to catch his breath then stared at a blue door. She'd gone in, it seemed.

He hesitated. He could no longer see the Jammu mosque now. He had no idea where he was. It seemed he'd found the local district. It was a world apart from the cosmopolitan Ku'Li that catered for the travelers and merchants. This was the real Ku'Li.

Above him were rows of colorful tattered drapes competing for space on cramped terraces. Spicy scents from some upstairs kitchen mixed with effusions of burning incense. The muggy mist of the bustling marketplace was gone. It was cooler here.

And save from the muffled Muslim chants that he could still discern, and the happy echoes of children playing nearby, it was quiet.

He pressed a hand against the blue door, still deciding what to do. He had no time to think. The blue panes swiveled open. Two giant arms emerged, seized him against his will and hurled him inside.

Chapter 33
The Spy from Ku'Li

The sweetness of burning incense teased his nostrils, luring him away from his dreams. Huang-Fu watched the swollen breasts fade into darkness. He heard the distinct sound of a frying pan in the background and awoke to an oppressing heat. There were voices too.

He blinked, lifting his head from the pink embroidered cushions. His lips were parched. He looked around. He was lying half-naked in a dim smoke-filled bedroom. Why, he couldn't remember. The blue sheets were soiled. It was sweat or something else. The room was filthy, its walls stained by grime and urine.

A colossal mustached Indian was leaning against the doorway. With his large, bulging eyes, he watched the canopy bed with expectation. The man had tucked his left thumb in the giant leather belt tied round his protruding belly. With the fat digits of his other hand, he preened his thick moustache.

Huang-Fu flipped to a sitting position. He stared through the faded red curtains.

"What happened to me?"

The stranger glared at him for a moment. Then he gestured to a shadow in the next room.

"What is it, Ekbal?" came a voice from behind.

"Bring the girl," said the mustached man.

Two stocky men moved into the bedroom. They presented the young girl. She looked exhausted. Huang-Fu remembered who she was.

The mustached man unfurled her sari to reveal three ferocious welts on her back.

"This is your doing," he croaked in broken Nanjing Hua.

Huang-Fu sat up. He rubbed his cloudy head, trying to recall, trying to assemble the pieces. He remembered nothing.

The mustached man they'd called Ekbal breathed heavily. He sat on a stool beside the bed and glowered at Huang-Fu.

"My men tell me you attacked her and tried to tear off her sari. And when she resisted, you stroke at her."

"What?"

Ekbal pointed a finger at him.

"Do you know what the penalty is for indecent behavior in the Zamorin lands? I could have you killed for this. The Arabs will not tolerate it! Neither will the Zamorin king!"

"But I did nothing..."

"My men followed you. They saw what you did. If your Ming ruler finds out about this he will castrate you. Or worse! Am I right?"

"You're wrong…"

"You're a criminal!"

"Look now, just listen. I saw her, yes, and then I ran after her but hey, I did not do anything! Your men are lying!"

"Says you. We will turn you into the authorities and let them decide."

"I did nothing!" protested Huang-Fu out of his wits.

He stared at the filthy bedroom understanding a little of the purpose it served but he had no recollection of even entering it. Let alone...

"She says you attacked her and my men saw you," repeated Ekbal, eyes bulging.

The mustached man now sifted through Huang Fu's belongings which lay scattered on the table.

"Card games? You play games, little Han? You like to take risks?"

Huang-Fu's heart thumped in his chest. He looked around for a weapon, anything.

"Yes, yes you do," continued the mustached man. "I know what kind of man you are. You're a trouble maker. That's why they took you aboard, am I right? They took you aboard because you are an idle man, or some criminal—"

"I'm no criminal!" spit Huang-Fu.

"Petty man without a life... I bet you were born in a stinking brothel somewhere in the most rotten part of the Middle Kingdom. You had nothing better to do than board a ship. They want you dead. They don't care if you make it or not."

"I'm no criminal, you son of a dog!"

The huge man laughed now. A vicious glow lit his round pupils.

"If you say so."

He sat back, observing Huang-Fu with a dark expression.

"See, men like you are the worse scum of the Middle Kingdom. They have to make their own rules, yes? Play their own games. That's the only way men like you can make it in life. Am I right?"

"Say whatever you like, you stinking boar. I'm leaving."

Huang-Fu sprang to his feet and bolted through the doorway. Ekbal signaled to his acolytes in the other room. The two men pounced and grabbed Huang-Fu by the shirt, forcing him back. He wrenched himself from their grip and stumbled to the ground. One of the men lunged forth to grab his ankles. The nimble Han flipped onto his palms landing a vigorous kick in the Indian's chin. The man cursed. Huang-Fu bounced up, evading the second man's fist. He ran to the front door, trying to unlock it. The door would not budge.

"Help!" he yelped. "Help me!"

They jiggled back onto their feet. He buckled under a blow, moaning and holding his jaw in place. Now they lifted him like a sack and held his arms back.

"Help!" he roared. But a vengeful row of steel knuckles silenced him instantly.

"Enough, enough. Take him in! Balraj, tie his hands. Good, very good. He won't be running away now."

They sat him down, his hands tied. Huang-Fu made a grimace and spat blood.

Ekbal leaned forward. Huang-Fu could smell his onion breath.

"Huang-Fu...that's your name isn't it? Don't let me do this to you again. You hear me? Don't try this again, understand? Or I'll kill you," he spat in a terrifying voice.

"Son of a bitch!" spit Huang-Fu.

"Ha ha, yes. You have spirit, little Han. Good. Very good. Listen, we can do business you and me."

"Swine!"

The giant man's hand clutched Huang-Fu's hair and tilted his head back with savage force.

"Now listen here, listen to me," warned Ekbal. "Is it true that the Ming have maps on board? Hey! Hey! Answer me!"

"What?"

"Tut... Don't play dumb with me," the man warned, giving Huang-Fu's head a good jerk. "I saw the papers you carry. You are a spy, yes?"

Huang-Fu closed his eyes with self-reproach and made a painful grimace.

"Answer me!"

"I have nothing to tell you."

"So you are a spy. See that, Balraj? Tut. Tut. Amazing what the Ming do to their own people. But that is good news for me. If they picked you for their dirty work, they must have their reasons. You are not so stupid as you look, little scum. They know that. I'll make you an offer."

"You devil..." replied Huang-Fu. "You tricked me and now you—"

"Careful. If you do what I say, I won't report you to the authorities. I'll let you go. But if you don't, see those two men here? This one is called Giri. You know why his name is Giri? Because he does not stop, he is like the mountain. And this one? Balraj. Strong as four men! Believe me, there is nowhere you can run in Ku'Li where they won't find you. And when they do... Tut, tut."

He shook his head to illustrate his point.

"I have bad evidence against you, little man. The Ming will not like what you have done. They are proud and arrogant, your people. They won't stand that you caused them to lose face. They'll let you rot here rather than put up with any more nonsense from a scum like you. You're just one man in many. No one they'll miss. They can pick up any one from their jailhouses to replace you. Yes? You know what I am saying, yes?"

"I'll kill you!"

The huge man roared with laughter.

"I'll make a deal with you. You get me as many maps as you can and I'll let you go. I swear this to you now, you'll go free as soon as you get me those maps."

"I don't know what you are talking about," protested Huang-Fu.

"The Ming maps. I want them!" thundered Ekbal.

"I've never seen those maps. I don't even know what they look like..."

"Don't you worry, little Han. *There is a spy on board your fleet who does.* All the spy needs is an accomplice to get them safety onshore. That's a start, isn't it? You will meet tomorrow morning, on the docks. My men will bring you there and show you the agreed meeting place."

Huang-Fu shook his forlorn head.

"You have the wrong man."

"Oh, no, no, no. I have the right man, little Han. You think I just picked you out of chance? Is that what you think? My men have been following you since you set foot on the port. For a Ming chump you are very sturdy on your feet. You'll think of something. You know, it's very rare that one of your crew men ventures as far as this district. But you did. You're not easily scared off. And you trust your instincts. That's good!"

"I got lost."

"Whatever you say. But it worked out very well for both of us."

"Not for me! You're a devil!"

"Yes, you would think that. But I see it differently. Someone has to take charge when the Zamorin rulers are naive and corrupt. I'm sick of those swine Arab merchants running my country. This is our land! Our land, you hear!"

He beat at his chest with every word.

"What are you planning to do with those maps?"

"Curious boy, aren't you? No, no, that's a very good. Shows you are thinking," he said, tapping his own head, "and that I was right about you. Well now, you see, I happen to know someone who will pay me a fortune for them."

"For maps?"

"The Ming know more about the world than anyone else. Now, I know nothing about sea travel but the Ming...ha! They have sea passages all mapped out and those sea passages are exactly what the foreigners want."

"The foreigners? Who?" asked Huang-Fu, suddenly suspicious.

Ekbal's eyes narrowed.

"You should know. The Ming call them Folangjiiii!"

He roared with laughter.

"Why is everyone so obsessed with these Folangji?" asked Huang-Fu.

"Durga knows I hope that you and I will live long enough to see them come."

"Come?"

"The men who will get rid of those filthy Arabs for us! Durga knows I hope to see that day!"

"You're crazy! This is crazy!"

"I tell you what's crazy, you stupid Han. The Arabs have mansions...private courtyards...ships, jewels! Tut. Look at this! Look at this shit hole! The Zamorin king doesn't see. He eats their words, the Arabs, the Ming...he eats all their words!"

"That's not my problem."

"You have no choice! You will do what I say. And if you don't come back, little Han, I will turn in this paper, your game cards and your name to the authorities."

"Get on those ships, huh... Now where have I heard that before," lamented Huang-Fu.

"Get up! Remember, I've got your papers and my men are watching you. Don't do anything stupid. You're dead if you do."

***

Ragged, bruised and his mouth parched, Huang-Fu sat behind a large warehouse, pondering gloomily over his fate. Giri and Balraj had retreated but he knew they were still there, watching him. They'd pounce on him if he tried anything.

He buried his face in his knees and waited for the contact. Swarms of buzzing flies pestered him. His clothes were filthy from yesterday's chase in the Hindu district. He had ripped his tunic during the wrestle with Ekbal's two men. They had his papers. He was at the mercy of thugs. And he was in a foreign land.

He eyed the port nervously, pondering over the deal. All he had to do was hand over the maps to Ekbal and they would return his papers. In exchange, they would drop their accusations. It seemed easy enough. But no matter what the Ming naval officers had done to him, he did not relish the idea of stealing imperial property. It smelled like treason.

"I had expected someone much older," said a voice beside him.

Huang-Fu stared. His eyes traveled up the long robe and into the sun's glaring rays as he tried to identify the shadow before him.

"Follow me into the warehouse," continued the voice. "We have only six days before the fleet departs. There is much to do."

Huang-Fu raised himself to his feet, still looking at the figure. He realized why the voice had startled him. He had heard it numerous times on board. And he recognized those eyes.

They crept inside an empty fruit warehouse. Even in the dim light, Huang-Fu could clearly see the spy. He shuddered.

"Now listen carefully," said this one, handing Huang-Fu a bundle of clothes. "They are five treasure ships from which navigation commands issue. There are then five map sets including starmaps. Put this on."

"You want me to dress as a soldier?"

"Quiet. I need you to have a solid reason to be on the bridge. No one will recognize you in that tunic. When you are done, put this cloak on."

Huang-Fu obeyed. It seemed that somewhere in the barbarian lands, there were people who would pay for those cursed maps? What a crazy world. What would it mean for the Ming fleet? What would Admiral Zheng He do if he knew that one of his crewmen, a petty gambler, had given maps away to the Folangji?

"We will take to the barges during the afternoon," said the spy.

"But it's too dangerous! The current—"

"Shut up! I know what I'm doing. The men will not expect intruders in those conditions. One by one, we will board the treasure ships and I will tell you what to look for. You'll sneak in, take the map and give them to me to hide in my cabin. When we're done, I shall find Ekbal and retrieve your papers."

There was a pause. Huang-Fu felt a mounting tightness in his throat. His heart raced. He had recognized the spy now. There was a sinking feeling in his chest as he realized the enormity of the situation. His accomplice was the last person they would ever suspect of treachery.

"And what do you get in return?" he asked, feeling terribly small.

There was a pause.

"Satisfaction," spit the spy.

"How much are the Folangji paying you?" continued Huang-Fu with reproach.

"You think money is what I am after? You poor simpleton! Now you listen to me. You try to tell Admiral Zheng He what you've seen today and I'll kill you. Is that understood?"

Huang-Fu nodded. He moved to a crate and hid, his limbs trembling as he changed into the uniform, discarding his dirty clothes. Still shaking, he followed the tall figure out of the warehouse and towards the barges.

Even if I tried to tell Admiral Zheng He about this, he realized, he would not believe me. In fact, he thought, reflecting on the spy's identity, no one would.

Chapter 34
Old Yu's Diary - Part Two

Time does pass so very quickly. We had but left Ku'Li that we already moored in Eastern African shores. Gone are some of the Arab envoys. Gone with them is the amber they left in their wake as they strolled like kings on the decks in their gilded garbs. Gone are their honeyed voices and their strange guttural utterances. They've regained their homes, leaving only memories of their stay among us. And memories do make one reflect.

I must apologize for my last entry. I said some awful words about the Omani woman. I don't regret any of them of course. Despite the fact she has now rejoined her home in Zanzibar, the unfavorable impression she made lingers until today.

Our giant ship has elegant but cramped lanes all along its decks. On a number of occasions I've felt watched. She would linger on the lower decks and pass my cabin to observe my work. It made me uneasy. All the more because she was always veiled save when in the presence of the other ladies. It was frightening at times to see this looming figure behind me.

She befriended none of the women on board. In fact, unlike the other women who congregated and sang songs, she preferred to remain alone, often shutting herself inside her cabin. Well, that is, when she was not creeping around putting her nose everywhere.

Come to think of it, I do remember that once, she awoke one of the interpreters only to hold a discussion with one of the Guangdong concubines. The two women were in conversation for hours and I hear that the interpreter blushed and fumed with embarrassment as they carried on. What possible questions could she have asked? I shudder.

And I remember that no sooner had we reached Ku'Li that our Omani lady, as we like to call her, declared that she would undertake a reconnaissance tour and that due to social rules governing her behavior, that she was going to need a male escort, so could not one of the ambassadors join her? Due to the unruly waters so frequent in this port, her fiancé was ill on that day and I was sent for him. Needless to say, a combination of excess *yang* and heat, just as I suspected...

To this request, she added that she would require the services of two interpreters for an undefined period of time. Of that, she was very specific. Oh, so not just one interpreter but two! And would you believe that our honorable admiral himself was incapable of refusing? It is a wonder we do not have an entire fleet at her disposition.

Following this imperious demand, which was met with little fuss, the veiled lady disappeared for hours. I insist that we remained a fortnight in Ku'Li and during the entire period of our visit to the port, she was nowhere to be seen.

No one knows where she went. When she returned and Zheng He, relieved that no harm had come to her, politely enquired about her little escapade, she ignored him and shut herself in her cabin as if nothing had happened. Who understands that woman?

Aside from her betrothed, who I admit is a delightful and good humored man, one of the most pleasant Arabs I have ever met—and I have met quite a few during our travels—the admiral is perhaps the only person who can converse with her.

But I am getting carried away with myself and giving the wrong impression. It is not so much shyness on her part that prevents her from engaging with others. It is conceit. That woman is fixated on an idea, or perhaps an objective. I once attributed her behavior to uncurbed selfishness. It was easy to make that judgment. But I like to keep an open mind.

There were a few things I had already begun to notice by the time we approached Malindi. Officially, I hear she speaks only Arabic and Persian. She has vague notions of our Nanjing dialect but I have evidence that her understanding is more profound than what she ever reveals. Of that I am certain!

Days before we moored in Malindi, one of the translators who assists me with cataloguing new herbs, overheard her speak with

Kareem on the upper deck. The translator found the conversation so curious that he shared it with me over dinner.

I will record what was said later. The seamstress has promised to resume her tale today. I am looking forward to hearing more. I am certain the admiral will also attend our little gathering. He showed me the embroidered cloth she gave him. I think he is mesmerized. Aren't we all?

Chapter 35
Chantefable Three: The Trader

Jun was not there. It was early afternoon and the portside upper deck, still wet from this morning's scrubbing was near empty. The admiral dismissed his guards and waited for the seamstress to arrive in the gardens as agreed. He glanced towards the lower deck, hoping to see a glimpse of her. Would she come today?

Eager for some entertainment, a crowd of officers approached. Seeing the admiral pace nervously, they looked at each other with bemused faces. Zheng He moved to a seat and pretended to observe the flower banks. His discomfort was short lived; Old Yu strolled up towards them.

"Early today," remarked the physician as he lit his pipe.

Zheng He tilted his head but refused to answer.

Old Yu smiled.

"And it is a lovely day today, isn't it? Pity a quarter of the crew is ill."

"A nasty epidemic," replied Zheng He, "but so far, I am still on my feet."

"And let's hope your luck holds, then. Ah, and what luck this is. Here she comes!"

A short woman with a blue cap and dark braided hair advanced towards the gardens, much to everyone's delight.

"And what surprises have you for us, today?" asked a coy officer, mirroring the anticipation they all felt.

The Southern woman smiled. She approached the gathering, beckoning everyone to come closer. The admiral's eyes lit up. He held his breath. No one spoke. They waited.

First she closed her eyes and stood among them, collecting her thoughts for a moment. Now she opened her eyes, gazing ahead, seeing but not seeing, ready to transport them into the world they longed to visit, a world of storytelling. And she began, in her strong voice.

Storyteller, storyteller, will you tell us more about this Bei Lan and the wise Jamma?

I will tell you, honored listener, about the day Bei Lan met Sonam.

In the village there existed an old man who lived not far from the Black Dragon Pool. Bei Lan soon learnt that he was the Dongba priest and that most of the villagers paid him their respect. He was their wise man.

The Mu family who ruled Nonguzhi, encouraged the villagers to show their allegiance to the Dongba priest. Sometimes Jamma went along with her friends to Bengshi village. This was the white sand old town from where the Ma clan once ruled. In Bengshi, the Ming had since built temples and the people prayed there regularly. They walked the distance in the morning and departed before nightfall.

But Bei Lan soon noticed that Jamma never saw the Dongba priest nor did she take part in his rituals or bother making the journey to Bengshi. It was hardly because Jamma refused to make the journey due to her old age, or lack of sight. She could have ridden to Bengshi on horseback. She could have.

But not only did Jamma remain stubbornly in Nonguzhi while her friends journeyed to Bengshi, she even considered the Dongba to be a charlatan and a thief.

"So you are a not a Buddhist then," asked Bei Lan one day, a little confused.

"Perhaps I am, and perhaps not," replied Jamma. "Would it matter?"

"I thought perhaps you disagreed with the Dongba's ways and...What I meant to ask is – where are you from? I see that sometimes, you dress in a blue apron like the Nakhi women and yet at other times, you wear a white skirt. I also notice that you do not visit the Dongba priest like they do."

"I've no wish to see those old men rub yak butter on my forehead. I don't need their blessings to go about my work."

"So you are not from here? All town folks save for the Hans follow the Dongba."

"Curious, are you? My people lived in Lugu Lake. I am not a Nakhi. Not the same thing! But we Mosuo, Nakhi and Bai people all have the same ancestors. We all come from the North West.

"Where is that?" asked Bei Lan, her eyes glowing with curiosity.

"Far. It is a long journey. I do not go there myself. But I will return there someday."

"What do you reproach the priest?" asked Bei Lan, hoping she would wrest an answer after having distracted Jamma.

"Nothing," spit Jamma.

The young woman began to brood. Jamma noticed that perhaps Bei Lan was used to hearing answers. She softened.

"I would have to go back many years ago to explain. And you would not understand. Before the priests, it was different. We had spirits, animal spirits."

"Animal spirits..."

"It is too complicated. And does it really matter? I will die soon anyway and then...there will be nothing left."

"What do you mean?"

They arrived in the Market Square when suddenly the old woman squinted and her ears seemed to rise on the side of her head as though to better capture sounds in the distance.

"Hush... Here, I want you to meet someone. I can hear his horse. Ah! There he is."

The conversation came to an abrupt end, much to Bei Lan's frustration. Jamma led them both to the same tanned horseman that had visited the village the month before. It was the very man her friends had been laughing about.

And what a man he was, honored listener.

As the two women approached, he sat idly on his saddle, his long auburn hair tossed over powerful shoulders. His lean frame stood firm despite the mellow sway of his mount.

He had about him, an air of agility and foresight. His features were sharper and darker than those of the Nonguzhi villagers. With skin as brown as *nanmu*, he must have stood a little taller than Bei Lan. But unlike her lithe frame, his limbs were as strong and taut as his U-Tsang mount.

As they neared, he tug at his reins and inclined his broad chest to greet them. Bei Lan saw, round his noble neck, a colored thread from where a jade pendant mounted on a silver disk hung proudly between tanned collarbones. But no adornment could compare in beauty with the man's long hair. Burnt to a warm mahogany by the mountain sun, it fell loose past his shoulders where it caressed the soft woolly curls of his vest. Beneath the rider's leather pants, Bei Lan noted how his tense limbs embraced the horse's flanks. She was horrified.

"This is Sonam," smiled Jamma, once she had confirmed the identity of the rider's horse with her fingers.

Bei Lan looked up. The young man's brows highlighted a raw, melancholy gaze. And in those black eyes were two tender lights glowing like primal moons. And how he stared...

"Hello Bei Lan."

"Hello..."

Jamma interrupted promptly.

"How was the journey?" she asked.

"Long. There was good weather. I have an advance of several days. I will remain here for six days before we leave."

Under Bei Lan's uncomfortable gaze, the old woman began to stroke the horse's mane.

"Have you anything for me," she asked. As she said this, she reached up and presented him with several taels. Sonam pocketed the coins and looked around him. He carefully reached down for his saddle bag and produced a tight bundle.

"It is fresh. The best from Pu'er. As old as you are, Jamma. The U-Tsang have never had better."

Jamma reached up to grab the tea parcel. Her fingers dug into the medicinal herbs. She wrinkled her pudgy nose, sniffed the tea and gave a satisfied grin. Then she hid the parcel in one of the many pockets of her blue apron.

"Stay then, Sonam. Bei Lan, why don't you take Sonam for some yak milk at the inn. I can make my own way home."

She tapped the young woman on the shoulder and added, "Sonam is a trader. He is tired from his journey. Keep him company." And before Bei Lan could protest, Jamma plodded home with her walking stick.

It took Bei Lan some time to overcome the shock of being with the stranger. The marketplace had soon filled up and there were other horsemen arriving today in Nonguzhi. Yet she had the sensation that she was alone with him.

He descended from his horse. She breathed something, not unlike incense, on his skin. She felt drawn to him in an alarming way and for a moment, she could not recall where the inn was.

He repeated his question, startling her from her thoughts.

"Oh, the inn... Yes, let's go this way. We will give your horse a drink too."

"So you are the newcomer," asked Sonam as Bei Lan organized a room for him.

She smiled quietly, moving to a table. He noticed her discomfort.

"I can see by your skin that you are not from here," he remarked, careful not to give her too much uninvited attention.

They sat at the inn and she ordered drinks for both of them. It was strange being with a man. She was not used to it. Under his seductive gaze, she was tempted to share everything – her real name, where she had come from and every single thought she had had since arriving in this foreign village – but she held her tongue.

Intrigued, Sonam saw Bei Lan smile as she placed her two hands delicately before her on the table. She was watching him eat.

"Jamma said that you are a trader. Where are you heading to?" she asked, finally.

"Lhasa."

"Is it...very far?"

He laughed at her question. His teeth were white and beautiful, like his entire face. He was a beautiful man. She remembered that she had never slept with a man. Not a single one. It was disorienting to be sitting with one of them. She felt dizzy.

***

On the ship, Jun's tale was interrupted by a furious protest. It was Old Yu. He had leapt from his stool with an alarmed expression and was now gesticulating, spectacles in hand.

"Now, now, where is this heading? On board tales ought not slip into debauchery!"

"Oh, you old fusser!" grunted one of the lieutenants as he slapped his own thigh.

"Let her finish! This is fun," enthused an officer.

"Please! Will you all be quiet!" shouted Zheng He. The urgency in the admiral's voice had startled them all. Much to Old Yu's surprise, Zheng He cleared his throat then gestured towards Jun, prompting her to resume.

"Everything is important to the story," explained Jun quietly.

"Is she going to reveal where she is from?" asked Old Yu.

"You will see," promised Jun. "But first, you must listen."

***

"Bei Lan."

She interrupted her thoughts only to see Sonam lean forth to mouth her name again. Her pulse quickened. She palmed her face to calm the rush of blood to her temples.

Sonam's quick eyes rested on her hands. He inferred that before settling in Nonguzhi, she had never worked in her life. His gaze seemed to bother her because she promptly hid her hands under the table. Then he noticed that she rubbed them across her lap as though wiping away something.

"Bei Lan. That's different. Is that your real name?"

"Yes...yes it is. Tell me," she asked, eager to change the subject, "what is it that you gave to Jamma?"

"It is tea. I am a tea-horse trader. Have you heard of them?"

"No. I see the riders often but I do not know what they do."

"I am surprised! You are in Nonguzhi. It is one of the stop points on the tea-horse route."

"I've not heard much about it," she admitted, a little embarrassed.

"Well, you see, there are many of us here. Muleteers, carriers, traders... I trade for the Ming," he added after hesitating. "They want good horses to fight the Mongols. Funny, isn't it?" he mused. "We U-Tsang people want tea to stay healthy. In exchange, we get the Ming all the horses they want. And so I make the journey to Lhasa to make the exchange."

"Where is Lhasa?"

"Far... In the Northwest. Very far from here," he said, gulping the yak milk and wiping his mouth with the back of his wrist.

She thought even this was the most sensual thing she had ever seen a man do.

"How long is your journey?" she asked.

Sonam observed her for a moment. Then he smiled and took out a little map that he held in one of his pockets. She eyed the map.

"Let's play a game, Bei Lan. I tell you three things about myself and you, you have to do the same. Is that fair?"

She shuddered at his directness. She pressed her hands to her lap and nodded.

"Why this game?" she asked.

"This way we trust each other. I like you," he said, surprised by the glow in her eyes.

"I like you too," she replied, meeting his gaze. Then she added, "That's one thing said already."

"Aha, you are a cunning one!" he laughed. He swept away one of the auburn strands from his face and unfolded the map, spreading it flat on the table. She distinguished names etched along a trail that stretched interminably, contouring what appeared to be a large mountain range and several rivers.

"This is us here," he said, pointing to a small spot beside a large mountain range. "And here, you would find Dali."

She nodded.

"So then...here comes another thing about me. Can I hold you to the rules of the game?"

She smiled. It was as if she had known him for years.

"Last month, I was here," he said, showing Pu'er. "This is where the good tea comes from. It grows in the six mountains. The tea leaves are fermented and compressed into those dark bricks you saw loaded on those yaks outside. Now, don't tell anyone this, but I sometimes handle an extra catty or two for Jamma. It is illegal. But she's an old friend."

"Is that it?" she laughed. "I was expecting more."

"I'm serious! It is illegal. Now, your turn..."

"...how is it illegal?"

Sonam frowned and replied in a mock injured tone. "This is no fair deal. I entrust you with some private information about my dealings with Jamma and you refuse to share the second thing about you."

He watched the alarm in her eyes.

"So come now, what is your real name?"

She shook her head vigorously.

"No, I can't tell you."

She paused. Sonam could see from her stiff movements and upright sitting position that she was taking this game far too seriously. At once, his expression changed from one of flirtation to one of concern. He did not want to be arrogant. And the last thing he wanted was to be accused of hassling her. But soon she was speaking again and her voice felt like a caress.

"I can tell you this," she shared. "Where I come from, I have never met a man like you."

He liked that. It was vague and she had not revealed much about herself but still, he liked that. It was all that mattered. There were both silent as their eyes met again.

"Now," she continued with a little more confidence. "Suppose we drop this game and you can teach me all about the tea-horse trade. It sounds fascinating... Is it dangerous?"

"Very. It is a very dangerous route. But I know it well."

"How many times have you done this?"

"Since I was a boy. I am from Zhongdian, very close to the U-Tsang border. My father's friends were in the trade. It was my father who first took me along one of his pilgrimages on the *chamadao*. These days, I begin the long trek from Pu'er. There, the mules and horses are loaded. Then I lead the men on. We continue past Dali until we reach Nonguzhi. Once in Nonguzhi, we rest and deal with the Ming eunuchs. They check our identity papers...they verify our loads, that sort of thing. After that, we continue on past Zhongdian, onto Deqin and finally, in U-Tsang."

"If it is a dangerous route, then why do you like it so much?" asked Bei Lan.

"Nothing else to do... I've no interest in being a priest... Besides, it's fun!"

He watched as the corner of her eyes slanted down beautifully with another warm smile.

"A priest? Who is asking you to be a priest?"

Sonam made a grim face. He finished his yak milk in one last draw. He gave the empty cup a pensive look before finally replying.

"My family are from a priest family. I was destined to be the next priest. It was my duty as my father's son. But I couldn't."

"Jamma does not like priests," volunteered Bei Lan.

"Well that's different. She's in competition with them."

"Jamma? In competition with the priests? What does that mean?"

"Never mind," dismissed Sonam. "But...anyhow, it's all true. My parents expected me to become a priest. I should have been a priest. I did not want to. So one morning, I saw a procession of traders, took off my ochre robe and I was off."

"You did that!"

"Yes, I changed my life. It takes a lot of courage to change one's life."

She nodded quietly. Sonam was still reflecting as he toyed with his yak milk goblet.

"I had been thinking about it for a while and one day it came to me – the thought of spending my life taking alms and leading the pilgrims like my father's done all his life, it frightened me. I much preferred riding horses through the *chamadao* and making a living."

She smiled again, wondering whether he had grown his hair so long as a protest against shaven heads.

"I know what you mean," she smiled. "I would not have liked to spend my life in a monastery either."

"Ah, yes that's another thing! I need open spaces! Closed doors do not suit me."

"Me neither," she replied with a sudden eagerness.

He watched her smile. He liked what she had said. He knew she kept a lot back but it did not bother him. There was much he had not told her either.

Soon after, Bei Lan paid the innkeeper and began to make her way back to Jamma's house. Her step was light and cheerful. She surprised him by turning back to wave at him as he led his horse to the stable. Then she appeared to blush before disappearing into the maze of streets.

He liked her. She was playful and could listen. But Sonam also knew, without being sure how, that like him, she was also sad inside. Perhaps he could see her sadness because it mirrored his.

He knew that his family was ashamed of him. His father, for one, had never forgiven him for failing to become a priest. Over the years, Sonam had learned to accept that he was no longer welcome in his father's home. The unpredictable *chamadao* kept his daredevil soul content for now but he longed to have his own family.

He wondered, though, what was Bei Lan's story? Who was she and where had she come from? His mind drifted to months ago when he had first asked Jamma about the young woman. No matter how much he had cajoled her, Jamma had revealed little of Bei Lan. She had only waved her stick to dismiss him. "Don't pester me, Sonam. If you really want to know, ask my daughter."

But Sonam knew that the Shaman had been gone for months now. He also remembered what Jamma had said. That she would never be back.

Later, as he lay naked on his mat, his hair spread around his pensive face, Sonam found himself pondering over the fair Bei Lan, long after the stars bejeweled the clear night sky.

Chapter 36
Conversation with Kareem

And now honored reader, let me share Shahrzad's confession to Kareem so that you may know more than Old Yu could ever tell you.

It began on a humid afternoon. The bamboo sails, taut under monsoon winds, carried the Ming fleet closer to the African shores. It was to moor at the port of Malindi and pass by Pemba Island.

It was Shahrzad who spoke first.

"There is something else I meant to tell you, Kareem. I can see a resemblance between you and San Bao, you know."

"What makes you believe that," Kareem mused, remembering her dark summation of the eunuch's personality. "I'm not at all cruel to you. Am I?"

"No, no. It's something else altogether. You see, the admiral is fond of stories. Would you believe it, Kareem? He is almost as entranced as you are with your book. Every three days, during his walk, he and the ship's senior research physician spend an awful amount of time listening to talk tales. From what I gather, they are lovely. They even rhyme at times. Why, that seamstress is very talented..."

Kareem ceased reading to contemplate her words.

"One must pass time, I suppose. The days are long. The admiral is not immune to boredom. Why should he not indulge in a little diversion? I do not see the resemblance."

"But...are you really bored, Kareem, or do you find yourself enthralled by *Hazar Afsanah*'s witty heroine? What was her name? I forget."

"Shahrazad. Her name is Shahrazad."

"Oh, yes. I forgot. Thank you. What a charming name," she joked. "*Hazar Afsanah*... Ah, you know what, it reminds me of those mischievous hours I spent in my parents' courtyard in Zanzibar... Hours of clandestine reading... Before my parents returned home, the maid would warn me. I would race to the courtyard and hide my precious *One Thousand Tales* beneath one of the veranda tiles. I'd then push the tile back in place and lock it down with a large stone pot. I wonder... Do you think it's still there?"

"Oh, I remember! I thought you were the most wicked little girl. You tried to make me read it and I would hear none of it. You were only eight then... Now look at me. My corruption is complete."

"That book is not all about naked pleasures, Kareem. I never saw *Hazar Afsanah* this way. Not at all. For me it was all about traveling and encountering women with a mind as vivacious as my own. And what is wrong with educating myself?"

"I am still astounded that you read this book at such a young age!"

"Well, at least, I read it in the original Persian edition. It is hardly the same in Arabic. Anyway, now I can no longer recount what I wanted to say..."

"The seamstress. Do you often wonder what her tales are about?" asked Kareem, gently returning to her concerns.

"Oh yes...the seamstress. You would be surprised. I can make out a few words..."

"Really?"

He felt a little envious of his companion's aptitude for languages.

"Yes, only vaguely...something about a village and an old woman... Oh, and a younger woman, a stranger of some sort. The seamstress has yet to finish her tale. She seems to interrupt it only to resume it on the following occasion... I wager that you, of all people, will not be surprised if I tell you that it keeps her auditors avid for more."

"Interesting... But I do not believe San Bao and I are at all similar. The admiral is bored and passing time while I am fond of good literature. Now if you will excuse me, my beloved Shahrzad, another beauty of that name beckons..."

He dropped his cheeky smile and resumed reading.

Shahrzad said nothing for a while. There was a long pause during which she was deep in thought. At last she replied.

"You're mistaken. The admiral is hardly bored. He is a very busy man. He almost never sleeps."

"Hmm..."

"Kareem..."

"What?"

"You're wrong. I still think that you and the admiral are very similar. Or rather I should say that as far as reading or listening to stories is concerned, *you are in the same situation.*"

Upon saying this, she faced him and leaned forward so that he at once sensed her gravity.

"Your heroine, whatever her name is, isn't she dragging her tale long enough for a purpose? I thought about that as a child and if I remember correctly, her tale is never completed because each night, she suspends it. She suspends it in a calculated way so that King Shahryar refrains from killing her. In fact, isn't it true that King Shahryar becomes so engrossed with her stories that he falls in love with her and spares her life? You see what I mean, don't you?"

Kareem's eyes widened.

"The admiral wants to kill the seamstress?"

"Of course not, my Eye. Very well, how shall I explain this? First, let us speak of you. What keeps you so enraptured? Why are you reading at all? Besides your curiosity and your desire to conclude each night's tale..."

Kareem sighed.

"I really don't know. Might I please continue to read, now?"

"Please do not. I can assure you that you will not be disappointed. You and San Bao are very alike. I'm sure of it. So think for a moment. Why are you reading this and not another book? Why are you not reading, say...the Qur'an?"

"I may well be debauched," said Kareem with a cheeky expression on his face. Then he recomposed himself. "Let's see now... It is because I want to know what happens to this Shahrazad. What else... It is a gripping story...very...very..."

Shahrzad shook her head vigorously.

"I honestly think you're mistaken all over again," she said.

"It is because you ask me confounding questions!"

"Maybe I haven't made myself clear. I should have examined the characters in your story first and then worked my way from there. It is the only way to better explain this..."

She paused.

"Very well. Let us suppose for a moment that this King Shahryar character is not so innocent. After all, he has since been cuckolded by his previous wife and eunuchs. So our king has been rendered highly suspicious of the women he sleeps with. This is, after all, the very reason why he is now taken to murdering each one of the harem girls he beds. Given his suspicious nature, it would not take him too long to deduce that his new bed partner, talented as she may be, is playing with him, that is to say, keeping him in suspense on her own volition to preserve her own life. He is not naive, our king. Have you considered that he may be well aware of her charade but nevertheless chooses to play along?"

Kareem seemed perplexed.

"You know, my dove, I never considered it that way. But yes, you could say that. You could say that he is playing along. My darling, you are ruining my reading pleasure but I will gracefully concede that he may be playing along."

"Excellent. So every night, aware that Shahrazad will engage him into yet another of her never ending tales, our king decides to willingly submit to the charade, spare the woman's life and dangle by her every rhyme...he does this despite knowing that she is playing with him and while he does relish the entertainment, he nevertheless allows himself to be played for a fool..."

"You think so? Now, hold on, he's not entirely a fool. Remember that this is a royal harem and the king, lucky man, receives significant nuptial delights in exchange. He does not lose out in the bargain! He is probably better off all things considered...that Shahrazad must be quite a nymph!"

But Shahrzad was not listening. Her voice became grave. "Precisely, Kareem... He allows himself another tale-filled night, at the expense of his dignity, because he is smitten, our King is!"

"Amazing," chirped Kareem, determined to finish this conversation and return to his book. "You may be right. He does fall in love with Shahrazad in the end...and yes, that is why he listened to her every night. So how does this make me akin to the Grand Admiral of your Eye? I am not at all in love with Shahrazad, you know."

"After all," he added with a twinkle in his eyes, "I have a Shahrzad of my own!"

He smiled at his own joke but his fiancée gently dismissed his advances.

"How very sweet of you, my beloved. But please, let us return to the Grand Admiral. Why then, do you think he *chooses* to listen to that woman's tale?"

Kareem experienced a sudden illumination. His eyes widened.

"Oh...now I see what you have been toying with," he whispered. "Because he is in love with her!"

Shahrzad glanced at him.

"In love, you think? Or?"

"You mean he does not find the seamstress attractive? Oh that's disappointing."

He glanced down at his book for inspiration but none came to him. At last, having suddenly lost interest, he shrugged his shoulders and began walking ahead of his fiancée to find a shaded seat.

"Really Kareem, you are not listening."

"It is because you always go off in tangents my precious dove. I have decided to give up," called out Kareem, determined to read once and for all.

They walked into the ship's gardens. Kareem reclined his broad mass onto a wooden bunk and gave an approving glance towards the surrounding flower pots. Shahrzad approached him. She had no intention to cease talking.

"Very well, I will tarry no longer. Let us resume what we were saying. The admiral is not in love with the seamstress but he is still very much intrigued by the seamstress. I give you that. Perhaps we should consider your situation and it would make better sense. What is it, Kareem, of my Eye, that intrigues *you* so much about this Shahrazad? The one in the book, of course..."

"Well I'm certainly not in love with her if that's what you're asking."

"But you still enjoy her stories very much. *Now, why is that?* Think."

"Well..." Kareem looked pained. He sighed and waved his arms frantically around him as though looking for some support. "I really don't know..."

"There must be something that holds your interest for long enough to wonder what will happen to her in the end..."

"No. I can think of nothing I've not told you already. She...she... Well, maybe she reminds me of you. Just a little. She's smart, cunning...troublesome...and very twisted! One wonders how she invents those tales. Yes, now that I think about it, I would say that is the reason." He looked triumphantly in her direction. "She reminds me of you."

Shahrzad nodded. She sat by his side for a few moments. Confused by her silence, Kareem turned towards her.

"Have I said something wrong? Is it the troublesome part?"

"No, no. You've confirmed my belief. Thank you, Kareem. I will trouble you no more."

They both remained on the wooden seat in the middle of the garden staring at the peach bougainvillea in silence. But Kareem refused to reopen his book. He recounted her words.

"Is that what you think, then? That this seamstress or maybe her tale, reminds him of someone he knows?" Her ideas unsettled him. He hesitated. "You might be right... But if you permit me, my Eye, it seems that you have forgotten one detail. There is a flaw in your parallel."

"What is that?"

"For good measure, if the admiral and I are as you say, in the same situation, then, just as the cunning Shahrazad tricks her king, wouldn't this...this seamstress be up to no good? Or perhaps a little cunning herself? I should think she would be playing the admiral for a fool... At least, according to what you said... See, in the book, Shahrazad is driven to tell her tales because she wants to live. It is her tales that keep her alive..."

"And so it is. What is troubling you so?"

"Well it's just this. By the same token, what could this seamstress want, do you think? Promotion? Money? What motivates her to drag on with her story? She is hardly the sort to want attention from the men on board. I hear she keeps very much to herself. From what I heard from the chef, even some crew men complained that she refuses to drink with them. What we have here is a very virtuous woman, my dove. Not some harem dilettante. But then, surely she must have a purpose, putting herself on display, day after day...don't you agree? So why is she doing this, huh? Why does she not finish her tale?"

He watched her body stiffen just as he finished speaking. Beneath her veil, the brows met forcefully.

"You are right, Kareem. That is the one thing I do not understand."

Chapter 37
Old Yu's Diary - Part Three

I think I scribed the discussion fairly well. And to think the translator who was working with Ma Huan at the time memorized the entire conversation before regaling me with it. This account proves to me that the Omani woman understands much more of our language than what I would have expected. This turned out to be a complete surprise. The other thing I have deduced is that the woman is a little crazy.

I remember thinking that the sooner she would get off this ship the better. I know this seems harsh but anyone would understand why I questioned her sanity once I explain it all. This I will do in the following pages.

So where do I start? The most disturbing of all incidents occurred, today before she left us. And I must say that I was not the only one who noticed. The admiral noticed it too. But of course, as always, nothing was spoken. It is a shame, really, as she is no longer with us and now I am beginning to regret the wasted time. Perhaps I should have summoned an interpreter myself and engaged *her* in an interrogation!

Unfortunately it is not the proper behavior for an old man like me. If only she had been ill, I could have had some words with her. But would you believe that she was not ill a single time during this trip. A true sailor! And judging from her gait the woman is as solid as a good Mongol steed.

But where was I?

It was dawn and the escort vessels had just moored not far from the lush and green Pemba Island. Crowds of men rushed forth on the beach. Zheng He prepared to dispatch the imperial barges to allow Kareem and Shahrzad to disembark with proper attention.

An odd thing happened then. I don't know who first noticed but a number of us began to congregate around the stern which overlooked the shore towards Zanzibar. There, on the beach, was an unsettling sight. Black men and women, shackled to each other via their necks and limbs stood, naked, save for a cloth round their loins. They were grossly treated and winced under the regular crack of a whip. I felt myself grow ill as I watched them being shoved by the dozen, onto a merchant dhow.

In disbelief, I rubbed the salt off my spectacles. I thought perhaps I had not seen clearly but judging from others who stared like me, in a manner that betrayed their own confusion and horror, the scene was real.

Squinting towards the island, I discerned a small table, laden with what appeared to be documents and over which a large man in a long flowing robe scrawled notes as other men inspected the pitiful black cargo. I am sure they were local merchants as all of them wore the traditional robe of Zanzibar which was so colorful as to be unmistakable.

"Omani slave traders," I heard the Grand Admiral whisper. I looked up to see Zheng He absorbed by the same sight.

For a while, I don't know for how long, we watched together and said nothing. The admiral struck me as being much moved by the scene. I noticed how tight his jaws were at the sight of those chains. Was he remembering his past?

"Are they coming with us?" I asked this question because our fleet had provided security for a growing number of foreign ships on our way across the Indian Ocean and I thought that perhaps I may get a better look at those dhows and their strange cargos once they were attached to the Ming fleet.

"No, Old Yu, they will follow the south-west monsoon and deliver their shipment to Arabia."

But his words were lost in the background as a distressed voice rose behind us.

"Are we not leaving?"

It was Shahrzad. We all turned round at once. Her reproachful voice rose so that even the soldiers began to pay her attention.

"One is tempted to believe you have never set foot outside the Middle Kingdom! Or have you never witnessed the most lucrative transactions of Zanzibar?"

All this Zheng He translated for me later. At the time, I could only make out that she was angry behind her veil. The resentment in that voice even shook the admiral. I had expected him to, but he did not put her back in her rightful place or at least try to save face with his well-known diplomatic manner. And that's when I realized, much later, that he had been more observant than me.

You see, the admiral did not respond to her provocation because he did not see it as a provocation.

Because while Shahrzad's words were full of spite, there was something unsaid that the admiral must have noticed. I think about it again now and I remember that her voice trembled all the while she spoke and that it was broken, almost hysterical. At that very moment, I could swear that I saw her grip onto Kareem as if she were about to swoon and pass out on the deck.

Chapter 38
The Ailing Seamstress

On return from Zanzibar, its water tankers once more full and its food supplies replenished, the Ming fleet ran south, skirting the African continent. So far, it had been on course, following the monsoon winds.

With the envoys safely back home, a delicate part of the journey awaited. Zheng He was to split the Ming fleet, sending each treasure ship on a different path to an unknown destination. In a matter of days, the Ming navigators would need to combine the very best of their skills further down the African coast and beyond. More so than before, they would need their starmaps.

Zheng He would not take part in the upcoming charting expeditions. Eagerly awaited in Beijing, he would remain a few days longer if only to assist his colleagues with planning their mission.

Two days before the admirals were due to disperse and when Zheng He had scheduled his return to Beijing, Old Yu dealt with increasing complaints from crew and passengers. After days of journeying in capricious seas and treacherous currents, passengers and crew had developed cold symptoms. Even Zheng He was not immune to the epidemic. Old Yu watched him closely, relieved that they were headed home.

But one particular patient also held Yu's attention. She was among the women who had consented to be examined by a male physician with little concern for her chastity. This, he remarked, seemed to arise from her trust in him. Old Yu had noted her sluggish movements and weakened state. She had been feverish since Sofala. She would often interrupt her enchanting tale, complaining of dizziness only to vanish in the lower decks for days.

And now Old Yu was tormented. Secretly, he wondered whether the new herbs he had tried on the seamstress, had not worsened her condition. Old Yu took malpractice seriously. He did not like making mistakes.

"Tell me, for how long have you had these pains?"

The Yunnan seamstress knew well how to hide her woes but today, the agony drained the blood from her face, leaving her lips blue. As she lay on her stomach with needles running down her back, Jun closed her eyes with relief. She was too tired to reply.

The physician frowned. He began to adjust the pins. He then pressed his finger on a node in her lower back.

"How does that feel? A little better?"

"It is not certain," replied the seamstress unintelligibly.

The physician shook his head. He wanted to help her but she did not make his job easy.

"Let me tell you, Daughter, you may be a wonderful storyteller but you say little that makes any sense otherwise."

For a good moment, he rubbed her neck and pressed his knuckle on her back, searching for a sensitive point. He watched her wince in silence.

"This damp weather is clearing up. Things will soon improve for you," said Old Yu.

"Not yet," whispered the seamstress, suddenly opening her eyes. Then she froze.

Old Yu withdrew the pins one by one, as though he had not heard. Jun's eyes roved to the left and then upwards. They stared. They seemed animated by a terrible notion. Old Yu did not notice. He removed the last two pins.

"Some very fine days ahead, I was told. We may all be on the deck listening to your wonderful tales," he cheered.

Jun continued to fixate the interior of the cabin with a frightening intensity. Her eyes gazed at the shelves before her, seeing but not seeing. Watching her limbs tense up, Old Yu jerked back, in disapproval.

"You ought to abandon the night shifts. That's why you are so exhausted. Take some rest. You ought not to sew into the night when you are in pain. And your pulse is weak..."

He shook his head. Was she even listening? He watched her rise from the couch, fumbling to put on her tunic. He thought she was embarrassed because she trembled with her head lowered. When she finished, she sat on the bench and stared at him with her moist, dark eyes. The color had returned to her face but she seemed agitated.

The pins may have worked a little, reflected Old Yu, somewhat relieved. Acupuncture was not a science he had practiced for long and he was still experimenting with the latest techniques.

"How do you know this?" she asked, stirring him from his thoughts.

"I am a physician."

She shook her head vigorously.

"About the weather to come...how do you know?" she insisted.

Old Yu looked surprised.

"The weather report is sent to me every morning. I use it for my patient's diagnosis. You see, the weather affects most of us...just in different ways, depending on the current balance or imbalance in our *qi*. So there is cold, wind, heat...our bodies exist in communion with the universe."

He watched her frown. She opened her mouth to reply but he continued, eager to impart his knowledge.

"If you are interested, you can ask one of the geomancers on board. They possess much insight into weather. They will perhaps wonder why you, of all people, would want to—"

"A storm is coming," blurted Jun. She continued to fix him with a frightening intensity.

But Old Yu shook his head, giving little thought to her outburst. He proceeded to write in his journal.

Based on his diagnosis, Jun had been ill for some years. She must have known she was unfit for the journey. How could she not? Old Yu sighed again. Why the Southerner would even register for the post was beyond his understanding.

He raised his head from his notes.

"That will do today. I need to see the other patients. Promise me, Daughter, that you will find the time to rest. Your condition will worsen if you do not rest. Do you understand?"

Jun gave no indication that she had understood. She stared fixedly at the old man in a manner he found odd. He sighed in exasperation.

"Alright, alright. Here, take your cape. Close the door behind you and let the other women know I'm finished. Send the next one in."

Having ushered her to the door, he sat back down, leaned over his desk and shuffled for his Arab spectacles. Once he had replaced these on his bulbous nose, he dipped his pen in ink to inscribe additional characters on Jun's patient card. Then he stopped short.

Jun had remained standing by the door. She appeared lost in thought.

"Jun... Did you hear what I said?"

The storyteller was startled from her contemplation.

"Jun?"

The seamstress made eye contact and smiled as though she took pity on the physician.

"I heard you. But you must hear me. There is a great storm coming. A very great storm... The admiral—"

"Very well, very well, I will see you later then. You go and rest my child. Go on."

When she had gone, Old Yu made a decision. Taking out his sealed imperial paper, he wrote a recommendation that Jun remain on Zheng He's ship on the return journey and that upon arrival at the Port of Guangdong, that the seamstress be provided with a eunuch escort home. It was the least he could do.

***

The very next morning, when Jun was about to begin her tale, an officer quietly pushed his way through the gathered audience. Looking very much terrified, he excused himself, demanding to speak at once with the admiral.

"Could this not wait..." replied this one, a little disappointed.

"No, it cannot."

It was soon agreed that any Chantefables should not go on without the admiral and as the crowd dispersed, much to Old Yu's disappointment, Zheng He followed his officer to the bridge. But no sooner had they entered the navigational cabin that furious shouts rose from the upper deck. The officer was seen flying out of the cabin, pursued by Zheng He himself. The admiral had brandished his sword. He was so unlike his composed self that his loud reprimands resonated beyond the bridge. Even the crew on the rigging deck below stared in astonishment.

Pipe in hand, the baffled Old Yu raised his nose towards the bridge to better observe the commotion.

"Traitor! I should kill you!" cried Zheng He, raising his sword above the officer's neck.

"Mercy!" cried the assistant navigator, flailing his arms about.

"What did you not understand? I ordered you to allow no one on the bridge! No one!" roared Zheng He.

"He was a cabin boy...just routine duties, I—"

"You ought to have advised me earlier! Did you even try to communicate to the peripheral ships?" charged Zheng He, seizing the officer by the collar.

"We have nothing," moaned another officer. "We tried everything. There are no starmaps on board the peripheral ships either. We have been looking for them for days..."

Zheng He continued to menace them both with his sword. He was out of himself.

"Are you telling me, Officers that somehow those starmaps have vanished into thin air with their whereabouts unaccounted for? Do you take me for a fool? We do not all wake up one morning to find starmaps gone!"

At this, Old Yu watched Zheng He pace back into the cabin where he heard some furious rummaging. Then again, rose the admiral's thundering voice.

"I will have your cabin searched, Officers, and if I find anything, you will answer to me!"

A look of defeat painted itself on the navigators' faces.

They understood Zheng He's fury. Without the starmaps, the ships could not gauge their bearings from Beijing. How would the admirals continue their expeditions? Lives and much money were at stake. Now they would lose face at court. The assistant's shoulders sank pitifully.

***

Two days later, the fleet still had not split. Old Yu had locked himself in his cabin to catalog new medicinal concoctions. He reflected on the dismal atmosphere on the treasure ship. With Zheng He concerned over the missing starmaps, a general tension reigned on board. They had found nothing.

What could be done? He remembered the look on Zheng He's face soon upon learning the terrifying news.

"Look for them Captain! Search everywhere! This could throw our journey and the entire charting project in jeopardy."

There had since been talks of cancelling the expeditions. Zheng He looked crushed. The task of reporting to Emperor Zhu Di would fall on his shoulders. To make matters worse, Old Yu noted how last evening the admiral was folded over with a persistent, rasping cough.

Old Yu pondered that perhaps the thief who had attacked them at the start of their journey may well have stolen the starmaps. He had shared his intuition with Zheng He who had nodded quietly, leaving no doubt that he suspected the same thing.

The thief's shadow loomed over the fleet. Only this morning, Zheng He himself had inspected every cabin and dispatched soldiers to search all treasure ships. But he had to come to reason. Neither the thief nor the starmaps could be found.

Old Yu could not work. Something bothered him. He abandoned his catalog and set out to replace herbs in their respective pots. Could things get worse than they already were? He frowned. He recalled that Jun had said something about a storm. A great storm, she had said.

Dear girl, inventing stories about the weather. Now, why would there be a storm if the geomancers had presaged otherwise? After all, over the last months, on every ship's altar, had they not been burning incense to the goddess Mazu? If anyone could appease the giant green-blue dragons that whipped up waves to monstrous proportions, it was her, the Celestial Goddess. Surely they were in good hands. Surely Jun was mistaken...

A storm was the last thing they needed.

Aside from inflicting damage, it would force them off course. The possibility of the treasure ship finding itself reefed in shallow waters was real now that they had no bearings. The thought frightened Old Yu.

It was fortunate that the geomancers remained adamant. No storms were presaged. And Jun was only a storyteller, was she not?

Still, Old Yu could not stifle a quick glance outside his cabin. If only to watch the skies...

And as he did, tentatively at first, sweat began to trickle down his forehead. Stumbling out onto the deck, he leaned against the railing, glancing out towards the sea in disbelief. At first he noticed little.

But already, the sun had disappeared and the ocean bed no longer glistened. As he looked ahead, far into the horizon, he saw then, the ominous gray vortex advancing in their direction.

The twisted mass of charcoal clouds tapered down into a giant finger pointing to the hapless fleet. It was one of those signs from the heavens, those that choke the light from the skies and warn all sailors to expect the dragons' wrath. Old Yu remained transfixed. A knowing look of terror descended upon his face.

"Mazu," he whispered, "help us. Help us..."

And as Old Yu turned around, he caught sight of Zheng He, ten feet across. The admiral stood alone at the railing, an icy resignation on his pale face.

Chapter 39
Tempest

The pigeons soared, carrying messages that would seal terror on all ships. One of the gray birds tilted its tiny head. It seemed to watch with alarm as the once turquoise waters turned black and a shadow enveloped the fleet below.

A deep sound broke through the silence, startling the bird in its flight. A drum sound rose from Zheng He's ship. It was followed by another. More drums joined in. Their distress call grew louder, more urgent.

It was the fleet's warning. The officers who struck these drums understood. They were beating the rhythm of impending death and as their muscles flexed, a deep frown etched across their solemn brows.

And along his shortened flight, the pigeon saw, the dotted path of lights springing to life on the ships below. One after the other, the dim glow of oil lanterns cascaded across the decks. The sturdier men moved to their posts, some tying themselves to masts. Bells were rung to issue orders and organize the crew.

The younger sailors had never seen such threat from the skies. They could only stare at the heavens, hoping that the many incense sticks the priests burnt on Mazu's altar would persuade the Celestial Goddess of the seas to save them.

Zheng He wiped sweat from his brow surveying the darkening clouds.

"Allah is great," he whispered. "We must surmount this monster but alas, I fear I have not the strength."

Close by, his assistant waited for instructions.

"Cancel our return, Officer," said Zheng He in a voice he wanted calm. But his breathing was labored and heavy.

"You are not leaving for Beijing, Admiral?"

"I am not leaving. Look up, young man. There is nowhere to go now."

He did not yet tell him about the missing starmaps. There was no need to.

"To your posts. What is our speed?"

"Two knots, Admiral." Uncertain, the navigator searched into his admiral's sunken eyes. Zheng He brushed past him, avoiding eye contact.

"Fold the sails, we stay in position. You know what to do."

"Yes, Admiral."

The men worked fast. They cast floating anchors on each side of the ships. This would, they hoped, increase the vessels' stability. Already the ocean's swells had risen by three feet.

"May Allah help us," said Zheng He. Turning to another officer, he motioned towards the large incense urns on the upper deck.

"Have those brought back inside. Do whatever you must, but keep the incense burning. Go now! Remember, without Her, we are lost! Hurry!"

The officers ran to execute the order. No sooner had the urns been carried away that a sudden light pierced the heavens. The electric web parted the blackened skies. The cries of thousands of anxious men rose from the ships. They wailed in terror invoking all the gods they knew. They prayed to Allah. They called out for the Goddess to save them. What little light remained had now dimmed. Screams tore through the darkness and were engulfed in the roaring thunder.

And then the heavens burst, pounding the fleet with thunderous might. Timber moaned under a furious wind. Even the proud masts of the treasure ship wobbled ominously. On the bridge, his face blanched by both fever and fear, Zheng He clung to the rattling railing. Pushing against a torrent of wind and rain, he hurried to the stern rudder post, shouting to his men along the way.

It was not what Jun had called, a storm. It was a cyclone. One like none of them had seen. It came fast. The fleet had scarce time to prepare. The sea appeared to rise, lifting smaller barges to level with the treasure ships.

The admiral watched with horror as escort vessels were swept up by rolling swells. Men who had failed to tie ropes round their waists flew high above the decks and disappeared into dark whirlpools of water. Men were flung on the flooded decks. Men were catapulted overboard. Bamboo sails were ripped from their battens, collapsing onto the rigging.

If these were sea-dragons, now they tore at the hull of the giant treasure ship. They pummeled from above as from below, clapping into the upper decks, flushing men to their death. The winds tore at the masts, rolling the mighty ship despite its anchors.

Zheng He bellowed to his men.

"Listen to me! If we collide onto a sister ship, we die. Hold steady!"

They worked in groups, steering the giant rudder at the stern post. Each group tired quickly from the colossal task and so they took turns. Zheng He issued orders to keep them from colliding into nearby vessels.

"Zhou Man's ship ahead, Admiral!" shouted the Captain, his red eyes bulging out in the darkness.

"Veer off starboard! Avoid them!"

"We'll soon drown! The current is pulling us in!"

"Do as I say! Veer now!"

And on and on it went. The noise was deafening. As thunder roared, the crew's bell signals grew faint. The men's shouts were lost, their screams engulfed by the spewing masses rising from the ocean's belly.

Somehow Zheng He continued to give orders in the darkness. He ignored what had happened to the other treasure ships. He prayed that the other admirals would know what to do. All he could see beyond were the larger horse and combat ships, swept by the giant billowing waves around them.

And then he gasped. He recognized the inverted hull of one of the horse ships. He saw it split in halves. In the intermittent light that followed, he watched in disbelief as the sealed compartments imploded, spewing hundreds of disoriented Mongol horses, into the raging ocean. The confused beasts struggled to keep their heads afloat but very soon they weakened and were swallowed into the sea.

In the thickening downpour, Zheng He lost sight of the surrounding ships.

They endured the sea-dragons for an entire night. And then it was dawn and silence followed. But it was short lived.

No sooner had they recovered their strengths, counted those missing, tended to the injured or ill and identified sunken ships that the chaotic forces lashed out once more.

***

Tonight I'm dead, cursed Huang-Fu, pressing his hand to his stomach.

He had felt the sting of guilt for some time since meeting the Ku'Li spy. The latter had coordinated his every movement. Together, they had seized all the starmaps because Huang-Fu had made a stupid mistake. The first map he had brought back had only enraged his contact. This one had flung the three-yard scroll into his face.

"You imbecile!"

Drink always managed to ire foul spirits.

"Never mind. Those damned Zamorins won't know the difference! Starmaps it is, then."

He had opened a box and pushed the rolled map into it, turning over the key.

"You fetch me the other starmaps for Ekbal. The expedition will be doomed, either way. I've done my work."

Terrified, Huang-Fu had obeyed. He'd scrub his face with soot from one of the oil lamps, descended into one of the vegetable barges and oared quietly to the ships. One by one. Since sampans shuttled in to and fro to bring fresh water from the port, no one questioned him as he climbed the gangplank. He hardly looked suspicious. Once he had scrubbed clean and removed his thick cloak, he appeared on deck in a soldier's uniform. A few times he was stopped and questioned but whenever he brandished documents stamped with Zhou Man's seal, he was left well alone.

He had forged ahead with the plan, giving no thought to the gravity of his actions. Before long, he possessed all the starmaps.

He was glad when at long last the fleet left Ku'Li's port. Glad when his papers were returned to him. Glad when he was promoted to the galleys on Zhou Man's ship. Glad again to know he was alive and far away from Ekbal's cronies.

But as the tempest neared and the dragons' wrath befell the treasure ship, Huang-Fu grew anxious. The guilt sent waves of nausea in his chest. He heard the thunder and blanched, taking it as a warning from the Heavens. One is never more superstitious than at sea.

Yet it had started days ago, while he peeled vegetables in the galley. He ruminated.

"I'm a traitor. Ekbal was right. I'm just scum."

He started losing at the games. Even his companions noticed. They saw how he eyed his cards with anxious dispassion, how his heart was no longer in the game.

And then these sea creatures had come to swallow him up, miserable traitor that he was.

During the eye of the cyclone, as he dragged away corpses and threw them at sea by the dozen, he promised himself that if he had to die, he'd die a noble man. Even if he looked like those bloated, rotting men, he'd save his honor. He would reveal his shameful secret.

But that's if I live tonight, he thought, cradled in the corner of his damp cabin. He felt the cold of his wet tunic as it clamped to his skin. One of the oil lamps had long been extinguished by the raging winds. In the screaming darkness, he managed to crawl on all fours, suppressing an urge to retch. He felt the ship roll towards starboard but he clung to the doorway, cursing the heavens. The torrential rains flooded in. Cards, mats and dice now floated together in a foul smelling slosh.

"Ping, we have to get out of here. The cabin's filling up!" he called out.

His friend was nowhere to be seen.

"Ping? It's too dangerous. We need to get to the rigging deck..."

The last oil lamp flickered to its end, startling him. Rising carefully, he waded in the darkness, clutching his painful stomach.

"Ping?"

He heard a thump.

"Ping?"

There was a splash. Then, surging from the back of the cabin, Ping was behind him, bearing him down, his lips pursed tight around the blade of a butcher's knife. Huang-Fu wriggled free then slipped. A savage jab in the shoulder sent him to his face. He swallowed a mouthful of salt water.

"Ping, what...What's got into you!"

Ping's knee came down on Huang-Fu's groin. His palm was hard on Huang-Fu's jaw, slamming him into the ground.

"Are you crazy?"

"It will be quick," blurted Ping as he held the knife with his other hand.

Huang-Fu saw the blade rising above his chest and panicked. He surged forth, wrestling Ping to the ground. The knife slipped. Huang-Fu watched it disappear into the rising waters.

"You mad?" he cried in disbelief.

Without responding, Ping leapt at the turbulent slosh. He felt around for the knife.

"What's wrong with you, Ping?" But he could no longer see him. The cabin dimmed. He heard Ping's breathing. It came fast. He knew he was close.

"Why are you doing this? Why?"

The blade shot past but he'd seen it. Evading the blow, he grabbed his friend's wrist, twisting it hard, ignoring Ping's yells. There was cracking sound as the elbow snapped. Ping screamed. With one hand, Huang-Fu had him pinned by the neck.

"I'm sorry!" cried Ping.

"You're sorry? You tried to kill me! Why?"

"He said you stole the fleet maps...said you were dangerous..."

"*He* did what? Damn it, Ping! I thought you were my friend!"

Ping could not reply. They both lost their balance. Huang-Fu understood. The treasure ship was now rolling to portside. A wave poured into the lower deck, submerging the little cabin. Huang-Fu lost his grip and slid. The torrent flushed Ping past the doorway and into the lower deck's corridor. Finding the railing, Huang-Fu held on.

"I can't swim Huang-Fu!"

Ping's head bobbed up and down only to disappear forever. Slowly, the portside began to rise. But it was too late. Ping had been flushed over the railing.

Huang-Fu remained stunned at what had just happened. The spy had tried to kill him. The bastard...

Knee deep in water, Huang-Fu flung himself forward, aiming for the staircase to the upper deck. Heaved by a giant wave, the ship pitched forward. The ground slipped under Huang-Fu's feet. He skidded across the planks and landed with a loud slam on his belly. In the blinding light, he found a rope. An icy splash of salt greeted him as he held on to the railing.

The fleet plunged into complete darkness. No one saw Huang-Fu run up the stairs. He staggered along the upper deck and onto the bridge.

***

At the bridge, Zheng He was exhausted. His fever burnt. He felt worse for not having slept the last three nights. His torn robe was drenched. I have to go on, he thought. Even if Hell has fallen from the Heavens.

Old Yu had begged him to rest earlier today but the admiral would not listen.

"Son of Ma Haji," had warned the physician just as he had almost forty years ago. "Do you want to live?"

Zheng He had said nothing. He had gulped down another cup of strong tea. He had tidied all loose furniture and secured away documents for the upcoming night. Old Yu was agitated.

"If you want to live, do not remain at the stern post tonight! You are burning with fever. Stay in your cabin."

"I can't do that, Old Yu."

"Stubborn old fool!"

Even Zheng He's assistant had offered to take over but the admiral had refused.

They were close to the end of the cyclone, he said. Indeed they were, but Zheng He had succumbed into a watery mirage.

Voices that he had once distinguished through the roaring storm, voices that had guided him in the darkness when he could barely see, all but faded. He saw nothing. He heard nothing. He swam. The men's shouts became murmurs, then whispers.

Perhaps it reflected his dearest wish or the games of a waning mind but he thought he saw her, then. She was bathing among the rose petals. Zheng He collapsed to his knees reaching towards Min Li.

***

On the other treasure ship, Huang-Fu burst through Zhou Man's cabin door. He knew the admiral was at the stern post. He stumbled inside the badly lit cabin, tripping against a broken stool. The room appeared empty. He looked in dismay at the wreckage. It seemed the heavens made no distinction between the upper and lower decks. A violent shatter startled him.

"What are you doing here?"

It was Yang Bao. He held a broken brandy bottle, ready to glass Huang-Fu.

"You're not answering, vermin? Lost your tongue? Answer when spoken to! What are you doing here?"

"I..."

"Speak up!"

"You...you tried to kill me..." said Huang-Fu, clenching his fists.

"That right?"

"I did what you asked and you tried to kill me!"

"Young fool! You stand for nothing and believe in nothing. Even your pathetic friends are prepared to betray you."

In response, Huang-Fu rammed his head forward. A violent kick propelled him back. Confused by the man's strength, he staggered onto his feet. How could he be so strong? As though sensing his thoughts, a wicked smile drew itself on Yang Bao's lips. And then Huang-Fu understood.

"It was you! You're the thief who broke into Admiral Zheng He's cabin!"

In response, Yang Bao took a swing with the broken bottle. Huang-Fu cried out, stumbling back. From the corner of his eye, he glimpsed the shiny metal of a blade leaning against a wooden cabinet. He fumbled towards the sword, stooping to avoid another swing. The glass bottle smashed onto the cabinet.

Yang Bao lunged forward. Huang-Fu dodged. He leapt across, reaching for the blade. His wet fingers slipped. A sharp blow landed across his kidneys.

"You don't get it do you?" shouted Yang Bao between blows. "We're all going to die! All of us! All for the glory of Ming!"

With one steel-like grip, he picked up the battered Huang-Fu and hurled him across the wall. Huang-Fu's head thumped against the hard wood. The walls spun. He skidded down, inanimate.

"Fucking fleet is cursed! Zhu Di can go to hell!" cursed the assistant admiral.

Almost unconscious, Huang-Fu watched as Yang Bao stooped to pick up a shard of glass.

"No one will miss you, little vermin," he said, raising his hand.

A flash of lightning illuminated the admiral's face. He was drunk. In the electric light, his bloodshot eyes appeared hideous.

"No, don't—"

Yang Bao hit him with the glass. Huang-Fu gave a yell.

"You came to get even didn't you? Came to tell on me..." breathed Yang Bao. "Rabid cur!"

And then Huang-Fu's rage surged in him. He spun to his palms, swinging his leg back with a grunt. The assistant admiral was not prepared for the savage blow to his flank. The wound Zheng He had inflicted upon him months ago, was still tender. He dropped the glass and folded over in pain. The little Han darted out, sword in hand.

"I'll crush you to pulp, I swear it!" cursed Yang Bao.

He kicked the stool aside and found his own sword. Then he bolted out of the cabin.

"I'll impale you, Huang-Fu! I'll impale you on that sword you've got in your hand!"

Yang Bao's raucous laugh was lost to the glacial torrent pounding the upper deck. Obscurity engulfed them.

As the wind howled in his ears and singed his bleeding face, Huang-Fu slinked past a row of cabins. If he could get to the rigging deck, he might stand a chance.

Again, the ship rolled to the portside. Yang Bao staggered out. His bulging eyes wandered into the darkness. He waited. A ray of light pierced the skies. He took note of the alley to his left. Darkness. No sign of Huang-Fu. He turned and ran past a row of cabins.

On the rigging deck, lightning struck one of the smaller masts. A loosened spar tore down one of the minor sails and collapsed onto the deck, killing two soldiers. But Yang Bao did not flinch. In the melee of sailors below, he had spotted Huang-Fu.

Near the prow, Huang-Fu clenched at the sword, his teeth chattering in the freezing rain. Crouched behind spare rigging, he could see Yang Bao running in his direction. There was nowhere to hide. But at least... His eyes rested on two sealed buckets whose contents he knew well. Crawling on his elbows, he reached the buckets. He removed both their lids.

Yang Bao's menacing silhouette surged forth through the rain. He had seen him. Huang-Fu raised one of the buckets. Yang Bao was closer. Closer still. Now!

Yang Bao tried to dodge the spewing mass. It was too late. The bucket knocked him off balance. A horrid stench filled his nostrils.

"Son of a bitch!"

Dripping in filth, Yang Bao leapt like a demon, swinging his sword over Huang-Fu's head. He snipped the Han's hair close to the skull. Huang-Fu cried out, sword in hand. Yang Bao met the clumsy attack with his own blade. The sword slipped from Huang-Fu's untrained hand. Undeterred, the little Han ran to the other bucket and kicked it down. Yang Bao skidded across the slippery dung.

Running back, Huang-Fu picked up his sword. A loud crash startled him. Ahead, lightning had struck the top of the main mast. Flames rose under the pounding rain as sailors ran across to salvage the largest sail on the ship.

"Vermin!" Yang Bao was back on his feet, angrier than before.

A knowing light flashed across Huang-Fu's eyes. He ran to the closest mast and began to climb.

Yang Bao chased after him. He looked up. As Huang-Fu raised himself to the next batten up, his foot slipped. For a moment, the boy hung, his legs swinging precariously.

"Ha! Ha! I told you I'd impale you!" cheered Yang Bao reaching up from below.

His heart thundering in his chest, Huang-Fu managed to swing across and find his footing. At last, he raised himself up towards the next batten.

"I'll come and get you. I'll finish you once and for all!"

Huang-Fu was now high enough. He looked down in Yang Bao's direction.

This one gazed up, ready to climb. He watched, mouth agape, unsure of the boy's intentions. The deluge blinded him. The alcohol dimmed his senses.

Huang-Fu's sword came down onto the stubborn timber. And again. A flash of light illuminated Yang Bao's raised face. With disbelief, he saw the sword cross the spar one last time. The timber gave way... but he could not hear it. All he saw was the snapping batten dropping from above, and with it, half a ton of bamboo canvas dragging down and into his eye.

***

The last Zheng He saw was the rising dawn. Before him, a gold disk pierced through a gray scattering of clouds, showering its generous rays on the emaciated fleet.

All strength had deserted him. The fever devoured his brow, blurring his vision. The warm daylight dimmed to nothingness. He lost consciousness.

Faces appeared in his dreams. They stirred from his tortured mind, those forgotten faces.

He was a little boy running from the Ming soldiers. He could see the terrifying figure of General Fu Youde, fierce from his Kunming victory. He remembered the punishment reserved for the young pubescent males lined up in their hundreds when Kunming had fallen. He remembered the grimace on his father's face when the Ming soldiers had murdered him. Then came the shame as he found himself, chained like an animal moving along the plains of Yunnan with hundreds other child prisoners with no name.

And then, somehow, he was swimming. He floated to the scented baths finding her breasts in his avid mouth. Sculpted across the alabaster walls, the emperor's stern face looked on. He was now in her chamber. Her eyes, they begged him. She mouthed words that he could not hear. Then she faded away, too late for him to reach her. She was gone.

He was now falling, deep into a cold tunnel of remorse. Was this the end? He felt the darkness of the ocean and breathed the smell of death.

Suddenly he lay in a cell, buried deep in the sea, alone and cold. Water poured in through cracks in the cell walls. Its level rose steadily. There was no escape. Death will find me now, he thought. He looked up. There was a passage above that led to sea. He could swim up if he wanted. Swim to the light, swim out. But he did not. He had no desire to. And still the water in the cell rose, but Zheng He refused to move. Let the water take me. He welcomed death.

And as he sunk within his dream, so too, aboard the ship, Zheng He's heart gave way. And after the crew men had dragged the admiral back to his chamber, the physicians took his six pulses but could not find the right beats. They shook their heads and listened on.

In his dream, the waters submerged him. Above him was immensity. It was silence; silence that rips through the soul; silence that makes even the hermit ache for touch. Death settled inside the cell, swift and fast. The light above dimmed. The admiral was dying.

In the cabin, the physicians released both Zheng He's wrists. They stood alarmed, looking at each other with disconcerted faces.

"Raise Old Yu!" ordered one of them to the sailors who had carried the admiral from the bridge. "Tell him to come at once! Hurry!"

And then he heard it. Something stirred ahead. In the ocean above, something moved fast towards him. It parted the waters with forceful sweeps. Unseen, it moved towards the cell. Zheng He closed his eyes. Too late, he thought, you come too late.

A slender hand emerged through the cell opening, its gentle fingers seeking him through the blue of the water. The fingers moved, as though blind, but guided by a secret knowledge. The hand was impelled by a tender purpose. And then, it found him. The hand grasped his arm. It pulled. It was a slight hand but it seemed energized by a tremendous force.

In the dim cell, Zheng He watched this hand pull him up towards the light. It seemed to say, swim up, swim up towards the light. So he swam. Legs frantically kicking...confused, because he could not see the owner of this hand, confused because he had not expected that the waters would now be so calm and peaceful. The maddening roar had ceased when his savior had appeared. He finally glanced up at the face shining above him. So strange that it was Jun.

She stared back at him beneath the water. Her eyes spoke and he understood. She had come for him. He had to follow her. All this she said with her eyes. All this she said as she held his hand. And Zheng He thought that he must be mad but still, he held on to her hand.

She was unapologetic for having touched the admiral. Because here, where they were now swimming, she was more powerful than he was. All this he sensed as he held on to her hand. She did not want him to die. She was going to save his life because she was his friend. All this he learnt, as he held on to her hand. Her eyes continued to speak to him, caressing his dark thoughts away. She smiled.

Her red robe was like a mist of silk as she swam up towards the light pulling the admiral behind her. Zheng He felt the strength radiating from her grasp. His eyes now wide open he let Jun raise him from his prison. All pain had left him. All fear had vanished.

And suddenly he was walking alongside the seamstress in a long tunnel. Her long-sleeved robe was already dry and now the silk floated about her like a faint breeze. He noticed that he was still holding her hand. She led ahead with her right arm stretched out before her, showing him the way, feeling the darkness with her open palm. It was an enchanting stroll. It took place nowhere. He liked this, to be blind and have the certainty that each step was carefully planned and carefully watched. He was at peace.

He realized, then, that he had shed his pride and placed his trust in her. She looked up triumphantly as if she had heard his thoughts. She smiled. It was perfect, this strong grasp. He wished he would never let go, that she could protect his soul forever. But now, something was shifting.

Old Yu staggered into the cabin. He leaned forward, pressing his ear to Zheng He's chest, listening for a sound. He reached out and tapped gently on Zheng He's hand.

"San Bao, old boy," whispered the physician, relieved by the admiral's moving lips.

The admiral seemed to be talking but no sound came out of his blue lips.

They had reached the large door at the end of the tunnel and he understood they must part. She released his hand and lowered her gaze. Her silk gown had vanished. In its place was the cotton tunic and apron she wore aboard.

His strength had returned. He felt alive. It was time.

Jun pushed opened a large gate. Light filled the dreamscape. Out there, he could hear a familiar voice calling him. Zheng He stepped into the blinding light. The voice became insistent but he wanted to ignore it. He turned around to say goodbye. But Jun was no longer there.

"Are you alright, San Bao?"

It was Old Yu. Zheng He blinked. Twice.

"Yes, yes. Where am I?"

"Aboard the Ming treasure ship, you fool." Then with much relief, Old Yu wiped a tear. "You gave us such a fright, my boy."

Chapter 40
The Inspired Navigator

When the admiral recovered from his illness and the destructive aftermath of the tempest was reported, he wept. Dozens of ships had sunk and with them thousands of people had been lost at sea. Fever spread, threatening to kill more of the crew. The loss of cargo amounted to more than a quarter of the fleet's worth. Minister Xia would be furious.

Despite their predicament, the admiral refused to give in to grief. A more pressing matter urged him to seek council. The fleet was erring because its navigators sailed blind. To make matters worse, his return was behind schedule. Beijing could wait no longer. Yet facing Zhu Di in these circumstances was out of the question.

In the navigation cabin, there reigned a stifling atmosphere as the senior admirals and navigators crammed around a large table and conferred over the missing starmaps. A mildewy smell rose from the damp carpet. Judging from the burnt incense sticks that a white robed eunuch replaced while discussions ensued, the men had argued for hours. As is the case when men cannot find a solution, the meeting had descended into riling and bickering.

Admiral Zheng He sat beside Admiral Zhou Man. The latter was still emotionally shaken after the horrendous death of his assistant admiral. Zheng He was far removed from the agitation in the room. He had long since drifted to the night of the tempest. In secret, he replayed his dream and questioned the identity of his savior.

Early this morning, he had visited one of the seers. He was eager to offer respects to a deity he felt indebted to after all these years and who, he believed, had visited him in his dream; Goddess Mazu. She was the Celestial Consort, the patron goddess of sailors. And she was his hope whenever he doubted and believed all was lost at sea.

The Taoist oracle had bled the chicken and leaned forward, observing the entrails through rising incense smoke. The moist morning air became infused with the smell of blood.

"You have seen Mazu," said the old man in a knowing tone.

"I saw someone that looked to be her."

"Tell me what you saw," replied the wrinkled sage, still peering into the dead pulp beneath his beard.

The admiral hesitated.

"She was...a woman, a woman draped in red silk. She came to me when I was asleep."

"What did she do?"

"I was drowning... She rescued me. She rescued me from death, she drove me out of a deep well."

The old seer grunted in acknowledgement.

"Only Mazu can see into your future. I cannot. But the signs do not lie. Grand Admiral, you are greatly burdened. You must trust and emerge from the depths of your troubled *shen*. If you do this, then Mazu will help you."

At that moment, Zheng He remembered something.

"Wise man," he confided, "I am not so sure it was Mazu."

The old man dripped chicken blood onto bark paper. Then he slowly burnt the paper.

"Mazu has the power to see into the hearts of men. She knows your intents, everything you conceal, she can see. Is that the woman you saw?"

"I don't know. I...I think so...What I do know is that I have lost more men in the last five days than I imagined possible."

"This great misery is not your doing," confided the Taoist sage. He grew abrupt as though tired of the Grand Admiral. Behind the role of seer, the old man revealed everything without bothering to hide what all along, those on board knew well.

"Mazu cannot help you unless you let her. Let her help you! Why, why must the admiral be so proud? Remember the saying, *pride goes before a fall*... The admiral must cast aside his pride."

Zheng He was weary of spiritual advice. There was little the oracle could say that could be reconciled with the practical situation.

"We are drifting into perhaps uncharted oceans," he replied. "I must return to Beijing soon but cannot in those conditions. My duty is with the fleet. We have lost our bearings and—"

"Then you must let Mazu guide you," repeated the sage, shutting his eyes.

"But how?"

The old man's eyes were sharp as he reflected. He closed them again, breathing the smoke in as though it were a message from the gods.

"Only she knows."

And now, seated among the admirals, among the navigators and the astronomers, the man who should have led the conference this morning could only stare quietly, repeating the seer's last words to himself. And as his assistant leaned over to ask him a question, Zheng He was no longer listening. A remarkable transformation took hold of his face. The white of his eyes bulged out. He seemed to be seeing something for the very first time so that it took his breath away. The others stared at him.

"What is it, San Bao?"

Zheng He leapt from his chair, bowing to excuse himself.

"I will return shortly, I ask you to please excuse me."

He rushed past the outraged whispers and the confused faces, elbowing his way out of the cabin. "Excuse me," was all he could say as Admiral Zhou Man rose from his high stool as though to demand an explanation.

How Zheng He found himself back into his living quarters he could not remember. The compelling force drove him with such violence that he could not hear nor see anything on his way. As he stepped onto the bridge, he had only one thought: find the cloth.

His eyes ran across the cabin fittings. He tried to recall where he had dismissed her gift. He surveyed the shelves near his desk, looking for a glimpse of white material. But there was nothing. I need to find that cloth or I'll go mad, he thought. The drawers caught his eye. He lunged towards the wooden cabinet, tugging at each drawer to reveal its content. Nothing in this one... He sighed. Nothing in that drawer either.

She may not be crazy but she's very, very cunning. Either that or she is a thief and a prankster...

He peered into the last compartment. It was not there either. The admiral sighed. What could he have done with the...

A flash of white caught his eye. It was on the desk all along. He had used it as a tablecloth months ago and forgot its existence since.

Afraid of what he would see, he reached for the fabric. He slowly raised it. It was the right length, a good three yards. He gazed at the reverse side and cursed. How had he not noticed this before?

He flipped the cloth to inspect the front. His eyes followed each line, each stitch.

And slowly, the pattern began to take shape. It was astonishing. From the moment she had given him the cloth, he knew he had seen something alike, and now... *And now*, he cursed, as he stared at it, completely stunned, *I know exactly where.*

***

The men in the meeting cabin were puzzled. Why had Zheng He felt a desire to evade their company? Surely the Grand Admiral knew better than to summon them only to breach etiquette with such carelessness. When they had ascertained that Zheng He was not merely outside taking some fresh air, the admirals set upon discussing among themselves.

Some of them wondered whether they ought to perhaps suspend the journey to the other continents. There was also the possibility of sailing as far as the Arab States and hoping that a local astronomer could be recruited for assistance. The issue of security was also a concern. Who had taken those maps and why? How had they done it?

"We're as good as lost. If we attempt to sail without proper bearings, we may reach cliffs south of the African continent and damage the fleet. These treasure ships do not do well in shallow waters."

"I agree with my colleague," said Zhou Man. "But I will not have us tarry. We shall need a plan very soon. You are aware that we have already lost twenty horse ships and seventeen battle ships since the heavens ripped through this fleet. We cannot afford to waste further time. Time is money!"

"Ming money," nodded Zheng He's assistant.

"Having the ministers screeching after us every time we propose to sail is one thing but this is sheer incompetence. Can you imagine if the word got out about this? That our entire fleet was incapacitated because we had no starmaps? They'd laugh at us!"

"What I want to know is where Admiral Zheng He has taken his attention," barked another admiral. "Given the circumstances, his absence—"

Another admiral had turned to his assistant, "Did you not tell me last month that we have on our ship, a young student astronomer who is capable of charting the entire starmap?"

"That is what I heard. But the young man is probably boasting."

"Yes, it is unlikely," retorted Zhou Man.

"Believe me, he affirmed that he had memorized a good part of it," said the admiral.

Zhou Man gave his colleague a doubtful glare. This one was about to answer when the cabin door was flung open, startling them all.

They all stared at Zheng He.

"I trust you have an explanation for leaving us at this time," grunted Zhou Man.

"It will not be necessary," replied Zheng He, barely looking at his colleagues. He approached the table with a grave expression.

They noticed that he had been running on the deck and was out of breath. He held what seemed like a dense silk cloth, bundled in his large fist. Right then and there, he spread out the cloth while all those round him peered over with knotted brows.

"Zheng He, my friend, will you kindly explain the meaning of this?" began Zhou Man as he stared at the curious length of fabric.

But one of the navigators promptly interrupted.

"Oh! Isn't this, here, *The Court of Eunuchs*?"

To which an astronomer, who'd been standing a little in retreat, approached and testified with great surprise, "And I recognize *The Celestial Market*...oh, *The Prince* and *The Concubine*," he pointed out.

"What in the heavens is this?" asked one of the admirals.

"It is an old starmap!" assured an Arab navigator. "It features all the constellations we need to make our journey. It is most incredible! Zheng He, may I ask where you found this?"

"You recognize it then," smiled Zheng He.

"Recognize it, sure I do! But what good is it without the names of each—"

"Flip the cloth over."

"What?"

"The names are stitched in blue on the other side of the fabric, see?"

The navigators promptly acquiesced, murmuring among themselves.

Zheng He turned to the assistant navigators.

"Have your men reproduce this map onto parchment and distribute it. You have four hours. In four hours, the Ming fleet will resume its journey to the continents."

"This is incredible!" they exclaimed, inspecting the thousand and four hundred stars stitched miraculously across the cloth.

"San Bao, where have you found this?" enquired Zhou Man with renewed impatience.

"You have four hours," repeated Zheng He.

Under the astounded glance of a dozen naval officers, he had once again abandoned the chamber and somehow followed his legs as quickly as he could, down the stairs, to the lower deck.

I have to find Jun, he thought, if only to thank her... He was enraptured by the incident and his step was light.

He finally reached Old Yu's cabin.

"Old Yu! You there?" he knocked, eager to enquire about Jun's whereabouts. He was startled by frantic yelling. The ship's captain was running towards him.

"Admiral! Admiral, we've found him! The starmap thief! Come quick!"

Chapter 41
The Traitor Among Us

Huang-Fu felt calm when the soldiers, alerted by Lieutenant Deng, had come to manacle him and drag him away. Of course, he did not want to die at sea but at least now, he would not die a traitor. He told himself that as an aspiring cavalry soldier, dying was the last thing that ought to frighten him anyway.

He was about to die for his deeds. His only regret, as he stared at that stubborn horizon of water stretching out before him, was that he would never return to the Middle Kingdom. He would never ride one of those fine horses that he'd tended to for months while the veiled Arab woman watched on. He remembered with amusement now, while the soldiers cursed him and pinned him down onto the reclined wooden plank, how attentively the Semuren had watched him with her large green eyes. In truth, she seemed to watch everything.

They pressed his arms tight against the wooden board, shackling both his wrists and his ankles. Like him, he reflected, the horses had been locked up and ached to run free. Unlike the other sailors, he found it hard to imagine the ocean as the door to freedom. To him it was like a prison. They covered his face with a thin cloth. The fabric's weave was so tight that he could barely breathe.

So then let's be done with it. He swallowed bitterly, embracing his fate. He closed his eyes waiting for the sword. But no blade came down. He waited, his breath coming in spasms beneath the cloth, his chest stretched out tight beneath his tunic. Deng's loud voice rose from above.

"Who did you talk to in Ku'Li? Who worked with you?"

Confused, Huang-Fu tried tilting his head towards the voice.

"Who worked with you?" roared the lieutenant. "I'll make you talk, you cursed swine!"

It came down flooding on his face, the water he dreaded, drowning him, suffocating his lung. For an interminable moment, air was denied to him. Huang-Fu coughed as Deng raised the water can.

"You'll talk now," said Deng, satisfied with himself.

The damp cloth was heavy. It pressed down on his face, blocking his airways. His breathing came fast like short sharp whistles through the fabric. But the air did not come.

Aboard the treasure ship, Zheng He watched from afar as Huang-Fu's questioning began.

"Is that him?" he asked, careful to dissimulate the fact that he recognized the rogue.

"Grand Admiral," replied the captain, "this is the very young man who took away our starmaps. We have two witnesses and one of them is Lieutenant Deng. He swears he saw this man kill Yang Bao."

"But it was an accident..."

"That's what we thought too but Lieutenant Deng assures us the boy had good use of Yang Bao's sword."

"Are you telling me this boy is Yang Bao's murderer?"

"And our thief, Admiral! He'd disguised himself in soldier's clothes to perform his deeds. One of the soldiers posted at the bridge on Zhou Man's ship recognized him."

"You mean...this young boy? We picked him up from..." It was too much. "Why, the miserable...We will teach him to sabotage the fleet!"

As Zheng He fumed, the men below continued hurling insults in the prisoner's direction. An angry crowd had now formed on the upper deck of the naval ship.

"Captain!"

"San Bao, at your command."

"The boy has Folangji connections. Do not kill him. He will be made to speak. Do what you must do. This can never happen again."

"Yes, San Bao!" shouted the Captain as he gave the signal. A drum was struck from the upper deck of the treasure ship.

Zheng He leaned forward.

On Zhou Man's ship, Lieutenant Deng vociferated anew.

"Who did you make contact with? Where is your accomplice?"

He paced nervously around the wooden plank, sending occasional kicks into Huang-Fu's chest.

"I'll make you talk, vermin," he whispered, kneeling close to Huang-Fu's ears. "Piece of shit that you are, you'd better tell me now who your accomplices are! I swear I'll make you speak. I'll make you regret that your swine of a mother gave birth to you."

Huang-Fu nearly passed out with the last blow in his rib.

"Now speak!" roared Deng.

The water gushed down once more in a deluge that stung his lungs. Huang-Fu jerked forward in a desperate struggle to breathe. No more, he thought. No more or this or I'll die.

"Yang Bao! It was Yang Bao!" he cried. The terror in his voice tore through the upper deck, muffled as it were by the pouring water and the soaked cloth.

Deng raised the can but to Huang-Fu, it felt as though more water submerged his face, refusing him any air, air that he wanted so badly. It was as though water had entered his airways, suffocating his lungs. He gagged. His hands and feet stiffened with panic. The metal bar rattled as he tried in vain to free himself from his shackles.

On the treasure ship, Zheng He remained tense, still pacing the upper deck.

"Has he spoken yet, Captain?"

"Not a word, Admiral. He refuses to speak."

"Then continue."

His stern gaze followed once more the proceeds on the ship below.

Again the can was raised above the prisoner. Huang-Fu could no longer breathe. His wet limbs trembled uncontrollably against the wooden board.

Zheng He watched as though in a bad dream, as the boy's body stiffened. Huang-Fu appeared to choke. He convulsed once more. And then suddenly the admiral gripped the railing. His anger had lifted. He felt a peculiar numbness as he confronted the raw scene below. Everywhere, cursing soldiers eyed the hapless prisoner with savage intent. Now the lieutenant filled his can anew.

Zheng He's horrified gaze traversed the unruly deck. Whether he saw it or imagined it, it was real; the bloodshot eyes, the tattered tunics reeking of sweat and excrement, the hirsute beards... How desperate they all were. Their tired limbs were burnt by sun and sea salt. They had gone several nights without sleep, in fear of the Heavens, in mourning for the death of their companions. Even as the fleet's carpenters scrambled to reassemble each ship, the men were haunted by the dismembered wreckage of sister ships floating all around them.

And now, after the great storm, they had joined together to denounce their fate. If the sea dragons would not be held accountable, then someone else would. Someone else had to pay.

The indignant voices rose to mass hysteria.

"Kill him!" they bellowed, raising their fists.

"Traitor!" shouted the others.

"Throw him overboard! Murderer!"

Something in Huang-Fu's limp body seized Zheng He with doubt. The admiral signaled frantically from the railing. Lieutenant Deng saw this and motioned towards Huang-Fu. Zheng He's breath halted. On the naval vessel, Lieutenant Deng lifted the damp cloth to assess whether the prisoner gave signs of life. And in that instant, the young Hue from the clearing glimpsed the sorrowful light in Huang-Fu's eyes.

Zheng He stood back, mouth agape. A truth he had long denied, forced itself before him. He saw its hideous reality. It singed his ears. It spoke to him in Min Li's broken voice. The voice he had ignored.

"*We are all his slaves*," she had said.

Then he heard his words. They were proud as always. *"I am no slave."*

And as he stared at Huang-Fu's torn limbs, Zheng He repeated those absurd words. He struggled to believe in them, struggled to persuade himself that she too, had acted upon nothing else than mere ambition and self-interest. Only he knew, now that it was not true. It had never been.

He turned to an officer.

"Stop them."

"Admiral?"

"Sound your cannons, send your soldiers to Zhou Man's ship and bring that boy up here."

"After they have killed him, Admiral?" asked the dumbfounded lieutenant.

"No. Now! Do it."

***

Huang-Fu stirred. He knew that voice. He scrutinized the cabin. Officers stood at the door while an older man in an admiral's uniform spoke with the ship's captain.

He had hoped for swift death. But death had not come. Now it appeared that he was about to meet Admiral Zheng He before dying. That was a curious honor. What could the Grand Admiral possibly want with him?

Huang-Fu raised himself on the stool where he'd been tied. He squinted through swollen pupils. The admiral turned around and approached him.

He came closer. Huang-Fu saw his face. He saw the dignified mouth with its firm, yet fleshy lips, the bright eyes where shone an intelligent light. He saw the fine high brow and the solemn, inscrutable jaw line. Huang-Fu gasped in disbelief. Life certainly knew how to deal him a strange hand.

The hermit from the inn, the man he had so insolently addressed months ago in the Tanggu winehouse was the very man who'd been leading this fleet all along. The so called fool that he'd quarreled with inside the inn was none other than the admiral that he'd secretly idolized for months. The Hue! They'd skinned him alive for this...

"Hold him," said Zheng He. "Now, you listen to me. Is it true? Did you kill Yang Bao?"

Huang-Fu nodded.

"Speak up!"

"I killed Yang Bao," he mouthed pitifully, his head slanting to the side.

"You killed Yang Bao, just as you killed those other thirty men on my ship! Why?"

"No! I never—"

"Traitor!" barked the captain, "You'll pay for this!"

It did not matter if they did not believe him. He was already as a good as dead.

"Why did you steal the maps?" asked Zheng He.

"They were going to kill me if I hadn't."

"Do not lie to me! Who? Who was going to kill you?"

"I'm not lying. They wanted the maps...they paid Yang Bao…they—"

"Leave Yang Bao out of this. Who? Who wanted the maps?"

"The Folangji... I met bad men in Ku'Li... They forced us to steal the maps... I... Look, I was in a bad state, I gambled... These men found me... They paid Yang Bao to—"

"What a fine ambassador you are. Have you no loyalty, even to yourself?" said Zheng He.

He moved back to his desk, retrieving a document from the first drawer. "I have here a report from your superior that you were chosen to advise on Folangji informers. Your merits are listed here – highly diligent, fit, capable – blah blah blah – trustworthy..." He shook his head. "This document is far too kind to you." He slammed the paper across Huang-Fu's face.

"It's no use, I can't read it."

"Well that's one area where you could put your clever wits to good use."

"I don't want to be a scholar. I wanted to join the cavalry," replied Huang-Fu, his ears burning with shame.

"You had your chance. And look what happened as soon as you were on the land. You were asked to pay close attention to foreign informers. Instead you say that you gambled with locals?"

Huang-Fu said nothing.

"I remain fascinated by the workings of your mind. And what? That they forced you to procure maps? What then prevented you from reporting these men? What?"

"Honorable Admiral, I am deeply sorry, I am a wretch. But please, hear me out…"

"I've had enough of listening to this cut-throat dog, San Bao. I say we hang him."

"I am not a traitor! Hear me out, Admiral."

"Shut up!" roared the captain.

Zheng He silenced his captain with one hand gesture.

"Speak then, Huang-Fu."

"I couldn't tell... No one would've believed me. I was afraid of Yang Bao. He attacked me because I was the only witness to his crime. He was a strong man to beat, Admiral…"

"How dare you!"

The captain pounded forward. He seized Huang-Fu's neck, with his giant hands.

"Captain! Captain, I will have you stop at once!" shouted Zheng He.

"This coward is sullying Yang Bao's name, Admiral!"

"He was a dangerous man," protested Huang-Fu. "His martial art technique was...like you'd never seen…He would have killed me if I hadn't…"

"Why? Why would he want to kill you?"

"Because I knew," whispered Huang-Fu. "I knew everything. They paid him, paid him to get maps for the Folang—"

"You expect us to believe that Yang Bao was in league with foreign spies? That's a far stretch," reproached Zheng He.

"Zheng He, let me cut this traitor's tongue, I've heard enough!"

"No, listen! I heard the reports about the thief on board, Admiral. I knew it was him."

"And you expect us to believe you!" bellowed the captain.

"You have to believe me! No, no, please, listen! Isn't it true that you wounded him, Admiral? You wounded the thief..."

Zheng He's eyes widened. He stood back.

"The boy could be saying the truth... Remove his shirt, captain."

"What?"

"Remove the boy's shirt."

The soldiers stripped off Huang-Fu's shirt. It was covered over in bruises and cuts but not a blemish lay on his skin where the jade-hilted sword had struck their thief.

"He drank brandy almost every day to calm his pain," said Huang-Fu.

"Captain, find me Old Yu. You shall ask him to examine Yang Bao's corpse."

"You don't believe what this swine is saying, do you, Admiral? He may not be the man we saw on the bridge but it makes no difference! He stole the maps!"

"Find me Old Yu, Captain."

When the captain had left, Zheng He stood in silence. Huang-Fu noticed that he seemed filled with self-reproach. The admiral paced the room for a long time before speaking.

"I sat in that inn for two nights," he began. "The first night, you did not even see me. But I was there. Long enough. I made a judgment about you. I pray to Allah I was not wrong. It is true I made the mistake of trying to change your life. You had little choice but to board. I take responsibility for that. Maybe I should have left you on the port..."

He turned around to face Huang-Fu.

"So unless you lied about Yang Bao, I will spare your life."

"The wretch you met is a reckless street thug...but he is not a bad man."

Without replying, the admiral approached. He bent forward and picked up Huang-Fu's wet tunic before handing it back to him. He nodded to the soldiers who untied the boy at once.

"Admiral, I...I remember what you told me in the inn, before we boarded. Admiral, you are no fool. I am the fool."

Zheng He did not know what to reply.

Moments later, Old Yu appeared. With his head lowered, the physician seemed troubled. He entered the room quietly, eyeing the soldiers with apprehension. Then he pressed his spectacles to his nose in disbelief. His eyes lingered on the prisoner's bloodied face, then back at his friend and again towards Huang-Fu. He seemed shocked. Finally, his shoulders sinking, he shook his head.

"Cursed Yang Bao," he said. Then he spit on the ground and shuffled away.

Chapter 42
A Daughter Returns

An unveiled Shahrzad glided along the inside patio of her home. She did not care if the full-length kaftan brushed the cold mosaic tiles. Her hair was loose, sending whiffs of bergamot and sandalwood along the path.

She walked with decisive steps, past the red wooden colonnade bordering the courtyard, past the blue Moroccan chest below the kitchen window, past the all-seeing mirrors in their carved cedar frames and past the palms in their generous earthen pots.

Shahrzad saw nothing, save for the green door ahead. She had made the decision today, the decision to walk through that green door. And now, she held her head high, her palms close to her chest as though sheltering her soul, sheltering her inner soul.

She neared the end of the corridor where two native servants guarded her father's bedroom. The local physician was here. He had not slept. Shahrzad gestured towards him.

"Leave," she ordered.

They obeyed. The first servant pushed the door to let her enter.

The old man breathed in death. He reeked of death. He dreamt of death. He did not see at first, the dark figure enter. With the afternoon light behind her, the blue silk kaftan dimmed to black. Then it glowed once more as Shahrzad turned around, closing the doors.

She inhaled the dusty smell, the damp heat, the pile of stained linen by the side of her father's bed. She saw how the sweaty robe clung to his frail frame. A raspy cough interrupted her thoughts. He had seen her. He was just too weak to move, too weak to welcome her back. Already, he raised one eyebrow as though to say, "See, I knew. I knew, you'd come. I knew all along you'd be back."

She swallowed hard.

"Father..."

"Sit... Sit," he whispered.

She sat by his side, refusing his outstretched hand, watching his contented smile fade. Yet he did not give up. What father ever does? He watched her. But Shahrzad had soon averted her eyes and resumed her silence.

"Ah, my daughter... Allah is great. You have something...to tell me...don't you? If you do…please...tell me. I don't know where...where you have gone for so long... I don't know."

She stood in a cold aloofness. She could hear the birds outside. The light pierced through the wooden blinds. It drew spots on her kaftan.

Then she sighed, breaching the silence of many years, expecting him to remember and to understand.

"Then I will tell you," she began. Her words were heavy. "Do you remember the day when the Sultan of Malindi first came to visit?"

The old man was silent. Why was she bringing up the Sultan? It seemed like too long ago. He squinted. He searched through memories, searched through the many receptions. There was a cluttering noise as Mustafa saw the gilded platters advancing towards the richly clad guests.

Reaching for another drink, the contented Malindi Sultan stared back at his host. Yes, Mustafa recalled that day. It was the day he and his daughter had laughed together for the last time. Why had he never thought of that?

He nodded quietly.

"You remember, then?" came her voice in a reproachful whisper. She exhaled her contempt. "I'm sure you remember."

Mustafa stared wide-eyed at the shadow over his bed. He looked into her grave face. He blinked. And then she was his dear girl again. She was smiling at him in that memory. Her voice was warmth. He remembered more. On that morning, before meeting with the Sultan, he watched from afar as she ran towards Kareem. They disappeared towards the stables.

Mustafa remembered. He was younger. His beard, not yet sparse, not yet gray. The jewels sparkled on his gilded broad-sleeved garb. He reclined on a rattan couch under the afternoon shade. He liked to entertain his rich guests in the center of his home, in the courtyard. Like him, they smiled, ecstatic with their new business agreement.

And then much later, they heard the clamoring as the heavy double doors of the entrance hall were slammed. They heard the quick steps. Mustafa shifted his weight, edging forward to grab a date. With a mellow smile, he appeased his guests. He presented a date to the Persian and cast a glance towards the front doors.

He glimpsed an intermittent vision gliding across the veranda, her somber face shielded behind the colonnades. There were whispers among his guests.

He wondered why she walked so hastily. He feared that something might be wrong with his sweet angel. Out of the corner of his eye, he saw his guest smile, heard him comment on the quality of Omani dates but Mustafa was not listening. He had just seen his daughter's blood-streaked face...

"You remember, Father, don't you? Of course you remember. I want to tell you what I saw that day but I don't know how to begin."

The unsettling memory surged in his mind. The gliding figure came closer. She was only several paces away. She had come to a stop after the last column, her body partly shielded by the stone, her hair loose around her unveiled face. And there! That red line on her forehead... How had it come about?

Her gaze was insolent. She observed the gilded party, the silver embroidered robes, the opulent chair where her father sat up, mouth agape, the gold jewelry...

One of the servants had rushed to her side. It was Shahrzad's nurse, old and gray haired but black as night. Amira wrapped a protective arm around Shahrzad. The soothing voice with its warm Swahili accent drew the guests' attention.

"My Eye, what is wrong? What is wrong? What happened to your face?"

But Shahrzad was not listening. She could hear nothing. All she saw, was *him*. She watched *him*. The disdain on her lips was unmistakable.

As the ailing man remembered this last vision, he nodded.

Above him, her voice rose. It was filled with hate.

"Well, if you must know, I shall tell you. I know about you, Father. I know everything! I shall never forget what I saw that day." She swallowed indignant tears. "Truly, I cannot be like you. What I saw that day..." She shook her head vigorously. "I can never be like you."

The tears ran down the old man's sunken cheeks. He nodded but his mouth was twisted in a painful rictus.

She had spoken. The raw violence she long held back had slammed the old man in the chest, hard. She watched her father's convulsive sobs and felt the shame of her outburst. She was surprised by her previous words. How easy it had been.

She sat by his side once more, preparing to start all over again. She wanted to start again. But she could not feel anything. She had been away too long, seething with resentment. Her pride forbade any forgiveness.

It was he who first spoke.

"You spent all this time hating me. All this time..."

"I did not hate you. I never hated you. But..."

"I love you, Shahrzad. You are all I have. All I have," he repeated.

"...so vile we both are. For years I struggled. I struggled with myself. And now I am telling you this. I don't want a part in this, any of it. I will put an end to this vile business when you are gone. And I shall..."

She shook her head with disgust. Her face grew tense.

"And Father, let me tell you something. There were moments in my anger when I thought about what you had done with your life, moments where I brooded over the darkest of thoughts. I have had thoughts..."

She observed his neck and saw how he struggled to breathe. The pulse quickened on his wiry neck. She knew that he understood what was coming. She heard contempt in her own voice as she continued.

"I had thoughts about killing you. Yes, that's right. There was murder in my heart. You think I am incapable of it, but you are wrong. I thought about it for months after what happened that day. Truth is, you repulsed me. No, don't look at me like that. You think

I couldn't do it? How wrong you are. If in those angry moments I had been sitting there, looking at your shriveled neck I could have easily reached forth and strangled the life out of you. But...what good would that do now?"

She stood.

"You know, Father...there were days and nights when it would have pleased me to put an end to your life. Yes, it is true... I considered it, only to see this wretched business closed. But you know what happened, then? You know why I could not kill you?"

She smiled.

"Well it's a crazy story. When I thought I had reached a point where I could no longer accept it, where you just had to die for your sins…a most peculiar thing happened. You know what it was?"

She emitted a nervous laugh.

His eyes widened. He held his breath and stared into the empty space above, listening to her every word. She laughed and shook her head.

"It was silly. I lost my khanjar! Just what I told you, an absurd tale! But when it happened, I saw it as a sign. Maybe...maybe Allah, peace be upon him, was trying to tell me something. He took away my dagger. At once, I realized what a good thing it was. I am a foolish woman. I have much to thank Him for."

She sighed and knelt at the bedside. Her face edged closer to his.

"You go to Him now. Only He knows whether I am mad or whether you are indeed a wretched man."

After those spiteful words, her face became tender.

"There is more I want to tell you," she whispered.

She reached for his hand. He clutched hers with all the weak strength he had left.

"Shahrzad," he lamented, broken by her words. "I...I have little time."

"Yes. It is right for you to talk of little time. But you see, Father, we all have such a short time. It should be treasured. It should be spent in good deeds."

She hesitated. Bitterness had merged with regret. Should she tell him? She had never told anyone, save Kareem. Although her fiancé often wished that he had remained in the dark. But her father was about to die. And she knew that they would never be able to speak to each other again. She saw that the old man wanted to hear more. His eyes betrayed the eagerness thumping in his chest and his claw-like grip was tight around her hand, urging her on.

Now, she realized. I will tell him now. And in a moment of trust, she understood that she had forgiven him.

So she began.

"Father, it is this. I am writing a book."

She waited for a reaction. Mustafa stared ahead in silence.

"You know...a story! Like those Persian tales I used to read... I am writing a story about a man. I am over halfway now."

She smiled, spurred on by her revelation.

"There's just one more thing...just someone I need to study. It is a woman, Father, a most intriguing woman. I need to discover a little more about her...and then, just a few more chapters...perhaps another trip to the Middle Kingdom…"

She interrupted herself.

The old man was dying. The light in his eyes was fading fast. As life slipped out of him, his body floated above and he observed this curious scene.

There sat his daughter, kneeling at his bedside. She beamed with rapture. Her eyes sparkled like two amber stones dancing under a glowing fire. It was a heartfelt, joyful smile. It was the smile of youth and hope, the smile of joyful escape.

"You go to him now, Father..."

Suddenly he saw her face more clearly than before, the face without the veil, her real face. There she was, the little Shahrzad he remembered, his own daughter. He recognized her again in that rare smile so full of secrets.

And now he understood. He understood how she had consumed the last years and where her mind had roamed, for comfort, for joy, for peace.

He saw well beyond her anger, beyond her bitterness. He recognized his child. The vision lifted his soul.

"Allah is great," he said, closing his eyes.

There was happiness, yet, in knowing that the long time stranger who now sat by his side had finally revealed her name. It was the very name on his lips when he expired.

Chapter 43
A Certain Box

Days later, even while he farewelled the other admirals and prepared for Beijing, Zheng He pondered over the embroidery and its origin. It nagged him.

He had no doubt that Jun had embroidered the cloth. Old Yu would confirm it. Yet if Jun had seen a starmap before, something Zheng He found entirely implausible, how could she have reproduced it with such clarity and, according to the navigators, such accuracy? The thought that a woman, one who had never sailed, could replicate more than two hundred constellations let alone name their stars, was aberrant.

Zheng He wanted to reveal this curious happenstance to someone else, if only to gain another opinion but there was no one he could trust with it. The political nature of such documents made it impossible for him to implicate Jun. It was dangerous. She could be arrested and accused of dabbling in affairs of the state. At worst, she could be accused of witchcraft. The admiral was conscious of the peril that would befall the woman he had grown to appreciate and so he remained silent.

Another vague notion stirred his mind. He was well aware that signs in themselves are divine gifts to guide men and that men should be thankful for those signs. Perhaps Jun had translated these divine signs through her artful embroidery, not understanding their meaning.

And so the more he thought about this notion and nursed it, the more Zheng He realized that there was something peculiar about his dream. The Taoist priest was wrong. In the dream, Zheng He had not seen Mazu. He had seen Jun. There was no question about it. He now had the firm conviction that it was the seamstress who had visited him in his dream and, Allah forgive him for thinking this, that it was she who had saved him.

And this made Zheng He even more uncomfortable. How is it that I feel I owe this woman something? How should I imagine that this woman, this complete stranger, for that is what she is, has crossed the dream realm to even help me?

Zheng He laughed. Just listen to me, he thought. And I know so little about her!

Not so, said a little voice. Not so.

Because there was one thing... He wandered to the back of the cabin where various boxes were stacked. He examined each box, searching for something. "Something made of *nanmu*..." he invoked as though prompting the object to reveal itself.

At last he found it. It was the box he had confiscated a few days after their departure. It rested on the edge of the shelf beside his books. The storm and the fleet's predicament had distracted him. But now he felt it again, the urge to discover its content. It gnawed at him stronger than before.

Zheng He ran his hand on the lid as though to wipe dust from the red paint. He could, if he wanted to, find out all there was to know about the seamstress. He believed the content of this mysterious box might explain his dream. It would dispel the aura around Jun, an aura he felt he was only attributing to her because of his curiosity.

Yes, it made perfect sense. There is no witchcraft about this woman, he reasoned with himself. The truth is that I am curious. This curiosity haunts me. It causes me to dream of her. I must find her and return this object.

***

In the plant lined corridor leading to the ship's bridge, Old Yu stooped to pick up a withered flower. Then he lit up a pipe and reflected on his find.

He was lamenting the state of the garden beds when a vision startled him. He had just seen Zheng He emerge from his cabin, a deep frown etched on his forehead. The navigator seemed to be in a great hurry as he fled down the stairs to the lower deck.

Old Yu raised his head towards the staircase to greet him.

"San Bao, my boy!"

"Ah, Old Yu," came the absent-minded reply.

"Missing Zhou Man, already?" asked the physician.

"Zhou man is quite capable, I assure you," dismissed the admiral. "No, I was resuming an errand I delayed for far too long. I would like to return this to our storyteller."

Old Yu noticed the navigator held a large wooden box under his arm.

"What is it?"

"It belongs to her," said Zheng He reluctant to say more. "Do you know where she is?"

Old Yu nodded quietly. He removed his glasses and began to wipe them, evading Zheng He's insistent gaze.

"I've not seen her for days," he finally answered. "It bothers me." He replaced his spectacles on his nose and sighed. "Not since the storm at least..."

Zheng He gave his physician an inquisitive glance. Old Yu inhaled another puff.

"How is your cough, Admiral? You sound well."

"Recovering, thank you. What do you mean? Where is Jun, Old Yu?"

In all reply, Old Yu squinted through his glasses and looked at the sea.

"A shame, really..." he said. "Now that everything's quietened around here, I was looking forward to listening to the end of this Yunnan tale. But the woman is gravely ill. More ill than before...What can you do?"

Zheng He eyed the box in his hand and pursed his lips.

"With your permission, Admiral," continued Old Yu, "we will have her escorted to her home as soon as we arrive in Guangdong."

Zheng He seemed saddened by the news. He was about to return to his cabin when he stopped, halfway through the steps. A firm resolve illuminated his face.

"Perhaps I should pay her a courtesy visit."

Old Yu was startled. He gaped at the admiral, pipe in hand.

"You would do that?"

Zheng He blushed.

"Only with your permission."

***

When Zheng He descended into the cramped lower deck, he at once felt the oppressive heat. Here, men and a few women lived, as best they could despite the pungent odors of excrement and urine. The confinement was such that the admiral could not stand straight. Being taller than most, he had to stoop as they traversed the male quarters. In a far corner, Jun shared a tiny, windowless cabin with six other women some of whom were concubines. She lay on a filthy mat curled up in a ball, her damp hair clinging to her pale face.

When the admiral approached, the other women sat up from their mats, looking at him with frightful eyes.

"She is sleeping," volunteered one of them in a Guangdong dialect. "Very very sick..."

"How long has she been like this?" asked Zheng He.

The concubine shrugged her shoulders.

"Old Yu," cringed the admiral, "this place is horrible! No wonder she is sick!"

"The cabins are airless in this area of the deck, Admiral."

Zheng He stared at the tiny seamstress.

He leaned forward, aware that she would be terrified if she awoke. He couldn't contain himself. Extending a hand, he touched the woman's cheek.

"Old Yu," he whispered, "she is burning!"

Old Yu shook his head. He had already tried everything to help her. It wasn't his fault was it? None of those damn herbs worked.

"We must move her!" cried Zheng He. "Lift her from here at once. You!" He called out to an officer on duty. "Fetch a stretcher from the hospital! We need to move this woman. Hurry!"

Old Yu was taken aback.

"Move her? Where to? All the female bunks are occupied. Surely you do not propose to move her to the men's quarters?"

"She cannot remain in this airless cabin for any longer! We need to do something, Old Yu!"

"Yes, yes. But there are no available rooms. Ever since the storm, I have used the spare cabins as a hospital. The bunks are full!"

"Well then," replied the admiral in an icy tone, "take her to my cabin."

Old Yu shook his head. The admiral was behaving very strangely.

Chapter 44
Chantefable Four: Sonam

It was odd seeing her in his cabin. There is something not quite right about this woman, he thought, watching her sleep. She haunts my dreams and knows astronomy. His gaze fell upon the wooden box. When they lifted her to his cabin, he had seen the key slip out of her little apron. It would be easy to push the key into the bronze lock...to take a look while she slept... And he was curious to know everything there was to know about Jun and about her wooden box.

All that remains for me to understand who this woman is, he mused, raising the object, is this box. That is all. I must open it.

***

When she finally came to, a warm glow illuminated her exhausted face. She watched him silently, observing his hesitation. The tall admiral sat on a stool, a low stool reserved for officers.

"Are you feeling a little better?" he asked. Then he took a deep breath. "I just want to... I want to thank you for..."

She closed her eyes. Had she heard? The sweat glistened down her temples and he grew concerned. He reached out to offer her some tea. Again, she opened her eyes but tilted her head away from the drink.

"I want to thank you for…" he repeated.

Then, remembering the reason he had tried to find her, he reached towards a low table.

"I have asked that all your belongings be placed here. See? Nothing is missing."

Jun continued to stare at him.

"Your box is here too," he added, hoping she would be pleased.

And then she spoke.

"You have come, Admiral. You have come to hear me finish my tale, have you not?"

"No, Jun."

"And yet...there is so much more..."

He smiled at her eagerness.

"Perhaps it is best that you rest."

"No," she replied, startling him. "It is best that you listen."

There was something about the way she had spoken. He was too stunned to refuse. And so he listened.

She began weakly but as her tale progressed the gentle voice acquired such strength that Zheng He knew not how such a fragile vessel could sustain it. He did not question or interrupt a single moment so enthralled was he with Jun's tale and secretly relieved that she was no longer feverish.

***

Now, honored listener, where did this ailing storyteller leave you last? Ah yes. You remember now. Bei Lan had met the handsome Sonam. And, oh, what a man he was!

Sonam was like what the people of the Middle Kingdom called a Kunlun. That is to say he was dark-skinned, with skin much darker than mine. He came from the villages to the east of the Hengduan Mountain range. He was a traveler. With the exception of the rainy period beginning in the fifth lunar month and ending in the seventh lunar month, he followed the *chamadao*, the tea horse road.

Like many who dared journey through this, the most dangerous mountain route in the world, Sonam was prosperous player in the trade between the Ming and the U-Tsang people.

Storyteller, what is this trade route you speak of? And why is it so important to this story? Honored listener, you must listen well.

It is a regulated trade. Only those with a license can take part in it. Together with salt and sugar, catties of tea from Yunnan, are carried across to U-Tsang. Once in Lhasa, tea catties are exchanged for horses and they in turn are brought back for the Ming army.

Bei Lan held her breath as Sonam described the beauty of the *chamadao*. She marveled at the lakes, the canyons and valleys of this famed road which skirted the foot of the Hengduan Mountain Range.

"You will not see the power of the Mountain God until you have lived through the capricious weather of the *chamadao*," Sonam had declared, his voice filled with passion.

He went on to describe how his face could burn from the sun one moment, only to be frosty the next and how he had to clothe himself well for the cold winds and snow.

But Bei Lan could scarcely imagine it. And for all the beauty around her, nested as they were in the mountainous heaven of Nonguzhi, the idea that such exulting landscape as that described by Sonam could exist, had soon driven her to obsession. She wanted to hear it...

Beyond Nonguzhi, he described the Jinsha River bend, flanked by canyons and valleys beyond which the blue sky seemed to stretch endlessly. For those who had never traveled the road, it was like reaching the heavens. And further along, just before Deqin, again there was a river crossing. There, the canyons and valleys dwarfed the traveler as though he were an invisible speck cradled in the realm of the Mountain God.

"It is the most beautiful thing you have ever seen," said Sonam. "But you must have courage to travel this road."

And then Sonam was on his way. But before he left, he lowered himself from his horse and slipped a flower in Bei Lan's hair. With a smile on her face, she waved goodbye and watched the graceful flick of his horse's tail as it moved out of the village square.

She remained there, watching him and a strange thing began to happen on this tired woman's face. It looked a little like hope when hope visits the disappointed. But no one in the village took any notice at the time. Though everyone knew just how bold Sonam was when he set his mind to something. When his dark fingers had brushed through the strands of her auburn hair to place the crimson flower, he had looked into her eyes and told Bei Lan that he would back.

And before long, true to his word, he was back. Sonam made the journey three times in a year and three times in a year, he found himself in Nonguzhi. Bei Lan began to learn to wait for him.

Soon, village women noticed that Sonam was planning his passage in Nonguzhi so that he could be assured to spend several days with Bei Lan. The women believed that perhaps Bei Lan would soon invite Sonam to her home but she did none of it.

"What's taking you so long, Bei Lan?"

"He is a good friend, Jamma."

"A good friend? What are you waiting for? An avalanche to swallow up the most virile man in the mountains? I'm telling you Sonam travels through plenty of villages on his way to Lhasa and if he is making a special pause in Nonguzhi you had better make your move before he decides to find a mountain lily and forgets all about you."

"I am happy being his friend, Jamma."

"Nonsense. You need a mountain horse ride, girl, that's what you need."

And on and on it went.

And one day, after Bei Lan had been friends with Sonam for two years, he returned from Lhasa as usual, tired after his long journey but eager to see the young woman. And soon one of Bei Lan's friend was running through the streets, looking for her.

"Come, come Sister," called out the young woman to whom she had taught her fine embroidery techniques.

"What is it?"

"Leave that laundry. Just come up, now! It's Sonam! He's back!"

Bei Lan's heart leapt in her chest.

She abandoned her laundry by the side of the Three Wells and ran up the broad steps and onto the Market Square to see for herself what her friend would not tell her.

When she arrived, flushed and panting from her race, a familiar figure in a fleecy sheep vest and leather trousers stood by the shade of an elm tree. Beside him, were not one, but two horses.

When he saw the color rise to Bei Lan's cheeks, Sonam smiled so that sunlight seemed to illuminate the square. He led the shorter of the two horses which was a beautiful dark brown color towards her. Bei Lan's face was radiant. She took the reins that Sonam presented her. He took her hand and set it on the horse's flank, stroking its mane with her palm.

It was a gift. Sonam had saved hard to purchase this horse and had brought it back all the way from U-Tsang. He let go of her hand so that together, they began to caress the horse in silence. She raised her face towards him.

"You must have courage," he said simply. "I will teach you."

Ah, storyteller, you alone, know well what those words meant for Bei Lan. She had more courage than what Sonam could have ever imagined. But what did he know of this strange woman from the North?

Soon enough, Sonam and Bei Lan spent much time together in the fields. He gave her his time and taught her how to ride. She fell off twice but over the days, her confidence grew until she was keeping her balance even when the horse trotted.

"It wasn't bad for a fortnight of riding," said Sonam with a smile, "but you will improve."

And all along, the gossip raged in the village.

"Yes, you will see," strutted Jamma to the other women. "Now the stubborn girl will make her move if she knows what's good for her."

But despite Jamma's wishful rants, the villagers all knew very well that Bei Lan had still not slept with the *chamadao* traveler. Before long, Bei Lan remained in Nonguzhi while Sonam left.

And three more years passed. Still Sonam had not become Bei Lan's *azhu*. And on the fifth year, when the month of his arrival arrived at last, Bei Lan was sitting by the shade of the elm tree waiting for him. All the village women grew more excited. They were thrilled that she had perhaps made a decision after months of pining for him.

In the Market Square, they watched Bei Lan rise and greet Sonam. They watched the two friends embrace each other and Sonam lead his horse to the inn. Soon enough they were riding away and the woman exchanged knowing glances at each other.

And then something unexpected happened. The very next day, Sonam was gone.

Jamma was out of herself when she heard the news.

"What! He did not stay for the whole ten days this time? What did you do to him? You want your children to shrivel in your womb, is that what you want?"

"We had a disagreement," said Bei Lan quite simply.

"Ah yes, still playing hard to get, Bei Lan. You must be as stupid as a stuffed up bamboo tube. Well he's forgotten you now. He'll be making all the village women very happy now, just you wait."

Despite this, Bei Lan kept firmly to herself.

But after several days of questioning, Jamma soon learn of what had transpired between Bei Lan and Sonam.

Jun began to cough violently. Zheng He watched with alarm as tiny specks of blood dotted her blouse. As he rose to summon Old Yu, an officer entered the cabin, followed by a eunuch.

The two naval officers began to speak aloud among themselves like most men do when an insignificant woman is in the room. They spoke of her while she lay in bed but she could hear their every word.

Zheng He was observing the eunuch.

"We can trust him," he nodded. "How long until we reach the port of Guangdong?" he asked, dabbing a cloth on Jun's forehead.

"Four hours," replied the soldier.

And then something happened. Jun understood that very soon, she was to leave the ship. Her face became terribly convulsed.

"Please please, hear my tale!"

"You must rest now," protested Zheng He. "I will call Old Yu, he knows what to do."

But Jun was in distress. She began to twist her bruised hands together and then she reached towards the admiral, tugged at his robe and pleaded that he remain. Zheng He signaled to the officer and this one rushed out to fetch Old Yu. The admiral was baffled.

"Jun. Jun! Listen, Old Yu will come to examine you. You can continue your tale later..."

He could not finish. Jun suddenly rose up. She reached with one hand and suddenly, breaching all protocol, she gripped the admiral's arm. Her skin burnt. As taken aback as he was, Zheng He did not let go, nor did he recoil in disgust as he had when Min Li's mother had grasped his ankles, decades ago. Sitting back down, he held Jun's hand to reassure her. And despite this, he watched her face contort. For some reason there was fear in her voice.

"Please... Please, hear the story..."

Zheng He did not know what to do. It was very early in the morning. He ought to get some sleep before his first meeting in the next couple of hours. But Jun did not let go.

"Admiral, you *must* listen. Not long to go now. Not long..."

Poor woman, he thought. This illness has made her lose her senses...

"Sit," pleaded Jun. "You sit here. I will finish soon. No more coughing, see? I am well."

He nodded. Perhaps telling this story allows her to remain strong, he thought. Whatever the reason, I can probably stay here for a while. Old Yu will arrive soon. And I am certain that she is bound to fall asleep...

"Very well. So tell me then, why did they quarrel? What caused their discord?"

"You already know this. You remember," she said in a haunting voice.

He frowned.

"That does not make any sense Jun," chided Zheng He.

"All that is to come is in your past," she insisted. "You see what comes next and you remember. It's all the same thing," she repeated nonsensically.

Then she closed her eyes and her voice changed. It was clear and smooth and the words rhymed again.

Bei Lan and Sonam kissed. His mouth was hard and demanding but his eyes begged and begged. "Bei Lan! Bei Lan!" they seemed to plead. "Do you not know, Sister, how much I pine for you? Long before I met you, the canyons and the valleys of the *chamadao* were beauty on earth for me and now... Now, I do not even look around me when I journey to Lhasa. I look back towards Nonguzhi and I look ahead whenever I return to you."

If Bei Lan understood what Sonam spoke with his eyes, she did not show it. But how she loved to hold him! How she loved his kisses on her eyes, cheeks and lips.

Today the kisses burnt and she decided that it was time to ask what she had wanted to ask ever since Sonam had brought the colt with him.

"You have told me about the *chamadao* many times," she began.

"Yes," replied the beaming Sonam, still ecstatic from being reunited with the woman he hoped would accept him and take him home.

"And now that I can even ride Mountain King," she continued, speaking of his horse, "will you not take me with you to see the river bend at Deqin? We could go at the edge of the rainy season when you are not engaged in trade. That way it would be just a short journey. I want to see the beauty as I cross the three rivers. I've longed to see it."

Sonam smiled. But he said nothing.

"I want to come with you, Sonam. I can gallop now. I'm very good."

"Ah," he sighed. "It is not possible."

He was smiling as he said this because he did not want to hurt her. This was his flower after all. He could not refuse her anything.

"Why not? Sonam...I want to come with you."

"It is too dangerous. You ride here but up there, the air is different. You will get sick. The terrain is rough and dangerous. I told you this many times," he said, almost sorry that he had even mentioned the *chamadao* in so many details.

He had aroused her envy when all he had wanted was her admiration.

She pouted. He reached out to hold her in his arms but she shrugged him off. Sonam was disconcerted.

When he attempted to gently reason with her, he was met with cold responses.

And then a curious thing happened. Bei Lan became so very quiet and would not speak to him. Together they strolled but she remained absent. She ceased replying to his questions and no longer laughed at his jokes.

So when Sonam saw that the woman he loved was so upset at him, he did what many spirited wanderers do when they are at loss and encounter a difficulty. He left.

And this was why when Jamma looked around for Sonam's horse in the Market Square, she did not see it.

***

It took Zheng He a long moment before he even noticed that Jun had ceased her tale.

For a while, he just sat there. He had, it seemed, forgotten all about having called Old Yu. He stared ahead, oblivious to his surroundings.

His eyes welled with tears.

"Did Sonam ever come back," he asked.

Jun closed her eyes and did not reply.

Zheng He waited, wondering whether she would resume her tale. But she didn't.

Bending forward, he neared his ear towards her face. Her breath was faint. Not a sound rose from her lips. She was asleep.

Four hours later, in the early morning, the admiral stood by as the ailing Jun boarded a barge with her eunuch escort.

He would forever remember his clumsiness during their last encounter on the bridge and how he, the powerful Grand Admiral had been lost for words before the seamstress.

"Thank you for your good work, Jun," he'd said, clutching his own hand.

She had nodded, too weak to reply.

"I wish you a good journey... May the path you walk on—"

Jun had tried to bow.

"Please," he said, reaching out to stop her. But he restrained himself, aware of the many witnesses.

"Goodbye Jun... The Ming fleet is indebted to you."

He thought that she had smiled back but he wasn't sure.

When the barge finally headed towards the port of Guangdong, he ran to the other side of the deck, eager to see Jun one last time. Before him, the vast gray skies stretched out towards Guangdong's early morning lights and a moist wind cooled the air, promising the fall of autumn rain. His searched through the scattering of ships on the calm sea. Through the many sampans, the couriers, the escort vessels, through the dozens of others, he found her.

She sat, hunched at the prow, her solemn gaze still fixed on the treasure ship. Her damp hair was matted to her expressionless face. Cradled in her arms, and pressed tightly across her much weakened chest, she held close her precious wooden box.

How sad, thought Zheng He.

"Who knows what the box contained..." he whispered.

And his brow darkened as he recounted something else. Because Beijing waited for him and he knew at once that when he had left it, he had also abandoned the woman he loved.

Chapter 45
Zhu Di's Campaign

Its broad triangular Ming banners flaming in its wake, a large battle ship cramped with a regiment of soldiers, sped towards the treasure ship. The dawn had not yet broken and already, Tanggu burst with life. Yet only the sinister outline of the imperial escort ship held the crew's attention. Where was the pomp, the glorious welcoming they were so accustomed to?

Zheng He stood on the bridge, flanked by his men. They watched the small military vessel as it came to a halt by the prow of the treasure ship. The admiral set a nonchalant palm on the hilt of his sword. Beside him, Old Yu wiped his glasses, wrinkling his nose.

"Are we at war?" asked the physician, gazing down with an incredulous expression at the imperial regiment below.

On the military ship, the captain stood stiff and upright while the attending officer ceremoniously rolled his drum. At last, the captain unfurled an imperial scroll.

"What in the heavens!" cursed Old Yu.

"Speak of a welcome..." whispered Zheng He. But he raised his hand to silence his men.

Below, the captain cleared his throat. He eyed the scroll and without much flourish, pronounced in a sonorous voice,

"His Imperial Highness, Zhu Di, the Son of Heaven and rightful heir of His late Highness, Hongwu, requests the presence of His Eminence Grand Admiral Zheng He without delay. The Honorable Grand Admiral is to be discharged at once from his duties as Commandant of the Treasure Fleet. The defense minister shall take command of the fleet—"

"What is the meaning of this charade? Could they not wait until you arrived in Beijing?" asked Old Yu. He placed a protective hand on the admiral's arm.

Zheng He said nothing. He had long dreaded his return to Beijing and the consequences of his actions. He ignored what secrets Zhu Di could have unearthed during his long absence. But one thing was certain; the emperor would have his vengeance.

For now Zheng He was convinced that Min Li had never betrayed him. I shall go to her, he thought. I shall let her know that I was wrong. But that's if I am still alive...

He watched as the imperial guards climbed onto the upper deck and approached him with their haughty arrogance.

They seized him.

"How dare you!" snapped Old Yu.

"Shut up old man!" warned the soldier. "This way, Admiral..."

"Do not worry, Old Yu, this is mere procedure," called out Zheng He.

"You cannot do this! You cannot lay your hands on the Honorable Zheng He!"

"Watch your tongue!"

"Old Yu, it is nothing. Please, do not concern yourself for me. Have Ma Huan collect all my travel logs. He knows what to do."

Old Yu stood there, his shoulders sunken, watching his friend descend towards the military ship. His place was not in the Imperial Palace. This would be the last time he would see Zheng He for many years.

***

What would Zhu Di do? He was unpredictable. As the heavily guarded procession made its way up the canal towards Beijing, Zheng He rehearsed the words he would deliver to his emperor.

For days as they journeyed back, escorted by Zhu Di's guards, all the way to the Imperial Palace, he had fixed Mecca, praying that the emperor would keep him alive, at least long enough for him to speak with Min Li. He recalled her tears and felt the sting of guilt mount in him.

Back in Beijing, he already sensed that something was wrong. Then as they entered the palace grounds, riding along the marble bridge and through the Gate of Supreme Harmony, none of the court was there to greet them. What a difference it was compared to his pompous return from the previous voyage. No ceremony, no greetings. But none of this troubled Zheng He. The Grand Admiral had but one preoccupation.

As they neared the three great Halls, he gazed longingly in the direction of the women's quarters. Where was Min Li now, he wondered. He would have dismounted and raced inside the Women's palace if only to find the concubine and hold her in his arms.

"What happened to the Hall of Supreme Harmony," he asked, upon noting the bamboo scaffolding and the workmen around the largest building.

None of the guards would answer.

"Are they decorating?" he asked once more.

"Fire damage," replied one of the palace servants passing by. Then he shuffled hurriedly along, refusing to say anything further. Zheng He stared at the eunuch in dismay before reluctantly following the guards into the Inner Palace.

They reached the end of a gilded corridor in the Palace of Heavenly Purity. Zheng He expected the guards to drag him inside but instead, the silent men withdrew. The lead officer paused.

"Admiral, I must warn you. His Highness is not well."

"Is my life in danger?" replied Zheng He, not even wincing.

"You will see for yourself. Please," said the guard as he motioned towards the main chamber.

The Grand Admiral entered into the sparsely furnished room. It was dim and cold. The bite of winter had set in yet the richest and most powerful man in the Middle Kingdom sat there, in a room that was barely heated. Zheng He noticed the lines etched across Zhu Di's forehead. He sighed and took a step towards his emperor.

"Son of Heaven—"

"You bald ass!"

Zheng He froze.

"You! Of all people!"

Under the impulse of a rasping cough, the emperor's robe shook like a tent. He reached across, drawing his jaguar skin coat tighter around his shoulders. The admiral noticed his extreme pallor.

"So you've decided to return. What month is this?"

"I am at fault. I implore your pardon, Your Highness. But Your Highness, I am late for a reason."

"It no longer matters! The Hanlin have won. I am ill. They've won! Don't you understand?"

Again, he succumbed to a violent cough. An attendant eunuch neared him with caution, presenting a wooden bowl. Zhu Di rose from his high chair and spit into the bowl as though he were ejecting venom.

Regaining his breath, the emperor's eyes roamed through the window's wooden lattice. It spanned across the quarters below where the terrible fire had propagated months ago. He turned to the Grand Admiral, his voice hoarse and dark.

"How ignorant you are of everything. No one's told you yet what has happened here? I'll tell you, Zheng He. The Heavens have cursed us. Don't look so confused. The Son of Heaven has been punished. And now, he was made a fool by his trusted eunuch. You chose to disobey my orders!"

Zheng He did not want to mention the starmaps.

"Your Majesty, I can explain my late coming. There were technical difficulties—"

"I expected you two months ago!"

"If you knew the reasons, Your Highness, you would not be so harsh..."

Zheng He's voice trailed. Zhu Di had burst into a devilish laugh. He seemed to choke at the effort.

Was this the drugs' effect or had Zhu Di gone mad? He was as petulant as a needy child.

The emperor continued to laugh, repeating senseless words. At last, overcome by a fainting spell, he stumbled back to his chair. He sat there, breathing heavily while two eunuchs wiped the sweat off his brow.

"Get away from me!" he spat.

Then he shot Zheng He a bitter look.

"Look at the man you betrayed. See what has befallen the Son of Heaven. It is what you wished for, after all. You're like the others!"

"Your Highness…"

The emperor raised an accusative index finger towards the admiral, shaking his head as he continued, "Ah, Zheng He, while you were away...while you were away..."

But he could not finish. He seemed out of breath. He gulped the strong brew presented to him.

Zheng He watched the dark liquid dribble down the sparse bristles in Zhu Di's beard. He cleared his throat.

"I heard the Mongols have taken to raid our borders again."

"Oh, so you have been updated!"

The admiral felt a familiar knot in his throat. He had to tread carefully with this matter.

"And that...Minister Xia has been imprisoned."

"I need him out of my way!" snapped Zhu Di.

"On what grounds, Your Highness?"

The emperor suddenly regained his vigor.

"Don't feign that you did not know. I had several reports that he was undercutting the fleets' resources and making it difficult for the expeditions. You knew this as well as I did. He has made his opinion of the eunuch expeditions exceedingly clear over these last ten years."

"Your Majesty, gossipers have piercing eyes and wagging tongues...undercutting? These were only rumors—"

"They are not!"

"Your Highness, Minister Xia is...difficult at times, I concede. But if you permit me, this is a very drastic measure. Prison, you say? Who is now in charge of the imperial treasury?"

Zhu Di stared back with bulging eyes.

"I am! And I'll do whatever I please. We are going to war!"

"I see. Is this why all the ministers I met since my arrival in the capital have cast me such murderous looks? All this time, it was about Minister Xia. I thought perhaps that...I had offended you."

"You have offended us," bit in Zhu Di. "More than you think," he added bitterly. "But we wish to give the Grand Admiral a chance to prove himself. After all..." He paused.

Zheng He froze. Was Zhu Di going to mention Min Li? Surely the emperor had raged for months following the banquet. Or perhaps, he thought, Zhu Di felt it would be beneath him to consider the admiral as a rival.

"I want to catch Arughtai. I want to humiliate him!" spat Zhu Di. "I will not tolerate him marauding around my cities and pillaging my caravans whenever he feels like it. Bad enough that he refuses to pay tribute to Ming. I won't have it! My father worked hard to secure this empire and rid it of the Mongols. I can't let his vision be soiled by conservative practices. The ministers are all pompous fools. They can go to hell."

"Where will you get the money?"

"Ha! There's plenty of gold. And are you forgetting that we have a salt monopoly. We will raise the money."

But the admiral had noticed something else upon arrival. Inflation was at a year's high. He had already been pestered several times by treasury officers to present the fleet's budget. The fleet's losses tormented him. Beijing would look harshly upon wasted resources.

He gripped his sword.

"We have a desertion problem do we not?"

He knew it was foolish to contradict his emperor. He had no desire for war but he had to remain pragmatic. The success of any military operation hinged on the army. And the army was weak. They were no match for the Mongols, least of all against Arughtai's ruthless tactics.

"Nothing that can't be solved," retorted Zhu Di. "You yourself made a conscription recommendation recently. The Minister of War remarked that it was out of place for low-lifers to join the cavalry but he relented. All this is a clear proof, is it not? That there are still young men in their right minds who are eager to be drafted; we just have to find them. Else we will enlist every first born in each family regardless of their name. I've already discussed it with Yang Shiqi."

"Or we could draw them from soldiers posted in other areas...so as not to waste—"

"Oh, indeed! Do you know, Zheng He, that Minister Xia made the same remark the other day? Something about our soldiers being wasted on the transport of food to the new capital. A charming Hanlin ploy to move the capital back to Nanjing. The yapping sons of bitches! Well, I like it here! I won't have those academics who know nothing about combat and military strategy telling me where to put my capital. We'll get those troop numbers to a healthy level before we set off for Mongolia."

"Mongolia? Your Highness, are we going to our ruin?"

"Whose side are you on, Zheng He? I am not dead yet."

"You are the sage, Your Highness. I am always on your side. But...is there perhaps a chance that Minister Xia's opinion contains a degree of validity?"

"No! The old fool is afraid. He has always been afraid. Do you think I will have a conservative foppish scholar run my armies? Never! I am the only remaining Ming general from my father's line. I will defend this empire, with or without Minister Xia's cooperation. Do you think I care for his biased accounts and his constant reprimands? From the very beginning he wanted to remain in Nanjing. Well I saw to it that we moved! And now, I need money to refurbish my armies and if he won't consent to this, he will remain in prison. This is my final word."

Now Zheng He understood. Zhu Di was ill and the more his health worsened, the more the emperor feared death and his empire's weakness. He was fighting a battle against death rather than against Arughtai. He wanted to prove that he was still a general to be reckoned with and he, as always, would have nothing stand in his way. Nothing, thought Zheng He bitterly.

"You can barely walk, Your Majesty," he reproached.

Zhu Di had regained his breath and was now rambling about military strategy. But Zheng He felt numb. He felt detached from the man he had served for over thirty years. He couldn't understand why. He now saw the emperor as just another egotistic man. A dangerous suggestion that maybe Jianwen should have been emperor flashed in his confused mind.

As Zhu Di continued to vent his past military strategies and the need to surprise Arughtai, he dribbled profusely.

"This is where I need your armament expertise," he gloated. "Your skills are too valuable, Zheng He, there's no one else I can trust with warfare strategy."

Zheng He could no longer listen. He stared at the cold walls with apprehension. Something did not seem right. Why had the emperor not even mentioned the question of Min Li?

"Listen, San Bao, I need you to oversee the perfection of our new weapon. It's a cannon. One of those our troops have brought back from Annam. These Annamese, ha! A calamity for our Southern armies. But one has to appreciate their genius for invention!"

His voice had risen with excitement.

"It remains a secret. But the eunuchs have been perfecting this weapon for months! So far it can shoot iron arrowheads to a distance of eighty steps. Eighty steps! We believe we can reach a hundred. All we need is someone to help us. You, Zheng He, are the ideal man for this. You'll start tomorrow. I need you to do this."

Zheng He frowned. It was unbelievable.

"You need me to... But, Your Majesty! I've just arrived. I...I will need to chart out the new navigational maps, to draft out report of the latest expeditions… Your Majesty, the remaining part of the fleet should be arriving next year...and I will need to—"

Zhu Di grabbed Zheng He by the arm.

"You were a fine soldier, remember? Remember the way we rode in the northern steppes, together?" He laughed forcefully and then smiled with a mad twinkle in his eyes. "And we have not forgotten all you did for your emperor. Do not forsake him, Zheng He. It is all settled. Zhu Gaozhi will remain here to guard the palace. He always was a fat, weakly mass. Can you blame him? Ha ha! We shall ride together. It will be like the old days!"

I haven't ridden a horse in years, thought Zheng He. My kidneys are weak. He demands too much. And then he saw the froth trickle from Zhu Di's lips. He extended his arms just in time to catch the collapsing emperor.

"Forgive me, Your Majesty!" he cried, as his hands touched the emperor's body.

Zhu Di's eyes rolled in their sockets.

"Terrible...terrible things..." he stuttered.

An epilepsy attack. Zheng He gestured to the attending eunuchs. They ran to summon the physicians.

Two physicians burst in. They carried with them their Taoist elixirs. One of them had a potion of musk and barus camphor under his cloak.

Zhu Di's jerked violently. One side of his body seemed paralyzed while the other side convulsed. The tip of his tongue hung out of his parted lips from which trickled a frothy pink liquid. He had bit his cheek.

Zheng He hesitated at the door. He heard one of the physicians call out, "His six pulses are normal. Hold him!" He heard the Son of Heaven, his emperor, wail and dribble.

The admiral took his leave. And as he did, he saw Zhu Gaozhi approach from the other end of the corridor. As always, the heir apparent had been summoned from his quarters in the event that his majesty found death.

He passed Zheng He without a word but the Grand Admiral, who was already overwhelmed with his own emotional demons, felt the sting of that princely glare.

It was unforgiving and implacable. It promised many things and yet, left them all unspoken. Zheng He knew that Zhu Gaozhi was Minister Xia's strongest supporter. And Zhu Gaozhi was no soldier. His father's urge to organize yet another Mongol campaign had all the more alienated the prince.

It did not matter that Zheng He did not support the new campaign. To the prince, he remained Zhu Di's ally. Zheng He's eyes glazed over as he realized how much Zhu Gaozhi hated him.

One day, Zhu Gaozhi will get rid of me, he thought, aware of his fragile position. It is just a matter of time, he thought as he walked away.

***

Zheng He had never felt so damaged by the energy of the palace. But today he knew where he could find some solace and forget his troubles.

He visualized her dark almond eyes and her small pouty lips. The warmth of her voice caressed his soul and transported him again in her chamber on that banquet night.

It was her smile that propelled him forward towards the Women's quarters. He wanted to go to her now, hold her and find some peace. He wanted to hear her laugh and feel joy. This time, I will be brave, he thought. She needs me and I will be brave. The emperor shall never know. I will make sure of it.

Immersed in happy thoughts, Zheng He began to plan his next year. He would travel to the Northern plains and help train the troops. And then he would persuade the emperor to let him go on another special expedition, just a small one of course, nothing extravagant. Somehow, he hoped to bring Min Li with him and to show her the world. The emperor would be far away at war. It would be perfect.

Zheng He's mind worked fast. They could never be together unless they deserted Beijing. Maybe they could both leave the Middle Kingdom. They could live in Melaka, perhaps? He liked the idea but did not know how to execute it. It certainly promised freedom. Yes, I will be a free man, like my father. I will revisit the

Arabian States and this time, I will pay homage to Mecca. All these thoughts made his head spin, enlivening his spirit.

So lost was he in this whirlwind of thoughts that the admiral passed through several corridors, unaware of his own bearings. It seemed that a few buildings had been modified during his absence. There was also a distinct smell. As though freshly cut wood had been used and the paintwork was different in some places. He could not be sure because his visits to the new palace had been few.

Yet there was no mistake. *Something* had changed. He frowned.

He reached a door and stopped abruptly. There should have been a corridor here, he remembered, perusing ahead at the empty courtyard. And then he began to worry. The emperor had spoken of terrible things, had he not? The punishment of the gods... The thought raised the hair on his head. It could only mean one thing.

There had been another fire.

He entered the new building. Ahead of him was a young eunuch wheeling a cart of dirty bath towels.

"Tell me, the concubine apartments, they are here, are they not?"

"Yes, Grand Admiral," replied the eunuch, bowing several times upon sighting Zheng He's red uniform. "That is to say, the previous ones no longer exist."

The eunuch left. Zheng He bit his lip, searching for someone who might have a little more information. A shadow stirred. His gaze fell upon the building adjacent to the new quarters, just in time to watch the disappearing train of a black robe hurrying towards the princess chambers.

He grabbed the hilt of his sword for balance and ran towards that figure.

"Your Highness! Princess Xia!"

Princess Xia's hurried limp came to a sudden halt. She turned to face him. Zheng He flinched at the severity of her traits. She seemed to have aged.

He bowed. Princess Xia shot him an inquisitive glance. She wore that same disgusted sneer that all too painfully reminded him he was not a man but which unknown to him, she also reserved for all men.

"Princess, I ask your forgiveness," he began.

"Well, well," she began, "so you have returned. What can that mean? Is it that you miss Beijing?"

"What terrible things does the emperor speak of? What has happened to this palace?"

"Hush! Isn't it evident?" she whispered with a devilish black smile. "The emperor is being poisoned. Why should he not go mad and speak of terrible things?"

The admiral frowned.

"Poisoned? But...who? How is it possible? They taste everything he eats? They..."

Princess Xia shrugged with disdain. "What poison has no antidote? They have their ways."

"But who...who would do such a thing?"

Her eyes were mocking. She raised an index finger to her black lips in a ponderous gesture.

"You are amusing, Zheng He. Come now, be truthful. This is the least of your concerns, isn't it? Let me tell you why you ran to me just then. It had nothing to do with the emperor's health! But look, you've changed your mind already. What were you about to ask me before you changed your mind?"

"I... How can you say such a thing? I pledge my life to my emperor. His health is very much of my concern..."

"Yes. I know you do. But when you ran to me a moment ago, you pined for an answer to a different question. Now think. What was it?"

"Well I...I did notice the palace had changed somewhat. And..."

Her eyes flashed with hatred. He regained his composure.

"But I understand that refurbishments may have been made while I was at sea. That is all. I ignore what you are talking about."

"Good. Leave me then. I will retire."

Zheng He watched as she prepared to leave. He felt his frustration mount.

"Wait!"

Princess Xia turned around.

"I could not hide from your perceptive powers, Princess Xia. I would like to see her. Please. I know that Min Li trusts you," he sighed, relieved from his secret. "That is why I followed you here. Where is she? I can't find her..."

For a moment Princess Xia appeared moved by such a revelation from a man whose pride she detested. But if she was taken by surprise, she did not let it show for very long.

"So you don't know?" she taunted.

"Where is she? Where can I find her?"

And still Princess Xia did not reply.

"What is it?"

Princess Xia's head tilted to the side. "How strange," she replied, "I should think the emperor would have told you about the great fire."

"I gathered that! What happened to—"

He could not continue. Princess Xia nodded at his thought. It was like a blade plunging into his chest.

"That's right. She died in the fire."

He blinked once.

There it was...the harrowing abyss from his dream and he had sunk deep into it. How cold it was. It was like wading through tunnels of icy waves. He could no longer hear or think as the waves submerged him lashing at him with force and drowning him deep.

The admiral's eyes watered and still, Princess Xia stared into them, refusing to release her forceful glare. Even as the tears flowed on his weary face, her gaze did not falter. He gasped for breath. The princess did not blink.

He could see it. He could see that she was satisfied.

But she wasn't finished. Before she took her leave, she whispered once more under a scorching breath.

"Your emperor needs you now, more than ever."

Chapter 46
Nonguzhi
December 1421

For days after arriving in the port of Guangdong the eunuch assisted the frail Jun into Yunnan. But the much weakened woman would never reach her native Nonguzhi. Her illness was too advanced.

Old Yu had been correct. The seamstress had been ill for years. Years ago while she still lived in Nonguzhi, she felt death draw near. She had looked at the wooden box and cursed herself for her cowardice. I shall do this one thing before I die she had pledged. This was then the one thing that had kept her alive on the fleet. It was the thought that one day, her work, everything she had done for Zheng He would be fruitful. And now it was done.

No sooner did they arrive in Dali that her breathing became labored and she sank into a deep sleep. They were only a short journey from Nonguzhi but after he observed the pallor of her cheeks and the sweat on her brow, the eunuch understood.

He did not abandon her. True to its promises of compensation, the Ming office had provided generously for the woman who, it appeared, had fallen gravely ill during the expedition. The eunuch hired an old nurse and for days, in one of the Dali hospitals, they took care of the seamstress.

And before she died, Jun called in the eunuch one last time and asked him to repeat her instructions.

"Good then," she whispered once he was finished. "Now take this box with you. Here, take it," she sighed, as though relieved to be parted from it.

She was cremated the day after her death. He organized a prompt ceremony and collected Jun's ashes in an earthen jar.

Then, moved by the strange message that he had been entrusted to deliver, the eunuch, rather than returning to Beijing, set off to the mountainous village of Nonguzhi.

Along his short journey, he retracted the very steps this mysterious woman had followed years ago. Riding her mule along this route, she had once traveled all the way to Tanggu, her wooden box saddled close. All the while in her tired eyes, there burnt a purpose so fierce that all the forces of nature could not, as much as they battled in her body, break her resolve.

No sooner had the dazed Han arrived in Nonghuzi that he asked to meet Jun's mother. Two young girls in white pleated skirts brought him to the old woman's home and he walked through a wooden door decorated with strange symbols such that he had never seen before. There, he traversed a stone-walled courtyard where hung colorful rugs and other ornaments that were also foreign to him.

He looked ahead. An old hunched woman stood inside the courtyard, waiting by the entrance. Beside her, cutting vegetables, was a much younger woman with fairer skin and the most beautiful soft features. But the dutiful eunuch only had eyes for Jun's mother.

The old woman stood. Her white orbits peered at the stranger. She sniffed the odorous satchel and understood that he was a eunuch. She heard him breathe and realized that he was young and that he was close enough to speak to.

"What do you want?" she asked.

"Greetings, wise one. Your daughter is no longer of this world," he replied, weary from his journey and conscious of the sad news that he was delivering.

Hearing this, the fairer woman gasped. But the old woman said nothing. She set a hand to her belly. It was so painful there, right there, on that spot. She felt it this very morning even before the stranger had arrived in the village. She sensed that her daughter would not return to her and she was right.

"Please go inside," she called out to the younger woman.

Now they were alone and the eunuch remained standing in the courtyard, casting a shadow on the colorful rugs.

Jun's mother sat her tired body on one of the stones skirting the white building.

"My daughter is gone..." she repeated, oblivious to the eunuch. She had tried to ignore her presentiment early this morning but the same Shaman blood flowed through her veins and she had to bring herself to reason. Jun had died. Tears trickled down her aggrieved face.

Finally her voice echoed in the courtyard.

"You are here?"

"I have not gone yet. I need to deliver a message."

"What is it?"

"Your daughter has expressed a wish before she left to rejoin her honorable ancestors."

Hearing this, the old woman raised her tear-streaked face. She stepped out into the center of the courtyard, shuffling forward. She was much shorter than him and had to raise her face to better hear the voice from above. Her expression was now stern and she seemed to squint.

Now, in the bright sunlight, the eunuch could better observe the old woman edging closer to him. He could see for example that there was a resemblance between her and Jun only that the woman was much darker and had tied her hair into a bun. He could also make out that she was blind and her eyes wandered before her like two souls belonging to a foreign universe. He took a step back.

"Well?" snapped the woman with all the authority of her years. "What is it? What do you want to tell me?"

"Your daughter..."

He suddenly remembered something and untied the load from his shoulder. He brought out a wooden box and hesitated. "She wished that you take this back."

She reached out her hand and felt the object's familiar contours. In an instant, her expression switched to dismay.

"She kept it, still? But why?"

"She told me it was the wrong time."

"The wrong time?"

Then she frowned.

"You did not open this box, I hope? Shame on you, if you did!"

Her voice resounded with such fury that the young man, for reasons he did not understand, took much fright.

"Wise woman, I promise you that I did not open this box. I swore to her that I would not. I was true to my word!"

"Very well, then. Speak!"

"She...she asked that you bring it with you to *the place where it belongs*. She did not tell me where... I thought, I thought you might know. But she said that you must wait. Now is not the time."

"When? I am an old woman, I may die soon enough!"

"In five years. You must wait for five new years from now and on the seventh month of the last year the time will come to begin your journey...to that place."

"That is all?" asked the blind woman.

"That is all," said the eunuch, confusing even himself.

The blind woman nodded. Then, much to the eunuch's surprise, a respectful expression appeared on her tired face.

"Very well," she said, "I will do what the great Shaman has asked."

Book Four: Earth

The Underground

"Earth overcomes Water"

Chapter 47
Hong's Great Task

Honored reader, there are many men whose lives entwine with history and yet whose deeds, no matter how remarkable, one never writes or reads about.

To learn about such men, you must return, you must go back to where our story began, back in the palace of Nanjing and you must learn of those you did not care for earlier; for it is them who have marked Min Li's story, a father and a son, men of earth and of labor.

***

After emperor Jianwen lost the battle to his uncle, the Prince of Yan, speculation ran rife that he had not died. It was believed he may have escaped out of Nanjing through secret tunnels underneath the imperial city. It was during a frantic search for his deposed nephew that Zhu Di himself made some startling discoveries about the Nanjing palace tunnels.

These tunnels ran several hundred yards from the periphery of the palace. Some were accessible from the outside of the palace and constituted an intricate den of alleys and secret passages.

How long had these tunnels existed? Zhu Di did not know. But he set about filling those tunnels and blocking the openings with multiple layers of tiles.

A secret contingency of military eunuchs were assigned to the underground. They worked at sealing passageways and mapping those that remained.

Because they possessed knowledge of the underground, these men posed a security threat to the emperor. On completion of their work, the eunuchs were never seen again.

After this murderous incident, not the least in a series of mass killings perpetrated by Zhu Di during the early years of his reign, word of the underground was never again spoken.

The subject may have resurfaced later. It was rumored that during one encounter with his sons, Zhu Di asserted that in Beijing, he planned to build a city within a city. The underground city would be well hidden and serve as a sort of storehouse. It would facilitate the transport of food and other goods between the imperial grounds and the rest of Beijing. There were also rumors of extending the underground tunnels into Beijing proper. If these rumors were true, then perhaps Zhu Di drew inspiration from the Nanjing tunnels.

It is not known whether Zhu Di carried out his designs.

Years later, in Beijing, it was the prince, Zhu Gaozhi, who supervised the construction of what would become the world's greatest palace complex. It was he, along with architect Nguyen Ann, who more than anyone, became acquainted with Zhu Di's endless ambition.

As Zhu Gaozhi often traveled on a sedan chair through the new Beijing construction grounds, he may well have met men whose role in the palace's construction would forever be forgotten years later.

Let us meet then, one such man; a genius in his own right.

His name was Jin Hong. Once a young soldier of six feet with a stocky, well-formed body, Hong had served as a eunuch in Zhu Di's army. Officially, he had died in an unfortunate underground accident, not long after the Prince of Yan's victory.

If anyone had suspected that this man, newly named Jin Hong, was a eunuch soldier, and that during his service to the emperor, he had worked at sealing Nanjing's underground tunnels, he would have been arrested.

It was Hong's astuteness that had saved him.

Determined to survive, he sought to shed his eunuch identity. To achieve this end was not easy but Hong was lucky. He was one of those eunuchs who had been castrated in his late teens. He somehow still grew hair on his chest and face.

But this was not the only reason why the soldier's new identity invited no suspicion. Prior to castration, he had been married in his native Yunnan and his wife had given him a son.

During his previous military service, Hong was one of the more proficient builders in his battalion. But no one knew of his private life. This became the key to his new identity.

And now, if he resembled the eunuch who had once served in Zhu Di's army, Hung could not have been a eunuch. After all, he had a son, a son who by virtue of his youthful features could pass as much younger than his age and attest to the fact that Hong was a virile man.

Hong was never questioned. He began to make a living as an artisan and carpenter moving from one province to the next. But Zhu Gaozhi was right in his assessment of the rising inflation and the cruel taxation imposed on the people. Hong faced much hardship. Then the famines came. Food and money became so scarce that the family moved several times, each time closer to Nanjing.

This was why, several years after the murder of his fellow soldiers in Nanjing, a destitute and emaciated Hong boldly approached the Ministry of Public Works for an occupation. His eye for detail and unsurpassed carpentry skills impressed the officials. Hong was soon appointed as one of hundreds of carpenters attached to the court.

As a testament of his manhood and to ease their financial hardship, Hung encouraged his son to come with him to the Nanjing imperial city.

"This is the only way for us," he told him. "If you work in the palace, our family will develop a good reputation and I will be able to keep my job as a carpenter. Times are bad. This is a good thing for us. Think of your family."

This was how Hung had come to recommend his newly castrated son, three years older than his declared age, as potential servant to the Nanjing palace.

***

In 1406, construction on the new Beijing imperial city began. One of Hung's primary appointments was as supervisor to a large group of carpenters. Together, they were responsible for the ample residential quarters in and around the new palace. They worked according to the plans of the great Annamese architect, Nguyen An. While there were well over six thousand carpenters in Beijing, Hong was responsible for seventy of these. His work so impressed his superiors, that several years later, he was asked to build what would be known as the concubine quarters.

Who were the men under Hong's supervision? This pitiful lot were none other than ex-convicts. They were men taken from the city's prisons and forced into this daunting project on the condition that after several years of intensive labor, they would be free. As they were employed for manual labor, their hands were not handcuffed. However, during the night, after the long arduous hours, they were forced to wear the humiliating cangue.

This yoke was a broad wooden frame with a hole in the center. The prisoner's hands were not only chained, but locked on each side of his head. The heavy weight of the yoke was a constant burden.

Hung knew well from past experience that innocent men are often punished or suffer unjust fates. He felt an understandable mixture of sympathy and repulsion for each of the convicts. Yet he stifled any feelings to avoid suspicion. He now had an occupation, a steady income of several piculs of rice a month, comfortable living quarters and more importantly, he was animated by a fervent passion for his craft.

Once, while inspecting the workers, Nguyen Ann himself had come close to Hong and nodded his approval. Inspired by the great architect, Hong intended to perform to his best ability. Yet despite the peace of mind his career offered, Hong was tormented.

No matter how successful he was at endorsing his new identity, no matter how impressed the Ministry of Works and Nguyen Ann himself were with Hong's work, our ex-soldier could not escape the ills plaguing many eunuchs in the Middle Kingdom.

It so happens that years ago, Hong's castration had left him prone to painful infections. Sometimes he felt a sharp pain in his abdomen. He would flinch from the sting in his groin, more so during the harsh summers when water was insufficient to abate the burning pain. Since certain foods worsened his condition, he was careful to avoid spices and ingested plenty of ginger, known for its warm, calming properties. He drank tea in moderate quantities and avoided the latrines when other workers were present unless he could be sure that he would remain unseen.

His pain would persist for days. At times, he would surrender to it, promising himself to seek medical help at the next opportunity, at the cost of revealing his deceit. But only as a eunuch could he hope to receive treatment from the infirmary, located in the north area of the construction site. Revealing that he was a eunuch was out of the question. Hong endured in silence. He did what best he could to hide his incontinence. In the sweaty stench surrounding him, it was easy.

From the overlooking hill to the north of the palace ground, the immense construction site resembled an arid field where swarms of insects toiled all day. The brown limbs of sun-wrecked men merged with wooden surrounds in a melee of constant movement. Convicts scurried in all directions, bending under loads, erecting, hammering, cutting wood, carving and digging. The construction seemed to never end. It is in this wretched arena, that over many years, the lowest of abject men toiled, suffered and died, pursuing what was then the largest palace complex known to the world.

When Zhu Di had found Dadu in 1380, it lay in ruins following the fall of the Mongols. And now a new city and a magnificent palace would rise like a phoenix from the ashes of the past as though to pronounce the glory of the Ming. The ancient capital, former crown of the Mongol empire, was but a skeleton of what was to come. In its place, Beijing would stand.

The new city and palace became a greedy sucking ground for the country's riches. Wall bricks came from Shandong province. Floor bricks were transported from Suzhou in Jiangsu province while the city had its own glazed tiles factory. Huge tree logs were carried from the far provinces as far as Annam all the way to the construction ground.

It is impossible to conceive the natural richness that flowed into this imperial city. *Nanmu* cedar from Sichuan, fir, elm oak, camphor, white marble from Fangshan County, colored stones and granite from Hebei Province, all were hauled over long distances to take their rightful place in the architecture of the palace.

Transportation was no easy feat but what paid men could not achieve, forced labor could. One winter morning, Hong was astounded to learn that a mass delivery of rocks had been sled across watered-down icy surfaces all the way from the northern Hebei province. He was struck by the enormity of the project. To be part of such a large scale construction project made him proud.

Because as much as Nguyen An was a proficient architect and engineer, Hong too, possessed many talents. One such talent was his aptitude for *dougong*.

Dougong was a traditional assembly going back to at least five thousand years ago where no nails were used in construction. Wooden brackets were fashioned and interlocked into place to build such structures as timber frames. Hong had long mastered a skill for mortise and tenon joinery. A tenon was a narrower piece of wood which inserted into a hole, or mortise from another piece of wood. Intricate wooden pieces with notches and inserts were linked onto one another to build frames. Hong's work was of such quality that the wooden pieces held without the need for glue or fasteners.

Once the pieces were assembled, Hong would dispatch them to the nearby palace grounds to be used in the beam and roof structure of each building.

Hong also oversaw *nanmu* orders for his unit. Woodcutters in the surrounding area cut and filed this wood to be employed almost everywhere in the new palace. Following the erection of each pavilion's wooden frames, Hong would step in to organize wooden panels for the walls while another department laid bricks.

Once each building had been erected, there were wooden walls to decorate, paint work to organize and latticed windows to carve out and embellish.

It was this creative aspect of woodwork which gave Hong the most enjoyment. Those who suffer from physical ailments often find art to be at once a pleasurable escape and a catharsis from pain. This was also true for Hong, but with a difference. He felt true pleasure in the knowledge that one day, a concubine would reside in this building, kneel at that window, perhaps admire that lattice pane, open that carved door and that he, the ex-soldier from the Northern Plains had fashioned this exquisite work.

The joy he derived from his art was also one of the reasons Hong dreaded fires. Sadly, fires would arise during the construction years. The dry winds, frequent in the spring, served as an accomplice to the flames. Often the blaze would destroy beautiful buildings that had been near completion and for which Hong and his unit had derived much pride.

While he never complained, these fires would set him back a few months.

Such then was Hong's life at the construction grounds; a blend of artful pleasure and bodily pain, of anticipation and dread, of joyful freedom and slavery.

Chapter 48
The Convict

Ten years into Beijing's reconstruction, while Hung bent over his workbench and carved an interior archway, one of the new convicts approached him.

His long gray beard reached to his navel. He had a self-important smug about him that put others on guard about his intentions. Under the cruel foreman's lash, this man, much like the other convicts, toiled for seventeen hours a day with little food or drink.

Yet while other broken men kept their eyes on their work, this particular convict had observed Hong for days.

Today after much deliberation, he had reached a decision. Dragging his tired frame towards his supervisor's work shed, the convict gave a furtive glance sideways and after ascertaining that no one would hear him, he addressed Hong.

"If you would help me to escape this wretched place, I will treat your health problem."

Hong at once raised his head from his workbench. He stifled an expression of surprise.

"Get back to work," he barked, dismissing the worker.

But the convict had already weighed his chances. He was not easily dissuaded.

"Lieutenant Liang, don't you remember me?" he asked, his tired eyes glazed over by the scorching summer sun.

Hong felt a panic mount in his chest. The sound of his real name rang in his ears like deafening thunder. He glanced around with apprehension, feeling himself grow weak at the knees. He had no recollection of the man who stood before him in his tattered clothes with his knees calloused and his reeking, cracked skin. A cold fear traversed Hong. He realized this convict could destroy his new life.

Calm yourself, he thought. No one will believe him.

"You must be mistaking me for someone else," Hong shrugged at last. "Now return to work before I knock your eye out."

"Now, now, you forgot me. That's all. I've lost weight. See? Look at my face. Look at my hands. You see these hands? This hard life would transform any man. Don't you forget that!"

"Why you insubordinate..." spat Hong, barely able to breathe.

But far from recoiling, the convict approached to have a closer look at his supervisor. Hong stepped back towards the darker corner of the workshop. He saw the face before him wrinkle as the man squinted to better observe him. Then the convict's voice rose with excitement. He pointed a finger towards Hong, his eyes gleaming with malice.

"It is you! I remember *you* very well, Liang. You were wounded in battle during the siege in Yingtian. I took care of you, remember? I was the attending camp physician at the time. You don't believe me, now? I tell you, your name is Liang, Lieutenant Liang! You have a scar on your left shoulder. See, right there..." He extended his wiry arm, threatening to lower Hong's sleeve and reveal the said scar.

Hong recoiled and stared at the man in disgust. His fear had boiled into anger. "Wounded!" he roared. "In a battle! Who do you take me for? Get back to work!"

The man grunted, shaking his tired head.

"As you wish. But if the pain persists, you know where to find me," he added with a knowing smile. "I will tell no one of your secret, *Liang*."

"I've had enough of your senseless dribble, you swine! Get out!"

The fat foreman appeared. "Is this wretch giving you trouble, Hong?"

He cracked his whip, sending a harsh warning towards the convict. This one gave Hong one last glance before shuffling away.

And as Hong returned to work, the smile on his face belied the turmoil within.

***

Hong's son, Zhijian, worked for the Fire and Water Department in the Nanjing capital. His unit dispatched charcoal to the various palace establishments. It also delivered oil for night time fuel and maintained a regular supply of firewood to the imperial kitchens. Every three months, Zhijian traveled from Nanjing to Beijing to see his father.

On this particular occasion, they had decided to meet for a meal. They sat under a tree on the northern hill overlooking the construction site. The area seemed to be a huge lump of coal and for this reason it had been nicknamed Jing Shan. It was interspersed with newly planted trees and looked a little barren.

Hong was anxious to speak with his son.

"What did you learn?" he asked. He noticed that Zhijian was less portly from his hard work. The birthmark on his cheek seemed less noticeable too.

"His name is Shen. He was a physician."

"That explains it," replied Hung in a disgruntled voice.

"But he is innocent, Father."

"What is he doing among the convicts then?"

"He was sent to prison after the death of some rich merchant's daughter. Shin told me the only reason he was arrested was because the merchant was keen to blame someone. These things happen."

"Humph! I could rid myself of him... I'll tell the directors he's been slacking on the site... I'll transfer the bastard... If he gives me any more trouble I'll—"

"You could transfer him, Father but he could still speak..."

Hong munched angrily on his pork-filled bun.

"You're right. And worse, they might believe him."

"He's not bothered you again, has he?"

"No, it's been months now and he's left me well alone."

"He must be a good man then," reflected Zhijian.

Hong paused for a long moment, thinking to himself. Either that, he pondered, or he already knows I'll help him. He knows I'm desperate. If he is a medical man it must be obvious to him.

He ate his second barbecued pork bun, observing his son. Zhijian seemed well settled in his new life at Nanjing but ever since starting his new job he had grown aloof.

Does he bear me a grudge, wondered Hong. Has he regretted following my advice and becoming a eunuch? At least they fared well. They had food to eat. Life could have been worse.

"Soon, Zhijian, you will be working in Beijing," he remarked proudly. "I saw the plans. The officials said this palace is set to become the largest and grandest structure in the world. Think of the honor of working in such a place."

"Yes, it will be an honor," replied Zhijian, a tired smile. "How is the palace construction faring? I notice a new building frame there." He pointed towards the far right. "I had not noticed it last year," he added. He seemed eager to show interest in his father's work.

"Ah, you should see the pavilion I've been working on!" said Hong. "To think that these spoilt princesses will never thank me for anything."

"They would not know you even existed," said Zhijian with a smile. Even so, a sad light clouded his eyes.

Hong noticed that his son's mind was elsewhere. He swallowed the last quarter of his bun and wiped his greasy hands on his worker's pants.

"It's beautiful isn't it?" he said at last, eyeing the constructions below.

"Yes, you should be very proud," replied the melancholy Zhijian. "It will be a fine palace."

From their hill picnic, they could discern the yellow glazed tiles which the workmen had begun laying for the first time on one of the buildings. The edifice would serve as a model for the others.

What a treasure, thought Hong. And just to imagine what it would look like once completed, a glowing maze of yellow tiles extending as far as the eye could see. Now, won't that be nice. Worth all the wretched pain, I think.

Then he remembered his visitor who seemed a little too quiet.

"Are you happy?" he asked with apprehension.

Zhijian smiled and continued to eat, avoiding the question.

"I think I have a friend," he said at last.

"That's good. That's very good. It's about time you started working your way up. That's what it is all about. You'll never get anywhere if you keep to yourself like this. What's his name, your friend? How long have you known him? Which department does he work in?"

"Well...she's... I mean, we...we've only spoken once...but I know of her."

On hearing his son speak so wishfully about a girl, Hung had never felt so guilty in his life. But he refused to feel bad. He had enough concerns to endure. So he grew a little impatient hearing about the young man's hopeless yearnings because they only reminded him of what he'd done to him.

"A servant girl? In the palace? What makes you think she likes you?" he asked.

"She likes everyone," replied the boy quite sure of himself. "I think... I think she is quite lonely," he added.

"Ahuh. Listen, I thought there were enough man friends around without you having to scurry after servant girls. Servant girls will not get you anywhere."

Zhijian remained expressionless.

Hong emitted another disapproving sigh and shook his head. To hell with his son's craving for girls. His pain had returned. It was unbearable. He had no control over what he was saying because he was constantly irritated by the stinging.

At last, the words rushed out and he felt relieved for saying them.

"Listen. You've made me think. I've reached a decision. This may sound crazy to you... But I am going to help that convict. If as you say he is innocent, then he deserves to be free."

Hong continued with passionate frenzy. The pain made him sweat and tremble.

"I've thought long and hard about this. And I think I've found a way to get him out. You must not tell a soul about this, Zhijian. This is what I'm going to do. Do you remember, what I told you years ago?"

He interrupted himself. Other workers had joined them on the hill.

Hong lowered his voice then whispered at length in his son's ears. Zhijian's eyes widened.

Hong then stood and faced the construction site. He was lost in thought.

"I can do it, you know. I'll double his ration. As long as he's kept alive it can work."

Zhijian frowned.

"There are guards everywhere—"

"We'll just have to try. We have to try! You are right, Zhijian. I cannot let this innocent man continue to live in such a wretched place. Convicts die here. A dozen die every day. They are treated like oxen... He never deserved it..."

Then realizing how desperate he had become, Hung buried his head in his hands.

"Cursed pain! I hope you never have to suffer this, Zhijian."

Before his son left three days later, Hong embraced him and said, "Remember, do not speak a word of this to anyone."

***

At first the convict had not believed him. The plan seemed absurd. He had looked upon the old palace ground map with distrust.

"What are these drawings?"

"Old tunnels. They existed long before the Yuan. According to the building directors, we will be extending one of these tunnels underneath the kitchen grounds for food supply. The underground chambers you see, here, they will be used to store ice and food during the hot summer months. Other approved extensions are to be dug here, here and here. You can see where the original tunnels are located."

"I don't follow you."

"Shen, it is simple," said Hong, pointing to the western area of the map. "Here is the palace carpentry area...and here is the—"

"I know where we are but—"

"Listen! All we have to do is reach an adjacent tunnel. We just have to tap into one and... Think about it. It might be possible that one of these old tunnels will extend far enough for you to escape."

The convict frowned, shaking his head.

"My good Liang, perhaps you were once a soldier but these years are long past. This is not a battlefield where you can just dig ditches wherever you please. This is a construction site in the middle of the imperial city! There is to be a moat twenty feet deep on the outskirts of the palace. Digging a tunnel underneath it will not work."

"Yes but the moat is not yet planned...it is quite safe."

"We won't be getting very far before your own foreman notices we're up to no good, Liang, cracking his whip and all... Have you seen my back?"

"Will you just listen? It is already arranged. Look around you. Our team will be redoing the wooden flooring to install heating pipes underneath the buildings. I can set aside a time for you to be located at the back of the building in the middle of the night. The doors are sealed and I will guard the entrance. Once you begin work, no one will question your absence. You can work undisturbed and..."

Shen stared at him.

"You want me to dig?"

"How else will you find the passage?"

"I may just die digging! You're a fool, Liang. It won't work. What if this tunnel does not even exist? And where did you get this map?"

Hong had doubted of course. He had looked at his tarnished parchment with a forlorn expression. Like many eunuchs, he could not read. What he understood were mere glimpses from the illustrations and from discussions with the directors. He looked again at the sketch. It was an old Yuan city plan. He could not even trust the scale.

And yet Hong's plan had worked. The following year, they had pierced through a tunnel. Shen could not believe it. The escape would take place the following month.

In that year, Hong had been appointed supervisor for the new Inner Palace quarters. There were over hundreds of thousands of workers in the new imperial city. Invested with Zhu Di's egotistical enthusiasm, they progressed at such an alarming rate that deaths from exhaustion and overwork were not uncommon.

Keen to help, Zhijian turned to Shin to help procure the future escapee with identity papers. Upon first hearing the illegal request, the Korean eunuch hesitated. In his eyes, Zhijian, now in his mid-twenties, was a reliable, humble and respectful man. He trusted him.

It was risky but due to his role, Shin had access to the authorization stationary and was in a position to help. All he would need to do is introduce the fabricated identity papers into the set of documents that were routinely stamped. Later, having access to the filing cabinets, he would retrieve the stamped documents. No one would notice. In fact, Shin found the little charade exciting. It gave him a thrill that was nothing short of a gambling wager.

At this time, a swarm of ambassadors had arrived in Nanjing. There was always much paperwork while envoys visited. During their stay, Shin organized lodgment and tributary identity papers. It would be easy with the mass of paper work, to generate a single set of false papers. Zhijian would be pleased, he thought.

What Shin did not realize was that Zhijian was in fact becoming more worldly. He had never revealed the real purpose of those documents.

Instead he had explained that his father needed to help a migrant relative from Annam. Feeling sympathy for the Annamese who had suffered a crippling defeat at the hands of the invading Ming a couple of years ago, and who, for this very reason, reminded him of his own bullied Korean countrymen, Shin had been unusually understanding. In fact, he had been only too happy to oblige.

Chapter 49
Trouble in the Purple Palace

Even while distracted by the convict's planned escape, Zhijian continued to dream daily of the beautiful Min Li. It was now one of his favorite occupations. He had been nicknamed "dreamer" by his many colleagues in the palace.

While he never dared approach her since their first encounter, he had, over the years, several occasions to see her either in the company of the other concubines or in the Imperial Gardens.

Now a sultry lady of nineteen, she was still very beautiful. But, and this was odd, Zhijian no longer saw a joyful light dance in her eyes. It seemed that over the last years, a shadow of doubt had veiled her face. He recognized it. After all, it was the same doubt he had felt when he was no longer a man. But in her case, it was much darker. When no one was looking and she thought herself alone, he would watch her expression dim into dark thoughts and it felt to him as though she was lonelier than she had ever been.

The Nanjing court relocation to Beijing was drawing near. Under the guidance of his assistant director, Zhijian began organizing the Fire and Water Department's new office in Beijing. The new department would be situated on the shores of Taiyi Lake, just outside the new Imperial Palace.

He already felt familiar with Beijing, having visited his father often. He had an appreciation of the palace's progress and how much things had changed in the new city. Meanwhile, according to his father, he seemed to have made no progress of his own.

"Have you been promoted yet?"

"No. I like my job, Father."

"The reason I pester you is that inflation is making everything expensive. Do you know how much the medicine our convict prescribed is costing me? We could do with a higher stipend. After all these years, and you are still a 7b eunuch? Maybe you could ask for a promotion? After all you have done, you probably deserve it."

"But I'm very happy with what I'm doing."

"Yes but you need to think of your income...and your family..."

"I'll see what I can do, Father."

"Good. How long will you be in Beijing this time?"

"Until next month. Why?"

"The escape is in four days."

Zhijian's eyes lit up.

"There is one problem," said Hong. "He will end up in the new Fire and Water Department. There is an old chute there, where the coal used to be stored."

He drew out a map. Zhijian noted that he radiated energy and was now in good health.

"He will surface in this area. It looks to be a courtyard outside the main office. I cannot be sure." His finger traced a circled area on the Western side of the palace.

Zhijian recognized it.

"I believe this area is not double-tiled," he said.

"One cannot be certain," continued Hong. "Can you see to it? Tomorrow perhaps?"

"I could. I'll have to see if I can shift the tiles."

"Excellent. If the opening is too narrow, you will need to enlarge it."

Zhijian nodded. He had expected his father to be thrilled but for the remainder of his visit, Hong was silent. Every now and then, he rubbed his chin, glancing uneasily in the direction of the construction site.

"I've enjoyed this," he cheered at last, slapping his thigh. "Even if it does not work, it was fun."

"What do you mean?" asked Zhijian, a frown on his face.

"The man does not stand a chance."

"I don't understand. Everything is ready. You, yourself said that the opening is in the Fire and Water Department."

"Yes. So what if I did?"

"Then what is the problem?"

"You're funny. This is still the middle of the imperial city, Zhijian. You think our physician friend can just sprout from a hole in the ground without raising attention? I know what you're thinking, I will remove the cangue. That's all good. But it won't matter that he has documents on him if he still reeks like a convict."

Hong watched his son's bemused expression before pursuing.

"Must I explain it? Sooner or later he will be spotted! Do you realize how many officers march through here on any one day? They'll find out. They'll take him back in. They may even kill him for knowing about those tunnels..."

Zhijian continued to stare at his father. He seemed disappointed.

"I see," he said at last.

"What? What do you see? Don't look at me this way."

"No, I understand now. You did all this, only to prove that you could..."

Hong looked away.

"It makes no difference. He's doomed, Zhijian."

***

He'd find an inn and drink to his heart's content. He'd order jug after jug and bring each one to his avid, parched mouth. He licked his lips, savoring the memory. But first he had to get out.

The tunnel was dark, almost fifteen feet under, but Shen could feel his way through it with his calloused palms. He had plodded for a while now, stopping often to regain his breath. Perhaps it was morning. Perhaps it was still dawn.

Hong had removed his cangue early into the night. A good man that Hong. A smart man. He'd even organized an extra bowl of barley. His last bowl of barley in that shit hole construction site. He was not even hungry and as always, it was disgusting and infested with insects. But he'd eaten it all.

"You'll need your strength, Shen," had observed Hong. And he had looked away. Perhaps he was sad to see him go. They understood that they would never see each other again. Hong was expert craftsman attached to the imperial city whereas he would soon be an escaped convict.

Before sunrise, before the guards could wonder where he was, Shen slipped into the tunnel. Hong replaced the tiled opening, plunging him deep into an unwelcomed darkness. He'd fallen, grazing his knee.

This wretched tunnel went on and he could not see the end of it. But Hong was a good man. Yes, he was. Not like those other Ming eunuchs. He'd been true to his word.

Shen dragged his bruised body along, supporting himself on his elbows. He could have stood but he was too weak. His bones ached. Even though it was no longer there, he could still feel the wretched cangue around his neck, like a spectral burden, digging into his burnt skin. But it did not matter.

I'll be free soon, he repeated to himself, his heart pounding in his bony chest. *Free as a bird, I'll get myself to an inn, is what I'll do.*

And then, he saw the light. Freedom, freedom was near. He saw the sun's rays cradled in the opening above. Was it already morning? He stood, catching his breath. His eyes glistened.

He mastered what was left of his strength and pushed against the dislodged tile above. Light filtered in, showering joy and disbelief on his sunken face. Free.

He peered outside, shivering in winter's cold breath. He shot an apprehensive glance at the courtyard... This was not what he had expected. Had Hong lied? He seemed locked in by four buildings. Horrified, he gripped onto the aperture's rim, breathing heavily, fearful of being seen. He saw a gate. But the compound was sealed. Left and right were guards. He was trapped. Cursed Hong.

Voices rose from one of the buildings. He had to hide. Hide where? Hide how?

Shen heaved himself out. He fumbled with the large tile, straining to replace it. At the far end of the courtyard, a figure stirred. He saw the outline of a soldier's uniform. He had to flee.

Shen was quick. He spotted a leafy shrub alongside the left building's porch and staggered across. *I'll die trying, yes I will.* His bare foot hit the edge of a tile. He collapsed onto the pavement five feet from the shrub and began to crawl.

The soldier neared. He had not seen the convict but he continued to advance, looking askance, sensing a presence. He was closer to the dislodged tile.

Shen held his breath.

The soldier leaned forward with a puzzled expression. He frowned. There was something liquid on that tile. He dipped his finger in the red clot. Was it blood? He raised his finger towards his nose with a grimace.

"Ah, officer!"

The soldier was startled. He stood and looked back towards the voice. Behind the shrub, Shen stiffened.

"Officer, it is important!"

The voice was soft and sweet. But it was still strong.

Shen watched the soldier turn and greet a round-faced eunuch.

"Officer, we need you to supervise a large supply of coal. This way please. Please wait for the director in the foyer."

The soldier seemed reluctant. He rubbed his tainted fingers on his pants and walked off.

When the soldier had gone, Shen watched the eunuch step furtively towards the uneven tile as though he had not seen it but knew it was there. He watched the eunuch extend a foot towards the tile. Slowly, the felt boot prodded along the opening, pushing the tile back into place. The eunuch pressed hard against the stone, smearing away traces of blood with his soles.

At last, just as Shen thought his heart would burst in his chest, the eunuch turned around...and smiled.

In three swift strides, he had crossed the courtyard and pushed a bundle of new clothes in Shen's hands.

"Inside! Quick!" he whispered.

"The soldiers—"

"I will take care of them. Hurry!"

Shen trembled but obeyed. He sneaked inside a lavatory and removed his torn clothes. Outside, the determined young man with the black winged hat surveyed the courtyard. Shen slipped on the clean tunic and the woolen coat.

"Are you ready? We must hurry!"

"Thank you..."

"Hush... Take these."

Shen clasped three bundles of rice and hid them in his tunic.

"How can I ever thank you?"

"You owe me nothing," replied Zhijian. "Thank you for helping my father."

***

And then Zhijian's world came apart.

It was early 1421, a fortnight since Zheng He had left for his sixth expedition. Much to his father's approval, Zhijian had recently accepted his new post as 5a intendant. As for Hong, he was now a reputed carpenter working outside the Beijing palace. Twice per year, he visited their family home in Yunnan.

It had begun like a normal day. Yet a dense silence stifled the palace.

It happened in the eunuch canteen while Zhijian shared a meal among the dwindling eunuch council. It was feared that the re-instated Eastern Depot saw these gatherings as political dissent. The eunuchs were more careful. They knew not who to trust. Shin and Zhijian had made a point to come along, only to find the atmosphere heavy with gloom.

When Zhijian sat at the table, several colleagues shot him a nervous glance. They then whispered among themselves. At first, Zhijian did not notice.

"Tried to kill him, they say. None of this is official but it would not surprise me."

"He never drank it though, too clever. The general is not easily fooled."

"She'll die of hunger, such a pity."

"Just as well she did not attempt this during the ambassadors' visit. Can you imagine if the emperor had died then?"

They shook their heads.

Zhijian looked up. The eunuchs were instantly silent. Now they stared back at him.

"Has someone been imprisoned?" he asked.

"It's nothing," waved Shin, eyeing the others nervously. "Just eat."

"Shin, we must tell him," reproached the eldest eunuch.

"Tell me what?" cried Zhijian, increasingly alarmed.

"Hush! It is not official. Zhu Di has not announced what will become of her but one of us had to deliver water this morning. And...she was there, in the back chamber. She has been denied any food. She'll starve, soon enough. It's only a matter of days, ten if she's lucky..."

"But... Who? Who is this?" asked Zhijian.

"No one!" barked Shin.

"For Heaven's sake tell him!"

Shin sighed.

"It's Li Guifei."

They all looked at him now. Zhijian was in shock. As he glanced at the table, he expected the eunuchs to laugh, revealing their distasteful prank. But there was no mockery in their eyes. Instead, he saw that they did care about him somehow. They knew what it felt like to want something and not have it. But they also knew that for Zhijian to want something was a rarity.

And now Zhijian was shaking his head and his eyes blinked wildly.

"But...there must be a mistake. Are you certain that it was her?"

"Her name has been removed from the concubine list. Or so we've been told. And her chamber is now occupied by another concubine. So you see, it has to be her..."

Zhijian shook his head.

"What has happened? Why her?"

"Well there's this rumor in the palace...but on your life you must swear to avoid the mention of it."

"I swear... What are the rumors? Tell me!" cried Zhijian, close to tears.

"Well...rumors is that she tried to poison the emperor. But that will be kept well under wraps. You know how things are around here. The emperor will refuse to make it known that a woman from his own Royal Chamber almost succeeded in taking his life...who knows how she did it..."

"I'd say she found a way to smuggle a poison from the marketplace..." suggested one.

"...or the palace apothecary—"

"You can be sure Princess Xia is behind this!" said Shin bitterly. Soon after, he bit his lip almost as though he regretted speaking.

But Zhijian was not listening. He could not breathe. His limbs stiffened. No. It was a lie. He did not want to accept it. He continued to stand there, a crushed expression on his pale face.

That night his heart raced. He could do nothing. He was but a low rank eunuch. He was powerless. If only I had been someone important, he thought, someone like Zheng He. Then I would have had the power to do something. Now for the first time, that thought haunted him.

Think what you could have done, after so many years as Shin's protégée. There may have been some hope if only, if only you had not idled your days in empty, useless daydreaming. You are an absolute fool.

The next day, his torment grew. Maybe she was already dead, he thought. If he wanted to help her, he would have to act quickly. For hours, he tried to concentrate on his work but he could not. More than ever, he dreaded the approach of sunset.

The thought nagged at him through the day and night. Min Li was locked up and *dian* after *dian*, she slowly starved to death. Each time he heard the sound of the damned *dian*, he felt his heart skip a beat and a numbing chill would race through him. Please hold on, Min Li. Please hold on.

What could be done?

***

Shin was also a troubled man. Since the previous night, he had in his possession, a gift from Princess Xia. It was always the same. She would bribe him to procure herself travel papers and leave the palace grounds through the Western gates. The emperor forbade this but Shin was weak.

"I hope I am not interrupting anything," she would always say as she arrived in his quarters, pouch in hand, ever ready to corrupt him.

She haunted him, her and her demonic lips. And every time, she wore one of those broad rim hats around which she draped dark blue silk to conceal her face from others. But he could still see those black lips as she spoke. Those lips, it was as though they were stained in putrid blood.

"And how was your last visit to Tanggu? Fruitful? I hear you lost again, Shin? Now, now, why the solemn face? We can certainly come to an arrangement now. Am I right?"

She was not permitted to leave the palace grounds unaccompanied. But Princess Xia always found ways to trap him. Because of his gambling habit, he needed money and rice and the princess somehow had plenty of it. She gave of her stipend and everything she gave, came with conditions. Often she was short so she gave him a little jewel or a trinket. She was a bottomless pit of bribes. He was weak. And she knew his dirty secret. Damn those women. Princess Xia was the worse. She knew what I was like, at once. How did she know? She had me spied and now I'm just putty in her hands.

In return for her silence, he obeyed her whims. She could leave whenever she wanted, unknown to the emperor, something he knew that Princess Xia was not permitted to do. These were the orders. Yet he had disobeyed them many times. The gifts saw to that. He lapped them up.

He had no choice. She could cease paying his debts, she could denounce his wretched habits, his frequent trips to the port of Tanggu, his love of game, oh, she could! If he let her, he would be finished. And now, this latest gift troubled him.

"Princess, I cannot."

"I am afraid that this is the only thing I can give you this once. Times are hard. Life is expensive in Beijing, Shin. We do what we can, don't we?"

"But I cannot take this...my life hangs upon it."

"Your life hangs upon your weak habits, you coward. I want an escort, a sedan chair and I want Xihuamen opened before nightfall. Take it! Take it and order your dickless minions to fetch me a sedan."

"Princess, this...this object cannot be sold. It...it is not of the court. Everyone will suspect it. And Princess, I beg you, if it is found on me, I am finished. Those...those gems..."

"You are hardly in a position to negotiate with me, Shin. Extract the gems and be done with it. Not another word!"

He could sell them and make a good profit but the very thought of that gift bothered him. It was...unusual. He shuddered at the thought. He would be found out. He would be accused of treachery. He could not keep it so close to the *Silijian*. He had to rid himself of it.

The opportunity arose the next afternoon, when Zhijian came to him, flustered, burning with a passion that the higher ranking eunuch had never seen in him before. The young man's eyes were at once alive yet absent. He spoke with erratic sentences as though in a fever. Now that Li Guifei is going to her death, the reality is too overwhelming for our young dreamer, thought Shin. And then he heard what Zhijian was saying.

"Leave the palace?"

"I've made my mind up. I must go. I will leave Beijing. Begin a new life..."

Shin could not believe it. The sickly boy went on, vomiting his woes. He wanted to desert, never be a palace eunuch again because he was not cut for it, not for that life, he added.

"I'm useless Shin. I want to regain Yunnan. Live in the country. I'll leave very soon."

He needed new papers and a new identity by this very afternoon.

"What will you do out there? In the country..." asked Shin.

"I can make a life. I'll find an occupation. Make a living like my father. His carpenter business is booming now. Will you help me?"

"I... Well, it's just, your sudden desire to leave the palace...it's...it's just so sudden young man. I...well, of course, I will help you. I respect your decision...however sudden it is..."

Perhaps it was to his advantage that Zhijian had remained such an unassuming eunuch. Shin knew that unlike the others, Zhijian never asked for anything, never used information to his advantage or tried to look more informed or more competent than others.

So then, Zhijian has been just as miserable as I have suspected, thought Shin. Surely I have to help him. This place is making him ill.

"Shin, I'm afraid I have nothing to give you in return. I will send you money when I reach home and setup my own business...will that do?"

And then Shin had a brilliant thought. He trusts me. I have nothing to lose in binding myself to him. It is my only chance. So he cleared his throat and looked around to ensure no one was by earshot.

"Listen, here Zhijian, maybe there is a way that you can repay me. There is something I need to get rid of. Something I would like you to take with you."

Chapter 50
The Revengeful Eunuch

Zhijian was not the only eunuch who brooded over Min Li's imprisonment. Another castrate was hard at work, seeking every detail about the one woman who had brought upon his demise.

The one bitch, as he liked to call her, who instead of doting on him like the other concubines, had brought about his shameful demotion.

The eunuch was no other than Ji Feng.

Honored reader, you have already learned that upon his dismissal, Ji Feng hired a palace eunuch to spy and report on Min Li. It came to pass that on the very evening following Min Li's imprisonment, Ji Feng's contact brought some pertinent news.

"She's been held in a back chamber...they have forbidden any food."

"Repeat what you say..." gasped Ji Feng.

"They took her last night. She's been sentenced to death by starvation."

"Can it be? I will curse you if you lie!"

"You owe me two silver coins already. And she will be dead in three days. Dead, I tell you. These whores do not last long."

"Ah, dead, you say! Here, take three. Ah, how this pleases me. Ah, sentenced to death, hmm? Pity they do not flay her! Ah, but starvation will have to do. The bitch had it coming."

Forgetting his upcoming transfer, he preoccupied himself with the thought of Min Li slowly dying in a prison. If only, ah, if only he could see it.

He had heard of the back chamber in the concubine quarters. At night, the room was not heated because the builders had failed to complete the piping under the floor. It had been a hasty job and one of the younger concubines had confided in him once that from that very room, there often arose muffled sounds at night and that finding it difficult to sleep, she had taken to read books.

To think that Min Li was now locked inside this chamber drew a smirk on Ji Feng's face. He wondered what torture she had endured and lusted at the thought of seeing her in great pain. The sense of justice resulting from Min Li's misfortune lessened the insult he felt.

The night before the great fire, while both Princess Xia and Zhijian made plans to leave the Imperial Palace, Ji Feng was drinking to his heart's content.

He intended to celebrate what he saw as rightful retribution by visiting a winehouse. It was in this very winehouse that a curious incident occurred.

At first, Ji Feng did not notice the conversation at the adjacent table. He was too absorbed by his wine. His contemplation was soon interrupted. A man in his sixties who had visibly drunk far too much was talking in uncontrolled bursts.

"Ha! He's dead...dead, I tell you. I go back a long, long way, my friend... Longer than you think! The offensive against Jianwen? I was there! I shook hands with the soldiers..."

His companion shrugged.

"I was only trying to say that we can never be certain what became of Jianwen. He could be in Siam as we speak! And besides, you're drunk."

"I'm a physician! I c...can treat my own ills," protested the man, barely able to sit still on his stool. "I may be old but I'm n...not stupid! Y...your problem is that y...you think you know ever...every...everything about me... B...but you don't! You don't!"

He cackled some more while his friend sighed.

"Alright, what is it I don't know? You've told me that story about the troops a thousand times now. So what?"

"I took care of them...all of them...the wounded, the sick... I c...could stitch a leg in no time."

"Aha, I knew that was coming. You're a useless physician when you drink, Shen, we all know that. Absolutely useless."

"Am not!"

"Do you need me to remind you of the last time you tried to treat a patient while drunk?"

"The mer...merchant's daughter? Ha! Hardly a case of reference. She was already dying!"

"You killed her. Now enough wine, you good for nothing swine."

"Am no swine, Chou! I helped b...build this very city!"

"Ha! As did half of Beijing! Now stop your whining. I'm taking you home."

"Aha, hee hee, but not every...not everyone knows of the tunnels...you forgot the tunnels," slurred the old man, a wicked glimmer in his eyes.

"I know, I know, you mentioned that before...underground tunnels... I'm no fool!"

"That's...that's how I esc...escaped. B...but no one knows! No one knows! Hee! Hee!"

Ji Feng, who had at first been irritated by the old man's drunken antics, now listened.

"Old man, you've drunk enough. Let me take you home," said Chou, rising from his seat.

"I'm not finished!" protested Shen, grabbing the wine carafe and holding on dearly to it.

Ji Feng continued to lend an ear, as Shen's voice lowered into a hushed, complicit tone.

"You want to come along, Chou? Hey? You want to? I can show...show you where I dug the tunnel. You'll see... I'll show you how I escaped. Five years ago!

"Hush! What's the matter with you! Not so loud!"

But it was too late for that. They now had Ji Feng's full attention. From what the Jurchen could make out, Chou was afraid. And the fear had nothing to do with his friend's poor conduct. No. Chou was afraid because Shen was telling the truth. Shen did not seem to be a lying drunk. Ji Feng knew when a man lied because he had practiced the art himself.

As the drunken man stumbled outside, his last words startled our wily eunuch.

"B...building sixty-four! I remember now! It was building six...sixty-four!"

Shen's rant could be heard even as he stepped out of the tavern. The two men disappeared into the streets of Beijing.

"Building sixty-four," mulled Ji Feng.

He recounted the conversation.

As absurd as it sounded, there was it seemed, a maintenance tunnel located straight below building sixty-four, a tunnel that reached out far enough outside the Imperial Palace for a convict like Shen—for he was obviously an ex-convict—to boast having escaped during the palace construction.

Ji Feng smiled. Oh, the delight. He had worked in the Imperial Palace long enough to know that building sixty-four was the very chamber where Min Li was now imprisoned.

What cruel irony that she would never see the light ever again.

He dropped a couple of taels in his empty plate, adjusted his winged eunuch hat and left.

The early hours of the morning saw him in the vicinity of the Imperial Palace. He had attempted to sleep but could not. A thought haunted him. What if Min Li did escape? He frowned. He wanted her to die. He thought of it all day. She could do it. She still had her huge, ugly feet and could even run if she wanted. She could run.

Not if he stopped her.

Chapter 51
In the Courtyard

The very next night, fire raged through the Imperial Palace. Like the flames, Ji Feng grew ever restless. Dark thoughts plagued him.

One particular fantasy made him sweat with delight. Like a dark force, it drew him closer to the palace even as ashes and cinders showered over the imperial city. As crowds gathered round him and Beijing townsfolk stared in alarm towards the rising smoke from the palace, Ji Feng thought of little else but of Min Li and of what he had overheard the night before.

Not even the noise, not even the deafening shrieks greeting this ominous celestial sign, even the intensity of a fire roaring like a hungry ghost, nothing could tear Ji Feng away from his most cherished thought.

It was simply that Ji Feng wished for no other thing more dearly than to kill Min Li with his own hands. He wanted to strangle her pretty neck and watch her gasp for air while her fearful eyes bulged out and begged for mercy. He relished the thought of finding the tunnel's entrance and following it through to building sixty-four.

There, unheard, unnoticed and never for a moment suspected by eunuchs or guards, he would emerge in the chamber and take his revenge.

He spit onto the ground at that thought. *And she will know why I have come. She will recognize me...*

She had been the eyes and ears of the emperor. Belying her lazy sensuality and her playful countenance, that woman knew almost everyone in the palace. Ah, yes, she would recognize him. And that, he told himself, a cruel smile etched on his lips, would be his first victory.

She would already be weak from her ordeal, famished from the hunger of the last days. She would have no strength to scream or fight him off. She would stumble in the darkness looking for a way out. He could imagine those wandering eyes screaming for help and longing for better days when she was but a budding peach in fanciful ribbons, strolling in the gardens and spoilt by every female in the palace.

Somehow, Ji Feng found himself lurking in the shadows by the tavern door, the very one where he had overheard Shen's secret the night before. Perhaps the astute eunuch understood that on account of his broken life, Shen thirsted for drink. And Ji Feng's instinct was right. Later, as the inn door opened, his savage gaze fell upon the unsuspecting physician. Hands behind his back, he proceeded to follow him into a winding alley until they were well away from sight.

And then when he was certain that they were alone, Ji Feng leapt out of the dark.

"Your name is Shen, is it not?"

The drunken man froze. He spun round, a look of dismay on his face. He heard the sinister voice and knew it spelt danger. He watched as Ji Feng approached like a phantom.

"You're that escaped convict! You will tell me where the escape tunnel begins!"

"Wh...what tunnel?" cried Shen.

He saw the gleam of a blade in the moonlight. In a flash, Ji Feng had brought the knife to his chest. "Tell me where this tunnel begins!" he screeched.

"I...I don't know what you are talking—"

The knife seared through his gut. Panic set in. Shen looked below his belt. He stared at the blood, poked his finger in, shell-shocked.

"Help me!" He could not finish. A cruel stab cut his breath short. There was blood. It choked him, oozed from his lips.

"Where? Speak up! Where is it? You will speak, vermin!"

Ji Feng pushed the blade against Shen's throat.

"Tell me where that tunnel begins, hmm? Or I'll slaughter you like the filthy convict you are!"

Shen spit blood.

"The Fire...the Fire and Water..."

Ji Feng smiled.

"Hmm, see now, it wasn't so hard, was it?"

He released Shen and stood back. He watched the blood flow from the physician stomach with a satisfied grin.

"Please!" pleaded Shen, raising one hand as he stumbled on his knees.

Ji Feng stared back with a grin.

"Well go home now, you old fool!"

Doubled over in pain, the physician staggered round to the corner. He hesitated then dived blindly into an alley, one hand pressed against his bleeding wound. Still watching, Ji Feng approached. His footfalls were silent. He liked watching. He saw Shen collapse onto his knees. He saw him attempt to get up. And then something monstrous surged in the castrate. He ran to the wounded man.

"You should have died long ago, you wretch!"

And before Shen could realize what was happening, Ji Feng had stabbed him in the back. And again. In that last strike, he twisted the blade with vengeance.

The physician collapsed on the pavement. Ji Feng's heart raced. He stepped back from the pool of blood, giddy with pleasure. The ghost in his loins surged under a savage impulse. He spit at the ground. He had made his decision.

In the Imperial Palace, the fire had surged to several feet. Ji Feng ran fast. He felt the night and its power. He embraced its dark presage. Because he knew well what had to happen tonight. It had to be tonight. It would be tonight or never.

***

Above him, hell ensued. Fifteen feet under but Zhijian could still hear the shrieks of women burning alive. He could hear the thundering clamor of collapsing wooden beams and the roaring flames advancing to consume the concubines.

He was not there but he could see it all; the Inner Palace defiled by the flames, the concubines devoured by the fire. Their screams spoke of agony, of horror. They would not cease. He shuddered. They reminded him that underneath it all, perhaps he was an ill-shaped monster. Yet, he pondered, as he moved stoically along, panting in the airless underground, what other means were there, except for this one?

His plan had almost worked. Yes, he had managed to distract the eunuchs of the Fire and Water Department and to slip unseen into the tunnel opening. But the fire... The fire had spread so fast. How could fire spread so fast? And now, because of him, many would die.

Zhijian tightened his grip on the inanimate form. He reminded himself that she was all that mattered. But his heart was heavy with despair.

He had only a short period of time to make it back before the director of the Fire and Water Department returned. They would find him gone from his post. They would find the dislodged tiles. They would find the underground. He had to move quickly. Hurry, he told himself. You must hurry. He ploughed forth.

Like a giant troll, he plodded along, feeling ahead with his free hand. He found the tunnel wall's sharp turn and pushed on, enlivened by the notion that he was halfway through. He was now heading straight towards the direction of Taiyi Lake. Back to the light.

The ascent would be difficult, he thought. He remembered his struggle years ago. He had examined the underground soon after the Imperial court was relocated from Nanjing. At that time, he had found it difficult to emerge out of it. And now, he was carrying her.

How long had he been underground now? He paused to catch his breath, leaning a lacerated palm against the cold earthen walls. His body trembled. The agony of those last two nights made his mind swoon... What to do, what to do...yet it had been easy. So easy! He recalled slinking into the imperial kitchens to inspect the ovens. As always, he was the insignificant odd job eunuch and no one had paid him attention.

And then he remembered running to the Western gates just as Princess Xia left. Back at the Fire Department, he had sounded the alarm, dispatching every staff member to attend to the fire. And then he had lifted the tiles and jumped.

Looking back now, Zhijian remembered something odd about Princess Xia. There was not a chance she could have guessed that he had started the fire. And yet as she passed through Xihuamen, she had observed him and pursed her lips. Maybe Shin was right and these women really were witches...

But not this one, he thought, holding Min Li tight. Not this one.

***

In the area between Taiyi Lake and the Imperial Palace wall, lay the Fire and Water Department. It was towards this compound that Ji Feng ran. He seemed to not notice the panic-stricken mob around the palace.

His bloodshot eyes stung by ash, Ji Feng pushed past a crowd. As he entered the Fire and Water Department, he verified the adjacent alley. Not a soul.

He slinked past the main building and into the courtyard. His hurried steps resonated on the tiles. He only needed to find the tunnel's entrance. Without a doubt, the opening must lie under one of the many tiles. But which one?

Ji Feng froze. In the corner of the courtyard, sheltered under the shadow of an eaved roof, two large tiles had been pushed to the side. It could only mean...

The Jurchen cursed. And then something began to happen, right there, in this infernal courtyard lit up by the orange flames.

He observed what seemed like a hand. The charred hand felt its way from an opening in the ground. Then and there, stubby fingers gripped onto the earthen ledge.

Emerging from that treacherous pit was a dirty, grimy eunuch – one Ji Feng remembered only too well – a eunuch with a sparse tuff of hair on his stupid round head and a vacant, boyish face. Now this eunuch's face was contorted with pain. Ji Feng watched him offload a large bundle.

And now Ji Feng understood.

He saw the violent writhing under the bundle. The grotesque woolen cloth was kicked aside. And then, horrified, crawling backwards on her palms, the female form began to scream. It was Min Li.

***

At once, Zhijian panicked. He lifted himself out of the tunnel.

"Please...please..." he whispered, pleading with his hands as he stood on his half-charred boots.

She was so beautiful. He watched the soft-skin lady with the glorious jet-black hair sit up on her hands. And in her eyes, there was a flash of recognition before she sat in silence on the hard tiles and stared back at him. She seemed to emerge from a nightmare.

"You are safe now..." whispered Zhijian.

She recoiled in horror. She had seen...*him*.

Ji Feng surged from behind, his face twisted with rage. He hurled himself on Zhijian. This one winced. He saw the fierce, sunken eyes. He saw the sharp yellow teeth.

"Filthy dog!" hissed Ji Feng. "Where did you think you were going, hmm?"

The two eunuchs lunged at each other. A deafening city noise blanketed the compound. Outside, people ran out onto the streets. A few hundred yards behind, the fire raged on, continuing to devour everything within the palace walls. Thick smoke rose above the city, raining debris and ash that the dry winds sifted with dust.

Zhijian met blow after blow, until he tasted blood. A final strike blinded him. He landed hard on the tiles. In his dimming vision, he saw Min Li's anguished face. Behind him, Ji Feng laughed.

But Zhijian's will was stronger. Slowly, he raised his head. Wiping the blood from his torn lips, he probed the courtyard. Ji Feng followed his gaze. They both fixed the large shifted tile. Ji Feng frowned. It was too late. Zhijian had already rolled across the ground. He leapt to his feet with the tile raised high before him.

The heavy stone came smashing onto Ji Feng's skull. The Jurchen stumbled forward, cursing under his breath. As he swooned, he saw Zhijian leap across and reach forth towards Min Li.

Ji Feng collapsed.

But he was not a man to easily desist from his rage. It did not take him long to regain his spirits, animated as they were by a lust for vengeance. As he came to, he saw no trace of Min Li or of the round-faced eunuch. Shaking with fury, his sweaty hair matted to his temples, he staggered upon his feet and ran out of the compound.

Book Five: Wood

Long Journey

"Wood overcomes Earth"

Chapter 52
The Mongolian Steppes

How does one battle an ever-shifting opponent? Zhu Di had sought an advantage against the Mongol riders of the North. He had, it seemed, the loyalty of an elite Mongol cavalry that he had bribed years ago. But as skilled as they proved in several battles, they were no match for the ruthless tactics of his loathed Mongol enemy.

In 1422, as the Ming troops were lured into the steppes, the reluctant soldiers faced freezing weather in a hostile land. The large, already disillusioned army was vulnerable.

Zhu Di's enemy was not organized. It was prone to internal strife and constant bickering. But where it lacked size and unity, its agility on the saddle and knowledge of the Northern terrain was unsurpassed. The steppe nomads were adept at surprising the larger Ming army. Without warning, a detachment of fierce riders would emerge, closing in fast. They attacked weaker points in Zhu Di's battalions then rode out again, only to disappear for days in the steppes. Small groups of Ming soldiers, often those crucial to lines of supply, were led into ambushes or else suffered sabotage at the hands of the steppe riders. The Mongols' repeated surprise attacks on small groups lessened their own casualties. But over time, the weakened Ming army would opt for retreat. This then, was the cat and mouse game that Zhu Di proposed to resume, even to his disadvantage.

Zheng He had been reluctant to submit further to his emperor's whims. The admiral would spend his last night with the troops before returning to Beijing.

"Your men have completed their training, Your Majesty. I have fulfilled your request and demand permission to withdraw."

The emperor knew well that the pressing problem of Japanese piracy demanded the admiral's attention. His majesty did not protest. Zheng He was soon released from his military obligations in Datong.

During the last months, the admiral had elected Huang-Fu as his assistant. Zheng He wanted to keep an eye over him. He wanted to know whether the young gambler would finally prove himself; whether he would endure the training.

Not surprisingly given his remarkable stunt on the fleet, Huang-Fu turned out to be one of the best recruits. He was always the first to rise and never too tired to complete his chores. He faced the dry cold of Datong with an enthusiasm that baffled the hardiest soldiers. Even in his heavy lamellar armor which he wore over a coarse leather brigandine, Huang-Fu moved with rare energy.

"Reckless but determined," had observed Zheng He with a rare smile.

Over the winter months at the Datong garrison, Huang-Fu had mastered the cavalry training, demonstrating unusual skill in both his spearmanship and archery. He was also a fine rider. It seemed the boy was grateful for the chance he had been given. Every day, he sought to prove that he deserved this honor and wished nothing more than approval from the only man who had ever placed any faith in him.

"We've shot across several feet further this time, even in the fog!" cheered Huang-Fu as he escorted the admiral at the end of the day.

They had made good progress with the Annamese cannons. Zhu Di would be pleased.

"Good work," smiled Zheng He. But deep down, he felt weary.

As he dragged his thick boots along the snowy slopes towards their tent, Zheng He realized another reason why he had chosen Huang-Fu's company. The boy's presence had kept him focused. It made forgetting easy. The admiral could pretend to be the man he had been before learning about Min Li's death. And now with his approaching departure, the reality set in.

"You know a soldier must marry, Huang-Fu," said Zheng He, hungry for conversation. "You'll be doing that, I hope, when you return to Beijing."

"I know my duty."

The young soldier smiled, adjusting his helmet as he entered the tent. He shook off the snow from his black fur-lined boots and hastened to remove the admiral's woolen coat. He began to brush off snowflakes from Zheng He's coat before putting it away on a high stool. The interior of the tent glowed under a warm coal fire. He rushed forth to rekindle it.

"Finding a wife is honorable. But right now, I've other things on my mind. I want to learn how to read and write properly," he cheered. He placed a pot above the fire, stirring over it as he spoke.

Zheng He seemed pleased.

"Now, that, is an honorable ambition. It may serve you some day. Might even keep you off the streets."

Huang-Fu laughed.

"I do not need the streets now. This is life for me," he smiled, sitting smug against the tent pole as he watched over the cooking pot.

"What about the Honorable Zheng He?"

Zheng He sat quietly, rubbing his hands together for warmth.

"The Grand Admiral has no plans," he said, after a moment of reflection.

"The Grand Admiral mocks me."

"You will soon learn, young man, that the more you acquire power among men, the more a puppet you suddenly become. That sounds obscure to you right now. But that is the truth. My destiny is to be decided by the man who sits on the dragon throne. Whatever he chooses for me is law."

Huang-Fu tilted his head a little confused. He raised the pot from the heat and walked across to where Zheng He was preparing to lie down for the night.

"I have prepared your medicine, Admiral. It is still very hot, please be careful."

Zheng He lowered himself on a fur spread while Huang-Fu presented the brew.

The admiral noticed the uneasy manner in Huang-Fu as this one watched him drink. He seemed troubled.

"I think you forgot to take it yesterday," observed the young man.

"Now you're starting to sound like Old Yu," remarked Zheng He between sips. "I'll be fine," he added, reaching across to put the cup away.

"Here, I'll take that, Admiral."

He then returned to Zheng He's improvised bed where he began to arrange the thick woolen blankets. Zheng He stared at him for a moment before losing patience.

"What are you doing? Leave that!"

"Honorable Zheng He, the geomancers have warned it would be colder tonight."

"I am well, Huang-Fu. Who will you fuss over when I leave Datong?" remarked the admiral in a tired voice. He pulled the rug closer to his chin and closed his eyes, indicating that he wanted to sleep.

Then, remembering something, he suddenly sat up.

"Huang-Fu, I may stir in my sleep and you'll take fright but don't trouble yourself like last time. I'm an old soldier now. These things happen."

Then after closing his eyes, his voice rose again, this time, muffled by the heavy blanket. "The past has a way of haunting you."

At this, Huang-Fu gave Zheng He an incredulous stare.

"The Grand Admiral has nightmares? What could the Grand Admiral have need to regret? I'm the rogue here. I've done some downright awful things."

"Yes, yes, so you have," jested Zheng He.

"But you know what I never understood?" asked Huang-Fu, a slight frown on his forehead. "How the Admiral resolved the problem... He never explained how he resolved the problem of the missing starmaps. That's always been a question in my mind."

Hearing this, Zheng He eyelids flicked open. He stared in the dim light, watching the strange shadows on the tent's taut canvass. An uneasy memory surged forth. Embroidery patterns seemed to dance before his eyes. He wondered where Jun was right now. And whether he would ever find out how she had stitched those constellations on her cloth.

Huang-Fu broke the silence.

"Aha! Was there perhaps a starmap I missed? I thought I was damn thorough."

"They should send you out to catch Arughtai," mused Zheng He, feigning to sleep.

Huang-Fu laughed.

"Honorable Zheng He..." he continued. "Now, I'm truly very curious. How did the Grand Admiral keep the expedition on course without starmaps?"

"You must learn not to ask questions when an old man has no wish to answer, my boy. It is very rude. I once knew a woman who was as rude as you and I almost threw her overboard."

"I'm not a woman!" protested Huang-Fu, raising his head from the tent pole with indignation.

"I am not sure she was one either," replied Zheng He feeling a surge of fondness. "Some people seem to be neither man nor woman," he added.

"In that case, I hope the admiral won't have nightmares about this woman."

"Shahrzad? Oh no, she is not frightening. A woman with a sharp mind should not be cause for men's fear." He thought for a moment and added, "There are other things...that are more frightening."

"Having a man like fat Ekbal threaten to cut your throat is pretty darn frightening," advanced Huang-Fu, remembering his ordeal in Ku'Li. He'd long shared his adventure with the admiral.

Zheng He did not reply. He changed position, turning his back towards the young soldier. Huang-Fu observed him with a kindly expression.

"Is it true what the other soldiers say?" he asked.

"What's that?"

"That the admiral was in love with a concubine?"

"Xiao Huang-Fu! Who told you this?"

"Ah, never mind," dismissed Huang-Fu, worried that he had gone too far and breached protocol. There was a pause while he toyed with the tassels on his boots, swinging the wet tuff that dangled from each of his laces in an attempt to keep awake.

Zheng He watched him.

"Yes, it's true. But I've only said this to you. Because I know your worse secrets. So now, you know mine," he said, suddenly relieved to have a confident.

Huang-Fu laughed.

"She must have been a woman of many talents to catch the admiral's eye."

"Yes. Yes, she was."

And curiously, Zheng He told Huang-Fu all he remembered about Min Li. He told him about the little girl in the pigtails, the agile-tongued concubine he had first met after his fourth expedition. He told him whatever he could about the baths without losing too much face. He told him about the night she had lured him to her chamber and about the fire that had taken her life on a night when he was not there. He left nothing out, so relieved was he to free his mind and soul and to have another man understand his grief. He would sleep a little better that night.

And as Huang-Fu listened, his disquiet grew. It hardly seemed fair that the man who had changed his life had so little power to change his. He wondered whether that was what the admiral had meant earlier when he mentioned that he was a puppet... Everything seemed so complicated.

***

In this 1422 campaign, Arughtai once again eluded Zhu Di and fled to Mongolia. Huang-Fu was soon back in Beijing, triumphant after his fling with the cavalry and, in his impulsive élan, determined to learn how to read and write.

As for Zhu Di, he was seething. All appeals to the U-Tsang rulers had been in vain. The emperor had hoped that the U-Tsang people would be able to appease the Mongols who had lately taken up Buddhism as their religion and held the U-Tsang Lamas in high regard. Gifts and honorary tokens delivered to the far Western lands by the recently dispatched eunuch had yielded no satisfactory response.

It seemed there was only so much that religious influence could achieve. Arughtai continued to offend the Ming. That is to say, the Mongol leader still refused to bow to Zhu Di and to send tributes to the Son of Heaven.

And then two years later, the audacious Arughtai once again launched an attack on Ming territory. It was 1424 and Zhu Di's health was failing. When the outraged emperor once again took to the Mongol steppes, Zheng He was long away on a special mission in the Southern Seas.

He had watched the man he once met as a child-prisoner, descend further into delusions. The scene he had witnessed following his arrival in 1421 seemed to be playing out again. Yet this time, Zheng He put aside feelings of reproach and allowed himself some sympathy for his emperor.

He remembered the last time he had seen him. Zhu Di had adjusted his helmet, pushed his sword in its scabbard and marched pitifully towards his horse. The admiral had followed him, conscious of the precarious state of his emperor's health.

"This is madness, Your Highness. You are ill. You can barely ride."

"I will seek your council when I need it, San Bao. You set your mind on those rabid pirates and I will deal with those Mongol dogs. What is it, now? You want your emperor to succumb to laziness and complacency. Would you have us loll about couches and read books all day like our indulgent heir?"

"Your Majesty, your strength is not what it used to be," protested Zheng He as he held steady the imperial steed.

"Strength? What has strength got to do with anything?" grunted the old general, adjusting his weight on the saddle. "Remember, Zheng He, we crushed Jianwen's troops not by strength, since after all, we were outnumbered three times. It was strategy that gave us victory! And now it is strategy that will win over the Mongols. I shall end it once and for all with this cursed Arughtai."

Then, his throat suddenly taken by a raspy cough, he said no more. He gave the signal and rode out of the palace gates with his young soldiers.

And while Zheng He was far away on a ship, Zhu Di's fever had him bedridden for days in the bitter cold of Shandong.

On August 12 1424, the great Yong Le emperor, Son of Heaven Zhu Di, former Prince of Yan, the man who had extended the Grand Canal, raised the imperial city of Beijing to its glory, restored the Great Wall, fought years to protect the Middle Kingdom from the Mongols, established the Eastern Depot and sponsored six of Zheng He's naval expeditions, gave his last breath. He was sixty-four years old.

The physicians were long aware of the prison conditions in which Zhu Di's finance minister languished. And so they were greatly surprised to hear the emperor's last words. They were reported to have been, "Xia loves me."

Chapter 53
The New Law

Beijing, November 1424

Several days after Zhu Di's death, Zheng He was at once summoned by Zhu Gaozhi. The admiral felt uneasy. He entered the Hall of Preserving Harmony, the very hall where Zhu Gaozhi had once argued with his father while this one boasted of his favorite eunuch. Rightly seated on the dragon throne was Zhu Gaozhi, Emperor Hongxi.

Zheng He watched the new emperor rise and walk towards him, dismissing the other court officials with a raised hand. He had just finished convening with his ministers. Now, he wished to speak with the admiral alone.

Zheng He bowed low several times. The time had come. Zhu Gaozhi would at last express the seething resentment the admiral had long sensed between them.

Yet the wrath did not come. Zhu Gaozhi was unlike his father in so many ways.

"Zheng He, you have served my father well and I, all Ming, we are indebted to you."

Again, Zheng He bowed three times. He knew not what those first words presaged. He waited for bad news.

"Come, come," said Zhu Gaozhi. "Let us not remain in this stifling hall. We shall take to the sunshine together."

They began a stroll towards the gardens. The two men walked side by side, silent in their mutual understanding.

"As you have heard, no trading ship shall leave The Middle Kingdom under our reign," came Zhu Gaozhi's soft voice.

"I understand," replied the admiral.

"There are to be no naval expeditions."

Zheng He's face remained expressionless.

The emperor smiled.

"However…upon reflecting upon his renowned expertise in governance, we have come to an arrangement. We wish to appoint the Honorable Zheng He to another post. It is a most privileged post."

"I am your dutiful servant, Your Highness."

Zheng He was inscrutable. He did not yet understand Zhu Gaozhi's motives. He understood that were it not to honor his father, Zhu Gaozhi could have humiliated him like some of the other eunuchs. Many of them had not been so lucky.

As for Zhu Gaozhi, he was reflecting on the question of what to do with Zheng He. Since there was no longer a fleet for him to lead, the admiral's role was no more.

Zhu Gaozhi spoke at last.

"I am sending you to Nanjing," he said simply.

Zheng He did not flinch.

"I will name you *Shoubei.* You, Grand Admiral," pronounced Zhu Goazhi, "will become Grand Commandant, Zheng He. A well-furnished mansion awaits you in Nanjing. I am entrusting the beautification of the city into your hands. We shall soon relocate the Imperial city back to Nanjing. Now that my father's trysts with the Mongols are discontinued, we must arrive at evidence. Beijing is ruining us."

And to indicate that the offer was not open to compromise and to speed up the execution of his order, he added. "I have already begun your transfer."

Zheng He bowed in silence.

His new appointment was, in all evidence, an honor. In Nanjing he would still serve in a high-ranking role. But in the context of his naval career, this new post would be a sort of prison. It would become all too conspicuous to the court that the fallen mariner now languished as a Nanjing bureaucrat.

But it was Zhu Gaozhi's next words that most injured the admiral.

"Perhaps it is best, given your extensive civil engineering experience that you, Admiral, be in charge of dismantling the fleet.

Much material could be used for our garrisons. We want nothing wasted."

The sting was well timed. The sting hurt his pride. The admiral had lost face. As though reading his thoughts, Zhu Gaozhi smiled. But the admiral recomposed himself.

"There is one thing I would like to request upon my departure, if I may, You Highness."

"Continue."

"His Majesty is fond of literature...of higher learning... His Majesty may therefore find great interest in my proposition."

"You note well," replied Zhu Gaozhi, amused by the admiral's spirited recovery. "What is it that the Grand Admiral wishes to propose?"

"Well, as His Majesty is no doubt aware, Nanjing houses the great Yong Le Encyclopedia."

"And so it does. It is the one endeavor I most treasure from my father," replied Zhu Gaozhi with sincerity.

"If you permit me, I propose to make a significant contribution to this body of work."

"Indeed! I had not known you were *also* a bookish man. The idea has merit. I suppose we could enrich our texts with naval and perhaps, combat history. That is your intention?"

"That is so, Your Majesty. And if I may, I had wish of appending the Encyclopedia with the travel logs produced during our recent voyage. I will work in close collaboration with Ma Huan. I believe that since expeditions have now been suspended, it would perhaps be wise for future generations to have at their disposal, accurate and rich accounts of what men before them have accomplished."

"Men like you, perhaps?"

Once again, Zheng He blushed.

"Your Majesty, I acknowledge my part in this achievement... But I cannot be credited for Ma Huan's work and for the knowledge other countries and their people have shared."

This only irked Zhu Gaozhi. The emperor's resentment grew all the more as the admiral continued to expound on his newly found intellectual passion.

He wants to trap me, thought Zhu Gaozhi. He understands too well my scholarly convictions and knows that this idea would please me and would please the Hanlin scholars.

"Your Highness, I promise that my engagement with this literary task will remain supervisory in nature. I will not falter from my duty as Nanjing Commandant. If His Majesty could do me the honor of overseeing this literary project, I will require nothing except the restitution of the documents that Ma Huan previously lodged with the library minister."

Zheng He paused to catch his breath. It was a bold request. He knew that.

The two men had stopped walking just as the emperor's patience had reached its limits. He faced the admiral with crisped jaws.

"Zheng He, your idea is excellent. Yes. It pleases me much."

Almost at once, Zheng He's traits relaxed. If the naval records were appended to an official encyclopedia, they would reach future generations. At least, his work would continue, if only in a different form, he thought.

But his smile faded with the emperor's next words.

"Alas, it would have proved a noteworthy contribution had you told me earlier."

"Earlier? Be assured, Your Highness, it is never too late..."

Zhu Gaozhi shook his head in what seemed disconsolation.

"Zheng He, I regret to inform you of the most unfortunate circumstance."

Noting Zheng He's increasingly ashen face, Zhu Gaozhi continued.

"I am afraid that your splendid, most excellent documents... How can I say this? It was an accident, you understand..."

Zheng He could not believe it. He knew the rest.

"A most unfortunate accident... And, I am certain of it, a misunderstanding," continued Zhu Gaozhi. "A member of my Grand Secretary had them burnt by mistake. All of them. Not a single one remains."

Chapter 54
The Visitor
Beijing, 1425

Beijing Marketplace

"My Lady, my lady! Come, come! We have the most beautiful silverware! Come look at this pretty bracelet!"

On a dusty afternoon in Beijing, a darkly clad figure weaved through crowds in the bustling markets. Wherever she went, she was flanked by two men.

They were of stocky built. They could have been thugs, possibly foreign judging from their hairy features and large noses. Underneath their hooded black robes, trimmed with silver embroidery, the men's powerful hands clutched at the khanjar attached to their waist. Concealed in the folds of their black leather boots were two further khanjars.

They were so armed because they were in a foreign land and were afraid. But mostly, they were afraid because this country no longer wished to deal with foreigners. It had closed itself. The two bodyguards towered above the crowd in the marketplace, eyeing each slanted eyed person with suspicion and readiness. Unlike her, they did not want to be here.

The woman wore a veil to shield herself from the assaults of the Beijing dust and because she liked her privacy. She was oblivious to her bodyguards. Her confident gait hinted that she would have gladly dismissed them.

A shorter man shuffled four paces behind the group. His cotton tunic hinted to the merchant class. He was a translator. Today he struggled to escort the woman and her two bodyguards. He scrutinized the passage before him, scrambled further, bounced ahead in the wrong direction and barely caught up with the shadowy form whose hands were forever probing and touching what the market vendors laid before her.

They had been in the imperial city streets since the morning. They explored these wonderful lanes which the translator explained were all named according to the wares and services being sold.

"Here, my Lady, we have the Scissors Lane...and over there, adjacent, is Paper Lane where you can buy pretty stationary...further up that block, you will find Hats Lane, then Silk Lane where—"

He knew his Arabic was poor and that it was the reason she persisted in ignoring him. She would pretend to listen then moved along in her preferred direction as though she had carefully considered what he had said and chosen to dismiss it.

The government had appointed him to keep an eye on the foreigner and monitor her movements. There were the new laws. At first she had refused any assistance from the translator but recognizing that he would make things a little easier for her should they be accosted by the eunuchs, she had relented.

Effectively, fourteen paces behind them, the translator knew that a eunuch had been appointed to keep close watch. He was from the Eastern Depot. They were now everywhere. He could smell their dried piss from here.

The little group entered into Silk Lane where already, eager voices rose to welcome the rich Arab woman.

"This is the latest peony design from Suzhou. Look, look, I have four colors. Which one do you want?"

Her hand reached out from under her veil but it was hard to see her expression. At last, she replied in near fluent Nanjing Hua.

"No thank you. I prefer the Zhejiang silk. Do you have any of that Phoenix pattern in the blue damask?"

"I have! Here! How about this one?"

"How much is it?"

Still fifteen feet away, the translator squeezed through. He passed two rows of sedan chair carriers and dodged a cart heaped with tinware. Brushing past a startled banner carrier, he finally reached the silk stand, out of breath.

"Fifty silver taels, my lady," he gasped as he waved his hands in the air to get her attention. "But they will only accept paper money!"

"What nonsense! What has happened to this country? Why will they not accept gold?"

"The emperor forbids it. Times are expensive and it is the only way to control—"

"But I have no paper money. Here, take this. It is all I have. No one needs to know."

And she shoved a couple of gold coins inside the silk vendor's reluctant hands.

The translator almost pulled his hair out. To his relief, the vendor, an old woman with blackened teeth, pushed the coins away.

"Will you not take it?" cried the Arab women in her unusually clear Nanjing Hua.

"My Lady, it is best to use paper money," intervened the wheezing translator. "We can get your gold exchanged if you like. Come this way..."

"Madness! Only a few years away from this city and prices have risen to ridiculous levels. And now, this foolish woman won't take my gold..."

While one of the thugs lifted her bail of silk, she pushed the gold into the translator's startled hands.

"Have it your way, then. Why don't you change this and pay him," she ordered. Then she disappeared into Medicine Lane, leaving the three men stranded in the crowd.

***

Shoubei

"The visitor is here to see you, San Bao."

"Let her in."

The servant ushered in a tall figure in a blue kaftan. She crossed the hallway into the carpeted meeting room, not least intimidated by Zheng He's grand mansion. A dense whiff of cinnamon mixed with amber emanated from the folds of her dress. It pervaded the scent of *nanmu* furniture, endowing the visitor with a potent aura.

Zheng He watched the familiar eyes sparkling beneath a black *hijab*. He knew it was her when she spoke.

"*As-Salaam wa alaikum.*"

"And peace be with you. Can it really be you?"

He stood, transfixed. He could hardly conceal his joy.

He found himself overwhelmed by a strange happiness. The happiness that overcomes some of us upon seeing, after a prolonged absence, those with whom we share a past however uneventful and for whom, unknown to us, a loyal flame has continued to burn. We are not even astounded to discover, once the person's memory is rekindled or if we perchance meet them again, that such a flame even existed. Instead, without questioning, we abandon ourselves to their warmth as though the ties that bind us had always been strong.

They were the casual acquaintance, the regular passerby and in those times, we could not see them but they were there. The elusive friend, the well-wisher, whoever they are, once, they existed in our life. And then, they are gone.

And the days, the months, the years are consumed. Much time passes and they are forgotten, often much to our relief because at the time, they often took too much space. We learn to accept the void.

If we later reminisce, we may endow them with qualities they never had. If we liked them only a little bit, we may remember the countless times when we were at fault and where we failed them. If we begrudge them, it is the opposite.

And suddenly, in a moment when we least expect it, they are there. Like a rock that has been washed ashore after years of oceanic roaming, sunsets after sunsets. The last thing we expect is to cling to that rock. All the unsaid of the past finds itself bursting to be spoken.

"Shahrzad! Welcome." His voice was warm.

"San Bao, the great San Bao. It is lovely to see you."

"How did you come to the Middle Kingdom? Come, sit. I will have tea brought at once."

"Thank you."

"My Arabic is no longer very good."

"My host is too humble." She had switched to the Nanjing Hua.

"Impressive!"

Zheng He sat there, staring at his friend. He leaned forward to offer her some apricots which she took kindly.

"So...how did you learn our language?"

"I have been here for nine months. Your government has been on the whole, amiable and even hospitable at times. I have even visited Chang'an."

"I am impressed. You must have come escorted, by land? From the Northwest, perhaps?"

She shook her head.

"No, I came to Sumatra on a dhow, after much arguing with my father's men. They were on their way to Java, you see. It wasn't difficult. My father had...business there. Ships today may not leave your ports but incoming ships are not forbidden. And since I was bored in Sumatra..."

Having said this, she paused to examine her friend's face. Then she took a sip of her tea.

"Be at rest, I am not alone. I have two very capable male bodyguards," she said with wicked amusement.

Zheng He's eyes scanned the corridor where the guards waited outside.

"Kareem hired them himself. Bless him. And then my name is recorded in your registers so when I leave, your people will check off my name…And if I do not leave because something has happened to me, well then, someone will find me!" She laughed. "Besides," she confided in a playful tone, "let us not pretend that one of the eunuchs from your security agency is not constantly on my heels. I am quite safe."

The admiral was listening avidly. He wondered why she had come to see him.

It appeared that she had just read his mind.

"This is the last journey I will ever make to the Middle Kingdom," she revealed. "So you could say that...I am a little like you. Soon, I will be – what's the word?"

"Settled," he offered.

She observed him for a moment.

"Settled? Yes, yes, in my case that would be the word to use. But in your case, it would be – stranded."

"You mock me," replied Zheng He with a playful tone. "My last voyage ended many years ago. I am definitely settled."

She took a sip from her tea and observed him with calculation.

"Are you quite sure that it was meant to be your last? And here I was thinking that maybe there was a touch of resentment for those new laws. And your new post, I mean you are literally stranded in Nanjing, are you not? We are friends, you can tell me, San Bao."

The eunuch stood.

"I am a different man, Shahrzad. Many things have changed for me. It would be easy to resent the emperor's decisions if they were baseless and not founded on sound principles. But Zhu Gaozhi has earned my respect. True, his advisors are the bane of the eunuchs and we've had to watch our backs these days. But – let me tell you a story."

"A story? Since when does the admiral tell stories? Last time I remembered you were quite fond of those rhyming tales a certain seamstress shared on your ship."

Zheng He felt himself blush. He laughed.

"It is not really a story. It actually took place many years ago. You see Zhu Gaozhi's younger brother is a very ambitious, spiteful man. He was always creating strife in Nanjing. He didn't take too well to being one of the younger sons.

"Zhu Gaoxu is his name. When he was younger, he would often accuse the prince, his brother, of secret meetings and all sorts of malfeasances. He sought to raise doubts about the heir's credibility. It reached a point where some of Zhu Gaozhi's close advisors were thrown into jail."

Zheng He stood.

"One of them was Grand Secretary Xie Jin, a man who had my highest esteem. Xie Jin was murdered by the Eastern Depot. Commander Ji Gang buried him in the snow until he died. I only found out two years later. And all this because of Zhu Gaoxu's vicious accusations! Zhu Gaoxu has always resented Xie Jin for advising Zhu Di in the selection of his heir."

"You mean Zhu Di had doubts?"

"Yes, between you and me, Zhu Gaozhi has never been a military strategist. Zhu Di saw him as idle and unfit. He rarely appreciated his son's qualities. He doted on his grandson. There was a time when even Zhu Gaoxu may well have had a chance at being heir apparent."

"It is a relief that he did not succeed. But continue..."

Zheng He reflected for a while longer before continuing.

"During this entire time, not once did Zhu Gaozhi flinch. He had every reason to. And one day, Zhu Gaoxu's antics went too far. Zhu Di threatened to have his younger son stripped of his princely title. And do you know what happened, Shahrzad? Zhu Gaozhi himself came to his brother's rescue. Yes, he did! He even cried. He pleaded and did his best to appeal on his younger brother's behalf."

"How generous of him..."

The admiral was staring ahead as he spoke as though trying to stir up visions of the past. He took a deep breath.

"I had actually forgotten all this. But being away from my ships gives me time to think. I have thought about people's past actions, including mine and one day, it came to me. When I remembered the way that Zhu Gaozhi had behaved, I realized what a good man he was. And you know, Shahrzad, he seems to genuinely care for the people of the Middle Kingdom. So no, I do not resent him. As for his close advisors, now, that is a different matter. An entirely different matter."

He smiled at his thoughts and changed the subject.

"So what are your hopes when you return to Zanzibar? Forgive my forwardness, but do you plan on having children?"

"If I can, yes, that would be a blessing. Speaking of children, I hear you have adopted almost half of Yunnan. Well, that is an exaggeration. But you spoil them, I hear."

Zheng He was silent. He smiled painfully. "It is the least I can do. A man like me cannot have his own children."

Shahrzad smiled knowingly.

"I wager they are very grateful to their adoptive father."

Zheng He nodded. The Omani knew nothing of Min Li's mother and the promise he had made before she went to her death in Hongwu's tomb. Yet Shahrzad's words had reminded him of Min Li. He decided that it was time to resume their unfinished conversation on the treasure ship.

"She is dead, you know."

Shahrzad's eyes widened through her veil. "Who is dead, Zheng He?"

"The woman you were so curious about many years ago. She died in a palace fire."

Shahrzad stifled an involuntary jerk of surprise. She sat up into her seat. She felt an initial joy from his trust but her empathy for her friend was so intense, that she slumped into her chair, as if beaten.

"I see."

Her voice was absent. She seemed to be thinking and focusing on something.

"Shahrzad, I was in love with her. You saw right through me didn't you? What pathetic little mask I put on and you could not be fooled. You were right. I was a coward. I could have saved her. I could have given her more attention. But I was so ashamed. I invented anything I could in my mind to despise her because...because I had to. Do you understand?"

Shahrzad was at loss for words.

Zheng He went on. "Even so I know there was little I could do. What kind of a life would she have led? Certainly in those days, even if Zhu Di had given his blessing, perhaps the Grand Admiral, Zheng He, could have used his imperial influence and lived with Guifei Min Li. He could have. Other eunuchs have consorts.

"But just look at the times we live in! We eunuchs have lost many of our privileges. Part of me is grateful that I am not treated as harshly as the others. Many of us have lost face. Why do you think they sent me here? I know the Hanlin council only too well. And now...I am only a memory of the person they grew to resent."

"It is so sad," whispered Shahrzad.

"Ah, let us not ruminate on the past," replied Zheng He, slapping his thigh as if to awaken himself from a dangerous journey into further introspection. "What will it all achieve? *Water spilled can never be retrieved*," he added. "Besides, I am so delighted to see you! I hope you will not regret coming here and having to put up with the ramblings of an old man. Just as well I did not bore you with astronomy and ship governance."

"Oh, no, that would have been very interesting!"

"Always so eager to learn," he smiled fondly.

Then he stood with sudden excitement.

"Ah, you know what, I almost forgot!"

"What is it?"

He did not reply at first and instead rummaged through the drawers of his desk. He produced a medium-sized lacquered box where he kept documents and unlocked it.

"I believe this belongs to you..."

He raised an object from the box just as Shahrzad shrieked in her chair.

"Oh! That… Where did you find it?"

In her bewilderment, she had switched to speaking in Arabic. She took the knife. Her hennaed hands cherished the curve of the sandalwood sheath. She drew out the blade, barely tarnished by time, as though to ascertain that it were one and the same.

"I saw your name engraved on the wooden handle, in Arabic calligraphy. I knew it was yours," replied Zheng He. "I hesitate to reveal how it was found..."

"Leave nothing out."

"One of the eunuchs, I prefer not to name him, who works here and keeps a tally on eunuch staff had the clarity to bring it to me. He thought perhaps I would recognize it as belonging to one of the envoys."

"Clever."

"Yes, but that's hardly the whole story. Do you know, Shahrzad, that your knife was actually stolen by one of the imperial city eunuchs?"

"A eunuch stole my knife? By the Prophet..."

"Yes. He eventually got what he deserved."

"What do you mean?"

"A very peculiar story... No one from the Eastern Depot could make much sense from it, from what I heard. But one morning of the year we left Beijing, this eunuch disappeared and failed to report to duty. Days after his disappearance, his body was found dead not far from the palace. My guess is that he was mugged and left for dead. I am sorry...but you did ask that I leave nothing out."

Shahrzad remained quiet but her eyes wandered, betraying her agile mind. "This eunuch – why was he killed, you say?"

"He must have run across some thieves while in the *hutong* district."

"Well that's no good. No good at all."

"Why?"

"Because, look! The blade is encrusted with gems. Why did they not take it?"

Zheng He could not bring himself to admit that the knife had been found plunged inside the eunuch's chest. He hesitated.

"I was given no further information."

"What a strange story indeed," said Shahrzad under her breath.

And she repeated this last phrase, something Zheng He found odd but smiled nevertheless. Then she remembered something.

"I wish you could travel too, San Bao."

"It would be wonderful. But as I said, I've no complaints. I am kept very busy."

Shahrzad leaned forward to whisper.

"Courage, my friend! This situation will not last long. It will end. What if I told you what I believe – that Zhu Gaozhi will not remain emperor for long. It would not surprise me if they planned to assassinate him by the end of the year... With the late emperor's blessing, I might add."

Zheng He gasped.

"What are you saying? Shahrzad, this is treason..."

"Not for me. We agree, don't we, that Zhu Di never intended for his son to rule. He had doubts. After what you told me, it would appear that he favored his grandson and that is the only reason why he allowed Zhu Gaozhi to inherit the throne. You would agree with this, wouldn't you?"

"Zhu Gaozhi gorges himself and spends far too long with his concubines. If anything will kill him, Shahrzad, it is his excesses."

Shahrzad shook her head.

"Perhaps. But I am prepared to wager that even your ministers have had enough of him. I am convinced they would want a stronger leader...like Zhu Gaozhi's son. I forget his name. But is he not a true military leader, like Zhu Di was? Besides—"

"How have your learnt all this?" frowned Zheng He, amused despite himself.

Shahrzad smiled. "Let's just say that I was given a visit into the palace. For old times sake."

"I do not believe it!"

"What do you not believe? That twice, I have used the hospitality of a prince...now an emperor? Or are you more concerned that I would sit here with you betraying my host after he showed me so much kindness and hospitality?"

"I am not sure. I scarcely know what to think with you. I just cannot imagine that someone would do this to Zhu Gaozhi. And besides, why are you telling me all this?"

"Because you are my friend."

Zheng He sighed.

"Do not concern yourself for me, Shahrzad. Even if I were to lose my title or my honor at court, I am already resigned to it. Besides I was thinking of journeying to the South soon. I wish to visit a village in Yunnan... It is a village where—"

Shahrzad was not listening. She wafted across the room. Without hesitation, as though this were her own mansion, she opened the doors and peered into the corridor where her Malindi servant waited. The man held a large cylindrical object in his hands. The object was concealed by a cloak but it appeared to be a cage.

"*Shukran.*"

She returned, placing the large object on the table. She looked at Zheng He with triumphant eyes. The admiral hesitated.

"What is this?"

Shahrzad administered a sharp tug on the black cloth and let it collapse on the floor.

"My father's messengers. Homing pigeons."

"They are beautiful, but..." He approached to examine the two white birds. "What does it mean?"

"If you do embark on a voyage and wish to meet me, release the first pigeon. I will wait for your message and make arrangements. Kareem and I will be glad to see you."

"And the second one?"

Shahrzad took a deep breath.

"I am offering you a chance to leave the Middle Kingdom. I offer you a life in Melaka."

"This is madness! Why would I leave the Middle Kingdom?"

"If you wish to leave, for whatever reason, send the second pigeon once you depart for your expedition. They will fly to Melaka. You do not need to worry about the rest. My friends in Melaka will be honored to come to your aid."

Zheng He shook his head vigorously.

"I will not be going anywhere! This is madness. It borders on treason!"

Shahrzad smiled.

"Alas, my time here has come to an end," she quipped lightly. "Embrace me, San Bao. There, my friend, and how tall you are still." She lowered her voice. "Know this. Know that I am sorry for your loss. But you have trusted me with your sad story and I would do anything to help you. Remember what I said about Zhu Gaozhi. If things do change for you, for good or for ill, you know what to do."

Now she was leaving. Zheng He felt himself grow sad but already filled with a dangerous tinge of excitement.

"Goodbye, San Bao. Perhaps it will be many more years until we see each other again. Take care of the homing pigeons. Oh, come now, there is no need to see me through the door. I know my way out. I have explored the world now!"

Halfway through the corridor, she hesitated. "Oh, that physician I met on board last time...the rude one, will he still be traveling with you?"

"I will not be going anywhere, Shahrzad."

"As you wish... But these are my last words, my friend. Bring him."

***

The Eyes and Ears of the Emperor

No sooner was Shahrzad's sedan procession out of sight that a black-clad rider with long leather boots and a scar on his right temple spurred his horse towards the mansion gates. The austere man gestured impatiently towards the gatekeeper who scrambled to meet him.

"Do you know who I am?" asked the rider.

He stroked his horse with a gloved hand. His broody eyes were sunken deep and he wore a gold insignia across his chest. The rider was none other than Yin Dao, service Captain of the Eastern Depot.

"Whoever you are, this is private property," began the gatekeeper preparing to use force.

"His majesty sends me here," replied the rider with assurance.

"How so?" asked the chubby gatekeeper with suspicion.

The rider extended his hand forward. The gatekeeper took one look at the seal on the man's ring and swallowed hard. Then he nodded apprehensively.

"You will answer my question or I will take you for questioning. Do you understand?"

The gatekeeper looked down and bowed in fear.

"Excellent. The woman, the one who was here, just then, who is she? Speak."

"What woman? I do not—"

"I saw her enter!"

"She...she is a friend, a friend of the *shoubei*..."

"A foreigner?" asked the rider, his tone loaded with hatred.

"Her—"

"Speak up! From where?"

"Her name is Shahrzad Haji. Her family lives in Zanzibar."

"What did she want?"

"I do not know..."

"I'll cut out your tongue before you lie again, you wretch!"

"Please my Lord, I am not privy to the admiral's business. I am only a gatekeeper."

"Don't fucking grovel, you cur. Here, take this. It is paper stamped with my address. You will dispatch a courier and advise me whenever the admiral receives unofficial visitors. I will pay the messenger. Don't try anything smart. I have other spies. They will know if you fail to alert me. Remember, your emperor's eyes and ears are everywhere. You will be rewarded for your loyalty."

The gatekeeper bowed. When he lifted his head, the rider was still there, brooding.

"Shahrzad Haji, you say? A Hui from the Arab lands?"

"Yes, yes my Lord. That is correct."

"Interesting."

Yin Dao sat erect on his mount. He observed the mansion through his narrowed pupils. Then he steered his horse towards the road and continued on his way, disappearing behind a rustling of mulberry trees.

Chapter 55
The Monastery

Beijing, June 1425

Princess Xia met her own eyes in the mirror. She advanced a trembling hand towards her cheek, pressing the damp cloth against the black paint on her mouth. Her once sensual lips pursed bitterly. She continued to wipe, cleaning off the black make-up.

There were not here yet. But they had seen her and they would come. They always did.

Her vacant stare traveled across her gaunt reflection. How tired she looked. The deep purple beneath her eyes forever marked the haunted years she had lived. Her lips curled down into a sneer. She gathered her spit with a vengeful expression and splattered the reflective surface. There. She pressed her palms flat on the table's ledge and rose with a painful grunt. For a moment she wavered before the stained mirror as the pain in her knee seared through her leg and up her hip.

The voices drew near.

There was now a peaceful glow in her eyes. Her traits relaxed. She gave a desolate glance towards the naked form on her bed. The maid had not stirred.

Fast footsteps rang in the hallway; three, maybe four men, all armed. Princess Xia wrapped her black silk cape across her shoulders. She limped, one hand on her hip. She reached the door just as the guards' voices rose from behind. Then she heard the metallic clink of their swords and knew. She would be dead by dawn.

They banged on the door. She knew they would storm through. They always did.

The maid awoke with a sudden jerk. She raised herself and reached for a blanket, eager to cover her naked limbs. She saw the princess by the door while outside, the guards' angry shouts rose to a loud pitch. She gasped.

"Princess Xia! Wh...what is happening?"

The princess set a finger across her lips. Her face was convulsed in fear.

"Hush... Sleep, my sweet."

And then the guards burst in.

***

The short, round eunuch from the *Silijian* bowed with reverence. He still did not understand why the *shoubei* had summoned him so urgently on his unexpected visit to Beijing.

"I intend to be brief with you, Shin," said Zheng He as he removed his sword and belt, placing them beside him. "That is your name, is it not?"

"Shin is my name. But... What is the meaning of this?"

Zheng He stood. He seemed agitated. He paced the room furiously, a deep frown etched across his brow.

"I had to meet you. The matter cannot wait, Shin."

"I will do my best to attend to the needs of the *shoubei*," bowed Shin.

"Very well," said Zheng He, watching the eunuch intently. "Then you would know that Princess Xia has been arrested by the Embroidered-uniform Guards. No one, it seems, is looking into this improper act. I thought you might know something."

Shin took a step back. His face had instantly grown pale.

"I know nothing, Admiral," he whimpered.

"Do not lie to me. You were the last person to see her. You two made a transaction...a sedan chair and two guards, do not lie."

The eunuch's eyeballs seem to swell from their sockets. He raised his chubby hands to his face, pressing them onto his cheeks in horror. His distressed pupils moved from side to side.

"They are watching us, Admiral," he whispered.

"Stop that. You think I ignore what goes on in the imperial city? The eunuch-led arrests? Your corrupt directorate? I know all about it. But why the princess? Why? What do you know, Shin? Does the emperor even suspect her arrest?"

Shin shook his head vigorously. He gulped.

"Honorable *Shoubei*, please..."

Zheng He grew impatient.

"Shin, I have already done my research. I came to Beijing as soon as I heard. You are the only one, the only one who knew that the princess had forbidden dealings outside the palace. You knew this. So if there is anything else you know, Shin, speak up now! Why did they take her?"

"Honorable *Shoubei*...I..."

Zheng He was now agitated. He seemed to hesitate. Then, as though he could no longer wait, he dug into his sleeve, trembling with a feverish passion. He withdrew a scrolled parchment, scribbled with tight ink and raised it to Shin's pale face.

"Can you read?"

Shin nodded pitifully.

It was unlike the dignified *shoubei* to be sweating and quivering with emotion but he did now. He shoved the scroll into Shin's reluctant face.

"Then read it! Read it all. Read it and tell me all you know!"

"What is it?"

Zheng He looked away.

"A message from a good friend. It arrived months after Zhu Di's death."

Perplexed, Shin stared at the message, perusing its content. And as he read, at first, shaking with fear then later, with arrested breath, his eyes dimmed with a knowing light.

—Honorable Zheng He

It is with great pleasure that I, Huang-Fu, announce to you my recent appointment in the cavalry. I still have to accustom myself to my new title, Lieutenant Liu, but aside from occasionally forgetting he is me or that I am him, I am grateful to you. My life has been changed with your help and I shan't forget.

I have made progress with my reading and writing. I even managed to find my future wife, a fair lady. No matter how lucky I feel, this letter is not the reason why I mention her.

Please let me explain, since her mother died and before our engagement, she spent years secluded in a monastery. In order to ease her into her new life, I have volunteered to accompany her frequently and pay a visit to the nuns of the Water Moon

Monastery. In one such visit a fortnight ago, I encountered a notable incident which, Honorable Zheng He, concerns you directly.

When we arrived at the Water Moon monastery that day, imagine my surprise when I caught sight of a yellow-curtained sedan and several imperial envoys posted at the gates. Oddly, when I asked the sedan carriers about the identity of their passenger, they would not tell me. I began to suspect some ill happenings but was wise enough to not let it show.

My betrothed had since disappeared to pay her visit. With a little persistence and after a card game or two, one of the guards finally revealed the identity of the visitor. The lady, Princess Xia, was at the monastery.

She later emerged from the convent, escorted by two servants of the court. What a frightening woman. Her face was veiled beneath the black gauze of a broad-rim hat. She was thin and walked with the aid of a cane. Her hair was as smooth as oil and black as a vampire cat. She looked uneasy as she climbed back inside her sedan.

What business had this strange princess in a monastery is something I could only speculate. I soon learned the truth about Princess Xia.

But before I reveal what I have learnt, forgive me for what I am about to say about our late emperor. Please dispose of this scroll upon reading it as my life may be in danger from the words it dares carry.

Five years following his ascent to the dragon throne, emperor Zhu Di's consort died. What you may remember is that upon the death of Empress Xu, Zhu Di attempted to marry his sister-in-law, Xu Miaojin. She refused. Zhu Di did not take the rejection well.

Then one fatal evening, he discovered that Princess Xia and Princess Xu Miaojin, were lovers. They had been lovers for three years.

The emperor was furious. In a fit of jealousy, he threatened to execute Princess Xia.

But Xu Miaojin, desperate to save the woman she loved, had him swear that he would never kill Xia for as long as he remained alive. The kindly woman sacrificed herself to the life of religious recluse as a pledge that the two women would never meet again.

From this moment on, Princess Xia lived as Zhu Di's prisoner. She was not permitted to leave the palace unless given imperial approval. The lovers were forbidden to meet.

But Princess Xia has since made herself familiar with one of the senior eunuchs from the Silijian. His name is Shin. With his help, she arranges monthly clandestine visits to the monastery and meets with her lover. It is believed that over the years, the princess has made large donations to the monastery.

Forgive me, I do not wish to scandalize the Honorable Zheng He with tales of lechery. Honorable Zheng He, if I am telling you all this, it is to leave no doubt about the identity of my source. I was afraid you would not believe me. I hope you will believe this woman.

Honorable Zheng He, before I left the monastery, I spoke with this old nun. Her Highness, Xu Miaojin has greatly aged and is on her deathbed. I was touched at once by her calm, inner peace. I remained there until dusk telling her of my good fortune and about you, until which time I felt it was time to accompany my betrothed back to her village. And as I was about to leave, she whispered these strange words, "Tell Zheng He that Princess Xia regrets not telling him about Li Guifei."

I was taken aback. How could this nun know about Li Guifei? And how had she learnt of your relation to the late emperor's courtesan? Confused, I pressed her to explain.

"She regrets the lie. But she would do any...anything to protect Min Li..."

I urged her to go on but the old woman grew tired and merely repeated *the fire*, *the fire* and made no sense.

"Min Li died in the palace fire. Is that what you mean?" I asked.

But the old nun shook her head as vigorously as her frail frame could let her. "They think...they think she is dead. Not so. Not so. She is alive. You go. You tell that to Zheng He. Go! Go now."

Honorable Zheng He, had this been any other nun from the monastery, I would have dismissed her words. But she is royalty and she is an intimate of Princess Xia.

My most Honorable Zheng He, Min Li never died in the palace fire.

I ought to have written earlier but I waited until after the Yong Le emperor mourning period. I hope you forgive my tardiness.

Your humble servant,
Lieutenant Liu, formerly Huang-Fu–

When he had finished reading, Shin lowered his face. He appeared stunned.

"How long have you had this letter?" he asked.

"It does not matter now. What do you know, Shin? Is it true?"

"If you are looking for the man who helped the princess visit her lover, then yes, that man is me."

"So it is true..." said Zheng He.

"...but if you want to know how you can help the princess, I'm afraid I can be of little use. As far as I know they've already killed her..."

Zheng He leapt. He seized Shin's collar, lifting the eunuch from his stool.

"Now you listen to me! I don't care that everyone thinks you're a fine fourth grade eunuch, Shin. If I find that you turned in the princess, I'll—"

"Honorable *Shoubei*! It wasn't me! I had nothing to do with it!"

"Do you realize what you've done?"

He shook Shin violently by the throat.

"Mercy! I had nothing to do with this...you must believe me! It is not what you think!"

"Then what is it? Why was Princess Xia arrested?" bellowed Zheng He, jerking Shin back with so much force that he collapsed onto the hard floor and skidded across the room.

Shin was wheezing with fear. He adjusted the rim of his collar, sweating profusely.

"She'd gone too far," he sobbed.

"How dare you! It was you! She would come to you! You would supply her with a sedan—"

"It was her fault! She'd gone too far with the blasphemy," cried Shin.

Zheng He froze.

"What blasphemy?"

Shin's voice became a whisper. He raised his hand before him, waving it, as though to calm the *shoubei*.

"Please..." he pleaded, rising to his feet. "That letter... It mentions a certain Min Li."

Zheng He blushed.

"You knew the Guifei?"

Shin shook his head.

"Not I. Not I. But what I am about to tell you does concern her."

Zheng He was listening. He watched as Shin adjusted his robe, eyeing the chamber as though fearful of onlookers.

"Is she alive then?" asked Zheng He. His voice was strained with emotion. "Tell me! Is she alive?" He looked down at the rolled parchment and picked it up from the floor, smoothing its edges with tenderness. "I dismissed this letter for almost a year. I thought the nun had lied. These nuns...they will invent such sordid tales..." His eyes were moist with tears. "Isn't that what happens in all erotic tales? Beautiful nuns enchant and corrupt men..." His voice trailed.

Shin shook his head. He had detected a glimmer of hope in the *shoubei*'s voice and it pained him because it reminded him of Zhijian.

"I ignore if Min Li is alive, Honorable *Shoubei*," he said finally. "I know nothing about that. It was so long ago... But the *shoubei* has asked me why the princess was imprisoned and I will tell him. I'll tell him everything I know."

Shin came closer. His face, hidden by the lengthened shadow of a setting sun, seemed burdened with secrets.

"She knew too much, the princess. She knew too much. And you know Princess Xia was not a spirit that one could tame. Oh that, she wasn't! The guards watched her. And they watched her...and... And one day, she went too far."

He paused. "Even I saw it...the writing on the palace wall before the eunuchs painted over it... Palace Damage they called it... By her own hand she tried to slander the emperor, by her own evil hand. They came for her that same day, I swear they did." He shook his head.

Zheng He frowned.

"What writing do you speak of?"

"Who knows why she did it? Maybe she'd written it from spite. After all, she could have run away years ago... She could have deserted the palace and rejoined her lover at the monastery. But the princess depended on her imperial stipend to live, depended on her base, lascivious habits, ah that, she did. This life ruined her. Every day she hated it and she bore hate wherever she went. She was a demon, I tell you, a demon!"

Shin's face convulsed as he said those words. There was a mixture of terror and revulsion in his eyes. Then he looked away. "But even then, even then, I did not turn her in, I swear it! No. She wrought it upon herself. Maybe she'd had enough of it all. Her little protégée had burnt to cinders. Now Xu Miaojin was dying. Soon she would have nothing left. That's why, you see, that's why I think she did it."

"What did she write about Zhu Gaozhi, Shin?"

Shin hesitated.

"She did not write about Zhu Gaozhi."

"But you said...the writing on the wall...the imperial blasphemy..."

Shin shook his head.

"Many years ago, in Nanjing, when she was only a child, the princess saw something she should not have. My guess is that's how she knew... Yes... I think that's how it happened. These little girls like to explore the palace..."

"She knew what? She saw what? You're not making any sense. What was it that she wrote?"

Shin looked away. He stood in the room's far corner, fearful of what he was about to say. His voice deepened, burdened by the revelation.

"The princess did not write about Zhu Gaozhi," he began. "She wrote about Zhu Di. Cursed the emperor in his grave, she did."

Zheng He was barely breathing. He listened.

"That woman slandered Zhu Di...said that he slept with his father's concubine and later with the very bastard daughter they bore together. But you didn't hear it from me."

The room had grown silent.

Shin turned around, watching the *shoubei* for a reaction. He continued, still trembling.

"Princess Xia said she saw it...saw Zhu Di in bed with Hongwu's concubine..."

Zheng He did not reply. He stared, transfixed.

Shin hesitated.

"Now you are going to ask me if it's all true. Well, it is. Min Li is not Hongwu's daughter. She never was. But you never heard it from me," he repeated.

Zheng He's voice rose from a distant world.

"Min Li is Zhu Di's daughter?"

He stood, squinting as though to better discern a vision in his memory. The vision took form. He saw a haggard face at his knees, a woman with long, black disheveled hair, who was calling out his name. She clung at his ankles.

He remembered years ago, in Nanjing palace, how Min Li's mother had said his nickname. He had long pondered over how this woman, Hongwu's concubine had somehow known his nickname. Without a doubt, Shin was telling the truth. Only a woman close to Zhu Di, only a woman who had shared Zhu Di's bed could have known about his favorite eunuch, the very eunuch who would help him depose of his nephew. Abandoned by Zhu Di to her dismal fate, the poor woman had gone mad.

"Honorable *Shoubei*—"

"Min Li is Zhu Di's daughter..." repeated Zheng He, still pacing the room.

"This is what I've been trying to say," continued Shin. "Princess Xia has known this for years. Oh, only a few of us know. Even Zhu Di knew nothing. It was never spoken." Shin shook his head for emphasis. "Never spoken..."

But Zheng He was elsewhere. He had lowered his gaze as though inspecting the carpeted hall. Shin sighed.

"So you see, Honorable *Shoubei*, it is not what you think. What could the guards care for Xia's visits to the monastery? Is that reason enough to arrest her? Ah, no. No, no. But if she defiles Zhu Di...then that, *that* is a reason to kill her... You've come...too late..."

Shin paused. He realized something was wrong then. Zheng He was frowning and the traits on his face intensified as though he were recounting something. According to Huang-Fu's letter, Zhu Di had promised Xu Miaojin that he would never kill Xia *for as long as he remained alive*...then how could the guards have known? Zheng He raised his face, struck by a powerful notion.

"Do you realize what you said, Shin?"

Without another word, he reached for his sword and replaced it swiftly under his belt. He was moving fast. Shin watched him adjust his jade buckle.

"This is part of Zhu Di's plan. It was always a part of Zhu Di's plan. They are loyal to Zhu Di," he called out as he lunged towards the door.

"What?" It was Shin's turn to be taken by surprise.

"The Embroidered-uniform Guards...they are loyal to Zhu Di. They are still following Zhu Di's orders."

Zheng He raced towards the Inner Palace, haunted by a single thought.

If Shahrzad's intuition was correct, Zhu Gaozhi's life was in danger.

Chapter 56
Hongxi and the Concubines

Zhu Gaozhi was sprawled on five embroidered cushions. The silk sheets barely covered his corpulent mass. He watched with abated breath as two tiny tongues darted out of a pair of plum colored lips, meeting each other playfully.

He ogled the first woman's breasts then turned his hungry gaze to the other. His eyes lingered on their hips and treasured the entwined limbs writhing before him. The younger one lowered her head to tease the breasts of her companion with an eager tongue. From the corner of her eye, she noticed Zhu Gaozhi's swelling member. She licked further down, circling the dark oily patch arched beneath her. Her accomplice moaned.

Squeezing a cushion in his avid digits, Zhu Gaozhi squealed.

"Excellent! You will taste her! I want you girls to show me the games you play in your chamber. I want to see it all! Don't be shy now," he cheered.

On this glorious afternoon, two of the most sensual Korean creatures reveled in the emperor's bed. Like most afternoons after holding court, Zhu Gaozhi enjoyed feeding his languorous passions in the company of agile women.

The younger concubine emitted delectable noises as she continued to savor the mound beneath her, forcing her tongue in the tender flesh. Enthused by this voluptuous assault, the other moaned like a wild cat and arched her back, piercing the musky air with her fierce nipples.

Zhu Gaozhi's lips parted lustfully. Through the narrowing slits that were his eyes, the smoke-filled room became a blur. The giddy

Son of Heaven licked his lips, eager to devour the glistening forms before him.

Panting like a hungry boar, he sat up on his elbows. The feline orgy unraveled in an urgent sweat. He clenched his heart, feeling his excitement mount. Now the girls hissed and sighed, kneading each other's breasts.

"This is what being the Son of Heaven is all about!" said Zhu Gaozhi. "You two are the most divine little sluts in my court. Look what you've done to me," he added, pulling the silk sheets aside to expose the erect jade member.

The women giggled with delight. They were both drunk and the aphrodisiac he had conscientiously added to their wine had only heightened their eagerness.

***

"Admiral, this part of the palace is sealed, you cannot enter."

"Let me in! This is not what you think. The emperor is in danger! Let me in, I say!"

"Grand Commandant! Have you gone completely mad?" reproached the head of the guards.

They raised their swords towards him, refusing him passage.

"Listen to me!" shouted Zheng He. I have a message for His Majesty. You must let me through at once!"

A voice rose from behind him.

"Honorable *Shoubei*, what is the meaning of this?"

It was Yin Dao.

Zheng He examined the guard's uniform. As he approached, the corridor became infused with a whiff of pungent tobacco. Yin Dao completed a short, half-mocking bow.

"Beijing is honored with your visit, Honorable *Shoubei*. But you have overstayed your welcome."

"Let me through! I have a message for His Highness."

"This palace would soon know chaos if it were to obey the *shoubei* of Nanjing. Remember, this is not a ship, Admiral. This is Beijing!"

"Captain, your duty is to protect the emperor, is it not?" retorted Zheng He. "I believe the emperor is in danger."

Yin Dao eyed the admiral coldly before gesturing to the other four guards.

"You will do your duty, Zheng He, and you will let me do mine. Guards! Escort the Honorable *Shoubei* to Wumen. His visit is officially over."

***

Zhu Gaozhi was now sweating. He crawled to the far side of the bed. The concubines sat there, waiting for him with hungry smiles.

"More wine!" moaned the younger nymph, turning her back towards him to reach for a goblet on a low table.

Without hesitation, Zhu Gaozhi stretched out his hand and grabbed the curved backside presented to him. He licked his lips.

"I'll give you wine, you drunken whore," he panted, preparing to plunge inside her.

"No, take me!" the second woman urged, pointing her breasts towards him.

A gut-wrenching shriek pierced the room. She raised her head. Zhu Gaozhi had released the younger concubine. He clutched at his heart and screamed.

The women glanced at each other, not comprehending. They sat up. With their sweaty black strands matting their faces and shoulders, they looked like ghosts. Their eyes mirrored the horror in Zhu Gaozhi's bulging eyes.

With harrowing violence, the emperor fell back on the bed. He rolled from side to side. His limbs jerked uncontrollably. The women shrieked. They watched his giant belly flop about and convulse as though demons possessed him. Out of the emperor's mouth poured a foamy white froth while his trembling hands clawed at his own throat.

The teary Guirens leapt from the bed and reached for their gowns. Zhu Gaozhi's face grew a violet shade. Then the rolling motion came to a halt. His arms flapped to his sides.

They had no time to dress. The Embroidered-uniform Guards burst in. Yin Dao was among them. Six eunuchs, armed to the teeth, invaded the nuptial chamber. Two of them reached for the screeching women and held their arms tight behind their backs.

Two others, physicians, knelt on each side of the emperor's body and listened for his pulse. They found no six pulses. Then one of them raised his angry face towards the women and pointed a finger in their direction.

"Murder! Our emperor murdered by these two concubines!"

The two drugged Guirens shook their heads, trembling.

Seething with rage, a fifth eunuch probed the room, scrutinizing every inch of carpet for indices that would unveil this hideous crime. At last, seizing the emperor's goblet, he brought it to his flared nostrils.

"Treason!" he hissed.

He nodded towards Yin Dao. They, alone, both knew of the poison's origin but there were to be no witnesses.

Yin Dao brandished his sword, undeterred by the women's screams. He sliced the breasts of one concubine who convulsed and nearly passed out while the guard behind her tightened his grip on her arms. Blood gushed from the two wounds. It spilt onto the carpet, soiling Yin Dao's boots. He cut her throat in one swift motion.

The other woman's shrieks pierced through the chamber.

"I'm innocent!"

But she could say no more. The blade swept across her belly. She collapsed to her knees wailing in her bloodbath. The sword came down severing her neck.

There were no witnesses.

Shortly after, the imperial physician pronounced the emperor dead.

***

It was set in motion, two days ago, soon after Princess Xia's murder. Two scholars had presumably appeared before the emperor. They reprimanded His Highness for his relentless pursuit of sexual relations during the period dedicated to mourning the late Zhu Di.

The outraged Zhu Gaozhi had promptly arrested them. Zhu Gaozhi was well known for his temper and now it was clear that the Son of Heaven, so driven was he by heated passions and excesses, had met death through the very pleasures he sought.

None of the court officials or high-ranking eunuchs questioned the report; after one year on the dragon throne, the Hongxi emperor had died. The cause of death was heart trouble.

Speculations were promptly dismissed. Had not the emperor suffered from sharp pains to the chest because of his love of rich foods? Two concubines had murdered him by raising him to excessive pleasure with aphrodisiac drugs. They had been justly punished.

A month later, on 26 June 1425, Xuande ascended the dragon throne.

Zheng He was taken aback. It seemed that all had gone according to Zhu Di's plan. Zhu Di's grandson would rule the Middle Kingdom.

But for now, honored reader, it is time we leave this festering Ming palace for more peaceful landscapes.

As the Eastern cities of the Middle Kingdom mourned the death of one great man and hailed the ascent of another, great changes were set in motion.

Far removed from the political intrigues of the Imperial Palace, in the South-western part of the Middle Kingdom, high up on the mountainous lands bordering U-Tsang, in a village where water rippled in every street, a blind old woman had ceased counting the days.

For too long now, she had consulted the almanacs and observed the days, months and years since her daughter's death. She had waited for this day, praying that she would not die of old age before it came. And it had come. It had come with the passing of the third Ming emperor. She would leave Yunnan and set off to Nanjing.

She would take the wooden box to the place where it belonged.

For this was what the Shaman had asked.

Chapter 57
The Wooden Box

August 1426

For days and nights, and over thousands of *li*, the Southern woman stubbornly rode on, refusing her guide's assistance. For days, they persisted across the dense rainforests of Yunnan, plodding through muddy roads and winding paths. After so long, the guide forgot to shake his head in disbelief.

He learnt to respect this strange old thing, riding head high, her nostrils perpetually inflated, staring ahead with vacant eyes as though floating through a maze of spirits. A grave purpose animated his client. Soon, they would reach the sprawling night lights of Nanjing and he knew that she would be pleased.

At times, he watched her extend her soft cheeks to feel the wind's caress. When she dismounted, she crouched to dig her withered hands into the soil and smell the earth. More often, she would stretch out her palm for signs in the trees and leaves.

Like her mother before her, she had been blind all her life. Yet it did not matter because the sounds of nature spoke to her in a language that others did not understand. She sensed the road through the gait of her steed, the sound of its hooves along the path, the smells of the forest and the angle of the sun on her hair and face. She was fearless about not seeing.

She had once raised a daughter alone. To this precious child she bestowed the art of gathering and preparing plants for healing. For Yunnan was wealthy in plants and rare herbs. On the Nakhis' sacred Haba Snow Mountain alone, there grew an unsurpassed range of rare medicinal plants, numbering over half of the many thousands to be found in Yunnan. But the true extent of their healing properties was unknown then, even from the emperor and the subjects of the Middle Kingdom.

The high-ranking Ming eunuchs would hire many physicians. They sent them off to travel far beyond the oceans and bring back medicinal plants from the other lands. Yet, unknown to them, Yunnan already detained so many remedies.

"This," she told her daughter, "is our sacred knowledge. We have cherished the secrets of nature for many generations."

It had been easy teaching her daughter. As young as five, the child had already shown evidence of the great sight.

It was unusual that unlike her mother and grandmother before her, the child had not been born blind. Yet in her, the great sight was strong and extended far, beyond the villages, beyond the forests of Yunnan, beyond the mountain peaks of the Middle Kingdom. It spanned as far as the Eastern cities, across the oceans, high up into the clouds and often, during rare moments that the girl could not control nor anticipate, the sight would leave the realm of the now and reach across time.

To protect her daughter, she warned her about the Dongba priests. They came from an old U-Tsang religion, one that had grown in influence and power. They were much stronger today, more so in Nonguzhi. Their power had grown because the Ming rulers were intent on pacifying the religious Mongols via the priests' influence. The priests had much to profit.

While not all Dongba priests were avid for power, she needed to be careful. Together they would hide the great secret, shield it from the jealousy of the priests, lest they be banished or tormented for it. She knew the great men could tarnish their reputation if they so wanted because to be sure, the two women were a great threat to Dongba legitimacy.

From the time Yunnan had fallen to the Ming, she had accepted the mere position of medicinal woman. She attended to the many women who, intent on protecting their virtue, shunned the male physicians. This allowed her to make a living. Yet she dared not speak of the sacred shamanistic legacy. She advised her grown daughter to find a humble occupation and not attract attention. Because the young woman was so skilled at the needle and thread and since these skills were valued even by the Ming, she had chosen to become a seamstress. Her mother gave her a name that the Ming would understand: Jun. It was a boy's name and it meant Truth.

And now if this old woman journeyed across the Middle Kingdom, it was to execute her daughter's last wish. The dying wish of a beloved, it had to be seen through.

Bundled up on her saddle was the wooden box her daughter had kept almost all her life. The old woman knew well and understood its contents.

After many days, they arrived into Anhui province. Here, the road skirted the eerie Huang Shan, the Yellow Mountain, and high above, where the lofty peaks pierced the heavens and vanished into the clouds, the misty air was moist and pure. In awe of the rising peaks behind him, the guide drew a long sigh. As the sun's rays waned and she felt weary knowing another day had passed, she heard him. She misunderstood. She lamented that they had not yet reached Yellow Mountain; until the rich dampness of the cold evening filled her nostrils and she smiled knowingly.

"I can smell the cold of marble," she said.

And the guide nodded.

"Huang Shan, Older Sister. We rest in Tunxi tonight. And tomorrow, onto Nanjing."

***

Zheng He studied at a lacquered table. The hair above his temples had grown ashen since Zhu Gaozhi's death. He had even lost a little weight. He had, on his brow, a gentle melancholic air that is often seen on those who wait years for their hopes to be fulfilled. Waiting bestows them with humility and gratitude.

Despite his cautious character, he had not burnt Huang-Fu's letter. He could not bring himself to destroy the one hope that still tied him to Min Li.

With Xuande on the dragon throne, the admiral also nurtured the hope of sailing again. Discussions for a potential journey had begun but all was uncertain. Even if an expedition were approved, it would still mean years of planning, shipbuilding and recruitment.

Since his first appointment as Zhu Gaozhi's personal representative, he had little choice but to oversee the government operations in Nanjing. It was almost farcical, that he, a military man, was in charge of sending Nanjing tributes to the capital. Recently they had appointed him to beautify the city, citing his engineering prowess as desirable. He supposed this was fortunate. Supervising the building of mosques appealed to him.

But it was the constant political clashes with the civil authorities who resented the *shoubei* and made no secret of this, which unsettled him in his new role. The chief censor of Nanjing made his work difficult.

For years at Zhu Di's service he had never had to watch his back. But now, with Xuande on the throne, it was different. He somehow believed that the hostility the civil authorities felt towards him had grown over the years. He knew how they worked. Shin kept him informed.

If they willed it, they could impeach him or accuse him of overstepping his military authority. Sometimes he wondered whether he was a mere puppet figure, dancing at the whims of both his emperor and the chief censor of Nanjing. But his resentment was not directed at the young emperor Xuande who he had grown to respect.

The distrust between the military and the civil authorities only reminded him of the high-ranking eunuchs' experience with the Hanlin ministers. This duality, this tendency to entrust leadership between clashing parties, this peculiarity of the Middle Kingdom, would it lead them into anarchy?

And now it seemed that foreigners were not the only ones to raise suspicion. Mistrust simmered within.

The admiral's thoughts were interrupted by a young courier. The man bowed. He seemed to hesitate as though unsure whether to trouble the *shoubei* with his message.

"Grand Commandant, you have a visitor. An old woman from the South... She says you will know her. She has come alone save for her guide."

"I cannot see them now..."

The courier handed him an identity paper.

"We tried to dismiss them but she refuses to leave the gates until she speaks with you. I have checked her papers, Grand Commandant, everything is in order. Forgive your servant, *Shoubei* but she insists on seeing you. Should I let her enter?"

Zheng He observed the document.

"Nonguzhi..." he whispered, perplexed.

He gave the document back and rose from his chair. There was time before his next appointment. He could meet with this intruder, whoever she was. He nodded to the courier.

When she entered, the admiral was astounded.

Such a tiny woman, he thought. Just look at her with that taut, dark skin and those little black eyes. He was amused that the very woman who was now kowtowing before him had previously defied his guards.

"Well, what is the meaning of this, old woman? What do you want?"

He continued to stare as she raised her frail face to his level. That strange old thing is blind, observed Zheng He. She was waiting for something. He realized what she wanted. He dismissed his assistant.

The soldier left the room, closing the doors behind him.

Zheng He's attention was again drawn towards the visitor. The frail woman cradled a wooden box in one arm, gently caressing its worn surface with the palm of her other hand.

She kowtowed again and, wasting no time, she presented the box.

Zheng He at once recognized it. Yet he could not recall where he had seen it.

He smiled, taken aback by the gift.

"Where did you get this?"

"It belonged to my daughter, Grand Commandant," replied the woman. "Her name was Jun."

"Your...your daughter? Jun was your daughter?"

He looked at the box with a flash of inspiration. "I remember. Your daughter boarded the Ming fleet, didn't she? Let's see... When was it?"

"...Five years and four moons ago."

"You are right," said Zheng He, more startled than before. "So then, Jun is your daughter?" he kept repeating. "I have long wished to know what became of her. Did she recover from her illness?"

His tone had grown more respectful and he blushed at the sudden familiarity in his voice.

The old woman tapped on the wooden floor with her cane and lowered her head.

"She sleeps forever, Grand Commandant."

"I am so sorry," replied Zheng He, touched by their mutual loss.

"Never mind that," snapped the old woman. "I did not journey all the way to Nanjing for you to mourn my daughter. I am too old for that. If I came here and pestered the Grand Commandant, it is for a better reason. I came to give him...her treasure."

Zheng He raised an incredulous eyebrow.

"Her treasure?"

He watched the old woman smile knowingly. Was she playing with him? There was no mistake. She was smiling as though she anticipated something.

"Please..." She reached forth with the key. "Open it".

As odd as it seemed, Zheng He took the key. He raised the foreign object in his hands. He had a fleeting memory of wanting to open it years ago. Ah, but he had resisted, hadn't he. How amazing that Jun had given it to him now. What a peculiar woman she was. He shook his head in disbelief.

Back then, he had not opened her box. He had given it back. And now, here it was this strange wooden thing, back in his tired old hands. It was almost silly. Almost as though...*she had planned it.*

He stared blankly at the box. Why should Jun have wished to give it to him? And what could be so precious about its contents that a gray-haired blind mother should travel all the way to Nanjing to deliver it?

An uneasy memory resurged. He had never spoken to anyone about the embroidered cloth. Nobody need to know. They would have thought him mad. He had tried to forget it but as he held the wooden box, the thought of that cloth forced itself in his mind.

Well, then, he thought, I best open this box once and for all. Whatever it is, it can't be harmful.

With careful fingers, the admiral inserted the metal key into the lock's groove. He pushed the key in. The bronze lock opened.

Before opening the box, he peered over at the old woman. She had not budged.

The lid seemed jammed. Pressing his fingers to the sides, he pushed it up, releasing effusions of dirt and incense into his startled lips.

Satisfied, he set a hand over the lid, ready to open it but not before casting another glance towards Jun's mother.

It was her gaze that alerted him. Her smile had vanished. The intense expression on her face chilled him. She was watching him with her blind eyes. She seemed to peer into the darkness, listening with disturbing intensity. She was waiting for something.

So then, he pondered, this box must not contain a mere trinket. It is, as I suspected, something important...something very important. His pulse quickened. Trembling a little, he lifted the lid.

He lifted the lid.

He lifted the lid. That was all he could do as he stared again at the content.

During all this time, he thought.

The old woman was blind yet she had sensed it. She had sensed how at first his eyes had narrowed to size up the toy and then instantly lit up in wonderment. It is true, she was blind. But somehow she had seen his lips part and the tears well up in his eyes.

I am the captain of the ship. He remembered, his eyes smiling and glistening with tears.

He blinked again, to be sure. It was still there, nested inside its wooden crate, his perfect ship. The little wooden model he had thought lost. He picked it up with trembling hands.

And suddenly, he was in the clearing again, surrounded by lush trees and wearing his white little cap. He played with his boat, as always, splashing into the puddles. And there she was, that little girl with her silver bracelets and her silly stories and he was sure, now, that her name was Jun. The embroidery...the stories that rhymed, now it all made sense to him. It was her all along. He sighed. It was crazy.

"How is this possible? Where did you find this?"

She heard the choking spasm in his voice. It was time to tell him.

"When the monk emperor, Hongwu, sent his demon soldiers into our village, we hid. She told us where to hide… she knew where it would be safe. They killed many people. They went on to Kunming... You remember, don't you? I felt for your pain, and for your family. But there was nothing to be done. The Yuan supporters were all massacred. And the little children were rounded up, little boys only ten, seven...some younger. She told me what she saw. She was so strong... My strong little one."

Zheng He lifted the flap below the bridge and gazed in astonishment at his secret cabin.

"You are telling me the truth. But tell me, how did she find it?"

"When the villages were raided nothing was left. Nothing! Hongwu's army burnt everything... But my little one, she was brave. She went looking for your home. She slept in the debris and she searched everything...and then one day, she found it. She kept it for you, Ma. She knew all along that you were alive."

Zheng He held the little boat in his two hands. His eyes searched for childhood memories. He recalled first a searing pain, deep in his loins. But he ignored it. There was much more than this. He had to find it. He prodded further into that past.

Then came the soldiers with their banners, he heard it all again, the screams, the murders... It was so long ago but he remembered the pillaging in Kunming. He remembered the death of his father...his family...there was something else. Jun. He saw it again now, the vision of that little girl in a full skirt with jingling bracelets on her arms. On that day, she was crying because the boys in his school had been teasing her. They ran after her in the village streets...mocking her.

Zheng He gasped.

"She was the story maker! I remember now... All the children would laugh..."

His voice became animated.

"There were silly children games. She would tell stories about things to come and they would laugh!"

He lowered his head as if acknowledging a shame he had long denied.

"I laughed too."

The old woman shook her head vigorously.

"Not stories, Zheng He! You must know this about the Mosuo. We have our own leaders. And do you know who she was? She was our Ssan-nyi, our great Shaman!"

"I do not understand."

"She was the guide for our souls. She walked in dreams."

"She walked in—"

"Honorable *Shoubei*, hers were not just made up stories like those told by the Dongba priests. Curse those wily charlatans!" She made an indignant sniff. "You call them stories. But they had meaning! Tell me something – why should she come on your ship when she was so ill, if her stories had no meaning?"

"Older Sister, what are you saying?" asked Zheng He, confused by her outburst.

At this, she grew silent. But with her cane she made a thunderous noise on the wooden floor. The resonant sound startled Zheng He, filling him with awe. He stood back. But the old woman advanced. She raised her hand out as though to touch him with every word.

"They told me you are a navigator, they call you San Bao. You look for meaning in the stars... The stars guide you on your journey. They tell you about the path to take, yes? Yes? This is the way of the Ssan-nyi. It is the same. The stars are your symbols. But...there are symbols in every story, Ma He. Did you ever think of that? You think I came all the way here just to give you a box with a child's toy in it? Humph!"

At this, she suddenly turned around and shriveled into a hunchback ball. She leaned heavily against her cane as if the effort of her words had drained her strength.

Zheng He watched as she adjusted her sheepskin cape and sighed. She sounded disappointed.

A wooden rhythm echoed through the mansion hall. It was the sound of her cane as she made her way out. She was leaving.

He repeated the old woman's last words to himself many times, hoping to draw their meaning. He did not want her to leave, there were questions to ask, things to understand, about Jun, about the embroidery...

A little hesitant, he clutched his boat in one hand, following after her, wondering how it was that she needed no assistance while he, master of the mansion, had lost his way among the seventy rooms.

There was something so convincing about this old woman. It was something that he respected. No. It wasn't that. He felt as if somehow, he *knew* her. That he had distinctly met her before, that he had somehow shared aspects of her life and could *remember* these.

That's ridiculous, he thought, even when I was a little boy, and living in the same area, I had never met Jun's mother.

They approached the courtyard where the horses waited. So how could I recognize her then? No, no, he was not mistaken. Somehow, he knew this old woman. He followed her quietly and watched as she prepared her horse. The dark man who rode with her had himself dismounted and was lifting her up on her saddle.

He too, had a large sheepskin coat and wore pants with colorful embroidered patterns.

Zheng He became absorbed by those enchanting patterns. They were like...like... He shook his head. But the possibility, the possibility that he could perhaps be right, consumed his mind and a joy surged within him. A joy he had not known for years.

He now understood the woman's last words. And with them, there existed the hope that everything he thought was lost could be regained.

For now he knew, without a doubt, that Jun's mother and the blind woman in Jun's tale, that is to say, the blind woman of Nonguzhi were one and the same. There was no doubt. "That's why I feel as if I know her and that's why she keeps insisting that Jun's tale had meaning!"

He tried to recall her tale. He searched his memory as Jun had searched in the debris. In a flash it came to him, visions of that passionate tale told by Jun on his last voyage. All along, she had been trying to tell him *something*...she had come aboard, ailing and dying to tell him *something*. Just like in the clearing, years ago, he had not been listening. Oh but yes, he had listened, he just had not understood. And now he saw a possibility, no, a treasure beyond imagination.

The meaning of Jun's story was the meaning he was ready to place in it. And only one made sense to him. Only one called out to him. It called out to him with a shrill so deafening that he thought he would go mad. All he could feel was immense joy and wonder. A wonderment so soothing that he dared no believe in it. To dare would be to risk again the loss of it and so he could not but remain in awe.

He was still following the old woman, his thoughts swirling in his mind. The Shaman had known more about him than he had realized. And not only that, she had sacrificed her last days to tell him something...

Zheng He's tears welled up again in his eyes. I remember that dark day when the physicians took me away, I called out to the little girl and promised that I would be her friend, did she know this too? Did she hear me?

The dark man in the sheepskin coat raised his arm in a signal and the horses began to move out towards the mansion gate.

Zheng He wanted to act quickly. But he dared not lift that last veil between the dream and the reality. He hastened his pace towards the horses.

Sensing the eunuch's steps behind them, the old woman smiled mischievously and, as if she knew this would only entice the *shoubei*, she spurred her horse. As they crossed the majestic gate, her clever ploy had the desired effect. Zheng He began to run behind the horses, huffing and puffing, eager to catch up to them.

"Wait! Wait! *Jamma*! Wait!"

The woman laughed. She tugged at the reins. The horses came to a halt.

Zheng He ran fast, still holding his wooden boat as though his life depended on it. His face was radiant and his eyes moist with tears. Forgetting all etiquette, he lunged forward just as they passed through the gates and gently pressed the blind woman's arm.

"Old Jamma! Please tell me..." he puffed, "*that young woman you took in, the stranger who came to live in your village*, is she...is she still there?"

And it was the blind woman who now beamed with happiness. She leaned towards him and it seemed to Zheng He that her breath blew on his face like a soothing breeze from the heavens.

"Admiral Zheng He," she began, with a rich white smile that lit up her sun washed face, "I was afraid that you might not ask me this question."

And there again, came that mischievous smile.

Chapter 58
The Eunuch's Last Voyage

The silent walls of Beijing palace greeted him on a cold morning. He eyed the imposing Meridian Gate, wondering what he would find behind it and what further imperial secrets he would unearth. He had not slept for days. He had traveled as soon as he could, driven to a feverish curiosity by Huang-Fu's letter and Jamma's visit. He hoped to understand something. How had Princess Xia known that Min Li was alive?

It was Shin who advised him about the laundries. He knew the maid who had served the princess for years.

Upon entering the office, the young woman seemed uneasy. She extended a frightful stare in Zheng He's direction. Zheng He nodded for the attending eunuch to leave and close the door behind him. He looked grave.

"Do you know who I am?" he asked, once they were alone.

"Yes," replied the timid maid, in awe of the giant man before her.

"Please sit down, I will not harm you. Sit here."

She moved tentatively towards the low stool. She may have been in her early twenties but years of manual work had ruined her. Her tiny hands were blistered. Her face was lined with worry lines. The admiral noticed the deep, dark circles beneath her eyes.

"Tell me, you were in Princess Xia's service, am I right?"

The maid's eyes widened. She hesitated.

"I...she—"

"Be at peace. I was a good friend of the princess, you can trust me. Princess Xia and I have long had...business together. I will not hurt you. And I will not let anyone hurt you. You can take my word that no harm will come to you."

He cleared his throat, wondering where to begin.

"I know that you had a difficult time since she...was taken away. I know that the guards have been asking you too many questions. I am not here to trouble you. I am not accusing you of anything. Please do not be troubled. The reason I am here is to ask you something about the princess that only her close chambermaid would know. Do you understand?"

She dared not look at the *shoubei*.

"How long were you with her before her arrest?"

"Since I was thirteen," she replied timidly.

"She trusted you?"

"Yes."

"You were close to the princess?"

The maid hesitated. Zheng He saw her shrivel in her seat and bow her head with shame.

"You attended to Princess Xia even at night? She trusted you?" rephrased Zheng He.

"Yes, Grand Admiral."

"Good. And did you ever notice anything strange about Princess Xia? Anything you found...odd?"

She nodded. Everything was strange about Princess Xia, admitted Zheng He. This did not advance him. He passed a hand through his hair, struggling to find the right words.

"What I want to know – what is your honorable name?" he interrupted.

"Mai."

"Very well, Mai. I want you to think back. Think back to Emperor Zhu Di's time. Do you remember the night of the fire?"

In his years as diplomat, he had dealt with foreigners long enough to notice subtle meanings beyond the spoken words. It was a fleeting expression in her face and it was there for only a moment but he saw it. She was terrified. He watched the deep heaving in her breast while her eyes stared ahead as though she could still see violent images from that night. Zheng He seized his chance.

"Mai, did you or Princess Xia notice anything on the night of the fire? Try to remember."

There again, the terror across her face. Her hands tightened on the edge of the stool.

"What did you see?"

She swallowed painfully. Her fearful eyes locked with his as if looking for support.

"It was the princess...she asked me to follow him..."

"Who?"

"There was a eunuch...a low grade eunuch. He...he was making for the gates just moments before the fire spread... Princess Xia ordered me to follow him."

"A eunuch... Did you follow him?"

"I did," whispered the maid looking down at her apron.

"And what happened? Please Mai, it is very important."

"He ran and ran. He vanished into the Fire and Water Department. It grew dark. I lost sight of him. The fire spread... The crowd outside was in tears... Eunuchs ran outside the palace... The smell...it was horrible. I tried to stay calm. Then I waited for him to come out of the building."

"Who was he, Mai?"

Mai looked pained. The horror of that night twisted her face.

"The eunuchs fled out of the department. They all rushed to the palace to help. But he never did... I thought I had lost him but later that night, I saw him again..."

She was now sobbing. Zheng He crouched down before her.

"Mai, you must not cry. You are quite safe."

Mai continued to weep, her words barely comprehensible. But Zheng He listened well.

And somehow, he managed to learn that as Mai roamed past the Fire and Water Department later in the night, she had heard voices in the courtyard of one of the *hutong*s nearby. The *hutong*s were near deserted because the smoke had driven people away. Under the glow of the palace lights, across the red stone wall ahead, she discerned two shadows.

She had crept forth and hidden low behind a large pot, only to recognize the eunuch from the gates. How different he seemed. Earlier, when the princess had given her orders, Mai had caught a glimpse of him, then. She had thought him young and fresh-faced.

But now... Now as she peered behind the bamboo to take a look at him, she saw a changed man. He seemed to have aged and witnessed the horrors of the world in one night. His clothes were ripped; his body limp against the wall. His face was battered and streaked with blood. Sweat and tears ran down his neck as he panted and clung to life. And right there, looming over the poor boy, she had seen a hideous man with limp black hair, clutching a knife in one hand. This man slashed at the young eunuch's face, asking the same question over and over again...

"Do you remember what he asked? Mai? What was the question?"

Zheng He had stopped breathing.

"It was – *where is she? Where have you hidden Min Li?*"

Zheng He froze.

Mai went on. The attacker could extract no response. And so before stabbing the poor eunuch to death, he had first cut out his tongue as punishment. Mai had covered her ears until finally, unable to control herself, she had screamed and run back towards the palace, startling the tall man away.

"By the Prophet..."

Zheng He stood.

"Mai, listen... Tell me more about this man. The man with the knife, what was he wearing? Did he have an insignia on his chest? What was it?"

"I do not remember…no, no, I do not think so."

Zheng He bit his lips. He wiped his face with a nervous hand. Whoever the eunuch was, he was dangerous. He may have even found Min Li...

"Did you speak of this to Princess Xia?"

Mai nodded.

Zheng He stood. He replayed the story in his mind. "Where is *Min Li?*" It was clear that she had not died the fire. Perhaps the eunuch had hidden her...and then he had been murdered for it. It was singular. A puzzling tale indeed...

Zheng He frowned.

"Did you know anything about this young man, Mai? Did you recognize him?"

She shook her head.

"Did Princess Xia know him perhaps?"

"No. But...she..."

The maid sighed, exhausted from years of silence. She hesitated. Zheng He's gaze was intense. He knelt before her once more.

"I am not here to speak to anyone about this. This is between us."

"Princess Xia had me swear I would never speak of this. She said it could ruin her."

"But why? How does this eunuch have anything to do with her?"

"She did not know him. But she learned... She told me that on that night, he had with him something she had given away... You see the Princess bribed eunuchs all the time..."

Mai hesitated, reluctant to say more. She took a deep breath.

"Princess Xia stole much...she did it to bribe the eunuchs..."

"Wait. You say she gave something away as bribe? And the eunuch was carrying it?"

"Well, she...she made me steal it! I...I..."

It came to Zheng He, like a flash of light.

"Just nod if I'm right. It was a knife, wasn't it? A curved foreigner's knife?"

Mai looked surprised now. She stared at the admiral and then nodded.

***

Later as Zheng He left the imperial city, two officers of the court approached him outside Wumen. They seemed to appear out of nowhere as though they had been lurking beneath the gate building, watching him from afar.

"Honorable *Shoubei*," the first one began, his words selective and few. "The *Silijian* has ear that you are planning a journey to Yunnan."

Zheng He eyed them in silence. He came to an abrupt halt, observing the young eunuchs with the calculated self-preservation he knew well.

The second officer continued in a voice that he wanted polished but his unnatural emphasis on words evinced a darker purpose.

"The *Silijian* Director advises the Honorable *Shoubei* to remain in Nanjing while the Hue rebel activists dissipate."

Zheng He froze.

"Who told you this? Who told you that I was leaving for Yunnan?"

The two men eyed each other in silence.

"Well, it is not so," said Zheng He, surprising himself as he spoke. *You see, Min Li*, he thought, *I do lie. And I will gladly lie for you.* "I've no plans to travel anywhere. You will go now and you will tell your director that the *Shoubei* is too taken with his duties to venture into the Southwest. Present him my respects."

They bowed in silence. With a swift motion, he tore up the document they had given him and walked off.

So then, thought Zheng He as he surveyed the congested traffic of hustlers and vendors in Beijing's market lanes and sat back in the privacy of his sedan, even my own home is sheltering spies. And how quickly these news circulated. It made him nauseous.

Even if he dismissed his servants under some pretext, he knew there was no way to be safe from the eyes of the Ming government. And the eunuch scapegoating machine was raging.

Let it, he shrugged. There is no turning back what is inevitable. *Trees have already been made into a boat.* He closed the curtains.

For now, nothing would stop him. I know there is a chance that she is alive, he thought. And if she is, then she is the woman from Nonguzhi. It has to be her.

A few days after his arrival in Nanjing, Zheng He handed a scrolled parchment to one of his trusted couriers.

"Ride. Take my swiftest horse and go as fast as you can. Go to the Datong garrisons. Give this to Lieutenant Liu. Tell him it is urgent. Go now, make haste!"

Now, he promised himself, as he watched the courier pass the gates and disappear behind the mulberry trees, I will find her.

Chapter 59
A Challenge for Ji Feng

Several years had passed since Ji Feng's plans were thwarted. After murdering Zhijian, he had resigned himself. He had not found Min Li.

Soon after journeying to Sichuan, he had almost forgotten about her.

This was partly because the villagers of his locality made his life difficult. Every day, they reminded him of his hatred for the western provinces. *A humid dump, that's all it is*, he seethed. *Beautiful forests, limpid lakes, all wasted on savages who have no education and little understanding of the hand that governs them. Little people.* That's how he saw the many different ethnic groups he encountered in this rural province. The place was so far removed from the prestigious city he was accustomed to.

On his arrival, his first lesson was an unpleasant experience with the unusually spicy local food, so popular in the region. His indignant mouth was overcome by the fire of chili peppers. He'd leapt from his stool at the shock while they jeered in his direction, pointing at the miserly government officer who wept tears over his meal. In his haste to find a jug of water, he'd knocked over the hot pots and their other unpalatable dishes.

As he scrambled out of the inn, cursing under his breath and sweating from the culinary assault he'd suffered, how they had laughed at him. Later, as he curled in pain, eager to find the lavatories and expel their demonic dishes from his burning gut, he had sworn that he would make these peasants pay for their ignobility.

The tables had soon turned. Sure, it was a matter of being accustomed to the spices but it was his post and the key role he played that had given him more confidence. Now, how they watched themselves as he passed.

After years of surviving at the edges of what he called civilized Han society, at the border between U-Tsang and Sichuan, Ji Feng knew better than to wallow in self-pity. He could use his powerful role and profit from it.

He had found the perfect scheme. It was simple really. The tea-horse trade was regulated by the eunuch agencies because it was highly profitable. So profitable, that it attracted many illegal traders.

There was, during a certain period, an overabundance of tea catties in comparison to horses available. In his early years in Baidu, the Mongols were at war with the Ming and horse trading was interrupted. But following Zhu Di's death and in the years that followed, trade renewed, albeit at an expensive rate, so that more catties were required for each horse, often a steed of poor to standard quality. It was in this climate that Ji Feng saw illegal horse trading flourish.

These illegal traders had no authority to sell Yunnan tea in U-Tsang, nor could they import horses and sell them for such a high profit. Illegal traders meant that the Ming government had less control over the supply of horses and over the tea trade. It meant more profit for the little people. Something Ji Feng would not tolerate.

Initially Ji Feng's indignation and his eagerness to assert his new power had made him intent on cracking down on the illegal traders. He confiscated their horses and their proceeds. But following some unsuccessful tryst with local traders who protected each other's interests, our calculating eunuch had found an alternative to policing.

Whenever he did send his officers to arrest the traffickers, he had them interrogated. Sometimes Ji Feng even devised his own tortures, so avid was he to consummate his cruel hatred for those he considered abject and inferior to himself.

Unknown to the Ming administration, he would taunt his captives for hours, exaggerating the evidence, their fate and their impending punishment until the poor men, broken and tormented, took fright and were more amenable to negotiate. This was how Ji

Feng had soon built an impressive list of connections in the region. They paid him a significant fee to continue their illegal activities.

Ji Feng's new business was thriving. The financial boost he gained from his ongoing charades kept him content in Baidu. But above all, Ji Feng was never happier than when he was profiting from those he saw as less cunning them himself. It appeared that deceit and the successful realization of his many schemes played a major role in his happiness.

Over the years, Ji Feng had limited contact with the other eunuchs, preferring instead to keep to himself. He nevertheless acquired the deserved reputation of sharp wits and superb organizational skills. His attention for fine detail and his unmatched ability to size up opportunities were again prized as they had been during his service to the palace.

During his years working for the *chamasi* in Sichuan, the self-castrate did not change much. While slimmer than the average eunuch, he had maintained a solid gait and a good appetite. Age had not whitened his hair. He wore it long such that in the humid weather, the long strands framing his face down to his shoulders appeared all the more greasy. In the pure air of the province, his skin condition did slightly clear up. Yet his internal vices and his excessive passions tempered this improvement.

For it must be said that during his time in Baidu, there churned, within Ji Feng, yet more rage and lust for vengeance. Honored reader, you would understand that Ji Feng would seethe, knowing that Min Li had escaped him. But it is the nature of humans to occupy themselves with beings who are in close proximity. And so Ji Feng's ruminations were not solely driven by Min Li.

In fact, there was a man, an illegal tea-horse trader who had taunted Ji Feng for months.

He was a shadow. He could vanish at whim, leaving no trace. People all over the province told tales of how he knew the *chamadao* like the back of his hand, of how he had crossed it many times since his teens. Ji Feng had sent a gang of locals to catch him on several occasions but to no avail. The villagers were on his side and did his best to protect and shelter the trader.

Ji Feng had never met this trader. What he knew of him, came through rumors; rumors that he was in Dali, then in Nonguzhi and then Lhasa. That he had brought back twenty horses last month and continued to make his numerous transactions unchecked by the *chamasi*. There were even assertions that he did not do it for the money. That it was a sport. A sport, hissed Ji Feng, galled by such claims. What kind of man would sport with the authorities at the risk of his life?

Ji Feng had found out.

They called him Sonam. In his mid-thirties, he was reputed to be a powerful figure, still virile and a fine horse rider. Some said that his jet black hair which he wore loose around his broad shoulders was as long as a horse's mane, that his taut arms could endure the traverse across the ropes of the widest ravines and his legs could run for *li*s even without a horse. His agility in dangerous terrain and his lifelong experience with the *chamadao*, gave him an advantage over the *chamasi*.

Sonam could have worked for the Ming if he had wanted to. They would have paid him well because he was a fine asset to the tea-horse trade and spoke several mountain dialects. But he was fiercely independent and wanted to remain free. He had once set about to cross the river canyons in the perilous mid-winter, a feat that would have cost the average man's life. In this mad endeavor, he had disappeared for months. For months, he was feared to have died in an avalanche only to be spotted again in Deqin in the next spring.

There was not a bend he did not know, nor a mountain village where the people had not heard of him and where he could not find shelter. The rumors spread in admiration and awe and the underlying rumor which also spread like wildfire, vexing Ji Feng to the core, was that perhaps the clever Sonam was far too quick for the officers of the *chamasi*.

Soon to be posted in Deqin, Ji Feng had been offered a substantial promotion if he could catch this man and deliver him to the authorities eager to punish the dissident. Initially amused and later infuriated, Ji Feng had laughed, cackling under his yellow teeth. But after months of searching in vain, he was no longer laughing.

What fuelled his rage, was that all the locals knew of his pledge to catch the legendary Sonam. Whenever Ji Feng set out for the town to eat his meals there was always an uninvited encounter with another Ming officer who, not without mockery, never failed to ask our sourly eunuch whether the Baidu *chamasi* had finally dealt with

Sonam. In response, our eunuch remained eloquently silent but as you already know, honored reader, he did not like to lose, more so in full view of others.

To these numerous enquirers who cast doubts over the effectiveness of his methods, Ji Feng would respond with a tenebrous smile as if he were assuring his colleagues and the curious locals, that the *chamasi* would have the last word, that it was only a matter of time, only a matter of time before they caught Sonam.

But months went by and Sonam was not found.

Until one day.

Chapter 60
His Own Worth

Huang-Fu was a man on a mission. He'd been summoned by Zheng He himself to find Min Li. He was good at it. For there was not a man he could not find.

And it was just as well because he would do anything to help Zheng He. So he journeyed from Datong to Nanjing. From Nanjing, he hired a guide and took a road less traveled to Kunming. From Kunming he found his way to Dali and then onto Nonguzhi. The entire journey took him months but he found the Nakhi village just as Zheng He had described.

He would spend two days and nights scouring the canals of Nonguzhi for a glimpse of her. On the second day, the young lieutenant roamed in the Market Square of Nonguzhi. To his surprise, he noted that it was a lazy, mellow Ku'Li. Here, too, the people were many and varied. They spoke many different tongues. Some could not even answer his questions as he tried in vain to describe the fair-skinned woman he had himself never seen.

Then, remembering Zheng He's letter, he had asked for Jamma. But they told him she had left to return to Lugu Lake, far to the north where her ancestors came from. And one of the villagers finally led him there, to the house where the Bei Lan he sought was thought to live. She lived alone, they told him, in Jamma's old house.

As he entered the courtyard, he saw someone. There was a graceful woman sitting in a corner before a large spinning loom. She had hung her woven fabrics on the line to dry and he noted the pink lotus flower pattern on one of them. It was exquisite work.

Upon seeing the Han, the woman was startled. She paused slack-jawed, and stood before her wooden frame.

"Who are you?"

She stood.

"What do you want?"

In another time, perhaps that voice had been lively and playful, thought Huang-Fu. He observed the long haired woman with the gentle bronzed skin who stood in a pleated white skirt before him. She wore a band of silver bracelets round her arms. A colored shawl draped her stately shoulders. She looked so beautiful even as she eyed him with suspicion. He felt that this woman could be Min Li.

"Are you Min Li?" he asked, tentative.

She winced and eyed him coldly.

"Get out," she said. "I don't know that name."

"You will not believe me but please, please hear me out. Zheng He sent me. Sent me to find—"

"Get out!"

"Don't you remember him? The admiral has not forgotten you, Min Li."

"My name is Bei Lan, Han officer!" spat the woman. She was more beautiful now as she advanced, threatening to stab him with a small knife. "Leave now before I set the Mu clan after you."

But Huang-Fu was a man of the streets. He sensed the pride in her words and glimpsed the tears welling up in her tender eyes.

"He thinks of you night and day and cannot find rest," he continued.

She stopped short, staring at him in silence, lips apart, knife in hand. A faint glow radiated from her sun-kissed face. Her lips curled in a tragic pout. She turned around, refusing to look at him.

"I know it has been a very long time but...he thought you were dead..." whispered Huang-Fu, watching her shoulders sink in as she put away the knife.

She would not look at him. She seemed to be thinking.

"What is your name?" she asked, in a firm voice.

"Huang-Fu."

She nodded.

"Huang-Fu, this man you speak of, is he not a navigator?"

"Yes, my Lady."

"I see... And is he not a man who has traveled to the ends of the earth?"

"Yes, that is him."

She raised her face and gazed far into the distance.

"I remember... A man who has journeyed through the oceans as far away as the shores of Africa... Is that him?"

"Yes! Yes, that is the man!" answered Huang-Fu.

"Then tell me this, Huang-Fu," she said, her blazing eyes suddenly on him. "If you believe it is the same man, then shouldn't he be standing here now, instead of you?"

Huang-Fu took a step back. He could not answer.

"Huang-Fu, you go back to this Zheng He. Tell him... Tell him the Min Li he seeks is dead."

Huang-Fu shook his head.

"But she never died! *You* never died!"

She stared at him quietly. Her face was veiled by a tremendous sorrow, an impenetrable mist that only dampened Huang-Fu's spirits.

"It was not the fire that killed me," she replied.

Then she moved into the house, closing the door behind her.

***

Zheng He had deliberated over many days. It would be treason to consider this journey, let alone allow the court to discover that Li Guifei was not dead.

"You must go to her."

"What! And lead the imperial guards to her? I cannot, Huang-Fu."

But Huang-Fu was right. He had to go. If he found her though, she would have to remain hidden. Perhaps he would even need to consider Shahrzad's offer and live abroad.

And now, his affairs in order, he was ready for a visit to Yunnan. There was not a moment that he did not think of it. Aside from Huang-Fu who had begun to plan their journey, he had told no one of his plans. And he had reasons not to. Future opportunities hinged on the admiral's reputation.

There was currently growing opposition to what was rumored to be an upcoming naval expedition. Following the Ming soldiers crushing defeat and their subsequent withdrawal from Annam,

Emperor Xuande had lost face. He sought to appease tributary vassals in the hope that they would not rebel like the Annamese.

Emperor Xuande had no choice. He had to restore the Middle Kingdom's prestige. He had to borrow from the pomp and splendor that his grandfather, Zhu Di, had flaunted years ago. He had to dispatch once again the mighty Ming fleet and re-assert Ming supremacy all over the world.

But the Hanlin scholars would have none of it. Minister Xia, again, fought bitterly against any maritime expedition. And Zheng He witnessed once more, court clashes that were only too familiar. Everything repeats itself, he thought.

He continued to hope that he may be able to find Min Li and journey soon. Two things he had wished dearly for years while he languished in Nanjing and his fleet lay dismantled in the docks of Longjiang.

In the current political climate, he wanted to sign a petition, along with the other admirals who pressed him to join his voice to theirs, in support of the expedition. But other fears held him back. Minister Xia would oppose it. I would be wasting my time, he thought. Xuande continued to sway between his grandfather's wishes and his own father's beliefs. He respected Minister Xia's opinion and it seemed now that he was prepared to listen to his scholar council.

Two days before his departure to Yunnan, Zheng He found himself visited by a man he knew well. He observed his colleague as this one slumped in a tall-back chair. Years had etched regret and dissatisfaction on Zhou Man's tired face.

"Do you know what they call us?" he began, muttering under his beard.

"No," replied Zheng He, his mind elsewhere.

About three days ago, he had made a second request to leave for Yunnan and it had been rejected by the Nanjing censor. He was however not deterred. He was determined to leave with or without the censor's approval.

"Rapacious."

"Rapacious? Ha!" laughed Zheng He. "Zhou Man, my friend, it is all talk, it will come to nothing. If the ministers desired to inculpate us, we would now be in prison."

"San Bao, and how do you suppose they imprison you? Why, the emperor would not have it. Think! You were his grandfather's protégé. No, he would never offend Zhu Di. Never."

The old man shook his head vigorously and pursued.

"No, they will know better than directly attack you. But... I am certain that they will find something. They will find something," he muttered, tapping his fist rhythmically onto the armchair as if pacing his thoughts.

His sharp eyes seem to prod into the space beyond, making connections between past and future events. Age had given him wisdom.

Zhou Man was a shadow of his past self. Years ago, an energetic towering figure on one of the treasure ships, he had commanded a detachment far into the unknown, towards lands that stretched further than the African coast and into the Pacific Ocean. When he had finally returned, in October 1423, the ministers had glowered at him, insisting that the expedition had proven a complete disaster. Indeed, Zhou Man's fleet had taken a battering and only a few ships had made it back to the Middle Kingdom.

It had been a few years since his return but still, the political climate had not been as kind to him as it had to Zheng He. The miserly fleet he had brought back at the time when Minister Xia lay imprisoned only deepened the ministers' opposition to maritime expeditions.

While Zheng He's spirit had been rekindled by warm childhood memories and a hopeful pining for his newly found beloved, his friend's bitterness showed on his face.

But far from resenting another one more fortunate than himself, Zhou Man was protective of his old friend, Zheng He. Zhou Man was confident in his past achievements. A man who knows his worth and is at peace with himself will wish no harm to befall others.

Zheng He heard him muttering under his breath.

"*The trees want to remain quiet, but the wind will not stop*. Trouble is brewing, San Bao..."

"What is the worst that may befall us, you think? Death?" asked Zheng He.

Only death frightened him because it would prevent him from ever reaching Min Li and coming to peace with himself.

"Dishonor," replied Zhou Man.

"I know all about dishonor," retorted Zheng He.

Zhou Man became impatient. He could see that Zheng He's mind was elsewhere.

"Do you know, San Bao, do you know what the palace eunuchs are saying back in Beijing?"

His voice had risen.

"What is that?"

"I did not come here for idle talk, my friend. Your reputation is not what it used to be."

Zheng He was now feeding the caged pigeons beside his desk.

"You already told me about my...about our reputation. Let's see... We are cruel, we are mercenary... We caused the economic woes of this country... What else?"

He smiled with a playfulness that Zhou Man had not seen for years before pursuing.

"We are despotic...and, what was that word you used? Ah, yes! Rapacious..."

Zheng He's eyes were on the pigeons as he spoke. Their wings were still bright and full of energy even after so many years. It gave him hope.

"Zhou Man, if it happens, it happens. There is nothing we can do. Old man, look at me. I was a prisoner. A partisan of the Mongols! They murdered my father. They could have easily killed me back then. I saw dozens of boys die after they were castrated. I could have easily been among those who died. Instead look at what happened. What I became later, the honor bestowed on me, everything – it was all chance. Anyone could have done it."

"Nothing to do with chance!" muttered Zhou Man.

"Now if the Hanlin ministers want to turn their hatred towards yet another scapegoat, I entrust my life into the hands of our emperor. And if—"

"Well that's just it. It's not the Hanlin," interrupted Zhou Man.

"What do you mean?"

"You heard me. It's not the damned ministers this time. You have rivals, Zheng He."

"Well I am cognizant of that. But who?"

"One of us! The eunuchs! Those who saw you rise before they did... Petty jealousy as always. You see, now, don't you? This is not the same battle anymore, Zheng He. Xuande has given his eunuchs a weapon. Now, they can read! They can write! He will not save you. Not this emperor. He cannot, old boy."

"I hope you realize what you are saying."

"Well how can he?" hissed Zhou Man. He leaned forward and continued to whisper. "They do what they want now. They do not even consult with the emperor! I've seen it with my own eyes! And now, you yourself know what will happen. Your position has always sparked resentment. They will ruin you."

Zheng He paced the room, troubled by more than he would say.

"If he finds out, the emperor will not allow it," he finally replied.

"Humph! Not if he finds out. You are right about that."

Zhou Man looked grave. He began to nod to himself, as though entertaining secret thoughts. Zheng He watched him in silence. At last, the old man spoke.

"So, San Bao...if the rumors are true, Xuande may have found a way to persuade Minister Xia. You could be embarking soon."

"If Xuande gives this order, I will undertake my last journey."

Zhou Man nodded.

"What will happen at sea do you think, my friend?" He seemed onto something.

"What do you mean?"

"Oh, you know. You know what I mean. You may be safe in the Middle Kingdom, Zheng He, but once you are on a Ming treasure ship far, far away on the ocean..." He raised his finger to make a point. "There is nothing, you understand now, nothing to stop the Inner Court eunuchs from having their way. Believe me you should cancel your trip. Remain here in Nanjing. Wait. Wait for those vultures to settle down."

There was a silence. If Zheng He was closely examining his friend's words, he did not show it. He remained motionless, revealing nothing, his face impassive.

"Thank you, Zhou Man."

The admiral began to take his leave but not before grunting one last time. Zheng He placed his arm on his friend's shoulder and then gave him a military salute for old times' sake. Zhou Man managed a smile. And then his eyes squinted with good humor.

"Do you know, Zheng He that Zhu Gaozhi lied to you? He never burnt your documents."

The admiral was genuinely surprised.

"No?"

"No, no, you see, he never did. Not him. He never did that to you, my friend. As much as he sought to make us lose face, he was far too respectful of knowledge. It did not matter where that knowledge came from, to Zhu Gaozhi, it was all the same. No. He never destroyed anything. Ah, but *they* will. It is only a matter of time..."

"I did not know that," frowned Zheng He. "So all this time..."

"Yes, can you believe it? Your journals were being kept in Beijing with the Ming Shilu..."

Zhou Man sighed.

"Ah, but times are not what they once were. You have enemies, Zheng He. Make it your final days' mission to tell the world what you have done...what *we* have done. Or our enemies will make sure it is all forgotten... Forgotten in the fire," he added with one last warning before ambling down the corridor.

***

The six senior guards convened secretly in one of the meeting rooms of the Eastern Depot. It was the very room Min Li had wanted to see six years ago but which Yin Dao, the Embroidered-uniform Guard had refused to show her. Today he was present amongst the six. He presided over their gathering.

At this instant, he had ceased speaking while his colleagues reviewed the scrolls. They were papers he had prepared meticulously over the last year. He waited for the men to finish, his dark brow intense. They had waved the tea ceremony and dived straight into perusing the report. The five men mulled over Yin Dao's scrawled characters, impressed but alarmed by his accusations. Finally the oldest of the guards pushed aside the leaflets before him and fell back on his seat with disgust.

"This proves nothing," he said.

Yin Dao sneered.

"The facts are clear," he replied. "I do not see what could cause you to refute the evidence. I can go over it for you."

He stood.

"Let us start from the beginning, shall we? The admiral met with the Zanzibar woman whose activities in the Middle Kingdom are dubious."

At this the long white-haired guard who had spoken earlier raised his voice.

"She is a harmless traveler...hardly a foreign spy. She may well have taunted our secret police a number of times but her behavior, even if disrespectful, remained impeccable. Illegal dabbling in the Beijing street markets is hardly a cause for concern."

"Impeccable, you say? I maintain that the woman's relation to the late emperor, Hongxi is highly suspicious. Did you not read my report?"

His felt boots tapped across the tiles as he paced the room.

"Let me say it again. She was invited into the Inner Court on a number of occasions. Why did Hongxi relent to let her access the Imperial Palace? Why did he give her a memorandum? We can never be too sure. But with the emperor dead now, we will never know and therefore, we can take no chances."

But another guard, an expert at weeding out lies, raised his voice in protest.

"You are gravely mistaken about this woman. From what I read, her visits go back much further. Her first visit was Yingtian. According to your own report, you yourself state that she was part of a tributary envoy in 1419 and again, she was present at the court in 1421. Now, Yin Dao, who else but Zhu Di was emperor in those days? Why do you assume that she dealt exclusively with Hongxi?"

"It was Hongxi who gave her access to the Inner Court. The memorandum was in his name. Did you not read this? She certainly knew him."

The men looked at each other.

"Pursue."

Yin Dao surveyed his companions to assess whether he had their attention.

"So now, this woman, this Hui, for that is what she is, she visits Admiral Zheng He, also a Hui. And not long afterwards, Admiral Zheng He receives an unknown visitor from Yunnan. An old woman, apparently but it could be a subterfuge. These South-western rebels are cunning..."

"Surely you are not insinuating that Admiral Zheng He is funding the recent Yunnan insurgents? His transactions are in order. They are all in the name of his adoptive children. Yin Dao, have you gone mad?"

"I insinuate nothing. But my agents inform me that Zheng He has disobeyed court advice and is now headed to Yunnan. What do you make of this? His relations are increasingly shady, wouldn't you say?"

"This is preposterous!" exclaimed the white-haired guard, slamming his fist on the table. "What are you suggesting? Why are you doing this? These are entirely disparate events! No relation!"

Another indignant guard spoke up.

"I have known Zheng He all my life. His reputation is intact. Zheng He is a diplomat, not a rebel! Do you realize the sort of accusations you are making?"

Yin Dao observed the other four men silently. They were undecided.

"I am only stating facts. Zheng He should know better than to venture into Yunnan, given the current political situation."

"Did you have him followed?"

"My men lost track of him. It appears his party took a less traveled route through the Stone forest. Shilin is a labyrinth. He could be anywhere."

"It may be a courtesy visit to his adopted family."

"My position on this matter is unchanged," replied Yin Dao.

"So what do you recommend? If you say Zheng He cannot be trusted, what do we do?"

Yin Dao shot the men a cold look.

"We continue to watch him. Even if it takes us years, we watch him. I have already put his mansion under surveillance."

"You did what?"

A collective murmur rose from the room.

"The Eastern Depot has no favorites," scorned Yin Dao.

"Have you thought this through? Do you really believe the emperor will consent to incarcerate one of the most powerful eunuchs the Middle Kingdom has ever known?"

Yin Dao glowered at them all. A menacing light lurked in his eyes.

"Xuande has no need to know about every suspect we eliminate," he said quietly. "Remember – our concern is his protection and the protection of the Middle Kingdom from dissidents and traitors."

He gave a long hard look around him, ready to placate any disagreement.

"We watch him. And if as I suspect, evidence amounts, we eliminate him. We should not weaken at the knees and indulge traitors, no matter who they are."

The men looked at one another.

"However," continued Yin Dao, "for our emperor's goodwill, and in the memory of his grandfather, be certain that if the *shoubei* should ever be condemned, he will officially die a natural death. On this, we all agree."

Chapter 61
Chamadao

Yunnan, 1428

Min Li felt alive.

She breathed in the mountain air, her senses overcome with an excitement she had never once felt and had scarcely imagined. She stole glances at the spectacular valley but dared not look down too long, lest she succumbed to the exhilarating dizziness and dive into the steep gorge, four thousand *li* below.

Mounted on her chestnut mare, she kept her eyes on the muleteers ahead as they plodded along the narrow path of the *chamadao*. Not all of them rode mules. Some went on foot, seemingly unburdened by the piles of compressed tea on their backs.

For two *lis* ahead, she could see a procession of yaks, sweating under their tea loads. Over the long journey to Lhasa, the heat and sweat of the animals would further ferment the leaves, turning them into the rich tea that Sonam had told her the U-Tsang people so loved to blend with their yak butter.

Behind her, casually trotting on the cliff edge that overlooked the turbulent rapids below, Sonam, his hair tied into a long ponytail, kept watch over the caravan. Occasionally, he would ride by her side. His eyes smiled, as if to say,

"I am honored to be traveling the *chamadao* with you."

This send shivers through her spine until she was even more out of breath with joy. She would smile back gratefully, her downturned eyes warming his heart more than the mountain sun, and her fair face, more beautiful than all the snow-capped mountains along the *chamadao*.

They had now traveled one hundred and twenty *lis* north of Nonguzhi and had reached the dramatic bend that Sonam called Tiger-Jump valley. Tiger-Jump valley or Tiger Leaping Gorge, as it would be later known, was a canyon on the Jinsha river which the Hans also called the Yangzi river. There, flanked by the spectacular Jade Dragon Snow Mountain and the Haba Snow Mountain, the Jinsha became animated into a series of thunderous rapids. Below, the waters flowed faster and faster, slamming into hard, polished rocks along their way.

The night before, while they rested in a Hue merchant village, Sonam had warned her that the cliff road at Tiger-Jump valley hung precariously over the top of the gorge so that it was very dangerous. She promised to be careful and dismissed his fears with a warm smile. But once they had entered the thirty *li* stretch of the Jinsha rapids, she realized that the scenery which unfolded beneath her was beyond anything she could have imagined.

It was beyond what her powerful emperor would ever know, beyond the luxurious Imperial Palaces where she had once lived, beyond the vastness of the imperial city markets that she had glimpsed while journeying from Nanjing to Beijing years ago. It surpassed the sweeping views of Nonguzhi's rooftops.

Nature's splendor, with its imposing mountains, its waterfalls and roaring waters, overwhelmed her. It took her breath away so that she wanted to be one with it, to absorb it within her. Nature was almighty.

"It is so beautiful, Sonam!" she cried, her voice mingled with fear and excitement.

"Keep your eyes on the road," he warned with a kind smile.

She did. But she also watched him whenever she could. And when her eyes rested on the noble Sonam, she was seized with admiration. She felt proud to ride alongside this free spirit, a man so sure of his mount, so protective of the caravan, and of her.

But what she liked most of all about the beautiful Sonam is that he had chosen to take her with him on his journey. This, even when he had long left this land, she would never forget.

They crossed the sixty *lis* in one long day, reaching a Nakhi hamlet by nightfall. Min Li waited in retreat as Sonam talked to the shelter guide in a strange dialect and organized their next camp. It was the fifth dialect she had heard him speak and this Nakhi tongue was not even similar to the one she was used to hearing in Nonguzhi. It was as though every ten *lis* of their journey, the people varied in some aspect of language and culture.

She realized then that this mountainous world comprised more languages and customs than most of the areas elsewhere in the Middle Kingdom. And they were lovely people. How many times had she heard the eunuchs refer to the southerners with the derogative Nanyang. Yet her experience taught her that the people of the South were unfairly called barbarians. True, life was hard in the mountains and the people adapted to the rudiments of the land but they were not barbarians.

They lived differently.

Along the way they attracted many curious onlookers. Villagers noticed her fair skin and wondered what she was doing, venturing into the *chamadao* and sleeping in coarse hamlets under the stars. But she did not mind. Her adventure took her well away from her years in the stern palace.

Even now, as the roaring waters of Tiger-Jump valley continued to echo through her temples, they seemed to wash away the dark years, these long years when she had been Zhu Di's slave, watching, being still and silent, living and breathing as the eyes and ears of her emperor.

Then a sad thought crossed her mind. She saw the admiral's face for a fleeting moment. The one thing these waters could never wash away was his breath on her skin and his tender embrace in the baths. Even today, she could still smell his amber scent and feel his mouth on her. But she had to bring herself to reason. The admiral would never come for her.

It was dark when Sonam and Min Li arrived at their hamlet some twenty *lis* from Zhongdian. No sooner had they dismounted and made themselves comfortable that a curious villager ran towards them. In the crepuscule he crept forward, panting from his race, anxious to speak with the U-Tsang tea-horse trader.

"Sonam!"

Sonam emerged from the hut.

"What is it?"

"Sonam, Sonam my friend, do not go to Deqin."

"What's got into you?"

The man was startled.

"Who is she?" he asked, peering over Sonam's shoulder into Min Li's alarmed face.

"Calm yourself, you can trust her. What is it? And why should I not go through Deqin."

"They will not let you through without papers. Security is tight. There are Han soldiers everywhere. They are doing license checks on everyone now. Stay here, Sonam, just for a little while."

Sonam laughed. "Is that why you've been running around? Now calm yourself," he added, kindly rubbing the man's shoulder. "Look at you. You'll only frighten her."

Then he leaned over and whispered. "Do not concern yourself. I am only passing through Deqin. I will not even stay the night."

"What?"

It was Min Li. She had been listening and was surprised by Sonam's revelation.

"I was going to tell you this but—"

"You are leaving me?" she cried in disbelief. "And where am I to go?"

"You will stay with friends until my return. Bei Lan, you will be exhausted by the time we reach Deqin. Once we reach Zhongdian, the path grows more dangerous. The traffic on the *chamadao* will also increase."

"But..."

"Deqin will be a good place for you to rest until I return. You will see, these are good people, they will take care of you until I come back."

She did not seem convinced. He watched her disappear into the hamlet. Then turning back to his friend, he spoke in a dialect that Min Li did not understand.

"Listen, she does not know that I've no papers. But I will have them soon, very soon. I've an agreement with a man in Deqin, you see. He knows who to speak to about the license. Soon it will not matter. Nothing will matter except her." He smiled.

"Sonam, Sonam, why not stay here for a bit longer. Just think, what if they recognize you there?"

The adventurer shook his head.

"I can take care of myself. Once I have seen this man, I will lead the caravan to the border and return to get my license. Out and back again, no one will see me."

"Aye my friend, but this is dangerous. There is now a reward for your arrest."

"Aha! How much now? Well then, it doesn't matter. Soon everything will be in order. She is worth it," Sonam added, his eyes glowing.

His friend sighed.

"Ah, I've almost forgotten!" exclaimed Sonam, digging into his leather pouch. "This is for you."

It was a bundle of coins, part of the proceeds from the sale of a horse.

He forced the bundle into his friend's protesting hands.

"Times are hard. Keep it safe."

The villager's eyes glistened.

"You are good man, Sonam."

Sonam watched his friend head back to the nearby hamlet before re-entering his own hut. He stopped short, contemplating Bei Lan as she lay quietly on her side. He could see that she was unsettled by the travel plans but it was better that way. Soon, everything would be in order.

He crouched in, shuffling on his knees to find a spot beside her. She did not stir but he knew she was deep in thought.

"I had secrets too once," she said, as though hinting that she understood he hid something.

Then she turned her head away to indicate that she was prepared to sleep and speak of nothing else.

Sonam did not reply. Still crouching, he began to adjust the fleece-lined blankets. He sat down beside her. He removed his sheepskin vest and covered her with it. He watched her smile and saw her raise the coat to her nose to inhale it. He smiled too. This was pleasant. There was much warmth from being close to her.

Yet a stubborn mountain stood between them. And even he, the intrepid Sonam, master of the *chamadao* could not traverse this mountain, even after all these years.

At last, he spoke.

"Bei Lan. Beiiiii Laaaan. What kind of a name is that? I do not even know your real name and how you even came to Nonguzhi."

He lowered his body across the mat, lying down beside her with a twinkle in his eyes.

"Jamma would not tell me...though I tried many times to get her to speak. Stubborn old woman," he joked.

He turned towards her. He had grown accustomed to the obscurity. And in the faint moonlight seeping through the open door, he could make out her gentle shoulders and the nape of her neck. She had braided her hair like the mountain girls and coiled it up into a bun while she lay on her side.

"Is your past so bad then?" he whispered.

"I promise to tell you when we return to Nonguzhi," she finally replied.

He lay quietly again.

"Sonam..."

"Yes? What is it, mysterious woman?"

"Thank you."

It hurt him. When she said those words, he wanted to reach out, hold her and become her *azhu*. But he did no such thing. The mountain remained and he could not pass through it. He felt uneasy smiling alone in the darkness, not really comprehending why she was thanking him. He let his shoulders collapse onto the mat and began to dream.

Chapter 62
Azhu

Zheng He burnt with an unrelenting fever. It nagged at him. It filled him with unease. Every night, despite his anticipation, he sensed dread, a dread he could not explain.

Huang-Fu warned him that it was the mountain air. That he was too old for the high lands. He did feel out of breath at times. He had not visited Yunnan for years and after leaving Dali, he remembered why. His head was giddy on most days as they approached Nonguzhi.

Still, the excitement of seeing her again raised his spirits. On numerous nights, he remained awake, listening to the calls of frogs and gazing wondrously at the stars. He floated, losing his mind up into the heavens. In the canopy above, every tree branch swaying under the moonlight appeared to him like the swish of long ebony strands. By day, if he perchance saw a fair woman, he raised himself upon his horse to see if it was Min Li.

He had hassled Huang-Fu countless times in the past month. How did she look like now? Was she happy? What did she do? Huang-Fu was brief. As in his first account...

"I know I found Min Li. A village, not far from Dali," he had said, avoiding the admiral's intense gaze.

"You did not bring her with you?"

"I tried to speak with her. She threatened to kill me at first. Held a knife at me..."

"Then you probably saw Min Li," said the admiral with a smile.

"I think I did. She spoke about your travels."

Huang-Fu had stressed those words. Then he had looked away. He had hesitated.

"But did you tell her that it was I who sent you and that I searched for her, Huang-Fu?"

"I did that."

Huang-Fu had sat there, sat there waiting. The young man's dark eyes were elusive as though he struggled with some truth, one he was not prepared to share.

Aside from Zhu Di, no one had ever dared judge the admiral. But on that day, Zheng He had felt the reproach in Huang-Fu's eyes. He saw it as the Han observed him, biting his cheek in silence.

Zheng He had sighed.

"I will have to disobey the censor then...and travel to Yunnan," he indicated, sealing their understanding.

Huang-Fu had nodded.

"It is her wish, Admiral."

Zheng He had sat in silence, contemplating the delicate situation with a deep frown.

"If I go to her, who knows what the officials will think. My mansion is riddled with spies, Huang-Fu. They will have the evidence they need against me then. I may as well sign my death sentence. But I'll do it, Huang-Fu. I'll do it! I will not let her down again."

And now, as they arrived in Nonguzhi and returned to the house where Huang-Fu had found Min Li, they found the white stone-walled courtyard deserted. Even the colorful trinkets by the gate were gone and the doors lay opened as though a soul had been released and flitted out.

When they asked to see the woman who once lived there, the village women told them Bei Lan had left. That she had been gone for months. That she could be anywhere. Zheng He was disconcerted. He did not know what to do.

And then as he pondered in silence, they reached a creek where he and Huang-Fu raised a tent. Not far from the gurgling creek, Zheng He was startled by a little green frog that seemed to stare straight at him. He froze.

He remembered how Jun had once talked about the little green frog of Nonguzhi. It was an old Nakhi animal spirit among the bear, the goat, the horse, the golden turtle and the tiger. Jun had interrupted her chantefable then to recount a tale of how a clever green frog had once tricked the conceited and foolish tiger, Soo Tan.

Zheng He now knew what the tale meant to him. It was about the strength of small things. It was about Jun's hidden power and how it had changed his life.

The admiral stooped to approach the little creature. On many occasions since his arrival in Nonguzhi he had noticed the two discs embroidered on each side of the cape worn by the Nakhi women. Jun had described these as the eyes of the frog. It was fascinating.

***

A strong gale iced Min Li's bones. The caravan progressed towards the snow-capped mountains. Sonam had been right. The traffic was increasing along the *chamadao*. They could no longer ride at ease, neck and neck, to exchange smiling glances or share their enthusiasm about the beautiful scenery.

They rode silently, their horse's heels trudging the rocky mountainous path while she tried to keep warm under the assaults of the chilly wind. The weather was unpredictable. In one day, they had experienced snow, rain, wind and unrelenting heat from the sun's intense rays. And the path was prone to landslides. Sonam had to keep watch well ahead. He was both anxious about her safety and about his fate in Deqin. The days became tense, busy with hundreds of horses passing them along their way.

She watched the processions thicken along the *chamadao*. The road was dense with people from numerous tribes. All spoke different dialects. Pilgrim monks journeyed alongside them, some destined for as far as Lhasa, while others sought to partake in celebrations at the foot of Meili Xue Mountain. There were Hue and Nakhi merchants, U-Tsang muleteers, both men and women riding on mules. Some went barely clothed, trudging on thin limbs and burdened with stacked tea catties on their bent wiry backs.

If the mountains had been more frightening since Zhongdian, it was nothing compared to the alarm she felt seeing so many people along the road. Given the relative isolation and quiet pace of Nonguzhi, she was not used to this. She now waited eagerly for the nights. He too, looked forward to those nights.

When they had drunk warm tea and huddled close by the warm glow of the fire, she would slowly let her guard down. At dusk, her face was radiant with a lovely honey color from so many days under the mountain sun. When she slept, she would nuzzle her face into his broad shoulders and he, sensing her behind him, would stop breathing, afraid of stirring her away and losing that closeness. But she never moved.

And one night he turned around and caught her pupils reflecting the moonlight. She had been watching him. Now she met his gaze with a playful expression, as if to say,

"I am watching you, Sonam. So there."

She was dressed in a long white skirt tied with many colorful woolen sashes. Underneath, he knew that she still wore her long trousers for warmth.

He moaned, torn by the hidden curves beside him. He had read the desire in her eyes.

"What is it, my *azhu*?" she asked, aware that she had called him lover for the very first time.

She waited for his reaction. But he showed no surprise.

Instead he sighed again, this time with frustration.

"If we were alone and it was not so damn cold, I would have taken off your evil tunic and your skirt."

"And I would let you," she smiled, pressing herself close to his naked chest. She loved breathing him in. He always smelt of incense and it excited every part of her. She emitted a chuckle, remembering the first time she had seen Zhu Di's hairy chest in that room. It was so long ago now. It was when it had all started. The interrogation room... On and on it went for years.

She pressed her face on Sonam's skin, sweeping away her memories with his deep scent. Without a word, he raised her mouth to his hungry lips. His kisses burned her, awakening a desire that thrilled them both. He wrapped her legs around his thighs and pulled her closer.

"Are you warmer, now?"

"Not quite. Hold me tighter."

He covered her face with ardent kisses while his hand reached out to caress her thighs and breasts. She giggled under his assault.

"So many things I have to tell you," she sighed, out of breath.

And then his playful hands had slipped under her tunic and were making their way to her aching skin. As he found her tender breasts, his face beamed with pleasure.

"Don't you want to know my name then, my *azhu*?" she whispered, caressing his hair.

"Please tell me..." he breathed.

And so she raised her face to whisper in his ear.

***

Zheng He watched the green frog. The glistening creature sat there with its bulging eyes, breathing avidly. Suddenly it leapt, springing up towards a red building on the outskirt of the village.

At once amused and in awe of the tiny creature, Zheng He hurried after it. He noticed that above the frog's landing were colorful markings painted on rough parchment. The notice was nailed to a door. The frog had settled at the doorstep, its hind legs springing up and down. Its throat swelled and pulsated.

Intrigued, Zheng He observed the markings on the parchment.

A villager wheeled past, his wooden cart loaded with maize. Zheng He called out to him.

"Whose house is this?"

The villager stared blankly, not understanding.

"What does this message say?" pressed Zheng He. He understood a little Malayalam and could read Arabic script but this was too unusual for him. It was colorful and looked like little drawings.

The man's eyes widened, terrified that he could not understand the giant Ming officer before him. Huang-Fu called for a translator. Finally, they found an old Nakhi woman to translate the Dongba writing. The woman dawdled along with a woven basket on her back and seemed reluctant to speak with them. After taking one glance at the parchment, she shrugged.

"It is a reward," she explained almost dismissively, "a reward to catch a man. We were forced to put it here."

"I see," replied Zheng He, still mulling over the sign. He watched the frog's pulsating throat. The creature had not budged.

Are you trying to tell me something, Jun, he thought.

"You know more than you will say. Is that not so?" he asked the old woman.

The woman returned the parchment with an indignant pout. Then she emitted an angry grunt and mumbled in her best Nanjing Hua.

"You can bark all you want, Officer. But no one in this village gives this notice any attention," she protested. "And I'll tell you why. This man is a good man! He's done nothing wrong." Satisfied with her courageous outburst, she adjusted her load and resumed her stroll down the street.

"Hold there! Who is this man you speak of?"

"His name is Sonam," replied the old woman sharply. Turning around, she glimpsed the fleeting expression on the tall man's face.

"Sonam, you say? Sonam?" asked Zheng He.

"That's what I said. Sonam."

She scrutinized him with curiosity.

"You are not from here," she observed. "If you were, you would know him. There are many men with this same name but there is only one Sonam who could be worth this much money. When you see him, you know him," she added with a certain pride.

"Sonam, the tea-horse trader?" asked Zheng He, recalling Jun's tale. His voice quivered with emotion.

"My, you are a strange one," muttered the woman.

"What is it, Admiral?" asked Huang-Fu, sensing the admiral's mood.

"Huang-Fu, I think this Sonam may know where Bei Lan is..." whispered Zheng He.

But the old woman's ears were sharp. She gave a piercing glance in their direction. Like all those in the village, she knew that Bei Lan and Sonam had left about a month ago. She was reluctant to betray their whereabouts.

"How do you know Bei Lan?" she asked.

They did not reply at first, exchanging nervous glances and refusing to say more.

Finally, Huang-Fu smiled taking her aside.

"Older Sister, we have traveled far to find Bei Lan. The man you see here has been looking for her for years."

Her pupils narrowed with suspicion.

"He is her...her...her adoptive father," continued Huang-Fu. Then he remembered something. "Bei Lan would weave pink and red lotus flowers. She was very good at it."

He watched the woman's traits relax. She nodded. Huang-Fu seized his chance.

"Older Sister, would you help us find Bei Lan?"

The woman gave another grunt.

"She is gone," she repeated, much to Huang-Fu's disappointment.

She turned to Zheng He.

"Sonam is long gone, Officer," she announced. "You won't catch him."

Disheartened, they watched her amble down the canal-lined street and disappear towards the marketplace.

"What shall we do now, Admiral?"

Zheng He was silent. He watched the green frog take several leaps towards the direction of Zhongdian in the north. To Huang-Fu's surprise, he continued to watch the frog.

Zheng He faced the northern road. He seemed lost in thought.

At last he sighed. He had resigned himself.

"How are your mountain skills, Huang-Fu?" he asked.

"My... Are you jesting with me?"

"No, I mean that," said Zheng He, eyeing the path beyond. Several *li*s ahead, lay the start of the *chamadao.*

A stern determination lined his brow as he sized up the challenge before him. He had confronted pirates, traversed the world's oceans, overcome treacherous seas and fierce winds but he knew nothing about the capricious mountainous terrain stretching beyond.

"It will take many days, perhaps over a month," he whispered, out of his depth.

Huang-Fu shook his head in protest.

"Oh no, you won't! It is madness, Admiral! No! I cannot let you do this."

"But that's what she wants me to do," answered Zheng He in a calm voice.

"What? Kill yourself? Is that it? No! This is not a ship! Things can go wrong... The air is bad up there!"

"Things can go wrong on a ship too, remember?"

"Yes but..."

"Lieutenant Liu, I did not know you to shirk before an adventure. Where is that fine gambling spirit?"

"Admiral, forgive me but if she's left with this Sonam, whoever he is, don't you think she must have given up waiting for you?"

The admiral contemplated this.

"I have not come all the way here to give up, Huang-Fu. But I may need your help. I cannot do this alone. That Sonam is wanted by the *chamasi*. What if Min Li is in danger? Even if you are right, even if she no longer waits for me, I need to know that she is safe. I owe her that. Do you understand?"

He placed a hand on the Han's shoulder.

"You are the only one I trust with this journey. Together we can cross the *chamadao*. I know we can."

Huang-Fu emitted a vexed sigh. He gazed at the winding path, horrified by the difficult traverse they would find and frowned. Zheng He saw his hesitation.

"I know this is beyond the duty of a cavalry officer. So I will ask you again. Will you help me, Lieutenant Lu?"

Huang-Fu shook his head. There was a half-mocking glow in his eyes as he replied.

"What choice do I have? You are my friend now, Admiral."

Chapter 63
Deqin

The Gate

Min Li and Sonam rode into the barren plains of white-tiled Deqin. A piercing blue sky stretched for miles around them. Though both their breaths were quickened by the cold thin air and their limbs weary after their five day journey from Zhongdian, still, Min Li noticed her *azhu* tense up on his saddle.

She followed the direction of his gaze past the rows of large wooden stupas lining the village gate. Her horse neared a bawdy archway, ornate with colorful prayer flags. As her eyes grew accustomed to flooding sunlight, she saw that the village of Deqin, overlooked by the snow-capped Meili Xue Shan was dotted with Han soldiers.

Well ahead, she noticed a row of familiar imperial banners and an officer's tent. With ruthless efficiency, undaunted by the seven thousand *li* altitude, the Hans were everywhere, checking papers and inspecting tea catties. There was not a doubt that these men were looking for something other than mere irregularities in the tea leaves.

And as the traders proceeded one by one through the checkpoint, Sonam shifted on his mount. His eyes roamed towards the plain where an escape could be assured if his ride was true and swift, and if the Han arrows did not pierce him. His heart still thundering in his chest, he was building up courage while surveying Min Li.

She, in turn, had seen the tension crisp his jaws. They had made a pact earlier on. She must reach the blue stupa-like house at the foot of the first hill where his friends would lodge her and he would travel towards Meili Xue Shan before continuing on to his business.

But twenty feet away from the checkpoint, a feeling of dread seized Min Li. It was not, as one would believe, because Sonam was in danger. Nor was it due to the sight of the numerous armed Han soldiers who formed a barrage and questioned each trader with pressing thoroughness.

For as her eyes searched further ahead, she grew aware, even before the vision formed, of a familiar chill running through her body and numbing her limbs.

Despite the spurious noise rising from the frustrated queue on the road, despite the crowds setting up tents on the sparse shrubby plains ahead, and the impatient muleteers and merchants who waited at the checkpoint, still, a deafening silence enveloped Min Li. It descended like a blanket of fear. Sonam attempted to attract her attention but she no longer saw him, no longer heard anything.

She grew aware of her sweaty hands tightening around the leather reins. In an instant, her body stiffened and her limbs pressed tight against her horse's flanks. It grew nervous and kicked, refusing to advance. And what she saw chilled her bones.

Because a few paces from the checkpoint, a man had fixed his mean gaze on her; a man whose mottled complexion and greasy long strands, she only too clearly remembered.

Calling out to two sturdy soldiers, this imperial officer began to take large pounding strides in her direction. And as he did so, her vision of his face sharpened, sharpened, and sharpened still, until Min Li was certain. It was Ji Feng.

At this moment, one of the soldiers had a flash of recognition. He called out to one of his companions, gesticulating towards Sonam. Meanwhile, Sonam tried in vain to attract Min Li's attention. But his *azhu* remained transfixed, the horror on her face mounting with every step Ji Feng made in her direction.

Sonam hesitated. The advancing officer had recognized him. He had no choice but to flee. If only Min Li could respond to his signal.

The soldiers were closer. There was no time. It was now or never. Sonam braced himself. He was about to gallop away, veering left to avoid the soldiers, when a thunderous voice startled him.

"Arrest her! Arrest this woman!"

Sonam winced. He forgot all plans to escape. He tugged at the reins. He tried to calm his panicking steed as it huffed and kicked. He looked with dismay while the soldiers rushed forth and Min Li brought a trembling hand to her face.

"Sonam! Go! Go now! Hurry!" she called out. Then seeing that he refused to budge, she hurled insults in his direction.

"You stupid man! As stupid as your mule! Go!"

Just like that. And he intuited that all along, she must have guessed his banal secret, must have known everything about his illegal trade and the noose that waited for him. For in her face, there flashed a knowing maturity he had never once seen in Bei Lan; it was the face of Min Li, one he hardly knew at all. She threw one final look of contempt in his direction and as a man, he felt deep down and despite all reason, that perhaps he had disappointed her. That he was not the *azhu* she wanted.

"Leave!" she screeched once more.

They reached her in that instant. She made scarce effort to fight back. The soldiers wrenched the reins from her hands and held her horse. With a vicious tug, they dragged her to the ground. She stumbled forward with a gasp, grazing her palms and knees. The Han soldiers raised her up. They held her arms back under Ji Feng's watchful eye.

For Sonam, this was too much. He stared, stunned to stone as the soldiers dragged Min Li away. Now she would not even look at him. Assailed by doubts, his spirit mortified by what he had just witnessed, Sonam gave Mountain King a strong kick and before long had turned back and retreated into the *chamadao.*

But Min Li's ruse had no effect.

Alerted by the soldiers, Ji-Feng turned towards the plain. A cruel rictus etched itself on his face. He gave a signal. A band of soldiers mounted their horses. They began their chase, bolting in unison, eager to be the one who would finally catch the intrepid Sonam.

***

Jun's Warning

If one only rested at night, one could traverse the steep two hundred *li* stretch from Nonguzhi to Tiger Leaping Gorge in a mere four days. Three days past the river gorge, with its swelling torrents and vertiginous depths, and they found that the towering pines, mountain orchids and colorful lilies gave way to more sparse terrain. Far behind were the snowy plateaux of Haba Snow Mountain and the imposing granite peaks of Jade Dragon Mountain.

Zheng He knew they were still days away from Deqin. As they reached Zhongdian with its scattering of monasteries, everywhere they looked were pilgrims bound for Meili Xue Shan. They had to scrutinize each face, squinting under the intense sunlight.

As he had done during their entire journey, Huang-Fu would meander through the crowds, scouring for a fair woman on horseback. Surely they would have caught up with her by now. It was bad enough that the admiral was so tall as to attract attention from the mountain people but none of the other travelers spoke in Nanjing Hua.

"Have you seen a fair woman with large eyes?" he would ask, gesticulating as he spoke.

And they would offer him salted pork and flat maize bread which he declined. But Huang-Fu did not give up and pressed on, short of bullying the other travelers. He looked much out of place in his coarse leather gabardine and his torn felt boots while all round him were clad in their colorful striped aprons and turbans.

"A tall, fair woman? Yes. Yes, young. Have you seen her?"

In his growing exasperation, he illustrated his words with obscene gestures and the frightened travelers pressed on, eager to avoid the odious Han.

"They can't understand a word I'm saying, Admiral," vented Huang-Fu as he rode back alongside Zheng He.

"Do not agitate yourself, Huang-Fu. We will find her." But the admiral seemed troubled.

A voice rose from behind them.

"A fair woman did you say? With broad cheeks and large eyes shaped like almonds?"

It was a thinly clothed muleteer, dark as night with wrinkled eyes and sparse white whiskers. He led a procession of three undernourished mules crushed by an impossibly high load of tea catties. He had spoken with a broken accent but Huang-Fu was overjoyed.

"Have you seen her?"

"She was with Sonam...only about a moon ago. I'd say they must be in Deqin by now."

"How do you know it was her?"

The man smiled with a knowing, cheeky glow in his tired eyes.

"Officer, I should know. This Sonam we speak of, he has never traveled with a woman before. It is her, no doubt. A very special woman!" croaked the muleteer. And he whacked his mule and advanced on the rocky track, one watchful eye on his dangerously swaying cargo.

They watched him from afar. Huang-Fu hesitated. He seemed restless.

"What do we do now, Admiral? Should we return to Nonguzhi?"

It seemed presumptuous on Zheng He's part to assert that Huang-Fu was wrong, that they should press on. On what grounds could he do so now? Min Li had probably fallen in love with Sonam. They came too late. What was there to do? Had he not already lost face?

Zheng He's eyes followed the muleteer in the distance. He pondered over how it was that one stranger could shatter his hopes and shame him before the pilgrims; shame him before the face of Meili Xue Shan.

Yet even now, an unsettling feeling clawed at his chest. After days through this perilous road that was the *chamadao*, the nagging dread had overwhelmed him. And the muleteer played no part in this. For a reason that eluded Zheng He, Jun's words echoed in his mind daily.

They rang in his ears. The words of warning she had spoken as she lay ailing in his cabin, years ago. At the time, he had thought them odd. Now... Now they frightened him.

Storyteller, what is this trade route you speak of? And why is it so important to this story? Honored listener, you must listen well.

She had said it as though...

"That man is mistaken," said Zheng He at last.

"What? But Admiral, we—"

"We must reach Deqin." His tone left no room for arguments.

And so they pressed ahead. Days of arduous trekking, sleeping in rundown hamlets and haggling for distasteful mountain food, did not diminish the admiral's resolve to find Min Li. The medicinal herbs Old Yu had prescribed were all but depleted. It was the thought of her that sustained him and lessened the aches in his tired body.

Now I know why you came aboard my ship, Jun, thought Zheng He whenever he stared out towards the snow-capped mountains. I fear that Min Li is in danger. So now, you must tell me. Where is she, Jun? Where is she?

***

In the Barn

Her head throbbed. She could smell fresh horse manure and hay. The rough bristles prickled her face and hands. As she moved, there was a clinking of a metal chain. Strange that she could not move her arms fully.

She opened her eyes, licking her parched lips. The soldiers were gone. She could hear the animals stirring behind their wooden enclosures.

She tried moving her numb iced toes, then her feet... As she rubbed one thigh against the other, she realized that she now only wore her long tunic. It was filthy. She knew not what had happened to the rest of her clothes. And there was another smell. It was sharp, metallic and nauseating. She knew that smell.

Min Li raised her head and discerned the coarse chains linking her wrists. A distasteful vision rose. She saw their boyish faces again. They jeered at her as one of them breathed heavily on top of her spread-eagled form. Not now... She resisted the memory, revolted by the humiliation it stirred in her. Her head ached. What was that smell? She looked down at her tunic. There was blood; a lot of blood.

At once, a female explanation entered her mind. It was her time. They had not fed her meat during her fifteen days in prison and now her *qi* was weak. The blood had flowed.

She lay back in thought. The village women in Nonguzhi used leaves to absorb the monthly blood but she had chosen to carry cloths with her along the *chamadao*. Had she remained safely in the village of Deqin she would have ensured that the blood did not stain her clothes. But now, here she was.

She closed her eyes. Again their teeth gleamed at her and their laughter compounded her shame. She could still feel the icy ale dribbling on her bare breasts. She pushed away the vision.

What would they do to her now? Bring her back to the palace? She would die rather than go back. They would have to kill her. And where was Sonam?

Her heart raced. She tried to stay still and relax but the high beams danced above her. Danced and danced until they faded.

***

Sonam's Friends

Zheng He understood Zhu Di now. He understood what Zhu Di had felt, then, when he set upon the Mongol ghosts, unrelenting. It was not the victory over the enemy that had mattered. It was proving himself. It was feeling that Zhu Di could still as an old general, make a difference to the destiny of the Middle Kingdom. And now Zheng He realized that he too wanted desperately to make a difference both for her and for himself.

"Remind me why we are doing this, Admiral?" would ask Huang-Fu almost every night as he tended to a withering fire.

"We are almost there. Courage."

But two days away from Deqin, as they entered an U-Tsang hamlet for the night, the two men were refused shelter into any of the dwellings.

"Greetings," began Zheng He but it almost seemed that the village men had come to an understanding. They had even warned their servants to keep the doors shut. There were no lodgments available. The hamlet seemed enclosed in a communal agreement. The two Han officers were not welcome. They would have to remain under the stars for the night.

When they had already asked a dozen families, tried without success to bargain with the serfs who ran errands and could possibly spare them some food, Huang-Fu was too disheartened by the rejection to persist.

"It's no use, they will not help us," he moaned, drawing a woolen coat closer to his freezing bones. "We may as well sit in the cold and die."

Zheng He looked around piercing the darkness with glassy eyes. He had run out of medicine.

"Come. We have yet to try this hut," he cheered in a weak voice.

"Admiral, it is all full! There are no shelters, we've already tried everything," replied Huang-Fu, chattering under the icy wind.

"I know you are tired, Lieutenant but so am I."

"It is too damp to even make a fire," said Huang-Fu.

"And yet there is smoke…"

"Where?"

"There! Can you see it? Rising from that abandoned monastery…up on that hill..."

"I can barely see anything," muttered Huang-Fu.

"Come."

They led their horses up along a steep winding path lined with thick shrubs and towards a row of short, broken stupas. The hill seemed deserted. They continued until they were within sight of a white building where a red light glowed faintly.

"Did you hear that?"

Huang-Fu reached for his sword. There was fierce whistling noise as the arrow flew. Zheng He surged forth. He pushed his friend to the side. Huang-Fu flinched, gripping his arm with a frown. It was merely grazed. The arrow had shot past very near them. Zheng He seized it to examine the tip.

"Was it poisoned?" cried Huang-Fu looking around with apprehension.

"It was intended as a warning."

Huang-Fu raised his own bow.

"A warning hey, I'll show him!"

"No, Huang-Fu!"

Huang-Fu stretched his bow in the direction of a shrub. They could now discern a form crouched atop the hill.

"Show yourself!" spit Huang-Fu, aiming his arrow.

There was a silence.

"Do not advance further, Huang-Fu. Remain where you are," whispered Zheng He between his teeth. His eyes pierced the darkness.

"We mean no harm," he called out. "Who are you?"

His voice echoed across the plain.

If diplomacy failed, Zheng He ignored what to do. There was no response for a moment. And suddenly a loud voice rose. It echoed across the plain, proud and solemn.

"What do you seek, Han officers?"

Zheng He looked up, scrutinizing the crouched form ahead.

"Are you wounded?" he asked, showing his goodwill. "Let us help you."

There was some hesitation as insect calls rose in the dark. In the monastery, the fire was now extinguished.

"Please...we are so tired. We need shelter. Whoever you are, if you would give us shelter, you will help the tea-horse trader, Sonam. We think he is in danger."

There was a rustling up in the bush as though the stranger was startled.

"What do you want with Sonam?" he answered.

"My friend, I need to find this man. I wish him no harm."

"I don't believe this!" cried Huang-Fu. "He almost killed us and you want to negotiate with him?" And he summarily raised his crossbow.

"Huang-Fu, lower your bow!"

It was too late. Huang-Fu released the arrow. In a flash, the stranger pounced from behind the shrub. He stood tall, feet apart, proud of his powerful form. With burning eyes, he pulled taut his crossbow. The feathered arrow flew in Huang-Fu's direction. Huang-Fu froze in disbelief. Somehow, the U-Tsang arrow met his in mid-air, spinning and swerving it flat to the damp ground.

"Bastard!" cursed Huang-Fu, reaching for his sword.

"Lieutenant Liu, lower your bow! He means no harm!" shouted Zheng He, pulling him back.

They looked up, squinting in the darkness. The man was no longer in sight.

"We mean no harm," repeated Zheng He.

"What do you want with Sonam?" called the imperious voice from afar.

"In truth," replied Zheng He, his ears burning with shame, "I want…I need to find a woman."

"A woman?"

"Her name is…Min Li. She…I…"

"Admiral, what are you doing?" whispered Huang-Fu. "Don't tell him that!"

"Min Li??" The voice seemed agitated. "You said Min Li?"

Zheng He listened. There was a long pause before the stranger continued.

"Then…then you must have been Min Li's first *azhu*…"

Again this was followed by a cold silence. Zheng He stood frozen, hardly breathing. He could discern a faint sound as though the stranger were wiping away tears.

"Min Li has been arrested in Deqin," said the stranger at last.

As horrified as Zheng He was by the revelation, he could not reply. The man had spoken then as though in grief. His voice seemed laden with sorrow. There was a long silence before it called out again, indignant and strong as though its owner had reached a decision and would let nothing stand in his way.

"And what makes you think Min Li needs you? Go! Go back from where you came! Go!"

Again, the dark silhouette rose up against the moonlit sky. Like an ethereal shadow, he loomed over them. The icy breeze lifted long silken strands above his proud shoulders.

"Tonight you can sleep here. Go back to the hamlet! Ask for Old Jetsan!"

Almost suddenly, he spun round and began to escalate the steep slope behind the monastery. Zheng He and Huang-Fu remained stunned by how fast he moved.

"He will open his door to you for the night," he called out.

But they could barely hear him now so fast were his agile steps along the rocky track. His voice faded until it was but an echo in the distance.

"Tell him Sonam sent you!"

Chapter 64
Ji Feng's Revenge

The grin on his face said it all.

What a surprise, mused Ji Feng. After all these years, sweet Guifei! You thought you had evaded me. But time, hmm, time has been on my side.

And again, the yellow teeth flashed for all the world to see and Ji Feng strode through Deqin like a man does when he discovers after many years that fortune favors him.

True, the riders had returned empty-handed after searching for days. Who knew where that cursed tea-horse trader was now hidden. But it no longer mattered.

Because the bitch was right here.

He looked out towards the hilly plain.

Sweet little Guifei... And no one, no one will ever find you now.

He hurried out of the main settlement and set upon his black horse. It was only the early afternoon. The night would be long. He had enjoyed it last time but she was weak now. It was too bad.

He rode into the plain. Alone. At his feet, the mountain sun projected a dark shadow that stretched and stretched. If it had stretched any further, it would have merged with another shadow.

For the bound heels of Mountain King and his U-Tsang rider were not far behind.

***

Several *li*s from the village of Deqin, in an area not frequented by pilgrims and travelers alike, there sat perched high on a rocky hill, a large mud brick building standing twelve feet high. Inside this barn were horses. It was a place where they held imperial stallions before these were led to the Eastern cities. Surrounding this hill, the plain was bare and desolate, extending for many *li*s. Below, the valley led back to Zhongdian.

Outside the barn, four soldiers gathered round a rectangular wooden slab that they had set upon a brick well. Seated on inverted boxes, unheard for *li*s afar, they swore, dealt cards, tossed dice, made lewd drunken gestures and smoked rolled mountain herbs. At their feet, on the dirt floor, lay empty ale kegs among heaped hay stacks. Further back, by the barn's wooden entrance was a one-wheeled cart filled with horse dung.

The soldiers seemed to have done nothing all day save for deal cards and drink ale. They were vermin of the coarser sort with grime from the tip of their fingers to the rim of their ears.

They had been hired to run errands for the officer of the *chamasi* and supervise the dispatch of horses to the East. But for days now, they kept watch outside the barn. They were sworn to silence, not only by Ji Feng but by their malicious deeds. For Ji Feng knew scum and scum by its nature, bound itself to Ji Feng.

The heavy barn door creaked open to reveal a fifth soldier, blinded by the glare of the afternoon sun. He adjusted his pants and stepped out towards the group.

"Sleeping?" asked one of the soldiers.

"Sleeping," replied the fifth soldier with a grunt. "Bitch is bleeding."

An ignorant laughter rose from the group. It was interrupted by the sound of horse's hooves. At once, the soldiers stood, dropping their cards to watch the horse advance.

The black-clad rider brought his steed to an open enclosure and dismounted swiftly. His black, greasy hair dangled on either side of face. He removed his eunuch cap, tied it to his horse and signaled towards the group.

"Anyone come?"

They shook their heads.

"Not a wild boar in sight," croaked one.

With a silent nod, Ji Feng strode past the soldiers who sat back to resume their game. But reaching the barn door, he paused. Almost as though he sensed an unfamiliar presence, he extended one last gaze towards the plain. Satisfied, he pushed the barn door and stepped in.

***

She ignored how long she lay there but the light's angle had now shifted above her. It might have been afternoon. The large wooden door at the far end of the building creaked open. It was greeted by the neighing of nervous horses.

Min Li sat up as best she could despite her chained wrists. There was an agitated clinking sound as she shifted hay around to dissimulate the blood. She stared wide-eyed towards the door, listening in for footsteps.

The sun's rays filtered into the barn. They illuminated the figure from the back so that at first, he appeared as a shadow to her. But she knew him by the way he moved. She had seen him countless times before.

Still the same hair and skin, still those cold, broody eyes peering through those dark, unwashed strands... He reached her and stopped. He said nothing but continued to stare at her, savoring his victory. She sat up. Her entire body trembled.

"Where is Sonam?" she cried, surprised at her own tired voice. She was exhausted.

He did not answer. He crouched down watching her tear-streaked face.

"Where is he? What you have done with him? Answer me!" she sobbed.

"It is not for you to ask questions, Li Guifei," he warned. "Here, as you know, I make all the decisions, hmm. I decide on your life. I decide whether you breathe or die."

A cry of despair escaped from her lips. She had an urge to get up and run but her legs felt like cotton. She rolled to the side, raising herself pitifully with her hands.

"Now, now, what do you think you are doing?" asked Ji Feng.

He mocked her frantic efforts.

"Where do you think you are going, hmm? This isn't the way to be. And look at that mess. Just look at you..."

She ignored him, raising herself to her feet.

It was true that she was weak. What had happened? How long had she been in the barn?

Ji Feng leapt. In a violent grip, he tug at her hair pulling her to him. Terror made her scream. He brought his sneering lips to her cheek.

"Li Guifei! Here, I decide where you can walk, and when. Do you hear? I alone decide if you can get up or remain still. Do you understand?"

"Then you will have to kill me!"

Ji Feng laughed. He observed her soiled tunic with satisfaction. How fragile she looked with her thin stalk legs protruding from that silly frock. And all those bruises on her thighs, had she noticed them? When all this was over, he would keep fond memories of her defilement.

Still gripping her hair, he moved to one corner of the barn.

She saw the axe hooked to the wall.

"No! Please don't! Please let me go!"

Ji Feng's talon like fingers curled around the axe handle.

Her screams rose up in the high ceiling barn. They distressed the horses. Their grunts and neighs intensified, angering Ji Feng.

"Why are you doing this? Please don't!" she sobbed.

"You know why. You thought you were clever, didn't you? You thought you could dishonor me, hmm? But I never forget, Min Li. I never forget."

She tried to wrestle free but he dragged her out of the barn, axe in hand. The sudden light greeted her. She blinked. Ji Feng, too, was startled. They both looked on.

The body of one soldier lay on the ground. There was another, on his back by the cart. Dead too.

Ji Feng froze. His men lay in their own blood, their bodies pierced by feathered arrows. The eunuch's jaws tightened. Still clutching the axe in one hand, he waited.

And then a rider appeared from behind a haystack. The rider held a crossbow in one arm and a quiver of arrows behind his back. He sat high on his saddle and looked insolently in Ji Feng's direction.

"Sonam! Sonam, I'm so sorry!" sobbed Min Li.

The U-Tsang arrow flew in Ji Feng's direction. The eunuch swung across to evade it, losing hold of Min Li. She ran towards the back of the cart.

"Get back here!" he roared.

Another arrow shot past. Enraged, Ji Feng aimed his axe at the passing horse. He missed.

Sonam prepared his last arrow. He spurred his horse. But the eunuch had retrieved his axe. With a vicious snarl, he hurled the spinning blade at Mountain King, startling the horse to its hind legs. Sonam tug frantically at his reins. It was too late. His leg slipped...

Min Li cried out. She saw the U-Tsang crossbow snap in two under the horse's hooves. And then Sonam was rolling down the steep slope, landing savagely on the cold rocks below.

Ji Feng gave a wicked grin.

"You're too late, Mountain Dog. Your whore, here, has met with much unpleasantness in your absence."

Sonam gave no answer. He crawled on his elbows reaching towards the fallen axe. Ji Feng noted the blood streaks behind Sonam's trailing leg. The trader's painful grimace confirmed a broken knee.

The eunuch continued his careful descent.

"If only you had found us eight days earlier, hmm...but now..."

He watched Sonam crawl, a mere foot away from the axe. And as the trader raised his face, Ji Feng began to laugh. His felt boot clamped down on the axe.

"What do you think you are doing, Mountain Dog? Hmm?"

He turned his face towards Min Li. "Shall we tell him, Li Guifei?"

Sonam was startled.

"Hmm, yes, that's right. Your peachy mountain girl was once the emperor's whore. What is it, now? You did not know this, hmm?"

Sonam rose. His fist came smashing into the eunuch's jaw. In turn, Ji Feng kicked. The trader doubled over, wincing from the pain.

"You think you're a hero, hmm? Ignorant fool! You did well to murder my men. You want to know why? I shall tell you why."

He sent further blows into Sonam's back.

"You did what was most honorable, Mountain Dog. Saved your face, hmm? You look confused. They were vile men, Sonam! You will never know how much I enjoyed watching them..."

A brown shadow shot past. Ji Feng shrieked. Mountain King kicked again. Blood oozed from Ji Feng's nostrils. He rolled across and seized the axe handle.

Sonam gave out a cry.

Blood splattered across Ji Feng's convulsed face. He wrenched the blade out of the horse's neck. For a while Mountain King lay on its flank, panting in a red pond. Then his lids tired.

Something desperate surged in Sonam. His eyes glazed over, he leapt, bearing the eunuch down to the ground. Ji Feng's eyes bulged out. His sunken cheeks swelled. He jerked in all directions. Then an ugly rictus formed slowly on his lips. He found Sonam's broken knee and kicked with all his might.

The trader winced, releasing his hold. A brutal kick from Ji Feng sent him to his face.

The eunuch was on his feet. In his sure hand, he held the axe smeared in horse's blood.

But Sonam no longer saw him. His eyes rested on the plain beyond. He sought the snow-capped mountains stretching out to Lhasa. He felt the warm earth under his ear. And then he heard the plea in Min Li's sobs and knew despair.

A tear fogged his vision before time stood still and the quiet swelled around him.

The axe flew down.

Min Li's cries tore through the valley.

***

They had reached Deqin. Their guide had assured them this barn was perhaps the only place where the man who had arrested Min Li could hope to hide her. The admiral saw the barn perched on the hill. He wondered what to do next.

And then he heard it. A long, harrowing scream echoed in the valley. It tore at him. It tore through the trees and extended its call far beyond the mountains, shaking the earth like a tragic tremor. It resembled a distressed animal but somehow, he knew that it was her voice.

"Admiral, it is her!" cried Huang-Fu.

"Remain here!" shouted Zheng He, scrambling up the hill.

High above, Ji Feng was on his feet. The bloodletting had revived him. He felt a thirst for vengeance, for time lost and for the damage to his dignity many years ago. He had not forgotten. Men like him never do.

This is what Zheng He saw, once he had climbed up and reached the place where a brown stallion rested beside a headless corpse.

As he approached, wincing in disbelief, Jun's warning echoed in his mind.

Honored listener, you must listen well.

Zheng He blinked. He saw the claw-like fingers curled around Min Li's neck. He saw the eunuch's contorted face bent forth over her swollen features.

"Stop! Stop, you coward! You are under arrest!"

He saw Min Li pant and cough as the eunuch released his grasp.

Ji Feng froze. He recognized a eunuch far more senior than himself. He observed the tall, sallow-faced man with his orange peel skin. The man before him had seen better days. He looked ridiculous, now, with his dirty uniform, this old naval officer, ambling forward under the weight of his swollen belly and his own sword.

In the past, Ji Feng would have groveled at this man's feet and perhaps tried to persuade him of his worth. He would have fought to place himself in favorable light for promotion.

"What is it, old man, hmm? Come to rescue your young bride?"

The eunuch revealed a gummy smile that horrified Zheng He.

"Whoever you are, you are under arrest!" he warned. But even now, he strained under an urge to weep and run towards Min Li. He wanted to hold her and tell her... He swallowed. What was there to say?

Ji Feng found the axe. His fingers tightened round the handle, ready to strike at the tall intruder. A wicked grin drew itself on his face as he peered through his hair at the approaching admiral.

"What's wrong, old man? Forgotten how to fight, hmm?"

Zheng He stumbled past the dead horse. He noted the headless trader who lay on his back. He drew out his sword. He felt a pang of self-doubt, the doubt of an old soldier who fears he cannot defeat an opponent. He turned his face in her direction. How he longed to hold her. But he merely gazed at her as though in fear that he would not be able to afterwards, when it was over; when he would be dead.

He blinked. Yes, it was her. It was Min Li. She had raised herself on her elbows. She stared at him, mirroring his disbelief. She tilted her head to the side too stunned to speak.

"Min Li..."

She did not reply. She screamed.

Zheng He spun round, evading the blunt metal. Ji Feng gave a sardonic laugh and swayed past, ready to strike anew. Zheng He saw red and struck. Ji Feng parried with a strength the admiral could not match.

"Now then, that was a dismal attempt but let us see what you can do, Grandpa."

Zheng He hesitated. Min Li's screams alerted him. He eclipsed a swipe of the axe. The blade lodged itself into the ground before Ji Feng, his black hair dangling before his face, yanked it up again, enraged at having missed. Zheng He struck but Ji Feng was too quick.

"I'll bury you. I'll bury you without your three treasures, old man."

The admiral's breath grew labored. He swiped at air. And then he tired. It seemed he only evaded the blows now. He no longer struck with his own sword. The long trek in the *chamadao* had exhausted him. His movements became slow and clumsy until he was doubled over.

This, Ji Feng noticed. With a savage grin, he ran to the concubine. He dragged her body to the shed. Min Li screamed. The rugged terrain lacerated her back. She fainted.

Ji Feng raised his axe.

There was a whistling sound as Huang-Fu's arrow shot past.

Ji Feng stumbled back, gripping his pierced thigh with a shriek. He gaped at the saddled archer.

Zheng He surged forth, leaping like a tiger. He drove the jade-hilted sword into the eunuch's chest. Anger twisted Ji Feng's face. He gave a hiss, as blood spattered through his teeth. Then he tumbled and rolled into the valley below.

A grisly silence descended upon the plain.

Long ago, aboard the treasure ship, an old seamstress from Yunnan had risked all to reach the admiral. She had begun a tale about a village where a broken stranger found refuge.

And as Zheng He dropped his sword and clutched at his torn shoulder, he realized that he had not been listening. Jun had not just sought to revive his hope, the hope that Min Li was alive; no, she had foretold the greater danger awaiting her.

Perhaps even now, he had been too late.

A knot burnt his throat. He fumbled to take Min Li into his arms and hold her close. He caressed the skin on her blistered face and adjusted the tattered shreds on her bruised body.

Then he pressed his face against hers and wept.

Chapter 65
The Lovers

In the summer of 1430, five years after ascending the dragon throne, Zhu Di's grandson, Emperor Xuande, ordered Zheng He to take command of the seventh fleet. With Minister Xia dead, the strongest opponent of the expedition was no more. The fleet was to be reassembled and dispatched.

Once again, more than 27000 men would embark. But this journey differed from what Zheng He had known. Unlike the other expeditions and despite the large size of the fleet, he was only in command of a mere three hundred men. Yet it did not alarm him. Only two aims pressed in his mind.

One was to follow Shahrzad's instructions and hope that she would help him and Min Li leave the Middle Kingdom. The second was to finally visit Mecca.

Faithful to Shahrzad's request, he had brought along Old Yu despite the physician's remonstrance and his warnings that the admiral ought to remain in Nanjing. Zheng He knew this was out of the question.

The reassembled fleet left from Fuzhou, in early 1432. It is believed that before the fleet's departure from the Middle Kingdom, Zheng He made a visit to the Three Peak Pagoda by the southern mountain of Changle County. Perhaps made aware that it was his last journey and conscious of what Zhou Man had told him, he erected a stone there to commemorate past naval achievements. This was his last legacy, a testament to all the expeditions he had once led. Perhaps the admiral knew he would never return to the Middle Kingdom.

He was now near the age Zhu Di had been when this one struggled across the Northern frontier, battling old Mongol foes. But for Zheng He, the only remaining battle, at least in our story, was to be safe from the machinations of court eunuchs.

On this, his last journey, he had brought with him two treasures.

First, there was Min Li.

She had only recently begun to speak to him, years since her encounter with Ji Feng.

On their return to Nanjing, Old Yu had examined her. He had informed Zheng He that Min Li had suffered so much during her captivity that not talking, not speaking of her ordeal in the mountains would allow her to forget and heal.

"*Water spilled can never be retrieved*, but let her heal."

And so Zheng He did not try to make her speak.

She had grown once again accustomed to the city's climate, regaining her delicate porcelain features. He was touched at how skilled she had become, eager to help with chores in the mansion. Once, while sitting quietly in the kitchen and exasperated by the new maid's clumsiness, she had taken over to teach her how to knead, executing each turn of the dough with expert finesse.

Like the Min Li he had met years ago, and much like a roaming ghost, she shape shifted seamlessly from one instant to the next. Was she, in a wilful moment, a playful child so eager to embrace him? Was she, on a sultry afternoon, a sensual woman given to brooding in solace? Or perhaps she was an ageless free-spirit traversing the hallways from one room to another like a whisper carried away in the breeze.

She was now at the summit of her beauty, a slender woman of four and thirty. Her hair, she wore it long, with the two side strands braided and coiled above her fine temples. At other times, she left those strands loose. In their intimate moments, her long hair snaked round her naked form all the way down where cradled in the scented warmth of her thighs, lay that delicious triangular mound.

Yet there were times when she appeared much older as she worked to beautify Zheng He's mansion with flowers, embroidery or, when engaged in her favorite occupation, drawing. For Min Li learned to heal through her drawings. She would sit for days on a stool, paintbrush in hand, tracing vertiginous mountainous landscapes, deep valleys, waterfalls and soaring falcons.

On completion of each drawing, she would pause. With her hands on her lap, she gave way to contemplation, sitting still before the easel, her expression grave and languorous. Sometimes her jaw would drop from the weight of these emotions and a broken expression haunted her face.

He startled her once. He called out her name and praised her latest drawing; the one with the caravan of horses along the cliff's edge. Beneath this soaring mountain dotted by tiny figures, water rapids smashed against large polished stones.

Again he called her. She did not reply. Instead she frowned and resumed her work. In the left corner, she added a striped tiger, leaping across the valley. Then, satisfied, she sighed and smiled, reaching her hand out to him.

But Zheng He had seen inside her heartache. He knew she was merely sketching memories that she refused to let go. And he understood that while she continued to hold on to the past and nursed her grief, she would not speak. No matter that she was happy with him and sought him out, longing to hold him and listen to him, yet, she was still holding on and still drawing tigers leaping across valley gorges.

In the first year, they had slept separately. Old Yu had warned that it was best for her to heal. But one night, she had tippy-toed into his room. Once there, she paused in the shadow, clutching the doorframe with a wicked grin.

He saw as he sat up that she wore nothing except her red silk *dudou*. Holding his breath, his eyes roved in sheer amazement over the thin straps round her alabaster neck then down to the satin of her shoulders. He held out his hand to her, so eager was he to welcome her again, after that cold night in the Nanjing baths. It had been so long. And soon, she was under the silk canopy and in his arms.

The night and her secrets had enveloped them and before long, she had returned as his secret concubine. They had all flooded back now, those memories he had once tried to forget. He remembered everything now. He allowed himself to remember.

He remembered the rose petals floating like candy around her ripe breasts as his fingers cupped each mound tenderly. He remembered the echoes of her wet tongue in his ear. He remembered the water muffling her giggles as he gorged himself on her perfect nipples. It had all come back, now as she lay in his bed beckoning him with her long slender arms. And it was perfect, this velvet embrace, this sweet scent from her ever moist skin and the honeydew in his mouth long after he had lingered in the secret of her thighs.

Yet, even then, she never spoke to him. Even as she arched her back and wrapped her thighs around his neck, moaning like a kitten, she never spoke, not yet anyway. For Zheng He, it had not mattered. To watch her smile gave him happiness. Just to know that she could feel pleasure in his arms and he in hers made him understand a truth about lovers that he had long doubted. And on that night, he felt a peace that as a man, he had never hoped to feel.

The second treasure that Zheng He had brought with him as he boarded the fleet and settled in his apartments with Min Li, were the two pigeons that years ago, Shahrzad had given him. They were his only ties to the world outside the Middle Kingdom. And he clung to them like a dear old friend.

And now, as they neared the Southern Seas, Min Li saw him reach for the cage and release one of the birds. The pigeon did not know that it was free at first. It remained perched high, on one of the masts, seemingly confused, flapping its wings aimlessly against the strong gale as if to ascertain that it could still fly.

For days, it remained perched on the bridge so that Zheng He worried that it would never fly off and return to Melaka. But then one day, it disappeared and he knew not what had happened to it.

During the dinner banquets on the treasure ship, Min Li, conscious of being recognized, would sit with the other concubines while he leisurely discussed past voyages with the other admirals. But the couple would never stay too long. He preferred to retire early, due to his health and perhaps also because he was weary of his new role. Because he saw that while the men on board respected him, times had changed. He was now too old.

But there was another reason why Zheng He liked to retire early. It was simply that one of the court officers, one who had introduced himself as an accountant, liked to examine him at length. Zheng He felt certain that he had seen this man before but he could not be sure.

And one night, that same man, seeing him retire with one arm around Min Li, stopped short to bar their way. With the pretext of wishing them a good night, he took a long hard look at the beautiful woman. It was dark and Min Li was so giddy with wine that she did not notice the shadow standing three feet ahead. Nor did she notice the vexation Zheng He felt seeing those cold eyes observe his beloved with unmasked insolence. She had buried her face in his arm and clung to him. Finally the accountant stepped aside to let them pass but the admiral's intuition warned him to remain vigilant.

Days later, they approached the eastern coast of Africa. As he prepared to release the second pigeon, the admiral sensed rapid footsteps on the staircase behind him. And right there, on the bridge, forbidden to all common officers, stood the accountant. As nonchalant as he appeared, his erect gait betrayed the rigidity and discipline of his purposes. A pungent smell rose to Zheng He's nostrils as the man drew closer. It often happens that even as we evolve from our turbid pasts, still its stench remains and this was none too true than for the accountant whose pores continued to emanate the rancid smell of death.

"Admiral," he observed, looking straight at him, "it is a dangerous game, you are playing here."

Zheng He cradled the bird in his hand, trembling with every fluttering of its feathers. He knew he was in the wrong. He would have used of his authority to release the bird and ignore the accountant but something in that man's tone left him hesitant. As he looked up, he felt the bird's pulse while its claws encircled his fingers. He felt the creature's fears as his very own. The wiry accountant gazed back at him with dark intent.

"Why only months ago," he continued, stressing every word as he leaned against the railing, "I found a similar pigeon with red markings on its feet. Odd, wouldn't you say?"

Zheng He continued to caress the bird, still shielding the message tied to one of its claws. The accountant's gaze became forceful.

"Put yourself in my position. I felt that this did not bode well," he said. "The empire is weary of spies. Admiral Zheng He, you would be aware that only Ming pigeons are to be used on the fleet. Security, you understand..."

Zheng He nodded.

"What did you do to the pigeon?" he asked, feeling the knot tighten in his throat.

The accountant smiled.

"I would have thought, Admiral, that you'd only have to ask and the lieutenant in charge of communication would dispatch messages on your behalf."

"What did you…?"

"I had to put it away. I am sorry."

"You—"

"Had I known you were the owner of this pigeon, Admiral, you can understand that I would have been more careful. Do you have relatives in Sumatra? Or in Melaka, perhaps?"

"Your impertinence is offensive," replied Zheng He, dismissing the question.

"Impertinence? Ah, yes. I may be only a lowly accountant but my loyalty to the emperor is without question. But you are right; it is not my place to rebuke the admiral. Please, accept my apology." At this, he bowed.

Then, as he moved back to his sleeping quarters, he stopped short.

"Kindly forward my respects to the Lady *Min Li*," he added with a chilling smile.

Zheng He watch the man walk leisurely across the lower deck. A crushing sense of doom fell upon him. Re-entering his cabin, he replaced the pigeon in its cage and sat on the edge of the canopied bed, brooding about the turn of events.

He considered his options. Even if he was unable to send this pigeon, there was a slim chance Shahrzad may still meet them in Zanzibar. But what if she was not there? What if her and Kareem had long returned to Oman? And given that the first pigeon had never made it to Melaka, none of her relatives would have been warned. They would have no choice but to return to the Middle Kingdom. He frowned.

"Who was that man you were speaking with?"

It was Min Li. She had not slept well. He stretched out his hand and smiled, if only to reassure her.

"The imperial accountant," he began but his smile faded. He was startled by her expression. He had not seen the same tension in Min Li's face for years. There was that icy veil across her eyes, one that was calculating and distant. She lowered her head and now paced up and down their cabin clutching at the jade beads of her silk belt. And how her hands trembled...

"And what were you speaking of?" she asked, turning abruptly towards him.

"Nothing…I…"

"Do not lie to me! What were you and him speaking of?"

"It is nothing. What is troubling you?"

He stared at her with disbelief.

And then, she could take no more. She knelt by the bedside, short of breath and pale as death. Her lips trembled as she spoke.

"Listen to me. This man, the man you were talking to, he is very dangerous."

"He is just the imperial accountant…a man who prides himself on fealty to the emperor. I was unfortunate enough to encounter this man in the midst of sending a message to my friend in Zanzibar. It is nothing."

He took both her hands with a kindly smile.

"It is nothing," he repeated, trying to allay his own fears.

But how cold were her hands and how terrified her eyes as she took in his words and realized the enormity of the lie.

"Is that what he told you?"

He watched her horrified expression.

"My love," she whispered at last. "Do you remember the man I told you of, the man I met years ago from the Eastern Depot…the torturer from the Zhenfusi…this man and the accountant, they are one and the same!"

"What?"

"Now you realize what this means," she sobbed, shaking her head. "I can never show my face. I will not attend any of the banquets from tonight. I will remain in this cabin…"

Zheng He sat up. He had said nothing but she could see the terror rising in his eyes as he brushed past her and took his turn pacing their cabin, his feet dragging on the dense carpet. His was the face of a tormented man, a man who had just realized the limits of his freedom.

He swallowed painfully. Those spies he had long sheltered in his mansion. They were but a token of the plot where he found himself. Along the gilded railing, down to its polished planks, from stern to prow, from the depth and richness of its holds through its infernal galleys and right up to the tip of its highest mast where fluttered the Ming banners, he saw it. This ship was a trap.

Now Shahrzad was their only chance.

"It will make no difference Min Li," he said at last. "It is too late for you to hide."

"What do you mean?"

"He recognized you, Min Li. He has called you by name. He knows who you are."

She pressed a hand to her lips. The blood had drained from her face.

"How…how long has he watched us? What do you think he will do? My love…are we…are we sailing to our death?"

Zheng He shook his head.

"I ignore what his designs are. Or even how he came to be on board... But remember how brave you were once, Min Li, and now, now you must draw from that same strength. You must have courage! We are to reach the shores of Africa, Min Li. After that, I do not know."

Again he shook his head. "I do not know. Only *He* knows. But I promise you this," he said, pulling her close and holding her tight. "No one, no one will dare lay a hand on you for as long as I am alive."

***

They were diverting part of the fleet to Mecca but due to the rigid security measures, he would not be permitted to disembark. His ship remained behind.

When they reached the Arabian Gulf, he watched, a little disheartened, as the naval detachment vanished into the night, cradled in the glistening lights of the Muslim port. He would never see Mecca.

"Considering your ailing health," said Old Yu, "it is probably best. Besides, there is still the return journey. You must preserve your strength if you are at all to visit Zanzibar and meet that dreadful Omani woman."

"Her name is Shahrzad," retorted Zheng He, a little wounded by Old Yu's cold distaste.

"I am sure she will be at her inquisitive best," quipped Old Yu. "Just don't expect me to be courteous with her."

Zheng He merely stifled a nervous laugh. He only hoped Shahrzad was there at all.

Chapter 66
The Sand of Time

The pensive man ambled across the dunes. He searched towards the dimming sunlight streaking the pink horizon. Ahead, like abandoned souls, graceful dhows danced along the glistening shore. In the cool of the evening, gentle foam sifted the sand along a deserted beach. Not quite deserted.

He squinted. Sitting on the sand was a familiar blue-clad figure. He sighed. As stern and impenetrable as the mountains, he thought.

Her long unruly locks were loose behind her dignified back. He inhaled the amber of her scent. It warmed yet pained him. She said not a word as he quietly sat by her side and removed his sandals.

"No sign of the red bamboo sails today," he observed, gazing ahead.

"It appears so," replied his wife.

"Shahrzad, mark my words. He will come. The ban has been lifted. We know this. Our partners in Palembang have confirmed it."

"I hope it is true, Kareem. It will be a blessing if he does come."

"But you cannot control the fate of this man."

She said nothing for a while, her ringed toe sinking deep into the cool sand. She looked down to watch the foam fizz at her feet before it retreated back out into sea.

When she finally spoke, her voice was tinted with regret.

"So what is it you have longed to tell me for months, Kareem?"

He felt the painful knot in his throat, sorry that he should have to say anything.

"I know it has been hard for you," she declared, her voice muffled by breaking waves.

Kareem knew it was difficult to persuade his headstrong wife. He rubbed his woolly beard with discomfort and leaned forward. Together they stared ahead at the undefined space. They endured the silence. His eyes welled up with tears.

"Perhaps," he began, "perhaps it would be better, if we should leave Zanzibar..."

She stared at him with surprise.

"Leave? You're not serious... I've lived here all my life."

"I know."

"My nurse is here."

"I know."

"My home is here."

"I know."

But Kareem's mood had sunk. He shook his head. "Shahrzad, you've never been the same. You know it. This place has tormented you long enough. Let us leave. Please."

She pouted in disgust, mulling over his words.

"As if leaving it would solve the problem," she retorted bitterly.

"Be reasonable."

"I am reasonable."

Kareem gave an exasperated sigh.

"What have you done since then, except run away? You barely talk to me now. Look what you and I have become. I was your best friend."

"You are still my best friend, Kareem."

"Please, please do not treat me like your father."

"Oh, Kareem..."

She saw his tears. She did not want to hurt him.

"Please, Shahrzad. Do you not see what you are doing?"

She contemplated for a moment. Her head rested on his shoulder while she tucked her arm under his.

"You are right." She paused, terrified of what she was about to say. But it was inevitable. "We should leave Zanzibar." She hesitated before adding, "As soon as it is over, I will leave. I promise."

At this, he recoiled. "When? When is it ever over? When you see *him* again? Is that it?"

"I need time, Kareem."

"Time? It has been years, Shahrzad! Years! We have been left behind. We have yet to build a family and live our lives. You have become a phantom. You've obsessed for too long now. Please, leave it alone and let us go. Let us go, my dove. Let us leave this place!"

She brooded at these words, aware of the distress, of the frustrated passion in his voice but torn by the tenacity of her own desires.

"I will sell the dhow business..." he continued. "We can setup a craft shop in Dhofar... We will sell our khanjars in the souks..."

As he spoke, her torment increased. She understood his true desires and its terrifying truth loomed before her eyes. She refused to look at him, merely nodding her head mechanically.

"I know what you wish for, Kareem," she said finally. "You want me to leave *it* here, don't you? You wish me to choose between you...between you and him. Am I right?"

Kareem did not reply. She nodded.

"I am right," she added, her voice trailing like a sad whisper.

"Shahrzad," admitted Kareem in a broken voice, "it has taken too much. I cannot live like this anymore."

She said nothing. He saw how difficult it was for her too. They were silent for a long time as she fixed the sea with a frightening intensity. At last, she took a deep breath and sighed.

"Very well, my love. I will do it. But let him come first. Let him moor on the Zanzibar shores one last time. I shall do this for myself. I shall ask him about *her* again. And I promise you, Allah strike me down if I lie, I will let *it* go. I'll do it, Kareem!"

Chapter 67
Shahrzad's Scar

"*As-Salaam wa alaikum*! Welcome my friend," cheered Kareem, stretching out his arms to embrace the tall man who strode towards him on the beach.

"*Wa alaikum as-Salaam*. It is good to see you, Kareem," said the admiral. Then his body stiffened as he whispered in Kareem's ear. "I am profoundly sorry that I could not warn you of my arrival."

"Warn me! I'd rise from my bed to greet you, San Bao," responded Kareem. Then, raising his voice in good cheer, he continued. "You must be tired. But that is not a problem, *insha'Allah*, everything is arranged..."

Kareem had noted the distant gaze in his friend's eyes. But he merely smiled, giving a friendly pat on the admiral's shoulder.

"How many years has it been already? What took you so long, my friend? But what did I tell her? *Insha'Allah*, the ships will be here, I told her. And I was right! Wasn't I? Allah, peace be upon him, favors us; the admiral graces us once more with his visit."

He reached forward, giving Zheng He a wholehearted embrace.

"I promised her that you would return!"

And he laughed. Zheng He finally spoke. His voice was cold and dignified.

"I must warn you, my visit will remain short. For security reasons we have also been asked to remain on the ship at night."

Kareem emitted a confused frown and dropped his arms by his side.

"Well...that's different. As you wish, San Bao. But Shahrzad will have something to say about that. And... Oh, here she is! The Eye of this island..."

"*As-Salaam wa alaikum*," said a familiar voice.

Zheng He could not speak. Disengaging himself from Kareem's embrace, he took a tentative step forward. He felt the relief as it surged in his chest. Shahrzad had set out alone to greet them. He had not seen her at first because her servants surrounded her.

Still standing a respectable distance away, Zheng He embraced the veiled woman, tears welling up his eyes.

"Shahrzad, what joy to see you," he began. He swallowed a hard lump in his throat.

He could say no more, but she quickly sensed that something was wrong.

"*Allah w akbar*," she whispered, holding tight his hand as if to allay his dark thoughts. "And what is this nonsense about you sleeping on board?" she asked. "Amira has prepared a bed for you in the west wing."

"That won't be necessary," protested Zheng He.

"Ah, my friend, you know how I like to get my way. Let me have a word with your council. They shall soon change their minds. Let all your party come along, we have enough rooms for all of the admirals. Don't we, Kareem?"

But Kareem did not answer. He had turned his body away from his guest as though in a daze. He seemed completely mesmerized by what he saw. On the shore, his employees held down a newly beached dhow. Now the boat had stabilized and the men assisted two long robed eunuchs as these stepped onto the sand.

"Shahrzad, look over there," whispered Kareem. "By the Prophet, I think you might know who this person is..."

And as the two eunuchs stepped aside, Shahrzad watched as a tiny figure walked for the first time on the shores of Africa. In this enchanting moment, a sandy breeze caressed the beauty's black hair and the silk of her pleated blue skirt fluttered with every step. The woman raised her face towards the admiral who, in turn, stretched out his hand in reassurance. Then as she neared the party, she bowed with rare grace.

"By the hand of Fatimah..." whispered Shahrzad.

"Shahrzad," said Zheng He, beaming with a love she had never imagined, "I want you to meet Min Li."

"You have spoiled years of my good work, my friend," she reproached, much to his confusion. "What miracle is this?"

Then, aware that he would not understand, she recomposed herself.

"Welcome," she said at last in perfect Beijing Hua. Then she bowed towards Min Li.

Min Li smiled. If truth be told, she was still troubled by Yin Dao. But she smiled because she had recognized the woman from the banquet. She smiled because she was in a place she had never seen. And she smiled because it was he who held her hand.

And as they walked quietly towards the town together, Shahrzad continued to stare at the Beijing woman. Her green eyes were moist with emotion and she seemed to question the admiral. Sensing this, he smiled again, revealing a familiar dimple in his cheeks.

"It is a long story. Perhaps Min Li will better share it with you."

***

During their entire stay in Shahrzad's family home, Min Li and Zheng He lacked of nothing. Zheng He wasted no time. As soon as they were well rested, he told the Zanzibar couple of his concerns.

"I will send a dhow immediately," said Kareem. "You do not have to worry, my friend. Leave it to me. Shahrzad's relatives will find you once you are in Melaka."

That left Yin Dao.

If they could somehow last the return journey without a confrontation with the guard, they may make it safely to Melaka. But all the cards were in Yin Dao's hand. There was no telling what he might do or who his accomplices were. Were the other admirals perhaps in league with him? Why had Yin Dao chosen to intercept them on the fleet? Zheng He ignored the answers to these questions but he could trust no one on board.

For days, he had quietly pondered over Zhou Man's last words and his insistence that the admiral remain close to the Middle Kingdom. His curious encounter with Yin Dao had further unsettled him. Prior to their arrival in Zanzibar, he had the clear presentiment that there was a purpose to Yin Dao's whereabouts on the fleet. If anything, he seemed to be observing the couple. Zheng He had spotted him a few times after the incident on the bridge and each time, it gave weight to his intuition. He even remembered having seen the man before, in Beijing. But he could not recall where.

He chose to put aside his growing fears so as to not spoil what little time he had left with his friends. He noted, with a certain wonder that Min Li had found it easy to forget their plight.

Min Li was in awe of Shahrzad. Now she was certain that it was Shahrzad whom she had once glimpsed walking in the corridors of the Inner Palace. Tall and demure, the Arab woman had impressed her.

Both women were quiet at first. Each seemed to examine the other, feeding their mutual curiosities. And then to Zheng He's surprise, they began to disappear, at first for a few moments and then for hours, even days, no doubt in Shahrzad's private quarters.

"Have you seen Min Li?" asked Zheng He one morning.

"Oh, don't trouble yourself, San Bao. She is in good hands," was Kareem's response.

"One must wonder what these two can find to converse about. I barely see Min Li these days," mused the admiral, collapsing in a seat under the shade of the veranda. He thanked a servant who had brought mint tea.

"Women can entertain themselves for hours, San Bao," replied Kareem in an evasive tone loaded with meaning.

"I suppose that this is one of the unfortunate consequences of Shahrzad having traveled far too long in the Middle Kingdom. Had she never learnt Beijing Hua, I might have had Min Li to myself," joked the admiral.

Kareem smiled.

Zheng He sipped his tea thoughtfully.

"I had not known Shahrzad to be like any other women," he finally observed, in reply to Kareem's earlier remark.

Kareem stared back at his friend. The joyful expression he usually sported had vanished.

"There may be truth in that, San Bao," he replied, after a long moment's reflection.

Then he reclined on his seat and closed his eyes, refusing to say more on the subject.

"You never told me how she got that scar," asked Zheng He.

Kareem was startled. His large fingers toyed with the rim of his teacup. Then he sprung up from his chair.

"Would you care to join me for a game of chess?"

"I would like that," smiled Zheng He, rising to his feet. "Kareem," he added, following this one in an opulent salon filled with embroidered poufs and low mosaic tables, "I hope I did not offend you."

"Nonsense! Sit, my friend. Let us play a good game of chess and fill our stomachs with sweet dates."

And despite this cheery declaration which was uttered in a dramatic manner, one his friend so often employed in public, Zheng He found that as the game of chess ensued, Kareem's mood turned sour. After staring at the pawns for far too long, unable to make a move, he suddenly broke his silence.

"Do you know why we, Arabs, call this island Zanzibar, San Bao?"

Zheng He raised an eyebrow.

"It comes from the Persian name, *Zendji-Bar*," Kareem said. "It means, Land of Blacks."

He abandoned the game and reclined on his couch, staring ahead behind his dark eyebrows.

"A very appropriate name. You see, that's why we are here. All of us. Well, except for a few."

"You mean the transportation of slaves from Africa to the Arab lands?"

"And further to the East... I'm sure you know of it. Someone once had a fine idea and the trade is progressing well. It does not matter whose idea it was, the Blacks, the Persians, us Arabs. It is not the business itself that is a tragedy. The business is only one part of it. No. It is the desire for black slaves. That is the worse part. Cheap labor appeals to all people, regardless of the land they live in. Someone always has to do the dirty work. And nobody likes to pay them. Greed, greed, my friend, is the greatest evil in this trade."

Zheng He looked at his friend who had dug his chin into his palm. His thick eyebrows now met as he fixated the chess board. But Kareem was no longer playing.

"Slavery. That's why many have come to the island of *Zendji-Bar*, San Bao."

"In the Middle Kingdom, slavery is forbidden. But everyone turns a blind eye. There is often a blur between one's slave and one's adopted son. Do you trade in slaves, my friend?"

"No! Shahrzad and I are against it."

"I thought as much," replied Zheng He. He remembered Shahrzad's frantic state on the treasure ship when they had approached Pemba many years ago. "I understand now why she lashed out at us. I have always wondered about that day."

"You remembered?"

Zheng He blushed.

"I understood that her father was a slave trader."

Kareem nodded and stood.

"The rich families take it for granted back in the Arabian lands. Either that or they turn a blind eye. So easily. For that matter, do you know what the geographer, Ibn Khaldun has to say about the Blacks?"

He paused and closed his eyes, collecting his thoughts. Zheng He listened as Kareem began to quote with dispassion.

"He says, *the negro nations are as a rule, submissive to slavery, because they have little that is human and possess attributes that are quite similar to those of dumb animals...*"

Kareem sighed.

"Ibn Khaldun said this. He once worked as a politician in Al-Andalus...even served illustrious leaders like the Sultan of Grenada. You don't have to be a petty, self-interested business man to believe the worst of others."

He pulled out a book on a nearby shelf and flipped a few pages until he found a familiar Arabic script.

"What about this quote: *When the Black is hungry, he thieves and when he is full, he fornicates.*"

He snapped the book shut.

"Charming isn't it? An Egyptian scholar, Al-Abshibi. Do you understand now? How can the unschooled businessman think otherwise when even scholars and historians think in those ways? Ibn Khaldun's words echo what a lot of we, Arabs have come to believe these days. After all, it befits our aims, does it not? That's how it is for many things, not just slavery. The people believe an idea when this idea serves their own interests. As Shahrzad would say, some personal convictions are mere artifice for selfish gain."

The impassioned Kareem sat back down. His eyes were ablaze.

"In this island, I have seen men that I thought were friends and decent Muslims, behave in vile ways. I have seen men turn into monsters in their lust for gain. They look upon the Blacks as Ibn Khaldun did. Why do they do this? They bow down to their greed and lust for power. They mock the natives, chaining them like beasts, even the young children."

He grew silent for a moment, gazing ahead as though the ugliness spread before him.

"And after many years, it has grown worse," he added with a grave tone. "Much worse. Of course, these shameful deeds happen in other parts. Please do not think it is just us, Arabs."

"But..." he continued, "people see what happens around them and sometimes they accept some deeds without questioning them. They are taught to accept these terrible things because it suits them. They think it is...a part of life... Tell me something, when you were a young boy, San Bao, you never thought of yourself as a slave, my friend, did you?"

"I...I suppose I was no better than a slave when Hongwu's generals captured us..."

Kareem nodded.

"It must have been difficult for you."

"I was afraid, night and day. I lost my father..."

They were both quiet.

"Kareem, tell me more about Shahrzad's father."

"Oh, he made a fortune from trading in black men. She never once imagined he could do something like that. You see, she grew up with the people of Zanzibar. Her beloved servants were mostly natives from the villages. They were part of her little family. The truth is, he masterminded it all. His methods were cruel, merciless. It was all about the money. It always is."

He emitted another deep sigh.

"I think the best way to explain everything is to tell you about the day...the day when she got the scar."

Zheng He leaned forward.

"It was so many years ago. She and I had been close since our teens and she was now a woman. She had seen the world! That's what she liked to say. She was always raving on about her travels to Nanjing and how much she longed to go back there. You made a strong impression on her, you know? She was always asking about San Bao. She wanted to know everything, everything about you. All the time, San Bao this, San Bao that."

Kareem paused. He rubbed an index finger on his lips as though to hide his shame.

"I was very jealous. Anyway, we liked to explore together and spend time at the beach on Pemba Island. I was entrusted with looking after my parents' home and with managing their accounts but I always found an excuse to go off with her. And then one day she had this crazy, crazy idea. She wanted to go to the other side of the island, where her dad's warehouses were. It was the first time she had expressed any interest in her father's work. All the time I had known her she was more interested in her books and her travels. And now her curiosity had grown to outrageous proportions. I told her it wasn't such a good idea..."

"You knew about the trade?"

"Well...yes. My father owned most of the dhows. He hired them out to traders. His company also carried out most of the maintenance. So I had been out on the beach in Pemba and seen... Well, I'd seen enough."

Zheng He nodded.

"So she was suddenly more interested in her father's business. What happened?"

"I just thought it would shock her. Besides, everyone was half naked. It was indecent."

"But she wouldn't listen."

"Ah, my friend, you know that Shahrzad does not take council from anyone. We took off with our horses. They were fierce Andalusian mares that her father had brought back from his last trip to Cordoba. I was wary. My plan was to skirt the shore and remain well away from the warehouse..."

"I did not know she could ride a horse," smiled Zheng He with wonder.

"She rides like a man. And of course she was way ahead of me, laughing behind her veil."

Kareem took a deep, sad breath. His voice came out muffled.

"There was a slave master on the shore. He was a man even I would not have hired. A real beast of a man and perhaps he was hired because as I said, someone has to do the dirty work. From the moment I saw him, it was clear. He hated the Blacks. I wasn't sure whether it was hatred as much as fear or perhaps it was fear and never anything else. It made him foam at the mouth whenever he wielded his whip. I lost count of all the obscenities he hurled at those unfortunates. He liked to show Shahrzad's father that he was in control and that the Blacks feared him. He would brandish his whip to make himself look more efficient. But that day it wasn't a man that Semi, that was his name, was taunting. It was a boy. He was...maybe twelve?"

Zheng He cleared the lump in his throat.

"A twelve year old boy?"

"...A skinny little thing. Oh, it was horrible. He was naked and in chains. I always remember those tears and the look of despair in the boy's eyes. It was as if during this moment, this horrible day, the boy had understood that he was very much alone in the world and that no one would help him."

Zheng He covered his mouth with his trembling hand. Kareem continued.

"I don't know how, but Semi derived pleasure from beating him. He roared like a madman and continued to beat him. It was horrible..."

"You don't have to tell me."

"I don't know what happened... I could hear the women wailing in the warehouse. I could hear the screams and... Then I saw Shahrzad's horse kicking a few paces ahead. It'd come to a stop long before I glimpsed that shocking scene. Animals sense things...

"Shahrzad seized the reins with both hands and gripped tight. She managed to calm it down. For a while, I hoped that she would not see... But then I watched her sit up...

"I remember catching up to her, suggesting that we return home. She wasn't listening to me. She just sat there. On another day, maybe she would have sported with the water. But she remained motionless, you know, sitting up like this on her saddle.

"I wondered where her mind was then and I realized that she must be calculating something. The perfumes, the Venetian glass, the jewels, the long trips abroad... Perhaps at this moment, she knew where all that came from. I felt sad for her. I think she had always believed her father dealt in cloves or other spices...maybe cinnamon. She understood now why he had always asked her to remain away from this side of the island.

"And then her eyes turned towards the boy. I don't know why, I had a really bad presentiment then. You see, I knew my Shahrzad. I knew what she would do next. And that's why at that moment I shouted at her. But—"

"She charged," whispered Zheng He.

Kareem nodded.

"She kicked the mare's flanks and darted in the direction of the warehouse. She led her horse towards Semi, threatening to knock him off his feet. The fool, he was still whipping the boy. You see, Semi had decided to teach him a lesson, and we'll never know why. He was one of those men who will always lash out at those who are weaker. Perhaps that is what he was taught all his life. I don't know. But I remember this clearly. He held the whip high and Shahrzad's horse pounced on him just as Semi cracked his weapon...He was taken by surprise and the leather flew out of his hand and whipped the air. It struck Shahrzad in the face like a wild sling. I knew she had been hit because she lost balance and I thought she might fall off her mare. But she held on.

"I yelled for her to turn back but Semi now realized who she was. I can still see his eyes bulging out of its sockets. I saw his rage. I bet he had never seen a woman ride a horse before. Everything went silent, then, except for the little boy. I wasn't sure what to do and like Semi I just stood there like an idiot. It was then that I saw Shahrzad pick up the whip. It had landed on the stone enclosure and she had only to reach out to grab the handle. It seemed so easy...

"I had a thought. I still ignore how I knew but I knew. Sometimes it is as if you know someone enough to predict how they would behave in a certain moment... And when that moment finally comes, you just know!

"I watched the horse's hooves dredging the sand. The animal's nostrils flared and puffed up sand and dirt. I saw Semi's jaw drop as he waved his palms ahead of him. I understood why. Shahrzad only had eyes for him. She still had the whip in one hand. Then she spurred her mare. She tracked him down as he ran on the sand. All this time, she held the reins in one hand and brandished the whip in the other. She gave him several blows."

"She hit him?" asked Zheng He dumbfounded.

"He never forgot it. But I don't think he told her father either. He knew better."

"And the scar was Semi's work..."

"The scar was Semi's work. Even Mustafa never found out. She trusts you, you see."

"What happened after this?"

"She shut out her own father. He was just another man to her now. You see, for Shahrzad, it matters little who you are – a father, a mother, a cousin – in the end, only your deeds can endear her to you. No matter that she loved him, she no longer held him in high regard. Now the reminder is here every day and every day she knows that the trade goes on. But she cannot stop it. What you do in your father's warehouse is one thing but the world abides to different rules. She is only a woman and most men will never listen to her. That's how it is, isn't it?"

Kareem paused for a moment. There was relief in his voice as he said the rest.

"We are thinking of leaving Zanzibar for Oman. It is hard for her. She has lived here all her life. She loves the people."

"What happened to the little boy?" asked Zheng He in a sorrowful voice.

Kareem's voice was muffled again.

"He died of kidney injuries. I would not have known but Shahrzad asked me to take care of him. So I organized that he be taken to the city hospital... I could not refuse her."

He stared gravely at his friend.

"You understand, don't you? It was not revenge. She did not hit Semi because of the blow to her face. She hit him because she wanted to protect the little boy. Wanted him to be safe..."

Zheng He nodded and Kareem noticed that the admiral's eyes were moist with tears.

Chapter 68
Arrest

It was a sad departure. He held Shahrzad's hand a long time before allowing himself to board the dhow that would take them to the treasure ship. And as the couples parted, he thought he saw Shahrzad raise her veil to wipe her tears. Long after, he watched Pemba's shore disappear until it was nothing but a black dot in the hazy horizon.

It was fortnights later, when they reached the port of Ku'Li that Zheng He who wary of Yin Dao, now observed everything with dread, noted that a great change had taken place aboard the treasure ship.

Old Yu had not reported an epidemic. There were no rotting compartments since the ship was in perfect condition. All cargo was in order and the floating farms around the ships could not be blamed for the pervading smell. Neither the galleys nor the stifling-hot lower deck compartments could account for the odor that now haunted Zheng He every moment of every day.

The scent of a certain man, for that is precisely what it was, had now spread insidiously across the decks until it seemed to Zheng He that every plank, every corridor, every carpet spread and every chamber was impregnated with the reek of tobacco.

And the cause was simple. Captain Yin Dao, who had since then sported only the common cotton scholar attire, was now fully decked into his dark blue military uniform. It was unmistakable; it came complete with its lion gilded *buzi*, its high felt boots and its long sharp sabre, the hilt of which left no question as to his rank and the importance of his mission. His very presence shamed those who had once dealt too lightly with the accountant.

Yin Dao gave no apology for his calculated deceit and paraded on the decks, puffing his addiction, encircled by a tightly knit group of the hardiest soldiers. It seemed that these soldiers had been at Yin Dao's service since the fleet's departure. All were well armed. All were animated by the same savage intransigence.

And all, without a doubt, were employed by the Eastern Depot.

With an assurance that left no question as to the decision he had made, Yin Dao began consulting with all the admirals and senior officers on the fleet, all, that is, except Zheng He.

Soon, all but the lowest of crew members ceased speaking to Zheng He. Whenever he spoke or offered his advice, he was met with evasive body language and barely listened to. When he attended evening banquets, all those present would quietly lower their gaze as he passed.

Aware of their discomfort, Zheng He would nod proudly and sit at his usual high-back chair, only to eat in silence, save for the deafening clicks of uneasy chopsticks. And as he raised each morsel of food to his lips, wondering if it might perchance be poisoned for all the seething venom in the room, he would become aware that though all eyes refused to meet his, their owners' thoughts were riveted on him.

Yin Dao's shadow blanketed the ship.

The trap was set.

In the days that followed, Min Li ceased to eat. Sickened and troubled, the admiral also shut himself in his cabin. He now prayed that they would soon reach Melaka where he hoped to arrange a subterfuge diplomatic visit and leave once and for all. This was their last hope. He was thankful that the treasure ships only sailed at slow speed. And now, he could only pray that Kareem's faster dhows would reach Melaka in time and that Shahrzad's relations would agree to come to the aid of complete strangers.

This was never to be.

In the early hours of the morning, as they departed the port of Ku'Li, six men came to find him. They pushed open the cabin door. As they stormed in, Min Li hastened to hide her nakedness. Trembling like a leaf, she managed to tie her sash before running towards Zheng He in tears. Two guards gripped her arms. There he was, vanquished, sitting by the bed. Three of them encircled him, ready to strike with their swords if he dared protest. One of them brandished an imperial order, sealed with red ink.

"Admiral Zheng He has been requested to present himself immediately to the Captain of the Eastern Depot."

Min Li gasped.

"Admiral Zheng He," continued the guards. "You are accused of treason. We have orders to arrest you," they recited, restraining him.

Zheng He remained silent. Behind him, Min Li gave a cry. She had just seen Yin Dao step inside their cabin. There was a cruel efficiency in his manner.

"Close the doors," he ordered.

The soldiers obeyed.

She took one glimpse at the Embroidered-uniform Guard and paled instantly. At once, the horrors of that early Beijing morning surfaced in her mind. She remembered the cells, the stench of urine and feces smeared against the walls while the cries of broken men echoed in the damp corridors of the Zhenfusi.

After all those years, it seemed that Yin Dao's eyes had sunken further. His face was speckled by the ravages of tobacco. She felt close to fainting. He met her gaze. His was a hard look. Then he turned and rested his implacable eyes on Zheng He. He spoke fast.

"Do you know who this woman is?"

"Yes. She is the woman I love."

"What is her name?" pressed Yin Dao.

Zheng He was startled.

"What is her name?"

"I thought you knew."

"I want to hear it from your own lips," spit Yin Dao.

"Her name is Min Li," replied Zheng He without shame.

"How very peculiar," mocked the Captain of the Eastern Depot. "I knew only one woman of that name... That woman, too, had unbound feet." He glanced down at Min Li before pursuing with calculated wonder. "But it turned out, would you believe...that the woman I knew was a traitor. She was sentenced to die by His Majesty, Zhu Di."

Yin Dao gave Min Li another hard glance and sneered.

"The woman I knew was fierce and spirited. She would stop at nothing to gain imperial privileges, even if it meant the death of her friends. But circumstances were not...how shall I say...in her favor. Isn't this so?"

Min Li did not reply.

The captain's attention shifted towards Zheng He.

"From what I remember, this woman tried to poison Emperor Zhu Di."

"Zheng He, I never—"

"Silence! And now you see how bad this looks for you, don't you, Admiral? You conspired with Hui foreigners, disobeyed orders to remain in Nanjing five years ago, were twice engaged in illegal naval proceedings and now...now, you fornicate with an imperial traitor!

"I shall not even ask how she came to escape her punishment or how she is even alive. But this is all I need to arrest you. Do you deny that this woman is your concubine?"

"Certainly not."

"Shameless old man..."

Min Li clasped her lover's arm.

When he saw this, Yin Dao emitted a disdainful smile.

"Guifei Min Li. I tried to help you once... I believe I was wrong. I should have never trusted you with state secrets."

He turned to the admiral.

"I know not to what design you destined your homing pigeon, three months ago. But I cannot allow you to remain a moment longer on this fleet. You are a miserable traitor. I will see what the Admiral Council has to say and if anyone is ready to speak in your favor. But we both know that outside the Middle Kingdom, those who endanger the fleet must be dealt with swiftly."

Zheng He could see Yin Dao's face clearly now. He noted the scar and the deep set eyes. He noted the tenebrous face as the impassioned guard spoke of treason and of law and of the danger Zheng He represented. He listened as Yin Dao appealed to imperial principles to justify his decision. And Zheng He understood. He understood that belying the guard's lengthy honorable speech, an erratic light danced in Yin Dao's eyes.

It was the same uneasy light he had seen when he had once tried to warn Zhu Gaozhi. Now he knew. It was Yin Dao who had not let him pass into the royal chamber. Because *he would not...*

"Have we met before, Captain Yin Dao?" he asked.

It felt like a slap in the guard's face. There was a fleeting light across his face. But the Captain of the Eastern Depot recomposed himself promptly. He weighed Zheng He's nuanced words much as a snake does.

And now Yin Dao knew well that he would pursue his aims to the bitter end. None should remain to question the cause of Zhu Gaozhi's death.

His next words were swift.

"As you have served Zhu Di well, you may have one request before your execution. If you are found guilty, Admiral Zheng He, how do you wish to die?"

Zheng He's complexion turned white.

In the deathly silence, Min Li squeezed his hand. Zheng He stared at her, refusing her sacrifice. She tightened her grip and remained there, watching her lover's faint smile. She saw nothing else.

***

At dusk, a small fleet detachment rejoined the Malabar Coast. The sailors lowered the anchor on the treasure ship. On the upper decks, four men sweated in the tropical heat, burdened by a large rectangular object. It had been fashioned at sea from pine wood to accommodate a man of longer height than average. Nothing was unusual about this wooden box save that inside lay the body of the admiral and his concubine. Yin Dao oversaw the procession as the coffin was lowered onto a smaller barge and steered onto the shore.

Old Yu remained there to organize the Hue burial into sacred ground. He had insisted that it was necessary.

The Admiral Council had deliberated on the question of Admiral Zheng He and whether he could be trusted. It was concubine Min Li, through her very presence, who had provided the evidence Yin Dao sought. She, together with her long history embodied all the treachery the Eastern Depot needed to persuade the council. Yin Dao had used this to bend the loyal admirals and slowly, they had relented.

Grand Admiral Zheng He was reported to have died and been buried at sea.

Chapter 69
Old Yu's Diary - Part Four

How strange this wondrous life is. I have seen perhaps as much as Zheng He in his lifetime. Perhaps more...

When I was a physician's assistant in Hongwu's army, all I wanted to do was prove myself and learn more. My curved knife meant the maiming of many young men and often, the death of hundreds. Castration is a depressing task. I took no joy in seeing boys maimed.

As soon as I could, I specialized in herbs and plants with the sole purpose of escaping my lot and traveling with Zheng He. I have been aboard ships and searched for plants and herbs in countless cities, speaking through translators in many tongues. I have healed many men, women and children, delivered hundreds of fleet babies and watched countless people die. I have survived naval battles, tempests at sea and slanderous attacks on my reputation as a physician.

I have made assumptions about people that were correct.

And then other, impertinent judgments that were wrong.

There was this Omani woman, you see. I am sure you remember what I wrote about her. Yes, how could you not. She was fascinating, wasn't she?

I often wondered why Zheng He had chosen to be her friend. Perhaps the truth is that I was jealous. After all, I was his personal physician. Why did he not confide in me? Of him, I really knew so little. But she understood many things about him.

Where do I begin?

It was in 1421. And she was always on the decks, following everyone, asking questions and peering over people's shoulders. It set me on edge you see, because she was veiled. We could not see her but she saw everything. It made me nervous.

And so I wrote about her in my journal. What I had not envisaged is that our paths would cross again, many years later, in quite an unexpected way.

It was in 1432, in Zanzibar, right after the admiral had been denied a visit to Mecca, that I saw her again. The admiral seemed stressed, weak even. I was pressed to look after him.

Min Li's help was indispensable because my vision was no longer what it had been. She helped me with the preparation of herbs, with the measures and concoctions. She was, it seems, very adept at these tasks.

But I digress.

And then one afternoon, while I rested in the courtyard of this magnificent house, the darkly veiled Omani woman came to me. She came and sat beside me and began to speak to me in my language. Of course I suspected all along that she spoke our Nanjing Hua. I had never been fooled for a moment.

Besides during their visit, she had spent hours entertaining Min Li, in her own bedroom. Heavens know what they could have spoken about. But the two were like best friends now.

Again, I digress. I will write now what transpired between us.

"So we meet again, Doctor," she flounced, gathering her robe and collapsing on the divan beside me.

"Why, yes, it appears we do. And you speak very well," I bowed respectfully.

"Thank you. The Middle Kingdom used to be my second home. And spending time aboard Ming ships, one learns many things. Wouldn't you agree?"

I shifted in my seat at this moment. You know how embarrassed I was, knowing that perhaps she suspected how much I resented her intrusions on board many years ago.

There was a silence, then, before she took to speaking again with a mild accent.

"Well Doctor, I must confess that I have thought long and hard about you."

To this, I was taken aback.

"About me?"

"Yes, you."

"You thought about me?"

"Why, yes! I needed to know if I could trust you," she replied, with a tone that I could not understand.

"Well, I suppose I took a long time to trust...err...to know you too...err..."

"Shahrzad."

"How did you say?"

"Shahrzad."

"Shalzat," I mouthed pitifully.

"That's good enough."

Then it appeared to me that she was smiling under her veil. But I can't be sure. In my pride, I interpreted that smile to mean that she was quite content speaking my language fluently while I could barely utter her Persian name.

We remained there for a good moment not knowing what else to say. But she was cunning and never wasted much time. She was ever ready to inflict burden upon others with her honesty.

"Old Yu," she began, "if ever the admiral were to encounter an incident...an unpleasant incident... How should I say this, an attack on his person... I hear that the Middle Kingdom is rife with eunuch accusations and that many have been—"

"This is inconceivable for one such as San Bao," I smiled, smug with assurance.

"Yes...but if that were the case, just if...then I wanted to ask you, as his physician to...help him."

"Oh?" I blushed.

"You see, I noticed that in one of your pouches, you carry certain derivatives of the poppy flower."

"You observe well."

"Oh, thank you. I have to tell you this; I read a lot about this flower in the libraries of Al-Andalus. I remember that you can use a large dose of it to kill a man."

"This discussion is most odd," I snapped, adjusting my spectacles on my nose. I frowned and looked away, eager to discourage her.

Shahrzad did not say a word and I thought she had been shamed to abandon the subject. But no, the woman was shameless. She was merely waiting until I had calmed myself.

At last, she took a deep breath and resumed with full force. "What I want to ask you, Old Yu, is to help give Zheng He a speedy death to spare him from dishonor and pain. Is this not something you care about?"

"It is good of you," I replied impatiently. "But I do not believe I would ever find myself in that situation."

"We never know, do we?"

"Anyhow," I answered tartly, "Admiral Zheng He is rather ill."

"Yes, I know."

"He is more likely to die a natural death," I advanced with scorn in my voice.

"You call kidney disease brought upon by castration, natural?"

You can see why I resented her. It seemed that she was now accusing me of being the very cause of the admiral's ailments.

"What I mean is that he is not likely to face any sort of accusation, much less execution," I replied, my face flushed with anger.

"Perhaps..." She appeared distracted. Then much to my displeasure she continued, unabated. "Old Yu, tell me, is it true that a certain dose of opium, you know, the brand you make, is it true that it does not kill a man but instead, induces a form of sleep...a deep sleep that looks a lot like death?"

"I have never tried this but that is possible," I shrugged, at once vexed and surprised that she had learned so much on the subject.

"Of course it is. When I was in Beijing you see, I spoke to a man, once, on Medicine Lane. The pulses are much slowed... The patient may appear to have ceased breathing... On appearance they look unconscious, dead even. But they are merely sleeping. I have read about that too."

I bit my lips. She really knew how to flaunt her cleverness. As I sat there, listening to her rant about her readings, I stewed on my seat. Perhaps she saw the frown on my face because she was silent again.

Then her voice rose up once more and I could not bear it.

"I would hate for Zheng He to suffer in any way," she said, speaking with a possessiveness that made me cringe.

"Well then, we should probably not talk about these things," I said, getting up and hurrying away as though she were a curse.

"Yes, yes of course. Well then, good day, Old Yu!" she called out from behind me with a tone that I swore was far too cheerful.

Old fool that I am! I look back on this conversation with wonderment. I see it differently now. Pride blinds you sometimes. And this is most true in our encounter with foreigners.

How could I have suspected that Shahrzad was so close to the truth? How could I have suspected that on the day of our departure from Ku'Li, the Admiral Council would summon me to witness and confirm the execution of Admiral Zheng He and his concubine, Min Li.?

Oh, it broke my old heart. I was older than him. I should have been dead before him. For the first time in years, I wanted to retch. I was horrified at the thought.

When I saw him last, he was not afraid. He thanked me for helping him along these years. I embraced him. I told him that he was like a younger brother to me and that it had been an honor. I took the little one's hand and rubbed it in mine. The poor child was white with fear. But she clung to him and did not want to leave him. When it was over and her delightful eyes were shut, I believe she was smiling and at peace. It is understandable. After all, what future was there for her without him?

I supervised the burial procession on the island long after the Ming ships had gone. And then when the time was right for me to leave, I secretly told the islanders to *open* the wooden box. I told them who they would find if they dared to follow my instructions and look inside. I told them that it was a man who would know them well for he had reached out to them many times and even spoke their tongue.

I remember something else, now. It brings a smile to my face. Moments after Zheng He confided that he would choose the sword, I asked him, shaking my head in protest, my old eyes burning with a fever that he had never known, "Son of Ma Haji, do you want to live?"

And for the first time since fifty years, he looked at me with that same childlike abandon I will always cherish.

Chapter 70
The Ming Storytellers

It had been eight years since Vasco de Gama's visit to Malindi in East Africa. The year was 1505. The Folangji now possessed Zanzibar. The Arabs and Persians remained for business but they no longer ruled this island.

Years before and months after San Bao's departure, Kareem and Shahrzad had left the island for Hormuz. They had sold her father's house and returned to the Arabian lands. After four generations, the Omani family had moved out.

Now the lovely stone house with its vast green internal courtyard, flanked on each side by broad colonnades, lay silent and still. Plants had emerged, persisting in their determined quest to overcome stone. The weather had been kind to the natural paint but stubborn ivy gripped the walls all along the veranda. Weeds grew, scattered between the courtyard tiles. Stone had cracked. The birds flew in and flew out. Leaves swirled. It was a quiet, desolate place.

The brown-haired soldier liked to come here and rest after his long shift at the fort. He would absorb the memories of the past and wonder who had lived here. He would idle on the steps to smoke a pipe and often leaned back against a column to watch the deserted courtyard.

Outside, the muezzin calls to prayer did not disturb him. They echoed through the corridors of this strange house and gave him what he sought, solitude, some respite from the life outside. He liked to take strolls and think back to his lovely girl who waited for him in Lisboa. Dear Isabel! Dear, lovely Isabel! How he would have liked to tell her of his journey so far...

How different customs were, here, in this curious land. The people seemed so wild and untamed. Did he suspect that in the coming years, the Folangji, for that is how his own people were called in the far East, would be pursuing what the Arabs had done for centuries and trade in African slaves? He did not.

He was proud to serve the Portuguese fleet. As an older lieutenant, in the years to come, he would be promoted and sent beyond, to the port of Macau in China. There, he would help secure Portuguese trade contracts with the Chinese. Did he know that the Chinese had ventured here, in Zanzibar, and that a Chinese admiral had visited this very house and spoken to his hosts in their own tongue? He did not.

He saw then, a large potted plant in the corner of the courtyard. It was strange, he thought, that weeds did not grow near this pot yet were present throughout the tiling elsewhere.

Curiosity took hold of him and out of intuition alone, and perhaps boredom, he found himself pushing against the large round pot. Boredom makes one do the strangest things. He pushed with an absent mind. He pushed as though it were a game at first. And then, seeing that the pot did indeed move he grew eager and more curious.

When he had pushed enough, he realized that the tile below was loose. He thought perhaps there might be something under it. The soldier crouched before this tile, and after straining for a while, he managed to lift it before peering underneath.

There were stories he would tell sweet Isabel when he returned home to Lisboa. But for now, he had no one to tell.

He reached inside the deep ditch, lined with smaller stones and thought perhaps it was a staircase. But it was not. It was just a ditch.

His probing hand found two books. He lifted them out. An expression formed on his lips, an expression a child makes when he discovers some long lost treasure. In this moment, he thought Isabel should have been with him, to discover the nostalgia in this house and travel through its secrets with him.

His eager hands and eyes traversed the first book. It was leather-bound, old and thick. It was richly decorated with gilded calligraphy and colorful vignettes. He recognized the script and understood that it was a set of Persian tales.

But the other book was different. A surge of wonderment and respect overwhelmed him. It was collection of over hundreds of pages, loosely bound together. Notes had been scribbled at the bottom of each page in different ink colors. In some pages, there were even sketches and maps. This manuscript seemed to have been created from all brands of papers, papers of various shades, each from a different place. It was meticulously handwritten, in Arabic.

For how many hours did he idle by the stone pot, lost in tarnished pages that he could not understand, his mind drifting to unknown places from a faraway time, he did not know. But long after the sun's golden shadow had bathed the courtyard tiles, and as the muezzin calls carried to his ears like a dream, the book and its mysterious scrawl lay open on his lap.

He heard his name in the distance. His fellow soldiers searched for him. Reluctantly, he rose to his feet and speedily replaced both the tile and the pot into place. Then, conscious of the elapsed time, the heels of his leather boots tapping hurriedly on the resonant tiles, he traversed the empty courtyard, still holding the Arabic manuscript under his arm.

But as he reached the majestic blue doors of the entrance hall, the brown-haired soldier had a fleeting thought and paused. His soulful eyes wondered ahead for one last glimpse of the wooden colonnades and their shadows.

Perhaps one day he would find someone who understood these beautiful pages. Someone with wisdom who could translate and share the story of men before his time... Who knows, perhaps this curious manuscript would give a voice to the ghosts of this grand mansion and reveal their story, their secrets. And someday, yes, someday when he returned to Lisboa, he may even share this story with sweet Isabel.

At that thought, the soldier smiled and crossed himself. Then stepping out, he shut the doors behind him, making a solemn promise to have courage, to give thanks every day, to be true, and finally, to return home...

All, for *The Ming Storytellers.*

END

Glossary

Azhu - the term for lover used by the Nakhi and Mosuo people; literally, *walk-in-friend*

Baba cake - deep-fried flaky pancake, often flavored with honey; Lijiang specialty

Beizi - a cloak that is either tied or buttoned at the front; often reveals the clothes beneath; sleeves can be broad or narrow; a *beizi* can be ankle length, above or below the knee

Buzi - embroidery piece at the front and back of military and civil officials' robes during the Ming dynasty; the highest ranking *buzi* features the lion for military officials and the celestial crane for civil officials

Chamadao - literally *cha-ma-dao* or tea horse path; an important road for allowing the Ming to trade with Tibet and exchange tea catties for horses; it consists of two main routes, one starting in Sichuan, the other in Pu'er, Yunnan; the two routes converge into a path leading to Lhasa

Chamasi - literally *cha-ma-si* or tea-horse-trade-bureau, they were established in several cities including Baidu in Sichuan and allowed the Ming government to verify tea-horse trading certificates and to regulate the tea horse trade

Confucian - relating to the philosophy of Confucius; insists on a hierarchical social order along with rules for etiquette and virtuous behavior according to one's social position

Dian - a time division that roughly equates to forty minutes, dividing a *geng* into three

Donganmen - the Eastern Gate of the Imperial City, consisting of a large building

Donghuamen - the Eastern Gate of the Imperial Palace, consisting of a large building

Dongba - Nakhi religion, headed by male Bon priests; known as a branch of Buddhism but likely derives from Tibetan pre-Buddhist practices with strong shamanistic elements

Dragon throne - the throne where the emperor of the Middle Kingdom resides

Dudou - the triangular shaped fabric fastened around the neck that many women of the Middle Kingdom wore as upper body undergarment

Durga - a fierce warrior goddess; a Hindu deity worshipped in Southern India
Eunuch - In the Middle Kingdom refers to a man or boy who has been fully castrated, including the removal of the glands
Eunuch palace grading - high-ranking eunuchs begin with rank 4, 1 is the highest level
Geng - a time division that equates to two hours
Grand Secretariat - officials acting as the highest executive institution in the Ming government; responsible for formulating imperial decrees, screening documents and drafting suggested policies for the emperor
Guifei - First or favorite concubine
Guiren - Fifth grade concubine; usually a beginner
Haji - one who has completed the pilgrimage to Mecca
Han - a member of the major ethnic group in the Middle Kingdom
Hanlin - pertaining to scholars or members of the Hanlin Academy, a scholarly and administrative institution; it held imperial examinations that bureaucrats needed to pass for acceding to higher ranks; Academy membership was restricted to an elite
Hazar Afsanah - original medieval Persian edition for *One Thousand Tales*, now known as One Thousand and One Nights
Hue - broad term used in the Middle Kingdom to denote a Muslim; ethnically can imply a Muslim of Han descent or of North-western origins, such as a Uyghur
Hun - nomadic, herdsmen people from the steppes of North Central Asia who invaded Europe from the 3rd to 5th century
Hutong - one of thousands of ancient alleys and city lanes surrounding the Beijing Imperial Palace and built mostly during the Yuan, Ming and Qing dynasties; the term originates from the Mongolian *hottog* which became hutong during the Yuan Dynasty
Jurchen - a member of an ethnic group originating from the Northeast or Manchuria
Kowtow- to prostate oneself, often touching the floor in reverence
Li - a measure of distance, roughly half a kilometer or third of a mile in the Ming Dynasty
Mazu - goddess of the sea worshipped in the Middle Kingdom by both Buddhists and Taoists, especially in Fujian and Guangdong but also in Annam; protector of fishermen and travelers; known for her ability to predict the future and heal the sick

Ming Code - also known as *Da Ming Lu*, Great Ming Code; a code of laws document compiled by emperor Hongwu, it greatly improved on the Tang Code

Ming Shilu - the *Veritable Records of the Ming*; imperial annals of the Ming Dynasty

Ministers - Hanlin educated officials who provided governance advice to the Ming emperor; there were six: Ministry of Revenue (Finance), Personnel, Rites, War, Works and Justice

Mosuo - a member of an ethnic group with strong matriarchal cultural heritage and with the same ethnic family as the Nakhi

Nakhi - member of an ethnic group found in a number of provinces but notably in Yunnan

Nanmu - literally *nan-mu* or Southern-wood; durable softwood used extensively in Ming Dynasty construction and originating from Vietnam, Sichuan and south of the Yangtze River

Oirat - member of a Western Mongolian tribe, often at war with Eastern Mongols from the 14th to 18th century

Qilin - mythical creature claimed to bring prosperity; the giraffe was identified as the qilin

Shoubei - Grand Commandant; title given to Zheng He under Emperor Zhu Gaozhi

Silijian - also known as the Directorate of Ceremonial; the administrative eunuch body of the imperial city

Son of Heaven - title given to the emperor of the Middle Kingdom

Weisuo - organization of military units; under this system, soldier roles were hereditary

Wumen - the Southern Gate of the Imperial Palace, also Meridian Gate, a large red building

Xihuamen - the Western Gate of the Imperial Palace, consisting of a building

Yang – from the Tao philosophy; Yin and Yang are opposite energies that exist in relation to the other; Yang is male, aggressive and sexually active, and heralds change while Yin is feminine, passive and dormant, and implies stability; Yang is represented by fire while Yin is represented by water

Yingtian - former name for Nanjing during the early Ming dynasty

Yuan Dynasty - the period when the Middle Kingdom came under Mongol rule

Zamorin - medieval title given to the feudal rulers of Southern India in present day Kerala
Zhenfusi - prison attached to the Eastern Depot at the Donganmen

Made in the USA
Las Vegas, NV
27 January 2022

42424096R00360